THE MORTAL INSTRUMENTS

City of Heavenly Fire

Book Six

CASSANDRA CLARE

WALKER
BOOKS

For Elias and Jonah

First published in Great Britain 2014 by Walker Books Ltd
87 Vauxhall Walk, London SE11 5HJ

2 4 6 8 10 9 7 5 3

Text © 2014 Cassandra Claire LLC
Cover photo-illustration © 2015 Cliff Nielsen
Spine landscape illustration © 2015 Nicolas Delort
Spine figure illustration © 2015 Pat Kinsella

This book has been typeset in Dolly

Printed and bound in Great Britain by Clays Ltd, St Ives plc

British Library Cataloguing in Publication Data:
a catalogue record for this book is available from the British Library

ISBN 978-1-4063-5581-9
ISBN 978-1-4063-6037-0 (non-trade edition)
ISBN 978-1-4063-6638-9 (Australia)

www.walker.co.uk

DISCOVER THE WORLD OF THE SHADOWHUNTERS, WHICH HAS CAPTIVATED 36 MILLION READERS

"The new queen of fantasy." *The Wall Street Journal*

"A cracking read." *Evening Standard*

"The Mortal Instruments series is a story world I love to live in. Beautiful." Stephenie Meyer

"A tale edged by lightning, driven by power and love." Tamora Pierce

"Cassie's writing makes my toes curl with envy. She is the rare writer who can write fast-paced dramatic fantasy with gorgeous language and memorable characters. It is rare to find someone who can do any one of those things well; to find someone who can do them all is just dangerous." Holly Black

"Hold on tight for a smart, sexy thrill ride." Libba Bray

"Clare's atmospheric setting is spot-on… Werewolves, vampires, angels and fairies all fit in this ambitious milieu. At the core, though, this is a compelling story about family secrets and coming-of-age identity crises. Fans of the smart/chic horror typified by *Buffy the Vampire Slayer* will instantly fall for this series." *Publishers Weekly*

"The story's sensual flavor comes from the wealth of detail: demons with facial piercings, diners serving locusts and honey, pretty gay warlocks, and cameo appearances from other urban fantasies' characters… Lush and fun." *Kirkus Reviews*

1 Entrance to Faerie Courts
2 St. Xavier's
3 Hunter's Moon
5 The Marble Cemetery
6 Taki's
7 Luke's pack headquarters
8 Garroway Books
4 Hotel Dumont/ Dumort
9 Magnus's apartment
11 Java Jones coffee shop
10 The Institute
12 Pandemonium
13 Clary & Jocelyn's apartment
14 Renwick Smallpox Hos

THE SHADOWHUNTER CHRONICLES

THE INFERNAL DEVICES

Clockwork Angel

Clockwork Prince

Clockwork Princess

THE MORTAL INSTRUMENTS

City of Bones

City of Ashes

City of Glass

City of Fallen Angels

City of Lost Souls

City of Heavenly Fire

THE SHADOWHUNTER'S CODEX

With Joshua Lewis

THE BANE CHRONICLES

With Sarah Rees Brennan and Maureen Johnson

** Digital exclusive **

TALES FROM THE SHADOWHUNTER ACADEMY

With Sarah Rees Brennan, Maureen Johnson
and Robin Wasserman

Also available as eBooks

Foreword

All the stories are true.

That's what Jace Wayland tells Clary Fray at the end of the first book of the Shadowhunters chronicles, *City of Bones*.

Jace means, of course, more than one thing by this. He means that everything she'd always been told didn't exist—vampires, werewolves, faeries, ghosts, and monsters of all shape, size, and intention—did exist after all and that, in fact, the world is full of them. He means that the stories we believe in our hearts—stories in which we are the heroes, stories in which there are good people who rise up to defeat the evil, stories in which there is always hope—are also true. Clary ends *City of Bones* feeling a true sense of wonder as she flies over New York City, seeing revealed below all the magic and enchantment that had been previously hidden from her.

All the stories are true.

When I set out to write *City of Bones*, I was in love with stories about vampires and faeries and warlocks, but I was also in love with the mythological tales of angels and demons. I was fascinated by *Paradise Lost* and Dante's *Inferno* and Mike Carey's *Lucifer*. I was fascinated with the way that human beings had grappled with the ideas of absolute evil and absolute good tempered with love and free will. I wanted to create a world that was rich in folklore, the tales people tell each other about things that go bump and bite in the night, but which also incorporated the existence of figures of myth—angels so powerful that one look at them would blind you. Demons so evil that their blood could change the nature of your soul from good to evil. I wanted to make real that which is so shrouded in myth and history that it has become symbolic: when Valentine frees Jace from his prison in the Silent City, he carries with him a sword and explains, "This is the blade with which the Angel drove Adam and Eve out of the garden. *And he placed at the east of the garden of Eden Cherubim, and a flaming sword which turned every way.*" Later, Simon comes into possession of the sword of the Archangel Michael. The idea that these objects of immense power and history were real things our heroes could touch and use delighted me.

The existence of angels and demons in the world of Shadowhunters is the ur-myth from which every other aspect of the stories is derived. Shadowhunters were created from the blood of angels. Faeries are part angel, part demon. Warlocks are the offspring of humans and demons. Werewolves and vampires are humans who bear demon diseases. I wanted to create a universe where myth and folklore dovetailed, where every story of magic could be explained.

All the stories are true.

The idea of Shadowhunters came to me in part from the stories of Nephilim in the Bible. The offspring of humans and angels, they were enormous monsters who laid waste to the earth. As writers often do, I adapted what seemed compelling to me from the myth—angels having children, when that is such a human thing to do! (Of course the Shadowhunters are only created from angel blood, but Raziel still seems to have a fatherly interest in them.) The idea of being part angel, partly a symbol of goodness, and yet being beset by all the weaknesses inherent to humanity: frailty, cruelty, greed, selfishness, despair. It seemed a way to take an ancient story and ring a twist on it that would allow any reader to imagine what it might mean to be part divine, to have immense power—and as Spider-Man likes to remind us, the immense responsibility that goes with it.

All the stories are true.

Of course, what Jace means ultimately is that stories are how we make sense of the world. The Mortal Instruments is the story of Clary above everything else: the story of a girl who starts out ordinary and becomes a hero. A girl who first is blind to the magic in the world all around her, but comes not just to see it, but to be able to master and control it. Clary is an artist and a shaper of runes, the magical language of angels, and in using that language she shapes her own story and her own destiny. Clary and her friends are heroes who *make* their stories true—as, in the end, do we all.

In God 'tis glory: And when men aspire,
'Tis but a spark too much of heavenly fire.
—John Dryden, "Absalom and Achitophel"

Acknowledgments

Them that I love, know that I love them. This time I want to thank my readers, who have stuck with me through this whole epic roller coaster of a saga, through cliff-hangers and angst and feels. I wouldn't trade you for all the glitter in Magnus's loft.

PROLOGUE:
FALL LIKE RAIN

The Los Angeles Institute, December 2007

On the day Emma Carstairs's parents were killed, the weather was perfect.

On the other hand the weather was usually perfect in Los Angeles. Emma's mother and father dropped her off on a clear winter morning at the Institute in the hills behind the Pacific Coast Highway, overlooking the blue ocean. The sky was a cloudless expanse that stretched from the cliffs of the Pacific Palisades to the beaches at Point Dume.

A report had come in the night before of demonic activity near the beach caves of Leo Carrillo. The Carstairs had been assigned to look into it. Later Emma would remember her mother tucking a windblown strand of hair behind her ear as she offered to draw a Fearless rune on Emma's father, and John Carstairs laughing and saying he wasn't sure how he felt about newfangled runes. He was fine with what was written in the Gray Book, thanks very much.

At the time, though, Emma was impatient with her parents,

hugging them quickly before pulling away to race up the Institute steps, her backpack bouncing between her shoulders as they waved good-bye from the courtyard.

Emma loved that she got to train at the Institute. Not only did her best friend, Julian, live there, but she always felt as if she were flying into the ocean when she went inside it. It was a massive structure of wood and stone at the end of a long pebbled drive that wound through the hills. Every room, every floor, looked out over the ocean and the mountains and the sky, rippling expanses of blue and green and gold. Emma's dream was to climb up onto the roof with Jules—though, so far they'd been foiled by parents—to see if the view stretched all the way to the desert in the south.

The front doors knew her and gave way easily under her familiar touch. The entryway and lower floors of the Institute were full of adult Shadowhunters, striding back and forth. Some kind of meeting, Emma guessed. She caught sight of Julian's father, Andrew Blackthorn, the head of the Institute, amid the crowd. Not wanting to be slowed down by greetings, she dashed for the changing room on the second floor, where she swapped her jeans and T-shirt for training clothes—oversize shirt, loose cotton pants, and the most important item of all: the blade slung over her shoulder.

Cortana. The name simply meant "shortsword," but it wasn't short to Emma. It was the length of her forearm, sparkling metal, the blade inscribed with words that never failed to cause a shiver down her spine: *I am Cortana, of the same steel and temper as Joyeuse and Durendal*. Her father had explained what it meant when he put the sword in her ten-year-old hands for the first time.

"You can use this for training until you're eighteen, when it becomes yours," John Carstairs had said, smiling down at her as her fingers traced the words. "Do you understand what that means?"

She'd shaken her head. "Steel" she'd understood, but not "temper." "Temper" meant "anger," something her father was always warning her she should control. What did it have to do with a blade?

"You know of the Wayland family," he'd said. "They were famous weapon makers before the Iron Sisters began to forge all the Shadowhunter blades. Wayland the Smith made Excalibur and Joyeuse, Arthur's and Lancelot's swords, and Durendal, the sword of the hero Roland. And they made this sword too, from the same steel. All steel must be tempered—subjected to great heat, almost enough to melt or destroy the metal—to make it stronger." He'd kissed the top of her head. "Carstairs have carried this sword for generations. The inscription reminds us that Shadowhunters are the Angel's weapons. Temper us in the fire, and we grow stronger. When we suffer, we survive."

Emma could hardly wait the six years until she would be eighteen, when she could travel the world to fight demons, when she could be tempered in fire. Now she strapped the sword on and left the changing room, picturing how it would be. In her imagination she was standing on top of the bluffs over the sea at Point Dume, fending off a cadre of Raum demons with Cortana. Julian was with her, of course, wielding his own favorite weapon, the crossbow.

In Emma's mind Jules was always there. Emma had known him for as long as she could remember. The Blackthorns and the Carstairs had always been close, and Jules was only a few months older; she'd literally never lived in a world without him in it. She'd learned to swim in the ocean with him when they'd both been babies. They'd learned to walk and then run together. She had been carried in his parents' arms and corralled by his older brother and sister when misbehaving.

And they'd misbehaved often. Dyeing the puffy white Blackthorn family cat—Oscar—bright blue had been Emma's idea when they were both seven. Julian had taken the blame anyway; he often did. After all, he'd pointed out, she was an only child and he was one of seven; his parents would forget they were angry with him a lot more quickly than hers would.

She remembered when his mother had died, just after Tavvy'd been born, and how Emma had stood holding Jules's hand while the body had burned in the canyons and the smoke had climbed toward the sky. She remembered that he'd cried, and remembered thinking that boys cried so differently from girls, with awful ragged sobs that sounded like they were being pulled out with hooks. Maybe it was worse for them because they weren't supposed to cry—

"Oof!" Emma staggered back; she'd been so lost in thought that she'd plowed right into Julian's father, a tall man with the same tousled brown hair as most of his children. "Sorry, Mr. Blackthorn!"

He grinned. "Never seen anyone so eager to get to lessons before," he called as she darted down the hall.

The training room was one of Emma's favorite rooms in the whole building. It took up almost an entire level, and both the east and the west walls were clear glass. You could see blue sea nearly everywhere you looked. The curve of the coastline was visible from north to south, the endless water of the Pacific stretching out toward Hawaii.

In the center of the highly polished wood floor stood the Blackthorn family's tutor, a commanding woman named Katerina, currently engaged in teaching knife-throwing to the twins. Livvy was following instructions obligingly as she always did, but Ty was scowling and resistant.

Julian, in his loose light training clothes, was lying on his back near the west window, talking to Mark, who had his head stuck in a book and was doing his best to ignore his younger half brother.

"Don't you think 'Mark' is kind of a weird name for a Shadow-hunter?" Julian was saying as Emma approached. "I mean, if you really think about it. It's confusing. 'Put a Mark on me, Mark.'"

Mark lifted his blond head from the book he was reading and glared at his younger brother. Julian was idly twirling a stele in his hand. He held it like a paintbrush, something Emma was always scolding him about. You were supposed to hold a stele like a stele, as if it were an extension of your hand, not an artist's tool.

Mark sighed theatrically. At sixteen he was just enough their senior to find everything Emma and Julian did either annoying or ridiculous. "If it bothers you, you can call me by my full name," he said.

"Mark Antony Blackthorn?" Julian wrinkled his nose. "It takes a long time to say. What if we got attacked by a demon? By the time I was halfway through saying your name, you'd be dead."

"In this situation are *you* saving *my* life?" Mark asked. "Getting ahead of yourself, don't you think, pipsqueak?"

"It could happen." Julian, not pleased to be called a pipsqueak, sat up. His hair stuck out in wild tufts all over his head. His older sister Helen was always attacking him with hairbrushes, but it never did any good. He had the Blackthorn hair, like his father and most of his brothers and sisters—wildly wavy, the color of dark chocolate. The family resemblance always fascinated Emma, who looked very little like either of her parents, unless you counted the fact that her father was blond.

Helen had been in Idris for months now with her girlfriend, Aline; they had exchanged family rings and were "very serious" about each other, according to Emma's parents, which mostly meant they looked at each other in a soppy way. Emma was determined that if she ever fell in love, she would not be soppy in that manner. She understood that there was some amount of fuss about the fact that both Helen and Aline were girls, but she didn't understand why, and the Blackthorns seemed to like Aline a lot. She was a calming presence, and kept Helen from fretting.

Helen's current absence did mean that no one was cutting Jules's hair, and the sunlight in the room turned the curling tips of it to gold. The windows along the east wall showed the shadowy sweep of the mountains that separated the sea from the San

Fernando Valley—dry, dusty hills riddled with canyons, cacti, and thornbushes. Sometimes the Shadowhunters went outside to train, and Emma loved those moments, loved finding hidden paths and secret waterfalls and the sleepy lizards that rested on rocks near them. Julian was adept at coaxing the lizards to crawl into his palm and sleep there as he stroked their heads with his thumb.

"Watch out!"

Emma ducked as a wooden-tipped blade flew by her head and bounced off the window, hitting Mark in the leg on the rebound. He tossed his book down and stood up, scowling. Mark was technically on secondary supervision, backing up Katerina, although he preferred reading to teaching.

"Tiberius," Mark said. "Do *not* throw knives at me."

"It was an accident." Livvy moved to stand between her twin and Mark. Tiberius was as dark as Mark was fair, the only one of the Blackthorns—other than Mark and Helen, who didn't quite count, because of their Downworlder blood—not to have the brown hair and blue-green eyes that were the family traits. Ty had curly black hair, and gray eyes the color of iron.

"No, it wasn't," said Ty. "I was aiming at you."

Mark took an exaggerated deep breath and ran his hands through his hair, which left it sticking up in spikes. Mark had the Blackthorn eyes, the color of verdigris, but his hair, like Helen's, was pale white-blond, as his mother's had been. The rumor was that Mark's mother had been a princess of the Seelie Court; she had had an affair with Andrew Blackthorn that had produced two children, whom she'd abandoned on the doorstep of the Los Angeles Institute one night before disappearing forever.

Julian's father had taken in his half-faerie children and raised them as Shadowhunters. Shadowhunter blood was dominant, and though the Council didn't like it, they would accept part-Downworlder children into the Clave as long as their skin could tolerate runes. Both Helen and Mark had been first runed at ten years old, and their skin held the runes safely, though Emma could tell that being runed hurt Mark more than it hurt an ordinary Shadowhunter. She noticed him wincing, though he tried to hide it, when the stele was set to his skin. Lately she'd been noticing a lot more things about Mark—the way the odd, faerie-influenced shape of his face was appealing, and the breadth of his shoulders under his T-shirts. She didn't know why she was noticing those things, and she didn't exactly like it. It made her want to snap at Mark, or hide, often at the same time.

"You're staring," Julian said, looking at Emma over the knees of his paint-splattered training gear.

She snapped back to attention. "At what?"

"At Mark—again." He sounded annoyed.

"Shut up!" Emma hissed under her breath, and grabbed for his stele. He grabbed it back, and a tussle ensued. Emma giggled as she rolled away from Julian. She'd been training with him so long, she knew every move he'd make before he made it. The only problem was that she was inclined to go too easy on him. The thought of anyone hurting Julian made her furious, and sometimes that included herself.

"Is this about the bees in your room?" Mark was demanding as he strode over to Tiberius. "You know why we had to get rid of those!"

"I assume you did it to thwart me," Ty said. Ty was small for his age—ten—but he had the vocabulary and diction of an eighty-year-old. Ty didn't tell lies usually, mostly because he didn't understand why he might need to. He couldn't understand why some of the things he did annoyed or upset people, and he found their anger either baffling or frightening, depending on his mood.

"It's not about *thwarting* you, Ty. You just can't have bees in your room—"

"I was studying them!" Ty explained, his pale face flushing. "It was important, and they were my friends, and I knew what I was doing."

"Just like you knew what you were doing with the rattlesnake that time?" said Mark. "Sometimes we take things away from you because we don't want you to get hurt; I know it's hard to understand, Ty, but we love you."

Ty looked at him blankly. He knew what "I love you" meant, and he knew it was good, but he didn't understand why it was an explanation for anything.

Mark bent down, hands on his knees, keeping his eyes level with Ty's gray ones. "Okay, here's what we're going to do..."

"Ha!" Emma had managed to flip Julian onto his back and wrestle his stele away from him. He laughed, wriggling under her, until she pinned his arm to the ground.

"I give up," he said. "I give—"

He was laughing up at her, and she was struck suddenly with the realization that the feeling of lying directly on top of Jules was actually sort of weird, and also the realization that, like Mark, he had a nice shape to his face. Round and boyish and really familiar, but she could almost see through the face he had now to the face he *would* have, when he was older.

The sound of the Institute doorbell echoed through the room. It was a deep, sweet, chiming noise, like church bells. From outside, the Institute looked to mundane eyes like the ruins of an old Spanish mission. Even though there were PRIVATE PROPERTY and KEEP OUT signs posted everywhere, sometimes people—usually mundanes with a slight dose of the Sight—managed to wander up to the front door anyway.

Emma rolled off Julian and brushed at her clothes. She had stopped laughing. Julian sat up, propping himself on his hands, his eyes curious. "Everything okay?" he said.

"Banged my elbow," she lied, and looked over at the others. Livvy was letting Katerina show her how to hold the knife, and Ty was shaking his head at Mark. *Ty.* She'd been the one to give Tiberius his nickname when he was born, because at eighteen months old she hadn't been able to say "Tiberius" and had called him "Ty-Ty" instead. Sometimes she wondered if he remembered. It was strange, the things that mattered to Ty and the things that didn't. You couldn't predict them.

"Emma?" Julian leaned forward, and everything seemed to explode around them. There was a sudden enormous flash of light, and the world outside the windows turned white-gold and red, as if the Institute had caught on fire. At the same time the floor under them rocked like the deck of a ship. Emma slid forward just as a terrible screaming rose from downstairs—a horrible unrecognizable scream.

Livvy gasped and went for Ty, wrapped her arms around him as if she could encircle and protect his body with her own. Livvy was one of the very few people Ty didn't mind touching him; he stood with his eyes wide, one of his hands caught in the sleeve of his sister's shirt. Mark had risen to his feet already; Katerina was pale under her coils of dark hair.

"You stay here," she said to Emma and Julian, drawing her sword from the sheath at her waist. "Watch the twins. Mark, come with me."

"No!" Julian said, scrambling to his feet. "Mark—"

"I'll be fine, Jules," Mark said with a reassuring smile; he already had a dagger in each hand. He was quick and fast with knives, his aim unerring. "Stay with Emma," he said, nodding toward both of them, and then he vanished after Katerina, the door of the training room shutting behind them.

Jules edged closer to Emma, slipped his hand into hers, and helped her to her feet; she wanted to point out to him that she was just fine and could stand on her own, but she let it go. She understood the urge to feel as if you were doing something, anything to help. Another scream suddenly rose from downstairs; there was the sound of glass shattering. Emma hurried across the room toward the twins; they were deadly still, like little statues. Livvy was ashen; Ty was clutching her shirt with a death grip.

"It's going to be okay," Jules said, putting his hand between his brother's thin shoulder blades. "Whatever it is—"

"You have no idea what it is," Ty said in a clipped voice. "You can't say it's going to be okay. You don't *know*."

There was another noise then. It was worse than the sound of a scream. It was a terrible howl, feral and vicious. *Werewolves?* Emma thought with bewilderment, but she'd heard a werewolf's cry before; this was something much darker and crueler.

Livvy huddled against Ty's shoulder. He raised his little white face, his eyes tracking from Emma to rest on Julian. "If we hide here," Ty said, "and whatever it is finds us, and they hurt our sister, then it's your fault."

Livvy's face was hidden against Ty; he had spoken softly, but Emma had no doubt he meant it. For all Ty's frightening intellect, for all his strangeness and indifference to other people, he was inseparable from his twin. If Livvy was sick, Ty slept at the foot of her bed; if she got a scratch, he panicked, and it was the same the other way around.

Emma saw the conflicting emotions chase themselves across Julian's face—his eyes sought hers, and she nodded minutely. The idea of staying in the training room and waiting for whatever had made that sound to come to them made her skin feel as if it were peeling off her bones.

Julian strode across the room and then returned with a recurve crossbow and two daggers. "You have to let go of Livvy now, Ty," he said, and after a moment the twins separated. Jules handed Livvy a dagger and offered the other one to Tiberius, who stared at it as if it were an alien thing. "Ty," Jules said, dropping his hand. "Why did you have the bees in your room? What is it you like about them?"

Ty said nothing.

"You like the way they work together, right?" Julian said. "Well, we have to work together now. We're going to get to the office and make a call out to the Clave, okay? A distress call. So they'll send backup to protect us."

Ty held his hand out for the dagger with a curt nod. "That's what I would have suggested if Mark and Katerina had listened to me."

"He would have," Livvy said. She had taken the dagger with more confidence than Ty, and held it as if she knew what she was doing with the blade. "It's what he was thinking about."

"We're going to have to be very quiet now," Jules said. "You two are going to follow me to the office." He raised his eyes; his gaze met Emma's. "Emma's going to get Tavvy and Dru and meet us there. Okay?"

Emma's heart swooped and plummeted like a seabird. Octavius—Tavvy, the baby, only two years old. And Dru, eight, too young to start physical training. Of course someone was going to have to get them both. And Jules's eyes were pleading.

"Yes," she said. "That's exactly what I'm going to do."

Cortana was strapped to Emma's back, a throwing knife in her hand. She thought she could feel the metal pulsing through her veins like a heartbeat as she slipped down the Institute corridor, her back to the wall. Every once in a while the hallway would open out into windows, and the sight of the blue sea and the green mountains and the peaceful white clouds would tease her. She thought of her parents, somewhere out on the beach, having no idea what was happening at the Institute. She wished they were here, and at the same time was glad they weren't. At least they were safe.

She was in the part of the Institute that was most familiar to her now: the family quarters. She slipped past Helen's empty bedroom, clothes packed up and her coverlet dusty. Past Julian's room, familiar from a million sleepovers, and Mark's, door firmly shut. The next room was Mr. Blackthorn's, and just beside it was the nursery. Emma took a deep breath and shouldered the door open.

The sight that met her eyes in the little blue-painted room made them widen. Tavvy was in his crib, his small hands clutching the bars, cheeks bright red from screaming. Drusilla stood in front of the crib, a sword—Angel knew where she'd gotten it—clutched in her hand; it was pointed directly at Emma. Dru's hand was shaking enough that the point of the sword was dancing around; her braids stuck out on either side of her plump face, but the look in her Blackthorn eyes was one of steely determination: *Don't you dare touch my brother.*

"Dru," Emma said as softly as she could. "Dru, it's me. Jules sent me to get you."

Dru dropped the sword with a clatter and burst into tears. Emma swept past her and seized the baby out of his crib with her free arm, heaving him up onto her hip. Tavvy was small for his age but still weighed a good twenty-five pounds; she winced as he clutched onto her hair.

"Memma," he said.

"Shush." She kissed the top of his head. He smelled like baby powder and tears. "Dru, grab onto my belt, okay? We're going to the office. We'll be safe there."

Dru took hold of Emma's weapons belt with her small hands; she'd already stopped crying. Shadowhunters didn't cry much, even when they were eight.

Emma led the way out into the hall. The sounds from below were worse now. The screams were still going on, the deep howling, the sounds of glass breaking and wood ripping. Emma inched forward, clutching Tavvy, murmuring over and over that everything was all right, he'd be all right. And there were more windows, and the sun slashed through them viciously, almost blinding her.

She *was* blinded, by panic and the sun; it was the only explanation for the wrong turn she took next. She turned down a corridor, and instead of finding herself in the hallway that she expected, she found herself standing atop the wide staircase that led down to the foyer and the large double doors that were the building's entrance.

The foyer was filled with Shadowhunters. Some, familiar to her as the Nephilim of the Los Angeles Conclave, in black, others in red gear. There were rows of statuary, now toppled over, in pieces and powder on the ground. The picture window that opened onto the sea had been smashed, and broken glass and blood were everywhere.

Emma felt a sick lurch in her stomach. In the middle of the foyer stood a tall figure in scarlet. He was pale blond, almost white-haired, and his face looked like the carved marble face of Raziel, only entirely without mercy. His eyes were coal black, and in one hand he carried a sword stamped with a pattern of stars; in the other, a goblet made of shimmering *adamas*.

The sight of the cup triggered something in Emma's mind. The adults didn't like to talk about politics around the younger Shadowhunters, but she knew that Valentine Morgenstern's son had taken on a different name and sworn vengeance against the Clave. She knew that he had made a cup that was the reverse of the Angel's Cup, that changed Shadowhunters into evil, demonic creatures. She had heard Mr. Blackthorn call the evil Shadowhunters the Endarkened Ones; he had said he'd rather die than be one.

This was him, then. Jonathan Morgenstern, whom everyone called Sebastian—a figure out of a fairy tale, a story told to frighten children, come to life. *Valentine's son.*

Emma put a hand to the back of Tavvy's head, pressing his face into her shoulder. She couldn't move. She felt as if lead weights were attached to her feet. All around Sebastian were Shadowhunters in black and red, and figures in dark cloaks—were they Shadowhunters, too? She couldn't tell—their faces were hidden, and there was Mark, his hands being held behind his back by a Shadowhunter in red gear. His daggers lay at his feet, and there was blood on his training clothes.

Sebastian raised a hand and crooked a long white finger. "Bring her," he said; there was a rustle in the crowd, and Mr. Blackthorn stepped forward, dragging Katerina with him. She was fighting, beating at him with her hands, but he was too strong. Emma watched in disbelieving horror as Mr. Blackthorn pushed her to her knees.

"Now," said Sebastian in a voice like silk, "drink of the Infernal Cup," and he forced the rim of the cup between Katerina's teeth.

That was when Emma found out what the terrible howling noise she had heard before was. Katerina tried to fight free, but Sebastian was too strong; he jammed the cup past her lips, and Emma saw her gasp and swallow. She wrenched away, and this time Mr. Blackthorn let her; he was laughing, and so was Sebastian. Katerina fell to the ground, her body spasming, and from her throat came a single scream—worse than a scream, a howl of pain as if her soul were being torn out of her body.

A laugh went around the room; Sebastian smiled, and there was something horrible and beautiful about him, the way there was something horrible and beautiful about poisonous snakes and great white sharks. He was flanked by two companions, Emma realized: a woman with graying brown hair, an axe in her hands, and a tall figure wrapped entirely in a black cloak. No part of him was visible except the dark boots that showed beneath the hem of his robe. Only his height and breadth made her think he was a man at all.

"Is that the last of the Shadowhunters here?" Sebastian asked.

"There is the boy, Mark Blackthorn," said the woman standing beside him, raising a finger and pointing at Mark. "He ought to be old enough."

Sebastian looked down at Katerina, who had stopped spasming and lay still, her dark hair tangled across her face. "Get up, sister Katerina," he said. "Go and bring Mark Blackthorn to me."

Emma watched, rooted to the spot, as Katerina rose slowly to her feet. Katerina had been the tutor at the Institute for as long as Emma could remember; she had been their teacher when Tavvy had been born, when Jules's mother had died, when Emma had first started physical training. She had taught them languages and bound up cuts and soothed scrapes and given them their first weapons; she had been like family, and now she stepped, blank-eyed, across the mess on the floor and reached out to seize Mark.

Dru gave a gasp, snapping Emma back to consciousness. Emma whirled, and placed Tavvy in Dru's arms; Dru staggered a little and then recovered, clutching her baby brother tight. "Run," Emma said. "Run to the office. Tell Julian I'll be right there."

Something of the urgency in Emma's voice communicated itself; Drusilla didn't argue, just clutched Tavvy more tightly and fled, her bare little feet soundless on the corridor floors. Emma spun back to stare down at the unfolding horror. Katerina was behind Mark, pushing him ahead, a dagger pressed to the space between his shoulder blades. He staggered and nearly stumbled in front of Sebastian; Mark was closer to the steps now, and Emma could see that he had been fighting. There were defensive wounds on his wrists and hands, cuts on his face, and there had doubtless been no time for healing runes. There was blood all over his right cheek; Sebastian looked at him, lip curling in annoyance.

"This one is not all Nephilim," he said. "Part faerie, am I correct? Why was I not informed?"

There was a murmur. The brown-haired woman said, "Does it mean the Cup will not work on him, Lord Sebastian?"

"It means I don't want him," said Sebastian.

"We could take him to the valley of salt," said the brown-haired woman. "Or to the high places of Edom, and sacrifice him there for the pleasure of Asmodeus and Lilith."

"No," Sebastian said slowly. "No, it would not be wise, I think, to do that to one with the blood of the Fair Folk."

Mark spat at him.

Sebastian looked startled. He turned to Julian's father. "Come and restrain him," he said. "Wound him if you desire. I shall have only so much patience with your half-breed son."

Mr. Blackthorn stepped forward, holding a broadsword. The blade was already stained with blood. Mark's eyes widened with terror. The sword rose up—

The throwing knife left Emma's hand. It flew through the air, and buried itself in Sebastian Morgenstern's chest.

Sebastian staggered back, and Mr. Blackthorn's sword hand fell to his side. The others were crying out; Mark leaped to his feet as Sebastian looked down at the blade in his chest, its handle protruding from his heart. He frowned.

"Ouch," he said, and pulled the knife free. The blade was slick with blood, but Sebastian himself looked unbothered by the injury. He cast the weapon aside, staring upward. Emma *felt* those dark, empty eyes on her, like the touch of cold fingers. She felt him take the measure of her, sum her up and know her, and dismiss her.

"It's a shame you won't live," he said to her. "Live to tell the Clave that Lilith has strengthened me beyond all measure. Perhaps Glorious could end my life. A pity for the Nephilim that they have no more favors they can ask of Heaven, and none of the puny instruments of war they forge in their Adamant Citadel can harm me now." He turned to the others. "Kill the girl," he demanded, flicking at his now bloody jacket with distaste.

Emma saw Mark lunge for the stairs, trying to get to her first, but the dark figure at Sebastian's side had already seized Mark and was drawing him backward with black-gloved hands; those arms went around Mark, held him, almost as if protecting him. Mark was struggling, and then he was lost to Emma's view as the Endarkened surged up the steps.

Emma turned and ran. She had learned to run on the beaches of California, where the sand shifted under her feet with every step, so on solid ground she was as fast as the wind. She hurtled down the hall, her hair flying out behind her, leaped and jumped down a short set of steps, spun to the right, and burst into the office. She slammed the door behind her and threw the bolt before turning to stare.

The office was a sizeable room, the walls lined with reference books. There was another library on the top floor as well, but this was where Mr. Blackthorn had run the Institute. There was his mahogany desk, and on it two telephones: one white and one black. The receiver was off the hook on the black phone, and Julian was holding the handset, shouting down the line: "You have to keep the Portal open! We're not all safe yet! Please—"

The door behind Emma boomed and echoed as the Endarkened threw themselves against it; Julian looked up with alarm, and the receiver fell from his fingers as he saw Emma. She stared back at him, and past him, to where the whole eastern wall was glowing. In the center was a Portal, a rectangular-shaped hole in the wall through which Emma could see whirling silver shapes, a chaos of clouds and wind.

She staggered toward Julian, and he caught her by the shoulders. His fingers gripped her skin tightly, as if he couldn't believe she was there, or real. "Emma," he breathed, and then his voice picked up speed. "Em, where's Mark? Where's my father?"

She shook her head. "They can't—I couldn't—" She swallowed. "It's Sebastian Morgenstern," she said, and winced as the door shuddered again under another assault. "We have to go back for them—" she said, turning, but Julian's hand was already around her wrist.

"The Portal!" he shouted over the sound of the wind and the battering at the door. "It goes to Idris! The Clave opened it! Emma—it's going to stay open for only another few seconds!"

"But Mark!" she said, though she had no idea what they could do, how they could fight their way past the Endarkened crowding the hallway, how they could defeat Sebastian Morgenstern, who was more powerful than any ordinary Shadowhunter. "We have to—"

"*Emma!*" Julian shouted, and then the door burst open and the Endarkened poured into the room. She heard the brown-haired woman shrieking after her, something about how the Nephilim would burn, they would all burn in the fires of Edom, they would burn and die and be destroyed—

Julian bolted toward the Portal, dragging Emma by one hand; after one terrified look behind her, she let him pull her along. She ducked as an arrow sailed past them and smashed through a window on her right. Julian seized her frantically, wrapping his arms around her; she felt his fingers knot into the back of her shirt as they fell forward into the Portal and were swallowed up by the tempest.

Part One

Bring Forth
a Fire

———◆———

Therefore will I bring forth a fire from the midst of thee,
it shall devour thee, and I will bring thee to ashes upon
the earth in the sight of all them that behold thee.
All they that know thee among the people shall be astonished
at thee: thou shalt be a terror, and never shalt thou be any more.
—Ezekiel 28:14

1

THE PORTION OF
THEIR CUP

"Picture something calming. The beach in Los Angeles—white sand, crashing blue water, you're strolling along the tide line..."

Jace cracked an eye open. "This sounds *very* romantic."

The boy sitting across from him sighed and ran his hands through his shaggy dark hair. Though it was a cold December day, werewolves didn't feel weather as acutely as humans, and Jordan had his jacket off and his shirtsleeves rolled up. They were seated opposite each other on a patch of browning grass in a clearing in Central Park, both cross-legged, their hands on their knees, palms up.

An outcropping of rock rose from the ground near them. It was broken up into larger and smaller boulders, and atop one of the larger boulders perched Alec and Isabelle Lightwood. As Jace looked up, Isabelle caught his eye and gave him an encouraging wave. Alec, noting her gesture, smacked her shoulder. Jace could see him lecturing Izzy, probably about not breaking Jace's concentration. He smiled to himself—neither of them really had a reason to be here, but they had come anyway, "for moral support."

Though, Jace suspected it had more to do with the fact that Alec hated to be at loose ends these days, Isabelle hated for her brother to be on his own, and both of them were avoiding their parents and the Institute.

Jordan snapped his fingers under Jace's nose. "Are you paying any attention?"

Jace frowned. "I was, until we wandered into the territory of bad personal ads."

"Well, what kind of thing *does* make you feel calm and peaceful?"

Jace took his hands off his knees—the lotus position was giving him wrist cramps—and leaned back on his arms. Chilly wind rattled the few dead leaves that still clung to the branches of the trees. Against the pale winter sky the leaves had a spare elegance, like pen and ink sketches. "Killing demons," he said. "A good clean kill is very relaxing. The messy ones are more annoying, because you have to clean up afterward—"

"No." Jordan held his hands up. Below the sleeves of his shirt, the tattoos that wrapped his arms were visible. *Shaantih, shaantih, shaantih.* Jace knew it meant "the peace that passes understanding" and that you were supposed to say the word three times every time you uttered the mantra, to calm your mind. But nothing seemed to calm his, these days. The fire in his veins made his mind race too, thoughts coming too quickly, one after another, like exploding fireworks. Dreams as vivid and saturated with color as oil paintings. He'd tried training it out of himself, hours and hours spent in the practice room, blood and bruises and sweat and once, even, broken fingers. But he hadn't managed to do much more than irritate Alec with requests for healing runes and, on one memorable occasion, accidentally set fire to one of the crossbeams.

It was Simon who had pointed out that his roommate meditated every day, and who'd said that learning the habit was what had calmed the uncontrollable fits of rage that were often part of the transformation into a werewolf. From there it had been a short jump to Clary suggesting that Jace "might as well try it," and here they were, at his second session. The first session had ended with Jace burning a mark into Simon and Jordan's hardwood floor, so Jordan had suggested they take it outside for the second round to prevent further property damage.

"No killing," Jordan said. "We're trying to make you feel peaceful. Blood, killing, war, those are all non-peaceful things. Isn't there anything else you like?"

"Weapons," said Jace. "I like weapons."

"I'm starting to think we have a problematic issue of personal philosophy here."

Jace leaned forward, his palms flat on the grass. "I'm a warrior," he said. "I was brought up as a warrior. I didn't have toys, I had weapons. I *slept* with a wooden sword until I was five. My first books were medieval demonologies with illuminated pages. The first songs I learned were chants to banish demons. I know what brings me peace, and it isn't sandy beaches or chirping birds in rain forests. I want a weapon in my hand and a strategy to win."

Jordan looked at him levelly. "So you're saying that what brings you peace is war."

Jace threw his hands up and stood, brushing grass off his jeans. "Now you get it." He heard the crackle of dry grass and turned, in time to see Clary duck through a gap between two trees and emerge into the clearing, Simon only a few steps behind her. Clary had her hands in her back pockets and she was laughing.

Jace watched them for a moment—there was something about looking at people who didn't know they were being watched. He remembered the second time he had ever seen Clary, across the main room of Java Jones. She'd been laughing and talking with Simon the way she was doing now. He remembered the unfamiliar twist of jealousy in his chest, pressing out his breath, the feeling of satisfaction when she'd left Simon behind to come and talk to him.

Things did change. He'd gone from being eaten up with jealousy of Simon, to a grudging respect for his tenacity and courage, to actually considering him a friend, though he doubted he'd ever say so out loud. Jace watched as Clary looked over and blew him a kiss, her red hair bouncing in its ponytail. She was so small—delicate, doll-like, he had thought once, before he'd learned how strong she was.

She headed toward Jace and Jordan, leaving Simon to scamper up the rocky ground to where Alec and Isabelle were sitting; he collapsed beside Isabelle, who immediately leaned over to say something to him, her black curtain of hair hiding her face.

Clary stopped in front of Jace, rocking back on her heels with a smile. "How's it coming along?"

"Jordan wants me to think about the beach," Jace said gloomily.

"He's stubborn," Clary said to Jordan. "What he means is that he appreciates it."

"I don't, really," said Jace.

Jordan snorted. "Without me you'd be bouncing down Madison Avenue, shooting sparks out of all your orifices." He rose to his feet, shrugging on his green jacket. "Your boyfriend's crazy," he said to Clary.

"Yeah, but he's hot," said Clary. "So there's that."

Jordan made a face, but it was good-natured. "I'm heading out," he said. "Got to meet Maia downtown." He gave a mock salute and was gone, slipping into the trees and vanishing with the silent tread of the wolf he was under the skin. Jace watched him go. *Unlikely saviors*, he thought. Six months ago he wouldn't have believed anyone who'd told him he was going to wind up taking behavioral lessons from a werewolf.

Jordan and Simon and Jace had struck up something of a friendship in the past months. Jace couldn't help using their apartment as a refuge, away from the daily pressures of the Institute, away from the reminders that the Clave was still unprepared for war with Sebastian.

Erchomai. The word brushed the back of Jace's mind like the touch of a feather, making him shiver. He saw an angel's wing, torn from its body, lying in a pool of golden blood.

I am coming.

"What's wrong?" Clary said; Jace suddenly looked a million miles away. Since the heavenly fire had entered his body, he'd tended to drift off more into his head. She had a feeling that it was a side effect of suppressing his emotions. She felt a little pang—Jace, when she had met him, had been so controlled, only a little of his real self leaking out through the cracks in his personal armor, like light through the chinks in a wall. It had taken a long time to break down those defenses. Now, though, the fire in his veins was forcing him to put them back up, to bite down on his emotions for safety's sake. But when the fire was gone, would he be able to dismantle them again?

He blinked, called back by her voice. The winter sun was high and cold; it sharpened the bones of his face and threw the shadows under his eyes into relief. He reached for her hand, taking a deep breath. "You're right," he said in the quiet, more serious voice he reserved only for her. "It is helping—the lessons with Jordan. It is helping, and I do appreciate it."

"I know." Clary curled her hand around his wrist. His skin felt warm under her touch; he seemed to run several degrees hotter than normal since his encounter with Glorious. His heart still pounded its familiar, steady rhythm, but the blood being pushed through his veins seemed to thrum under her touch with the kinetic energy of a fire just about to catch.

She went up on her toes to kiss his cheek, but he turned, and their lips brushed. They'd done nothing more than kiss since the fire had first started singing in his blood, and they'd done even that carefully. Jace was careful now, his mouth sliding softly against hers, his hand closing on her shoulder. For a moment they were body to body, and she felt the thrum and pulse of his blood. He moved to pull her closer, and a sharp, dry spark passed between them, like the zing of static electricity.

Jace broke off the kiss and stepped back with an exhale; before Clary could say anything, a chorus of sarcastic applause broke out from the nearby hill. Simon, Isabelle, and Alec waved at them. Jace bowed while Clary stepped back slightly sheepishly, hooking her thumbs into the belt of her jeans.

Jace sighed. "Shall we join our annoying, voyeuristic friends?"

"Unfortunately, that's the only kind of friends we have." Clary bumped her shoulder against his arm, and they headed up toward the rocks. Simon and Isabelle were side by side, talking quietly. Alec was sitting a little apart, staring at the screen of his phone with an expression of intense concentration.

Jace threw himself down next to his *parabatai*. "I've heard that if you stare at those things enough, they'll ring."

"He's been texting Magnus," said Isabelle, glancing over with a disapproving look.

"I haven't," Alec said automatically.

"Yes, you have," said Jace, craning to look over Alec's shoulder. "*And* calling. I can see your outgoing calls."

"It's his birthday," Alec said, flipping the phone shut. He looked smaller these days, almost skinny in his worn blue pullover, holes at the elbows, his lips bitten and chapped. Clary's heart went out to him. He'd spent the first week after Magnus had broken up with him in a sort of daze of sadness and disbelief. None of them could really believe it. She'd always thought Magnus loved Alec, really loved him; clearly Alec had thought so too. "I didn't want him to think that I didn't—to think that I forgot."

"You're pining," said Jace.

Alec shrugged. "Look who's talking. 'Oh, I love her. Oh, she's my sister. Oh why, why, why—'"

Jace threw a handful of dead leaves at Alec, making him splutter.

Isabelle was laughing. "You know he's right, Jace."

"Give me your phone," Jace said, ignoring Isabelle. "Come on, Alexander."

"It's none of your business," Alec said, holding the phone away. "Just forget about it, okay?"

"You don't eat, you don't sleep, you stare at your phone, and I'm supposed to *forget* about it?" Jace said. There was a surprising amount of agitation in his voice; Clary knew how upset he'd been that Alec was unhappy, but she wasn't sure Alec knew it. Under normal circumstances Jace would have killed, or at least threatened, anyone who hurt Alec; this was different. Jace liked to win, but you couldn't win out over a broken heart, even someone else's. Even someone you loved.

Jace leaned over and grabbed the phone out of his *parabatai*'s hand. Alec protested and reached for it, but Jace held him off with one hand, expertly scrolling through the messages on the phone with the other. *"Magnus, just call me back. I need to know if you're okay—"* He shook his head. "Okay, no. Just no." With a decisive move he snapped the phone in half. The screen went blank as Jace dropped the pieces to the ground. "There."

Alec looked down at the shattered pieces in disbelief. "You BROKE my PHONE."

Jace shrugged. "Guys don't let other guys keep calling other guys. Okay, that came out wrong. Friends don't let friends keep calling their exes and hanging up. Seriously. You have to stop."

Alec looked furious. "So you broke my brand-new phone? Thanks a lot."

Jace smiled serenely and lay back on the rock. "You're welcome."

"Look on the bright side," Isabelle said. "You won't be able to get texts from Mom anymore. She's texted me six times today. I turned my phone off." She patted her pocket with a significant look.

"What does she want?" Simon asked.

"Constant meetings," Isabelle said. "Depositions. The Clave keeps wanting to hear what happened when we fought Sebastian at the Burren. We've all had to give accounts, like, fifty times. How Jace absorbed the heavenly fire from Glorious. Descriptions of the Dark Shadowhunters, the Infernal Cup, the weapons they used, the runes that were on them. What we were wearing, what Sebastian was wearing, what *everyone* was wearing ... like phone sex but boring."

Simon made a choking noise.

"What we think Sebastian wants," Alec added. "When he'll come back. What he'll do when he does."

Clary leaned her elbows on her knees. "Always good to know the Clave has a well-thought-out and reliable plan."

"They don't want to believe it," said Jace, staring at the sky. "That's the problem. No matter how many times we tell them what we saw at the Burren. No matter how many times we tell them how dangerous the Endarkened are. They don't want to believe that Nephilim could really be corrupted. That Shadowhunters could kill Shadowhunters."

Clary had been there when Sebastian had created the first of the Endarkened. She had seen the blankness in their eyes, the fury with which they'd fought. They terrified her. "They're not Shadowhunters anymore," she added in a low voice. "They're not *people*."

"It's hard to believe that if you haven't seen it," Alec said. "And Sebastian has only so many of them. A small force, scattered— they don't want to believe he's really a threat. Or if he is a threat, they'd rather believe it was more a threat to us, to New York, than to Shadowhunters at large."

"They're not wrong that if Sebastian cares about anything, it's about Clary," Jace said, and Clary felt a cold shiver at her spine, a mixture of disgust and apprehension. "He doesn't really have emotions. Not like we do. But if he did, he'd have them about her. And he has them about Jocelyn. He *hates* her." He paused, thoughtful. "But I don't think he'd be likely to strike directly here. Too ... obvious."

"I hope you told the Clave this," Simon said.

"About a thousand times," said Jace. "I don't think they hold my insights in particularly high regard."

Clary looked down at her hands. She had been deposed by the Clave, just like the rest of them; she'd given answers to all their questions. There were still things about Sebastian she hadn't told them, hadn't told anyone. The things he'd said he wanted from her.

She hadn't dreamed much since they'd come back from the Burren with Jace's veins full of fire, but when she did have nightmares, they were about her brother.

"It's like trying to fight a ghost," Jace said. "They can't track Sebastian, they can't find him, they can't find the Shadowhunters he's turned."

"They're doing what they can," Alec said. "They're shoring up the wards around Idris and Alicante. All the wards, in fact. They've sent dozens of experts to Wrangel Island."

Wrangel Island was the seat of all the world's wards, the spells that protected the globe, and Idris in particular, from demons and demon invasion. The network of wards wasn't perfect, and demons slipped through sometimes anyway, but Clary could only imagine how bad the situation would get if the wards didn't exist.

"I heard Mom say that the warlocks of the Spiral Labyrinth have been looking for a way to reverse the effects of the Infernal

Cup," said Isabelle. "Of course it would be easier if they had bodies to study…"

She trailed off; Clary knew why. The bodies of the Dark Shadowhunters killed at the Burren had been brought back to the Bone City for the Silent Brothers to examine. The Brothers had never gotten the chance. Overnight the bodies had rotted away to the equivalent of decade-old corpses. There had been nothing to do but burn the remains.

Isabelle found her voice again: "And the Iron Sisters are churning out weapons. We're getting thousands more seraph blades, swords, *chakhrams*, everything … forged in heavenly fire." She looked at Jace. In the days immediately following the battle at the Burren, when the fire had raged through Jace's veins violently enough to make him scream sometimes with the pain, the Silent Brothers had examined him over and over, had tested him with ice and flame, with blessed metal and cold iron, trying to see if there was some way to draw the fire out of him, to contain it.

They hadn't found one. The fire of Glorious, having once been captured in a blade, seemed in no hurry to inhabit another, or indeed to leave Jace's body for any kind of vessel. Brother Zachariah had told Clary that in the earliest days of Shadowhunters, the Nephilim had sought to capture heavenly fire in a weapon, something that could be wielded against demons. They had never managed it, and eventually seraph blades had become their weapons of choice. In the end, again, the Silent Brothers had given up. Glorious's fire lay curled in Jace's veins like a serpent, and the best he could hope for was to control it so that it didn't destroy him.

The loud beep of a text message sounded; Isabelle had flicked on her phone again. "Mom says to get back to the Institute now," she said. "There's some meeting. We have to be at it." She stood up, brushing dirt from her dress. "I'd invite you back," she said to Simon, "but you know, banned for being undead and all."

"I did remember that," Simon said, getting to his feet. Clary scrambled up and reached a hand down to Jace. He took it and stood.

"Simon and I are going Christmas shopping," she said. "And none of you can come, because we have to get you presents."

Alec looked horrified. "Oh, God. Does that mean I have to get you guys presents?"

Clary shook her head. "Don't Shadowhunters do ... you know, Christmas?" She thought back suddenly to the rather distressing Thanksgiving dinner at Luke's when Jace, on being asked to carve the turkey, had laid into the bird with a sword until there had been little left but turkey flakes. Maybe not?

"We exchange gifts, we honor the change of the seasons," said Isabelle. "There used to be a winter celebration of the Angel. It observed the day the Mortal Instruments were given to Jonathan Shadowhunter. I think Shadowhunters got annoyed with being left out of all the mundane celebrations, though, so a lot of Institutes have Christmas parties. The London one is famous." She shrugged. "I just don't think we're going to do it ... this year."

"Oh." Clary felt awful. Of course they didn't want to celebrate Christmas after losing Max. "Well, let us get you presents, at least. There doesn't have to be a party, or anything like that."

"Exactly." Simon threw his arms up. "I have to buy Hanukkah presents. It's mandated by Jewish law. The God of the Jews is an angry God. And very gift-oriented."

Clary smiled at him. He was finding it easier and easier to say the word "God" these days.

Jace sighed, and kissed Clary—a quick good-bye brush of lips against her temple, but it made her shiver. Not being able to touch Jace or kiss him properly was starting to make her jump out of her own skin. She'd promised him it would never matter, that she'd love him even if they could never touch again, but she hated it anyway, hated missing the reassurance of the way they had always fit together physically. "See you later," Jace said. "I'm going to head back with Alec and Izzy—"

"No, you're not," Isabelle said unexpectedly. "You broke Alec's phone. Granted, we've all been wanting to do that for weeks—"

"ISABELLE," Alec said.

"But the fact is, you're his *parabatai*, and you're the only one who hasn't been to see Magnus. Go talk to him."

"And tell him what?" Jace said. "You can't *talk* people into not breaking up with you... Or maybe you can," he added hastily, at Alec's expression. "Who can say? I'll give it a try."

"Thanks." Alec clapped Jace on the shoulder. "I've heard you can be charming when you want to be."

"I've heard the same," Jace said, breaking into a backward jog. He was even graceful doing that, Clary thought gloomily. And sexy. Definitely sexy. She lifted her hand in a halfhearted wave.

"See you later," she called. *If I'm not dead from frustration by then.*

The Frays had never been a religiously observant family, but Clary loved Fifth Avenue at Christmastime. The air smelled like sweet roasted chestnuts, and the window displays sparkled with silver and blue, green and red. This year there were fat round crystal snow-flakes attached to each lamppost, sending back the winter sunlight in shafts of gold. Not to mention the huge tree at Rockefeller Center. It threw its shadow across them when she and Simon draped them-selves over the gate at the side of the skating rink, watching tourists fall down as they tried to navigate the ice.

Clary had a hot chocolate wrapped in her hands, the warmth spreading through her body. She felt almost normal—this, coming to Fifth to see the window displays and the tree, had been a winter tradition for her and Simon for as long as she could remember.

"Feels like old times, doesn't it?" he said, echoing her thoughts as he propped his chin on his folded arms.

She chanced a sideways look at him. He was wearing a black topcoat and scarf that emphasized the pallor of his skin. His eyes were shadowed, indicating that he hadn't fed on blood recently. He looked like what he was—a hungry, tired vampire.

Well, she thought. Almost *like old times.* "More people to buy presents for," she said. "Plus, the always traumatic what-to-buy-someone-for-the-first-Christmas-after-you've-started-dating question."

"What to get the Shadowhunter who has everything," Simon said with a grin.

"Jace mostly likes weapons," Clary said. "He likes books, but they have a huge library at the Institute. He likes classical music..." She brightened. Simon was a musician; even though his band was terrible, and was always changing their name—currently they were Lethal Soufflé—he did have training. "What would you give someone who likes to play the piano?"

"A piano."

"*Simon.*"

"A really huge metronome that could also double as a weapon?"

Clary sighed, exasperated.

"Sheet music. Rachmaninoff is tough stuff, but he likes a challenge."

"Good idea. I'm going to see if there's a music store around here." Clary, done with her hot chocolate, tossed the cup into a nearby trash can and pulled her phone out. "What about you? What are you giving Isabelle?"

"I have absolutely no idea," Simon said. They had started heading toward the avenue, where a steady stream of pedestrians gawking at the windows clogged the streets.

"Oh, come on. Isabelle's easy."

"That's my girlfriend you're talking about." Simon's brows drew together. "I think. I'm not sure. We haven't discussed it. The relationship, I mean."

"You really have to DTR, Simon."

"What?"

"Define the relationship. What it is, where it's going. Are you boyfriend and girlfriend, just having fun, 'it's complicated,' or what? When's she going to tell her parents? Are you allowed to see other people?"

Simon blanched. "What? Seriously?"

"Seriously. In the meantime—perfume!" Clary grabbed Simon by the back of his coat and hauled him into a cosmetics store. It was massive on the inside, with rows of gleaming bottles everywhere. "And something unusual," she said, heading for the fragrance area. "Isabelle isn't going to want to smell like everyone else. She's going to want to smell like figs, or vetiver, or—"

"Figs? Figs have a smell?" Simon looked horrified; Clary was about to laugh at him when her phone buzzed. It was her mother.

WHERE ARE YOU?

Clary rolled her eyes and texted back. Jocelyn still got nervous when she thought Clary was out with Jace. Even though, as Clary had pointed out, Jace was probably the safest boyfriend in the world since he was pretty much banned from (1) getting angry, (2) making sexual advances, and (3) doing anything that would produce an adrenaline rush.

On the other hand, he *had* been possessed; she and her mother had both watched while he'd stood by and let Sebastian threaten Luke. Clary still hadn't talked about everything she'd seen in the apartment she'd shared with Jace and Sebastian for that brief time out of time, a mixture of dream and nightmare. She'd never told her mother that Jace had killed someone; there were things Jocelyn didn't need to know, things Clary didn't want to face herself.

"There is so much in this store I can picture Magnus wanting," Simon said, picking up a glass bottle of body glitter suspended in some kind of oil. "Is it against some kind of rule to buy presents for someone who broke up with your friend?"

"I guess it depends. Is Magnus your closer friend, or Alec?"

"Alec remembers my name," said Simon, and he set the bottle back down. "And I feel bad for him. I understand why Magnus did it, but Alec is *so* wrecked. I feel like if someone loves you, they should forgive you, if you're really sorry."

"I think it depends what you did," Clary said. "I don't mean Alec—I just mean in general. I'm sure Isabelle would forgive you for anything," she added hastily.

Simon looked dubious.

"Hold still," she announced, wielding a bottle near his head. "In three minutes I'm going to smell your neck."

"Well, I never," said Simon. "You've waited a long time to make your move, Fray, I'll say that for you."

Clary didn't bother with a smart retort; she was still thinking of what Simon had said about forgiveness, and remembering someone else, someone else's voice and face and eyes. Sebastian sitting across from her at a table in Paris. *Do you think you can forgive me? I mean, do you think forgiveness is possible for someone like me?*

"There are things you can never forgive," she said. "I can never forgive Sebastian."

"You don't love him."

"No, but he's my brother. If things were different—" *But they're not different.* Clary abandoned the thought, and leaned in to inhale instead. "You smell like figs and apricots."

"Do you really think Isabelle wants to smell like a dried fruit plate?"

"Maybe not." Clary picked up another bottle. "So, what are you going to do?"

"When?"

Clary looked up from pondering the question of how a tuberose was different from a regular rose, to see Simon looking at her with puzzlement in his brown eyes. She said, "Well, you can't live with Jordan forever, right? There's college..."

"You're not going to college," he said.

"No, but I'm a Shadowhunter. We keep studying after eighteen, we get posted to other Institutes—that's our college."

"I don't like the thought of you going away." He shoved his hands into the pockets of his coat. "I can't go to college," he said. "My mother's not exactly going to pay for it, and I can't take out student loans. I'm legally dead. And besides, how long would it take everyone at school to notice they were getting older but I wasn't? Sixteen-year-olds don't look like college seniors, I don't know if you've noticed."

Clary set the bottle down. "Simon..."

"Maybe I should get my mom something," he said bitterly. "What says 'Thanks for throwing me out of the house and pretending I died'?"

"Orchids?"

But Simon's joking mood had gone. "Maybe it's not like old times," he said. "I would have gotten you pencils usually, art supplies, but you don't draw anymore, do you, except with your stele? You don't draw, and I don't breathe. Not so much like last year."

"Maybe you should talk to Raphael," Clary said.

"*Raphael?*"

"He knows how vampires live," Clary said. "How they make lives for themselves, how they make money, how they get apartments—he does know those things. He could help."

"He could, but he wouldn't," said Simon with a frown. "I haven't heard anything from the Dumort bunch since Maureen took over from Camille. I know Raphael is her second in command. I'm pretty sure they still think I have the Mark of Cain; otherwise they would have sent someone after me by now. Matter of time."

"No. They know not to touch you. It would be war with the

Clave. The Institute's been *very* clear," said Clary. "You're protected."

"Clary," Simon said. "None of us are protected."

Before Clary could answer, she heard someone call out her name; thoroughly puzzled, she looked over and saw her mother shoving her way through a crowd of shoppers. Through the window she could see Luke, waiting outside on the sidewalk. In his flannel shirt he looked out of place among the stylish New Yorkers.

Breaking free of the crowd, Jocelyn caught up to them and threw her arms around Clary. Clary looked over her mother's shoulder, baffled, at Simon. He shrugged. Finally Jocelyn released her and stepped back. "I was so worried something had happened to you—"

"In *Sephora?*" Clary said.

Jocelyn's brow furrowed. "You haven't heard? I would have thought Jace would have texted you by now."

Clary felt a sudden cold wash through her veins, as if she'd swallowed icy water. "No. I—What's going on?"

"I'm sorry, Simon," Jocelyn said. "But Clary and I have to get to the Institute right away."

Not much had changed at Magnus's since the first time Jace had been there. The same small entryway and single yellow bulb. Jace used an Open rune to get in through the front door, took the stairs two at a time, and buzzed Magnus's apartment bell. Safer than using another rune, he figured. After all, Magnus could be playing video games naked or, really, doing practically anything. Who knew what warlocks got up to in their spare time?

Jace buzzed again, this time leaning firmly on the doorbell. Two more long buzzes, and Magnus finally yanked the door open, looking furious. He was wearing a black silk dressing gown over a white dress shirt and tweed pants. His feet were bare. His dark hair was tangled, and there was the shadow of stubble on his jaw. "What are you doing here?" he demanded.

"My, my," said Jace. "So unwelcoming."

"That's because you're not welcome."

Jace raised an eyebrow. "I thought we were friends."

"No. You're Alec's friend. Alec was my boyfriend, so I had to put up with you. But now he's not my boyfriend, so I don't have to put up with you. Not that any of you seem to realize it. You must be the—what, fourth?—of your lot to bother me." Magnus counted off on his long fingers. "Clary. Isabelle. Simon—"

"*Simon* came by?"

"You seem surprised."

"I didn't think he was that invested in your relationship with Alec."

"I don't *have* a relationship with Alec," said Magnus flatly, but Jace had already shouldered past him and was in his living room, looking around curiously.

One of the things Jace had always secretly liked about Magnus's apartment was that it rarely looked the same way twice. Sometimes it was a big modern loft. Sometimes it looked like a French bordello, or a Victorian opium den, or the inside of a spaceship. Right now, though, it was messy and dark. Stacks of old Chinese food cartons littered the coffee table. Chairman Meow lay on the rag rug, all four legs sticking straight out in front of him like a dead deer.

"It smells like heartbreak in here," said Jace.

"That's the Chinese food." Magnus threw himself onto the sofa and stretched out his long legs. "Go on, get it over with. Say whatever you came here to say."

"I think you should get back together with Alec," said Jace.

Magnus rolled his eyes up to the ceiling. "And why is that?"

"Because he's miserable," said Jace. "And he's sorry. He's sorry about what he did. He won't do it again."

"Oh, he won't sneak around behind my back with one of my exes planning to shorten my life *again*? Very noble of him."

"Magnus—"

"Besides, Camille's dead. He *can't* do it again."

"You know what I mean," said Jace. "He won't lie to you or mislead you or hide things from you or whatever it is you're actually upset about." He threw himself into a wingback leather chair and raised an eyebrow. "So?"

Magnus rolled onto his side. "What do you care if Alec's miserable?"

"What do I *care*?" Jace said, so loudly that Chairman Meow sat bolt upright as if he'd been shocked. "Of course I care about Alec; he's my best friend, my *parabatai*. And he's unhappy. And so are you, by the look of things. Take-out containers everywhere, you haven't done anything to fix up the place, your cat looks dead—"

"He's not dead."

"I care about Alec," Jace said, fixing Magnus with an unswerving gaze. "I care about him more than I care about myself."

"Don't you ever think," Magnus mused, pulling at a bit of peeling fingernail polish, "that the whole *parabatai* business is rather cruel? You can choose your *parabatai*, but then you can never unchoose them. Even if they turn on you. Look at Luke and Valentine. And though your *parabatai* is the closest person in the world to you in some ways, you can't fall in love with them. And if they die, some part of you dies too."

"How do you know so much about *parabatai*?"

"I know Shadowhunters," said Magnus, patting the sofa beside him so that the Chairman leaped up onto the cushions and nudged at Magnus with his head. The warlock's long fingers sank into the cat's fur. "I have for a long time. You are odd creatures. All fragile nobility and humanity on one side, and all the thoughtless fire of angels on the other." His eyes flicked toward Jace. "You especially, Herondale, for you have the fire of angels in your blood."

"You've been friends with Shadowhunters before?"

"Friends," said Magnus. "What does that mean, really?"

"You'd know," said Jace, "if you had any. Do you? Do you have friends? I mean, besides the people who come to your parties. Most people are afraid of you, or they seem to owe you something or you slept with them once, but friends—I don't see you having a lot of those."

"Well, this is novel," said Magnus. "None of the rest of your group has tried insulting me."

"Is it working?"

"If you mean do I suddenly feel compelled to get back together with Alec, no," said Magnus. "I have developed an odd craving for pizza, but that might be unrelated."

"Alec said you do that," said Jace. "Deflect questions about yourself with jokes."

Magnus narrowed his eyes. "And I'm the *only* one who does that?"

"Exactly," Jace said. "Take it from someone who knows. You hate talking about yourself, and you'd rather make people angry than be pitied. How old are you, Magnus? The real answer."

Magnus said nothing.

"What were your parents' names? Your father's name?"

Magnus glared at him out of gold-green eyes. "If I wanted to lie on a couch and complain to someone about my parents, I'd hire a psychiatrist."

"Ah," said Jace. "But my services are free."

"I heard that about you."

Jace grinned and slid down in his chair. There was a pillow with a pattern of the Union Jack on the ottoman. He grabbed it and put it behind his head. "I don't have anywhere to be. I can sit here all day."

"Great," Magnus said. "I'm going to take a nap." He reached out for a crumpled blanket lying on the floor, just as Jace's phone rang.

Magnus watched, arrested midmotion, as Jace dug around in his pocket and flipped the phone open.

It was Isabelle. "Jace?"

"Yeah. I'm at Magnus's place. I think I might be making some headway. What's up?"

"Come back," Isabelle said, and Jace sat up straight, the pillow tumbling to the floor. Her voice was tightly strained. He could hear the sharpness in it, like the off notes of a badly tuned piano. "To the Institute. Right away, Jace."

"What is it?" he asked. "What's happened?" And he saw Magnus sit up too, the blanket dropping from his hand.

"Sebastian," Isabelle said.

Jace closed his eyes. He saw golden blood, and white feathers scattered across a marble floor. He remembered the apartment, a knife in his hands, the world at his feet, Sebastian's grip on his wrist, those fathomless black eyes looking at him with dark amusement. There was a buzzing in his ears.

"What is it?" Magnus's voice cut through Jace's thoughts. He realized he was already at the door, the phone back in his pocket. He turned. Magnus was behind him, his expression stark. "Is it Alec? Is he all right?"

"What do you care?" said Jace, and Magnus flinched. Jace didn't think he'd ever seen Magnus flinch before. It was the only thing that kept Jace from slamming the door on the way out.

There were dozens of unfamiliar coats and jackets hanging in the entryway of the Institute. Clary felt the tight buzzing of tension in her shoulders as she unzipped her own wool coat and hung it on one of the hooks that lined the walls.

"And Maryse didn't say what this was about?" Clary demanded. The edges of her voice had been rubbed thin by anxiety.

Jocelyn had unwound a long gray scarf from around her neck,

and barely looked as Luke took it from her to drape it on a hook. Her green eyes were darting around the room, taking in the gate of the elevator, the arched ceiling overhead, the faded murals of men and angels.

Luke shook his head. "Just that there'd been an attack on the Clave, and we needed to get here as quickly as possible."

"It's the 'we' part that concerns me." Jocelyn wound her hair up into a knot at the back of her head, and secured it with her fingers. "I haven't been in an Institute in years. Why do they want me here?"

Luke squeezed her shoulder reassuringly. Clary knew what Jocelyn feared, what they all feared. The only reason the Clave would want Jocelyn here was if there was news of her son.

"Maryse said they'd be in the library," Jocelyn said. Clary led the way. She could hear Luke and her mother talking behind her, and the soft sound of their footsteps, Luke's slower than they had once been. He hadn't entirely recovered from the injury that had nearly killed him in November.

You know why you're here, don't you, breathed a soft voice in the back of her head. She knew it wasn't really there, but that didn't help. She hadn't seen her brother since the fight at the Burren, but she carried him in some small part of her mind, an intrusive, unwelcome ghost. *Because of me. You always knew I hadn't gone away forever. I told you what would happen. I spelled it out for you.*

Erchomai.

I am coming.

They had reached the library. The door was half-open, and a babble of voices spilled through. Jocelyn paused for a moment, her expression tight.

Clary put her hand on the doorknob. "Are you ready?" She hadn't noticed till then what her mother was wearing: black jeans, boots, and a black turtleneck. As if, without thinking of it, she had put on the closest thing she had to fighting gear.

Jocelyn nodded at her daughter.

Someone had pushed back all the furniture in the library, clearing a large space in the middle of the room, just atop the mosaic of the Angel. A massive table had been placed there, a huge slab of marble balanced on top of two kneeling stone angels. Around the table were seated the Conclave. Some members, like Kadir and Maryse, Clary knew by name. Others were just familiar faces. Maryse was standing, ticking off names on her fingers as she chanted aloud. "Berlin," she said. "No survivors. Bangkok. No survivors. Moscow. No survivors. Los Angeles—"

"Los Angeles?" said Jocelyn. "That was the Blackthorns. Are they—"

Maryse looked startled, as if she hadn't realized Jocelyn had come in. Her blue eyes swept over Luke and Clary. She looked drawn and exhausted, her hair scraped back severely, a stain—red wine or blood?—on the sleeve of her tailored jacket. "There were survivors," she said. "Children. They're in Idris now."

"Helen," said Alec, and Clary thought of the girl who had fought with them against Sebastian at the Burren. She remembered her in the nave of the Institute, a dark-haired boy clinging to her wrist. *My brother, Julian.*

"Aline's girlfriend," Clary blurted out, and saw the Conclave look at her with thinly veiled hostility. They always did, as if who she was and what she represented made them almost unable to see her. *Valentine's daughter. Valentine's daughter.* "Is she all right?"

"She was in Idris, with Aline," said Maryse. "Her younger brothers and sisters survived, although there seems to have been an issue with the eldest brother, Mark."

"An issue?" said Luke. "What's going on, exactly, Maryse?"

"I don't think we'll know the whole story until we get to Idris," said Maryse, smoothing back her already smooth hair. "But there have been attacks, several in the course of two nights, on six

Institutes. We're not sure yet how the Institutes were breached, but we know—"

"Sebastian," said Clary's mother. She had her hands jammed into the pockets of her black trousers, but Clary suspected that if she hadn't, Clary would have been able to see that her mother's hands were tightened into fists. "Cut to the point, Maryse. My son. You wouldn't have called me here if he wasn't responsible. Would you?" Jocelyn's eyes met Maryse's, and Clary wondered if this was how it had been when they'd both been in the Circle, the sharp edges of their personalities rubbing up against each other, causing sparks.

Before Maryse could speak, the door opened and Jace came in. He was flushed with the cold, bareheaded, fair hair tousled by the wind. His hands were gloveless, red at the tips from the weather, scarred with Marks new and old. He saw Clary and gave her a quick smile before settling into a chair propped against the wall.

Luke, as usual, moved to make peace. "Maryse? Is Sebastian responsible?"

Maryse took a deep breath. "Yes, yes he was. And he had the Endarkened with him."

"Of course it's Sebastian," said Isabelle. She had been staring down at the table; now she raised her head. Her face was a mask of hatred and rage. "He said he was coming; well, now he's come."

Maryse sighed. "We assumed he'd attack Idris. That was what all the intelligence indicated. Not Institutes."

"So he did the thing you didn't expect," said Jace. "He always does the thing you don't expect. Maybe the Clave should plan for *that*." Jace's voice dropped. "I told you. I told you he'd want more soldiers."

"Jace," said Maryse. "You're not helping."

"I wasn't trying to."

"I would have thought he'd attack here first," said Alec. "Given what Jace was saying before, and it's true—everyone he loves or hates is here."

"He doesn't *love* anyone," Jocelyn snapped.

"Mom, stop," Clary said. Her heart was pounding, sick in her chest; yet at the same time there was a strange sense of relief. All this time waiting for Sebastian to come, and now he had. Now the waiting was over. Now the war would start. "So what are we supposed to do? Fortify the Institute? *Hide?*"

"Let me guess," said Jace, his voice dripping sarcasm. "The Clave's called for a Council. Another meeting."

"The Clave has called for immediate evacuation," said Maryse, and at that, everyone went silent, even Jace. "All Institutes are to empty out. All Conclaves must return to Alicante. The wards around Idris will be doubled after tomorrow. No one will be able to come in or get out."

Isabelle swallowed. "When do we leave New York?"

Maryse straightened up. Some of her usual imperious air was back, her mouth a thin line, her jaw set with determination. "Go and pack," she said. "We leave tonight."

2

STAND OR FALL

Waking was like being plunged into a bath of icy water. Emma sat up straight, torn out of sleep, her mouth opening on a scream. "Jules! *Jules!*"

There was movement in the darkness, a hand on her arm, and a sudden light that stung her eyes. Emma gasped and scrabbled backward, pushing herself among the cushions—she was lying on a bed, she realized, pillows stacked behind her back and the sheets twisted around her body in a sweaty tangle. She blinked the darkness out of her eyes, trying to focus.

Helen Blackthorn was leaning over her, blue-green eyes worried, a witchlight glowing in her hand. They were in a room with a steeply gabled roof, slanting down hard on either side, like in a fairytale cabin. A big four-poster wooden bed was in the center of the room, and in the shadows behind Helen, Emma could see furniture looming: a big square wardrobe, a long sofa, a table with rickety legs. "W-where am I?" Emma gasped.

"Idris," Helen said, stroking her arm in a soothing manner. "You made it to Idris, Emma. We're in the attic of the Penhallows' house."

"M-my parents." Emma's teeth chattered. "Where are my parents?"

"You came through the Portal with Julian," said Helen gently, not answering her question. "All of you made it through somehow—it's a miracle, you know. The Clave opened the way, but Portal travel is hard. Dru came through holding on to Tavvy, and the twins came through together, of course. And then, when we'd almost given up hope, you two. You were unconscious, Em." She brushed Emma's hair back from her forehead. "We were so worried. You should have seen Jules—"

"What's *happening?*" Emma demanded. She pulled back from Helen's touch, not because she didn't like Helen but because her heart was pounding. "What about Mark, and Mr. Blackthorn—"

Helen hesitated. "Sebastian Morgenstern has attacked six Institutes over the past few days. He's either killed everyone or Turned them. He can use the Infernal Cup to make Shadowhunters—not themselves anymore."

"I saw him do it," Emma whispered. "To Katerina. And he Turned your father, too. They were going to do it to Mark, but Sebastian said he didn't want him because he had faerie blood."

Helen flinched. "We have reason to think Mark's still alive," she said. "They were able to track him to a point where he disappeared, but the runes indicate he's not dead. It's possible that Sebastian may be holding him hostage."

"My—my parents," Emma said again, through a dryer throat this time. She knew what it meant that Helen hadn't answered her question the first time she'd asked it. "Where are they? They weren't in the Institute, so Sebastian couldn't have hurt them."

"Em..." Helen exhaled. She looked young suddenly, almost as young as Jules. "Sebastian doesn't just attack Institutes; he murders or takes Conclave members from their own homes. Your parents—the Clave tried to track them, but they couldn't. Then their bodies washed up in Marina del Rey, on the beach, this morning. The Clave doesn't know what happened exactly, but..."

Helen's voice trailed off into a meaningless string of words, words such as "positive identification" and "scars and markings on the bodies" and "no evidence recovered." Things like "in the water for hours" and "no way to transport the corpses" and "given all the proper funeral rites, burned on the beach as they had both requested, you understand—"

Emma screamed. It was a scream with no words at first, rising higher and higher, a scream that tore her throat and brought the taste of metal into her mouth. It was a scream of loss so immense there was no speech for it. It was the wordless cry of having the sky over your head, the air in your lungs, ripped away from you forever. She screamed, and screamed again, and tore at the mattress with her hands until she gouged through it, and there were feathers and blood stuck under her fingernails, and Helen was sobbing, trying to hold her, saying, "Emma, Emma, please, Emma, please."

And then there was more illumination. Someone had turned on a lantern in the room, and Emma heard her name, in a soft urgent familiar voice, and Helen let her go and there was Jules, leaning against the edge of the bed, and holding something out to her, something that gleamed gold in the new harsh light.

It was Cortana. Unsheathed, lying bare across his palms like an offering. Emma thought she was still screaming, but she took the sword, the words flashing across the blade, burning across her eyes: *I am Cortana, of the same steel and temper as Joyeuse and Durendal.*

She heard her father's voice in her head. *Carstairs have carried this sword for generations. The inscription reminds us that Shadowhunters are the Angel's weapons. Temper us in the fire, and we grow stronger. When we suffer, we survive.*

Emma choked, pushing back on the screams, forcing them down and into silence. This was what her father had meant: Like Cortana, she had steel in her veins and she was meant to be strong. Even if her parents were not there to see it, she would be strong for them.

She hugged the sword against her chest. As if from a distance she heard Helen exclaim and reach for her, but Julian, Julian who always knew what Emma needed, tugged Helen's hand back. Emma's fingers were around the blade, and blood was running down her arms and chest where the tip sliced at her collarbone. She didn't feel it. Rocking back and forth, she clutched the sword like it was the only thing she had ever loved, and let the blood spill down instead of tears.

Simon couldn't quite shake a feeling of déjà vu.

He'd been here before, standing just outside the Institute, watching the Lightwoods disappear through a shimmering Portal. Though then, back before he had ever borne the Mark of Cain, the Portal had been created by Magnus, and this time it was under the oversight of a blue-skinned warlock woman named Catarina Loss. That time, he'd been summoned because Jace had wanted to talk to him about Clary before he disappeared into another country.

This time Clary was disappearing with them.

He felt her hand on his, her fingers lightly ringing his wrist. The whole of the Conclave—nearly every Shadowhunter in New York City—had come through the gates of the Institute and passed through the shimmering Portal. The Lightwoods, as guardians of the Institute, would go last. Simon had been here since the start of twilight, bars of red sky sliding down behind the buildings of the New York skyline, and now witchlight lit the scene in front of him, picking out small glimmering details: Isabelle's whip, the spark of fire that jumped from Alec's family ring as he gestured, the glints in Jace's pale hair.

"It looks different," Simon said.

Clary looked up at him. Like the rest of the Shadowhunters,

she was dressed in what Simon could only describe as a cloak. It seemed to be what they broke out during cold winter weather, made of a heavy, velvety black material that buckled across the chest. He wondered where she'd gotten it. Maybe they just issued them. "What does?"

"The Portal," he said. "It looks different from when Magnus did it. More—blue."

"Maybe they all have different senses of style?"

Simon looked over at Catarina. She seemed briskly efficient, like a hospital nurse or kindergarten teacher. Definitely not like Magnus. "How's Izzy?"

"Worried, I think. Everyone's worried."

There was a short silence. Clary exhaled, her breath floating white on the winter air.

"I don't like you going," Simon said, at exactly the same time that Clary said, "I don't like going and leaving you here."

"I'll be fine," Simon said. "I have Jordan looking after me." Indeed, Jordan was there, sitting on top of the wall that ran around the Institute and looking watchful. "And no one's tried to kill me in at least two weeks."

"Not funny." Clary scowled. The problem, Simon reflected, was that it was difficult to reassure someone that you'd be fine when you were a Daylighter. Some vampires might want Simon on their side, eager to benefit from his unusual powers. Camille had attempted to recruit him, and others might try, but Simon had the distinct impression that the vast majority of vampires wanted to kill him.

"I'm pretty sure Maureen's still hoping to get her hands on me," Simon said. Maureen was the head of the New York vampire clan and believed that she was in love with Simon. Which would have been less awkward if she hadn't been thirteen years old. "I know the Clave warned people not to touch me, but…"

"Maureen wants to touch you," Clary said with a sideways grin. "Bad touch."

"Silence, Fray."

"Jordan will keep her off you."

Simon looked ahead meditatively. He had been trying not to stare at Isabelle, who had greeted him with only a brief wave since he'd arrived at the Institute. She was helping her mother, her black hair flying in the brisk wind.

"You could just go up and talk to her," Clary said. "Instead of staring like a creeper."

"I'm not staring like a creeper. I'm staring subtly."

"I noticed," Clary pointed out. "Look, you know how Isabelle gets. When she's upset, she withdraws. She won't talk to anyone but Jace or Alec, because she hardly trusts anyone. But if you're going to be her boyfriend, you have to show her you're one of those people she can trust."

"I'm not her boyfriend. At least, I don't think I'm her boyfriend. She's never used the word 'boyfriend,' anyway."

Clary kicked him in the ankle. "You two need to DTR more than any other people I've ever met."

"Defining relationships over here?" said a voice from behind them. Simon turned and saw Magnus, very tall against the dark sky behind them. He was soberly dressed, jeans and a black T-shirt, his dark hair partly in his eyes. "I see that even as the world plunges into darkness and peril, you two stand around discussing your love lives. Teenagers."

"What are you doing here?" Simon said, too surprised for a smart comeback.

"Came to see Alec," Magnus said.

Clary raised her eyebrows at him. "What was that about teenagers?"

Magnus held up a warning finger. "Don't overstep yourself,

biscuit," he said, and moved past them, disappearing into the crowd around the Portal.

"Biscuit?" said Simon.

"Believe it or not, he's called me that before," Clary said. "Simon, look." She turned toward him, tugging his hand out of his jeans pocket. She looked down at it and smiled. "The ring," she said. "Handy when it worked, wasn't it?"

Simon looked down as well. A hammered gold ring in the shape of a leaf encircled his right ring finger. It had once been a connection to Clary. Now, with hers destroyed, it was only a ring, but he kept it regardless. He knew it was a little close to having half of a BFF necklace, but he couldn't help it. It was a beautiful object, and still a symbol of the connection between them.

She squeezed his hand hard, raising her eyes to his. Shadows moved in the green of her irises; he could tell she was afraid. "I know it's just a Council meeting—" Clary started to say.

"But you're staying in Idris."

"Only until they can figure out what happened with the Institutes, and how to protect them," said Clary. "Then we'll come back. I know phones and texting and all that, that doesn't work in Idris, but if you need to talk to me, tell Magnus. He'll find a way to get me a message."

Simon felt his throat tighten. "Clary—"

"I love you," she said. "You're my best friend." She let go of his hand, her eyes shining. "No, don't say anything, I don't want you to say anything." She turned and almost ran back toward the Portal, where Jocelyn and Luke were waiting for her, three packed duffel bags at their feet. Luke glanced across the courtyard at Simon, his expression thoughtful.

But where was Isabelle? The crowd of Shadowhunters had thinned. Jace had moved to stand beside Clary, his hand on her shoulder; Maryse was near the Portal, but Isabelle, who had been with her—

"Simon," said a voice at his shoulder, and he turned to see Izzy, her face a pale smudge between dark hair and dark cloak, looking at him, her expression half-angry, half-sad. "I guess this is the part where we say good-bye?"

"Okay," Magnus said. "You wanted to talk to me. So talk."

Alec looked at him, wide-eyed. They had gone around the side of the church and were standing in a small, winter-burned garden, among leafless hedges. Thick vines covered the stone wall and rusted gate nearby, now so denuded by winter that Alec could see the mundane street through the gaps in the iron door. A stone bench was nearby, its rough surface crusted with ice. "I wanted—What?"

Magnus looked at him darkly, as if he had done something stupid. Alec suspected that he had. His nerves were jangling together like wind chimes, and he had a sick feeling in the pit of his stomach. The last time he had seen Magnus, the warlock had been walking away from him, vanishing into a disused subway tunnel, getting smaller and smaller until he disappeared. *Aku cinta kamu*, he'd said to Alec. "I love you," in Indonesian.

It had given Alec a spark of hope, enough that he'd called Magnus dozens of times, enough to keep him checking his phone, checking the mail, even checking the windows of his room—which seemed strange and empty and unfamiliar without Magnus in it, not his room at all—for magically delivered notes or messages.

And now Magnus was standing in front of him, with his raggedy black hair and slit-pupilled cat eyes, and his voice like dark molasses, and his cool, sharp beautiful face that gave nothing whatsoever away, and Alec felt like he had swallowed glue.

"Wanted to talk to me," Magnus said. "I assumed that was the meaning of all those phone calls. And why you sent all your stupid friends over to my apartment. Or do you just do that to everyone?"

Alec swallowed against the dryness in his throat and said the first thing that came into his head. "Aren't you ever going to forgive me?"

"I—" Magnus broke off and looked away, shaking his head. "Alec. I *have* forgiven you."

"It doesn't seem like it. You seem angry."

When Magnus looked back at him, it was with a gentler expression. "I'm worried about you," he said. "The attacks on the Institutes. I just heard."

Alec felt dizzy. Magnus forgave him; Magnus was worried about him. "Did you know we were leaving for Idris?"

"Catarina told me she'd been summoned to make a Portal. I guessed," Magnus said wryly. "I was a little surprised you hadn't called or texted to tell me you were going away."

"You never answer my calls or texts," said Alec.

"That hasn't stopped you before."

"Everyone gives up eventually," Alec said. "Besides. Jace broke my phone."

Magnus huffed out a breath of laughter. "Oh, Alexander."

"What?" Alec asked, honestly puzzled.

"You're just—You're so—I really want to kiss you," Magnus said abruptly, and then shook his head. "See, this is why I haven't been willing to see you."

"But you're here now," Alec said. He remembered the first time Magnus had ever kissed him, against the wall outside his apartment, and all his bones had turned to liquid and he'd thought, *Oh, right, this is what it's supposed to be like. I get it now.* "You could—"

"I can't," Magnus said. "It's not working, it wasn't working. You have to see that, don't you?" His hands were on Alec's shoulders; Alec could feel Magnus's thumb brush against his neck, over his collar, and his whole body jumped. "Don't you?" Magnus said, and kissed him.

Alec leaned into the kiss. It was utterly quiet. He heard the crunch of his boots on the snowy ground as he moved forward,

Magnus's hand sliding around to steady the back of his neck, and Magnus tasted like he always did, sweet and bitter and familiar, and Alec parted his lips, to gasp or breathe or breathe Magnus in, but it was too late because Magnus broke away from him with a wrench and stepped backward and it was over.

"What," Alec said, feeling stunned and strangely diminished. "Magnus, what?"

"I shouldn't have done that," Magnus said, all in a rush. He was clearly agitated, in a way Alec had rarely seen him, a flush along his high cheekbones. "I forgive you, but I can't be with you. I can't. It doesn't work. I'm going to live forever, or at least until someone finally kills me, and you're not, and it's too much for you to take on—"

"Don't tell me what's too much for me," said Alec with deadly flatness.

Magnus so rarely looked surprised that the expression seemed almost foreign on his face. "It's too much for most people," he said. "Most mortals. And not easy on us, either. Watching someone you love age and die. I knew a girl, once, immortal like me—"

"And she was with someone mortal?" said Alec. "What happened?"

"He died," Magnus said. There was a finality to the way he said it that spoke of a deeper grief than words could paint. His cat's eyes shone in the dark. "I don't know why I thought this would ever work," he said. "I'm sorry, Alec. I shouldn't have come."

"No," Alec said. "You shouldn't."

Magnus was looking at Alec a little warily, as if he had approached someone familiar on the street only to find out they were a stranger.

"I don't know why you did," Alec said. "I know I've been tor-turing myself for weeks now about you, and what I did, and how I shouldn't have done it, shouldn't ever have talked to Camille. I've been sorry and I've understood and I've apologized and apologized, and *you haven't ever been there*. I did all that without you. So it makes me wonder what else I could do, without you." He looked at Magnus meditatively. "It was my fault, what happened. But it was your fault too. I could have learned not to care that you're immortal and I'm mortal. Everyone gets the time they get together, and no more. Maybe we're not so different that way. But you know what I can't get past? That you never tell me anything. I don't know when you were born. I don't know anything about your life—what your real name is, or about your family, or what the first face you ever loved was, or the first time your heart was broken. You know everything about me, and I know nothing about you. That's the real problem."

"I told you," Magnus said softly, "on our first date that you would have to take me as I came, no questions—"

Alec waved that away. "That's not a fair thing to ask, and you know—you knew—I didn't understand enough about love then to understand that. You act like you're the wronged party, but you had a hand in this, Magnus."

"Yes," Magnus said after a pause. "Yes, I suppose I did."

"But that doesn't change anything?" Alec said, feeling the cold air stealing under his rib cage. "It never does, with you."

"I can't change," Magnus said. "It's been too long. We petrify, you know, immortals, like fossils turn to stone. I thought when I met you that you had all this wonder and all this joy and everything was new to you, and I thought it would change me, but—"

"Change yourself," Alec said, but it didn't come out angry, or stern, as he had intended it, but soft, like a plea.

But Magnus only shook his head. "Alec," he said. "You know my dream. The one about the city made of blood, and blood in the streets, and towers of bone. If Sebastian gets what he wants, that will be this world. The blood will be Nephilim blood. Go to Idris. You're safer there, but don't be trusting, and don't let your guard down. I need you to live," he breathed, and turned around, very abruptly, and walked away.

I need you to live.

Alec sat down on the frozen stone bench and put his face in his hands.

"Not good-bye forever," Simon protested, but Isabelle just frowned.

"Come here," she said, and tugged at his sleeve. She was wearing dark red velvet gloves, and her hand looked like a splash of blood against the navy fabric of his jacket.

Simon pushed the thought away. He wished he wouldn't think about blood at inopportune times. "Come where?"

Isabelle just rolled her eyes and pulled him sideways, into a shadowed alcove near the front gates of the Institute. The space wasn't a large one, and Simon could feel the heat from Isabelle's body—warmth and cold didn't affect him since he'd become a vampire, unless it was the heat of blood. He didn't know if it was because he'd drunk Isabelle's blood before, or if it was something deeper, but he was aware of the pulse of blood through her veins the way he was of no one else's.

"I wish I were coming with you to Idris," he said without preamble.

"You're safer here," she said, though her dark eyes softened. "Besides, we're not going forever. The only Downworlders who can go to Alicante are Council members because they're going to have a meeting, figure out what we're all going to do, and probably send us back out. We can't hide in Idris while Sebastian rampages around outside it. Shadowhunters don't do that."

He stroked a finger down her cheek. "But you want me to hide here?"

"You've got Jordan to watch you here," she said. "Your own personal bodyguard. You're Clary's best friend," she added. "Sebastian knows that. You're hostage material. You should be where he isn't."

"He's never shown any interest in me before. I don't see why he'd start now."

She shrugged, pulling her cloak tighter around herself. "He's never shown any interest in anyone but Clary and Jace, but that doesn't mean he won't start. He's not stupid." She said it grudgingly, as if she hated to give Sebastian even that much credit. "Clary would do anything for you."

"She'd do anything for you, too, Izzy." And at Isabelle's doubtful look, he cupped her cheek. "Okay, so if you won't be gone all that long, what's all this about, then?"

She made a face. Her cheeks and mouth were rosy, the cold bringing the red to the surface. He wished he could press his cold lips to hers, so full of blood and life and warmth, but he was conscious of her parents watching. "I heard Clary when she was saying good-bye to you. She said she loved you."

Simon stared. "Yes, but she didn't mean it *that* way—Izzy—"

"I know that," Isabelle protested. "Please, I know that. But it's just that she says it so easily, and you say it back so easily, and I've never said it to anyone. Not anyone who wasn't related to me."

"But if you say it," he said, "you could get hurt. That's why you don't."

"So could you." Her eyes were big and black, reflecting the stars. "Get hurt. I could hurt you."

"I know," Simon said. "I know and I don't care. Jace told me once you'd walk all over my heart in high-heeled boots, and it hasn't stopped me."

Isabelle gave a little gasp of startled laughter. "He said that? And you stuck around?"

He leaned in toward her; if he had breath, it would have stirred her hair. "I would consider it an honor."

She turned her head, and their lips brushed together. Hers

were achingly warm. She was doing something with her hands—unfastening her cloak, he thought for a moment, but surely Isabelle wasn't about to start taking her clothes off in front of her entire family? Not that Simon was sure he'd have the fortitude to stop her. She was Isabelle, after all, and she had almost—*almost*—said she loved him.

Her lips moved against his skin as she spoke. "Take this," she whispered, and he felt something cold at the back of his neck, and the smooth glide of velvet as she drew back and her gloves brushed his throat.

He glanced down. Against his chest gleamed a blood-red square. Isabelle's ruby pendant. It was a Shadowhunter heirloom, enchanted to detect the presence of demonic energy.

"I can't take this," he said, shocked. "Iz, this must be worth a fortune."

She squared her shoulders. "It's a loan, not a gift. Keep it until I see you again." She brushed her gloved fingers across the ruby. "There's an old story that it came into our family by way of a vampire. So it's fitting."

"Isabelle, I—"

"Don't," she said, cutting him off, though he didn't know exactly what he'd been about to say. "Don't say it, not now." She was backing away from him. He could see her family behind her, all that was left of the Conclave. Luke had gone through the Portal, and Jocelyn was in the middle of following him. Alec, coming around the side of the Institute with his hands in his pockets, glanced over at Isabelle and Simon, raised an eyebrow, and kept walking. "Just don't—don't date anyone else while I'm gone, okay?"

He stared after her. "Does that mean we're dating?" he said, but she only quirked a smile and then turned and dashed toward the Portal. He saw her take Alec's hand, and they stepped through together. Maryse followed, and then Jace, and then, finally, Clary was the last, standing beside Catarina, framed by sizzling blue light.

She winked at Simon and stepped through. He saw the whirl of the Portal as it caught her, and then she was gone.

Simon put his hand to the ruby at his throat. He thought he could feel a beat inside the stone, a shifting pulse. It was almost like having a heart again.

3

BIRDS TO THE MOUNTAIN

Clary set her bag down by the door and looked around.

She could hear her mother and Luke moving around her, putting down their own luggage, turning on the witchlights that illuminated Amatis's house. Clary braced herself. They still had little idea how Amatis had been taken by Sebastian. Though the place had already been examined by Council members for dangerous materials, Clary knew her brother. If the mood had taken him, he would have destroyed everything in the house, just to show that he could—turned the sofas to kindling, shattered the glass in the mirrors, blown the windows to smithereens.

She heard her mother give a small exhale of relief and knew Jocelyn must have been thinking what Clary was: Whatever had happened, the house looked fine. There was nothing in it to indicate that harm had come to Amatis. Books were stacked on the coffee table, the floors were dusty but uncluttered, the photographs on the walls were straight. Clary saw with a pang that there was a recent photograph near the fireplace of her, Luke, and Jocelyn at Coney Island, arms around one another, smiling.

She thought of the last time she had seen Luke's sister, Sebastian forcing Amatis to drink from the Infernal Cup as she screamed in protest. The way the personality had faded out of her eyes after she had swallowed its contents. Clary wondered if that was what it was like to watch someone die. Not that she hadn't seen death, too. Valentine had died in front of her. Surely she was too young to have so many ghosts.

Luke had moved to look at the fireplace, and the photos hanging around it. He reached out to touch one that showed two blue-eyed children. One of them, the younger boy, was drawing, while his sister looked on, her expression fond.

Luke looked exhausted. Their Portal travel had taken them to the Gard, and they had walked down through the city to Amatis's house. Luke still winced often from the pain of the wound in his side that hadn't quite healed, but Clary doubted that the injury was what was affecting him. The quiet in Amatis's house, the homey rag rugs on the floor, the carefully arranged personal mementoes—everything spoke of an ordinary life interrupted in the most terrible way possible.

Jocelyn moved over to put her hand on Luke's shoulder, murmuring soothingly. He turned in the circle of her arms, putting his head against her shoulder. It was more comforting than in any way romantic, but Clary still felt as if she had stumbled on a private moment. Soundlessly she plucked up her duffel bag and made her way up the stairs.

The spare room hadn't changed. Small; the walls painted white; the windows, like portholes, circular—there was the window Jace had crawled through one night—and the same colorful quilt on the bed. She dropped her bag onto the floor near the nightstand. The nightstand, where Jace had left a letter in the morning, telling her he was going and he wasn't coming back.

She sat down on the edge of the bed, trying to shake off the web of memories. She hadn't realized how hard it would be to be back in Idris. New York was home, normal. Idris was war and devastation. In Idris she had seen death for the first time.

Her blood was humming, pounding hard in her ears. She wanted to see Jace, to see Alec and Isabelle—they would ground her, give her a sense of normalcy. She was able, very faintly, to hear her mother and Luke moving around downstairs, possibly even the clink of cups in the kitchen. She swung herself off the bed and went to the foot, where a square trunk rested. It was the trunk Amatis had brought up for her when she had been here before, telling her to go through it to find clothes.

She knelt down now and opened it. The same clothes, carefully packed away between layers of paper: school uniforms, practical sweaters and jeans, more formal shirts and skirts, and beneath that a dress Clary had first thought was a wedding gown. She drew it out. Now that she was more familiar with Shadowhunters and their world, she recognized it for what it was.

Mourning clothes. A white dress, simple, and a close-fitting jacket, with silver mourning runes worked into the material—and there, at the cuffs, an almost invisible design of birds.

Herons. Clary laid the clothes carefully on the bed. She could see, in her mind's eye, Amatis wearing these clothes when Stephen Herondale had died. Putting them on carefully, smoothing down the fabric, buttoning the jacket close, all to mourn a man to whom she'd no longer been married. Widow's clothes for someone who had not been able to call herself a widow.

"Clary?" It was her mother, leaning in the doorway, watching her. "What are those—Oh." She crossed the room, touched the fabric of the dress, and sighed. "Oh, Amatis."

"She never did get over Stephen, did she?" asked Clary.

"Sometimes people don't." Jocelyn's hand moved from the dress to Clary's hair, tucked it back with quick motherly precision.

"And Nephilim—we do tend to love very overwhelmingly. To fall in love only once, to die of grief over love—my old tutor used to say that the hearts of Nephilim were like the hearts of angels: They felt every human pain, and never healed."

"But you did. You loved Valentine, but now you love Luke."

"I know." Jocelyn's look was faraway. "It wasn't until I spent more time in the mundane world that I started to realize that it wasn't how most human beings thought of love. I realized that you might have it more than once, that your heart could heal, that you could love over and over again. And I always loved Luke. I might not have known it, but I always did love him." Jocelyn pointed at the clothes on the bed. "You should wear the mourning jacket," she said. "Tomorrow."

Startled, Clary said, "To the meeting?"

"Shadowhunters have died and been turned Dark," said Jocelyn. "Every Shadowhunter lost is someone's son, brother, sister, cousin. Nephilim are a family. A dysfunctional family, but..." She touched her daughter's face, her own expression hidden in the shadows. "Get some sleep, Clary," she said. "Tomorrow is going to be a long day."

After the door shut behind her mother, Clary put on her nightgown and then clambered obediently into bed. She shut her eyes and tried to sleep, but sleep wouldn't come. Images kept bursting behind her eyelids like fireworks: angels falling from the sky; golden blood; Ithuriel in his chains, with his blinded eyes, telling her of the images of runes he had given her through her life, the visions and dreams of the future. She remembered her dreams of her brother with black wings that spilled blood, walking across a frozen lake...

She threw the coverlet off. She felt hot and itchy, too strung-up to sleep. After getting out of bed, she padded downstairs in search of a glass of water. The living room was half-lit, dim witchlight spilling down the corridor. Murmurs came from beyond the door.

Someone was awake, and talking in the kitchen. Clary moved down the corridor warily, until soft overheard whispers began to take on shape and familiarity. She recognized her mother's voice first, taut with distress. "But I just don't understand how it could have been in the cupboard," she was saying. "I haven't seen it since—since Valentine took everything we owned, back in New York."

Luke spoke: "Didn't Clary say that Jonathan had it?"

"Yes, but then it would have been destroyed with that foul apartment, wouldn't it?" Jocelyn's voice rose as Clary moved to stand in the doorway of the kitchen. "The one with all the clothes Valentine bought for me. As if I were coming back."

Clary stood very still. Her mother and Luke were sitting at the kitchen table; her mother had her head down on one hand, and Luke was rubbing her back. Clary had told her mother everything about the apartment, about how Valentine had maintained it with all Jocelyn's things there, determined that one day his wife would come back and live with him. Her mother had listened calmly, but clearly the story had upset her much more than Clary had realized.

"He's gone now, Jocelyn," said Luke. "I know it might seem half-impossible. Valentine was always such a huge presence, even when he was in hiding. But he really is dead."

"My son isn't, though," said Jocelyn. "You know, I used to take this box out and cry over it, every year, on his birthday? I dream sometimes, of a boy with green eyes, a boy who was never poisoned with demon blood, a boy who could laugh and love and be human, and that is the boy I wept over, but that boy never existed." *Take it out and cry over it,* Clary thought—she knew what box her mother meant. A box that was a memorial to a child that had died, though he still lived. The box had contained locks of his baby hair, photographs, and a tiny shoe. The last time Clary had seen it, it had been in her brother's possession. Valentine must have given it to him, though she could never understand why

Sebastian had kept it. He was hardly the sentimental sort.

"You're going to have to tell the Clave," Luke said. "If it's something that has to do with Sebastian, they'll want to know."

Clary felt her stomach go cold.

"I wish I didn't have to," Jocelyn said. "I wish I could throw the whole thing into the fire. I hate that this is my fault," she burst out. "And all I've ever wanted was to protect Clary. But the thing that frightens me most for her, for all of us, is someone who wouldn't even be alive if it weren't for me." Jocelyn's voice had gone flat and bitter. "I should have killed him when he was a baby," she said, and leaned back, away from Luke, so that Clary saw what was on the surface of the kitchen table. It was the silver box, just as she remembered it. Heavy, with a simple lid, and the initials J.C. carved into the side.

The morning sun sparkled off the new gates in front of the Gard. The old ones, Clary guessed, had been destroyed in the battle that had wrecked much of the Gard and scorched the trees along the hillside. Past the gates she could see Alicante below, shimmering water in the canals, the demon towers reaching up to where sunlight made them glitter like mica sparkling in stone.

The Gard itself had been restored. Fire had not destroyed the stone walls or towers. A wall still ran around it, and the new gates were made of the hard, clear *adamas* that formed the demon towers. They seemed to have been hand-wrought, their lines curving in to circle around the symbol of the Council—four Cs in a square, standing for Council, Covenant, Clave, and Consul. The curvature of each C held a symbol of one of the branches of Downworlders. A crescent moon for the wolves, a spell book for the warlocks, an elf arrow for the Fair Folk, and for the vampires, a star.

A star. She hadn't been able to think of anything that symbolized vampires, herself. Blood? Fangs? But there was something simple and elegant about the star. It was bright in the darkness, a darkness that would never be illuminated, and it was lonely the way only things that could never die were lonely.

Clary missed Simon with a sharp pain. She was exhausted after a night of little sleep, and her emotional resources were low. It didn't help that she felt as if she were the center of a hundred hostile stares. There were dozens of Shadowhunters milling around the gates, most of them unfamiliar to her. Many were shooting Jocelyn and Luke covert glances; a few were coming up to greet them, while others stood back looking curious. Jocelyn seemed to be keeping her calm with a certain amount of effort.

More Shadowhunters were coming up the path along the Gard Hill. With relief Clary recognized the Lightwoods—Maryse in front, with Robert beside her; Isabelle, Alec, and Jace following. They were wearing white mourning clothes. Maryse looked especially somber. Clary couldn't help but notice that she and Robert were walking side by side but apart, not even their hands touching.

Jace broke away from the group and moved over toward her. Gazes followed him as he went, though he seemed not to notice. He was famous in a strange sort of way among the Nephilim— Valentine's son, who had not really been his son. Kidnapped by Sebastian, rescued by the blade of Heaven. Clary knew the story well, as did everyone else close to Jace, but the rumors had grown like coral, adding layers and colors of story.

"... angel blood..."

"... special powers..."

"... heard that Valentine taught him tricks..."

"... fire in his blood..."

"... not right for Nephilim..."

She could hear the whispers, even as Jace moved among them.

It was a bright winter day, cold but sunny, and the light picked the gold and silver threads out of his hair and made her squint as he came up to her at the gate. "Mourning clothes?" he said, touching the sleeve of her jacket.

"You're wearing them," she pointed out.

"I didn't think you had any."

"Amatis's," she said. "Listen—I have to tell you something."

He let her draw him aside. Clary described the conversation she had overheard between her mother and Luke about the box. "It's definitely the box I remember. It's the one my mother had when I was growing up, and the one that was in Sebastian's apartment when I was there."

Jace raked a hand through the light strands of his hair. "I thought there was something," he said. "Maryse got a message from your mother this morning." His gaze was inward. "Sebastian Turned Luke's sister," he added. "He did it on purpose, to hurt Luke and hurt your mother through Luke. He hates her. He must have come to Alicante to get Amatis, that night we fought at the Burren. He as much as told me he was going to do it, back when we were bound. He said he was going to kidnap a Shadowhunter from Alicante, just not which one."

Clary nodded. It was always strange to hear Jace talk about the self he had been, the Jace who had been Sebastian's friend—more than his friend, his ally. The Jace who had worn her Jace's skin and face but had been someone else entirely.

"He must have brought the box with him then, left it in her house," Jace added. "He would have known that your family would find it one day. He would have thought of it as a message, or a signature."

"Is that what the Clave thinks?" Clary asked.

"It's what I think," Jace said, focusing on her. "And you know we both can read Sebastian better than they can, or ever will. They don't understand him at all."

"Aren't they lucky." The sound of a bell echoed through the air, and the gates slid open. Clary and Jace joined the Lightwoods, Luke, and Jocelyn in the tide of Shadowhunters pouring through. They passed through the gardens outside the fortress, up a set of stairs, then through another set of doors into a long corridor that ended at the Council chamber.

Jia Penhallow, in Consul robes, stood at the entrance to the chamber as Shadowhunter after Shadowhunter came through. It was built like an amphitheater: a half circle of tiered benches facing a rectangular raised dais in the front of the room. There were two lecterns on the dais, one for the Consul and one for the Inquisitor, and behind the lecterns two windows, massive rect-angles, looked out over Alicante.

Clary moved to sit with the Lightwoods and her mother, while Robert Lightwood broke away from them and headed down the cen-ter aisle to take up the place of the Inquisitor. On the dais, behind the lecterns, were four tall chairs, the back of each inscribed with a sym-bol: spell book, moon, arrow, star. The seats for the Downworlders of the Council. Luke eyed his but seated himself next to Jocelyn. This was not a full Council meeting, with Downworlder attendance. Luke wasn't here in an official capacity. In front of the seats a table had been erected, draped with blue velvet. Atop the velvet lay some-thing long and sharp, something that glimmered in the light from the windows. The Mortal Sword.

Clary glanced around. The flood of Shadowhunters had slowed to a trickle; the room was nearly filled to its echoing roof. There had once been more entrances than through the Gard. Westminster Abbey had had one, she knew, as had the Sagrada Família and Saint Basil the Blessed, but they had been sealed when Portals were invented. She couldn't help but wonder if some kind of magic kept the Council room from overflowing. It was as full as she had ever seen it, but there were still empty seats when Jia Penhallow stepped up onto the stage and clapped her hands sharply.

"Will the Council please come to attention," she said.

Silence fell quickly; many of the Shadowhunters were straining forward. Rumors had been flying around like panicked birds, and there was an electricity in the room, the crackling current of people desperate for information.

"Bangkok, Buenos Aires, Oslo, Berlin, Moscow, Los Angeles," said Jia. "Attacked in quick succession, before the attacks could be reported. Before warnings could be given. Every Conclave in these cities has had its Shadowhunters captured and Turned. A few—pitifully few, the very old or very young—were simply killed, their bodies left for us to burn, to add to the voices of lost Shadowhunters in the Silent City."

A voice spoke from one of the front rows. A woman with black hair, the tattooed silver design of a koi fish standing out on the dark skin of her cheek. Clary rarely saw Shadowhunters with tattoos that weren't Marks, but it wasn't unheard of. "You say 'Turned,'" she said. "But do you not mean 'slain'?"

Jia's mouth tightened. "I do not mean 'slain,'" she said. "I mean 'Turned.' We speak of the Endarkened, the ones Jonathan Morgenstern—or as he prefers to be known, Sebastian—Turned from their purpose as Nephilim using the Infernal Cup. Every Institute was issued reports of what happened at the Burren. The existence of the Endarkened is something we have known of now for some time, even if there were perhaps those who did not want to believe it."

A murmur went around the room. Clary barely heard it. She was aware that Jace's hand was around hers, but she was hearing the wind on the Burren, and seeing Shadowhunters rising from the Infernal Cup to face Sebastian, the Marks of the Gray Book already fading from their skin...

"Shadowhunters don't fight Shadowhunters," said an older man in one of the front rows. Jace murmured into her ear that he was the head of the Reykjavík Institute. "It is blasphemy."

"It *is* blasphemy," Jia agreed. "Blasphemy is Sebastian Morgenstern's creed. His father wanted to cleanse the world of Downworlders. Sebastian wants something very different. He wants Nephilim reduced to ashes, and he wants to use Nephilim to do it."

"Surely if he was able to turn Nephilim into—into monsters, we ought to be able to find a way to turn them back," said Nasreen Choudhury, the head of the Mumbai Institute, regal in her rune-decorated white sari. "Surely we should not give up so easily on our own."

"The body of one of the Endarkened was found at the Berlin site," said Robert. "He was injured, probably left for dead. The Silent Brothers are examining him right now to see if they can glean any information that might lead to a cure."

"Which Endarkened?" demanded the woman with the koi tattoo. "He had a name before he was Turned. A Shadowhunter name."

"Amalric Kriegsmesser," said Robert after a moment's hesitation. "His family has already been told."

The warlocks of the Spiral Labyrinth are also working on a cure. The whispered omnidirectional voice of a Silent Brother echoed in the room. Clary recognized Brother Zachariah standing with his hands folded near the dais. Beside him was Helen Blackthorn, dressed in white mourning clothes, looking anxious.

"They're warlocks," said someone else in a dismissive tone. "Surely they won't do any better than our own Silent Brothers."

"Can't Kriegsmesser be interrogated?" interrupted a tall woman with white hair. "Perhaps he knows Sebastian's next move, or even a manner of curing his condition—"

Amalric Kriegsmesser is barely conscious, and besides, he is a servant of the Infernal Cup, said Brother Zachariah. *The Infernal Cup controls him completely. He has no will of his own and therefore no will to break.*

The woman with the koi tattoo spoke out again: "Is it true that Sebastian Morgenstern is invulnerable now? That he can't be killed?"

There was a murmur in the room. Jia spoke, raising her voice, "As I said, there were no Nephilim survivors from the first of the attacks. But the last attack was on the Institute in Los Angeles, and six survived. Six children." She turned. "Helen Blackthorn, if you please, bring the witnesses out."

Clary saw Helen nod, and disappear through a side door. A moment later she returned; she was walking slowly now, and carefully, her hand on the back of a thin boy with a mop of wavy brown hair. He couldn't have been older than twelve. Clary recognized him immediately. She had seen him in the nave of the Institute the first time she had met Helen, his wrist clamped in his older sister's grip, his hands covered in wax where he had been playing with the tapers that decorated the interior of the cathedral. He had had an impish grin and the same blue-green eyes as his sister.

Julian, Helen had called him. Her little brother.

The impish grin was gone now. He looked tired and dirty and frightened. Skinny wrists stuck out of the cuffs of a white mourning jacket, the sleeves of which were too short for him. In his arms he was carrying a little boy, probably not more than three years old, with tangled brown curls; it seemed to be a family trait. The rest of the children wore similar borrowed mourning clothes. Following Julian was a girl of about ten, her hand firmly clasped in the hold of a boy the same age. The girl's hair was dark brown, but the boy had tangled black curls that nearly obscured his face. Fraternal twins, Clary guessed. After them came a girl who might have been eight or nine, her face round and very pale between brown braids. All of the Blackthorns—for the family resemblance was striking—looked bewildered and terrified, except perhaps Helen, whose expression was a mixture of fury and grief.

The misery on their faces cut at Clary's heart. She thought of her power with runes, wishing that she could create one that would soften the blow of loss. Mourning runes existed, but only to honor the dead, in the same way that love runes existed, like wedding rings, to symbolize the bond of love. You couldn't make someone love you with a rune, and you couldn't assuage grief with it either. So much magic, Clary thought, and nothing to mend a broken heart.

"Julian Blackthorn," said Jia Penhallow, and her voice was gentle. "Step forward, please."

Julian swallowed and nodded, handing the little boy he was holding to his older sister. He stepped forward, his eyes darting around the dais. He was clearly scouring the space for someone. His shoulders had just begun to slump when another figure darted out onto the stage. A girl, also about twelve, with a tangle of dark blond hair that hung down around her shoulders. She wore jeans and a T-shirt that didn't quite fit, and her head was down, as if she couldn't bear so many people looking at her. It was clear that she didn't want to be there—on the stage or perhaps even in Idris—but the moment he saw her, Julian seemed to relax. The terrified look vanished from his expression as she moved to stand beside Helen, her face tucked down and away from the crowd.

"Julian," said Jia in the same gentle voice, "would you do something for us? Would you take up the Mortal Sword?"

Clary sat up straight. She had held the Mortal Sword; she had felt the weight of it. The cold, like hooks in your skin, dragged the truth out of you. You couldn't lie holding the Mortal Sword, but the truth, even a truth you wanted to tell, was agony.

"They can't," she whispered. "He's just a kid—"

"He's the oldest of the children who escaped the Los Angeles Institute," Jace said under his breath. "They don't have a choice."

Julian nodded, his thin shoulders straight. "I'll take it."

Robert Lightwood passed behind the lectern then and went

to the table. He took up the Sword and returned to stand in front of Julian. The contrast between them was almost funny—the big, barrel-chested man and the lanky, wild-haired boy.

Julian reached a hand up and took the Sword. As his fingers closed around the hilt, he shuddered, a ripple of pain that was quickly forced down. The blond girl behind him started forward, and Clary caught a glimpse of the look on her face—pure fury—before Helen caught at her and pulled her back.

Jia knelt down. It was a strange sight, the boy with the Sword, bracketed on one side by the Consul, her robes spreading out about her, and on the other by the Inquisitor. "Julian," Jia said, and though her voice was low, it carried throughout the Council room. "Can you tell us who is on the stage here with you today?"

In his clear boy's voice Julian said, "You. The Inquisitor. My family—my sister Helen, and Tiberius and Livia, and Drusilla and Tavvy. Octavian. And my best friend, Emma Carstairs."

"And they were all with you when the Institute was attacked?"

Julian shook his head. "Not Helen," he said. "She was here."

"Can you tell us what you saw, Julian? Without leaving anything out?"

Julian swallowed. He was pale. Clary could imagine the pain he was feeling, the weight of the Sword. "It was in the afternoon," he said. "We were practicing in the training room. Katerina was teaching us. Mark was watching. Emma's parents were on a routine patrol at the beach. We saw a flash of light; I thought it was lightning, or fireworks. But—it wasn't. Katerina and Mark left us and went downstairs. They told us to stay in the training room."

"But you didn't," Jia said.

"We could hear the sounds of fighting. We split up—Emma went to get Drusilla and Octavian, and I went to the office with Livia and Tiberius to call the Clave. We had to sneak by the main entrance to get there. When we did, I saw him."

"Him?"

"I knew he was a Shadowhunter, but not. He was wearing a red cloak, covered in runes."

"What runes?"

"I didn't know them, but there was something wrong with them. Not like the Gray Book runes. It gave me a sort of sick feeling to look at them. And he pushed his hood back—he had white hair, so I thought he was old at first. Then I realized it was Sebastian Morgenstern. He was holding a sword."

"Can you describe the sword?"

"Silver, with a pattern of black stars on the blade and the handle. He took it out and he—" Julian's breath skittered, and Clary could almost feel it, feel his horror at the recollection warring with the compulsion to tell it, to relive it. She was leaning forward, her hands in fists, hardly aware that her nails were digging into her palms. "He held it to my father's throat," Julian went on. "There were others with Sebastian. They were wearing red too—"

"Shadowhunters?" Jia said.

"I don't know." Julian's breath was coming short. "Some wore black cloaks. Others wore gear, but their gear was red. I've never seen red gear. There was a woman, with brown hair, and she was holding a cup that looked like the Mortal Cup. She made my father drink out of it. He fell down and screamed. I could hear my brother screaming too."

"Which brother?" asked Robert Lightwood.

"Mark," said Julian. "I saw them start to move into the entryway, and Mark turned around and shouted for us to run upstairs and get out. I fell on the top step, and when I looked down, they were swarming all over him—" Julian made a gagging sound. "And my father, he was standing up, and his eyes were black too, and he started moving toward Mark like the rest of them, like he didn't even know him—"

Julian's voice cracked, just as the blonde girl wrenched herself free of Helen's grasp and hurtled forward, throwing herself between Julian and the Consul.

"Emma!" Helen said, stepping forward, but Jia held out a hand to keep her back. Emma was white-faced and gasping. Clary thought she had never seen so much anger contained in such a small form.

"Leave him alone!" Emma shouted, throwing her arms out wide, as if she could shield Julian behind her, though she was a head shorter. "You're torturing him! Leave him alone!"

"It's okay, Emma," Julian said, though the color was starting to come back into his face now that they were no longer questioning him. "They have to do it."

She turned on him. "No, they don't. I was there too. I saw what happened. Do it to me." She held out her hands, as if begging for the Sword to be put into them. "I'm the one who stabbed Sebastian in the heart. I'm the one who saw him not die. You should be asking *me*!"

"No," Julian began, and then Jia said, still gently:

"Emma, we *will* question you, next. The Sword is painful, but not harmful—"

"Stop it," Emma said. "Just stop it." And she walked over to Julian, who was holding the Sword tightly. It was clear he had no intention of trying to hand it over. He was shaking his head at Emma, even as she laid her hands over his, so that both of them were holding the Sword together.

"I stabbed Sebastian," Emma said, in a voice that rang out through the room. "And he pulled the dagger out and laughed. He said, 'It's a shame you won't live. Live to tell the Clave that Lilith has strengthened me beyond all measure. Perhaps Glorious could end my life. A pity for the Nephilim that they have no more favors they can ask of Heaven, and none of the puny instruments of war they forge in their Adamant Citadel can harm me now.'"

Clary shuddered. She heard Sebastian through Emma's words,

and could almost see him, standing in front of her. Chatter had burst out among the Clave, drowning what Jace said to her next.

"Are you sure you didn't miss the heart?" Robert demanded, his dark eyebrows drawn together.

It was Julian who answered. "Emma doesn't miss," he said, sounding as offended as if they had just insulted him.

"I know where the heart is," Emma said, stepping back from Julian and casting a look of anger—more than anger, hurt—at the Consul and the Inquisitor. "But I don't think you do."

Her voice rose, and she spun and ran off the dais, practically elbowing her way past Robert. She disappeared through the door from which she had come, and Clary heard her own breath rush out through her teeth—wasn't anyone going to go after her? Julian clearly wanted to, but, trapped between the Consul and Inquisitor, carrying the weight of the Mortal Sword, he couldn't move. Helen was looking after her with an expression of raw pain, her arms cradling the youngest boy, Tavvy.

And then Clary was on her feet. Her mother reached for her, but she was already running down the sloping aisle between the rows of seats. The aisle turned into wooden steps; Clary clattered up them, past the Consul and Inquisitor, past Helen, and through the side door after Emma.

She nearly knocked over Aline, who was hovering near the open door, watching what was going on in the Council room and scowling. The scowl disappeared when she saw Clary, and was replaced by a look of surprise. "What are you doing?"

"The little girl," Clary said breathlessly. "Emma. She ran back here."

"I know. I tried to stop her, but she pulled away from me. She's just..." Aline sighed and glanced at the Council room, where Jia had begun to question Julian again. "It's been so hard on them, Helen and the others. You know their mother died, only a few years ago.

All they've got now is an uncle in London."

"Does that mean they're going to move the kids to London? You know, when this is all over," Clary said.

Aline shook her head. "Their uncle's been offered the leadership of the Los Angeles Institute. I think the hope is that he'll take over the job and raise the kids. I don't think he's agreed yet, though. He's probably in shock. I mean, he lost his nephew, his brother—Andrew Blackthorn isn't dead, but he might as well be. In a way, it's worse." Her voice was bitter.

"I know," Clary said. "I know exactly what that's like."

Aline looked at her more closely. "I suppose you do know," she said. "It's just—Helen. I wish I could do more for her. She's eating herself up with guilt because she was here with me and not in Los Angeles when the Institute was attacked. And she's trying so hard, but she can't be a mom to all those kids, and their uncle hasn't gotten here yet, and then there's Emma, Angel help her. She doesn't even have a scrap of family left—"

"I'd like to talk to her. To Emma."

Aline tucked a lock of hair behind her ear; the Blackthorn ring shimmered on her right hand. "She won't talk to anyone but Julian."

"Let me try," Clary urged. "Please."

Aline looked at the determined expression on Clary's face and sighed. "Down the hall—the first room on the left."

The hall curved away from the Council room. Clary could hear the voices of the Shadowhunters fading as she walked. The walls were smooth stone, lined with tapestries that depicted various glorious scenes from Shadowhunter history. The first door that appeared on her left was wooden, very plain. It was partly ajar, but she rapped quickly before opening it, so as not to surprise whoever was inside.

It was a simple room, with wooden wainscoting and a jumble of chairs, hastily assembled. It felt to Clary like a hospital waiting room. It had that heavy sense in the air, of an impermanent place where people spent their anxiety and grief in unfamiliar surroundings.

In the corner of the room was a chair propped against a wall, and in the chair was Emma. She looked smaller than she had from a distance. She was only wearing a short-sleeved T-shirt and on her bare arms were Marks, the Voyance rune on her left hand—so she was left-handed like Jace—which lay on the hilt of an unsheathed shortsword lying across her lap. Up close Clary could see that her hair was a pale blonde, but tangled and dirty enough that it had looked darker. From between the tangles the girl glared up at Clary defiantly.

"What?" she said. "What do you want?"

"Nothing," Clary said, pushing the door shut behind her. "Just to talk to you."

Emma's eyes narrowed in suspicion. "You want to use the Mortal Sword on me? Interrogate me?"

"No. I've had it used on me, and it's awful. I'm sorry they're using it on your friend. I think they should find another way."

"I think they should trust him," said Emma. "Julian doesn't lie." She looked at Clary challengingly, as if daring her to disagree.

"Of course he doesn't," Clary said, and took a step into the room—she felt as if she were trying not to frighten off some kind of wild creature in the forest. "Julian's your best friend, isn't he?"

Emma nodded.

"My best friend is a boy too. His name is Simon."

"So where is he?" Emma's eyes flicked behind Clary, as if she expected Simon to materialize suddenly.

"He's in New York," said Clary. "I miss him a lot."

Emma looked as if this made enormous sense. "Julian went to New York once," she said. "I missed him, so when he got back, I made him promise he wouldn't go anywhere without me again."

Clary smiled, and moved closer to Emma. "Your sword is beautiful," she said, pointing at the blade across the girl's lap.

Emma's expression softened fractionally. She touched the blade, which was etched with a delicate pattern of leaves and runes. The crossbar was gold, and across the blade were carved words: *I am Cortana, of the same steel and temper as Joyeuse and Durendal.* "It was my father's. It's been passed down through the Carstairs family. It's a famous sword," she added proudly. "It was made a long time ago."

"'Of the same steel and temper as Joyeuse and Durendal,'" said Clary. "Those are both famous swords. You know who owns famous swords?"

"Who?"

"Heroes," Clary said, kneeling down on the ground so she could look up into the girl's face.

Emma scowled. "I'm not a hero," she said. "I didn't do anything to save Julian's father, or Mark."

"I'm so sorry," said Clary. "I know how it is to watch someone you care about go Dark. Get turned into someone else."

But Emma was shaking her head. "Mark didn't go Dark. He got taken away."

Clary frowned. "Taken away?"

"They didn't want him to drink from the Cup because of his faerie blood," said Emma, and Clary recalled Alec saying that there was a faerie ancestor in the Blackthorn family tree. As if anticipating Clary's next question, Emma said wearily, "Only Mark and Helen have faerie blood. They had the same mother, but she left them with Mr. Blackthorn when they were small. Julian and the others had a different mom."

"Oh," Clary said, not wanting to press too hard, not wanting this damaged girl to think that she was just another adult who saw Emma as a source of answers for her questions and nothing else. "I know Helen. Does Mark look like her?"

"Yeah—Helen and Mark have pointy ears a little, and light hair. None of the rest of the Blackthorns are blond. They all have brown hair except Ty, and no one knows why he has black hair. Livvy doesn't have it, and she's his twin." A little color and animation had come back into Emma's face; it was clear she liked to talk about the Blackthorns.

"So they didn't want Mark to drink from the Cup?" said Clary. Privately she was surprised that Sebastian would care one way or the other. He'd never had Valentine's obsession with Downworlders, though it wasn't as if he liked them. "Maybe it doesn't work if you have Downworlder blood."

"Maybe," said Emma. Clary reached out and put her hand over one of Emma's. She dreaded the answer but couldn't keep herself from asking the question. "He didn't Turn your parents, did he?"

"No—no," Emma said, and now her voice was shaking. "They're dead. They weren't at the Institute; they were investigating a report of demon activity. Their bodies washed up on the beach after the attack. I could have gone with them, but I wanted to stay back at the Institute. I wanted to train with Jules. If I'd just gone with them—"

"If you had, you'd be dead too," said Clary.

"How would you know?" Emma demanded, but there was something in her eyes, something that wanted to believe it.

"I can see what a good Shadowhunter you are," Clary said. "I see your Marks. I see your scars. And how you hold your sword. If you're that good, I can only imagine they were really good too. And something that could have killed them both isn't something you could have saved them from." She touched the sword lightly. "Heroes aren't always the ones who win," she said. "They're the ones who lose, sometimes. But they keep fighting, they keep coming back. They don't give up. That's what makes them heroes."

Emma drew in a shaky breath, just as a rapping noise sounded at the door. Clary half-turned as it opened, letting in light from the hall outside, and Jace. He caught her eye and smiled, leaning in the doorway. His hair was very dark gold, his eyes a shade lighter. Clary sometimes thought she could see the fire inside him, lighting his eyes and skin and veins, moving just under the surface. "Clary," he said.

Clary thought she heard a small squeak from behind her. Emma was clutching her sword, looking between Clary and Jace with very large eyes.

"The Council's over," he said. "And I don't think Jia's any too pleased you came running back here."

"So I'm in trouble," Clary said.

"As usual," Jace said, but his smile took any sting out of it. "We're all leaving. Are you ready to go?"

She shook her head. "I'll meet you at your house. You guys can fill me in on what happened at the Council then."

He hesitated. "Get Aline or Helen to come with you," he said finally. "The Consul's house is just down the street from the Inquisitor's." He zipped his jacket up and slipped out of the room, closing the door behind him.

Clary turned back to Emma, who was still staring at her.

"You know Jace Lightwood?" said Emma.

"I— What?"

"He's famous," Emma said with obvious amazement. "He's the best Shadowhunter. The *best*."

"He's my friend," Clary said, noting that the conversation had taken an unexpected turn.

Emma gave her a superior look. "He's your boyfriend."

"How did you—"

"I saw the way he looked at you," said Emma, "and anyway, everyone knows Jace Lightwood has a girlfriend and she's Clary Fairchild. Why didn't you tell me your name?"

"I guess I didn't think you'd know it," Clary said, reeling.

"I'm not stupid," Emma said, with an air of annoyance that had Clary straightening up quickly before she could laugh.

"No, you're not. You're really smart," said Clary. "And I'm glad you know who I am, because I want you to know you can come talk to me anytime. Not just about what happened at the Institute—about whatever you want. And you can talk to Jace, too. Do you need to know where to find us?"

Emma shook her head. "No," she said, her voice soft again. "I know where the Inquistor's house is."

"Okay." Clary folded her hands, mostly to keep herself from reaching out and hugging the girl. She didn't think Emma would appreciate it. Clary turned toward the door.

"If you're Jace Lightwood's girlfriend, you should have a better sword," Emma said suddenly, and Clary glanced down at the blade she'd strapped on that morning, an old one she'd packed with her belongings from New York.

She touched the hilt. "This one isn't good?"

Emma shook her head. "Not good at all."

She sounded so serious that Clary smiled. "Thanks for the advice."

4

DARKER THAN GOLD

When Clary knocked on the door of the Inquisitor's house, it was opened by Robert Lightwood.

For a moment she froze, unsure what to say. She had never had a conversation with Jace's adoptive father, had never known him well at all. He had been a shadow in the background, usually behind Maryse with his hand on her chair. He was a big, dark-haired man with a neatly trimmed beard. She could not imagine him being friends with her own father, though she knew he had been in Valentine's Circle. There were too many lines on his face, and there was too hard a set to his jaw, for her to imagine him young.

When he looked at her, she saw that his eyes were a very dark blue, so dark, she had always thought they were black. His expression didn't change; she could feel disapproval radiating off him. She suspected Jia wasn't the only one annoyed that she'd run out of the Council meeting after Emma. "If you're looking for my children, they're upstairs," was all he said. "Top floor."

She passed by him, into the extremely grand front room. The house, the one officially designated to the Inquisitor and his or her family, was grand in its scope, with high ceilings and heavy, expensive-looking furniture. It was a large enough space to have interior archways, a massive grand staircase, and a chandelier that hung down from the ceiling, glowing with dim witchlight. She wondered where Maryse was, and if she liked the house.

"Thanks," Clary said.

Robert Lightwood shrugged and disappeared into the shadows without another word. Clary took the stairs two at a time, passing several landings before she reached the top floor, which was up a flight of steep attic stairs that led to a corridor. A door down the hall was half-open; she could hear voices from the other side.

With a perfunctory knock she stepped inside. The walls of the attic room were painted white, and there was a massive armoire in the corner, both doors flung open—Alec's clothes, practical and a little shabby, hanging on one side, and Jace's, crisp in blacks and grays, on the other. Their gear was neatly folded along the bottom.

Clary almost smiled; she wasn't entirely sure why. There was something about Alec and Jace's sharing a room that she found endearing. She wondered if they kept each other up at night talking, the way she and Simon always had.

Alec and Isabelle were perched on the sill of the window. Behind them Clary could see the colors of sunset sparking off the water of the canal below. Jace was sprawled on one of the single beds, his boots rather defiantly planted on the velvet coverlet.

"I think they mean they can't just wait around for Sebastian to attack more Institutes," Alec was saying. "That would be hiding. Shadowhunters don't hide."

Jace rubbed his cheek against his shoulder; he looked tired, his pale hair rumpled. "Feels like hiding," he said. "Sebastian's out there; we're in here. Double-warded. All the Institutes emptied out. No one to protect the world from demons. *Who will watch the watchers?*"

Alec sighed and rubbed a hand over his face. "Hopefully it won't be for long."

"Hard to imagine what would happen," Isabelle said. "A world with no Shadowhunters. Demons everywhere, Downworlders attacking one another."

"If I were Sebastian—" Jace started.

"But you're not. You're not Sebastian," Clary said.

They all looked over at her. Alec and Jace looked absolutely nothing alike, Clary thought, but every once in a while there was a similarity in the way they glanced or gestured that reminded her that they'd been raised together. They both looked curious, a little concerned. Isabelle seemed more tired, and upset.

"You all right?" Jace said by way of greeting, giving her a lopsided smile. "How's Emma?"

"Wrecked," Clary said. "What happened after I left the meeting?"

"The interrogation was mostly over," said Jace. "Sebastian's obviously behind the attacks, and he has a sizeable force of Endarkened warriors backing him up. Nobody knows exactly how many, but we have to assume all of the missing have been Turned."

"Still, we have greater numbers by far," said Alec. "He has his original forces, and the six Conclaves he Turned; we have everyone else."

There was something in Jace's eyes that turned them darker than gold. "Sebastian knows that," he murmured. "He'll know his forces, down to the last warrior. He'll know exactly what he can match and what he can't."

"We have the Downworlders on our side," said Alec. "That's the whole point of tomorrow's meeting, isn't it? Talk to the representatives, strengthen our alliances. Now that we know what Sebastian's doing, we can strategize around it, hit him with the Night's Children, the Courts, the warlocks..."

Clary's eyes met Jace's in silent communication. *Now that we know what Sebastian's doing, he'll do something else. Something we don't expect yet.*

"And then everyone talked about Jace," said Isabelle. "So, you know, the usual."

"About Jace?" Clary leaned against the footboard of Jace's bed. "What about him?"

"There was a lot of back-and-forth about whether Sebastian's basically invulnerable now, and if there are ways to wound and kill him. Glorious could have done it because of the heavenly fire, but currently the only source of heavenly fire is..."

"Jace," Clary said grimly. "But the Silent Brothers have tried *everything* to separate Jace from the heavenly fire, and they can't do it. It's in his *soul*. So what's their plan, hitting Sebastian over the head with Jace until he passes out?"

"Brother Zachariah said pretty much the same thing," Jace said. "Maybe with less sarcasm."

"Anyway, they wound up talking about ways to capture Sebastian without killing him—if they can destroy all the Endarkened, if he can be trapped somewhere or somehow, it might not matter as much if he can't be killed," Alec said.

"Put him in an *adamas* coffin and drop it into the sea," Isabelle said. "That's my suggestion."

"Anyway, when they were done talking about me, which was of course the best part," Jace said, "they went back pretty quickly to talking about ways to cure the Endarkened. They're paying the Spiral Labyrinth a fortune to try to unravel the spell Sebastian used to create the Infernal Cup and enact the ritual."

"They need to stop obsessing about curing the Endarkened and start thinking about how to defeat them," Isabelle said in a hard voice.

"A lot of them know people who were Turned, Isabelle," said Alec. "Of course they want them back."

"Well, I want my little brother back," said Isabelle, her voice rising. "Don't they understand what Sebastian did? He *killed* them. He killed what was human about them, and he left demons walking around in skin-suits that look like people we used to know, that's all—"

"Keep it *down*," Alec said, in his determined-older-brother tone. "You know Mom and Dad are in the house, right? They'll come up."

"Oh, they're here," said Isabelle. "About as far away from each other, bedroom-wise, as you could possibly be, but they're here."

"It's not our business where they sleep, Isabelle."

"They're our *parents*."

"But they have their own lives," said Alec. "And we have to respect that and stay out of it." His expression darkened. "A lot of people split up when they have a child who dies."

Isabelle gave a little gasp.

"Izzy?" Alec seemed to realize he'd gone too far. Mentions of Max seemed to devastate Isabelle more than they did any of the other Lightwoods, even Maryse.

Isabelle turned and ran out of the room, slamming the door behind her.

Alec shoved his fingers into his hair, causing it to stick up like duck fluff. "Goddammit," he swore, and then flushed—Alec hardly ever swore, and usually when he did, he muttered. He shot Jace an almost apologetic look and went after his sister.

Jace sighed, swung his long legs off the bed, and stood up. He stretched like a cat, cracking his shoulders. "Guess that's my cue to walk you home."

"I can find my way back—"

He shook his head, grabbing his jacket off the bedpost. There was something impatient about his movements, something prowling and watchful that made Clary's own skin prickle. "I want to get out of here anyway. Come on. Let's go."

***

"It's been an hour. At least an hour. I swear," Maia said. She was lying on the couch in Jordan and Simon's apartment, her bare feet in Jordan's lap.

"Shouldn't have ordered Thai," said Simon absently. He was sitting on the floor, fiddling with the Xbox controller. It hadn't been working for several days. There was a Duraflame log in the fireplace. Like everything else in the apartment the fireplace was poorly maintained, and half the time the room would fill with smoke when they used it. Jordan was always complaining of the cold, the cracks in the windows and walls, and the landlord's disinterest in fixing anything. "They never come on time."

Jordan grinned good-naturedly. "What do you care? You don't eat."

"I can drink now," Simon pointed out. It was true. He'd trained his stomach to accept most liquids—milk, coffee, tea—though solid food still made him retch. He doubted the drinks did anything much for him in the way of nutrition; only blood seemed to do that, but it made him feel more human to be able to consume something in public that wouldn't send everyone screaming. With a sigh he dropped the controller. "I think this thing is broken. Permanently. Which is great, because I have no money to replace it."

Jordan looked at him curiously. Simon had brought all his savings from home when he'd moved in, but that hadn't been much. Fortunately, he also had few expenses. The apartment was on loan from the Praetor Lupus, who also provided Simon's blood. "I've got money," Jordan said. "We'll be fine."

"That's your money, not mine. You're not going to be watching me forever," Simon said, staring into the blue flames of the fireplace. "And then what? I'd be applying for college soon if—everything hadn't happened. Music school. I could learn, get a job. No one's going to employ me now. I look sixteen; I always will."

"Hm," Maia said. "I guess vampires don't really have jobs, do they? I mean, some werewolves do—Bat's a DJ, and Luke owns that bookstore. But vampires are all in clans. There aren't really vampire scientists."

"Or vampire musicians," said Simon. "Let's face it. My career is now professional vampire."

"I'm actually kind of surprised the vampires haven't been rampaging through the streets, eating tourists, what with Maureen leading them," said Maia. "She's pretty bloodthirsty."

Simon made a face. "I assume some of the clan are trying to control her. Raphael, probably. Lily—she's one of the smartest of the vampire clan. Knows everything. She and Raphael were always thick as thieves. But I don't exactly have vampire friends. Considering what a target I am, sometimes I'm surprised I have *any* friends."

He heard the bitterness in his own voice and glanced across the room at the pictures Jordan had tacked up on the wall—pictures of himself with his friends, at the beach, with Maia. Simon had thought of putting up his own photos. Though he hadn't taken any from his house, Clary had some. He could have borrowed them, made the apartment more his own. But though he liked living with Jordan and felt comfortable there, it wasn't home. It didn't feel permanent, as if he could make a life there.

"I don't even have a bed," he said out loud.

Maia turned her head toward him. "Simon, what is this about? Is it because Isabelle left?"

Simon shrugged. "I don't know. I mean, yes, I miss Izzy, but—Clary says the two of us need to DTR."

"Oh, define the relationship," Maia said at Jordan's puzzled look. "You know, when you decide if you're actually girlfriend and boyfriend. Which you should do, by the way."

"Why does everyone know this acronym but me?" Simon

wondered aloud. "Does Isabelle *want* to be my girlfriend?"

"Can't tell you," said Maia. "Girl code. Ask her."

"She's in Idris."

"Ask her when she gets back." Simon was silent, and Maia added, more gently, "She'll come back, and Clary, too. It's just a meeting."

"I don't know. The Institutes aren't safe."

"Neither are you," said Jordan. "That's why you have me."

Maia looked at Jordan. There was something odd in the look, something Simon couldn't quite identify. There had been something off between Maia and Jordan for some time now, a distance from Maia, a question in her eyes when she looked at her boyfriend. Simon had been waiting for Jordan to say something to him, but Jordan hadn't. Simon wondered if Jordan had noticed Maia's distance—it was obvious—or if he was stubbornly in denial.

"Would you still be a Daylighter?" Maia asked, turning her attention to Simon. "If you could change it?"

"I don't know." Simon had asked himself the same question, then pushed it away—there was no point obsessing over things you couldn't change. Being a Daylighter meant that you had gold in your veins. Other vampires wanted it, for if they drank your blood, they too could walk in the sun. But just as many wanted you destroyed, for it was the belief of most vampires that Daylighters were an abomination to be rooted out. He remembered Raphael's words to him on the roof of a Manhattan hotel. *You had better pray, Daylighter, that you do not lose that Mark before the war comes. For if you do, there will be a line of enemies waiting their turn to kill you. And I will be at the head of it.*

And yet. "I would miss the sun," he said. "It keeps me human, I think."

The light from the fire sparked off Jordan's eyes as he looked at Simon. "Being human's overrated," he said with a smile.

Maia swung her feet off his legs abruptly. Jordan looked over at her, worried, just as the doorbell rang.

Simon was on his feet in a flash. "Takeout," he announced. "I'll go get it. Besides," he added over his shoulder as he headed down the hall to the front door, "no one's tried to kill me in two weeks. Maybe they got bored and gave up."

He heard the murmur of voices behind him but didn't listen; they were talking to each other. He reached for the knob and swung the door open, already fumbling for his wallet.

And there was a throb against his chest. He glanced down to see Isabelle's pendant flash bright scarlet, and threw himself backward, just missing a hand thrust out to grab him. He yelled out loud—there was a looming figure dressed in red gear in the doorway, a Shadowhunter man with ugly splashes of runes on both cheeks, a hawk-like nose, and a broad, pale forehead. He snarled at Simon and advanced.

"Simon, get *down!*" Jordan shouted, and Simon threw himself flat and rolled to the side just as a crossbow bolt exploded along the hallway. The Dark Shadowhunter spun sideways with almost unbelievable speed; the bolt embedded itself in the door. Simon heard Jordan curse in frustration, and then Maia in wolf form sprang past him, leaping at the Endarkened.

There was a satisfying howl of pain as her teeth sank into his throat. Blood sprayed out, filling the air with a salty red mist; Simon inhaled it, tasting the bitter tang of demon-tainted blood as he rose to his feet. He stepped forward just as the Endarkened seized hold of Maia and threw her down the hall, a thrashing, howling ball of teeth and claws.

Jordan shouted. Simon was making a noise low in his own throat, a sort of vampire hiss, and he could feel his fang teeth snap out. The Endarkened stepped forward, pouring blood but still steady. Simon felt a pang of fear low in his gut. He had seen them fight at the Burren, Sebastian's soldiers, and he knew that they were stronger, faster, and harder to kill than Shadowhunters. He hadn't really thought about how much harder to kill they were than *vampires*.

"Get out of the way!" Jordan grabbed Simon by the shoulders and half-threw him after Maia, who had scrambled to her feet. There was blood on her ruff, and her wolf eyes were dark with rage. "Get out, Simon. Let us deal with this. *Get out!*"

Simon stood his ground. "I'm not going—he's here for me—"

"*I know that!*" Jordan shouted. "I'm your Praetor Lupus guard! Now *let me do my job!*"

Jordan swung around, bringing up his crossbow again. This time the bolt sank into the Dark Shadowhunter's shoulder. He staggered back and let loose a string of curses in a language Simon didn't know. German, he thought. The Berlin Institute had been hit—

Maia sprang past Simon, and she and Jordan closed in on the Dark Shadowhunter. Jordan glanced back once at Simon, his hazel eyes fierce and wild. Simon nodded and darted back into the living room. He slammed open the window—it gave with a fierce shriek of swollen wood and an explosion of old paint chips—and climbed out onto the fire escape, where Jordan's wolfsbane plants, withered by winter air, crowded the metal ledge.

Every part of him screamed that he shouldn't be leaving, but he had promised Isabelle, promised he would let Jordan do his work as bodyguard, promised he wouldn't make himself a target. He clasped one hand around Izzy's pendant, warm under his fingers as if it had lain recently against her throat, and headed down the metal steps. They were clanging and slippery with snow; he almost fell several times before he reached the last rung and dropped to the shadowy pavement below.

And was immediately surrounded by vampires. Simon had time to recognize only two of them as part of the Hotel Dumort clan—delicate dark-haired Lily and blond Zeke, both grinning like fiends—before something was thrown over his head. Fabric pulled tight around his throat, and he choked, not because he needed air but because of the pain of having his throat compressed.

"Maureen sends her regards," said Zeke into his ear.

Simon opened his mouth to scream, but darkness claimed him before he could make a sound.

"I didn't realize you were quite so famous," said Clary as she and Jace made their way down the narrow pavement that ran alongside Oldway Canal. It was turning to evening—darkness had only just fallen—and the streets were full of people hurrying to and fro, wrapped in thick cloaks, their faces cold and closed-off.

Stars were beginning to come out, a soft prickle of light across the eastern sky. They illuminated Jace's eyes as he looked over at Clary curiously. "Everyone knows Valentine's son."

"I know, but—when Emma saw you, she acted like you were her celebrity crush. Like you were on the cover of *Shadowhunters Weekly* every month."

"You know, when they asked me to pose, they said it would be tasteful..."

"As long as you were holding a strategically placed seraph blade, I don't see the problem," Clary said, and Jace laughed, a cut-off sound that indicated that she had surprised the amusement out of him. It was her favorite laugh of his. Jace was always so controlled; it was still a delight to be one of the few people who could get under his carefully constructed armor and surprise him.

"You liked her, didn't you?" Jace said.

Thrown, Clary said, "Liked who?" They were passing through a square she recalled—cobblestoned, with a well in the center, covered now with a stone circle, probably to keep the water from freezing.

"That girl. Emma."

"There was something about her," Clary acknowledged. "The way she stood up for Helen's brother, maybe. Julian. She'd do anything for him. She really loves the Blackthorns, and she's lost everyone else..."

"She reminded you of you."

"I don't think so," Clary said. "I think maybe she reminded me of *you*."

"Because I'm tiny, blonde, and look good in pigtails?"

Clary bumped him with her shoulder. They had reached the top of a street lined with stores. The stores were closed now, though witchlight glowed through the barred windows. Clary had the sense of being in a dream or fairy tale, a sense that Alicante never failed to give her—the vast sky overhead, the ancient buildings carved with scenes out of legends, and over everything the clear demon towers that gave Alicante its common name: the City of Glass. "Because," she said as they passed a store with loaves of bread stacked in the window, "she lost her blood family. But she has the Blackthorns. She doesn't have anyone else, no aunts or uncles, no one to take her in, but the Blackthorns will. So she'll have to learn what you did: that family isn't blood. It's the people who love you. The people who have your back. Like the Lightwoods did for you."

Jace had stopped walking. Clary turned around to look at him. The crowd of pedestrians parted around them. He was standing in front of the entrance to a narrow alley by a shop. The wind that blew up the street ruffled his blond hair and his unzipped jacket; she could see the pulse in his throat. "Come here," he said, and his voice was rough.

Clary took a step toward him, a little warily. Had she said something that had upset him? Though, Jace was rarely angry at her, and when he was, he was straightforward about it. He reached out, took her hand gently, and led her after him as he ducked around the corner of the building and into the shadows of a narrow passage that wound toward a canal in the distance.

There was no one else in the passageway with them, and its narrow entrance blocked the view from the street. Jace's face was all angles in the dimness: sharp cheekbones, soft mouth, the golden eyes of a lion.

"I love you," he said. "I don't say it often enough. I love you."

She leaned back against the wall. The stone was cold. Under other circumstances it might have been uncomfortable, but she didn't care at the moment. She pulled him toward her carefully until their bodies were lined up, not quite touching, but so close that she could feel the heat radiating off him. Of course he didn't need to zip his jacket, not with the fire burning through his veins. The scent of black pepper and soap and cold air clung around him as she pressed her face into his shoulder and breathed him in.

"Clary," he said. His voice was a whisper and a warning. She could hear the roughness of longing in it, longing for the physical reassurance of closeness, of any touch at all. Carefully he reached around her to place the palms of his hands against the stone wall, caging her into the space made by his arms. She felt his breath in her hair, the light brush of his body against hers. Every inch of her seemed supersensitized; everywhere he touched she felt as if tiny needles of pleasure-pain were being dragged across her skin.

"Please don't tell me you pulled me into an alley and you're touching me and you *don't* plan on kissing me, because I don't think I could take it," she said in a low voice.

He closed his eyes. She could see his dark lashes feathering against his cheeks, remembered the feel of mapping the shape of his face under her fingers, of the full weight of his body on hers, the way his skin felt against her skin.

"I don't," he said, and she could hear the dark roughness under the usual smooth glide of his voice. Honey over needles. They were close enough together that when he breathed in, she felt the expansion of his chest. "We can't."

She put her hand against his chest; his heart was beating like trapped wings. "Take me home, then," she whispered, and she leaned up to brush her lips against the corner of his mouth. Or at least she meant it as a brush, a butterfly touch of lips on lips, but he leaned down toward her, and his movement changed the angle swiftly; she pressed up against him harder than she'd meant to, her lips sliding to center against his. She felt him breathe out in surprise against her mouth, and then they were kissing, really kissing, exquisitely slow and hot and intense.

Take me home. But this was home, Jace's arms surrounding her, the cold wind of Alicante in their clothes, her fingers digging into the back of his neck, the place where his hair curled softly against the skin. His palms were still flat against the stone behind her, but he moved his body against hers, gently pressing her up against the wall; she could hear the harsh undertone of his breathing. He wouldn't touch her with his hands, but she could touch him, and she let her hands go freely, over the swell of his arms, down to his chest, tracing the ridges of muscle, pressing outward to grip his sides until his T-shirt was rucking up under her fingers. Her fingertips touched bare skin, and then she was sliding her hands up under his shirt, and she hadn't touched him like this in so long, had nearly forgotten how his skin was soft where it wasn't scarred, how the muscles in his back jumped under her touch. He gasped into her mouth; he tasted like tea and chocolate and salt.

She had taken control of the kiss. Now she felt him tense as he took it back, biting at her lower lip until she shuddered, nipping at the corner of her mouth, kissing along her jawbone to suck at the pulse point at her throat, swallowing her racing heartbeat. His skin burned under her hands, *burned*—

He broke away, reeling back almost drunkenly, hitting the

opposite wall. His eyes were wide, and for a dizzy moment Clary thought she could see flames in them, like twin fires in the darkness. Then the light went out of them and he was only gasping as if he had been running, pressing the heels of his palms against his face.

"Jace," she said.

He dropped his hands. "Look at the wall behind you," he said in a flat voice.

She turned—and stared. Behind her, where he had been leaning, were twin scorch marks in the stone, in the exact shape of his hands.

The Seelie Queen lay upon her bed and looked up at the stone ceiling of her bedchamber. It was wreathed with dangling trellises of roses, thorns still intact, each one perfect and blood-red. Every night they withered and died, and every morning they were replaced, as fresh as the day before.

Faeries slept little, and rarely dreamed, but the Queen liked her bed to be comfortable. It was a wide couch of stone, with a feather mattress laid on top, and covered with thick swathes of velvet and slippery satin.

"Have you ever," said the boy in the bed beside her, "pricked yourself on one of the thorns, Your Majesty?"

She turned to look at Jonathan Morgenstern sprawled among the covers. Though he had asked her to call him Sebastian, which she respected—no faerie would allow another to address them by their true name either. He was on his stomach, head pillowed on his crossed arms, and even in the dim light the old whip weals across his back were visible.

The Queen had always been fascinated by Shadowhunters—they were part angel, as were the Fair Folk; certainly there should be a kinship between them—but had never thought she would find one whose personality she could stand for more than five minutes, until Sebastian. They were all so dreadfully self-righteous. Not Sebastian. He was most unusual for a human, and for a Shadowhunter especially.

"Not so often as you cut yourself on your wit, I think, my dearest," she said. "You know I do not wish to be called 'Your Majesty' but only 'Lady,' or 'my lady,' if you must."

"You do not seem to mind it when I call you 'beautiful one,' or 'my beautiful lady.'" His tone was not repentant.

"Hmm," she said, raking her slim fingers through the mass of his silvery hair. He had lovely coloring for a mortal: hair like a blade, eyes like onyx. She recalled his sister, so very different, not nearly so elegant. "Was your sleep refreshing? Are you weary?"

He rolled over onto his back and grinned up at her. "Not quite spent, I think."

She leaned to kiss him, and he reached up to twine his fingers in her red hair. He looked at a curl of it, scarlet against the scarred skin of his knuckles, and touched the curl to his cheek. Before she could speak another word, a knock came at the door of her bedchamber.

The Queen called out, "What is it? If it is not a matter of importance, be off with you, or I shall have you fed to the nixies in the river."

The door opened, and one of the younger Court ladies came in—Kaelie Whitewillow. A pixie. She curtsied and said, "My lady, Meliorn is here, and would speak with you."

Sebastian quirked a pale eyebrow. "A Queen's work is never done."

The Queen sighed and rolled from the bed. "Bring him in," she said, "and bring me one of my dressing gowns as well, for the air is chill."

Kaelie nodded and left the room. A moment later Meliorn entered, and bowed his head. If Sebastian thought it odd that the Queen greeted her courtiers standing naked in the middle of her bedchamber, he did not evince it by any quirk of expression. A mortal woman would have been embarrassed, might have tried to cover herself, but the Queen was the Queen, eternal and proud, and she knew she was as glorious out of clothes as she was in them. "Meliorn," she said. "You have news from the Nephilim?"

He straightened. Meliorn wore, as he usually did, white armor in a design of overlapping scales. His eyes were green and his hair was very long and black. "My lady," he said, and glanced behind her at Sebastian, who was sitting up on the bed, the coverlet tangled around his waist. "I have much news. Our new forces of Dark Ones have been situated at the fortress of Edom. They await further orders."

"And the Nephilim?" the Queen asked as Kaelie came back into the room carrying a dressing gown woven of the petals of lilies. She held it up, and the Queen slipped into it, wrapping the silken whiteness about herself.

"The children who escaped the Los Angeles Institute have given enough information that they know that Sebastian is behind the attacks," said Meliorn rather sourly.

"They would have guessed it anyway," said Sebastian. "They do have a regrettable habit of blaming me for everything."

"The question is, were our people identified?" the Queen demanded.

"They were not," said Meliorn with satisfaction. "The children assumed all the attackers to be Endarkened."

"That is impressive, considering the presence of faerie blood in that Blackthorn boy," said Sebastian. "One might have thought they'd be attuned to it. What are you planning on doing with him, anyway?"

"He has faerie blood; he is ours," said Meliorn. "Gwyn has claimed him to join the Wild Hunt; he will be dispatched there." He turned to the Queen. "We have need of more soldiers," he said. "The

Institutes are emptying: The Nephilim are fleeing to Idris."

"What of the New York Institute?" Sebastian demanded sharply. "What of my brother and sister?"

"Clary Fray and Jace Lightwood have been sent to Idris," said Meliorn. "We cannot attempt to retrieve them quite yet without showing our hand."

Sebastian touched the bracelet on his wrist. It was a habit of his the Queen had noted, something he did when he was angry and trying not to show it. The metal was written on in an old language of humans: *If I cannot reach Heaven, I will raise Hell.* "I want them," he said.

"And you shall have them," said the Queen. "I have not forgotten that was part of our bargain. But you must be patient."

Sebastian smiled, though it did not reach his eyes. "We mortals can be overhasty."

"You are no ordinary mortal," said the Queen, and turned back to Meliorn. "My knight," she said. "What do you advise your Queen?"

"We need more soldiers," Meliorn said. "We must take another Institute. More weapons would be a boon as well."

"I thought you said all the Shadowhunters were in Idris?" Sebastian said.

"Not quite yet," said Meliorn. "Some cities have taken longer than expected to evacuate all the Nephilim—the Shadowhunters of London, Rio de Janeiro, Cairo, Istanbul, and Taipei remain. We must have at least one more Institute."

Sebastian smiled. It was the sort of smile that transformed his lovely face, not into something lovelier but into a cruel mask, all teeth, like a manticore's grin. "Then I shall have London," he said. "If that does not go against your wishes, my Queen."

She could not help but smile. It had been so many centuries since a mortal lover had made her smile. She bent to kiss him, and felt his hands slide over the petals of her gown. "Take London, my love, and turn it all to blood," she said. "My gift to you."

"You're all right?" Jace asked, for what felt to Clary like the hundredth time. She was standing on the front step of Amatis's house, partly illuminated by the lights from the windows. Jace was just below her, his hands jammed into his pockets, as if he were afraid to let them free.

He had stared at the burn marks he'd made on the wall of the shop for a long time, before tugging his shirt down and practically yanking Clary out into the crowded street, as if she shouldn't be alone with him. He'd been taciturn the rest of the way home, his mouth set in a tense line.

"I'm *fine*," she assured him. "Look, you burned the wall, not me." She did an exaggerated twirl, as if she were showing off a new outfit. "See?"

There were shadows in his eyes. "If I hurt you—"

"You didn't," she said. "I'm not that fragile."

"I thought I was getting better at controlling it, that working with Jordan was helping." Frustration curled through his voice.

"You are; it is. Look, you were able to concentrate the fire in your hands; that's progress. I was touching you, kissing you, and I'm not hurt." She put her hand against his cheek. "We work through this together, remember? No shutting me out. No epic sulks."

"I was figuring I could sulk for Idris in the next Olympics," Jace said, but his voice was already softening, the edge of hard self-loathing filed away, wryness and amusement taking its place.

"You and Alec could go for pair sulking," said Clary with a smile. "You'd get the gold."

He turned his head and kissed the palm of her hand. His hair brushed the tops of her fingers. Everything around them seemed still and quiet; Clary could almost believe they were the only people in Alicante. "I keep wondering," he said against her skin, "what the guy who owns that store is going to think when he comes to work in the morning and sees two handprints burned into his wall."

"'I hope I have insurance for this'?"

Jace laughed, a small puff of air against her hand.

"Speaking of which," said Clary, "the next Council meeting is tomorrow, right?"

Jace nodded. "War council," he said. "Only select members of the Clave." He wiggled his fingers irritably. Clary felt his annoyance—Jace was an excellent strategist and one of the Clave's best fighters, and would have greatly resented being left out of any meeting that was about battles. Especially, she thought, if there was going to be discussion about using the heavenly fire as a weapon.

"Then maybe you can help me out with something. I need an armaments shop. I want to buy a sword. A really good one."

Jace looked surprised, then amused. "What for?"

"Oh, you know. Killing." Clary made a hand gesture she hoped conveyed her murderous intentions toward all things evil. "I mean, I've been a Shadowhunter for a while now. I should have a proper weapon, right?"

A slow grin spread over his face. "The best blade shop is Diana's on Flintlock Street," he said, eyes alight. "I'll pick you up tomorrow afternoon."

"It's a date," Clary said. "A weapons date."

"So much better than dinner and a movie," he said, and disappeared into the shadows.

5

MEASURE OF REVENGE

Maia looked up as the door to Jordan's apartment banged open and he raced inside, almost skidding on the slippery hardwood floor. "Anything?" he asked.

She shook her head. His face fell. After they'd killed the Endarkened, she'd called the pack to come help them deal with the mess. Unlike demons, Endarkened didn't just evaporate when you killed them. Disposal was required. Normally they would have summoned the Shadowhunters and Silent Brothers, but the doors to the Institute and the Bone City were closed now. Instead Bat and the rest of the pack had showed up with a body bag, while Jordan, still bleeding from the fight with the Endarkened, had gone to look for Simon.

He hadn't come back for hours, and when he had, the look in his eyes had told Maia the whole story. He had found Simon's phone, smashed to pieces, abandoned at the bottom of the fire escape like a mocking note. Otherwise there'd been no sign of him at all.

Neither of them had slept after that, of course. Maia had gone back to wolf pack headquarters with Bat, who had promised—if a little hesitantly—that he would tell the wolves to look for Simon, and try (emphasis on try) to reach the Shadowhunters in Alicante. There were lines open to the Shadowhunter capital, lines that only the heads of packs and clans could use.

Maia had returned to Jordan's apartment at dawn, despairing and exhausted. She was standing in the kitchen when he came in, a wet paper towel pressed to her forehead. She took it away as Jordan looked at her, and felt the water run down her face like tears. "No," she said. "No news."

Jordan slumped against the wall. He was wearing only a short-sleeved T-shirt, and the inked designs of lines from the Upanishads were darkly visible around his biceps. His hair was sweaty, plastered to his forehead, and there was a red line on his neck where the strap of his weapons pack had cut into the skin. He looked miserable. "I can't believe this," he said, for what felt to Maia like the millionth time. "I lost him. I was responsible for him, and I goddamned lost him."

"It's not your fault." She knew it wouldn't make him feel any better, but she couldn't help saying it. "Look, you can't fight off every vampire and baddie in the tristate area, and the Praetor shouldn't have asked you to try. When Simon lost the Mark, you asked for backup, didn't you? And they didn't send anyone. You did what you could."

Jordan looked down at his hands, and said something under his breath. "Not good enough." Maia knew she should go over to him, put her arms around him, comfort him. Tell him he wasn't to blame.

But she couldn't. The weight of guilt was as heavy on her chest as an iron bar, words unsaid choking her throat. It had been that way for weeks now. *Jordan, I have to tell you something. Jordan, I have to. Jordan, I.*

Jordan—

The sound of a ringing phone cut through the silence between them. Almost frantically Jordan dug into his pocket and yanked his mobile out; he flipped it open as he put it to his ear. "Hello?"

Maia watched him, leaning so far forward that the countertop cut into her rib cage. She could hear only murmurs on the other end of the phone, though, and was nearly screaming with impatience by the time Jordan closed the phone and looked over at her, a spark of hopefulness in his eyes. "That was Teal Waxelbaum, second in command at the Praetor," he said. "They want me at headquarters right away. I think they're going to help look for Simon. Will you come? If we head out now, we should be there by noon."

There was a plea in his voice, under the current of anxiety about Simon. He wasn't stupid, Maia thought. He knew something was wrong. He knew—

She took a deep breath. The words crowded her throat—*Jordan, we have to talk about something*—but she forced them back down. Simon was the priority now.

"Of course," she said. "Of course I'll come."

The first thing Simon saw was the wallpaper, which wasn't that bad. A bit dated. Definitely peeling. Serious mold problem. But overall, not the worst thing he'd ever opened his eyes to. He blinked once or twice, taking in the heavy stripes that cut through the floral pattern. It took him a second to realize that those stripes were, in fact, bars. He was in a cage.

He quickly rolled onto his back and stood, not checking to see how high the cage was. His skull made contact with the bars on top, knocking his gaze downward as he cursed out loud.

And then he saw himself.

He was wearing a flowing, puffy white shirt. Even more troubling was the fact that he also appeared to be wearing a pair of very tight leather pants.

Very tight.

Very leather.

Simon looked down at himself and took it all in. The billows of the shirt. The deep, chest-exposing V. The tightness of the leather.

"Why is it," he said after a moment, "that whenever I think I've found the most terrible thing that could happen to me, I'm always wrong."

As if on cue the door opened, and a tiny figure rushed into the room. A dark shape closed the door instantly behind her, with Secret Service–like speed.

She tiptoed up to the cage and squeezed her face between two bars. "Siiimon," she breathed.

Maureen.

Simon would normally have at least tried to ask her to let him out, to find a key, to assist him. But something in Maureen's appearance told him that would not be helpful. Specifically, the crown of bones she was wearing. Finger bones. Maybe foot bones. And the bone crown was bejeweled—or possibly bedazzled. And then there was the ragged rose-and-gray ball gown, widened at the hips in a style that reminded him of those costume dramas set in the eighteenth century. It was not the kind of outfit that inspired confidence.

"Hey, Maureen," he said cautiously.

Maureen smiled and pressed her face harder into the opening.

"Do you like your outfit?" she asked. "I have a few for you. I got you a frock coat and a kilt and all kinds of stuff, but I wanted you to wear this one first. I did your makeup too. That was me."

Simon didn't need a mirror to know he was wearing eyeliner. The knowledge was instant, and complete.

"Maureen—"

"I'm making you a necklace," she said, cutting him off. "I want you to wear more jewelry. I want you to wear more *bracelets*. I want things around your *wrists*."

"Maureen, where am I?"

"You're with me."

"Okay. Where are *we*?"

"The hotel, the hotel, the hotel..."

The Hotel Dumort. At least that made some kind of sense.

"Okay," he said. "And why am I ... in a cage?"

Maureen started humming a song to herself and ran her hand along the bars of the cage, lost in her own world.

"Together, together, together ... now we're together. You and me. Simon and Maureen. Finally."

"Maureen—"

"This will be your room," she said. "And once you're ready, you can come out. I've got things for you. I've got a bed. And other things. Some chairs. Things you'll like. And the band can play!"

She twirled, almost losing her balance under the strange weight of the dress.

Simon felt he should probably choose his next words very carefully. He knew he had a calming voice. He could be sensitive. Reassuring.

"Maureen ... you know ... I like you..."

On this, Maureen stopping spinning and gripped the bars again.

"You just need time," she said with a terrifying kindness in her voice. "Just time. You'll learn. You'll fall in love. We're together now. And we'll rule. You and me. We will rule my kingdom. Now that I'm queen."

"Queen?"

"Queen. Queen Maureen. Queen Maureen of the night. Queen Maureen of the darkness. Queen Maureen. Queen Maureen. Queen Maureen of the dead."

She took a candle that burned in a sconce on the wall and suddenly poked it between the bars and in Simon's general direction.

She tipped it ever so slightly, and smiled as the white wax dropped in tear-like forms to the rotted remains of the scarlet carpet on the floor. She bit her lower lip in concentration, turning her wrist gently, pooling the drips together.

"You're ... a queen?" Simon said faintly. He'd known Maureen was the leader of the New York vampire clan. She'd killed Camille, after all, and taken her place. But clan leaders weren't called kings or queens. They dressed normally, like Raphael did, not in costumey getups. They were important figures in the community of the Night's Children.

But Maureen, of course, was different. Maureen was a child, an undead child. Simon remembered her rainbow arm warmers, her little breathy voice, her big eyes. She'd been a little girl with all the innocence of a little girl when Simon had bitten her, when Camille and Lilith had taken her and changed her, injecting an evil into her veins that had taken all that innocence and corrupted it into madness.

It was his fault, Simon knew. If Maureen hadn't known him, hadn't followed him around, none of this would have happened to her.

Maureen nodded and smiled, concentrating on her wax pile, which was now looking like a tiny volcano. "I need ... to do things," she said abruptly, and dropped the candle, still burning. It snuffed itself out as it hit the ground, and she bustled toward the door. The same dark figure opened it the instant she approached. And then Simon was alone again, with the smoking remains of the candle and his new leather pants, and the horrible weight of his guilt.

Maia had been silent the whole way to the Praetor, as the sun had risen higher in the sky and the surroundings had turned from the crowded buildings of Manhattan to the traffic-clogged Long Island Expressway, to the pastoral small towns and farms of the North

Fork. They were close to the Praetor now, and could see the ice-blue waters of the Sound on their left, rippling in the cool wind. Maia imagined plunging into them, and shuddered at the thought of the cold.

"Are you all right?" Jordan had hardly spoken most of the way either. It was chilly inside his truck, and he wore leather driving gloves, but they didn't conceal his white-knuckle grip on the wheel. Maia could feel the anxiety rolling off him in waves.

"I'm fine," she said. It wasn't true. She was worried about Simon, and she was still fighting the words she couldn't say that choked her throat. Now wasn't the right time to say them, not with Simon missing, and yet every moment she didn't say them felt like a lie.

They swung onto the long white drive that stretched into the distance, toward the Sound. Jordan cleared his throat. "You know I love you, right?"

"I know," Maia said quietly, and fought the urge to say "Thank you." You weren't supposed to say "Thank you" when someone said they loved you. You were supposed to say what Jordan was clearly expecting—

She looked out the window and started, jerked out of her reverie. "Jordan, is it *snowing*?"

"I don't think so." But white flakes were drifting past the windows of the truck, building up on the windshield. Jordan brought the truck to a stop and rolled one of the windows down, opening his hand to catch a flake. He drew it back, his expression darkening. "That's not snow," he said. "That's ash."

Maia's heart lurched as he shoved the truck back into gear and they pitched forward, spinning around the corner of the drive. Up ahead of them, where the Praetor Lupus headquarters should have been rising, gold against the gray noon sky, was a gout of black smoke. Jordan swore and slewed the wheel to the left; the truck bumped into a ditch and sputtered out. He kicked his door open and jumped down; Maia followed a second later.

The Praetor Lupus headquarters had been built on a huge parcel of green land that sloped down to the Sound. The central building was built of golden stone, a Romanesque manor house surrounded by arched porticoes. Or it had been. It was a mass of smoking wood and stone now, charred like bones in a crematorium. White powder and ashes blew thickly across the gardens, and Maia choked on the stinging air, bringing up a hand to shield her face.

Jordan's brown hair was thickly snowflaked with ash. He stared around him, his expression shocked and uncomprehending. "I don't—"

Something caught Maia's eye, a flicker of movement through the smoke. She grabbed Jordan's sleeve. "Look—there's someone there—"

He took off, skirting the smoking ruin of the Praetor building. Maia followed him, though she couldn't help but hang back in horror, staring at the charred remnants of the structure that protruded from the earth—walls holding up a no-longer-existing roof, windows that had blown out or melted, glimpses here and there of white that could have been brick or bones...

Jordan stopped ahead of her. Maia moved up to stand beside him. Ash was clinging to her shoes, the grit of it in among the laces. She and Jordan were in the main body of the burned-out buildings. She could see the water in the near distance. The fire hadn't spread, though there were charred dead leaves and blowing ash here, too—and in among the clipped hedgerows, there were bodies.

Werewolves—of all ages, though mostly young—lay sprawled along the manicured paths, their bodies being slowly covered by ash as if they were being swallowed by a blizzard.

Werewolves had an instinct to surround themselves with others of their kind, to live in packs, to draw strength from one another.

This many dead lycanthropes felt like a tearing ache, a hole of loss in the world. She remembered the words from Kipling, written on the walls of the Praetor. *For the strength of the pack is the wolf, and the strength of the wolf is the pack.*

Jordan was gazing around, his lips moving as he murmured the names of the dead—*Andrea, Teal, Amon, Kurosh, Mara.* At the edge of the water Maia suddenly saw something move—a body, half-submerged. She broke into a run, Jordan on her heels. She skidded through the ash, to where the grass gave way to sand, and dropped down beside the corpse.

It was Praetor Scott, corpse bobbing facedown, his gray-blond hair soaked, the water around him stained pinkish red. Maia bent down to turn him over, and nearly gagged. His eyes were open, staring sightlessly at the sky, his throat sliced wide open.

"Maia." She felt a hand on her back—Jordan's. "Don't—"

His sentence was cut off by a gasp, and she whirled around, only to feel a sense of horror so intense that it nearly blacked out her vision. Jordan stood behind her, one hand outstretched, a look of utter shock on his face.

From the center of his chest protruded the blade of a sword, its metal stamped with black stars. It looked utterly bizarre, as if someone had taped it there, or as if it were some sort of theatrical prop.

Blood began to spread out in a circle around it, staining the front of his jacket. Jordan gave another bubbling gasp and slid to his knees, the sword retracting, slipping back out of his body as he collapsed to the ground and revealed what was behind him.

A boy carrying a massive black and silver sword stood looking at Maia over Jordan's kneeling body. The hilt was slicked with blood—in fact, he was bloody all over, from his pale hair to his boots, spattered with it as if he had stood in front of a fan blowing scarlet paint. He was grinning all over his face.

"Maia Roberts and Jordan Kyle," he said. "Have I heard a lot about *you*."

Maia dropped to her knees, just as Jordan slumped sideways. She caught him, easing him down into her lap. She felt numb all over with horror, as if she were lying at the icy bottom of the Sound. Jordan was shuddering in her arms, and she put them around him as blood ran out of the corners of his mouth.

She looked up at the boy standing over her. For a dizzy moment she thought he had stepped out of one of her nightmares of her brother, Daniel. He was beautiful, like Daniel had been, though they could not have looked more different. Daniel's skin had been the same brown as hers, while this boy looked like he had been carved out of ice. White skin, sharp pale cheekbones, salt-white hair that fell over his forehead. His eyes were black, shark's eyes, flat and cold.

"Sebastian," she said. "You're Valentine's son."

"Maia," Jordan whispered. Her hands were over his chest, and they were soaked in blood. So was his shirt, and the sand under them, the grains of it clumped together by sticky scarlet. "Don't stay—run—"

"Shh." She kissed his cheek. "You'll be all right."

"No, he won't," Sebastian said, sounding bored. "He's going to die."

Maia's head jerked up. "Shut up," she hissed. "Shut up, you—you *thing*—"

His wrist made a fast snapping motion—she had never seen anyone else move that fast, except maybe Jace—and the tip of the sword was at her throat. "Quiet, Downworlder," he said. "Look how many lie dead around you. Do you think I would hesitate to kill one more?"

She swallowed but didn't lean away. "Why? I thought your war was with the Shadowhunters—"

"It's rather a long story," he drawled. "Suffice it to say that the London Institute is annoyingly well protected, and the Praetor has paid the price. I was going to kill *someone* today. I just wasn't sure who when I woke up this morning. I do love mornings. So full of possibilities."

"The Praetor has nothing to do with the London Institute—"

"Oh, you're wrong there. There's quite a history. But it's unimportant. You're correct that my war is with the Nephilim, which means I am also at war with their allies. This"—and he swung his free hand back to indicate the burned ruins behind him—"is my message. And you will deliver it for me."

Maia began to shake her head, but felt something grip her hand—it was Jordan's fingers. She looked down at him. He was bone white, his eyes searching hers. *Please*, they seemed to say. *Do what he asks.*

"What message?" she whispered.

"That they should remember their Shakespeare," he said. "'*I'll never pause again, never stand still, till either death hath closed these eyes of mine, or fortune given me measure of revenge.*'" Lashes brushed his bloody cheek as he winked. "Tell all the Downworlders," he said. "I am in pursuit of vengeance, and I will have it. I will deal this way with any who ally themselves with Shadowhunters. I have no argument with your kind, unless you follow the Nephilim into battle, in which case you will be food for my blade and the blades of my army, until the last of you is cut from the surface of this world." He lowered the tip of his sword, so that it brushed down the buttons of her shirt, as if he meant to slice it off her body. He was still grinning when he drew the sword back. "Think you can remember that, wolf girl?"

"I..."

"Of course you can," he said, and glanced down at Jordan's body, which had gone still in her arms. "Your boyfriend's dead, by the way," he added. He slid his sword into the scabbard at his waist and walked away, his boots sending up puffs of ash as he went.

Magnus hadn't been inside the Hunter's Moon since it had been a speakeasy during the years of Prohibition, a place where mundanes had gathered quietly to drink themselves blackout drunk. Sometime in the 1940s it had been taken over by Downworlder owners, and had catered to that clientele—primarily werewolves—ever since. It had been seedy then and was seedy now, the floor covered with a layer of sticky sawdust. There was a wooden bar with a flecked countertop, marked with decades of rings left by damp glasses and long claw scratches. Sneaky Pete, the bartender, was in the middle of serving a Coke to Bat Velasquez, the temporary head of Luke's Manhattan wolf pack. Magnus squinted at him thoughtfully.

"Are you eyeing up the new wolf pack leader?" asked Catarina, who was squeezed into the shadowy booth beside Magnus, her blue fingers curled around a Long Island Iced Tea. "I thought you were over werewolves after Woolsey Scott."

"I'm not eyeing him up," Magnus said loftily. Bat wasn't bad-looking, if you liked them square-jawed and broad-shouldered, but Magnus was deep in thought. "My mind was on other things."

"Whatever it is, don't do it!" said Catarina. "It's a bad idea."

"And why do you say that?"

"Because they're the only kind you have," she said. "I have known you a long time, and I am absolutely certain on this subject. If you are planning to become a pirate again, it's a bad idea."

"I don't repeat my mistakes," Magnus said, offended.

"You're right. You make all new and even worse mistakes," Catarina told him. "Don't do it, whatever it is. Don't lead a werewolf uprising, don't do anything that might accidentally contribute to the apocalypse, and don't start your own line of glitter and try to sell it at Sephora."

"That last idea has real merit," Magnus remarked. "But I'm not contemplating a career change. I was thinking about..."

"Alec Lightwood?" Catarina grinned. "I've never seen anyone get under your skin like that boy."

"You haven't known me forever," Magnus muttered, but it was halfhearted.

"Please. You made me take the Portal job at the Institute so you wouldn't have to see him, and then you showed up anyway, just to say good-bye. Don't deny it; I saw you."

"I didn't deny anything. I showed up to say good-bye; it was a mistake. I shouldn't have done it." Magnus tossed back a slug of his drink.

"Oh, for goodness' sake," Catarina said. "*What* is this about, really, Magnus? I've never seen you so happy as you were with Alec. Usually when you're in love, you're miserable. Look at Camille. I hated her. Ragnor hated her—"

Magnus put his head down on the table.

"*Everyone* hated her," Catarina went on ruthlessly. "She was devious *and* mean. And so your poor sweet boyfriend got suckered by her; well, really, is that any reason to end a perfectly good relationship? It's like siccing a python on a bunny rabbit and then being angry when the bunny rabbit loses."

"Alec is not a bunny rabbit. He's a Shadowhunter."

"And you've never dated a Shadowhunter before. Is that what this is?"

Magnus pushed himself away from the table, which was a relief, because it smelled like beer. "In a sense," he said. "The world is changing. Don't you feel it, Catarina?"

She looked at him over the rim of her drink. "I can't say that I do."

"The Nephilim have endured for a thousand years," said Magnus. "But something is coming, some great change. We have always accepted them as a fact of our existence. But there are warlocks old enough to remember when the Nephilim did not walk the earth. They could be wiped away as quickly as they came."

"But you don't really think—"

"I've dreamed about it," he said. "You know I have true dreams sometimes."

"Because of your father." She set her drink down. Her expression was intent now, no humor in it. "He could just be trying to frighten you."

Catarina was one of the few people in the world who knew who Magnus's father really was; Ragnor Fell had been another. It wasn't something Magnus liked to tell people. It was one thing to have a demon for a parent. It was another thing when your father owned a significant portion of Hell's real estate.

"To what end?" Magnus shrugged. "I am not the center of whatever whirlwind is coming."

"But you're afraid Alec will be," said Catarina. "And you want to push him away before you lose him."

"You said not to do anything that might accidentally contribute to the apocalypse," Magnus said. "I know you were joking. But it's less funny when I can't rid myself of the feeling that the apocalypse is coming, somehow. Valentine Morgenstern nearly wiped out the Shadowhunters, and his son is twice as clever and six times as evil. And he will not come alone. He has help, from demons greater than my father, from others—"

"How do you know that?" Catarina's voice was sharp.

"I've looked into it."

"I thought you were done helping Shadowhunters," said Catarina, and then she held up a hand before he could say anything. "Never mind. I've heard you say that sort of thing enough times to know you never really mean it."

"That's the thing," Magnus said. "I've looked into it, but I haven't found anything. Whoever Sebastian's allies are, he's left no tracks of their alliance behind. I keep feeling like I'm about to discover something, and then I find myself grasping at air. I don't think I *can* help them, Catarina. I don't know if anyone can."

Magnus looked away from her suddenly pitying expression, across the bar. Bat was leaning against the counter, playing with his phone—the light from the screen cast shadows across his face. Shadows that Magnus saw on every mortal face—every human, every Shadowhunter, every creature doomed to die.

"Mortals die," said Catarina. "You have always known that, and yet you've loved them before."

"Not," Magnus said, "like this."

Catarina inhaled in surprise. "Oh," she said. "Oh..." She picked up her drink. "Magnus," she said tenderly. "You are impossibly stupid."

He narrowed his eyes at her. "Am I?"

"If that's the way you feel, you should be with him," she said. "Think of Tessa. Did you learn nothing from her? About what loves are worth the pain of losing them?"

"He's in Alicante."

"So?" said Catarina. "You were supposed to be the warlock representative on the Council; you unloaded that responsibility onto me. I'm unloading it back. Go to Alicante. It sounds to me like you'll have more to say to the Council than I ever could, anyway." She reached into the pocket of the nurse's scrubs she was wearing; she had come directly from her work at the hospital. "Oh, and take this."

Magnus plucked the crumpled piece of paper from her fingertips. "A dinner invitation?" he said in disbelief.

"Meliorn of the Fair Folk wishes for all the Council Downworlders to meet for supper the night before the great Council," she said. "Some kind of gesture of peace and goodwill, or maybe he just wants to annoy everyone with riddles. Either way it should be interesting."

"Faerie food," Magnus said glumly. "I hate faerie food. I mean, even the safe kind that doesn't mean you'll be stuck dancing reels for the next century. All those raw vegetables and beetles—"

He broke off. Across the room Bat had his phone pressed to his ear. His other hand gripped the counter of the bar.

"There's something wrong," Magnus said. "Something pack-related."

Catarina set her glass down. She was very used to Magnus, and knew when he was probably right. She looked over at Bat as well, who had snapped his phone shut. He had paled, his scar standing out, livid on his cheek. He leaned over to say something to Sneaky Pete behind the bar, then put two fingers into his mouth and whistled.

It sounded like the whistle of a steam train, and cut through the low murmur of voices in the bar. In moments every lycanthrope was on his or her feet, surging toward Bat. Magnus stood up too, though Catarina caught at his sleeve. "Don't—"

"I'll be fine." He shrugged her off, and pushed through the crowd, toward Bat. The rest of the pack stood in a loose ring around him. They tensed mistrustfully at the sight of the warlock in their midst, shoving to get close to their pack leader. A blonde female werewolf moved to block Magnus, but Bat held up a hand.

"It's all right, Amabel," he said. His voice wasn't friendly, but it was polite. "Magnus Bane, right? High Warlock of Brooklyn? Maia Roberts says I can trust you."

"You can."

"Fine, but we have urgent pack business here. What do you want?"

"You got a call." Magnus gestured toward Bat's phone. "Was it Luke? Has something happened in Alicante?"

Bat shook his head, his expression unreadable.

"Another Institute attack, then?" Magnus said. He was used to being the one with all the answers, and hated not knowing anything. And while the New York Institute was empty, that didn't mean the other Institutes were unprotected—that there might not have been a battle—one Alec might have decided to involve himself in—

"Not an Institute," Bat said. "That was Maia on the phone. The Praetor Lupus headquarters were burned to the ground. At least a hundred werewolves are dead, including Praetor Scott and Jordan Kyle. Sebastian Morgenstern has taken his fight to us."

6

BROTHER LEAD
AND SISTER STEEL

"Don't throw it—please, please don't throw it—oh, God, he threw it," said Julian in a resigned voice as a wedge of potato flew across the room, narrowly missing his ear.

"Nothing's damaged," Emma reassured him. She was sitting with her back against Tavvy's crib, watching Julian give his littlest brother his afternoon meal. Tavvy had reached the age where he was very particular about what he liked to eat, and anything that didn't pass muster was hurled to the floor. "The lamp got a little potatoed, that's all."

Fortunately, though the rest of the Penhallows' house was quite elegant, the attic—where "the war orphans," the collective term that had been applied to the Blackthorn children and Emma since they'd arrived in Idris, were now living—was extremely plain, functional and sturdy in its design. It took up the whole top floor of the house: several connected rooms, a small kitchen and bathroom, a haphazard collection of beds and belongings strewn everywhere. Helen slept downstairs with Aline, though she was up every day; Emma had been given her own room and so had Julian, but he was hardly ever in it. Drusilla and Octavian were still waking up every night screaming, and Julian had taken to sleeping on the floor of their room, pillow and blanket piled up next to Tavvy's crib. There was no high chair to be had, so Julian sat on the floor opposite the toddler on a food-covered blanket, a plate in one hand and a despairing look on his face.

Emma came over and sat down opposite him, heaving Tavvy up onto her lap. His small face was scrunched with unhappiness. "Memma," he said as she lifted him.

"Do the choo-choo train," she advised Jules. She wondered if she should tell him he had spaghetti sauce in his hair. On second thought, probably better not.

She watched as he zoomed the food around before placing it in Tavvy's mouth. The toddler was giggling now. Emma tried to shove down her sense of loss: She remembered her own father patiently separating out the food on her plate during the phase she'd gone through where she refused to eat anything that was green.

"He's not eating enough," Jules said in a quiet voice, even as he made a piece of bread and butter into a chugging train and Tavvy reached for it with sticky hands.

"He's sad. He's a baby, but he still knows something bad happened," Emma said. "He misses Mark and your dad."

Jules scrubbed tiredly at his eyes, leaving a smear of tomato sauce on one cheekbone. "I can't replace Mark or my dad." He put a slice of apple in Tavvy's mouth. Tavvy spat it out with a look of grim pleasure. Julian sighed. "I should go check on Dru and the twins," he said. "They were playing Monopoly in the bedroom, but you never know when that's going to go south."

It was true. Tiberius, with his analytical mind, tended to win most games. Livvy never minded but Dru, who was competitive, did, and often any match would end in hair-pulling on both sides.

"I'll do it." Emma handed Tavvy back and was about to rise to her feet when Helen came into the room, looking somber. When she saw the two of them, somberness turned to apprehension. Emma felt the hair on the back of her neck rise.

"Helen," Julian said. "What's wrong?"

"Sebastian's forces attacked the London Institute."

Emma saw Julian tense. She almost felt it, as if his nerves were her nerves, his panic her panic. His face—already too thin—seemed to tighten, though he kept the same careful, gentle grasp on the baby. "Uncle Arthur?" he asked.

"He's all right," Helen said quickly. "He was injured. It'll delay his arrival in Idris, but he's all right. In fact, everyone from the London Institute is all right. The attack was unsuccessful."

"How?" Julian's voice was barely a whisper.

"We don't know yet, not exactly," said Helen. "I'm going over to the Gard with Aline and the Consul and the rest, to try to figure out what happened." She knelt down and stroked her hand over Tavvy's curls. "It's *good* news," she said to Julian, who looked more stunned than anything else. "I know it's scary that Sebastian attacked again, but he didn't win."

Emma met Julian's eyes with hers. She felt as if she ought to be thrilled at the good news, but there was a tearing feeling inside her—a terrible jealousy. Why did the inhabitants of the London Institute get to live when her family died? How had they fought better, done more?

"It's not fair," Julian said.

"Jules," said Helen, standing up. "It's a defeat. That means something. It means we *can* defeat Sebastian and his forces. Take them down. Turn the tide. It will make everyone less afraid. That's important."

"I hope they catch him alive," said Emma, her eyes on Julian's. "I hope they kill him in Angel Square so we can all watch him die, and I hope it's slow."

"*Emma*," said Helen, sounding shocked, but Julian's blue-green eyes echoed Emma's own fierceness back to her without a hint of disapproval. Emma had never loved him so much as she did in that moment, for reflecting back to her even the darkest feelings in the depths of her own heart.

The weapons shop was gorgeous. Clary never thought she would have described a weapons shop as gorgeous before—maybe a sunset, or a clear night view of the New York skyline, but not a shop full of maces, axes, and sword-canes.

This one was, though. The metal sign that hung outside was in the shape of a quiver, the name of the store—Diana's Arrow—inscribed on it in curling letters. Inside the shop were blades displayed in deadly fans of gold and steel and silver. A massive chandelier hung from a ceiling painted with a rococo design of golden arrows in flight. Real arrows were displayed on carved wooden stands. Tibetan longswords, their pommels decorated with turquoise, silver, and coral, hung on the walls alongside Burmese *dha* blades with hammered metal tangs in copper and brass.

"So what brought this on?" Jace asked curiously, taking down a *naginata* carved with Japanese characters. When he set it on the floor, the blade rose over his head, his long fingers curving around the shaft to hold it steady. "This desire for a sword?"

"When a twelve-year-old tells you the weapon you have sucks, it's time to change it up," said Clary.

The woman behind the counter laughed. Clary recognized her as the woman with the tattoo of the fish who had spoken out at the Council meeting. "Well, you've come to the best place."

"Is this your shop?" Clary asked, reaching to test the point of a long sword with an iron hilt.

The woman smiled. "I'm Diana, yes. Diana Wrayburn."

Clary reached for the rapier, but Jace, having leaned the *naginata* against the wall, shook his head at her. "That claymore would be taller than you. Not that that's hard."

Clary stuck her tongue out at him and reached for a short-sword hanging on the wall. There were scratches along the blade—scratches that on closer examination she could see were clearly letters in a language she didn't know.

"Those are runes, but not Shadowhunter runes," said Diana. "That's a Viking sword—very old. And very heavy."

"Do you know what it says?"

"'Only the Worthy,'" said Diana. "My father used to say you could tell a great weapon if it had either a name or an inscription."

"I saw one yesterday," Clary recalled. "It said something like 'I am of the same steel and temper as Joyeuse and Durendal.'"

"Cortana!" Diana's eyes lit up. "The blade of Ogier. That *is* impressive. Like owning Excalibur, or Kusanagi-no-Tsurugi. Cortana is a Carstairs blade, I think. Is Emma Carstairs, the girl who was at the Council meeting yesterday, the one who owns it now?"

Clary nodded.

Diana pursed her lips. "Poor child," she said. "And the Blackthorns, too. To have lost so many in a single sweeping blow— I wish there was something I could do for them."

"Me too," Clary said.

Diana gave her a measured look and ducked down behind the counter. She came up a moment later with a sword about the length of Clary's forearm. "What do you think of this?"

Clary stared at the sword. It was undoubtedly beautiful. The cross-guard, grip, and pommel were gold chased with obsidian, the blade a silver so dark it was nearly black. Clary's mind ran quickly through the types of weapons she had been memorizing in her lessons—falchions, sabres, backswords, longswords. "Is it a *cinque-dea*?" she guessed.

"It's a shortsword. You might want to look at the other side," said Diana, and she flipped the sword over. On the opposite side of the blade, down the center ridge, ran a pattern of black stars.

"Oh." Clary's heart thumped painfully; she took a step back and nearly bumped into Jace, who had come up behind her, frowning. "That's a Morgenstern sword."

"Yes, it is." Diana's eyes were shrewd. "Long ago the Morgensterns commissioned two blades from Wayland the Smith—a matched set. A larger and a smaller, for a father and his son. Because Morgenstern means Morning Star, they were each named for a different aspect of the star itself—the smaller, this one here, is called Heosphoros, which means dawn-bringer, while the larger is called Phaesphoros, or light-bringer. You have doubtless seen Phaesphoros already, for Valentine Morgenstern carried it, and now his son carries it after him."

"You know who we are," Jace said. It wasn't a question. "Who Clary is."

"The Shadowhunter world is small," said Diana, and she looked from one of them to the other. "I'm on the Council. I've seen you give testimony, Valentine's daughter."

Clary looked doubtfully at the blade. "I don't understand," she said. "Valentine would never have given up a Morgenstern sword. How do you have it?"

"His wife sold it," Diana said. "To my father, who owned this shop in the days before the Uprising. It was hers. It should be yours now."

Clary shuddered. "I've seen two men bear the larger version of that sword, and I hated them both. There are no Morgensterns in this world now who are dedicated to anything but evil."

Jace said, "There's you."

She glanced over at him, but his expression was unreadable.

"I couldn't afford it, anyway," Clary said. "That's gold, and black gold, and *adamas*. I don't have the money for that kind of weapon."

"I'll give it to you," said Diana. "You're right that people hate the Morgensterns; they tell stories of how the swords were created to contain deadly magic, to slay thousands at once. They're just stories, of course, no truth to them, but still—it's not the sort of item I could sell elsewhere. Or would necessarily want to. It should go to good hands."

"I don't want it," Clary whispered.

"If you flinch from it, you give it power over you," said Diana. "Take it, and cut your brother's throat with it, and take back the honor of your blood."

She slid the sword across the counter to Clary. Wordlessly Clary picked it up, her hand curling around the pommel, finding that it fit her grip—fit it exactly, as if it had been made for her. Despite the steel and precious metals in the sword's construction, it felt as light as a feather in her hand. She raised it up, the black stars along the blade winking at her, a light like fire running, sparking along the steel.

She looked up to see Diana catch something out of the air: a glimmer of light that resolved itself into a piece of paper. She read down it, her eyebrows knitting together in concern. "By the Angel," she said. "The London Institute's been attacked."

Clary almost dropped the blade. She heard Jace suck in his breath beside her. "*What?*" he demanded.

Diana looked up. "It's all right," she said. "Apparently there's some kind of special protection laid on the London Institute, something even the Council didn't know about. There were some injuries, but no one was killed. Sebastian's forces were rebuffed. Unfortunately, none of the Endarkened were captured or killed either." As Diana spoke, Clary realized that the shop owner was wearing white mourning clothes. Had she lost someone in Valentine's war? In Sebastian's attacks on the Institutes?

How much blood had been spilled by Morgenstern hands?

"I—I'm so sorry," Clary gasped. She could see Sebastian, see him clearly in her head, red gear and red blood, silver hair and silver blade. She reeled back.

There was a hand on her arm suddenly, and she realized she was breathing in cold air. Somehow she was outside the weapons shop, on a street full of people, and Jace was beside her. "Clary," he was saying. "It's all right. Everything is all right. The London Shadowhunters, they all escaped."

"Diana said there were injuries," she said. "More blood spilled because of Morgensterns."

He glanced down at the blade, still clutched in her right hand, her fingers bloodless on the hilt. "You don't have to take the sword."

"No. Diana was right. Being afraid of everything Morgenstern, it—it gives Sebastian power over me. Which is exactly what he wants."

"I agree," Jace said. "That's why I bought you this."

He handed her a scabbard, dark leather, worked with a pattern of silver stars.

"You can't walk up and down the street with an unsheathed weapon," he added. "I mean, you can, but it's likely to get us some odd looks."

Clary took the sheath, covered the blade, and tucked it through her belt, closing her coat over it. "Better?"

He brushed a strand of red hair back from her face. "It's your first real weapon, one that belongs to you. The Morgenstern name isn't cursed, Clary. It's a glorious old Shadowhunter name that goes back hundreds of years. *The morning star.*"

"The morning star isn't a star," Clary said grumpily. "It's a planet. I learned that in astronomy class."

"Mundane education is regrettably prosaic," said Jace. "Look," he said, and pointed up. Clary looked, but not at the sky. She looked at him, at the sun on his light hair, the curve of his mouth when he smiled. "Long before anyone knew about planets, they knew there were bright rips in the fabric of the night. The stars. And they knew there was one that rose in the east, at sunrise, and they called it the morning star, the light-bringer, the herald of dawn. Is that so bad? To bring light to the world?"

Impulsively Clary leaned up and kissed his cheek. "Okay, fine," she said. "So that was more poetic than astronomy class."

He dropped his hand and smiled at her. "Good," he said. "We're going to do something else poetic now. Come on. I want to show you something."

Cold fingers against Simon's temples woke him up. "Open your eyes, Daylighter," said an impatient voice. "We do not have all day."

Simon sat up with such alacrity that the person opposite him jerked back with a hiss. Simon stared. He was still surrounded by the bars of Maureen's cage, still inside the rotting room in the Hotel Dumort. Across from him was Raphael. He wore a buttoned white shirt and jeans, the glint of gold visible at his throat. Still—Simon had only ever seen him look neat and pressed, as if he were going to a business meeting. Now his dark hair was mussed, his white shirt ripped and stained with dirt.

"Good morning, Daylighter," Raphael said.

"What are *you* doing here?" Simon snapped. He felt filthy and sick and angry. And he was still wearing a puffy shirt. "Is it actually morning?"

"You were asleep, now you are awake—it's morning." Raphael seemed obscenely cheerful. "As for what I am doing here: I am here for you, of course."

Simon leaned back against the bars of the cage. "What do you mean? And how did you get in here, anyway?"

Raphael looked at him pityingly. "The cage unlocks from the outside. It was easy enough for me to get in."

"So is this just loneliness and a desire for bro-type companionship, or what?" Simon inquired. "The last time I saw you, you asked me to be your bodyguard, and when I said no, you strongly implied that if I ever lost the Mark of Cain, you would kill me."

Raphael smiled at him.

"So is this the killing part?" Simon asked. "I have to say, it's not that subtle. You'll probably get caught."

"Yes," Raphael mused. "Maureen would be very unhappy at your demise. I once broached the mere topic of selling you to unscrupulous warlocks, and she was not amused. It was unfortunate. With its healing powers, Daylighter blood brings a high price." He sighed. "It would have been quite an opportunity. Alas, Maureen is too foolish to see things from my point of view. She would rather keep you here dressed up like a doll. But then, she is insane."

"Are you supposed to say that sort of thing about your vampire queen?"

"There was a time I wanted you dead, Daylighter," Raphael replied conversationally, as if he were telling Simon that there had once been a time when he'd considered buying Simon a box of chocolates. "But I have a greater enemy. You and I, we are on the same side."

The bars of the cage were pressing uncomfortably into Simon's back. He shifted. "Maureen?" he guessed. "You always wanted to be the vampire leader, and now she's taken your place."

Raphael curled his lip in a snarl. "You think this is only a power play?" he said. "You do not understand. Before Maureen was Turned, she was terrified and tortured to the point of madness. When she rose, she clawed her way free of her coffin. There was no one to teach her. No one to give her first blood. Like I did for you."

Simon stared. He remembered the graveyard suddenly, coming up out of the earth into the cold of the air and the dirt, and the hunger, tearing hunger, and Raphael tossing him a bag full of blood. He had never thought of it as a favor or a service, but he would have torn into any living creature he had encountered if he hadn't had that first meal. He almost had torn into Clary. It was Raphael who had stopped that from happening.

It was Raphael who had carried Simon from the Dumort to the Institute; had laid him, bleeding, down on the front steps when they could go no farther; and had explained to Simon's friends what had happened. Simon supposed Raphael could have tried to hide it, could have lied to the Nephilim, but he had confessed and taken the consequences.

Raphael had never been particularly nice to Simon, but in his own way he had a strange sort of honor.

"I made you," Raphael said. "My blood, in your veins, made you a vampire."

"You've always said I was a terrible vampire," Simon pointed out.

"I do not expect your gratitude," Raphael said. "You have never wanted to be what you are. Neither did Maureen, one can guess. She was made insane by her Turning, and she is still insane. She murders without a thought. She does not consider the dangers of exposing us to the human world by too careless a slaughter. She does not think that perhaps, if vampires killed without need or consideration, one day there would be no more food."

"Humans," corrected Simon. "There would be no more humans."

"You *are* a terrible vampire," Raphael said. "But in this we are aligned. You desire to protect humans. I desire to protect vampires. Our goal is one and the same."

"So kill her," said Simon. "Kill Maureen and take over the clan."

"I cannot." Raphael looked grim. "The other children of the clan love her. They do not see the long road, the darkness on the horizon. They see only having the freedom to kill and consume at will. Not to bend to the Accords, not to follow an outside Law. She has given them all the freedom in the world, and they will end themselves with it." His tone was bitter.

"You actually care what happens to the clan," Simon said, surprised. "You would make a pretty good leader."

Raphael glared at him.

"Though I don't know how you'd look in a bone tiara," Simon added. "Look, I understand what you're saying, but how can I help you? In case you didn't notice, I'm trapped in a cage. If you free me, you'll get caught. And if I leave, Maureen will find me."

"Not in Alicante, she will not," said Raphael.

"Alicante?" Simon stared. "You mean—capital of Idris, Alicante?"

"You are not very smart," Raphael said. "Yes, that is the Alicante I mean." At Simon's stunned expression, he smiled thinly. "There is a vampire representative to the Council. Anselm Nightshade. A retiring sort, the leader of the Los Angeles clan, but a man who knows certain ... friends of mine. Warlocks."

"Magnus?" said Simon in surprise. Raphael and Magnus were both immortals, both residents of New York and fairly high-ranking representatives of their Downworlder branches. And yet he had never really considered how they might know each other, or how well.

Raphael ignored Simon's question. "Nightshade has agreed to send me as the representative in his place, though Maureen does not know it. So I shall go to Alicante, and sit on the Council for their great meeting, but I require you to come with me."

"Why?"

"They do not trust me, the Shadowhunters," said Raphael simply. "But they trust you. Especially the New York Nephilim. Look at you. You wear Isabelle Lightwood's necklace. They know you are more like another Shadowhunter than you are like the Night's Children. They will believe what you say if you tell them that Maureen has broken the Accords and must be stopped."

"Right," Simon said. "They trust me." Raphael looked at him with wide, guileless eyes. "And this has nothing to do with your not wanting the clan to find out you turned Maureen in, because they like her, and then they'd turn on you like weasels."

"You know the children of the Inquisitor," he said. "You can testify directly to him."

"Sure," Simon said. "No one in the clan will care that I ratted on their queen and got her killed. I'm sure my life will be fantastic when I get back."

Raphael shrugged. "I do have supporters here," he said. "Someone had to let me into this room. Once Maureen is taken care of, it is likely we can return to New York with few negative consequences."

"Few negative consequences." Simon snorted. "You're a comfort."

"You are in danger anyway, here," said Raphael. "If you did not have your werewolf protector, or your Shadowhunters, you would have met eternal death many times over. If you do not wish to come with me to Alicante, I will be happy to leave you here in this cage, and you may be Maureen's plaything. Or you can join your friends in the Glass City. Catarina Loss is waiting downstairs to make a Portal for us. It is your choice."

Raphael was leaning back, one leg bent, his hand dangling loosely over his knee as if he were relaxing in the park. Behind him, through the bars of the cage, Simon could see the outline of another vampire standing by the door, a dark-haired girl, her features in shadow. The one who had let Raphael in, he guessed. He thought of Jordan. *Your werewolf protector.* But this, this clash of clans and loyalties, and above all Maureen's murderous desire for blood and death, was too much to lay at Jordan's door.

"Not much of a choice, is it?" Simon said.

Raphael smiled. "No, Daylighter. Not much at all."

The last time Clary had been in the Hall of Accords, it had been nearly destroyed—its crystal roof shattered, its marble floor cracked, its central fountain dry.

She had to admit the Shadowhunters had done an impressive job of patching it up since then. The roof was back in one piece, the marble floor clean and smooth and veined with gold. The arches soared overhead, the light that shone down through the roof illuminating the runes carved into them. The central fountain with its mermaid statue glimmered under the late afternoon sunlight, which turned the water to bronze.

"When you get your first real weapon, it's traditional to come here and bless the blade in the fountain waters," said Jace. "Shadowhunters have been doing it for generations." He moved forward, under the dull gold light, to the fountain's edge. Clary remembered dreaming of dancing with him here. He looked back over his shoulder and gestured for her to join him. "Come here."

Clary moved up to stand beside him. The central statue in the fountain, the mermaid, had scales made of overlapping bronze and copper gone green with verdigris. The mermaid held a pitcher, from which water poured, and her face was set in a warrior's grin.

"Put the blade in the fountain and repeat after me," said Jace. "*Let the waters of this fountain wash this blade clean. Consecrate it to my use alone. Let me use it only in the aid of just causes. Let me wield it in righteousness. Let it guide me to be a worthy warrior of Idris. And let it protect me that I may return to this fountain to bless its metal anew. In Raziel's name.*"

Clary slipped the blade into the water and repeated the words after him. The water rippled and shimmered around the sword, and she was reminded of another fountain, in another place, and Sebastian sitting behind her, looking at the distorted image of her own face. *You have a dark heart in you, Valentine's daughter.*

"Good," Jace said. She felt his hand on her wrist; the water of the fountain splashed up, making his skin cool and wet where it touched hers. He drew back her hand with the sword in it, and released her so that she could lift the blade up. The sun was even farther down now, but there was enough of it to strike sparks off the obsidian stars along the central ridge. "Now give the sword its name."

"Heosphoros," she said, sliding it back into its scabbard and tucking the scabbard into her belt. "The dawn-bringer."

He huffed out a laugh, and bent to feather a kiss against the corner of her mouth. "I should get you home—" He straightened up.

"You've been thinking about him," she said.

"You might have to be more specific," Jace said, though she suspected he knew what she meant.

"Sebastian," she said. "I mean, more than usual. And something's bothering you. What is it?"

"What isn't?" He started to walk away from her, across the marble floor toward the great double doors of the Hall, which were propped open. She followed him, stepped out onto the wide ledge above the staircase that led down to Angel Square. The sky was darkening to cobalt, the color of sea glass.

"Don't," Clary said. "Don't shut yourself off."

"I wasn't going to." He exhaled harshly. "It just isn't anything new. Yeah, I think about him. I think about him all the time. I wish I didn't. I can't explain it, not to anyone but you, because you were there. It was like I was him, and now, when you tell me things like that he left that box in Amatis's house, I know exactly *why*. And I hate that I know it."

"Jace—"

"Don't tell me I'm not like him," he said. "I am. Raised by the same father—we both have the benefits of Valentine's *special* education. We speak the same languages. We learned the same style of fighting. We were taught the same morals. Had the same pets. It changed, of course; it all changed when I turned ten, but the foundations of your childhood, they stay with you. Sometimes I wonder if all of this is my fault."

That jolted Clary. "You can't be serious. Nothing you did when you were with Sebastian was your choice—"

"I *liked* it," he said, and there was a rough undercurrent to his voice, as if the fact rasped at him like sandpaper. "He's brilliant, Sebastian, but there are holes in his thinking, places where he doesn't *know*—I helped him with that. We would sit there and we would talk about how to burn the world down, and it was exciting. I wanted it. Wipe it all clean, start again, a holocaust of fire and blood, and afterward, a shining city on a hill."

"He made you think you wanted those things," Clary said, but her voice shook slightly. *You have a dark heart in you, Valentine's daughter.* "He made you give him what *he* wanted."

"I liked giving it," said Jace. "Why do you think I could so easily think of ways to break and destroy, but I now can't think of any way to fix it? I mean, what does that qualify me for, exactly? A job in Hell's army? I could be a general, like Asmodeus or Sammael."

"Jace—"

"They were the brightest servants of God, once," Jace said. "That's what happens when you fall. Everything that was bright about you becomes dark. As brilliant as you once were, that's how evil you become. It's a *long* way to fall."

"You haven't fallen."

"Not yet," he said, and then the sky exploded in spangles of red and gold. For a dizzy moment Clary remembered the fireworks that

had painted the sky the night they had celebrated in Angel Square.
Now she stepped back, trying to get a better view.

But this was no celebration. As her eyes adjusted to the brightness, she saw that the light was the demon towers. Each had lit like a
torch, burning red and gold against the sky.

Jace had gone white. "The battle lights," he said. "We have to
get to the Gard." He reached for her hand and began to tug her down
the stairs.

Clary protested. "But my mother. Isabelle, Alec—"

"They'll all be on their way to the Gard too." They had reached
the foot of the steps. Angel Square was filling with people flinging
open the doors of their houses, emptying into the streets, all of
them running toward the lighted path that ran up the side of the
hill and to the Gard at the top. "That's what the red-and-gold signal
means. 'Get to the Gard.' That's what they'll expect us to do—" He
ducked away from a Shadowhunter who was running past them
while strapping on an arm guard. "What's going on?" Jace shouted
after him. "Why the alarm?"

"There's been another attack!" an older man in worn gear
shouted back over his shoulder.

"Another Institute?" Clary called. They were back at a shop-
lined street she remembered visiting with Luke before; they were
running uphill, but she didn't feel breathless. Silently she thanked
the past few months of training.

The man with the arm guard turned around and jogged uphill
backward. "We don't know yet. The attack's ongoing."

He spun back around and redoubled his speed, dashing up the
curving street toward the bottom of the Gard path. Clary concentrated on not crashing into anyone in the crowd. They were a moving, jostling flood of people. She kept her hand in Jace's as they ran,
her new sword tapping against the outside of her leg as she went, as
if to remind her it was there—there and ready to be used.

The path that led up to the Gard was steep, packed dirt. Clary tried to run carefully—she was wearing boots and jeans, her gear jacket zipped over the top, but it wasn't quite as good as being all in gear. A pebble had worked its way into her left boot somehow and was stabbing into the pad of her foot by the time they reached the front gate of the Gard and slowed, staring.

The gates were thrown open. Within them was a wide courtyard, grassy in the summers, though it was bare now, surrounded by the interior walls of the Gard. Against one wall was a massive, swirling square of whirling air and emptiness.

A Portal. Within it, Clary thought she could glimpse hints of black and green and burning white, even a patch of sky dotted with stars—

Robert Lightwood loomed up in front of them, blocking their way; Jace nearly crashed into him, and let go of Clary's hand, righting himself. The wind from the Portal was cold and powerful, blowing through the fabric of Clary's gear jacket, lifting her hair. "What's going on?" Jace demanded tersely. "Is this about the London attack? I thought that was rebuffed."

Robert shook his head, his expression grim. "It seems that Sebastian, having been foiled in London, has turned his attention elsewhere."

"Where—?" Clary began.

"The Adamant Citadel is besieged!" It was Jia Penhallow's voice, rising over the shouts of the crowd. She had moved to stand by the Portal; the swirl of air within and without it made her cloak flap open like the wings of a great black bird. "We go to the aid of the Iron Sisters! Shadowhunters who are armed and ready, please report to me!"

The courtyard was full of Nephilim, though not as many as Clary had thought at first. It had seemed like a flood as they'd bolted up the hill to the Gard, but she saw now that it was more like a group of forty to fifty warriors. Some were in gear, some in street clothes. Not all were armed. Nephilim in the service of the Gard were darting back and forth to the open door of the armory, adding weapons to a pile of swords, seraph blades, axes, and maces heaped by the side of the Portal.

"Let us go through," Jace said to Robert. All in gear and wrapped in the gray of the Inquisitor, Robert Lightwood reminded Clary of the hard, rocky side of a cliff: craggy and unmovable.

Robert shook his head. "There's no need," he said. "Sebastian has attempted a sneak attack. He has only twenty or thirty Endarkened warriors with him. There are enough warriors for the job without us sending our children through."

"I am *not a child*," Jace said savagely. Clary wondered what Robert thought when he looked at the boy he had adopted—if Robert saw Jace's father in Jace's face, or still searched for remnants of Michael Wayland that weren't there. Jace scanned Robert Lightwood's expression, suspicion darkening his gold eyes. "What are you doing? There's something you don't want me to know."

Robert's face set into hard lines. At that moment a blonde woman in gear brushed by Clary, speaking excitedly to her companion: "... told us that we can try to capture the Endarkened, bring them back here. See if they can be cured. Which means maybe they can save Jason."

Clary looked daggers at Robert. "You're not. You're *not* letting people whose relatives were taken in the attacks go through. You're not telling them the Endarkened can be saved."

Robert gave her a grim look. "We don't know that they can't be."

"*We* know," Clary said. "They can't be saved! They're not who they were! They're not *human*. But when these soldiers see the faces of people they know, they'll hesitate, they'll *want* it to not be true—"

"And they'll be slaughtered," Jace said bleakly. "Robert. You have to stop this."

Robert was shaking his head. "This is the will of the Clave. This is what they want to see done."

"Then why even send them through?" Jace demanded. "Why not just stay here and stab fifty of our own people to death? Save the time?"

"Don't you dare joke," Robert snapped.

"I wasn't joking—"

"And don't you tell me *fifty* Nephilim can't defeat *twenty* Endarkened warriors." Shadowhunters were beginning to go through the Portal, guided by Jia. Clary felt a tickle of panic run down her spine. Jia was letting through only those who were completely outfitted in gear, but quite a few were very young or very old, and many had come unarmed and were simply seizing up weapons from the pile provided by the armory, before passing through.

"Sebastian's expecting exactly this response," Jace said desperately. "If he's come with only twenty warriors, then there's a reason, and he'll have backup—"

"He can't have backup!" Robert's voice rose. "You cannot open a Portal to the Adamant Citadel unless the Iron Sisters allow it. They're allowing us, but Sebastian must have come over land. Sebastian didn't expect us to be watching for him at the Citadel. He knows we know he can't be tracked; he doubtless thought we were watching only Institutes. This is a gift—"

"Sebastian doesn't give gifts!" Jace shouted. "You're being blind!"

"We are not blind!" Robert roared. "You may be frightened of him, Jace, but he is just a boy; he is not the most brilliant military mind ever to exist! He fought you at the Burren, *and he lost!*"

Robert turned and wheeled away, striding toward Jia. Jace looked as if he had been slapped. Clary doubted anyone had ever accused him of being frightened before.

He turned to look at her. The movement of Shadowhunters

toward the Portal had slowed; Jia was waving people away. Jace touched the shortsword at Clary's hip. "I'm going through," he said.

"They won't let you," Clary said.

"They don't need to *let* me." Under the red-and-gold lights of the towers, Jace's face looked as if it had been cut out of marble. Behind him Clary could see more Shadowhunters coming up the hill. They were chatting among themselves as if this were any ordinary fight, any situation that could be handled by sending fifty or so Nephilim to the place of attack. They hadn't been at the Burren. They hadn't seen. They didn't *know.* Clary met Jace's eyes with hers.

She could see the lines of tension on his face, deepening the angles of his cheekbones, setting his jaw. "The question is," he said, "is there any chance *you'd* agree to stay here?"

"You know there's not," she said.

He took a shuddering breath. "Right. Clary, this could be dangerous, really dangerous—" She could hear people murmuring around them, excited voices, rising against the night on puffs of exhaled air, people chattering that the Consul and Council had been meeting to discuss the London attack just as Sebastian popped into sudden existence on the tracking map, that he had only been there a short time and with few reinforcements, that they had a real chance to stop him, that he had been foiled in London and would be again—

"I love you," she said. "But don't try to stop me."

Jace reached to take her hand. "All right," he said. "Then we run, together. Toward the Portal."

"We run," she agreed, and they did.

7

CLASH BY NIGHT

The volcanic plain spread out like a pale moonscape before Jace, reaching to a line of distant mountains, black against the horizon. White snow dusted the ground: thick in some places; crisp, thin ice in others. Deadly sharp rocks sliced through the ice and snow, along with the bare branches of hedges and frozen moss.

The moon was behind clouds, the velvet dark sky pricked here and there with stars, dulled by a sheen of cloud. Light blazed up all around them, though, from seraph blades—and, Jace saw as his eyes adjusted, light from what looked like a bonfire burning in the distance.

The Portal had deposited Jace and Clary a few feet from each other, in the snow. They were side by side now, Clary very silent, her coppery hair dusted with white flakes. All around them were cries and shouts, the sound of seraph blades being ignited, the murmur of the names of angels.

"Stay close to me," Jace murmured as he and Clary neared the top of the ridge. He had caught up a longsword from the pile by the Portal just before leaping in, Jia's cry of dismay following them through the shrieking winds. Jace had half-expected her or Robert to follow them through, but instead the Portal had closed up immediately after them, like a door slamming shut.

The unfamiliar blade was heavy in Jace's hand. He preferred to use his left arm, but the sword had a right-handed grip. The weapon was dented around the sides, as if it had seen quite a few battles. He wished he had one of his own weapons in his hand—

It appeared all at once, rising up in front of them like a fish breaking the surface of water with a sudden silver glint. Jace had seen the Adamant Citadel before only in pictures. Carved out of the same stuff as seraph blades, the Citadel glowed against the night sky like a star; it was what Jace had mistaken for the light of a bonfire. A circular wall of *adamas* ringed it, with no opening in the wall except a single gate, formed of two huge blades plunged into the ground at angles, like an open pair of scissors.

All around the Citadel the volcanic ground stretched away, black and white like a chessboard—half volcanic rock and half snow. Jace felt the hairs rise on the back of his neck. It was like being at the Burren again, though he remembered that only the way one might remember a dream: Sebastian's dark Nephilim, in their red gear, and the Nephilim of the Clave, in black, blade to blade, the sparks of battle rising into the night, and then the fire of Glorious, wiping out all that had gone before.

The earth of the Burren had been dark, but now Sebastian's warriors stood out like drops of blood against the white ground. They were waiting, red under the light of the stars, their dark blades in their hands. They stood between the Nephilim who had come through the Portal, and the gates of the Adamant Citadel. Though the Endarkened were at a distance, and though Jace could not see any of their faces clearly, he could somehow *feel* them smiling.

And he could feel too the unease in the Nephilim around him, the Shadowhunters who had come through the Portal so confident, so ready for battle. They stood and looked down at the Endarkened, and Jace could feel the hesitation in their bravado. At last—too late—they felt it: the alienness, the difference of the Endarkened. These were not Shadowhunters who had temporarily strayed from the path. They were not Shadowhunters at all.

"Where is he?" Clary whispered. Her breath was white in the cold. "Where's Sebastian?"

Jace shook his head; many of the red-geared Shadowhunters had their hoods up, and their faces were invisible. Sebastian could have been any one of them.

"And the Iron Sisters?" Clary searched the plain with her gaze. The only white was snow. There was no sign of the Sisters in their robes, familiar from many *Codex* illustrations.

"They'll stay inside the Citadel," Jace said. "They have to protect what's inside it. The arsenal. Presumably that's what Sebastian's here for—the weapons. The Sisters will have surrounded the interior armory with their bodies. If he manages to get through the gates, or his Endarkened do, the Sisters will destroy the Citadel before they let him have it." His voice was grim.

"But if Sebastian knows that, if he knows what the Sisters will do—" Clary began.

A scream cut the night like a knife. Jace started forward before realizing the scream was coming from behind them. Jace whirled to see a man in worn gear go down with the blade of a Dark Shadowhunter in his chest. It was the man who had called out to Clary in Alicante, before they had reached the Gard.

The Dark Shadowhunter whirled, grinning. There was a cry from the Nephilim, and the blonde woman Clary had heard speaking excitedly at the Gard stepped forward. "Jason!" she cried, and Clary realized she was speaking to the Endarkened warrior, a thickset man with the same blonde hair she had. "Jason, please." Her voice trembled as she moved forward, stretching out her hand to the Endarkened, who drew another blade from his belt, looking at her expectantly.

"Please, *no*," Clary said. "Don't—don't go near him—"

But the blonde woman was only a step away from the Dark Shadowhunter. "Jason," she whispered. "You're my brother. You're one of us, a Nephilim. You don't have to do this—Sebastian can't force you. Please—" She looked around, desperate. "Come with us. They're working on a cure; we'll fix you—"

Jason laughed. His blade flashed out, a sideways slash. The blonde Shadowhunter's head fell. Blood fanned out, black against the white snow, as her body slumped to the ground. Someone was screaming over and over, hysterically, and then someone else cried out and gestured wildly behind them.

Jace looked up and saw a line of Endarkened advancing from behind, from the direction of the closed Portal. Their blades flashed out in the moonlight. The Nephilim began to stumble down the ridge, but it was no longer an orderly progression—there was panic among them; Jace could feel it, like the taste of blood on the wind. "Hammer and anvil!" he shouted, hoping they would understand. He seized Clary with his free hand and yanked her back, away from the headless body on the ground. "It's a trap," he shouted at her over the noise of the fighting. "Get to a wall, somewhere you can make a Portal! Get us out of here!"

Her green eyes widened. He wanted to grab her, kiss her, cling on to her, protect her, but the fighter in him knew he had brought her into this life. Encouraged her. Trained her. When he saw the understanding in her eyes, he nodded and let her go.

Clary pulled away from his grip, sliding past an Endarkened warrior who was facing off against a staff-wielding Silent Brother in bloody parchment robes. Her boots skidded on the snow as she darted toward the Citadel. The crowd swallowed her up just as an Endarkened warrior drew his weapon free and lunged for Jace.

Like all Endarkened Shadowhunters, his motions were blindingly swift, almost feral. As he rose up with his blade, he seemed to blot out the moon. And Jace's blood rose up too, shooting like fire through his veins as his awareness narrowed: There was nothing else in the world, only this moment, only the weapon in his hand. He leaped toward the Dark Shadowhunter, his sword outstretched.

Clary bent to retrieve Heosphoros from where it had fallen in the snow. The blade was smeared with blood, the blood of a Dark Shadowhunter who was even now darting away from her, flinging himself back into the battle churning on the plain.

It had happened now a half dozen times. Clary would attack, attempt to engage one of the Endarkened in a fight, and they would drop their weapons, back away, turn from her as if she were a ghost, and hurry away. The first time or two she had wondered if they were afraid of Heosphoros, confused by a blade that looked so much like Sebastian's. She suspected something else now. Sebastian had probably told them not to touch her or hurt her, and they were obeying.

It made her want to scream. She knew she should fling herself after them when they ran, end them with a blade to the back, or a slice to the throat, but she couldn't bring herself to do it. They still *looked* like Nephilim, human enough. Their blood ran red onto the snow. It still felt like cowardice to attack someone who could not attack back.

Ice crunched behind her, and she spun, her blade out. Everything had happened in a rush: the realization that there were twice as many Endarkened as they had counted on, that they were besieged on two sides, Jace's plea to her to make a Portal. She was fighting her way through a desperate crowd now. Some Shadowhunters had scattered, and some had planted themselves where they were, determined to fight. As a mass they were being slowly pushed down the hill toward the plain, where the battle was at its thickest, bright seraph blades flashing out against dark knives, a mix of black and white and red.

For the first time Clary had cause to bless her small size. She was able to dart through the crowd, her gaze catching on desperate tableaux of fighting. There, a Nephilim barely older than she was waged a desperate battle against one of the Endarkened, twice the Shadowhunter's size, who forced her down into the blood-slicked snow; a blade swung out, and then a shriek, and a seraph blade darkened forever. A dark-haired young man in black Shadowhunter gear stood over the body of a dead warrior in red. He held a bloody sword in one hand, and tears were running down his face, unchecked. Nearby a Silent Brother, a sight unexpected but welcome in his parchment robes, crushed the skull of a Dark Shadowhunter with one blow from his wooden staff; the Endarkened crumpled in silence. A man fell to his knees, wrapping his arms around the legs of a woman in red gear; she looked at him dispassionately, then drove her sword down between his shoulder blades. None of the warriors moved to stop her.

Clary burst out on the other side of the crowd and found herself beside the Citadel. Its walls were shining with an intense light. Through the arch of the scissor gate, she thought she could see the glow of something red-gold like fire. She scrabbled for the stele at her belt, took hold of it, put the tip to the wall—and froze.

Only feet from her, a Dark Shadowhunter had slipped away from the battle and toward the Citadel gates. He carried a mace and flail under his arm; with a grinning glance back at the battle, he ducked through the Citadel gate—

And the scissors closed. There was no scream, but the sickening crunch of bone and gristle was audible even through the noise of battle. A gout of blood sprayed across the closed gate, and Clary realized it was not the first. There were other stains, fanned across the Citadel wall, darkening the ground beneath—

She turned away, her stomach clenching, and pressed her stele harder against the stone. She began to force her mind to thoughts of Alicante, trying to visualize the grassy space before the Gard, trying to push away the distractions all around her.

"Drop the stele, Valentine's daughter," said a cold, even voice.

She froze. Behind her stood Amatis, sword in hand, the sharp tip pointing directly at Clary. There was a feral grin on her face. "That's right," she said. "Drop the stele to the ground and come with me. I know someone who'll be *very* pleased to see you."

"Move, Clarissa." Amatis jabbed Clary in the side with the tip of her sword—not hard enough to cut through her jacket, but enough to make Clary uncomfortable. Clary had dropped her stele; it lay feet away in the filthy snow, shining with a tantalizing glimmer. "Stop dawdling."

"You can't hurt me," Clary said. "Sebastian's given orders."

"Orders not to kill you," Amatis agreed. "He never said anything about hurting you. I'll happily turn you over to him with all your fingers missing, girl. Don't think I won't."

Clary glared before turning around and letting Amatis herd her toward the battle. Her gaze was darting among the Endarkened, looking for a familiar fair head in the sea of scarlet. She needed to know how much time she had before Amatis threw her down at Sebastian's feet and the chance to fight or run was over. Amatis had taken Heosphoros, of course, and the Morgenstern blade now dangled at the older woman's hip, the stars along the ridge winking in the dim light. "I bet you don't even know where he is," Clary said.

Amatis jabbed her again, and Clary lurched forward, almost stumbling over the dead body of a Dark Shadowhunter. The ground was a churned-up mass of snow and dirt and blood. "I am Sebastian's first lieutenant; I always know where he is. That is why I am the one he trusts to bring you to him."

"He doesn't trust you. He doesn't care about you, or anything. Look." They had reached the bump of a small ridge; Clary slowed to a stop and swept her arm out, indicating the battlefield. "Look how many of you are falling—Sebastian just wants cannon fodder. Just wants to use you up."

"Is that what you see? I see dead Nephilim." Clary could see Amatis out of the corner of her eye. Her gray-brown hair floated on the cold air, and her eyes were hard. "You think the Clave is not overmatched? Look. Look there." She jabbed with a finger, and Clary looked, unwillingly. The two halves of Sebastian's army had closed in and were encircling the Nephilim in their midst. Many of the Nephilim were fighting with skill and viciousness. They were, in their own strange way, lovely to watch in battle; the light of their seraph blades traced patterns on the dark sky. Not that it changed the fact that they were doomed. "They did what they always do when there's an attack outside Idris and a Conclave is not near. They sent through the Portal whoever arrived at the Gard first. Some of these warriors have never fought in a real battle before. Some of them have fought in too many. None of them are prepared to kill an enemy that bears the faces of their sons, lovers, friends, *parabatai*." She spat the last word. "The Clave does not understand our Sebastian or his forces, and they will be dead before they do."

"Where did they come from?" Clary demanded. "The Endarkened. The Clave said there were only twenty of them, and there was no way for Sebastian to hide their numbers. How—"

Amatis threw her head back and laughed. "As if I'd tell you. Sebastian has allies in more places than you know, little one."

"Amatis." Clary tried to keep her voice steady. "You're one of us. Nephilim. You're Luke's sister."

"He's a Downworlder, and no brother of mine. He should have killed himself when Valentine told him to."

"You don't mean that. You were happy to see him when we came to your house. I know you were."

This time the jab of the blade's tip between her shoulder

blades was more than uncomfortable: It hurt. "I was trapped then," Amatis said. "Thinking I needed the approval of the Clave and the Council. The Nephilim took everything from me." She turned to glare at the Citadel. "The Iron Sisters took my mother. Then an Iron Sister presided over my divorce. They cut my marriage Marks in two, and I cried with the pain of it. They have no hearts in them, only *adamas*, and the Silent Brothers too. You think they are kind, that the Nephilim are kind, because they are good, but goodness is not kindness, and there is nothing crueler than virtue."

"But we can *choose*," Clary said, but how could you explain to someone who didn't understand that their choices had been taken away, that there was such a thing as free will?

"Oh, for Hell's sake, be quiet—" Amatis broke off, stiffening.

Clary followed her gaze. For a moment she couldn't see what the other woman was staring at. She saw the chaos of fighting, blood in the snow, the spark of starlight on blades and the harsh glow of the Citadel. Then she realized that the battle seemed to be resolving itself into an odd sort of pattern—something was cutting a path through the middle of the crowd, like a ship slicing through water, leaving chaos in its wake. A slender black-clad Shadowhunter with bright hair, moving so fast, it was like watching fire spring from ridge to ridge in a forest, catching everything ablaze.

Only in this case the forest was Sebastian's army, Endarkened falling one by one. Falling so quickly, they barely had time to reach for their weapons, much less raise them. And as they fell, others began to fall back, confused and uncertain, so that Clary could see the space that was being cleared in the middle of the battle, and who stood in the center of it.

Despite everything, she smiled. "Jace."

Amatis sucked in a breath of surprise—it was a moment's distraction, but it was all Clary needed to swing forward and hook her leg around Amatis's ankles the way Jace had taught her, and then she swept Amatis's feet out from under her. Amatis fell, her sword skittering out of her hand, across the frozen ground. Amatis was bending to spring back up when Clary tackled her—not gracefully but effectively, knocking her back into the snow. Amatis hit out at her, snapping Clary's head back, but Clary's hand was at the older woman's belt, snatching Heosphoros free, and then jamming the razor-sharp tip against Amatis's throat.

Amatis froze.

"That's right," Clary said. "Don't even think about moving."

"Let me go!" Isabelle screamed at her father. "Let me *go*!"

When the demon towers had gone red and gold with the warning to get to the Gard, she and Alec had scrambled to seize their gear and their weapons and hurtle up the hill. Isabelle's heart pounded, not from the exertion but from excitement. Alec was grim and practical as always, but Isabelle's whip was singing to her. Maybe this might be it, a real battle; maybe this might be the time they faced Sebastian again on the field, and this time she would kill him.

For her brother. For Max.

Alec and Isabelle had been unprepared for the crush of people in the Gard courtyard, or the speed with which Nephilim were being ushered through the Portal. Isabelle had lost her brother in the crowd but had pushed toward the Portal—she had seen Jace and Clary there, about to step through, and she'd redoubled her speed—until suddenly two hands had come out of the crowd and seized hold of her arms.

Her father. Isabelle kicked against him and yelled for Alec, but Jace and Clary were already gone, into the Portal whirlpool. Snarling, Isabelle fought, but her father had height and build and years of training on her.

He let her go just as the Portal gave one last whirl and slammed closed, disappearing into the blank wall of the armory.

The remaining Nephilim in the courtyard went quiet, waiting for instructions. Jia Penhallow announced that enough of them had gone through to the Citadel, that the others should wait inside the Gard in case reinforcements were needed; there was no need to stand in the courtyard and freeze. She understood how badly everyone wanted to fight, but plenty of warriors had been dispatched to the Citadel, and Alicante still required a force to guard it.

"See?" said Robert Lightwood, gesturing at his daughter in exasperation as she whirled to face him. She was pleased to see that there were bleeding scratches on his wrists where she'd clawed at him. "You're needed here, Isabelle—"

"Shut up," she hissed at him through her teeth. "Shut up, you lying *bastard*."

Astonishment wiped his expression blank. Isabelle knew from Simon and Clary that a certain amount of shouting at one's parents was expected in mundane culture, but Shadowhunters believed in respect for elders and a governance of one's emotions.

Only, Isabelle didn't feel like governing her emotions. Not right now.

"Isabelle—" It was Alec, skidding into place beside her. The crowd around was thinning, and she was distantly aware that many of the Nephilim had already gone inside the Gard. The ones who were left were looking away awkwardly. Other people's family fights were not Shadowhunter business. "Isabelle, let's go back to the house."

Alec reached for her hand; she jerked it out of his with an irritated movement. Isabelle loved her brother, but never had she more wanted to punch him in the head. "No," she said. "Jace and Clary went through; we should get to go with them."

Robert Lightwood looked weary. "They weren't meant to go," he said. "They did it against strict orders. It doesn't mean you should follow."

"They knew what they were doing," Isabelle snapped. "You need more Shadowhunters facing Sebastian, not less."

"Isabelle, I don't have time for this," said Robert, looking exasperatedly at Alec as if he expected his son to side with him. "There are only twenty Endarkened there with Sebastian. We sent fifty warriors through."

"Twenty of them is like a hundred Shadowhunters," said Alec in his quiet voice. "Our side could be slaughtered."

"If anything happens to Jace and Clary, it'll be your fault," Isabelle said. "Just like Max."

Robert Lightwood recoiled.

"*Isabelle.*" Her mother's voice cut through the sudden, terrible silence. Isabelle whipped her head around and saw that Maryse had come up behind them; she, like Alec, looked stunned. A small distant part of Isabelle felt guilty and sick, but the part of her that seemed to have taken the reins, that was bubbling up inside her like a volcano, felt only a bitter triumph. She was tired of pretending everything was all right. "Alec's right," Maryse went on. "Let's go back to the house—"

"No," Isabelle said. "Didn't you hear the Consul? We're needed here, at the Gard. They might want reinforcements."

"They'll want adults, not children," said Maryse. "If you're not going to go back, then apologize to your father. Max's—What happened to Max was no one's fault but Valentine's."

"And maybe if you hadn't been on Valentine's side once, there wouldn't have *been* a Mortal War," Isabelle hissed at her mother. Then she rounded on her father. "I'm tired of pretending I don't know what I know. I know you cheated on Mom." Isabelle couldn't stop the words now; they kept coming, like a flood. She saw Maryse go white, Alec open his mouth to protest. Robert looked as if she had hit him. "Before Max was born. I know. She told me. With some woman who died in the Mortal War. And you were going to leave too, leave all of us, and you only stayed because Max was born, and I bet you're glad he's dead, aren't you, because now you don't have to stay."

"Isabelle—" Alec began, in horror.

Robert turned to Maryse. "You *told* her? By the Angel, Maryse, when?"

"You mean it's true?" Alec's voice shook with revulsion.

Robert turned to him. "Alexander, please—"

But Alec had turned his back. The courtyard was almost entirely empty of Nephilim now. Isabelle could see Jia standing in the distance, near the entrance to the armory, waiting for the last of them to come inside. She saw Alec go over to Jia, heard the sound of him arguing with her.

Isabelle's parents were both looking at her as if their worlds were toppling over. She had never thought of herself as being able to destroy her parents' world before. She had expected her father to shout at her, not to stand there in his Inquisitor's gray, looking wrecked. Finally he cleared his throat.

"Isabelle," he said hoarsely. "Whatever else you think, you must believe—you can't really think that when we lost Max, that I—"

"Don't talk to me," Isabelle said, stumbling away from both of them, her heart thudding brokenly in her chest. "Just—don't talk to me."

She turned and fled.

Jace hurtled through the air, collided with a Dark Shadowhunter, and rode the Endarkened One's body down to earth, dispatching him with a vicious scissoring blow. Somehow he had acquired a second blade; he wasn't sure where. Everything was blood and fire singing in his head.

Jace had fought before, many times. He knew the chill of battle as it descended, the world around him slowing to a whisper, every movement he made precise and exact. Some part of his mind was able to push away the blood and pain and stink of it behind a wall of clear ice.

But this wasn't ice; this was fire. The burn that coursed through his veins drove him on, sped his movements so that he felt as if he were flying. He kicked the headless corpse of the Dark Shadowhunter into the path of another, a red-clad figure flying toward him. She stumbled, and he sliced her neatly in half. Blood erupted across the snow. He was already soaked in it: he could feel his gear, heavy and sodden, against his body, and could smell the salt-iron tang, as if blood infused the air he was breathing.

He neatly jumped the dead Endarkened's body and strode toward another of them, a brown-haired man with a tear in the sleeve of his red gear. Jace raised the sword in his right hand, and the man flinched, surprising him. The Dark Shadowhunters didn't seem to feel much fear, and they died without screaming. This one, though, had his face twisted with fear—

"Really, Andrew, there's no need to look like that. I'm not going to do anything to you," said a voice behind Jace, sharp and clear and familiar. And just a touch exasperated. "Unless you don't move out of the way."

The brown-haired Shadowhunter darted hastily away from Jace, who turned, already knowing what he would see.

Sebastian stood behind him. He had arrived seemingly out of nowhere, though that didn't surprise Jace. He knew Sebastian still possessed Valentine's ring, which allowed him to appear and disappear at will. He wore red gear, worked all through with gold runes— runes of protection and healing and good luck. Gray Book runes, the kind his followers couldn't wear. The red made his pale hair look paler, his grin a white slice across his face as his gaze scanned Jace from his head to his boots.

"My Jace," he said. "Been missing me?"

In a flash Jace's swords were up, both tips hovering just over Sebastian's heart. He heard a murmur from the crowd around him. It seemed that both the Dark Shadowhunters and their Nephilim counterparts had paused their fighting to watch what was going on. "You can't actually think I missed you."

Sebastian raised his eyes slowly, his amused gaze meeting Jace's. Eyes black like his father's. In their lightless depths Jace saw himself, saw the apartment he had shared with Sebastian, the meals they had eaten together, jokes they had traded, battles they'd shared. He had subsumed himself in Sebastian, had given over his will entirely, and it had been pleasurable and easy, and down in the darkest depths of his treacherous heart, Jace knew that part of him wanted it again.

It made him hate Sebastian even more.

"Well, I can't imagine why else you're here. You know I can't be killed with a blade," Sebastian said. "The brat from the Los Angeles Institute must have told you that, at least."

"I could slice you apart," Jace said. "See if you can survive in tiddlywink-size pieces. Or cut off your head. It might not kill you, but it would be fun watching you try to find it."

Sebastian was still smiling. "I wouldn't try," he said, "if I were you."

Jace exhaled, his breath a white plume. *Don't let him stall you,* his brain screamed, but the curse of it was that he knew Sebastian, knew him well enough that he couldn't trust that Sebastian was bluffing. Sebastian hated to bluff. He liked to have the advantage and know it. "Why not?" Jace growled through clenched teeth.

"My sister," said Sebastian. "You sent Clary off to make a Portal? Not very clever, separating yourselves. She is being held some distance from here by one of my lieutenants. Harm me, and her throat will be cut."

There was a murmuring from the Nephilim behind him, but

Jace couldn't listen. Clary's name pounded in the blood in his veins, and the place where Lilith's rune had once connected him to Sebastian burned. They said it was better to know your enemy, but how did it help to know that your enemy's one weakness was your weakness too?

The murmuring of the crowd rose to a roar as Jace began to lower his blades; Sebastian moved so quickly that Jace saw only a blur as the other boy whipped around and kicked out at Jace's wrist. The sword fell from his right hand's numb grasp, and he threw himself backward, but Sebastian was faster, drawing the Morgenstern blade and slashing out at Jace with a blow that Jace managed to evade only by twisting his whole body to the side. The tip of the sword sliced a shallow gash across his ribs.

Now some of the blood on his gear was his own.

He ducked as Sebastian slashed out at him again, and the sword whistled past his head. He heard Sebastian curse and came up with his own blade swinging. The two clashed together with the sound of ringing metal, and Sebastian grinned. "You can't win," he said. "I'm better than you, always have been. I might be the best."

"Modest, too," Jace said, and their swords slid apart with a grinding noise. He moved back, just enough to get range.

"And you can't hurt me, not really, because of *Clary*," Sebastian went on, relentless. "Just like she couldn't hurt me because of you. Always the same dance. Neither of you willing to make the sacrifice." He came at Jace with a side swing; Jace parried, though the force of Sebastian's blow sent a shock up his arm. "You'd think, with all your obsession with *goodness*, that one of you would be willing to give up the other for a greater cause. But no. Love is essentially selfish, and so are both of you."

"You don't know either of us," Jace gasped; he was breathing hard now, and knew he was fighting defensively, fending off Sebastian rather than attacking. The Strength rune on his arm was burning, flaring up the last of its power. That was bad.

"I know my sister," said Sebastian. "And not now, but soon enough I'll know her *every* way you can know someone." He grinned again, feral. It was the same look he'd worn so long ago, on a summer night outside the Gard, when he'd said, *Or maybe you're just angry because I kissed your sister. Because she wanted me.*

Nausea rose up in Jace, nausea and rage, and he flung himself at Sebastian, forgetting for a moment the rules of swordplay, forgetting to keep the weight of his grip evenly distributed, forgetting balance and precision and everything but hate, and Sebastian's grin widened as he stepped out of the way of the attack and neatly kicked Jace's leg out from under him.

He went down hard, his back colliding with the icy ground, knocking the breath out of him. He heard the whistle of the sword before he saw it, and rolled to the side as the Morgenstern blade slashed into the ground where he'd been a second before. The stars swung crazily overhead, black and silver, and then Sebastian was standing over him, more black and silver, and the sword came down again, and he rolled to the side, but he wasn't fast enough this time and he felt it drive down into him.

The agony was instant, clear and clean as the blade slammed into his shoulder. It was like being electrified—Jace felt the pain through his entire body, his muscles contracting, his back arcing off the ground. Heat seared through him, as if his bones were being fused to charcoal. Flame gathered and coursed through his veins, up his spine—

He saw Sebastian's eyes widen, and in their darkness he saw himself reflected, sprawled on the red-black ground, and his shoulder was *burning*. Flames licked up from the wound like blood. They sparked upward, and a single spark ran up along the Morgenstern blade, blazing into the hilt.

Sebastian swore and jerked his hand back as if he had been

stabbed. The sword clanged to the ground; he lifted his hand and stared at it. And even through his daze of pain, Jace could see that there was a black mark, a burn across the palm of Sebastian's hand, in the shape of the grip of a sword.

Jace began to struggle up onto his elbows, though the movement sent a wave of pain through his shoulder so severe, he thought he might pass out. His vision darkened; when it came back again, Sebastian was standing over him with a snarl twisting his features, the Morgenstern sword back in his hand—and the two of them were surrounded by a ring of figures. Women, gowned in white like Greek oracles, their eyes leaping orange flames. Their faces were tattooed with masks, as delicate and winding as vines. They were beautiful and terrible. They were Iron Sisters.

Each of them held a sword of *adamas*, point-down. They were silent, their mouths set in grim lines. Between two of them stood the Silent Brother whom Jace had seen earlier, fighting on the plain, his wooden staff in hand.

"In six hundred years we have not abandoned our Citadel," said one of the Sisters, a tall woman whose hair fell in black ropes to her waist. Her eyes blazed, twin furnaces in the darkness. "But the heavenly fire calls us, and we come. Move away from Jace Lightwood, Valentine's son. Harm him again, and we destroy you."

"Neither Jace Lightwood nor the fire in his veins will save you, Cleophas," Sebastian said, sword still in hand. His voice was steady. "The Nephilim have no savior."

"You did not know to fear the heavenly fire. Now you do," said Cleophas. "Time to retreat, boy."

The tip of the Morgenstern sword lowered toward Jace—lowered—and with a cry Sebastian lunged forward. The sword whistled past Jace and buried itself in the earth.

The earth seemed to howl as if mortally wounded. A tremor ripped through the ground, spreading out from the tip of the

Morgenstern sword. Jace's vision was coming and going, consciousness bleeding out of him like the fire that bled from his wound, but even as the darkness came down, he saw the triumph on Sebastian's face, and heard him begin to laugh as with a sudden terrible wrenching the earth tore itself apart. A great black rift opened beside them. Sebastian leaped into it and vanished.

"It's not that simple, Alec," Jia said tiredly. "Portal magic is complicated, and we've heard nothing from the Iron Sisters to indicate that they need our assistance. Besides, after what happened in London earlier today, we need to be here, on alert—"

"I'm telling you, I *know*," Alec said. He was shivering, despite his gear. It was cold on the Gard Hill, but it was more than that. In part it was shock, at what Isabelle had said to his parents, at the look on his father's face. But more of it was apprehension. Cold foreboding was dripping down his spine like ice. "You don't understand the Endarkened; you don't understand what they're like—"

He doubled over. Something hot had lanced through him, through his shoulder down through his guts, like a spear of fire. He hit the ground on his knees, crying out.

"Alec—Alec!" The Consul's hands were on his shoulders. He was distantly aware of his parents running toward him. His vision swam with agony. Pain, overlapping and doubled because it wasn't his pain at all; the sparks under his rib cage didn't burn in his body but in someone else's.

"Jace," he ground out between his teeth. "Something's happened—the fire. You have to open a Portal, *quickly*."

Amatis, flat on her back on the ground, laughed. "You won't kill me," she said. "You haven't got the backbone."

Clary, breathing hard, nudged the tip of the sword under Amatis's chin. "You don't know what I'm capable of."

"Look at me." Amatis's eyes glittered. "Look at me and tell me what you see."

Clary looked, already knowing. Amatis didn't look exactly like her brother, but she had the same jawline, the same trustworthy blue eyes, the same brown hair touched with gray.

"Mercy," Amatis said, raising her hands as if to ward off Clary's blow. "Will you give it to me?"

Mercy. Clary stood frozen, even as Amatis looked up at her with obvious amusement. *Goodness is not kindness, and there is nothing crueler than virtue.* She knew she should cut Amatis's throat, wanted to, even, but how to tell Luke she had killed his sister? Killed his sister while she'd lain on the ground, begging for mercy?

Clary felt her own hand shake, as if it were disconnected from her body. Around her the sounds of battle had dimmed: she could hear shouts and murmurs but didn't dare turn her head away to see what was going on. She was focused on Amatis, on her own grip on the hilt of Heosphoros, of the thin trickle of blood that ran from beneath Amatis's chin, where the tip of Clary's sword had pierced the skin—

The earth erupted. Clary's boots slipped in the snow, and she was flung to the side; she rolled, barely managing not to slice herself on her own blade. The fall knocked the breath from her, but she scrambled back, clutching Heosphoros as the ground shook around her. *Earthquake,* she thought wildly. She clutched at a rock with her free hand as Amatis rolled to her knees, looking around with a predatory grin.

There were screams all around, and an awful ripping noise. As Clary stared in horror, the ground tore itself in half, a massive crack opening in the earth. Rocks, dirt, and jagged chunks of ice rained down into the gap as Clary scrambled to get away from it. It was widening quickly, the jagged crack becoming a vast chasm with sheer sides that dropped away into shadow.

The ground was beginning to stop shaking. Clary heard Amatis laugh. She looked up and saw the older woman rise to her feet, grinning mockingly at Clary. "Give my brother all my love," Amatis called, and jumped into the chasm.

Clary jolted to her feet, her heart pounding, and ran to the edge of the crack. She stared down over it. She could see only a few feet of sheer earth and then darkness—and shadows, moving shadows. She turned to see that everywhere across the battlefield the Endarkened were running toward the chasm and leaping into it. They reminded her of Olympic divers, sure and determined, confident of their landing.

The Nephilim were scrambling to get away from the chasm as their red-clad enemies dashed past them, throwing themselves into the pit. Clary's gaze tracked among them, anxious, looking for one particular black-clad figure, one head of bright hair.

She stopped. There, just at the right of the chasm, some distance from her, were a group of women dressed in white. The Iron Sisters. Through gaps between them, Clary could see a figure on the ground, and another, this one in parchment robes, bent over him—

She broke into a run. She knew she shouldn't run with an unsheathed blade, but she didn't care. She pounded across the snow, darting out of the way of running Endarkened, weaving through the Nephilim, and here the snow was bloody and soaked and slippery, but she ran on anyway, until she burst through the circle of the Iron Sisters and reached Jace.

He was on the ground, and her heart, which had felt as if it were exploding inside her chest, slowed its beating slightly when she saw that his eyes were open. He was very pale, though, and breathing harshly enough that she could hear it. The Silent Brother was kneeling next to him, long pale fingers unsnapping the gear at Jace's shoulder.

"What's going on?" Clary asked, looking around wildly. A

dozen Iron Sisters gazed back, impassive and silent. There were more Iron Sisters as well, on the other side of the chasm, watching unmoving as the Endarkened threw themselves into it. It was eerie. "What happened?"

"Sebastian," Jace said through gritted teeth, and she dropped down beside him, across from the Silent Brother, as his gear peeled away and she saw the gash in his shoulder. "Sebastian happened."

The wound was weeping fire.

Not blood but fire, tinged gold like the ichor of angels. Clary took a ragged breath and looked up to see Brother Zachariah looking back at her. She caught a single glimpse of his face, all angles and pallor and scars, before he drew a stele from his robe. Instead of setting it to Jace's skin, as she would have expected, he set it to his own and carved a rune into his palm. He did it quickly, but Clary could feel the power that came from the rune. It made her shudder.

Stay still. This will end the hurt, he said in his soft omnidirectional whisper, and placed his hand over the fiery gash on Jace's shoulder.

Jace cried out. His body half-lifted off the ground, and the fire that had bled like slow tears from his wound rose as if gasoline had been poured on it, searing up Brother Zachariah's arm. Wildfire consumed the parchment sleeve of Zachariah's robe; the Silent Brother jerked away, but not before Clary saw that the blaze was rising, consuming him. In the depths of the flame, as it wavered and crackled, Clary saw a shape—the shape of a rune that looked like two wings joined by a single bar. A rune she had seen before, standing on a rooftop in Manhattan: the first rune not from the Gray Book that she had ever visualized. It flickered and disappeared, so quickly that she wondered if she had imagined it. It seemed to be a rune that appeared to her in times of stress and panic, but what did it mean? Was it meant to be a way to help Jace—or Brother Zachariah?

The Silent Brother fell back silently into the snow, collapsing like a burned tree shivering to ashes.

A murmur tore through the ranks of the Iron Sisters. Whatever was happening to Brother Zachariah, it wasn't supposed to be happening. Something had gone horribly wrong.

The Iron Sisters moved toward their fallen brother. They blocked Clary's view of Zachariah as she reached for Jace. He was bucking and spasming on the ground, his eyes closed, his head tilted back. She looked around wildly. Through the gaps between the Iron Sisters she could see Brother Zachariah, thrashing on the ground: His body was shimmering, sizzling with fire. A cry burst from his throat—a human noise, the cry of a man in pain, not the silent mind-whisper of the Brothers. Sister Cleophas caught at him—parchment robes and fire, and Clary could hear the Sister's voice rising, "Zachariah, Zachariah—"

But he was not the only one wounded. Some of the Nephilim were grouped around Jace, but many of the others were with their injured comrades, administering healing runes, searching their gear for bandages.

"Clary," Jace whispered. He was trying to struggle up onto his elbows, but they wouldn't hold him. "Brother Zachariah—what's happened? What did I do to him—"

"Nothing, Jace. Lie still." Clary sheathed her blade and fumbled his stele from his weapons belt with numb fingers. She reached to press the tip to his skin, but he writhed away from her, his body jerking.

"No," he gasped. His eyes were huge and burning gold. "Don't touch me. I'll hurt you, too."

"You won't." Desperate, she threw herself on top of him, the weight of her body bearing him backward into the snow. She reached for his shoulder as he twisted under her, his clothes and skin blood-slippery and fire-hot. Her knees slid to either side of his hips as she threw her full weight against his chest, pinning him down. "Jace," she said. "Jace, please." But his eyes wouldn't focus on her, his hands spasming against the ground. "*Jace*," she said, and put the stele to his skin, just over his wound.

And she was on the ship again with her father, with Valentine, and she was throwing everything she had, every bit of strength, every last atom of will and energy into crafting a rune, a rune that would burn down the world, that would reverse death, that would make the oceans fly up into the sky. Only, this time it was the simplest of runes, the rune every Shadowhunter learned in their first year of training:

Heal me.

The *iratze* took shape on Jace's shoulder, the color spiraling from the tip so black that the light coming from the stars and the Citadel seemed to vanish into it. Clary could feel her own energy vanishing into it too as she drew. Never had she felt more like the stele was an extension of her own veins, that she was writing in her own blood, as if all the energy in her was being drawn out through her hand and fingers, her vision darkening as she fought to keep the stele steady, to finish the rune. The last thing she saw was the great burning whirl of a Portal, opening onto the impossible sight of Angel Square, before she slid into nothingness.

8

STRENGTH IN WHAT REMAINS

Raphael stood, hands in his pockets, and looked up at the demon towers, shimmering dark red. "Something's going on," he said. "Something unusual."

Simon wanted to snap back that the unusual thing that was going on was that he'd just been kidnapped and taken to Idris for the second time in his life, but he was feeling too nauseated. He'd forgotten the way a Portal seemed to take you apart when you went through it and reassemble you on the other side with important pieces missing.

Also, Raphael was right. Something was going on. Simon had been in Alicante before, and he remembered the roads and the canals, the hill rising over it all with the Gard at the top. He remembered that on ordinary nights the streets were quiet, lit by the pale glow of the towers. But there was noise tonight, largely coming from the Gard and the hill, where lights were dancing as if a dozen bonfires had been lit. The demon towers were glowing an eerie red-gold.

"They change the color of the towers to convey messages," said Raphael. "Gold for marriages and celebrations. Blue for the Accords."

"What does red mean?" Simon asked.

"Magic," said Raphael, his dark eyes narrowed. "Danger."

He turned in a slow circle, looking around the quiet street, the large houses by the canal side. He was about a head shorter than Simon. Simon wondered how old he'd been when he'd been Turned. Fourteen? Fifteen? Only a little older than Maureen. Who had Turned him? Magnus knew but had never told.

"The Inquisitor's house is there," Raphael said, and pointed at one of the largest of the houses, with a pointed roof and balconies out over the canal. "But it is dark."

Simon couldn't deny that fact, though his unbeating heart gave a little leap as he looked at the place. Isabelle was living there now; one of those windows was her window. "They must all be up at the Gard," he said. "They do that, for meetings and things." He had no fond memories of the Gard himself, having been imprisoned there by the last Inquisitor. "We could go up there, I guess. See what's going on."

"Yes, thank you. I am aware of their 'meetings and things,'" Raphael snapped, but he looked uncertain in a way Simon couldn't recall him looking before. "Whatever is happening, it is Shadowhunter business. There is a house, not far from here, that has been granted to the vampire representative on the Council. We may go there."

"Together?" Simon said.

"It is a very large house," Raphael said. "You will be at one end of it and I at the other."

Simon raised his eyebrows. He wasn't entirely sure what he had expected would happen, but spending the night in a house with Raphael hadn't occurred to him. It wasn't that he thought Raphael was going to kill him in his sleep. But the thought of sharing living quarters with someone who seemed to dislike him intensely and always had was odd.

Simon's vision was clear and precise now—one of the few

things he really liked about being a vampire—and he could see details even at a distance. He saw her before she could have seen him. She was walking along quickly, her head down, her dark hair in the long braid she often wore it in when fighting. She was in gear, and her boots tapped against the cobblestones as she walked.

You're a heartbreaker, Isabelle Lightwood.

Simon turned to Raphael. "Go away," he said.

Raphael smirked. "*La belle Isabelle*," he said. "It is hopeless, you know, you and she."

"Because I'm a vampire and she's a Shadowhunter?"

"No. She's just—how do you say it—out of your league?"

Isabelle was halfway down the street now. Simon gritted his teeth. "Salt my game, and I'll stake you. I mean it."

Raphael shrugged innocently but didn't move. Simon turned away from him and stepped out of the shadows, into the street.

Isabelle halted instantly, her hand going to the whip coiled at her belt. A moment later she blinked in shock, her hand dropping, her voice uncertain: "*Simon?*"

Simon felt suddenly awkward. Maybe she wouldn't appreciate his suddenly appearing in Alicante like this—this was her world, not his. "I—" he began, but he got no further, because Isabelle had launched herself at him and thrown her arms around him, nearly knocking him off his feet.

Simon let himself close his eyes and bury his face against her neck. He could feel her heart beating, but violently pushed aside any thoughts of blood. She was soft and strong in his arms, her hair tickling his face, and holding her, he felt normal, wonderfully normal, like any teenage boy in love with a girl.

In love. He jerked back with a start and found himself looking at Izzy from a few inches away, her huge dark eyes shining. "I can't believe you're here," she said, breathless. "I was wishing you were and thinking about how long it would be before I could see you, and—*Oh, my God, what are you wearing?*"

Simon looked down at his puffy shirt and leather pants. He was vaguely aware of Raphael, somewhere in the shadows, snickering. "It's kind of a long story," he said. "Do you think we could go inside?"

Magnus turned the silver box with the initials on it over in his hands, his cat's eyes gleaming in the witchlit dimness of Amatis's cellar.

Jocelyn was gazing at him with a look of curious anxiety. Luke couldn't help thinking about all the times Jocelyn had taken Clary to Magnus's loft when Clary had been a child, all the times the three of them had sat together, an unlikely trio, as Clary grew up and older and began to remember what she was supposed to forget. "Anything?" Jocelyn asked.

"You have to give me time," Magnus said, poking the box with a finger. "Magical booby-traps, curses, the like, they can be pretty subtly hidden."

"Take your time," said Luke, leaning back against a table shoved into a cobwebby corner. Long ago it had been his mother's kitchen table. He recognized the pattern of careless knife marks across the wooden top, even the dent in one of the legs he'd made when he'd kicked it as a teenager.

It had been Amatis's for years. It had been hers when she'd been married to Stephen and had sometimes hosted dinner parties at the Herondale house. It had been hers after the divorce, after Stephen had moved out to the countryside manor house with his new wife. The whole cellar in fact was stacked with old furniture: items Luke recognized as having belonged to their parents, paintings and knickknacks from the time Amatis had been married. He wondered why she had hidden them away down here. Perhaps she hadn't been able to bear to look at them.

"I don't think there's anything wrong with it," Magnus said

finally, setting the box back on the shelf where Jocelyn had shoved it, unwilling to have the item in the house but unwilling to throw it away, either. He shivered and rubbed his hands together. He was swathed in a gray and black coat that made him look like a hard-boiled detective; Jocelyn hadn't given him a chance to hang his coat up when he'd arrived on their doorstep, just grabbed him by the arm and dragged him down to the cellar. "No snares, no traps, no magic at all."

Jocelyn looked a bit sheepish. "Thanks," she said. "For looking at it. I can be a bit paranoid. And after what just happened in London—"

"What *did* happen in London?"

"We don't know that much," said Luke. "We got a fire-message about it this afternoon from the Gard, but not a lot of details. London was one of the few Institutes that hadn't emptied yet. Apparently Sebastian and his forces tried to attack. They were rebuffed by some kind of protection spell, something even the Council didn't know about. Something that warned the Shadowhunters what was coming and led them to safety."

"A ghost," Magnus said. A smile hovered around his mouth. "A spirit, sworn to protect the place. She's been there for a hundred and thirty years."

"*She?*" Jocelyn said, leaning back against a dusty wall. "A ghost? Really? What was her name?"

"You would recognize her last name, if I told it to you, but she wouldn't like that." Magnus's gaze was faraway. "I hope this means she's found peace." He snapped back to attention. "Anyway," he said. "I hadn't meant to drag the conversation in this direction. It isn't why I came to you."

"I guessed as much," said Luke. "We appreciate the visit, though I admit I was surprised to see you on our doorstep. It's not where I thought you'd go."

I thought you'd go to the Lightwoods' hung in the air between them, unsaid.

"I had a life before Alec," Magnus snapped. "I'm the High Warlock of Brooklyn. I am here to take a Council seat on behalf of Lilith's Children."

"I thought Catarina Loss was the warlock representative," said Luke, surprised.

"She was," Magnus admitted. "She made me take her place so I could come here and see Alec." He sighed. "She in fact made this particular pitch to me while we were in the Hunter's Moon. And that's what I wanted to talk to you about."

Luke sat down on the rickety table. "Did you see Bat?" he asked. Bat tended to set up office in the Hunter's Moon during the days, rather than the police station; it was unofficial, but everyone knew that was where to find him.

"Yes. He'd just gotten a call from Maia." Magnus ran a hand through his black hair. "Sebastian doesn't exactly appreciate being rebuffed," he said slowly, and Luke felt his nerves tighten. Magnus was clearly hesitant to impart bad news. "It looks like after he attempted to attack the London Institute and was unsuccessful, he turned his attention to the Praetor Lupus. Apparently he doesn't have much use for lycanthropes—can't turn them into Endarkened—so he burned the place to the ground and murdered them all. He killed Jordan Kyle in front of Maia. He let her live so she could deliver a message."

Jocelyn hugged her arms around herself. "My God."

"What was the message?" Luke said, finding his voice.

"It was a message to Downworlders," said Magnus. "I talked to Maia on the phone. She had me memorize it. Apparently he said, 'Tell all the Downworlders that I am in pursuit of vengeance, and I will have it. I will deal this way with any who ally themselves with Shadowhunters. I have no argument with your kind, unless you follow the Nephilim into battle, in which case you will be food for my blade and the blades of my army, until the last of you is cut from the surface of this world.'"

Jocelyn made a ragged sound. "He sounds just like his father, doesn't he?"

Luke looked at Magnus. "Are you going to deliver that message at the Council?"

Magnus tapped at his chin with a glittery fingernail. "No," he said. "But I'm not going to conceal it from the Downworlders, either. My loyalty is not to Shadowhunters over them."

Not like yours. The words hung between them, unspoken.

"I have this," Magnus said, taking a piece of paper from his pocket. Luke recognized it, since he had one of his own. "Will you be at the dinner tomorrow night?"

"I will. Faeries take invitations like that very seriously. Meliorn and the Court would be insulted if I didn't go."

"I plan to tell them then," Magnus said.

"And if they panic?" said Luke. "If they abandon the Council and the Nephilim?"

"It's not as if what happened at the Praetor can be concealed."

"Sebastian's message could," said Jocelyn. "He's trying to frighten the Downworlders, Magnus. He's trying to make them stand back while he destroys the Nephilim."

"It would be their right," said Magnus.

"If they do, do you think that the Nephilim will ever forgive them?" said Jocelyn. "The Clave is not forgiving. They are more unforgiving than God himself."

"Jocelyn," said Luke. "It's not Magnus's fault."

But Jocelyn was still looking at Magnus. "What," she said, "would Tessa tell you to do?"

"Please, Jocelyn," Magnus said. "You hardly know her. She would preach honesty; she usually does. Concealing the truth never works. When you live long enough, you can see that."

Jocelyn looked down at her hands—her artist's hands, that Luke had always loved, agile and careful and stained with ink. "I am not a Shadowhunter anymore," she said. "I fled from them. I told you both that. But a world without Shadowhunters in it—I am afraid of that."

"There was a world before the Nephilim," said Magnus. "There will be one after."

"A world we can survive in? My son—" Jocelyn began, and broke off as a hammering sound came from upstairs. Someone was pounding on the front door. "Clary?" she wondered aloud. "She might have forgotten her key again."

"I'll get it," Luke said, and stood up. He exchanged a brief look with Jocelyn as he left the cellar, his mind whirling. Jordan dead, Maia grieving. Sebastian trying to pit Downworlders against Shadowhunters.

He drew the front door open, and a blast of cold night air came in. Standing on the doorstep was a young woman with pale curling blond hair, dressed in gear. Helen Blackthorn. Luke barely had time to register that the demon towers above them were glowing bloodred when she spoke.

"I've come with a message from the Gard," she said. "It's about Clary."

"Maia."

A soft voice out of the silence. Maia turned over, not wanting to open her eyes. There was something terrible waiting out there in the darkness, something that she could escape if she just slept and slept forever.

"*Maia.*" He was looking at her out of the shadows, pale eyes and dark skin. Her brother, Daniel. As she watched, he tore the wings from a butterfly and let its body fall, twitching, to the ground.

"Maia, please." A light touch on her arm. She bolted upright, her whole body recoiling. Her back hit a wall and she gasped, peeling her eyes open. They were sticky, her eyelashes fringed with salt. She had been crying in her sleep.

She was in a half-lit room, a single window looking out onto a winding downtown street. She could see the leafless boughs of trees through the smeared glass and the edge of something metal—a fire escape, she guessed.

She glanced down—a narrow bed with an iron headboard and a thin blanket that she had kicked to the foot. Her back against a brick wall. A single chair by the bed, old and splintered. Bat sat in it, his eyes wide, slowly lowering his hand.

"I'm sorry," he said.

"Don't," she ground out. "Don't touch me."

"You were screaming," he said. "In your sleep."

She hugged her arms around herself. She was wearing jeans and a tank top. The sweater she had been wearing on Long Island was missing, and the skin on her arms prickled with gooseflesh. "Where are my clothes?" she said. "My jacket, my sweater—"

Bat cleared his throat. "They were covered in blood, Maia."

"Right," she said. Her heart was drumming in her chest.

"You remember what happened?" he asked.

She closed her eyes. She remembered it all: the drive, the truck, the burning building, the beach covered in bodies. Jordan collapsing against her, his blood running down on and around her like water, mixing with the sand. *Your boyfriend's dead.*

"Jordan," she said, though she already knew.

Bat's face was grave; there was a greenish cast to his brown eyes that made them shine in the half-light. It was a face she knew well. He was one of the first werewolves she'd ever met. They'd dated until she'd told him she thought she was too new to the city, too jittery, too much not over Jordan for a relationship. He'd broken up with her the next day; surprisingly they had stayed friends. "He's dead," he said. "Along with almost all the Praetor Lupus. Praetor Scott, the students—a few survived. Maia, why were you there? What were you doing at the Praetor?"

Maia told him about Simon's disappearance, the phone call to Jordan from the Praetor, their frantic drive to Long Island, the discovery of the Praetor in ruins.

Bat cleared his throat. "I do have some of Jordan's things. His keys, his Praetor pendant—"

Maia felt as if she couldn't catch her breath. "No, I don't want— I don't want his things," she said. "He would have wanted Simon to have the pendant. When we find Simon, he should have it."

Bat didn't push the issue. "I do have some good news," he said. "We heard from Idris: your friend Simon's all right. He's there, actually, with the Shadowhunters."

"Oh." Maia felt the tight knot around her heart loosen slightly with relief.

"I should have told you right away," he apologized. "It's just—I was worried about you. You were in bad shape when we brought you back to headquarters. You've been sleeping since then."

I wanted to sleep forever.

"I know you already told Magnus," added Bat, his face strained. "But explain it to me again, why Sebastian Morgenstern would target lycanthropes."

"He said it was a message." Maia heard the flatness in her own voice as if from a distance. "He wanted us to know that it was because werewolves are allies with the Shadowhunters, and that this was what he planned to do to all the Nephilim's allies."

"I'll never pause again, never stand still, till either death hath closed these eyes of mine, or fortune given me measure of revenge."

"New York is empty of Shadowhunters now, and Luke is in Idris with them. They're putting up extra wards. Soon we'll barely be able to get messages in and out." Bat shifted in his chair; Maia sensed there was something he wasn't telling her.

"What is it?" she said.

His eyes darted away.

"Bat..."

"Do you know Rufus Hastings?"

Rufus. Maia remembered the first time she'd been to the Praetor Lupus, a scarred face, an angry man exiting Prateor Scott's office in a rage. "Not really."

"He survived the massacre. He's here in the station, with us. He's been filling us in," said Bat. "And he's been talking to the others about Luke. Saying that he's more of a Shadowhunter than a lycanthrope, that he doesn't have pack loyalty, that the pack needs a new leader now."

"*You're* the leader," she said. "You're second in command."

"Yeah, and I was put in that position by Luke. That means I can't be trusted either."

Maia slid to the edge of the bed. Her whole body ached; she felt it as she put her bare feet on the cold stone floor. "No one's listening to him, are they?"

Bat shrugged.

"That's ridiculous. After what's happened, we need to be unified, not to have someone trying to split us up. Shadowhunters are our allies—"

"Which is why Sebastian targeted us."

"He'd target us anyway. He's no friend to Downworlders. He's Valentine Morgenstern's *son*." Her eyes burned. "He might be trying to get us to abandon the Nephilim temporarily, so he can go after them, but if he managed to wipe them off the earth, all he'd do is come for us next."

Bat clasped and unclasped his hands, then seemed to come to a decision. "I know you're right," he said, and went over to a table in the corner of the room. He returned with a jacket for her, socks and boots. He handed them over. "Just—do me a favor and don't say anything like that this afternoon. Emotions are going to be running pretty high as it is."

She shrugged the jacket on. "This afternoon? What's this afternoon?"

He sighed. "The funeral," he said.

"I'm going to *kill* Maureen," Isabelle said. She had both doors of Alec's wardrobe open and was flinging clothes onto the floor in heaps.

Simon was lying barefoot on one of the beds—Jace's? Alec's?—having kicked off his alarming buckled boots. Though his skin didn't really bruise, it felt amazing to be on a soft surface after having spent so many hours on the hard, dirty floor of the Dumort. "You'll have to fight your way through all the vampires of New York to do it," he said. "Apparently they love her."

"No accounting for taste." Isabelle held up a dark blue sweater Simon recognized as Alec's, mostly from the holes in the cuffs. "So Raphael brought you here so you could talk to my dad?"

Simon propped himself up on his elbows to watch her. "Do you think that'll be okay?"

"Sure, why not. My dad loves talking." She sounded bitter. Simon leaned forward, but when she raised her head, she was smiling at him and he thought he must have imagined it. "Although, who knows what will happen, with the attack on the Citadel tonight." She worried at her lower lip. "It could mean they cancel the meeting, or move it earlier. Sebastian's obviously a bigger problem than they thought. He shouldn't even be able to get that close to the Citadel."

"Well," Simon said. "He is a Shadowhunter."

"No, he's not," Isabelle said fiercely, and yanked a green sweater down from a wooden hanger. "Besides. He's a man."

"Sorry," Simon said. "It must be nerve-racking, waiting to see how the battle turns out. How many people did they let through?"

"Fifty or sixty," Isabelle said. "I wanted to go, but—they wouldn't let me." She had the guarded tone in her voice that meant they were closing in on a subject she didn't want to talk about.

"I would have worried about you," he said.

He saw her mouth quirk into a reluctant smile. "Try this on," she said, and tossed him the green sweater, slightly less frayed than the rest.

"Are you sure it's okay for me to borrow clothes?"

"You can't go around like *that*," she said. "You look like you escaped from a romance novel." Isabelle laid a hand dramatically against her forehead. "Oh, Lord Montgomery, what do you mean to do with me in this bedroom when you have me all alone? An innocent maiden, and unprotected?" She unzipped her jacket and tossed it to the floor, revealing a white tank top. She gave him a sultry look. "Is my virtue safe?"

"I, ah—what?" Simon said, temporarily deprived of vocabulary.

"I know you are a dangerous man," Isabelle declared, sashaying toward the bed. She unzipped her trousers and kicked them to the floor. She was wearing black boy shorts underneath. "Some call you a rake. Everybody knows you are a devil with the ladies with your poetically puffed shirt and irresistible pants." She pounced onto the bed and crawled over to him, eyeing him like a cobra considering making a snack out of a mongoose. "I pray you will consider my innocence," she breathed. "And my poor, vulnerable heart."

Simon decided this was a lot like role-playing in D&D, but potentially much more fun. "Lord Montgomery considers nothing but his own desires," he said in a gravelly voice. "I'll tell you something else. Lord Montgomery has a very large estate ... and pretty extensive grounds, too."

Isabelle giggled, and Simon felt the bed shake under them.

"Okay, I didn't expect you to get *quite* so into this."

"Lord Montgomery always surpasses expectations," Simon said, seizing Isabelle around the waist and rolling her over so she was beneath him, her black hair spread out onto the pillow. "Mothers, lock up your daughters, then lock up your maidservants, then lock up yourselves. Lord Montgomery is on the prowl."

Isabelle framed his face between her hands. "My lord," she said, her eyes shining. "I fear I can no longer withstand your manly charms and virile ways. Please do with me as you will."

Simon wasn't sure what Lord Montgomery would do, but he knew what *he* wanted to do. He bent down and pressed a lingering kiss to her mouth. Her lips parted under his, and suddenly everything was all sweet dark heat and Isabelle's lips brushing over his, first teasing, then harder. She smelled, as she always did, dizzyingly of roses and blood. He pressed his lips to the pulse point at her throat, mouthing over it gently, not biting, and Izzy gasped; her hands went to the front of his shirt. He was momentarily concerned about its lack of buttons, but Isabelle grasped the material in her strong hands and ripped the shirt in half, leaving it dangling off his shoulders.

"Goodness, that stuff rips like paper," she exclaimed, reaching to pull her tank top off. She was halfway through the action when the door opened and Alec walked into the room.

"Izzy, are you—" he began. His eyes flew wide, and he backed up fast enough to smack his head into the wall behind him. "*What* is he doing here?"

Isabelle tugged her tank top back down and glared at her brother. "You don't knock now?"

"It—It's *my* bedroom!" Alec spluttered. He seemed to be deliberately trying not to look at Izzy and Simon, who were indeed in a very compromising position. Simon rolled quickly off Isabelle, who sat up, brushing herself off as if for lint. Simon sat up more slowly, trying to hold the torn edges of his shirt together. "Why are all my clothes on the floor?" Alec said.

"I was trying to find something for Simon to wear," Isabelle explained. "Maureen put him in leather pants and a puffy shirt because he was being her romance-novel slave."

"He was being her *what*?"

"Her romance-novel slave," Isabelle repeated, as if Alec were being particularly dense.

Alec shook his head as if he were having a bad dream. "You know what? Don't explain. Just—put your clothes on, both of you."

"You're not going to leave—are you?" Isabelle said in a sulky tone, sliding off the bed. She picked up her jacket and shrugged it on, then tossed Simon the green sweater. He happily swapped it for the poet shirt, which was in ribbons anyway.

"No. It's my room, and besides, I need to talk to you, *Isabelle*." Alec's voice was terse. Simon grabbed up jeans and shoes from the floor and went into the bathroom to change, deliberately taking plenty of time with it. When he came back out, Isabelle was sitting on the rumpled bed, looking strained and tense.

"So they're opening the Portal back up to bring everyone through? Good."

"It is good, but what I felt"—Alec put his hand unconsciously over his upper arm, near his *parabatai* rune—"that isn't good. Jace isn't dead," he hastened to add as Isabelle paled. "I would know if he were. But something happened. Something with the heavenly fire, I think."

"Do you know if he's okay now? And Clary?" Isabelle demanded.

"Wait, back up," Simon interrupted. "What's this about Clary? And Jace?"

"They went through the Portal," Isabelle said grimly. "To the battle at the Citadel."

Simon realized he had unconsciously reached for the gold ring on his right hand and was gripping it with his fingers. "Aren't they too young?"

"They didn't exactly have permission." Alec was leaning back against the wall. He looked tired, the shadows under his eyes bruise-blue. "The Consul tried to stop them, but she didn't have time."

Simon turned on Isabelle. "And you didn't tell me?"

Isabelle wouldn't meet his eyes. "I knew you'd freak out."

Alec was looking from Isabelle to Simon. "You didn't tell him?" he said. "About what happened at the Gard?"

Isabelle crossed her arms over her chest and looked defiant. "No. I bumped into him in the street, and we came upstairs, and— and it's none of your business."

"It is if you do it in my bedroom," said Alec. "If you're going to use Simon to make yourself forget you're angry and upset, fine, but do it in your own room."

"I wasn't using him—"

Simon thought about Isabelle's eyes, shining when she'd seen him standing in the street. He'd thought it was happiness, but he realized now it had more likely been unshed tears. The way she'd been walking toward him, her head down, her shoulders curved in, as if she'd been holding herself together.

"You were, though," he said. "Or you would have told me what happened. You didn't even mention Clary or Jace, or that you were worried, or *anything*." He felt his stomach clench as he realized how deftly Isabelle had deflected his questions and distracted him with kissing, and he felt stupid. He'd thought she was glad to see him specifically, but maybe he could have been anyone.

Isabelle's face had gone very still. "Please," she said. "It's not like you *asked*." She had been fiddling with her hair; now she reached up and began twisting it, almost savagely, into a knot on the back of her head. "If you're both going to stand there blaming me, maybe you should just go—"

"I'm not blaming you," Simon began, but Isabelle was already on her feet. She snatched the ruby pendant, pulled it none too gently over his head, and dropped it back around her own neck. "I never should have given it to you," she said, her eyes bright.

"It saved my life," Simon said.

That made her pause. "Simon..." she whispered.

She broke off as Alec suddenly clutched at his shoulder with a gasp. He slid to the floor. Isabelle ran to him and knelt down by his side. "Alec? *Alec!*" Her voice rose, tinged with panic.

Alec pushed aside his jacket, shoved down the collar of his shirt, and craned to see the mark on his shoulder. Simon recognized the outlines of the *parabatai* rune. Alec pressed his fingers to it; they came away smudged with something dark that looked like a smear of ash. "They've come back through the Portal," he said. "And there's something wrong with Jace."

It was like returning to a dream, or a nightmare.

After the Mortal War, Angel Square had been full of bodies. Shadowhunter bodies, laid out in neat rows, each corpse with its eyes bound in the white silk of death.

There were bodies in the square again, but this time there was also chaos. The demon towers were shining down a brilliant light on the scene that greeted Simon when, having followed Isabelle and Alec through the winding streets of Alicante, he finally reached the Hall of Accords. The square was full of people. Nephilim in gear lay on the ground, some writhing in pain and calling out, some alarmingly still.

The Accords Hall itself was dark and shut tight. One of the larger stone buildings on the square was open and blazing with lights, double doors thrown wide. A stream of Shadowhunters was going in and out.

Isabelle had risen up on tiptoe and was scanning the crowd

anxiously. Simon followed her gaze. He could make out a few familiar figures: the Consul moving anxiously among her people, Kadir
from the New York Institute, Silent Brothers in their parchment
robes directing people wordlessly toward the lighted building. "The
Basilias is open," Isabelle said to a haggard-looking Alec. "They
might have taken Jace in there, if he was hurt—"

"He was hurt," Alec said shortly.

"The Basilias?" Simon asked.

"The hospital," Isabelle said, indicating the lighted building.
Simon could feel her thrumming with nervous, panicked energy. "I
should—we should—"

"I'll go with you," Simon said.

She shook her head. "Shadowhunters only."

Alec said, "Isabelle. Come on." He was holding the shoulder
marked by his *parabatai* rune stiffly. Simon wanted to say something to him, wanted to say that his best friend had also gone
into the battle and was also missing, wanted to say that he understood. But maybe you could only understand *parabatai* if you were
a Shadowhunter. He doubted Alec would thank him for saying he
understood. Rarely had Simon felt so keenly the divide between
Nephilim and those who were not Nephilim.

Isabelle nodded and followed her brother without another
word. Simon watched them go across the square, past the statue
of the Angel, looking down on the aftermath of the battle with sad
marble eyes. They went up the front steps of the Basilias and were
lost to even his vampire sight.

"Do you think," said a soft voice at his shoulder, "that they
would mind much if we fed on their dead?"

It was Raphael. His curly hair was a mussed halo around his
head, and he wore only a thin T-shirt and jeans. He looked like a
child.

"The blood of the recently deceased is not my favorite vintage," he went on, "but it is better than bottled blood, would you not agree?"

"You have an incredibly charming personality," said Simon. "I hope someone's told you that."

Raphael snorted. "Sarcasm," he said. "Tedious."

Simon made an uncontrollable, exasperated noise. "You go ahead then. Feed on the Nephilim dead. I'm sure they're really in the mood for that. They might let you live five, ten seconds even."

Raphael chuckled. "It looks worse than it is," he said. "There are not so many dead. Quite a lot injured. They were overmatched. They will not forget, now, what it means to fight the Endarkened."

Simon narrowed his eyes. "What do you know about the Endarkened, Raphael?"

"Whispers and shadows," said Raphael. "But I make it my business to know things."

"Then if you know things, tell me where Jace and Clary are," said Simon, without a lot of hope. Raphael was rarely helpful unless it was useful to him.

"Jace is in the Basilias," said Raphael, to Simon's surprise. "It appears the heavenly fire in his veins was finally too much for him. He nearly destroyed himself, and one of the Silent Brothers along with him."

"*What?*" Simon's anxiety sharpened from the general to the specific. "Is he going to live? Where's Clary?"

Raphael cast him a look out of dark, long-lashed eyes; his smile was lopsided. "It does not do for vampires to fret overmuch for the lives of mortals."

"I swear to God, Raphael, if you don't start being more helpful—"

"Very well, then. Come with me." Raphael moved farther into the shadows, keeping to the inside edge of the square. Simon hurried to catch up with him. He caught sight of a blond head and a dark head bent together—Aline and Helen, tending to one of the wounded—and thought for a moment of Alec and Jace.

"If you are wondering what would happen if you drank Jace's blood now, the answer is that it would kill you," said Raphael. "Vampires and heavenly fire do not mix. Yes, even you, Daylighter."

"I wasn't wondering that." Simon scowled. "I was wondering what happened at the battle."

"Sebastian attacked the Adamant Citadel," said Raphael, moving around a tight knot of Shadowhunters. "Where the weapons of the Shadowhunters are forged. The place of the Iron Sisters. He tricked the Clave into believing he had a force of only twenty with him, when in fact he had more. He would have killed them all and taken the Citadel most likely, if not for your Jace—"

"He isn't my Jace."

"And Clary," said Raphael, as if Simon hadn't spoken. "Though I do not know the details. Only what I have overheard, and there seems much confusion among the Nephilim themselves as to what happened."

"How did Sebastian manage to trick them into thinking he had fewer warriors than he did?"

Raphael shrugged a thin shoulder. "Shadowhunters forget sometimes that not all magic is theirs. The Citadel is built on ley lines. There is old magic, wild magic, that existed before Jonathan Shadowhunter, and will exist again—"

He broke off, and Simon followed his gaze. For a moment Simon saw only a sheet of blue light. Then it subsided and he saw Clary lying on the ground. He heard a roaring sound in his ears, like rushing blood. She was white and still, her fingers and mouth tinged a dark bluish purple. Her hair hung in lank straggles around her face, and her eyes were circled with shadows. She wore torn and bloody gear, and by her hand lay a Morgenstern sword, its blade stamped with stars.

Magnus was leaning over her, his hand on her cheek, the tips of his fingers glowing blue. Jocelyn and Luke knelt on the other side of Clary. Jocelyn looked up and saw Simon. Her lips shaped his name. He couldn't hear anything over the roaring in his ears. Was Clary dead? She looked dead, or nearly.

He started forward, but Luke was already on his feet, reaching for Simon. He caught at Simon's arms, pulled him back from where Clary lay on the ground.

Simon's vampire nature gave him unnatural strength, strength he'd barely learned how to use yet, but Luke was just as strong. His fingers dug into Simon's upper arms. "What happened?" Simon said, his voice rising. "Raphael—?" He whipped around to look for the vampire, but Raphael was gone; he had melted into the shadows. "Please," Simon said to Luke, looking from his familiar face to Clary. "Let me—"

"Simon, no," Magnus barked. He was tracing his fingertips over Clary's face, leaving blue sparks in their wake. She didn't move or react. "This is delicate—her energy is extremely low."

"Shouldn't she be in the Basilias?" Simon demanded, looking over at the hospital building. Light was still pouring from it, and to his surprise he saw Alec standing on the steps. He was staring at Magnus. Before Simon could move or signal to him, Alec turned abruptly and went back inside the building.

"Magnus—" Simon began.

"Simon, *shut up*," Magnus said through gritted teeth. Simon twisted out of Luke's grasp only to trip and fetch up against the side of a stone wall.

"But Clary—" he started.

Luke looked haggard, but his expression was firm. "Clary exhausted herself making a healing rune. But she's not wounded, her body's whole, and Magnus can help her better than the Silent Brothers can. The best thing you can do is stay out of the way."

"Jace," Simon said. "Alec felt something happen to him through the *parabatai* bond. Something to do with the heavenly fire. And Raphael was babbling about ley lines—"

"Look, the battle was bloodier than the Nephilim expected. Sebastian wounded Jace, but the heavenly fire rebounded on him, somehow. It nearly destroyed Jace as well. Clary saved Jace's life, but there's still work for the Brothers to do, healing him." Luke looked at Simon with tired blue eyes. "And why were you with Isabelle and Alec? I thought you were going to stay behind in New York. Did you come because of Jordan?"

The name brought Simon up short. "Jordan? What does he have to do with anything?"

For the first time Luke seemed truly taken aback. "You don't know?"

"Know what?"

Luke hesitated a long moment. Then he said, "I have something for you. Magnus brought it from New York." He reached into his pocket and drew out a medallion on a chain. The medallion was gold, stamped with a wolf's paw and the Latin inscription *Beati Bellicosi*.

Blessed are the warriors.

Simon knew it instantly. Jordan's Praetor Lupus pendant. It was flaked and stained with blood. Dark red like rust, it clung to the chain and the medallion's face. But if anyone knew what was rust and what was blood, it was a vampire. "I don't understand," Simon said. The roaring was back in his ears again. "Why do you have this? Why are you giving it to me?"

"Because Jordan wanted you to have it," said Luke.

"Wanted?" Simon's voice rose. "Don't you mean 'wants'?"

Luke took a deep breath. "I'm sorry, Simon. Jordan's dead."

9

THE ARMS YOU BEAR

Clary woke to the fading afterimage of a rune against her closed eyelids—a rune like wings connected by a single bar. Her whole body hurt, and for a moment she lay still, afraid of the pain that moving would bring. Memories crept back slowly—the icy lava plain in front of the Citadel, Amatis laughing and daring Clary to hurt her, Jace cutting his way through a field of the Endarkened; Jace on the ground bleeding fire, Brother Zachariah lurching back from the blaze.

Her eyes flew open. She had half-expected to wake up somewhere entirely foreign, but instead she was lying in the small wooden bed in Amatis's spare room. Pale sunshine poured through the lace curtains, making patterns on the ceiling.

She began to struggle to sit up. Near her someone had been singing softly—her mother. Jocelyn broke off immediately and leaped up to lean over her. She looked as if she had been up all night: She was wearing an old shirt and jeans, and her hair was scraped back into a bun with a pencil stuck through it. A wash of familiarity and relief went through Clary, quickly followed by panic.

"Mom," she said as Jocelyn leaned over her, pressing the back of her hand to Clary's forehead as if checking for fever. "Jace—"

"Jace is fine," Jocelyn said, taking her hand away. At Clary's suspicious look Jocelyn shook her head. "He really is. He's in the Basilias now, along with Brother Zachariah. He's recovering."

Clary looked at her mother, hard.

"Clary, I know I've given you reason not to trust me in the past, but please believe me, Jace is *perfectly all right*. I know you'd never forgive me if I didn't tell you the truth about him."

"When can I see him?"

"Tomorrow." Jocelyn sat back on the chair beside the bed, revealing Luke, who had been leaning against the wall of the bedroom. He smiled at Clary—a sad, loving, protective smile.

"Luke!" she said, relieved to see him. "Tell Mom I'm fine. I can go to the Basilias—"

Luke shook his head. "Sorry, Clary. No visitors for Jace right now. Besides, today you have to rest. We heard what you did with that *iratze*, at the Citadel."

"Or at least, what people saw you do. I'm not sure I'll ever understand it exactly." The lines at the corners of Jocelyn's mouth deepened. "You nearly killed yourself healing Jace, Clary. You're going to have to be careful. You don't have endless reserves of energy—"

"He was dying," Clary interrupted. "He was bleeding fire. I had to save him."

"*You* shouldn't have had to!" Jocelyn tossed a stray lock of red hair out of her eyes. "What were you doing at that battle?"

"They weren't sending enough people through," Clary said in a subdued tone. "And everyone was talking about how when they got there, they were going to rescue the Endarkened, they were going to bring them back, find a cure—but I was at the Burren. You were too, Mom. You know there's no rescuing the Nephilim that Sebastian's taken with the Infernal Cup."

"Did you see my sister?" Luke said, his voice gentle.

Clary swallowed, and nodded. "I'm sorry. She's—she's Sebastian's lieutenant. She's not herself anymore, not even a little bit."

"Did she hurt you?" Luke demanded. His voice was still calm, but a muscle jumped in his cheek.

Clary shook her head; she couldn't bring herself to speak, to lie, but she couldn't tell Luke the truth, either.

"It's all right," he said, misunderstanding her distress. "The Amatis that is serving Sebastian is no more my sister than the Jace who served Sebastian was the boy you loved. No more my sister than Sebastian is the son your mother ought to have had."

Jocelyn put out her hand, took Luke's, and kissed the back of it lightly. Clary averted her eyes. Her mother turned back to her a moment later. "God, the Clave—if only they would *listen*." She blew out a frustrated breath. "Clary, we understand why you did what you did last night, but we thought you were safe. Then Helen showed up on our doorstep and told us you'd been injured in the Citadel battle. I nearly had a heart attack when we found you in the square. Your lips and fingers were blue. Like you'd drowned. If it hadn't been for Magnus—"

"Magnus healed me? What's he doing here, in Alicante?"

"This isn't about Magnus," said Jocelyn with asperity. "This is about you. Jia's been beside herself, thinking she let you go through the Portal and you could have been killed. It was a call for experienced Shadowhunters, not children—"

"It was Sebastian," Clary said. "They didn't understand."

"Sebastian's not your responsibility. Speaking of which—" Jocelyn reached under the bed; when she straightened, she was holding Heosphoros. "Is this yours? It was in your weapons belt when they brought you home."

"Yes!" Clary clapped her hands together. "I thought I'd lost it."

"It's a Morgenstern sword, Clary," her mother said, holding it as if it were a piece of moldy lettuce. "One I sold years ago. Where did you get it?"

"The weapons shop where you sold it. The lady who owns the store now said no one else would buy it." Clary snatched Heosphoros out of her mother's hand. "Look, I *am* a Morgenstern. We can't pretend I don't have any of Valentine's blood in me. I need to figure out a way to be partly a Morgenstern and to have that be all right, not to pretend I'm someone else—someone with a made-up name that doesn't mean anything."

Jocelyn recoiled slightly. "Do you mean 'Fray'?"

"It's not exactly a Shadowhunter name, is it?"

"No," her mother said, "not exactly, but it doesn't mean nothing."

"I thought you picked it randomly."

Jocelyn shook her head. "You know the ceremony that must be performed on Nephilim children when they're born? The one that confers the protection that Jace lost when he came back from the dead, the one that allowed Lilith to get to him? Usually the ceremony is performed by an Iron Sister and a Silent Brother, but in your case, because we were hiding, I couldn't officially do that. It was done by Brother Zachariah, and a female warlock stood in as the Iron Sister. I named you—after her."

"Fray? Her last name was 'Fray'?"

"The name was an impulse," said Jocelyn, not quite answering the question. "I—liked her. She had known loss and pain and grief, but she was strong, like I want you to be strong. That's all I've ever wanted. For you to be strong and safe and not have to suffer what I suffered—the terror and the pain and the danger."

"Brother Zachariah—" Clary suddenly bolted upright. "He was there last night. He tried to heal Jace, but the heavenly fire burned him. Is he all right? He isn't dead, is he?"

"I don't know." Jocelyn looked a little bewildered at Clary's vehemence. "I know he was taken to the Basilias. The Silent Brothers have been very secretive about everyone's condition; they certainly wouldn't speak about one of their own."

"He said the Brothers owed the Herondales because of old ties," said Clary. "If he dies, it will be—"

"No one's fault," Jocelyn said. "I remember when he put the protection spell on you. I told him I never wanted you to have anything to do with Shadowhunters. He said it might not be my choice. He said that the pull of the Shadowhunters is like a riptide—and he was right. I thought we had fought free, but here we are, back in Alicante, back in a war, and there sits my daughter with blood on her face and a Morgenstern blade in her hands."

There was an undertone to her voice, shadowed and tense, that made Clary's nerves spark. "Mom," she said. "Did something else happen? Is there something you're not telling me?"

Jocelyn exchanged a look with Luke. He spoke first: "You already know that yesterday morning, before the battle at the Citadel, Sebastian tried to attack the London Institute."

"But no one was hurt. Robert said—"

"So Sebastian turned his attention elsewhere," Luke went on firmly. "He left London with his forces and attacked the Praetor Lupus on Long Island. Almost all the Praetorians, including their leader, were slaughtered. Jordan Kyle—" His voice cracked. "Jordan was killed."

Clary wasn't aware that she had moved, but suddenly she was no longer under the covers. She had swung her legs over the side of the bed and was reaching for the scabbard of Heosphoros on the nightstand. "Clary," her mother said, reaching to place her long fingers on Clary's wrist, restraining her. "Clary, it's over. There's nothing you can do."

Clary could taste tears, hot and salty, burning the back of her throat, and under the tears the rougher, darker taste of panic. "What about Maia?" she demanded. "If Jordan's hurt, is Maia all right? And Simon? Jordan was his guard! *Is Simon all right?*"

"I'm fine. Don't worry, I'm fine," said Simon's voice. The bedroom door opened, and to Clary's utter astonishment Simon came in, looking surprisingly shy. She dropped Heosphoros's scabbard onto the coverlet and launched herself to her feet, barreling into Simon so hard that she banged her head into his collarbone. She didn't notice if it hurt or not. She was too busy holding on to Simon as if they'd both just fallen out of a helicopter and were hurtling downward. She was grabbing fistfuls of his creased green sweater, mashing her face awkwardly into his shoulder as she fought not to cry.

He held her, soothing her with awkward boy-pats to her back and shoulders. When she finally let him go and stepped back, she saw that the sweater and jeans he was wearing were both a size too big for him. A metal chain hung around his throat.

"What are you doing here?" she demanded. "Whose *clothes* are you wearing?"

"It's a long story, and Alec's, mostly," Simon said. His words were casual, but he looked strained and tense. "You should have seen what I had on before. Nice pajamas, by the way."

Clary looked down at herself. She was wearing a pair of flannel pajamas, too short in the leg and tight in the chest, with fire trucks on them.

Luke raised an eyebrow. "I think those were mine when I was a kid."

"You can't seriously tell me there wasn't anything else you could have put me in."

"If you insist on trying to get yourself killed, I insist on being the one who chooses what you wear while you recover," Jocelyn said with a tiny smirk.

"The pajamas of vengeance," Clary muttered. She grabbed up jeans and a shirt from the floor and looked at Simon. "I'm going to change. And by the time I get back, you better be ready to tell me something about how you're here besides 'long story.'"

Simon muttered something that sounded like "bossy," but Clary was already out the door. She showered in record time, enjoying the feel of the water sluicing away the dirt of the battle. She was still worried about Jace, despite her mother's reassurances, but the sight of Simon had lifted her spirits. Maybe it didn't make sense, but she was happier that he was where she could keep an eye on him, rather than back in New York. Especially after Jordan.

When she got back to the bedroom, her damp hair tied back in a ponytail, Simon was perched on the nightstand, deep in conversation with her mother and Luke, recounting what had happened to him in New York, how Maureen had kidnapped him and Raphael had rescued him and brought him to Alicante.

"Then I hope Raphael intends to attend the dinner held by the representatives of the Seelie Court tonight," Luke was saying. "Anselm Nightshade would have been invited, but if Raphael is standing in for him at the Council, then he should be there. Especially after what's happened with the Praetor, the importance of Downworlder solidarity with Shadowhunters is greater than ever."

"Have you heard from Maia?" Simon asked. "I hate the thought that she's alone, now that Jordan's dead." He winced a little as he spoke, as if the words—"Jordan's dead"—hurt to say.

"She's not alone. She's got the pack taking care of her. Bat's been in touch with me—she's physically fine. Emotionally, I don't know. She's the one Sebastian gave his message to, after he killed Jordan. That can't have been easy."

"The pack is going to find itself having to deal with Maureen," said Simon. "She's thrilled the Shadowhunters are gone. She's going to make New York her bloody playground, if she gets her way."

"If she's killing mundanes, the Clave will have to dispatch someone to deal with her," said Jocelyn. "Even if it means leaving Idris. If she's breaking the Accords—"

"Shouldn't Jia hear about all this?" Clary said. "We could go talk to her. She's not like the last Consul. She'd listen to you, Simon."

Simon nodded. "I promised Raphael I'd talk to the Inquisitor and the Consul for him—" He broke off suddenly, and winced.

Clary looked at him harder. He was sitting in a weak shaft of daylight, his skin ivory pale. The veins under the skin were visible, as stark and black as ink marks. His cheekbones looked sharp, the shadows under them harsh and indented. "Simon, how long has it been since you've eaten anything?"

Simon flinched back; she knew he hated being reminded of his need for blood. "Three days," he said in a low voice.

"Food," Clary said, looking from her mother to Luke. "We need to get him food."

"I'm fine," Simon said, unconvincingly. "I really am."

"The most reasonable place to get blood would be the vampire representative's house," said Luke. "They have to provide it for the use of the Night's Children's Council member. I would go myself, but they're hardly going to give it to a werewolf. We could send a message—"

"No messages. Too slow. We'll go now." Clary threw her closet open and grabbed for a jacket. "Simon, can you make it there?"

"It's not that far," Simon said, his voice subdued. "A few doors down from the Inquisitor's."

"Raphael will be sleeping," said Luke. "It's the middle of the day."

"Then we'll wake him up." Clary shrugged the jacket on and zipped it. "It's his job to represent vampires; he'll have to help Simon."

Simon snorted. "Raphael doesn't think he *has* to do anything."

"I don't care." Clary seized up Heosphoros and slid it into the scabbard.

"Clary, I'm not sure you're well enough to go out like this—" Jocelyn began.

"I'm fine. Never felt better."

Jocelyn shook her head, and the sunlight caught the red glints in her hair. "In other words there's nothing I can do to stop you."

"Nope," Clary said, shoving Heosphoros into her belt. "Nothing whatsoever."

"The Council member dinner is tonight," Luke said, leaning back against the wall. "Clary, we're going to have to leave before you get back. We're putting a guard on the house to make sure you return home before dark—"

"You have *got* to be kidding me."

"Not at all. We want you in, and the house closed up. If you don't come home before sunset, the Gard will be notified."

"It's a police state," Clary grumbled. "Come on, Simon. Let's go."

Maia sat on the beach at Rockaway, looking out at the water, and shivered.

Rockaway was crowded in summer, but empty and windswept now, in December. The water of the Atlantic stretched away, a heavy gray, the color of iron, under a similarly iron-colored sky.

The bodies of the werewolves Sebastian had killed, Jordan's among them, had been burned among the ruins of the Praetor Lupus. One of the wolves of the pack approached the tide line and cast the contents of a box of ashes onto the water.

Maia watched as the surface of the sea turned black with the remains of the dead.

"I'm sorry." It was Bat, sitting down beside her on the sand. They watched as Rufus stepped up to the shoreline and opened another wooden box of ashes. "About Jordan."

Maia pushed her hair back. Gray clouds were gathering on the horizon. She wondered when it would start to rain. "I was going to break up with him," she said.

"What?" Bat looked shocked.

"I was going to break up with him," Maia said. "The day Sebastian killed him."

"I thought everything was going great with you guys. I thought you were happy."

"Did you?" Maia dug her fingers into the damp sand. "You didn't like him."

"He hurt you. It was a long time ago, and I know he tried to make up for it, but—" Bat shrugged. "Maybe I'm not so forgiving."

Maia exhaled. "Maybe I'm not either," she said. "The town I grew up in, all these spoiled thin rich white girls, they made me feel like crap because I didn't look like them. When I was six, my mom tried to throw me a Barbie-themed birthday party. They make a black Barbie, you know, but they don't make any of the stuff that goes with her—party supplies and cake toppers and all that. So we had a party for me with a blonde doll as the theme, and all these blonde girls came, and they all giggled at me behind their hands." The beach air was cold in her lungs. "So when I met Jordan and he told me I was beautiful, well, it didn't take that much. I was totally in love with him in about five minutes."

"You are beautiful," Bat said. A hermit crab inched its way along the sand, and he poked it with his fingers.

"We were happy," Maia said. "But then everything happened, and he Turned me, and I hated him. I came to New York and I hated him, and then he showed up again and all he wanted was for me to forgive him. He wanted it so badly and he was so sorry. And I knew, people do crazy things when they get bitten. I've heard of people who've killed their families—"

"That's why we have the Praetor," said Bat. "Well. Had them."

"And I thought, how much can you hold someone accountable for what they did when they couldn't control themselves? I thought I should forgive him, he just wanted it so damn much. He'd done everything to make up for it. I thought we could go back to normal, go back to the way we used to be."

"Sometimes you can't go back," Bat said. He touched the scar on his cheek thoughtfully; Maia had never asked him how he had gotten it. "Sometimes too much has changed."

"We couldn't go back," Maia said. "At least, I couldn't. He wanted me to forgive him so much that I think sometimes he just looked at me and he saw forgiveness. Redemption. He didn't see *me*." She shook her head. "I'm not someone's absolution. I'm just Maia."

"But you cared about him," Bat said softly.

"Enough that I kept putting off breaking up with him. I thought maybe I'd feel differently. And then everything started happening: Simon got kidnapped, and we went after him, and I was still going to tell Jordan. I was going to tell him as soon as we got to the Praetor, and then we arrived and it was"—she swallowed—"a slaughterhouse."

"They said when they found you, you were holding him. He was dead and his blood was washing out with the tide, but you were holding on to his body."

"Everyone should die with someone holding on to them," Maia said, taking a handful of sand. "I just—I feel so guilty. He died thinking I was still in love with him, that we were going to stay together and everything was fine. He died with me lying to him." She let the grains trickle out through her fingers. "I should have told him the truth."

"Stop punishing yourself." Bat stood up. He was tall and muscular in his half-zipped anorak, the wind barely moving his short hair. The gathering gray clouds outlined him. Maia could see the rest of the pack, gathered around Rufus, who was gesturing while he talked. "If he hadn't been dying, then yes, you should have told him the truth. But he died thinking he was loved and forgiven. There are much worse gifts you could give someone than that. What he did to you was terrible, and he knew it. But few people are all good or all bad. Think of it as a gift you gave to the good in him. Wherever Jordan's going—and I do believe we all go somewhere—think of it as the light that will bring him home."

If you are leaving the Basilias, understand that it is against the advice of the Brothers that you do so.

"Right," Jace said, pulling on his second gauntlet and flexing his fingers. "You've made that pretty clear."

Brother Enoch loomed over him, glowering, as Jace bent down with slow precision to do up the laces on his boots. He was sitting on the edge of the infirmary bed, one of a line of white-sheeted cots that ran the length of the long room. Many of the other cots were taken up with Shadowhunter warriors, recovering from the battle at the Citadel. Silent Brothers moved among the beds like ghostly nurses. The air smelled of herbs and strange poultices.

You should take another night to rest, at least. Your body is spent, and the heavenly fire still burns within you.

Finished with his boots, Jace looked up. The arched ceiling above was painted with an interlaced design of healing runes in silver and blue. He'd been staring up at it for what felt like weeks, though he knew it had been only a night. The Silent Brothers, keeping all visitors away, had hovered over him with healing runes and poultices. They had also run tests on him, taking blood, hair, even eyelashes—touching him with a series of blades pressed to his skin: gold, silver, steel, rowan wood. He felt fine. He had a strong feeling that keeping him in the Basilias was more about studying the heavenly fire than it was about healing him.

"I want to see Brother Zachariah," he said.

He is well. You need not worry yourself about him.

"I want to see him," he said. "I nearly killed him at the Citadel—"

That was not you. That was the heavenly fire. And it did anything but harm him.

Jace blinked at the odd choice of words. "He said when I met him that he believes that a debt is owed the Herondales. I'm a Herondale. He'd want to see me."

And then you intend to depart the Basilias?

Jace stood up. "There's nothing wrong with me. I don't need to be in the infirmary. Surely you could be using your resources more fruitfully on the actually wounded." He caught his jacket off a hook by the bed. "Look, you can either bring me to Brother Zachariah or I can wander around yelling for him until he turns up."

You are a great deal of trouble, Jace Herondale.

"So I've been told," Jace said.

There were arched windows between the beds; they cast wide spokes of light across the marble floor. The day was beginning to dim: Jace had woken in the early afternoon, with a Silent Brother by his bed. He'd jerked upright, demanding to know where Clary was, as recollections of the night before poured through him: he recalled the pain when Sebastian had stabbed him, recalled the fire blazing up the blade, recalled Zachariah burning. Clary's arms around him, her hair falling down around them both, the cessation of pain that had come with darkness. And then—nothing.

After the Brothers had reassured him that Clary was all right, safe at Amatis's, he'd asked after Zachariah, whether the fire had harmed him, but had received only irritatingly vague answers.

Now he followed Enoch out of the infirmary hall and into a narrower, white-plastered corridor. Doors opened off the corridor. As they passed one, Jace caught a quick glimpse of a writhing body tied to a bed, and heard the sound of screaming and cursing. A Silent Brother stood over a thrashing man dressed in the remnants of red gear. Blood spattered the white wall behind them.

Amalric Kriegsmesser, said Brother Enoch without turning his head. *One of Sebastian's Endarkened. As you know, we have been attempting to reverse the spell of the Infernal Cup.*

Jace swallowed. There didn't seem anything to say. He had seen the ritual of the Infernal Cup performed. In his heart of hearts he didn't believe the spell could be reversed. It created too fundamental a change. But then neither had he ever imagined that a Silent Brother could be as human as Brother Zachariah had always seemed. Was that why he was so determined to see him? He remembered what Clary had told him Brother Zachariah had said once, when she'd asked him if he'd ever loved anyone enough to die for them:

Two people. There are memories that time does not erase. Ask your friend Magnus Bane, if you do not believe me. Forever does not make loss forgettable, only bearable.

There had been something about those words, something that spoke of a sorrow and a sort of memory that Jace did not associate with the Brothers. They had been a presence in his life since he was ten: pale silent statues who brought healing, who kept secrets, who did not love or desire or grow or die but only *were*. But Brother Zachariah was different.

We are here. Brother Enoch had paused in front of an unremarkable white-painted door. He lifted a broad hand and knocked. There was a sound from inside, as of a chair scraping back, and then a male voice:

"Come in."

Brother Enoch swung the door open and ushered Jace inside. The windows were west-facing, and it was very bright in the room, the light of the sun as it went down painting the walls with pale fire. There was a figure at the window: a silhouette, slender, not in the robes of a Brother—Jace turned to look at Brother Enoch in surprise, but the Silent Brother had already left, closing the door behind him.

"Where's Brother Zachariah?" Jace said.

"I'm right here." A quiet voice, soft, a little out of tune, like a piano that hadn't been played in years. The figure had turned from the window. Jace found himself looking at a boy only a few years older than himself. Dark hair, a sharp delicate face, eyes that seemed young and old at the same time. The runes of the Brothers marked his high cheekbones, and as the boy turned, Jace saw the pale edge of a faded rune at the side of his throat.

A *parabatai*. Like he was. And Jace knew too what that faded rune meant: a *parabatai* whose other half was dead. He felt his sympathy leap toward Brother Zachariah, as he imagined himself without Alec, with only that faded rune to remind him where once he had been bonded to someone who knew all the best and worst parts of his soul.

"Jace Herondale," said the boy. "Once more a Herondale is the bringer of my deliverance. I should have anticipated."

"I didn't—that's not—" Jace was too stunned to think of anything clever to say. "It's not possible. Once you're a Silent Brother, you can't change back. You—I don't understand."

The boy—Zachariah, Jace supposed, though not a Brother anymore—smiled. It was a heartbreakingly vulnerable smile, young and gentle. "I am not sure I entirely understand either," he said. "But I was never an ordinary Silent Brother. I was brought into the life because there was a dark magic upon me. I had no other way to save myself." He looked down at his hands, the unlined hands of a boy, smooth the way few Shadowhunters' hands were smooth. The Brothers could fight as warriors, but rarely did. "I left everything I knew and everything I loved. Didn't leave it entirely, perhaps, but erected a wall of glass between myself and the life I'd had before. I could see it, but I could not touch, could not be a part of it. I began to forget what it was like to be an ordinary human."

"We're not ordinary humans."

Zachariah looked up. "Oh, we tell ourselves that," he said. "But I have made a study of Shadowhunters now, over the past century, and let me tell you that we are more human than most human beings. When our hearts break, they break into shards that cannot be easily fit back together. I envy mundanes their resilience sometimes."

"More than a century old? You seem pretty ... resilient to me."

"I thought I would be a Silent Brother forever. We—they don't die, you know; they fade after many years. Stop speaking, stop moving. Eventually they are entombed alive. I thought that would be my fate. But when I touched you with my runed hand, when you were wounded, I absorbed the heavenly fire in your veins. It burned away the darkness in my blood. I became again the person I was before I took my vows. Before even that. I became what I have always wanted to be."

Jace's voice was hoarse. "Did it hurt?"

Zachariah looked puzzled. "I'm sorry?"

"When Clary stabbed me with Glorious, it was—agonizing. I felt as if my bones were melting down to ashes inside me. I kept thinking about that when I woke up—I kept thinking about the pain, and whether it hurt when you touched me."

Zachariah looked at him in surprise. "You thought about me? About whether I was in pain?"

"Of course." Jace could see their reflections in the window behind Zachariah. Zachariah was as tall as he was, but thinner, and with his dark hair and pale skin he looked like a photo negative of Jace.

"Herondales." Zachariah's voice was a breath, half laughter, half pain. "I had almost forgotten. No other family does so much for love, or feels so much guilt for it. Don't carry the weight of the world on you, Jace. It's too heavy for even a Herondale to bear."

"I'm not a saint," Jace said. "Maybe I should bear it."

Zachariah shook his head. "You know, I think, the phrase from the Bible: '*Mene mene tekel upharsin*'?"

"'You have been weighed in the balance and have been found wanting.' Yes, I know it. The Writing on the Wall."

"The Egyptians believed that at the gate of the dead your heart was weighed on scales, and if it weighed more than a feather, your path was the path to Hell. The fire of Heaven takes our measure, Jace Herondale, like the scales of the Egyptians. If there is more evil in us than good, it will destroy us. I only just lived, and so did you. The difference between us is that I was only brushed by the fire, whereas it entered your heart. You carry it in you still, a great burden and a great gift."

"But all I've been trying to do is get rid of it—"

"You cannot rid yourself of this." Brother Zachariah's voice had become very serious. "It is not a curse to be rid of; it is a weapon you have been entrusted with. You *are* the blade of Heaven. Make sure you are worthy."

"You sound like Alec," Jace said. "He's always on about responsibility and worthiness."

"Alec. Your *parabatai*. The Lightwood boy?"

"You..." Jace indicated the side of Zachariah's throat. "You had a *parabatai* too. But your rune is faded."

Zachariah looked down. "He is long dead," he said. "I was—When he died, I—" He shook his head, frustrated. "For years I have spoken only with my mind, though you hear my thoughts as words," he said. "The process of shaping language in the ordinary way, of finding speech, does not come easily to me now." He raised his head to look at Jace. "Value your *parabatai*," he said. "For it is a precious bond. All love is precious. It is why we do what we do. Why do we fight demons?

Why are they not fit custodians of this world? What makes us better? It is because they do not build, but destroy. They do not love, but hate only. We are human and fallible, we Shadowhunters. But if we did not have the capacity to love, we could not guard humans; we must love them to guard them. My *parabatai*, he loved like few ever could love, with all and everything. I see you are like that too; it burns more brightly in you than the fire of Heaven."

Brother Zachariah was looking at Jace, with a fierce intensity that felt as if it would strip the flesh off his bones. "I'm sorry," Jace said quietly. "That you lost your *parabatai*. Is there anyone—anyone left for you to go home to?"

The boy's mouth curved a little at the corner. "There is one. She has always been home for me. But not so soon. I must stay, first."

"To fight?"

"And love and grieve. When I was a Silent Brother, my loves and losses were muted slightly, like music heard from a distance, true in tune but muffled. Now—now it has all come upon me at once. I am bowed under it. I must be stronger before I can see her." His smile was wistful. "Have you ever felt that your heart contained so much that it must surely break apart?"

Jace thought of Alec wounded in his lap, of Max still and white on the floor of the Accords Hall; he thought of Valentine, his arms around Jace as Jace's blood soaked the sand underneath them. And lastly he thought of Clary: her sharp bravery that kept him safe, her sharper wit that kept him sane, the steadiness of her love.

"Weapons, when they break and are mended, can be stronger at the mended places," said Jace. "Perhaps hearts are the same."

Brother Zachariah, who was now just a boy like Jace himself, smiled at him a little sadly. "I hope that you are right."

"I can't believe Jordan's dead," Clary said. "I just saw him. He was sitting on the wall at the Institute when we went through the Portal."

She was walking beside Simon along one of the canals, heading toward the center of the city. The demon towers rose around them, their brilliance reflected in the canal waters.

Simon glanced sidelong at Clary. He kept thinking of the way she'd looked when he'd seen her the night before, blue and exhausted and barely conscious, her clothes ripped and bloody. She looked like herself again now, color in her cheeks, her hands in her pockets, the hilt of her sword protruding from her belt. "Neither can I," he said.

Clary's eyes were distant and bright; Simon wondered what she was remembering—Jordan teaching Jace to control his emotions in Central Park? Jordan in Magnus's apartment, talking to a pentagram? Jordan the first time they'd ever seen him, ducking under a garage door to audition for Simon's band? Jordan sitting on the sofa in his and Simon's apartment, playing Xbox with Jace? Jordan telling Simon that he was sworn to protect him?

Simon felt hollow inside. He'd spent the night sleeping fitfully, waking up out of nightmares in which Jordan appeared and stood looking at him silently, hazel eyes asking Simon to help him, save him, while the ink on his arms ran like blood.

"Poor Maia," she said. "I wish she were here; I wish we could talk to her. She's had such a hard time, and now this—"

"I know," Simon said, almost choking. Thinking about Jordan was bad enough. If he thought about Maia, too, he'd fall apart.

Clary responded to the abruptness in his tone by reaching out for his hand. "Simon," she said. "Are you all right?"

He let her take his hand, loosely interlacing their fingers. He saw her glance down at the gold faerie ring he always wore.

"I don't think so," he said.

"No, of course not. How could you be? He was your—" *Friend? Roommate? Bodyguard?*

"Responsibility," Simon said.

She looked taken aback. "No—Simon, you were his. He was your guard."

"Come on, Clary," Simon said. "What do you think he was doing at the Praetor Lupus headquarters? He never went there. If he was there, it was because of me, because he was looking for me. If I hadn't gone and gotten myself kidnapped—"

"Gotten yourself kidnapped?" Clary snapped. "What, you volunteered to have Maureen kidnap you?"

"Maureen didn't kidnap me," he said in a low voice.

She looked at him, puzzled. "I thought she kept you in a cage at the Dumort. I thought you said—"

"She did," Simon said. "But the only reason I was outside where she could get at me was because I was attacked by one of the Endarkened. I didn't want to tell Luke and your mother," he added. "I thought they'd freak out."

"Because if Sebastian sent a Dark Shadowhunter after you, it was because of me," said Clary tightly. "Did he want to kidnap you or kill you?"

"I didn't really get a chance to ask him." Simon shoved his hands into his pockets. "Jordan told me to run, so I ran—right into some of Maureen's clan. She was having the apartment watched, evidently. I suppose that's what I get for running off and leaving him. If I hadn't, if I hadn't been taken, he never would have gone out to the Praetor, and he never would have been killed."

"Stop it." Simon looked over in surprise. Clary sounded genuinely angry. "Stop blaming yourself. Jordan didn't get himself assigned to you at random. He wanted the job so he could be near Maia. He knew the risks in guarding you. He took them on voluntarily. It was his choice. He was looking for redemption. Because of what happened between him and Maia. Because of what he *did*. That was what the Praetor was, for him. It saved him. Guarding you, people like you, saved him. He'd turned into a monster. He'd hurt Maia. He'd turned her into a monster too. What he did wasn't forgivable. If he hadn't had the Praetor, if he hadn't had you to take care of, it would have eaten him up until he killed himself."

"Clary—" Simon was shocked at the darkness in her words.

She shivered, as if she were shaking off the touch of spiderwebs. They had turned onto a long street by a canal, lined with grand old houses. It reminded Simon of pictures of rich neighborhoods in Amsterdam. "That's the Lightwoods' house, there. The high Council members have houses on this street. The Consul, the Inquisitor, the Downworlder representatives. We just have to figure out which one is Raphael's—"

"There," Simon said, and indicated a narrow canal house with a black door. A star had been painted on the door in silver. "A star for the Night's Children. Because we don't see the light of the sun." He smiled at her, or tried to. Hunger was burning up his veins; they felt like hot wires under his skin.

He turned away and mounted the steps. The door knocker was in the shape of a rune, and heavy. The sound it made as it dropped reverberated inside the house.

Simon heard Clary come up the stairs behind him just as the door opened. Raphael stood inside, carefully out of the light that spilled in through the open door. In the shadows Simon could make out only the general shape of him: his curly hair, the white flash of his teeth when he greeted them. "Daylighter. Valentine's daughter."

Clary made an exasperated noise. "Don't you ever call anyone by their name?"

"Only my friends," said Raphael.

"You have friends?" Simon said.

Raphael glared. "I assume you are here for blood?"

"Yes," Clary said. Simon said nothing. At the sound of the word "blood" he'd started to feel slightly faint. He could feel his stomach contracting. He was beginning to starve.

Raphael cast a glance at Simon. "You look hungry. Perhaps you should have taken my suggestion in the square last night."

Clary's eyebrows went up, but Simon just scowled. "If you want me to talk to the Inquisitor for you, you're going to have to give me blood. Otherwise I'll pass out on his feet, or eat him."

"I suspect that would go over poorly with his daughter. Though she already seemed none too pleased with you last night." Raphael disappeared back into the shadows of the house. Clary glanced at Simon.

"I take it you saw Isabelle yesterday?"

"You take it right."

"And it didn't go well?"

Simon was spared answering by Raphael's reappearance. He was carrying a stoppered glass bottle full of red liquid. Simon took it eagerly.

The scent of the blood came through the glass, billowy and sweet. Simon yanked the stopper out and swallowed, his fang teeth snapping out, despite the fact that he didn't need them. Vampires weren't meant to drink out of bottles. His teeth scraped against his skin as he wiped the back of his hand across his mouth.

Raphael's brown eyes glittered. "I was sorry to hear about your werewolf friend."

Simon stiffened. Clary put a hand on his arm. "You don't mean that," Simon said. "You hated me having a Praetorian Guard."

Raphael hummed thoughtfully. "No guard, no Mark of Cain. All your protections stripped away. It must be strange, Daylighter, to know that you can truly die."

Simon stared at him. "Why do you try so hard?" he said, and took another swallow from the bottle. It tasted bitter this time, a little acidic. "To make me hate you? Or is it just that you hate me?"

There was a long silence. Simon realized that Raphael was barefoot, standing just at the edge of the sunlight where it lay in a stripe along the hardwood floor. Another step forward, and the light would char his skin.

Simon swallowed, tasting the blood in his mouth, feeling slightly unsteady. "You don't hate me," he realized, looking at the white scar at the base of Raphael's throat, where sometimes a crucifix rested. "You're *jealous*."

Without another word Raphael shut the door between them.

Clary exhaled. "Wow. That went well."

Simon didn't say anything, just turned and walked away, down the steps. He paused at the bottom to finish his bottle of blood, and then, to her surprise, tossed it. It flew partway down the street and hit a lamppost, shattering, leaving a smear of blood on the iron.

"Simon?" Clary hurried down the steps. "Are you all right?"

He made a vague gesture. "I don't know. Jordan, Maia, Raphael, it's all—it's too much. I don't know what I'm supposed to do."

"You mean, about talking to the Inquisitor for him?" Clary moved to catch up with Simon as he began walking aimlessly down the street. The wind had come up, ruffling his brown hair.

"About anything." He wobbled a little as he walked away from her. Clary squinted suspiciously. If she hadn't known better, she would have guessed he was drunk. "I don't belong here," he said. He had stopped in front of the Inquisitor's residence. He cocked his head back, staring up at the windows. "What do you think they're doing in there?"

"Having dinner?" Clary guessed. The witchlight lamps were starting to come on, illuminating the street. "Living their lives? Come on, Simon. They probably knew people who died in the battle last night. If you want to see Isabelle, tomorrow is the Council meeting and—"

"She knows," he said. "That her parents are probably breaking up. That her father had an affair."

"He *what*?" Clary said, staring at Simon. "When?"

"Long time ago." Simon's voice was definitely slurred. "Before Max. He was going to leave but—he found out about Max, so he stayed. Maryse told Isabelle, years ago. Not fair, to put all that on a little girl. Izzy's strong, but still. You shouldn't do that. Not to your child. You should—carry your own burdens."

"Simon." She thought of his mother, turning him away from her door. *You shouldn't do that. Not to your child.* "How long have you known? About Robert and Maryse?"

"Months." He moved toward the front gate of the house. "I always wanted to help her, but she never wanted me to say anything, do anything—your mother knows, by the way. She told Izzy who Robert had the affair with. It wasn't anyone she'd ever heard of. I don't know if that makes it worse or better."

"What? Simon, you're wobbling. Simon—"

Simon crashed into the fence around the Inquisitor's house with a loud rattling noise. "Isabelle!" he called, tipping his head back. "*Isabelle!*"

"Holy—" Clary grabbed Simon by the sleeve. "Simon," she hissed. "You're a vampire, in the middle of Idris. Maybe you shouldn't be *shouting for attention*."

Simon ignored this. "Isabelle!" he called again. "Let down your raven hair!"

"Oh, my God," Clary muttered. "There was something in that blood Raphael gave you, wasn't there? I'm going to kill him."

"He's already dead," Simon observed.

"He's undead. Obviously he can still die, you know, again. I'll re-kill him. Simon, come on. Let's head back, and you can lie down and put ice on your head—"

"Isabelle!" Simon shouted.

One of the upper windows of the house swung open, and Isabelle leaned out. Her raven hair *was* unbound, tumbling around her face. She looked furious, though. "Simon, shut up!" she hissed.

"I won't!" Simon announced mutinously. "For you are my lady fair, and I shall win your favor."

Isabelle dropped her head into her hands. "Is he drunk?" she called down to Clary.

"I don't know." Clary was torn between loyalty to Simon and an urgent need to get him out of there. "I think he may have gotten some expired blood or something."

"I love you, Isabelle Lightwood!" Simon called, startling everyone. Lights were going on all through the house, and in neighboring houses as well. There was a noise from down the street, and a moment later Aline and Helen appeared; both looked frazzled, Helen in the middle of tying her curly blond hair back. "I love you, and I won't go away until you tell me you love me too!"

"Tell him you love him," Helen called up. "He's scaring the whole street." She waved at Clary. "Good to see you."

"You, too," Clary said. "I'm so sorry about what happened in Los Angeles, and if there's anything I can do to help—"

Something came fluttering down from the sky. Two things: a pair of leather pants, and a puffy white poet shirt. They landed at Simon's feet.

"Take your clothes and go!" Isabelle shouted.

Above her another window opened, and Alec leaned out. "What's going on?" His gaze landed on Clary and the others, his eyebrows drawing together in confusion. "What is this? Early caroling?"

"I don't carol," said Simon. "I'm Jewish. I only know the dreidel song."

"Is he all right?" Aline asked Clary, sounding worried. "Do vampires go crazy?"

"He's not crazy," said Helen. "He's drunk. He must have consumed the blood of someone who'd been drinking alcohol. It can give vampires a sort of—contact high."

"I hate Raphael," Clary muttered.

"Isabelle!" Simon called. "Stop throwing clothes at me! Just because you're a Shadowhunter and I'm a vampire doesn't mean we can never happen. Our love is forbidden like the love of a shark and a—and a shark hunter. But that's what makes it special."

"Oh?" Isabelle snapped. "Which one of us is the shark, Simon? *Which one of us is the shark?*"

The front door burst open. It was Robert Lightwood, and he did not look pleased. He stalked down the front walk of the house, kicked the gate open, and strode up to Simon. "What's going on here?" he demanded. His eyes flicked to Clary. "Why are you shouting outside my house?"

"He's not feeling well," Clary said, catching at Simon's wrist. "We're going."

"No," Simon said. "No, I—I need to talk to him. To the Inquisitor."

Robert reached into his jacket and drew out a crucifix. Clary stared as he held it up between himself and Simon. "I speak to the Night's Children Council representative, or to the head of the New York clan," he said. "Not to any vampire who comes to knock at my door, even if he is a friend of my children. Nor should you be in Alicante without permission—"

Simon reached out and plucked the cross out of Robert's hand. "Wrong religion," he said.

Helen made a whistling noise under her breath.

"And I was sent by the representative of the Night's Children to the Council. Raphael Santiago brought me here to speak to you—"

"Simon!" Isabelle hurried out of the house, racing to place herself between Simon and her father. "What are you doing?"

She glared at Clary, who grabbed Simon's wrist again. "We *really* need to go," Clary muttered.

Robert's gaze went from Simon to Isabelle. His expression changed. "Is there something going on between you two? Is that what all the yelling was about?"

Clary looked at Isabelle in surprise. She thought of Simon, comforting Isabelle when Max died. How close Simon and Izzy had become in the past months. And her father had no idea.

"He's a friend. He's friends with all of us," Isabelle said, crossing her arms over her chest. Clary couldn't tell if she was more annoyed with her father or with Simon. "And I'll vouch for him, if that means he can stay in Alicante." She glared at Simon. "But he's going back to Clary's now. Aren't you, Simon?"

"My head feels round," Simon said sadly. "So round."

Robert lowered his arm. "*What*?"

"He drank some drugged blood," said Clary. "It isn't his fault."

Robert turned his dark blue gaze on Simon. "I'll talk to you tomorrow at the Council meeting, *if* you've sobered up," he said. "If Raphael Santiago has something he wants you to speak to me about, you can say it in front of the Clave."

"I don't—" Simon began.

But Clary cut him off with a hasty: "Fine. I'll bring him with me to the Council meeting tomorrow. Simon, we have to get back before dark; you know that."

Simon looked mildly dazed. "We do?"

"Tomorrow, at the Council," Robert said shortly, turned, and stalked back into his house. Isabelle hesitated a moment—she was in a loose dark shirt and jeans, her pale feet bare on the narrow stone path. She was shivering.

"Where did he get spiked blood?" she asked, indicating Simon with a wave of her hand.

"Raphael," Clary explained.

Isabelle rolled her eyes. "He'll be all right tomorrow," she said. "Put him to bed." She waved to Helen and Aline, who were leaning on the gateposts with unabashed curiosity. "See you at the meeting," she said.

"Isabelle—" Simon began, starting to wave his arms wildly, but, before he could do any more damage, Clary grabbed the back of his jacket and hauled him toward the street.

Because Simon kept ranging off down various alleys, and insisted on trying to break into a closed candy shop, it was already dark by the time Clary and Simon reached Amatis's house. Clary looked around for the guard Jocelyn had said would be posted, but there was no one visible. Either he was exceptionally well concealed or, more likely, he had already set off to report to Clary's parents on her lateness.

Gloomily Clary mounted the steps to the house, unlocked the door, and manhandled Simon inside. He had stopped protesting and starting yawning somewhere around Cistern Square, and now his eyelids were drooping. "I hate Raphael," he said.

"I was just thinking the same thing," she said, turning him around. "Come on. Let's get you lying down."

She shuffled him over to the sofa, where he collapsed, slumping down against the cushions. Dim moonlight filtered through the lace curtains that covered the large front windows. Simon's eyes were the color of smoky quartz as he struggled to keep them open.

"You should sleep," she told him. "Mom and Luke will probably be back any minute now." She turned to go.

"Clary," he said, catching at her sleeve. "Be careful."

She detached herself gently and headed up the stairs, taking her witchlight rune-stone to illuminate her way. The windows along the upstairs corridor were open, and a cool breeze blew down the hall, smelling of city stone and canal water, lifting her hair away from her face. Clary reached her bedroom and pushed the door open—and froze.

The witchlight pulsed in her hand, casting bright spokes of light across the room. There was someone sitting on her bed. A tall someone, with white-fair hair, a sword across his lap, and a silver bracelet that sparked like fire in the witchlight.

If I cannot reach Heaven, I will raise Hell.

"Hello, sister mine," Sebastian said.

10

These Violent Delights

Clary's own harsh breathing was loud in her ears.

She thought of the first time that Luke had ever taken her swimming, in the lake at the farm, and how she had sunk so far down into the blue-green water that the world outside had disappeared and there was only the sound of her own heartbeat, echoing and distorted. She had wondered if she had left the world behind, if she would always be lost, until Luke had reached down and pulled her back, sputtering and disoriented, into the sunlight.

She felt that way now, as if she had tumbled into another world, distorted and suffocating and unreal. The room was the same, the same worn furniture and wood walls and colorful rug, dimmed and bleached by moonlight, but now Sebastian had sprung up in the middle of it like some exotic poisonous flower growing in a bed of familiar weeds.

In what felt like slow motion, Clary turned to run back out through the open door—only to find it banging shut in her face. An invisible force seized hold of her, spinning her around and slamming her up against the bedroom wall, her head hitting the wood. She blinked away tears of pain and tried to move her legs; she couldn't. She was pinned against the wall, paralyzed from the waist down.

"My apologies for the binding spell," Sebastian said, a light, mocking tone to his voice. He lay back against the pillows, stretching his arms up to touch the headboard in a catlike arch. His T-shirt had ridden up, baring his flat, pale stomach, traced with the lines of runes. There was something that was clearly meant to be seductive about the pose, something that made nausea twist in her gut. "It took me a little while to set up, but you know how it is. One can't take risks."

"Sebastian." To her amazement her voice was steady. She was very aware of every inch of her skin. She felt exposed and vulnerable, as if she were standing without gear or protection in front of flying broken glass. "Why are you here?"

His sharp face was thoughtful, searching. A serpent sleeping in the sun, just waking, not dangerous quite yet. "Because I've missed you, little sister. Have you missed me?"

She thought about screaming, but Sebastian would have a dagger in her throat before she got a sound out. She tried to still the pounding of her heart: she had survived him before. She could do it again.

"Last time I saw you, you had a crossbow in my back," she said. "So that would be a no."

He traced a lazy pattern in the air with his fingers. "Liar."

"So are you," she said. "You didn't come here because you miss me; you came because you want something. What is it?"

He was suddenly on his feet—graceful, too fast for her to catch the movement. White-pale hair fell into his eyes. She remembered standing at the edge of the Seine with him, watching the light catch his hair, as fine and fair as the feathery stems of a dandelion clock. Wondering if Valentine had looked like that, when he was young.

"Maybe I want to broker a truce," he said.

"The Clave isn't going to want to broker a truce with you."

"Really? After last night?" He took a step toward her. The realization that she couldn't run surged back up inside her; she bit back a scream. "We are on two different sides. We have opposing armies. Isn't that what you do? Broker a truce? Either that or fight till one of you loses enough people that you give up? But then, maybe I'm not interested in a truce with *them*. Maybe I'm only interested in a truce with you."

"Why? You don't forgive. I know you. What I did—you wouldn't forgive it."

He moved again, a sharp flicker, and suddenly he was pressed against her, his fingers wrapped around her left wrist, pinioning it over her head. "Which part? Destroying my house—our father's house? Betraying me and lying to me? Breaking my bond with Jace?" She could see the flicker of rage behind his eyes, feel his heart pounding.

She wanted nothing more than to kick out at him, but her legs simply wouldn't move. Her voice shook. "Any of it."

He was so close, she felt it when his body relaxed. He was hard and lean and whippet-thin, the sharp edges of him pressing into her. "I think you may have done me a favor. Maybe you even meant to do it." She could see herself in his uncanny eyes, the irises so dark they almost melded with the pupils. "I was too dependent on our father's legacy and protection. On Jace. I had to stand on my own. Sometimes you must lose everything to gain it again, and the regaining is the sweeter for the pain of loss. Alone I united the Endarkened. Alone I forged alliances. Alone I took the Institutes of Buenos Aires, of Bangkok, of Los Angeles..."

"Alone you murdered people and destroyed families," she said. "There was a guard stationed in front of this house. He was meant to be protecting me. What did you do to him?"

"Reminded him he ought to be better at his job," Sebastian said. "Protecting my sister." He raised the hand that wasn't pinioning her wrist to the wall, and touched a curl of her hair, rubbing the strands between his fingers. "Red," he said, his voice half-drowsy, "like sunset and blood and fire. Like the leading edge of a falling star, burning up when it touches the atmosphere. We are *Morgensterns*," he added, a dark ache in his voice. "The bright stars of morning. The children of Lucifer, the most beautiful of all God's angels. We are so much lovelier when we fall." He paused. "Look at me, Clary. Look at me."

She looked at him, reluctantly. His black eyes were focused on her with a sharp hunger; they contrasted starkly with his salt-white hair, his pale skin, the faint flush of pink along his cheekbones. The artist in Clary knew he was beautiful, the way panthers were beautiful, or bottles of shimmering poison, or the polished skeletons of the dead. Luke had told Clary once that her talent was to see the beauty and horror in ordinary things. Though Sebastian was far from ordinary, in him, she could see both.

"Lucifer Morningstar was Heaven's most beautiful angel. God's proudest creation. And then came the day when Lucifer refused to bow to mankind. To humans. Because he knew they were lesser. And for that he was cast down into the pit with the angels who had taken his side: Belial, and Azazel, and Asmodeus, and Leviathan. And Lilith. My mother."

"She's not your mother."

"You're right. She's more than my mother. If she were my mother, I'd be a warlock. Instead I was fed on her blood before I was born. I am something very different from a warlock; something better. For she was an angel once, Lilith."

"What's your point? Demons are just angels who make poor life decisions?"

"*Greater* Demons are not so different from angels," he said. "We are not so different, you and I. I've said it to you before."

"I remember," she said. "'You have a dark heart in you, Valentine's daughter.'"

"Don't you?" he said, and his hand stroked down through her curls, to her shoulder, and slid finally to her chest, and rested just over her heart. Clary felt her pulse slam against her veins; she wanted to push him away, but forced her right arm to remain at her side. The fingers of her hand were against the edge of her jacket, and under her jacket was Heosphoros. Even if she couldn't kill him, maybe she could use the blade to put him down long enough for help to arrive. Maybe they could even trap him. "Our mother cheated me," he said. "She denied me and hated me. I was a child and she hated me. As did our father."

"Valentine raised you—"

"But all his love was for Jace. The troubled one, the rebellious one, the broken one. I did everything our father ever asked of me, and he hated me for it. And he hated you, too." His eyes were glowing, silver in the black. "It's ironic, isn't it, Clarissa? We were Valentine's blood children, and he hated us. You because you took our mother from him. And me because I was exactly what he created me to be."

Clary remembered Jace then, bloody and torn, standing with the Morgenstern blade in his hand on the banks of Lake Lyn, shouting at Valentine: Why *did you take me? You didn't need a son. You* had *a son.*

And Valentine, his voice hoarse: *It wasn't a son I needed. It was a soldier. I had thought Jonathan might be that soldier, but he had too much of the demon nature in him. He was too savage, too sudden, not subtle enough. I feared even then, when he was barely out of infancy, that he would never have the patience or the compassion to follow me, to lead the Clave in my footsteps. So I tried again with you. And with you I had the opposite trouble. You were too gentle. Too empathic. Understand this, my son—I loved you for those things.*

She heard Sebastian's breath, harsh in the quiet. "You know," he said, "that what I'm saying is the truth."

"But I don't know why it matters."

"Because we are *alike*!" Sebastian's voice rose; her flinch let her ease her fingers down another millimeter, toward the hilt of Heosphoros. "You are mine," he added, controlling his voice with obvious effort. "You have always been mine. When you were born, you were mine, *my sister*, though you did not know me. There are bonds that nothing can erase. And that is why I am giving you a second chance."

"A chance at what?" She moved her hand downward another half inch.

"I am going to win this," he said. "You know. You were at the Burren, and the Citadel. You have seen the power of the Endarkened. You know what the Infernal Cup can do. If you turn your back on Alicante and come with me, and pledge your loyalty, I will give you what I have given to no one else. Not ever, for I have saved it for you."

Clary let her head fall back against the wall. Her stomach was twisting, her fingers just touching the hilt of the sword in her belt. Sebastian's eyes were fixed on her. "You'll give me what?"

He smiled then, exhaling, as if the question were, somehow, a relief. He seemed to blaze for a moment with his own conviction; looking at him was like watching a city burn.

"Mercy," he said.

The dinner was surprisingly elegant. Magnus had dined with faeries only a few times before in his life, and the décor had always tended toward the naturalistic—tree-trunk tables, cutlery made of elaborately shaped branches, plates of nuts and berries. He had always been left with the feeling, afterward, that he would have enjoyed the whole business more if he had been a squirrel.

Here in Idris, though, in the house provided to the Fair Folk, the table was set with white linens. Luke, Jocelyn, Raphael, Meliorn, and Magnus were eating from plates of polished mahogany; the decanters were crystal, and the cutlery—in deference to both Luke and the faeries present—was made not from silver or iron but from delicate saplings. Faerie knights stood guard, silent and motionless, at each of the exits to the room. Long white spears that gave off a dim illumination were by their sides, casting a soft glow across the room.

The food wasn't bad either. Magnus speared a piece of a really quite decent coq au vin and chewed thoughtfully. He didn't have much of an appetite, it was true. He was nervous—a state he loathed. Somewhere out there, past these walls and this required dinner party, was Alec. No more geographical space separated them. Of course, they hadn't been far from each other in New York either, but the space that had separated them hadn't been made up of miles but of Magnus's life experiences.

It was strange, he thought. He'd always thought of himself as a brave person. It took courage to live an immortal life and not close off your heart and mind to any new experiences or new people. Because that which was new was almost always temporary. And that which was temporary broke your heart.

"Magnus?" said Luke, waving a wooden fork almost under Magnus's nose. "Are you paying attention?"

"What? Of course I am," Magnus said, taking a sip of his wine. "I agree. One hundred percent."

"Really," Jocelyn said dryly. "You agree that the Downworlders should abandon the problem of Sebastian and his dark army and leave it to the Shadowhunters, as a Shadowhunter issue?"

"I told you he was not paying attention," said Raphael, who had been served a blood fondue and appeared to be enjoying it immensely.

"Well, it is a Shadowhunter issue—" Magnus began, and then he sighed, setting down his wineglass. The wine was quite strong; he was beginning to feel light-headed. "Oh, all right. I wasn't listening. And no, of course I don't believe that—"

"Shadowhunter lapdog," snapped Meliorn. His green eyes were narrowed. The Fair Folk and warlocks had always enjoyed a somewhat difficult relationship. Neither liked Shadowhunters much, which provided a common enemy, but the Fair Folk looked down upon warlocks for their willingness to perform magic for money. Meanwhile the warlocks scorned the Fair Folk for their inability to lie, their hide-bound customs, and their penchant for pettily annoying mundanes by curdling their milk and stealing their cows. "Is there any reason you wish to preserve amity with the Shadowhunters, besides the fact that one of them is your lover?"

Luke coughed violently into his wine. Jocelyn patted him on the back. Raphael simply looked amused.

"Get with the times, Meliorn," said Magnus. "No one says 'lover' anymore."

"Besides," added Luke. "They broke up." He scrubbed the back of his hand over his eyes and sighed. "And really, ought we to be gossiping right now? I don't see how anyone's personal relationships enter into this."

"Everything is about personal relationships," said Raphael, dipping something unpleasant-looking into his fondue. "Why do you Shadowhunters have this problem? Because Jonathan Morgenstern has sworn vengeance against you. Why has he sworn vengeance? Because he hates his father and mother. I've no wish to offend you," he added, nodding toward Jocelyn. "But we all know it's true."

"No offense taken," said Jocelyn, though her tone was frigid. "If it were not for me and for Valentine, Sebastian would not exist, in any sense of the word. I take full responsibility for that."

Luke looked thunderous. "It was Valentine who turned him into a monster," he said. "And yes, Valentine was a Shadowhunter. But it is not as if the Council is endorsing and supporting him, or his son. They are actively at war with Sebastian, and they want our help. All races, lycanthropes and vampires and warlocks and, yes, the Fair Folk, have the potential to do good or do evil. Part of the purpose of the Accords is to say that all of us who do good, or hope to do it, are united against those who do evil. Regardless of bloodlines."

Magnus pointed his fork at Luke. "That," he said, "was a beautiful speech." He paused. He was definitely slurring his words. How had he gotten so drunk on so little wine? He was usually much more careful than that. He frowned.

"What kind of wine is this?" he asked.

Meliorn leaned back in his chair, crossing his arms. There was a glint in his eyes as he replied. "Does the vintage not please you, warlock?"

Jocelyn set her glass down slowly. "When faeries answer questions with questions," she said, "it's never a good sign."

"Jocelyn—" Luke reached to put his hand on her wrist.

He missed.

He stared muzzily at his hand for a moment, before lowering it slowly to the table. "What," he said, enunciating each word carefully, "have you done, Meliorn?"

The faerie knight laughed. The sound was a musical blur in Magnus's ears. The warlock went to set his wineglass down, but realized he had already dropped it. The wine had run out across the table like blood. He glanced up and over at Raphael, but Raphael was facedown on the table, still and unmoving. Magnus tried to shape his name through numb lips, but no sound came.

Somehow he managed to struggle to his feet. The room was swaying around him. He saw Luke sink back against his chair; Jocelyn rose to her feet, only to crumple to the ground, her stele rolling from her hand. Magnus lurched to the door, reached to open it—

On the other side stood the Endarkened, dressed all in red gear. Their faces were blank, their arms and throats decorated with runes, but none Magnus was familiar with. These runes were not the runes of the Angel. They spoke of dissonance, of the demonic realms and dark, fell powers.

Magnus turned away from them—and his legs gave out beneath him. He fell to his knees. Something white rose up before him. It was Meliorn, in his snowy armor, bending to one knee to look Magnus in the face. "Demon-fathered one," he said. "Did you really think we would ever ally with your kind?"

Magnus heaved a breath. The world was darkening at the edges, like a photograph burning, curling in at the sides. "The Fair Folk don't lie," he said.

"Child," said Meliorn, and there was almost sympathy in his voice. "Not to know after all these years that deception can hide in plain sight? Oh, but you are an innocent, after all."

Magnus tried to raise his voice to protest that he was anything but innocent, but the words would not come. The darkness did, however, and drew him down and away.

Clary's heart wrenched in her chest. She tried again to move her feet, to kick out, but her legs remained frozen in place. "You think I don't know what you mean by mercy?" she whispered. "You'll use the Infernal Cup on me. You'll make me one of your Endarkened, like Amatis—"

"No," he said, a strange urgency in his tone. "I won't change you if you don't want it. I will forgive you, and Jace as well. You can be together."

"Together with you," she said, letting just the edge of the irony of it touch her voice.

But he didn't appear to register it. "Together, with me. If you swear loyalty, if you promise it in the name of the Angel, I will believe you. When all else changes, you alone I will preserve."

She moved her hand down another inch, and now she was holding the hilt of Heosphoros. All she needed was to tighten her fist... "And if I don't?"

His expression hardened. "If you refuse me now, I will Turn everyone you love to Endarkened Ones, and then Turn you last, that you might be forced to watch them change when you can still feel the pain of it."

Clary swallowed against a dry throat. "That's your mercy?"

"Mercy is a condition of your agreement."

"I won't agree."

His lowered lashes scattered light; his smile was a promise of terrible things. "What's the difference, Clarissa? You will fight for me regardless. Either you keep your freedom and stand with me, or you lose it and stand with me. Why not be with me?"

"The angel," she said. "What was its name?"

Taken aback, Sebastian hesitated for a moment before he replied. "The angel?"

"The one whose wings you cut off and sent to the Institute," she said. "The one you killed."

"I don't understand," he said. "What's the difference?"

"No," she said, slowly. "You don't understand. The things you've done are too terrible to ever be forgiven, and you don't even know they're terrible. And that's why not. That's why *never*. I will never forgive you. I will never love you. *Never*."

She saw each word hit him like a slap. As he drew breath to reply, she swung the blade of Heosphoros out at him, up toward his heart.

But he was faster, and the fact that her legs were pinned in place by magic shortened her reach. He whipped away; she reached out, trying to pull him toward her, but he yanked his arm away easily. She heard a rattle and realized distantly that she had pulled his silver bracelet free. It clattered to the ground. She slashed toward him again with her blade; he jerked back, and Heosphoros cut a clean slice across his shirtfront. She saw his lip curl in pain and anger. He caught her by the arm and swung her hand up to slam it against the door, sending a jolt of numbness up to her shoulder. Her fingers went loose, and Heosphoros fell from her grasp.

He glanced down at the fallen blade and then back up at her, breathing hard. Blood edged the fabric where she had cut his shirt; not enough for the wound to slow him down. Disappointment shot through her, more painful than the ache in her wrist. His body pinned hers to the door; she could feel the tension in every line of him. His voice was knifelike. "That blade is Heosphoros, the Dawn-Bringer. Where did you find it?"

"In a weapons shop," she gasped. Feeling was coming back to her shoulder; the pain was intense. "The woman who owned the place gave it to me. She said nobody else would ever—would ever want a Morgenstern blade. Our blood is *tainted*."

"But it is *our blood*." He pounced on the words. "And you took the sword. You wanted it." She could feel the heat burning off him; it seemed to shimmer around him, like the flame of a dying star. He bent his head until his lips touched her neck, and spoke against her skin, his words matching the tempo of her pulse. She closed her eyes with a shudder as his hands ran up her body. "You lie when you tell me you'll never love me," he said. "That we're different. You lie just like I do—"

"Stop," she said. "Get your hands off me."

"But you're mine," he said. "I want you to—I need you to—" He took a gasping breath; his pupils were blown wide; something about it terrified her more than anything else he had ever done. Sebastian in control was frightening; Sebastian out of control was something too horrible to contemplate.

"Let her go," said a clear, hard voice from across the room. "Let her go and stop touching her, or I will burn you down to ashes."

Jace.

Over Sebastian's shoulder she saw him, suddenly, where there had been no one standing a moment ago. He was in front of the window, the curtains blowing behind him in the breeze off the canal, and his eyes were as hard as agate stones. He was wearing gear, his blade in his hand, still with the shadow of fading bruises on his jaw and neck, and his expression as he looked at Sebastian was one of absolute loathing.

Clary felt Sebastian's whole body tighten against hers; a moment later he had spun away from her, slamming his foot down on her sword, his hand flying to his belt. His smile was a razor slice, but his eyes were wary. "Go ahead and try it," he said. "You got lucky at the Citadel. I wasn't expecting you to burn like that when I cut you. My mistake. I won't make it twice."

Jace's eyes flicked to Clary once, a question in them; she nodded that she was all right.

"So you admit it," said Jace, circling a little closer to them. The tread of his boots was soft on the wooden floor. "The heavenly fire surprised you. Threw you off your game. That's why you fled. You lost the battle at the Citadel, and you don't like to lose."

Sebastian's razor smile grew a little brighter, a little brittler. "I didn't get what I came for. But I did learn quite a bit."

"You didn't break the walls of the Citadel," said Jace. "You didn't get into the armory. You didn't Turn the Sisters."

"I didn't go to the Citadel for arms and armor," Sebastian sneered. "I can get those easily. I came for you. The two of you."

Clary looked sideways at Jace. He was standing, expressionless and unmoving, his face as still as stone.

"You couldn't have known we'd be there," she said. "You're lying."

"I'm not." He practically radiated, like a torch burning. "I can see you, little sister. I can see everything that happens in Alicante. In the day and in the night, in darkness and in light, *I can see you.*"

"Stop it," Jace said. "It's not true."

"Really?" Sebastian said. "How did I know Clary would be *here*? Alone, tonight?"

Jace went on, prowling toward them, like a cat on the hunt. "How didn't you know that I would be here, too?"

Sebastian made a face. "Hard to watch two people at once. So many irons in the fire..."

"And if you wanted Clary, why not just take her?" Jace demanded. "Why spend all this time talking?" His voice dripped contempt. "You want her to *want* to go with you," he said. "No one in your life has done anything but despise you. Your mother. Your father. And now your sister. Clary wasn't born with hate in her heart. You made her hate you. But it wasn't what you wanted. You forget we were bonded, you and I. You forget I've seen your dreams. Somewhere inside that head of yours, there is a world of flames, and there is you looking down at it from a throne room, and in that room are two thrones. So who occupies that second throne? Who sits beside you in your dreams?"

Sebastian gave a gasping laugh; there were red spots on his cheeks, like fever. "You are making a mistake," he said, "talking to me like this, angel boy."

"Even in your dreams you are not companionless," Jace said, and now his voice was that voice Clary had first fallen in love with, the voice of the boy who had told her a story about a child and a falcon and the lessons he had learned. "But who could you find who would understand you? You don't understand love; our father taught you too well. But you understand blood. Clary is your blood. If you could have her beside you, watching the world burn, it would be all the approval you ever needed."

"I never desired approval," said Sebastian through gritted

teeth. "Yours, hers, or anyone's."

"Really?" Jace smiled as Sebastian's voice rose. "Then why have you given us so many second chances?" He had stopped prowling and stood opposite them, his pale gold eyes shining in the dim light. "You said it yourself. You stabbed me. You went for my shoulder. You could have gone for the heart. You were holding back. For what? For me? Or because in some tiny part of your brain you know that Clary would never forgive you if you ended my life?"

"Clary, do you wish to speak for yourself on this matter?" said Sebastian, though he never took his eyes from the blade in Jace's hands. "Or do you require him to give answers for you?"

Jace cut his eyes toward Clary, and Sebastian did as well. She felt the weight of both gazes on her for a moment, black and gold.

"I'll never want to come with you, Sebastian," she said. "Jace is right. If the choice was to spend my life with you or die, I'd rather die."

Sebastian's eyes darkened. "You'll change your mind," he said. "You'll mount that throne beside me of your own accord, when the end comes to the end. I've given you your chance to come willingly now. I've paid in blood and inconvenience to have you with me by your own choice. But I will take you unwilling, just the same."

"No!" Clary said, just as a loud crash sounded from downstairs. The house was suddenly full of voices.

"Oh, dear," said Jace, his voice dripping sarcasm. "I just might have sent a fire-message to the Clave when I saw the body of the guard you killed and shoved under that bridge. Foolish of you not to dispose of it more carefully, Sebastian."

Sebastian's expression tightened, so momentarily that Clary imagined most people would never have noticed it. He reached for Clary, his lips shaping words—a spell to free her from whatever force held her clamped to the wall. She pushed, shoved at him, and then Jace leaped at them, his blade driving down—

Sebastian spun away, but the blade had caught him: It drew a line of blood down his arm. He cried out, staggering back—and paused. He grinned as Jace stared at him, white-faced.

"The heavenly fire," Sebastian said. "You don't know how to control it yet. Works sometimes and not other times, eh, little brother?"

Jace's eyes blazed up in gold. "We'll see about that," he said, and lunged for Sebastian, sword slicing through the darkness with light.

But Sebastian was too quick for it to matter. He strode forward and plucked the sword out of Jace's hand. Clary struggled, but Sebastian's magic kept her pinned in place; before Jace could move, Sebastian swung Jace's sword around and plunged it into his own chest.

The tip sank in, parting his shirt, then his skin. He bled red, human blood, as dark as rubies. He was clearly in pain: His teeth bared in a rictus grin, his breath coming unevenly, but the sword kept moving, his hand steady. The back of his shirt bulged and tore as the tip of the sword broke through it, on a gout of blood.

Time seemed to stretch out like a rubber band. The hilt slammed up against Sebastian's chest, the blade protruding from his back, dripping scarlet. Jace stood, shocked and frozen, as Sebastian reached for him with bloody hands and pulled him close. Over the sound of feet pounding up the stairs, Sebastian spoke:

"I can feel the fire of Heaven in your veins, angel boy, burning under the skin," he said. "The pure force of the destruction of ultimate goodness. I can still hear your screams on the air when Clary plunged the blade into you. Did you burn and burn?" His breathless voice was dark with poisonous intensity. "You think you have a weapon you can use against me, now, don't you? And perhaps with fifty years, a hundred, to learn to master the fire, you could, but time is exactly what you don't have. The fire rages, uncontrolled, inside you, far more likely to destroy you than it is to ever destroy me."

Sebastian raised a hand and cupped the back of Jace's neck, pulling him closer, so close their foreheads almost touched.

"Clary and I are alike," he said. "And you—you are my mirror. One day she will choose me over you, I promise you that. And you will be there to see it." With a swift darting motion, he kissed Jace on the cheek, fast and hard; when he drew back, there was a smear of blood there. "*Ave*, Master Herondale," Sebastian said, and twisted the silver ring on his finger—there was a shimmer, and he vanished.

Jace stared for a wordless moment at the place where Sebastian had been, then started toward Clary; suddenly freed by Sebastian's disappearance, her legs had collapsed under her. She hit the ground on her knees and threw herself forward immediately, scrabbling for the blade of Heosphoros. Her hand closed around it and she drew it close, curling her body around it as if it were a child that needed protecting.

"Clary—Clary—" Jace was there, sinking to his knees beside her, and his arms were around her; she rocked into them, pressing her forehead to his shoulder. She realized his shirt, and now her skin, was wet with her brother's blood, as the door burst open, and the guards of the Clave poured into the room.

"Here you go," said Leila Haryana, one of the newest of the pack's wolves, as she handed over a stack of clothes to Maia.

Maia took them gratefully. "Thanks—you have no idea what it means to have clean clothes to wear," she said, glancing through the pile: a tank top, jeans, a wool jacket. She and Leila were about the same size, and even if the clothes didn't quite fit, it was better than going back to Jordan's apartment. It had been a while since Maia had lived at pack headquarters, and all her things were at Jordan and Simon's, but the thought of the apartment without either of the boys in it was a dreary one. At least here she was surrounded by other werewolves, surrounded by the constant hum of voices, the smell of take-out Chinese and Malaysian food, the sound of people cooking in the kitchen. And Bat was there—not getting in her space, but always around if she wanted someone to talk to or just sit silently with, watching the traffic go by on Baxter Street.

Of course there were also downsides. Rufus Hastings, huge and scarred and fearsome in his black leather biker clothes, seemed to be everywhere at once, his grating voice audible in the kitchen as he muttered over lunch about how Luke Garroway wasn't a reliable leader, he was going to marry an ex-Shadowhunter, his loyalties were in question, they needed someone they could depend on to put werewolves first.

"No problem." Leila fiddled with the gold clip in her dark hair, looking awkward. "Maia," she said. "Just a word to the wise—you might want to tone down the whole loyalty-to-Luke thing."

Maia froze. "I thought we were all loyal to Luke," she said, in a careful tone. "And to Bat."

"If Luke were here, maybe," said Leila. "But we've barely heard from him since he left for Idris. The Praetor isn't a pack, but Sebastian threw the gauntlet down. He wants us to choose between the Shadowhunters and going to war for them and—"

"There's always going to be war," Maia said in a low furious voice. "I'm not blindly loyal to Luke. I *know* Shadowhunters. I've met Sebastian, too. He hates us. Trying to appease him, it isn't going to work—"

Leila put her hands up. "Okay, okay. Like I said, just advice. Hope those fit," she added, and headed off down the hall.

Maia wiggled into the jeans—tight, like she'd figured—and the shirt, and shrugged on Leila's jacket. She grabbed her wallet from the table, shoved her feet into her boots, and headed down the hall to knock on Bat's door.

He opened it shirtless, which she hadn't been expecting. Aside from the scar along his right cheek, he had a scar on his right arm, where he'd been shot with a bullet—not silver. The scar looked like a moon crater, white against his dark skin. He raised an eyebrow. "Maia?"

"Look," she said. "I'm going to tell off Rufus. He's filling everyone's head with crap, and I'm tired of it."

"Whoa." Bat held up a hand. "I don't think that's a good idea—"

"He's not going to stop unless someone tells him to," she said. "I remember running into him at the Praetor, with Jordan. Praetor Scott said Rufus had snapped another werewolf's leg for no reason. Some people see a power vacuum and they want to fill it. They don't care who they hurt."

Maia spun on her heel and headed downstairs; she could hear Bat making muffled cursing noises behind her. A second later he joined her on the steps, hastily pulling a shirt on.

"Maia, I really don't—"

"There you are," she said. She had reached the lobby, where Rufus was lounging against what had once been a sergeant's desk. A group of about ten other werewolves, including Leila, were grouped around him.

"... have to show them that we're stronger," he was saying. "And that our loyalties lie with ourselves. The strength of the pack is the wolf, and the strength of the wolf is the pack." His voice was as gravelly as Maia remembered it, as if something had injured his throat a long time ago. The deep scars on his face were livid against his pale skin. He smiled when he saw Maia. "Hello," he said. "I believe we've met before. I was sorry to hear about your boyfriend."

I doubt that.

"Strength is loyalty and unity, not dividing people with lies," Maia snapped.

"We've only just been reunited, and you're calling me a liar?"

Rufus said. His demeanor was still casual, but there was a flicker of tension under it, like a cat readying itself to pounce.

"If you're telling people that they should stay out of the Shadowhunters' war, then you're a liar. Sebastian isn't going to stop with the Nephilim. If he destroys them, then he'll come for us next."

"He doesn't care about Downworlders."

"He just slaughtered the Praetor Lupus!" Maia shouted. "He cares about destruction. He *will* kill us all."

"Not if we don't join with the Shadowhunters!"

"That's a lie," Maia said. She saw Bat pass a hand over his eyes, and then something struck her hard in the shoulder, knocking her backward. She was caught off her guard enough to stumble, and then steadied herself on the edge of the desk.

"Rufus!" Bat roared, and Maia realized that Rufus had hit her in the shoulder. She clamped her jaw shut, not wanting to give him the satisfaction of seeing the pain on her face.

Rufus stood smirking amid the suddenly frozen group of werewolves. Murmurs ran around the group as Bat strode forward. Rufus was enormous, towering over even Bat, his shoulders as thick and broad as a plank. "Rufus," Bat said. "I'm the leader here, in Garroway's absence. You have been a guest among us but are not of our pack. It's time for you to get out."

Rufus narrowed his eyes at Bat. "Are you throwing me out? Knowing I have nowhere to go?"

"I'm sure you'll find somewhere," Bat said, starting to turn away.

"I challenge you," Rufus said. "Bat Velasquez, I challenge you for the leadership of the New York pack."

"No!" Maia said in horror, but Bat was already straightening his shoulders. His eyes met Rufus's; the tension between the two werewolves was as palpable as a live wire.

"I accept your challenge," Bat said. "Tomorrow night, in

Prospect Park. I'll meet you there."

He spun on his heel and stalked out of the station. After a frozen moment Maia dashed after him.

The cold air hit her the minute she reached the front steps. Icy wind was swirling down Baxter Street, cutting through her jacket. She clattered down the stairs, her shoulder aching. Bat had nearly reached the corner of the street by the time she caught up with him, grabbing his arm and spinning him around to face her.

She was aware that other people on the street were staring at them, and wished for a moment for the Shadowhunters' glamour runes. Bat looked down at her. There was an angry line between his eyes, and his scar stood out, livid on his cheek. "Are you crazy?" she demanded. "How could you accept Rufus's challenge? He's *huge*."

"You know the rules, Maia," said Bat. "A challenge has to be accepted."

"Only if you're challenged by someone in your own pack! You could have turned him down."

"And lost all the pack's respect," said Bat. "They never would have been willing to follow my orders again."

"He'll kill you," Maia said, and wondered if he could hear what she was saying under the words: that she'd just watched Jordan die, and didn't think she could stand it again.

"Maybe not." He drew from his pocket something that clanked and jingled, and pressed it into her hand. After a moment she realized what it was. Jordan's keys. "His truck's parked around the corner," Bat said. "Take it and go. Stay away from the station until this is resolved. I don't trust Rufus around you."

"Come with me," Maia begged. "You never cared about being pack leader. We could just go away until Luke comes back and sorts all this out—"

"Maia." Bat put his hand on her wrist, his fingers curling gently around her palm. "Waiting for Luke to get back is pretty much exactly what Rufus wants us to do. If we leave, we're abandoning the pack to him, basically. And you know what he'll choose to do, or not do. He'll let Sebastian slaughter the Shadowhunters without lifting a finger, and by the time Sebastian decides to come back and pick us all off like the last pieces on a chessboard, it'll be too late for everyone."

Maia looked down at his fingers, gentle on her skin.

"You know," he said, "I remember when you told me you needed more space. That you couldn't be in a real relationship. I took you at your word and I gave you space. I even started dating that girl, the witch, what was her name—"

"Eve," Maia supplied.

"Right. Eve." Bat looked surprised that she remembered. "But that didn't work out, and anyway, maybe I gave you too much space. Maybe I should have told you how I felt. Maybe I should—"

She looked up at him, startled and bewildered, and saw his expression change, the shutters going up behind his eyes, hiding his brief vulnerability.

"Never mind," he said. "It's not fair to lay all this on you right now." He let go of her and stepped back. "Take the truck," he said, backing away from her into the crowd, heading toward Canal Street. "Get out of town. And look after yourself, Maia. For me."

Jace set his stele down on the arm of the sofa and traced a finger over the *iratze* he had drawn on Clary's arm. A silver band glittered at his wrist. At some point, Clary didn't remember when, he had picked up Sebastian's fallen bracelet and clipped it onto his own wrist. She didn't feel like asking him why. "How's that?"

"Better. Thanks." Clary's jeans were rolled up above her knees; she watched as the bruises on her legs began to fade slowly. They were in a room in the Gard, some kind of meeting space, Clary guessed. There were several tables and a long leather sofa, angled in front of a low-burning fire. Books lined one of the walls. The room was illuminated by the firelight. The unshaded window gave out onto a view of Alicante and the shining demon towers.

"Hey." Jace's light golden eyes searched her face. "Are you all right?"

Yes, she meant to say, but the reply stuck in her throat. Physically she was fine. The runes had healed her bruises. She was all right, Jace was all right—Simon, knocked out by the spiked blood, had slept through it all and was currently still sleeping in another room in the Gard.

A message had been sent to Luke and Jocelyn. The dinner they were attending was warded for safety, Jia had explained, but they would receive it on leaving. Clary ached to see them again. The world felt unsteady under her feet. Sebastian was gone, for the moment at least, but still she felt torn apart, bitter and angry and vengeful and *sad*.

The guards had let her pack a bag of her things before she'd left Amatis's house—a change of clothes, her gear, her stele, drawing pad, and weapons. Part of her wanted to change her clothes desperately, to get rid of Sebastian's touch on the fabric, but more of her didn't want to leave the room, didn't want to be alone with her memories and thoughts.

"I'm fine." She rolled the legs of her jeans down and stood up, walked over to the fireplace. She was aware of Jace watching her from the sofa. She put her hands out as if warming them at the fire, though she wasn't cold. In fact, every time the thought of her brother crossed her mind, she felt a surge of anger like liquid fire rip through her body. Her hands were shaking; she looked at them with a strange detachment, as if they were a stranger's hands.

"Sebastian's afraid of you," she said. "He played it off, especially at the end, but I could tell."

"He's afraid of the heavenly fire," corrected Jace. "I don't think he's exactly sure what it does, any more than we are. One thing's for certain, though—it doesn't hurt him just to touch me."

"No," she said, without turning around to look at Jace. "Why did he kiss you?" It wasn't what she'd meant to say, but she kept seeing it in her head, over and over, Sebastian with his bloody hand curling around the back of Jace's neck, and then that strange and surprising kiss on the cheek.

She heard the creak of the leather sofa as Jace shifted his weight. "It was a sort of quote," he said. "From the Bible. When Judas kissed Jesus in the garden of Gethsemane. It was a sign of his betrayal. He kissed him and said 'Hail, master' to him, and that was how the Romans knew who to arrest and crucify."

"That was why he said '*Ave*, master,' to you," said Clary, realizing. "'Hail, master.'"

"He meant he planned to be the instrument of my destruction. Clary, I—" She turned to look at Jace as he broke off. He was sitting on the edge of the couch, running a hand through his messy blond hair, his eyes fixed on the floor. "When I came into the room and saw you there, and him there, I wanted to kill him. I should have attacked him immediately, but I was afraid it was a trap. That if I moved toward you, either of you, he would find a way to kill you or hurt you. He's always twisted everything I've ever done. He's clever. Cleverer than Valentine. And I've never been—"

She waited, the only sound in the room the crackle and pop of the damp wood in the fireplace.

"I've never been afraid of anyone like this," he finished, biting off the words as he spoke them.

Clary knew what it cost Jace to say it, how much of his life had been spent expertly hiding fear and pain and any perceived vulnerability. She wanted to say something in reply, something about how he shouldn't be afraid, but she couldn't. She was afraid as well, and she knew they both had good reason to be. There was no one in Idris who had better reason than they did to be terrified.

"He risked a lot, coming here," Jace said. "He let the Clave know he can get in through the wards. They'll try to shore them up again. It might work, it might not, but it'll probably inconvenience him. He wanted to see you badly. Badly enough to make it worth the risk."

"He still thinks he can convince me."

"Clary." Jace rose to his feet and moved toward her, his hand outstretched. "Are you—"

She flinched, away from his touch. Startled light flared in his golden eyes.

"What's wrong?" He glanced down at his hands; the faint glow of the fire in his veins was visible. "The heavenly fire?"

"Not that," she said.

"Then—"

"Sebastian. I should have told you before, but I just—I couldn't."

He didn't move, just looked at her. "Clary, you can tell me anything; you know you can."

She took a deep breath and stared into the fire, watching the flames—gold and green and sapphire blue—chase each other. "In November," she said. "Before we came to the Burren, after you'd left the apartment, he realized I'd been spying. He crushed my ring, and then he—he hit me, pushed me through a glass table. Knocked me to the ground. I almost killed him then, almost shoved a piece of glass through his throat, but I realized that if I did, I'd be killing you, and so I couldn't do it. And he was so delighted. He laughed and he shoved me down. He was pulling at my clothes and reciting pieces of the Song of Solomon, telling me about how brothers and sisters used to marry to keep royal bloodlines pure, how I *belonged* to him. Like I was a piece of monogrammed luggage with his name stamped on me..."

Jace looked shocked in a way she had rarely seen him shocked;

she could read the levels of his expression: hurt, fear, apprehension. "He ... Did he...?"

"Rape me?" she said, and the word was awful and ugly in the stillness of the room. "No. He didn't. He ... stopped." Her voice fell to a whisper.

Jace was as white as a sheet. He opened his mouth to say something to her, but she could hear only the distorted echo of his voice, as if she were underwater again. She was shaking all over, violently, though it was warm in the room.

"Tonight," she said, finally. "I couldn't move, and he pushed me up against the wall, and I couldn't get away, and I just—"

"I'll kill him," Jace said. Some color had washed back into his face, and he looked gray. "I'll cut him into pieces. I'll cut his hands off for touching you—"

"Jace," Clary said, feeling suddenly exhausted. "We have a million reasons to want him dead. Besides," she added with a mirthless laugh, "Isabelle already cut his hand off, and it didn't work."

Jace closed his hand into a fist, drew it up against his stomach, and dug it into his solar plexus as if he could cut off his own breath. "All that time I was connected to him, I thought I knew his mind, his desires, what he wanted. But I didn't guess, I didn't *know*. And you didn't tell me."

"This isn't about you, Jace—"

"I know," he said. "I *know*." But his hand was so tightly fisted that it was white, the veins standing out in a stark topography across the back of it. "I know, and I don't blame you for not telling me. What could I have done? How am I not completely useless here? I was just standing five feet from him, and I have fire in my veins that ought to be able to kill him, and I tried and it didn't work. I couldn't make it *work*."

"*Jace.*"

"I'm sorry. It's just—you know me. I only have two reactions to bad news. Uncontrollable rage and then a sharp left turn into boiling self-hatred."

She was silent. Above everything else she was tired, so tired. Telling him what Sebastian had done had been like lifting an impossible weight, and now all she wanted was to close her eyes and disappear into the darkness. She had been so angry for so long—anger always under the surface of everything. Whether she was shopping for presents with Simon or sitting in the park or alone at home trying to draw, the anger was always with her.

Jace was visibly struggling; he wasn't trying to hide anything from her, at least, and she saw the quick flicker of emotions behind his eyes: rage, frustration, helplessness, guilt, and, finally, sadness. It was a surprisingly quiet sadness, for Jace, and when he spoke at last, his voice was surprisingly quiet too. "I just wish," he said, not looking at her but at the floor, "that I could say the right thing, do the right thing, to make this easier for you. Whatever you want from me, I want to do it. I want to be there for you in whatever the right way is for you, Clary."

"There," she said softly.

He looked up. "What?"

"What you just said. That was perfect."

He blinked. "Well, that's good, because I'm not sure I have an encore in me. What *part* of it was perfect?"

She felt her lip quirk slightly at the side. There was something so Jace about his reaction, his strange mixture of arrogance and vulnerability, of resilience and bitterness and devotion. "I just want to know," she said, "that you don't think any differently of me. Any less."

"No. *No*," he said, appalled. "You're brave and brilliant, and you're perfect and I love you. I just love you and I always have. And the actions of some lunatic aren't going to change that."

"Sit down," she said, and he sat down on the creaking leather sofa, his head tipped back, looking up at her. The reflected firelight clustered like sparks in his hair. She took a deep breath and walked over to him, settled herself carefully in his lap. "Could you hug me?" she said.

He put his arms around her, held her against him. She could feel the muscles in his arms, the strength in his back as he put his hands on her gently, so gently. He had hands made for fighting, and yet he could be so gentle with her, with his piano, with all the things he cared about.

She settled against him, sideways in his lap, her feet on the sofa, and leaned her head against his shoulder. She could feel the rapid beat of his heart. "Now," she said. "Kiss me too."

He hesitated. "Are you sure?"

She nodded. "Yes. *Yes*," she said. "God knows we haven't exactly been able to do all that much lately, but every time I kiss you, every time you touch me, it's a victory, if you ask me. Sebastian, he did what he did because—because he doesn't understand the difference between loving and having. Between giving yourself and taking. And he thought that if he could *make* me give myself, then he'd have me, I'd be his, and to him that's love, because he doesn't know anything else. But when I touch you, I do it because I want to, and that's all the difference. And he doesn't get to have that or take it away from me. He doesn't," she said, and she leaned up to kiss him, a light touch of lips to lips, bracing her hand against the back of the sofa.

She felt him draw in his breath at the slight spark that jumped between their skins. He brushed his cheek against hers, the strands of their hair tangling together, red and gold.

She settled back down against him. The flames leaped in the grate, and some of their warmth soaked into Clary's bones. She was resting against the shoulder that was marked with the white star of the men of the Herondale family, and she thought of all those who had gone before Jace, whose blood and bones and lives had made him what he was.

"What are you thinking?" he said. He was drawing his hand through her hair, letting the loose curls slip between his fingers.

"That I'm glad I told you," she said. "What are you thinking?"

He was silent for a long moment, as the flames rose and fell. Then he said, "I was thinking of what you said about Sebastian being lonely. I was trying to remember what it was like to be in that house with him. He took me for a lot of reasons, sure, but half of it was just to have company. The company of someone who he thought might understand him, because we'd been raised the same. I was trying to remember if I'd ever actually liked him, liked spending time with him."

"I don't think so. Just from being there, with you, you never seemed at ease, not exactly. You were you, but not you. It's hard to explain."

Jace looked at the fire. "Not that hard," he said. "I think there's a part of us, separate even from our will or our minds, and it was that part he couldn't touch. It was never really exactly me, and he knew that. He wants to be liked, or really loved, for what he is, genuinely. But he doesn't think he has to change to be worthy of being loved; instead he wants to change the whole world, change humanity, make it into something that loves him." He paused. "Sorry about the armchair psychology. Literally. Here we are in an armchair."

But Clary was deep in thought. "When I went through his things, at the house, I found a letter he'd written. It wasn't finished, but it was addressed to 'my beautiful one.' I remember thinking it was weird. Why would he be writing a love letter? I mean, he understands sex, sort of, and desire, but romantic love? Not from what I've seen."

Jace drew her up against him, fitting her more neatly against the curve of his side. She wasn't sure who was soothing whom, just that his heart beat steadily against her skin, and the soap-sweat-metal smell of him was familiar and comforting. Clary softened against him, exhaustion catching her up and dragging her down, weighting her eyelids. It had been a long, long day and night, and a long day before that. "If my mom and Luke get here while I'm sleeping, wake me up," she said.

"Oh, you'll be woken up," Jace said drowsily. "Your mother will think I'm trying to take advantage of you and chase me around the room with a fireplace poker."

She reached up to pat his cheek. "I'll protect you."

Jace didn't reply. He was already asleep, breathing steadily against her, the rhythms of their heartbeats slowing to match each other. She lay awake as he slept—looking into the leaping flames and frowning, the words "my beautiful one" echoing in her ears like the memory of words heard in a dream.

11

THE BEST IS LOST

"Clary. Jace. Wake up."

Clary raised her head and almost yelped as a twinge shot through her stiff neck. She'd fallen asleep curled up against Jace's shoulder; he was asleep too, wedged into the corner of the sofa with his jacket wadded up under his head as a pillow. The hilt of his sword dug uncomfortably into Clary's hip as he groaned and straightened up.

The Consul stood over them, dressed in Council robes, unsmiling. Jace scrambled to his feet. "Consul," he said, in as dignified a voice as he could muster with his clothes rumpled and his light hair sticking out in every possible direction.

"We nearly forgot the two of you were in here," Jia said. "The Council meeting has begun."

Clary got to her feet more slowly, working out the cricks in her back and neck. Her mouth was as dry as chalk, and her body ached with tension and exhaustion. "Where's my mother?" she said. "Where's Luke?"

"I'll wait for you in the hall," Jia said, but she didn't move.

Jace was sliding his arms into his jacket. "We'll be right along, Consul."

There was something in the Consul's voice that made Clary look at her again. Jia was pretty, like her daughter Aline, but at the moment there were sharp lines of tension at the corners of her mouth and eyes. Clary had seen that look before.

"What's going on?" she demanded. "There's something wrong, isn't there? Where's my mother? Where's Luke?"

"We're not sure," Jia said quietly. "They never responded to the message that we sent to them last night."

Too many shocks, delivered too quickly, had left Clary numb. She didn't gasp or exclaim, only felt a coldness spread through her veins. She seized up Heosphoros from the table where she'd left it, and shoved it through her belt. Without another word she pushed past the Consul, into the hallway outside.

Simon was waiting there. He looked rumpled and exhausted, pale even for a vampire. She reached to squeeze his hand, fingers brushing across the gold leaf ring on his finger as she did.

"Simon's coming to the Council meeting," Clary said, her look daring the Consul to say anything in return.

Jia simply nodded. She looked like someone who was too tired to argue anymore. "He can be the Night Children's representative."

"But Raphael was going to stand in for the representative," Simon protested, alarmed. "I'm not prepared—"

"We haven't been able to reach any of the Downworld representatives, Raphael included." Jia began to make her way down the hall. The walls were wood, with the pale color and sharp scent of freshly cut lumber. This must have been part of the Gard that had been rebuilt after the Mortal War—Clary had been too tired to notice the night before. Runes of angelic power were cut into the walls at intervals. Each glowed with a deep light, illuminating the window-less corridor.

"What do you mean, you haven't been able to reach them?" Clary demanded, hurrying after Jia. Simon and Jace followed. The corridor curved, leading deeper into the heart of the Gard. Clary could hear a dull roar, like the sound of the ocean, just ahead of them.

"Neither Luke nor your mother came back from their appointment at the house of the Fair Folk." The Consul paused in a large antechamber. There was a good deal of natural light here, pouring through windows made up of alternating squares of plain and colored glass. Double doors stood before them, blazoned with the triptych of the Angel and the Mortal Instruments.

"I don't understand," Clary said, her voice rising. "So they're still there? At Meliorn's?"

Jia shook her head. "The house is empty."

"But—what about Meliorn, what about *Magnus*?"

"Nothing is certain yet," Jia said. "There is no one in the house, nor are any of the representatives responding to messages. Patrick is out searching the city now with a team of guards."

"Was there blood in the house?" Jace asked. "Signs of a struggle, anything?"

Jia shook her head. "No. The food was still on the table. It was as if they just—vanished into thin air."

"There's more, isn't there?" Clary said. "I can tell by your expression that there's more."

Jia didn't answer, just pushed the door of the Council room open. Noise poured out into the antechamber. This was the sound Clary had been hearing, like the crash of the ocean. She hurried past the Consul and paused in the doorway, hovering uncertainly.

The Council room, so orderly only a few days before, was full of shouting Shadowhunters. Everyone was standing, some in groups and some apart. Most of the groups were arguing. Clary couldn't make out the words, but she could see the angry gestures. Her eyes scanned the crowd for familiar faces—no Luke, no Jocelyn, but there were the Lightwoods, Robert in his Inquisitor's robes beside Maryse; there were Aline and Helen, and the crowd of Blackthorn children.

And there, down in the center of the amphitheater, were the four carved wooden seats of the Downworlders, set around the lecterns in a half circle. They were empty, and splashed across the floorboards in front of them was a single word, scrawled in a crooked hand, in what looked like sticky gold paint:

Veni.

Jace moved past Clary, into the room. His shoulders were tight as he stared down at the scrawl. "That's ichor," he said. "Angel blood."

In a flash Clary saw the library at the Institute, the floor slicked with blood and feathers, the angel's hollow bones.

Erchomai.

I am coming.

And now the single word: *Veni.*

I have come.

A second message. Oh, Sebastian had been busy. *Stupid,* she thought, so stupid of her to think he'd come only for her, that it hadn't been part of something larger, that he hadn't wanted more, more destruction, more terror, more upheaval. She thought of his smirk when she'd mentioned the battle at the Citadel. Of course it had been more than an attack; it had been a distraction. Turning the gaze of the Nephilim outward from Alicante, making them search the world for him and his Endarkened, panicking them over the wounded and dead. And in the meantime Sebastian had found his way to the heart of the Gard and painted the floor in blood.

Near the dais was a group of Silent Brothers in their bone-colored robes, faces hidden by hoods. Her memory sparking, Clary turned to Jace. "Brother Zachariah—I never got a chance to ask you if you knew whether he was all right?"

Jace was staring at the writing on the dais, a sick look on his face. "I saw him in the Basilias. He's all right. He's—different."

"Good different?"

"Human different," Jace said, and before Clary could ask him what he meant, she heard someone call her name.

Down in the center of the room, she saw a hand rise out of the crowd, waving toward her frantically. Isabelle. She was standing with Alec, a little distance from their parents. Clary heard Jia call out after her, but she was pushing through the crowd already, Jace and Simon at her heels. She sensed curious stares being cast in her direction. Everyone knew who she was, after all. Knew who they all were. Valentine's daughter, Valentine's adopted son, and the Daylighter vampire.

"Clary!" Isabelle called as Clary, Jace, and Simon pulled free of the staring onlookers and nearly fell into the Lightwood siblings, who had managed to clear a small space for themselves in the middle of the crowd. Isabelle shot an irritated glance at Simon before reaching out to hug Jace and Clary. As soon as she released Jace, Alec pulled him over by the sleeve and hung on, his knuckles whitening around the fabric. Jace looked surprised, but said nothing.

"Is it true?" Isabelle said to Clary. "Sebastian was at your house last night?"

"At Amatis's, yes—how did you know?" Clary demanded.

"Our father's the Inquisitor; of course we know," said Alec. "Rumors about Sebastian being in the city were all everyone was talking about before they opened up the Council room and we saw—this."

"It's true," Simon added. "The Consul asked me about it when she woke me up—like I'd know anything. I slept through it," he added as Isabelle shot him an inquiring look.

"Did the Consul say anything to you about *this*?" Alec demanded, sweeping an arm toward the grim scene below. "Did Sebastian?"

"No," Clary said. "Sebastian doesn't exactly share his plans."

"He shouldn't have been able to get to the Downworld representatives. Not only is Alicante guarded, but each of their safe houses is warded," said Alec. There was a pulse going in his throat like a hammer; his hand, where it rested on Jace's sleeve, was shaking with a fine tremor. "They were at dinner. They should have been *safe*." He let go of Jace and jammed his hands into his pockets. "And Magnus—Magnus wasn't even supposed to be here. Catarina was coming instead of him." He looked at Simon. "I saw you with him in Angel Square on the night of the battle," he said. "Did he say why he was in Alicante?"

Simon shook his head. "He just shooed me away. He was healing Clary."

"Maybe this is a bluff," Alec said. "Maybe Sebastian is trying to make us think he's done something to the Downworld representatives to throw us off—"

"We don't *know* that he's done anything to them. But—they are missing," Jace said quietly, and Alec looked away, as if he couldn't bear to meet their gazes.

"*Veni*," Isabelle whispered, looking at the dais. "Why...?"

"He's telling us he has power," Clary said. "Power none of us even begin to understand." She thought of the way he'd appeared in her room and then disappeared. Of the way the ground had opened under his feet at the Citadel, as if the earth were welcoming him in, hiding him from the threat of the world above.

A sharp report rang out through the room, the bell that called the Council to order. Jia had moved to the lectern, an armed Clave guard in hooded robes on either side of her.

"Shadowhunters," she said, and the word echoed as clearly through the room as if she'd used a microphone. "Please be silent."

The room subsided gradually into quiet, though from the rebellious looks on quite a few faces, it was an uncooperative quiet.

"Consul Penhallow!" called out Kadir. "What answers do you have for us? What is the meaning of this—this desecration?"

"We're not sure," said Jia. "It happened in the night, in between one watch of guards and another."

"This is vengeance," said a thin, dark-haired Shadowhunter whom Clary recognized as the head of the Budapest Institute. Lazlo Balogh, she thought his name was. "Vengeance for our victories in London and at the Citadel."

"We didn't have victories in London and at the Citadel, Lazlo," said Jia. "The London Institute turned out to be protected by a force even we were unaware of, one we cannot replicate. The Shadowhunters there were warned and led to safety. Even then, a few were injured: None of Sebastian's forces were harmed. At best it could be called a successful retreat."

"But the attack on the Citadel," Lazlo protested. "He did not enter the Citadel. He did not reach the armory there—"

"But neither did he lose. We sent through sixty warriors, and he killed thirty and injured ten. He had forty warriors, and he lost perhaps fifteen. If it hadn't been for what happened when he wounded Jace Lightwood, his forty would have slaughtered our sixty."

"We're Shadowhunters," said Nasreen Choudhury. "We are used to defending that which we must defend with our last breaths, our last drops of blood."

"A noble idea," said Josiane Pontmercy, from the Marseilles Conclave, "but perhaps not entirely practical."

"We were too conservative in the number we sent to face him at the Citadel," said Robert Lightwood, his booming voice carrying through the room. "We have estimated since the attacks that Sebastian has four hundred Endarkened warriors on his side. Simply given the numbers, a head-to-head battle now between his forces and *all* Shadowhunters would mean that he would lose."

"So what we need to do is fight him as soon as possible, before he Turns any other Shadowhunters," said Diana Wrayburn.

"You can't fight what you can't find," said the Consul. "Our attempts to track him continue to prove fruitless." She raised her voice. "Sebastian Morgenstern's best plan now is to lure us out in small numbers. He needs us to send out scouting parties to hunt demons, or to hunt him. We must stay together, here, in Idris, where he cannot confront us. If we split up, if we leave our homeland, then we will lose."

"He'll wait us out," said a blond Shadowhunter from the Copenhagen Conclave.

"We have to believe he doesn't have the patience for that," said Jia. "We have to assume he will attack, and when he does, our superior numbers will defeat him."

"There's more than patience to be considered," said Balogh. "We left our Institutes, we came here, with the understanding that we would be returning once we had held a Council with the Downworld representatives. Without us out in the world, who will protect it? We have a *mandate*, a mandate from Heaven, to protect the world, to hold back the demons. We cannot do that from Idris."

"All the wards are at full strength," said Robert. "Wrangel Island is working overtime. And given our new cooperation with Downworlders, we will have to rely on them to keep the Accords. That was part of what we were going to discuss at the Council today—"

"Well, good luck to you with that," said Josiane Pontmercy, "considering that the representatives of Downworld are missing."

Missing. The word fell into the silence like a pebble into water, sending out ripples through the room. Clary felt Alec stiffen, minutely, at her side. She hadn't been letting herself think about it, hadn't been letting herself believe that they could really be gone. It was a trick Sebastian was playing on them, she kept telling herself. A cruel trick, but nothing more.

"We don't know that!" Jia protested. "Guards are out searching now—"

"Sebastian wrote on the floor in front of their very seats!" shouted a man with a bandaged arm. He was the head of the Mexico City Institute and had been at the Citadel battle. Clary thought his last name was Rosales. "*Veni.* 'I am come.' Just as he sent us a message with the death of the angel in New York, now he strikes at us in the heart of the Gard—"

"But he didn't strike at us," Diana interrupted. "He struck at the representatives of Downworld."

"To strike at our allies is to strike at us," called Maryse. "They *are* members of the Council, with all the attendant rights that represents."

"We don't even know what happened to them!" snapped someone in the crowd. "They could be perfectly all right—"

"Then *where are they*?" shouted Alec, and even Jace looked startled to hear Alec raise his voice. Alec was glowering, his blue eyes dark, and Clary was suddenly reminded of the angry boy she had met in the Institute what felt like so long ago. "Has anyone tried to track them?"

"We have," said Jia. "It hasn't worked. Not all of them can be tracked. You cannot track a warlock, or the dead—" Jia broke off with a sudden gasp. Without warning the Clave guard on her left had come up behind her and seized her by the back of her robes. A shout ran through the assembly as he yanked her back, placing the blade of a long, silver dagger against her throat.

"Nephilim!" he roared, and his hood fell away, showing the blank eyes and swirling, unfamiliar Marks of the Endarkened. A roar began to rise from the crowd, cut off quickly as the guard dug his blade farther into Jia's throat. Blood bloomed around it, visible even from a distance.

"Nephilim!" the man roared again. Clary's mind struggled

to place him—he seemed somehow familiar. He was tall, brown-haired, probably around forty. His arms were thickly muscled, the veins standing out like ropes as he struggled to hold Jia still. "Stay where you are! Do not approach, or your Consul dies!"

Aline screamed. Helen had hold of her, visibly restraining her from running forward. Behind them the Blackthorn children huddled around Julian, who was carrying his youngest brother in his arms; Drusilla had her face pressed against his side. Emma, her hair bright even at a distance, stood with Cortana out, protecting the others.

"That's Matthias Gonzales," said Alec in a shocked voice. "He was head of the Buenos Aires Institute—"

"Silence!" roared the man behind Jia—Matthias—and an uneasy silence fell. Most Shadowhunters stood, like Jace and Alec, with their hands halfway to their weapons. Isabelle was clutching the handle of her whip. "Hear me, Shadowhunters!" Matthias cried, his eyes burning with a fanatic light. "Hear me, for I was one of you. Blindly following the rule of the Clave, convinced of my safety within the wards of Idris, protected by the light of the Angel! But there is no safety here." He jerked his chin to the side, indicating the scrawl on the floor. "None are safe, not even Heaven's messengers. That is the reach of the power of the Infernal Cup, and of he who holds it."

A murmur ran through the crowd. Robert Lightwood pushed forward, his face anxious as he looked at Jia, and the blade at her throat. "What does he want?" he demanded. "Valentine's son. What does he want from us?"

"Oh, he wants many things," said the Endarkened Shadowhunter. "But for now he will content himself with the gift of his sister and adoptive brother. Give him Clarissa Morgenstern and Jace Lightwood, and avert disaster."

Clary heard Jace suck in his breath. She looked at him, panicking; she could feel the gaze of the whole room on her, and felt as if she were dissolving, like salt in water.

"We are Nephilim," Robert said coldly. "We do not trade away our own. He knows that."

"We of the Infernal Cup have in our possession five of your allies," was the reply. "Meliorn of the Fair Folk, Raphael Santiago of the Night's Children, Luke Garroway of the Moon's Children, Jocelyn Morgenstern of the Nephilim, and Magnus Bane of the Children of Lilith. If you do not give us Clarissa and Jonathan, they will be put to the deaths of iron and silver, of fire and rowan. And when your Downworld allies learn that you have sacrificed their representatives because you would not give up your own, they will turn on you. They will join with us, and you will find yourselves fighting not just he who holds the Infernal Cup, but all of Downworld."

Clary felt a wave of dizziness, so intense that it was almost sickness, pass over her. She had known—of course she had known, with a creeping knowledge that was not certainty and could not be dismissed—that her mother and Luke and Magnus were in danger, but to hear it was something else. She began to shiver, the words of an incoherent prayer repeating over and over in her head: *Mom, Luke, be all right, please be all right. Let Magnus be all right, for Alec. Please.*

She heard Isabelle's voice in her head too, saying that Sebastian could not fight them and all of Downworld. But he had found a neat way to turn it back on them: If harm came to the Downworld representatives now, it would seem the Shadowhunters' fault.

Jace's expression had gone bleak, but he met her eyes with the same understanding that had lodged like a needle in her heart. They could not stand back and let this happen. They would go to Sebastian. It was the only choice.

She started forward, meaning to call out, but she found herself jerked back by a hard grip on her wrist. She turned, expecting Simon, and saw to her surprise that it was Isabelle. "Don't," Isabelle said.

"You are a fool and a follower," snapped Kadir, his eyes angry as he regarded Matthias. "No Downworlders will hold us accountable for not sacrificing two of our children to Jonathan Morgenstern's pyre of corpses."

"Oh, but he will not kill them," said Matthias with vicious glee. "You have his word on the Angel that no harm will come to the Morgenstern girl or the Lightwood boy. They are his family, and he desires them by his side. So there is no sacrifice."

Clary felt something brush her cheek—it was Jace. He had kissed her, quickly, and she remembered Sebastian's Judas kiss the night before and whirled to catch at him, but he was gone already, away from all of them, striding out onto the aisle of stairs between the benches. "I will go!" he shouted, and his voice rang through the room. "I will go, willingly." His sword was in his hand. He threw it down, where it clattered on the steps. "I will go with Sebastian," he said, into the silence that followed. "Just leave Clary out of it. Let her stay. Take me alone."

"Jace, *no*," Alec said, but his voice was drowned by the clamor that ran through the room, voices rising like smoke and curling up toward the ceiling, and Jace stood calmly, with his hands out, showing he had no weapons, his hair shining under the light of the runes. A sacrificial angel.

Matthias Gonzales laughed. "There will be no bargain without Clarissa," he said. "Sebastian demands her, and I deliver what my master demands."

"You think we're fools," Jace said. "Actually, I know better than that. You don't *think* at all. You're a mouthpiece for a demon, that's all you are. You don't care about anything anymore. Not family or blood or honor. You're no longer human."

Matthias sneered. "Why would anyone want to be human?"

"Because your bargain is worthless," said Jace. "So we give ourselves up, and Sebastian returns his hostages. Then what? You've been at such pains to tell us how much better he is than the Nephilim, how much stronger, how much cleverer. How he can strike at us here in Alicante, and all our wards and all our guards can't keep him out. How he'll destroy us all. If you want to bargain with someone, you offer them a chance to *win*. If you were human, you'd know that."

In the silence that followed, Clary thought you could have heard a drop of blood strike the floor. Matthias was still, his blade still pinned against Jia's throat, his lips shaping words as if he were whispering something, or reciting something he had heard—

Or listening, she realized, listening to words being whispered into his ear...

"You cannot win," Matthias said finally, and Jace laughed, that sharp acerbic laugh Clary had first fallen in love with. Not a sacrificial angel, she thought, but an avenging one, all gold and blood and fire, confident even in the face of defeat.

"You see what I mean," Jace said. "Then what does it matter if we die now or die later—"

"You cannot *win*," said Matthias, "but you can *survive*. Those of you who choose it can be changed by the Infernal Cup; you will become soldiers of the Morning Star, and you will rule the world with Jonathan Morgenstern as your leader. Those who choose to remain the children of Raziel may do so, as long as you remain in Idris. The borders of Idris will be sealed, closing it away from the rest of the world, which will belong to us. This land granted you by the Angel, you will keep, and keeping within its borders, you will be safe. That, you can be promised."

Jace glared. "Sebastian's promises mean nothing."

"His promises are all you have," said Matthias. "Keep your alliance with Downworlders, stay within the borders of Idris, and you will survive. But this offer stands only so long as you give yourselves willingly up to our master. You and Clarissa both. There is no negotiation."

Clary looked slowly around the room. Some of the Nephilim looked anxious, others fearful, others full of rage. And others were calculating. She remembered the day when she had stood up in the Hall of Accords in front of these same people and showed them the Binding rune that could win their war. They had been grateful, then. But this was also the same Council who had voted to cease searching for Jace when Sebastian had taken him, because one boy's life had not been worth their resources.

Especially when that boy had been Valentine's adopted son.

She had thought once that there were good people and bad people, that there was a side of light and a side of darkness, but she no longer thought that. She had seen evil, in her brother and her father, the evil of good intentions gone wrong and the evil of sheer desire for power. But in goodness there was also no safety: Virtue could cut like a knife, and the fire of Heaven was blinding.

She moved away from Alec and Isabelle, felt Simon catch at her arm. She turned and looked at him, and shook her head. *You have to let me do this.*

His dark eyes pleaded with her. "Don't," he whispered.

"He said both of us," she whispered back. "If Jace goes to Sebastian without me, Sebastian will kill him."

"He'll kill you both anyway." Isabelle was nearly crying with frustration. "You can't go, and Jace can't either—*Jace!*"

Jace turned to look at them. Clary saw his expression change as he realized she was struggling to get to him. He shook his head, mouthing the word: "No."

"Give us time," Robert Lightwood called. "Give us some time to cast a vote, at least."

Matthias drew the knife away from Jia's throat and held it aloft; his other arm circled her, his hand gripping the front of her robes. He raised the knife toward the ceiling, and light sparked off it at the gesture. "Time," he sneered. "Why should Sebastian give you time?"

A sharp singing noise cut the air. Clary saw something bright shoot past her, and heard the noise of metal striking metal as an arrow slammed into the knife Matthias held above Jia's head, knocking it free of his grasp. Clary whipped her head sideways and saw Alec, his bow raised, the string still vibrating.

Matthias let out a roar and staggered back, his hand bleeding. Jia darted away from him as he dived for his fallen blade. Clary heard Jace call out *"Nakir!"* He had drawn a seraph blade from his belt and its light illuminated the hall. "Get out of my *way!*" he shouted, and began to shoulder his way down the steps, toward the dais.

"No!" Alec, dropping his bow, flung himself over the back of the row of benches, and dived on top of Jace, knocking him to the ground just as the dais went up in flames like a bonfire doused with gasoline. Jia cried out and leaped from the platform into the crowd; Kadir caught her and lowered her gently as all the Shadowhunters turned to stare at the rising flames.

"What the hell," Simon whispered, his fingers still clasped around Clary's arm. She could see Matthias, a black shadow at the heart of the flames. They were clearly not harming him; he seemed to be laughing, throwing up his arms over and over as if he were a conductor directing an orchestra of fire. The room was full of shrieks and the stink and crackle of burning wood. Aline had run to clutch at her bleeding mother, weeping; Helen was watching helplessly as, along with Julian, she tried to shield the younger Blackthorns from what was happening below.

No one was shielding Emma, though. She was standing apart from the group, her small face white with shock as, over the already horrible sounds filling the room, Matthias's cries pierced the din: "Two days, Nephilim! You have two days to decide your fate! And then you will all burn! You will burn in the fires of Hell, and the ashes of Edom will cover your bones!"

His voice rose to an unearthly shriek and was suddenly silenced, as the flames dropped away and he disappeared along with them. The last of the embers licked across the floor, their glowing tips barely touching the message still scrawled in ichor across the dais.

Veni.

I HAVE COME.

It had taken Maia two minutes of deep breathing outside the apartment door before she could bring herself to slide the key into the lock.

Everything in the hallway seemed normal, eerily so. Jordan's coats, and Simon's, hung on pegs in the narrow entranceway. The walls were decorated with street signs bought from flea markets.

She moved into the living room, which seemed frozen in time: The TV was on, the screen showing dark static, the two game controllers still on the couch. They'd forgotten to turn off the coffeepot. She went and flipped the switch, trying as hard as she could to ignore all the pictures of herself and Jordan stuck to the fridge: them on the Brooklyn Bridge, drinking coffee at the Waverly Place diner, Jordan laughing and showing off his fingernails, which Maia had painted blue and green and red. She hadn't realized how *many* pictures he'd taken of them, as if he'd been trying to record every second of their interactions, lest they slip through his memories like water.

She had to steel herself again before she could go into the bedroom. The bed was still mussed and untucked—Jordan had never been particularly neat—his clothes scattered around the room. Maia went across the room to the bureau where she'd kept her own belongings and stripped off Leila's clothes.

With relief she threw on her own jeans and T-shirt. She was reaching to pull out a coat when the doorbell rang.

Jordan had kept his weapons, issued to him by the Praetor, in the trunk at the foot of the bed. She flung the trunk open and scooped up a heavy iron vial with a cross carved into the front.

She flung on her coat and stalked into the living room, the vial in her pocket, her fingers wrapped around it. She reached out and yanked the front door open.

The girl who stood on the other side had dark hair falling sheer to her shoulders. Against it her skin was dead white, her lips dark red. She wore a severely tailored black suit; she was a modern Snow White in blood, char, and ice. "You called me," she said. "Jordan Kyle's girlfriend, am I correct?"

Lily—she's one of the smartest of the vampire clan. Knows everything. She and Raphael were always thick as thieves.

"Don't act like you don't know, Lily," Maia snapped. "You've been here before; I'm pretty sure you grabbed Simon from this apartment for Maureen."

"And?" Lily crossed her arms, making her expensive suit crackle. "Are you going to invite me in, or not?"

"I'm not," said Maia. "We're going to talk here, in the hallway."

"Dull." Lily leaned back against the wall with its peeling paint, and made a face. "Why did you summon me here, werewolf?"

"Maureen is crazy," said Maia. "Raphael and Simon are gone. Sebastian Morgenstern is murdering Downworlders to make a point to the Nephilim. And maybe it's time for the vampires and lycanthropes to talk. Even to ally."

"Well, aren't you as cute as a bug's ear," Lily said, and stood up straight. "Look, Maureen's crazy, but she's still the clan leader. And I can tell you one thing. She isn't going to parley with some jumped-up pack member who's lost the plot because her boyfriend died."

Maia tightened her grip on the bottle in her hand. She yearned to throw the contents in Lily's face, so much so that it frightened her.

"Call me when you're the pack leader." There was a dark light in the vampire girl's eyes, as if she were trying to tell Maia something without saying the words. "And we'll talk then."

Lily turned and clicked off down the hallway on her high heels. Slowly Maia loosened her grip on the bottle of holy water in her pocket.

"Nice shot," Jace said.

"You don't need to make fun of me." Alec and Jace were in one of the Gard's dizzying array of meeting rooms—not the same room Jace had been in earlier with Clary, but another more austere room in an older part of the Gard. The walls were stone, and there was one long bench that ran across the west wall. Jace was kneeling on it, his jacket thrown aside, the right sleeve of his shirt rolled up.

"I'm not," Jace protested as Alec set the tip of his stele to the bare skin of Jace's arm. As the dark lines began to spiral out from the *adamas*, Jace couldn't help but remember another day, in Alicante, Alec bandaging Jace's hand, telling him angrily: *You can heal slow and ugly, like a mundane.* Jace had put his hand through a window that day; he'd deserved everything Alec had said to him.

Alec exhaled slowly; he was always very careful with his runes, especially the *iratzes*. He seemed to feel the slight burn, the sting against the skin that Jace felt, though Jace had never minded the pain—the map of white scars that covered his biceps and ran down to his forearm attested to that. There was a special strength to a rune given by your *parabatai*. It was why they had sent the two of them away, while the rest of the Lightwood family met in the Consul's offices, so that Alec could heal Jace as quickly and efficiently as possible. Jace had been rather startled; he'd half-expected them to make him sit through the meeting with his wrist blue and swelling up.

"I'm not," Jace said again, as Alec finished and stepped back to examine his handiwork. Already Jace could feel the numbing of the *iratze* spreading through his veins, soothing the pain in his arm, sealing his split lip. "You hit Matthias's knife from halfway across an amphitheater. Clean shot, didn't hit Jia at all. And he was moving around, too."

"I was motivated." Alec slid his stele back into his belt. His dark hair hung raggedly into his eyes; he hadn't gotten it properly cut since he and Magnus had broken up.

Magnus. Jace closed his eyes. "Alec," he said. "I'll go. You know I'll go."

"You're saying that like you think it'll reassure me," said Alec. "You think I want you to give yourself up to Sebastian? Are you crazy?"

"I think it might be the only way to get Magnus back." Jace spoke into the darkness behind his eyelids.

"And you're willing to barter Clary's life too?" Alec's tone was acid. Jace's eyes flew open; Alec was looking at him steadily, but without expression.

"No," Jace said, hearing the defeat in his own voice. "I couldn't do that."

"And I wouldn't ask it," said Alec. "This—this is what Sebastian's trying to do. Drive wedges between all of us, using the people we love as hooks to pull us apart. We shouldn't let him."

"When did you get so wise?" Jace said.

Alec laughed, a short, brittle laugh. "The day I'm wise is the day you're careful."

"Maybe you've always been wise," Jace said. "I remember when I asked if you wanted to be *parabatai*, and you said you needed a day to think about it. And then you came back and said yes, and when I asked you why you agreed to do it, you said it was because I needed someone to look after me. You were right. I never thought about it again, because I never had to. I had you, and you've always looked after me. Always."

Alec's expression tightened; Jace could almost see the tension thrumming through his *parabatai*'s veins. "Don't," Alec said. "Don't talk like that."

"Why not?"

"Because," Alec said. "That's how people talk when they think they're going to die."

"If Clary and Jace are delivered to Sebastian, then they will be delivered to their deaths," said Maryse.

They were in the offices of the Consul, likely the most plushly decorated room in all the Gard. A thick rug was underfoot, the stone walls spread with tapestries, a massive desk standing diagonally across the room. On one side of it was Jia Penhallow, the cut on her throat sealing as her *iratzes* took effect. Behind her chair stood her husband, Patrick, his hand on her shoulder.

Facing them were Maryse and Robert Lightwood; to Clary's surprise, she, Isabelle, and Simon had been allowed to stay in the room as well. It was her own and Jace's fate they were discussing, she supposed, but then the Clave had never before seemed to have much in the way of a problem with deciding people's fates without their input.

"Sebastian says he won't hurt them," said Jia.

"His word's worthless," Isabelle snapped. "He lies. And it doesn't mean anything if he swears on the Angel, because he doesn't care about the Angel. He serves Lilith, if he serves anyone."

There was a soft click, and the door opened, admitting Alec and Jace. Jace and Alec had tumbled down quite a few stairs, and Jace had gotten the worst of it, with a split lip and a wrist that had either been broken or twisted. It looked back to normal now, though; he tried to smile at Clary as he came in, but his eyes were haunted.

"You have to understand how the Clave will see it," Jia said. "You fought Sebastian at the Burren. They were told, but they didn't *see*, not until the Citadel, the difference between Endarkened warriors and Shadowhunters. There has never been a race of warriors more powerful than Nephilim. Now there is."

"The reason he attacked the Citadel was to gather information," said Jace. "He wanted to know what the Nephilim were capable of: not just the group we could scramble together at the Burren, but warriors sent to fight by the Clave. He wanted to see how they stood up against his forces."

"He was taking our measure," said Clary. "He was weighing us in the balance."

Jia looked at her. "*Mene mene tekel upharsin*," she said softly.

"You were right when you said Sebastian doesn't want to fight a big battle," said Jace. "His interest is to fight a lot of small battles where he can Turn a bunch of Nephilim. Add to his forces. And it might have worked, to stay in Idris, let him bring the battle here, break the tide of his army on the rocks of Alicante. Except now that he's taken the Downworld representatives, staying here won't work. Without us watching, with Downworld turning against us, the Accords will fall apart. The world—will fall apart."

Jia's gaze went to Simon. "What do you say, Downworlder? Was Matthias correct? If we refuse to ransom Sebastian's hostages, will it mean war with Downworld?"

Simon looked startled to be addressed in such an official capacity. Consciously or unconsciously, his hand had gone to Jordan's medallion at his throat; he held it as he spoke. "I think," he said with reluctance, "that though there are some Downworlders who would be reasonable, the vampires wouldn't. They already believe Nephilim set a light price on their lives. Warlocks..." He shook his head. "I don't really understand warlocks. Or faeries—I mean, the Seelie Queen seems to look out for herself. She helped Sebastian with these." He held up his hand, where his ring glimmered.

"It seems likely that was less about helping Sebastian than about her own insatiable desire to know everything," Robert said. "It is true, she did spy on you, but Sebastian was not known to be our enemy then. More tellingly, Meliorn has sworn up and down that the Fair Folk's loyalty is to us and that Sebastian is their enemy, and faeries cannot lie."

Simon shrugged. "Anyway, my point is that I don't understand how they think. But the werewolves love Luke. They'll be desperate to get him back."

"He used to be a Shadowhunter—" Robert began.

"That makes it worse," said Simon, and it wasn't Simon, Clary's oldest friend, talking but someone else, someone knowledge-able about Downworld politics. "They see the way Nephilim treat Downworlders who were once Nephilim as evidence of the fact that Shadowhunters believe Downworld blood is tainted. Magnus told me once about a dinner he was invited to at an Institute for Downworlders and Shadowhunters alike; afterward the Shadowhunters threw out all the plates. Because Downworlders had touched them."

"Not all Nephilim are like that," Maryse said.

Simon shrugged. "The first time I ever came to the Gard, it was because Alec brought me," he said. "I trusted that the Consul only wanted to talk to me. Instead I was thrown into prison and starved. Luke's own *parabatai* told him to kill himself when Luke was Turned. The Praetor Lupus has been burned to the ground by someone who, even if he is an enemy of Idris, is a Shadowhunter."

"So you are saying, yes, it will be war?" asked Jia.

"It's already war, isn't it?" said Simon. "Weren't you just injured in a battle? I'm just saying—Sebastian is using the cracks in your alliances to break you, and he's doing it well. Maybe he doesn't understand humans, I'm not saying he does, but he does under-stand evil and betrayal and selfishness, and that's something that applies to everything with a mind and a heart." He closed his mouth abruptly, as if afraid that he'd said too much.

"So you think that we should do as Sebastian asks, send Jace and Clary to him?" asked Patrick.

"No," Simon said. "I think he always lies, and sending them

won't help anything. Even if he swears, he lies, like Isabelle said." He looked at Jace, and then Clary. "*You* know," he said. "You know him better than anyone; you know he never means what he says. Tell them."

Clary shook her head, mutely. It was Isabelle who answered for her: "They can't," she said. "It would seem like they were begging for their lives, and neither of them are going to do that."

"I've already volunteered," said Jace. "I said I would go. You *know* why he wants me." He threw his arms wide. Clary wasn't surprised to see that the heavenly fire was visible against the skin of his forearms, like golden wires. "The heavenly fire injured him at the Burren. He's afraid of it, so he's afraid of me. I saw it on his face, in Clary's room."

There was a long silence. Jia slumped back in her chair. "You're right," she said. "I don't disagree with any of you. But I cannot control the Clave, and there are those among them who will choose what they see as safety, and yet others who hate the idea that we allied with Downworlders in the first place and will welcome a chance to refuse. If Sebastian wished to splinter the Clave into factions, and I am sure he did, he chose a good way to do it." She looked around at the Lightwoods, at Jace and Clary, the Consul's steady dark gaze resting on each of them in turn. "I would love to hear suggestions," she added, a little dryly.

"We could go into hiding," Isabelle said immediately. "Disappear to a place where Sebastian will never find us; you can report back to him that Jace and Clary fled despite your attempts to keep us. He can't blame you for that."

"A reasonable person wouldn't blame the Clave," said Jace. "Sebastian's not reasonable."

"And there isn't anywhere we can hide from him," Clary said. "He found me in Amatis's house. He can find me anywhere. Maybe Magnus could have helped us, but—"

"There are other warlocks," said Patrick, and Clary chanced a glimpse at Alec's face. It looked like it had been carved out of stone.

"You can't count on them helping us, no matter what you pay them, not now," Alec said. "That's the point of the kidnapping. They won't come to the aid of the Clave, not until they see whether we come to their aid first."

There was a knock on the door and in came two Silent Brothers, their robes glimmering like parchment in the witchlight. "Brother Enoch," said Patrick, by way of greeting, "and—"

"Brother Zachariah," said the second of them, drawing his hood down.

Despite what Jace had hinted at in the Council room, the sight of the now-human Zachariah was a shock. He was barely recognizable, only the dark runes on the arches of his cheekbones a reminder of what he had been. He was slender, almost slight, and tall, with a delicate and very human elegance to the shape of his face, and dark hair. He looked perhaps twenty.

"Is that," Isabelle said in a low, amazed voice, "*Brother Zachariah?* When did he get hot?"

"Isabelle!" Clary whispered, but Brother Zachariah either hadn't heard her or had great self-restraint. He was looking at Jia, and then, to Clary's surprise, said something in a language she didn't know.

Jia's lips trembled for a moment. Then they tightened into a hard line. She turned to the others. "Amalric Kriegsmesser is dead," she said.

It took Clary, numb from a dozen shocks in as many hours, several seconds to remember who that was: the Endarkened who had been captured in Berlin and brought to the Basilias while the Brothers searched for a cure.

"Nothing we tried on him worked," said Brother Zachariah. His spoken voice was musical. He sounded British, Clary thought;

she'd only ever heard his voice in her mind before, and telepathic communication apparently wiped out accents. "Not a single spell, not a single potion. Finally we had him drink from the Mortal Cup."

It destroyed him, said Enoch. *Death was instantaneous.*

"Amalric's body must be sent through a Portal to the warlocks in the Spiral Labyrinth, to study," Jia said. "Perhaps if we act quickly enough, she—*they* can learn something from his death. Some clue to a cure."

"His poor family," said Maryse. "They will not even see him burned and buried in the Silent City."

"He is not Nephilim anymore," said Patrick. "If he were to be buried, it would be at the crossroads outside Brocelind Forest."

"Like my mother was," said Jace. "Because she killed herself. Criminals, suicides, and monsters are buried at the place where all roads cross, right?"

He had his false bright voice on, the one Clary knew covered up anger or pain; she wanted to move closer to him, but the room was too full of people.

"Not always," said Brother Zachariah in his soft voice. "One of the young Longfords was at the battle at the Citadel. He found himself forced to kill his own *parabatai*, who had been Turned by Sebastian. Afterward he turned his sword on himself and cut his wrists. He will be burned with the rest of the dead today, with all attendant honors."

Clary remembered the young man she had seen at the Citadel, standing over a dead Shadowhunter in red gear, weeping as the battle raged around him. She wondered if she should have stopped, spoken to him, if it would have helped, if there was anything she could have done.

Jace looked as if he were going to throw up. "This is why you have to let me go after Sebastian," he said. "This can't keep happening. These battles, fighting the Endarkened—he'll find worse things to do. Sebastian always does. Being Turned is worse than dying."

"*Jace*," Clary said sharply, but Jace shot her a look, half-desperate and half-pleading. A look that begged her not to doubt him. He leaned forward, hands on the Consul's desk.

"Send me to him," Jace said. "And I'll try to kill him. I have the heavenly fire. It's our best chance."

"It's not an issue of *sending* you anywhere," said Maryse. "We can't send you to him; we don't know where Sebastian is. It's an issue of letting him take you."

"Then let him take me—"

"Absolutely not." Brother Zachariah looked grave, and Clary remembered what he had said to her, once: *If the chance comes before me to save the last of the Herondale bloodline, I consider that of higher importance than the fealty I render the Clave.* "Jace Herondale," he said. "The Clave can choose to obey Sebastian or defy him, but either way you cannot be given up to him in the way he will expect. We must surprise him. Otherwise we are simply delivering to him the only weapon that we know he fears."

"Do you have another suggestion?" asked Jia. "Do we draw him out? Use Jace and Clary to capture him?"

"You can't use them as bait," Isabelle protested.

"Maybe we could separate him from his forces?" suggested Maryse.

"You can't trick Sebastian," Clary said, feeling exhausted. "He doesn't care about reasons or excuses. There's only him and what he wants, and if you get between those two things, he'll destroy you."

Jia leaned across the table. "Maybe we can convince him he wants something else. Is there anything else we could offer him as a bargaining chip?"

"No," Clary whispered. "There's nothing. Sebastian is..." But how did you explain her brother? How could you explain staring into the dark heart of a black hole? *Imagine if you were the last Shadowhunter left on earth, imagine if all your family and friends were dead, imagine if there were no one left who even believed in what you were. Imagine if you were on the earth in a billion, billion years, after the sun had scorched away all the life, and you were crying out from inside yourself for just one single living creature to still draw breath alongside you, but there was nothing, only rivers of fire and ashes. Imagine being that lonely, and then imagine there was only one way you could think of to fix it. Then imagine what you would do to make that thing happen.* "No. He won't change his mind. Not ever."

A murmur of voices broke out. Jia clapped her hands for silence. "Enough," she said. "We're going around in circles. It is time for the Clave and Council to discuss the situation."

"If I might make a suggestion." Brother Zachariah's eyes swept the room, thoughtful under dark lashes, before coming to rest on Jia. "The funeral rites for the Citadel dead are about to begin. You will be expected there, Consul, as will you, Inquisitor. I would suggest that Clary and Jace remain at the Inquisitor's house, considering the contention surrounding them, and that the Council gather after the rites."

"We have a right to be at the meeting," said Clary. "This decision concerns us. It's *about* us."

"You will be summoned," said Jia, her gaze not resting on Clary or Jace, but skipping past them, sweeping over Robert and Maryse, Brother Enoch and Zachariah. "Until then, rest; you will need your energy. It could be a long night."

12

THE FORMAL NIGHTMARE

The bodies were burning on orderly rows of pyres that had been set up along the road to Brocelind Forest. The sun was beginning to set behind a cloudy white sky, and as each pyre went up, it burst in orange sparks. The effect was oddly beautiful, although Jia Penhallow doubted that any of the mourners gathered on the plain thought so.

For some reason a rhyme she had learned as a child was repeating itself in her head.

> *Black for hunting through the night*
> *For death and mourning the color's white*
> *Gold for a bride in her wedding gown*
> *And red to call enchantment down.*
> *White silk when our bodies burn,*
> *Blue banners when the lost return.*
> *Flame for the birth of a Nephilim,*
> *And to wash away our sins.*
> *Gray for knowledge best untold,*

Bone for those who don't grow old.
Saffron lights the victory march,
Green will mend our broken hearts.
Silver for the demon towers,
And bronze to summon wicked powers.

Bone for those who don't grow old. Brother Enoch, in his bone-colored robes, was striding up and down the line of pyres. Shadowhunters stood or knelt or cast into the orange flames handfuls of the pale white Alicante flowers that grew even in the winter.

"Consul." The voice at her shoulder was soft. She turned to see Brother Zachariah—the boy who had once been Brother Zachariah, at least—standing at her shoulder. "Brother Enoch said you wished to speak to me."

"Brother Zachariah," she began, and then paused. "Is there another name by which you wish to be called? The name you had before you became a Silent Brother?"

"'Zachariah' will do fine for now," he said. "I am not yet ready to reclaim my old name."

"I have heard," she said, and paused, for the next bit was awkward, "that one of the warlocks of the Spiral Labyrinth, Theresa Gray, is someone whom you knew and cared for during your mortal life. And for someone who has been a Silent Brother as long as you have, that must be a rare thing."

"She is all I have left from that time," said Zachariah. "She and Magnus. I would have wished to talk to Magnus, if I could have, before he—"

"Would you like to go to the Spiral Labyrinth?" Jia interrupted.

Zachariah looked down at her with startled eyes. He looked about the same age as her daughter, Jia thought, his lashes impossibly long, his eyes both young and old at the same time. "You're releasing me from Alicante? Aren't all warriors needed?"

"You have served the Clave for more than a hundred and thirty years. We can ask no more of you."

He looked back at the pyres, at the black smoke smearing the air. "How much does the Spiral Labyrinth know? Of the attacks on the Institutes, the Citadel, the representatives?"

"They are students of lore," said Jia. "Not warriors or politicians. They know of what happened at the Burren. We have discussed Sebastian's magic, possible cures for the Endarkened, ways to strengthen the wards. They do not ask beyond that—"

"And you do not tell," said Zachariah. "So they do not know of the Citadel, the representatives?"

Jia set her jaw. "I suppose you will say I must tell them."

"No," he said. He had his hands in his pockets; his breath was visible on the cold clear air. "I will not say that."

They stood side by side, in the snow and silence, until, to her surprise, he spoke again:

"I will not go to the Spiral Labyrinth. I will stay in Idris."

"But don't you want to see her?"

"I want to see Tessa more than I want anything else in the world," said Zachariah. "But if she knew more of what was happening here, she would want to be here and fight beside us, and I find that I do not want that." His dark hair fell forward as he shook his head. "I find that as I waken from being a Silent Brother, I am capable of not wanting that. Perhaps it is selfishness. I am not sure. But I am sure that the warlocks in the Spiral Labyrinth are safe. Tessa is safe. If I go to her, I will be safe as well, but I will also be hiding. I am not a warlock; I cannot be a help to the Labyrinth. I can be a help here."

"You could go to the Labyrinth and return. It would be complicated, but I could request—"

"No," he said quietly. "I cannot see Tessa face-to-face and keep from telling her the truth about what is happening here. And more than that, I cannot go to Tessa and present myself to her as a mortal man, as a Shadowhunter, and not tell her the feelings I had for her when I was—" He broke off. "That my feelings are unchanged. I cannot offer her that, and then return to a place where I might be killed. Better she thinks there never was a chance for us."

"Better you think it as well," said Jia, looking at his face, at the hope and longing that was painted there clearly for anyone to see. She looked over at Robert and Maryse Lightwood, standing a distance apart from each other in the snow. Not far away was her own daughter, Aline, leaning her head against Helen Blackthorn's curly blond one. "We Shadowhunters, we put ourselves in danger, every hour, every day. I think sometimes we are reckless with our hearts the way we are with our lives. When we give them away, we give every piece. And if we do not get what we so desperately need, how do we live?"

"You think she might not still love me," said Zachariah. "After all this time."

Jia said nothing. It was, after all, exactly what she thought.

"It is a reasonable question," he said. "And perhaps she does not. As long as she is alive and well and happy in this world, I will find a way to be happy as well, even if it is not beside her." He looked over at the pyres, at the lengthening shadows of the dead. "Which body is that of young Longford? The one who killed his *parabatai*?"

"There." Jia pointed. "Why do you want to know?"

"It is the worst thing I can imagine ever having to do. I would not have been brave enough. Since there is someone who was, I wish to pay my respects to him," said Zachariah, and he walked away across the snow-dusted ground toward the fires.

"The funeral's over," Isabelle said. "Or at least, the smoke's stopped rising." She was perched on the windowsill of her room in the Inquisitor's house. The room was small and white-painted, with flowered curtains. Not very Isabelle, Clary thought, but then it would have been hard to replicate Isabelle's powder-and-glitter-strewn room in New York on short notice.

"I was reading my *Codex* the other day." Clary finished buttoning up the blue wool cardigan she'd changed into. She couldn't stand to keep on for one more second the sweater she'd been wearing all yesterday, had slept in, and that Sebastian had touched. "And I was thinking. Mundanes kill one another all the time. We—they—have wars, all kinds of wars, and slaughter one another, but this is the first time Nephilim have ever had to kill other Shadowhunters. When Jace and I were trying to convince Robert to let us go through to the Citadel, I couldn't understand why he was being so stubborn. But I think I kind of get it now. I think he couldn't believe that Shadowhunters could really pose a threat to other Shadowhunters. No matter what we told them about the Burren."

Isabelle laughed shortly. "That's charitable of you." She pulled her knees up to her chest. "You know, your mom took me to the Adamant Citadel with her. They said I would have made a good Iron Sister."

"I saw them at the battle," said Clary. "The Sisters. They were beautiful. And scary. Like looking at fire."

"But they can't get married. They can't be with anyone. They live forever, but they don't—they don't have lives." Isabelle rested her chin on her knees.

"There's all different ways of living," said Clary. "And look at Brother Zachariah—"

Isabelle glanced up. "I heard my parents talking about him on the way to the Council meeting today," she said. "They said what happened to him was a miracle. I've never heard of anyone ending being a Silent Brother before. I mean they can die, but reversing the spells, it shouldn't be possible."

"A lot of things shouldn't be possible," Clary said, raking her fingers through her hair. She wanted a shower, but she couldn't bear the thought of standing there alone, under the water. Thinking about her mother. About Luke. The idea of losing either of them, never mind both of them, was as terrifying as the idea of being abandoned out at sea: a tiny speck of humanity surrounded by miles of water around and below, and empty sky above. Nothing to moor her to earth.

Mechanically she started to divide her hair into two braids. A second later Isabelle had appeared behind her in the mirror. "Let me do that," she said gruffly, and took hold of the strands of Clary's hair, her fingers working the curls expertly.

Clary closed her eyes and let herself be lost for a moment in the sensation of someone else taking care of her. When she had been a little girl, her mother had braided her hair every morning before Simon had come to pick her up for school. She remembered his habit of undoing the ribbons while she was drawing, and hiding them in places—her pockets, her backpack—waiting for her to notice and throw a pencil at him.

It was impossible, sometimes, to believe that her life had once been so ordinary.

"Hey," Isabelle said, nudging her. "Are you okay?"

"I'm fine," Clary said. "I'm fine. Everything's fine."

"Clary." She felt Isabelle's hand on her hand, slowly unclosing Clary's fingers. Her hand was wet. Clary realized that she had been gripping one of Isabelle's hairpins so tightly that the ends had dug into her palm and blood was running down her wrist. "I don't—I don't even remember picking that up," she said numbly.

"I'll take it." Isabelle pulled it away. "You're not fine."

"I have to be fine," Clary said. "I *have* to be. I have to stay in control and not fall apart. For my mom and for Luke."

Isabelle made a gentle, noncommittal noise. Clary was aware that the other girl's stele was sweeping over the back of her hand,

and the flow of blood was slowing. She still felt no pain. There was only the darkness at the edge of her vision, the darkness that threatened to close in every time she thought about her parents. She felt like she was drowning, kicking at the edges of her own consciousness to keep herself alert and above the water.

Isabelle suddenly gasped and jumped back.

"What is it?" Clary asked.

"I saw a face, a face at the window—"

Clary seized Heosphoros from her belt and started to make her way across the room. Isabelle was right behind her, her silver-gold whip uncurling from her hand. It slashed forward, and the tip curled around the handle of the window and yanked it open. There was a yelp, and a small, shadowy figure fell forward onto the rug, landing on hands and knees.

Isabelle's whip snapped back into her grasp as she stared, wearing a rare look of astonishment. The shadow on the floor uncurled, revealing a diminutive figure clad in black, the smudge of a pale face, and a tousle of long blonde hair, coming free from a careless braid.

"*Emma?*" Clary said.

The southwest part of the Long Meadow in Prospect Park was deserted at night. The moon, half-full, shone down on the distant view of Brooklyn brownstones beyond the park, the outline of bare trees, and the space that had been cleared on the dry winter grass by the pack.

It was a circle, roughly twenty feet across, hemmed in by standing werewolves. The whole of the downtown New York pack was there: thirty or forty wolves, young and old.

Leila, her dark hair bound back in a ponytail, stalked to the center of the circle and clapped once for attention. "Members of the pack," she said. "A challenge has been issued. Rufus Hastings has challenged Bartholomew Velasquez for the seniority and leadership of the New York pack." There was a muttering in the crowd; Leila raised her voice. "This is an issue of temporary leadership in the absence of Luke Garroway. No discussion of replacing Luke as leader will be had at this time." She clasped her hands behind her back. "Please step forward, Bartholomew and Rufus."

Bat stepped forward into the circle, and a moment later Rufus followed. Both were dressed unseasonably in jeans, T-shirts, and boots, their arms bare despite the chill air.

"The rules of the challenge are these," said Leila. "Wolf must fight wolf without weapons save the weapons of tooth and claw. Because it is a challenge for leadership, the fight will be a fight to death, not to the blood. Whoever lives will be leader, and all other wolves will swear loyalty to him tonight. Do you understand?"

Bat nodded. He looked tense, his jaw set; Rufus was grinning all over, his arms swinging at his sides. He waved away Leila's words. "We all know how it works, kid."

Her lips compressed into a thin line. "Then you may begin," she said, though as she moved back into the circle with the others, she muttered, "Good luck, Bat" under her breath just loudly enough for everyone to hear her.

Rufus didn't seem bothered. He was still grinning, and the moment Leila stepped back into the circle with the pack, he lunged.

Bat sidestepped him. Rufus was big and heavy; Bat was lighter and a shade faster. He spun sideways, just missing Rufus's claws, and came back with an uppercut that snapped Rufus's head back. He pressed his advantage quickly, raining down blows that sent the other wolf stumbling back; Rufus's feet dragged along the ground as a low growl began in the depths of his throat.

His hands hung at his sides, his fingers clenched in. Bat swung again, landing a punch to Rufus's shoulder, just as Rufus turned and slashed out with his left hand. His claws were fully extended, massive and gleaming in the moonlight. It was clear he had sharpened them somehow. Each one was like a razor, and they raked across Bat's chest, slicing open his shirt, and his skin with it. Scarlet bloomed across Bat's rib cage.

"First blood," Leila called, and the wolves began to stamp, slowly, each raising their left foot and bringing it down in a regular beat, so that the ground seemed to echo like a drum.

Rufus grinned again and advanced on Bat. Bat swung and hit him, landing another punch to the jaw that brought blood to Rufus's mouth; Rufus turned his head to the side and spit red onto the grass—and kept coming. Bat backed up; his claws were out now, his eyes gone flat and yellow. He growled and flung out a kick; Rufus grabbed his leg and twisted, sending Bat to the ground. He flung himself after Bat, but the other werewolf had already rolled away, and Rufus landed on the ground in a crouch.

Bat staggered to his feet, but it was clear that he was losing blood. Blood had rolled down his chest and was soaking the waistband of his jeans, and his hands were wet with it. He slashed out with his claws; Rufus turned, taking the blow on his shoulder, four shallow cuts. With a snarl he seized Bat's wrist and twisted. The sound of snapping bone was loud, and Bat gasped and pulled back.

Rufus lunged. The weight of him bore Bat to the ground, slamming Bat's head hard against a tree root. Bat went limp.

The other wolves were still pounding the earth with their feet. Some of them were openly weeping, but none moved forward as Rufus sat up on Bat, one hand pressing him flat to the grass, the other raised, the razors of his fingers gleaming. He moved in for the killing blow—

"Stop." Maia's voice rang out through the park. The other wolves looked up in shock. Rufus grinned.

"Hey, little girl," he said.

Maia didn't move. She was in the middle of the circle. Somehow she had pushed past the line of wolves without them noticing. She wore cords and a denim jacket, her hair pulled tightly back. Her expression was severe, almost blank.

"I want to issue a challenge," she said.

"Maia," Leila said. "You know the law! 'When ye fight with a wolf of the pack, ye must fight him alone and afar, Lest others take part in the quarrel, and the pack be diminished by war.' You cannot interrupt the battle."

"Rufus is about to deliver the death blow," Maia said unemotionally. "Do you really feel like I need to wait that five minutes before I issue my challenge? I will, if Rufus is too scared to fight me with Bat still breathing—"

Rufus leaped off Bat's limp body with a roar, and advanced on Maia. Leila's voice rose in panic:

"Maia, get out of there! Once there's first blood, we can't stop the fight—"

Rufus lunged at Maia. His claws tore the edge of her jacket; Maia dropped to her knees and rolled, then came up onto her knees, her claws extended. Her heart was slamming against her rib cage, sending wave after wave of icy-hot blood through her veins. She could feel the sting of the cut on her shoulder. *First blood.*

The werewolves began to stamp the earth again, though this time they weren't silent. There was muttering and gasping in the ranks. Maia did her best to block it out, ignore it. She saw Rufus step toward her. He was a shadow, outlined by moonlight, and in that moment she saw not just him but also Sebastian, looming over her on the beach, a cold prince carved out of ice and blood.

Your boyfriend's dead.

Her fist clenched against the ground. As Rufus threw himself at her, razor claws extended, she rose and flung her handful of dirt and grass into his face.

He staggered back, choking and blinded. Maia stepped

forward and slammed her boot down on his foot; she felt the small bones shatter, heard him scream; in that moment, when he was distracted, she jammed her claws into his eyes.

A scream ripped from his throat, quickly cut off. He slumped backward, collapsing onto the grass with a loud crash that made her think of a tree falling. She looked down at her hand. It was covered in blood and smears of liquid: brain matter and vitreous humor.

She dropped to her knees and threw up in the grass. Her claws slid back in, and she wiped her hands on the ground, over and over, as her stomach spasmed. She felt a hand on her back and looked up to see Leila leaning over her. "Maia," she said softly, but her voice was drowned out by the pack chanting the name of their new leader: "Maia, Maia, Maia."

Leila's eyes were dark and concerned. Maia rose to her feet, wiping her mouth on the sleeve of her jacket, and hurried across the grass to Bat. She bent down beside him and touched her hand to his cheek. "Bat?" she said.

With an effort he opened his eyes. There was blood on his mouth, but he was breathing steadily. Maia guessed he was already healing from Rufus's blows. "I didn't know you fought dirty," he said with a half smile.

Maia thought of Sebastian and his glittering grin and the bodies on the beach. She thought of what Lily had told her. She thought of the Shadowhunters behind their wards, and of the fragility of the Accords and Council. *It's going to be a dirty war,* she thought, but that wasn't what she said out loud.

"I didn't know your name was Bartholomew." She picked up his hand, held it in her own bloody one. All around them the pack was still chanting. "Maia, Maia, Maia."

He closed his eyes. "Everyone's got their secrets."

* * *

"It almost doesn't seem to make a difference," said Jace, curled into the window seat in his and Alec's attic room. "It all feels like prison."

"Do you think that's a side effect of the fact that armed guards are standing all around the house?" Simon suggested. "I mean, just a thought."

Jace shot him an irritable look. "What is it about mundanes and their overwhelming compulsion to state the obvious?" he asked. He leaned forward, staring through the panes of the window. Simon might have been exaggerating slightly, but only slightly. The dark figures standing at cardinal points surrounding the Inquisitor's house might have been invisible to the untrained eye, but not to Jace's.

"I'm not a mundane," Simon said, an edge to his voice. "And what is it about Shadowhunters and their overwhelming compulsion to get themselves and everyone they care about killed?"

"Stop arguing." Alec had been leaning against the wall, in classical thinking pose, with his chin propped on his hand. "The guards are there to protect us, not keep us in. Have some perspective."

"Alec, you've known me for seven years," said Jace. "When have I ever had perspective?"

Alec glowered at him.

"Are you still mad because I broke your phone?" Jace said. "Because you broke my wrist, so I'd say we're even."

"It was sprained," Alec said. "Not broken. *Sprained*."

"Now who's arguing?" said Simon.

"Don't talk." Alec gestured at him with an expression of vague disgust. "Every time I look at you, I keep remembering coming in here and seeing you draped all over my sister."

Jace sat up. "I didn't hear about *this*."

"Oh, come on—" said Simon.

"Simon, you're blushing," observed Jace. "And you're a vampire and almost never blush, so this better be *really* juicy. And weird. Were bicycles involved in some kinky way? Vacuum cleaners? Umbrellas?"

"Big umbrellas, or the little kind you get with drinks?" Alec asked.

"Does it *matter*—" Jace began, and then broke off as Clary came into the room with Isabelle, holding a small girl by the hand. After a moment of shocked silence, Jace recognized her: Emma, the girl whom Clary had run off to comfort during the Council meeting. The one who'd looked at him with barely concealed hero worship. Not that he *minded* hero worship, but it was a bit odd to have a child dropped suddenly into the middle of what had, admittedly, begun to be a somewhat awkward conversation.

"Clary," he said. "Did you kidnap Emma Carstairs?"

Clary gave him an exasperated look. "No. She got here on her own."

"I came in through one of the windows," Emma supplied helpfully. "Like in *Peter Pan*."

Alec started to protest. Clary held her free hand up to stop him; her other hand was now on Emma's shoulder. "Everyone just be quiet for a second, okay?" Clary said. "She's not supposed to be here, yeah, but she came for a reason. She has information."

"That's right," Emma said in her small, determined voice. She was actually only about a head shorter than Clary, but then Clary was tiny. Emma would probably be tall one day. Jace tried to remember her father, John Carstairs—he was sure he'd seen him at Council meetings, and thought he recalled a tall, fair-haired man. Or had his hair been dark? The Blackthorns he remembered, of course, but the Carstairs had faded out of his memory.

Clary returned his sharp look with one that said: *Be nice.* Jace closed his mouth. He'd never given much thought to whether he liked children or not, though he'd always liked playing with Max.

Max had been surprisingly adept at strategy for such a little boy, and Jace had always liked setting him puzzles. The fact that Max had worshipped the ground he walked on hadn't hurt either.

Jace thought of the wooden soldier he'd given to Max, and closed his eyes in sudden pain. When he opened them again, Emma was looking at him. Not the way she'd looked at him when he'd found her with Clary in the Gard, that sort of startled half-impressed, half-frightened *You're Jace Lightwood* look, but with a little bit of worry. In fact, her whole posture was a mix of confidence that he was fairly sure she was faking, and clear fright. Her parents were dead, he thought, had died days ago. And he remembered a time, seven years before, when he'd faced the Lightwoods himself with the knowledge in his heart that his father had just died, and the bitter tang of the word "orphan" in his ears.

"Emma," he said as gently as he could. "How did you get to the window?"

"I climbed over the rooftops," she said, pointing out the window. "It wasn't that hard. Dormer windows are almost always bedrooms, so I climbed down to the first one, and—it was Clary's." She shrugged, as if what she'd done hadn't been either risky or impressive.

"It was mine, actually," said Isabelle, who was looking at Emma as if she were a fascinating specimen. Isabelle sat down on the trunk at the foot of Alec's bed, stretching out her long legs. "Clary lives over at Luke's."

Emma looked confused. "I don't know where that is. And everyone was talking about all of you being here. That's why I came."

Alec looked down at Emma with the half-fond, half-worried look of a much older brother. "Don't be afraid—" he began.

"I'm *not* afraid," she snapped. "I came here because you need help."

Jace felt his mouth quirk up involuntarily at the corner. "What kind of help?" he asked.

"I recognized that man today," she said. "The one who threatened the Consul. He came with Sebastian, to attack the Institute." She swallowed. "That place he said we would all burn in, Edom—"

"It's another word for 'Hell,'" said Alec. "Not a real place, you don't have to be worried—"

"She's not worried, Alec," Clary said. "Just listen."

"It *is* a place," said Emma. "When they attacked the Institute, I heard them. I heard one of them say that they could take Mark to Edom, and sacrifice him there. And when we escaped through the Portal, I heard her calling after us that we'd burn in Edom, that there was no real escape." Her voice shook. "The way they talked about Edom, I know it was a real place, or a real place to them."

"Edom," said Clary, remembering. "Valentine called Lilith something like that; he called her 'my Lady of Edom.'"

Alec's eyes met Jace's. Alec nodded, and slipped out of the room. Jace felt his shoulders relax minutely; in among the clamor of everything, it was good to have a *parabatai* who knew what you were thinking, without you having to say it. "Have you told anyone else about this?"

Emma hesitated, and then shook her head.

"Why not?" said Simon, who had been quiet until that moment. Emma looked at him, blinking; she was only twelve, Jace thought, and had probably barely encountered Downworlders up close before. "Why not tell the Clave?"

"Because I don't trust the Clave," said Emma in a small voice. "But I trust you."

Clary swallowed visibly. "Emma..."

"When we got here, the Clave questioned all of us, especially Jules, and they used the Mortal Sword to make sure we weren't lying. It hurts, but they didn't care. They used it on Ty and Livvy. They used it on *Dru.*" Emma sounded outraged. "They would probably have used it on Tavvy if he could talk. And it hurts. The Mortal Sword hurts."

"I know," Clary said, quietly.

"We've been staying with the Penhallows," Emma said. "Because of Aline and Helen, and because the Clave wants to keep an eye on us too. Because of what we saw. I was downstairs when they came back from the funeral, and I heard them talking, so—so I hid. A whole group of them, not just Patrick and Jia, but a lot of the other Institute heads too. They were talking about what they should do, what the Clave should do, whether they should turn over Jace and Clary to Sebastian, as if it was their choice. Their decision. But I thought it should be *your* decision. Some of them said it didn't matter whether you wanted to go or not—"

Simon was on his feet. "But Jace and Clary offered to go, practically begged to go—"

"We would have told them the truth." Emma pushed her tangled hair out of her face. Her eyes were enormous, brown shot through with bits of gold and amber. "They didn't have to use the Mortal Sword on us, we would have told the Council the truth, but they used it anyway. They used it on Jules until his hands—his hands were burned from it." Her voice shook. "So, I thought you should know what they were saying. They don't want you to know that it's not your choice, because they know Clary can make Portals. They know she can get out of here, and if she escapes, they think they'll have no way to bargain with Sebastian."

The door opened, and Alec came back into the room, carrying a book bound in brown leather. He was holding it in such a way as to obscure the title, but his eyes met Jace's, and he gave a slight nod, and then a glance toward Emma. Jace's heartbeat sped up; Alec had found something. Something he didn't like, judging from his grim expression, but something nonetheless.

"Did the Clave members you overheard give any sense of when they were going to decide what to do?" Jace asked Emma, partly to distract her, as Alec sat down on the bed, sliding the book behind him.

Emma shook her head. "They were still arguing when I left. I crawled out the top floor window. Jules told me not to, because I'd get killed, but I knew I wouldn't. I'm a good climber," she added with a tinge of pride. "And he worries too much."

"It's good to have people worry about you," said Alec. "It means they care. It's how you know they're good friends."

Emma's gaze went from Alec to Jace, curious. "Do you worry about him?" she asked Alec, surprising a laugh out of him.

"All the time," he said. "Jace could get himself killed putting his pants on in the morning. Being his *parabatai* is a full-time job."

"I wish I had a *parabatai*," Emma said. "It's like someone who's your family, but because they want to be, not because they have to be." She flushed, suddenly self-conscious. "Anyway. I don't think anyone should be punished for saving people."

"Is that why you trust us?" Clary asked, touched. "You think we save people?"

Emma toed the carpet with her boots. Then she looked up. "I knew about you," she said to Jace, blushing. "I mean, *everyone* knows about you. That you were Valentine's son, but then you weren't, you were Jonathan Herondale. And I don't think that meant anything to most people—most of them call you Jace Lightwood—but it made a difference to my dad. I heard him say to my mom that he'd thought the Herondales were all gone, that the family was dead, but you were the last of them, and he voted in the Council meeting for the Clave to keep looking for you because, he said, 'The Carstairs owe the Herondales.'"

"Why?" Alec said. "What do they owe them for?"

"I don't know," Emma said. "But I came because my dad would have wanted me to, even if it was dangerous."

Jace huffed a soft laugh. "Something tells me you don't care if things are dangerous." He crouched down, putting his eyes on a level with Emma's. "Is there anything else you can tell us? Anything else they said?"

She shook her head. "They don't know where Sebastian is. They don't know about the Edom thing—I mentioned it when I was holding the Mortal Sword, but I think they just thought it was another word for 'Hell.' They never asked me if I thought it was a real place, so I didn't say."

"Thanks for telling us. It's a help. A huge help. You should go," he added, as gently as he could, "before they notice you're gone. But from now on the Herondales owe the Carstairs. Okay? Remember that."

Jace stood up as Emma turned to Clary, who nodded and led her over to the window where Jace had been sitting earlier. Clary bent down and hugged the younger girl before reaching over to unlatch the window. Emma clambered out with the agility of a monkey. She swung herself up until only her dangling boots were visible, and a moment later those were gone too. Jace heard a light scraping overhead as she darted across the roof tiles, and then silence.

"I like her," Isabelle said finally. "She kind of reminds me of Jace when he was little, and stubborn, and acted like he was immortal."

"Two of those things still apply," said Clary, swinging the window shut. She sat down on the window seat. "I guess the big question is, do we tell Jia or anyone else on the Council what Emma told us?"

"That depends," said Jace. "Jia has to bow to what the whole Clave wants; she said so herself. If they decide that what they want is to toss us into a cage until Sebastian comes for us—well, that pretty much squanders any upper hand this information might give us."

"So it depends on if the information's actually useful or not," said Simon.

"Right," said Jace. "Alec, what did you find out?"

Alec pulled the book out from behind him. It was an *encyclopedia daemonica*, the sort of book every Shadowhunter library would have. "I thought Edom might be a name for one of the demon realms—"

"Well, everyone's been theorizing that Sebastian might be in a different dimension, since he's untrackable," said Isabelle. "But the demon dimensions—there are millions of them, and people can't just *go* there."

"Some are better known than others," said Alec. "The Bible and the Enochian texts mention quite a few, disguised and subsumed, of course, into stories and myths. Edom is mentioned as a wasteland—" He read out loud, his voice measured. "*And the streams of Edom shall be turned into pitch, and her soil into sulfur; her land shall become burning pitch. Night and day it shall not be quenched; its smoke shall go up forever. From generation to generation it shall lie waste; none shall pass through it forever and ever.*" He sighed. "And of course there's the legends about Lilith and Edom, that she was banished there, that she rules the place with the demon Asmodeus. That's probably why the Endarkened were talking about sacrificing Mark Blackthorn to her in Edom."

"Lilith protects Sebastian," said Clary. "If he was going to go to a demon realm, he'd go to hers."

"'*None shall pass through it forever and ever*' doesn't sound very encouraging," said Jace. "Besides, there's no way to get to the demon realms. Traveling from place to place in this world is one thing—"

"Well, there is a way, I think," said Alec. "A pathway that the Nephilim can't close, because it lies outside the jurisdiction of our Laws. It's old, older than Shadowhunters—old, wild magic." He sighed. "It's in the Seelie Court, and it is guarded by the Fair Folk. No human being has set foot on that pathway in more than a hundred years."

13

PAVED WITH GOOD INTENTIONS

Jace was prowling the room like a cat. The others watched him, Simon with one eyebrow cocked. "There's no other way to get there?" Jace asked. "We can't try to Portal?"

"We're not demons. We can Portal only within a dimension," said Alec.

"I know that, but if Clary experimented with the Portal runes—"

"I won't do it," Clary interrupted, putting her hand protectively over the pocket where her stele rested. "I won't put you all in danger. I Portaled myself and Luke to Idris and nearly got us killed. I'm not risking it."

Jace was still prowling. It was what he did when he was thinking; Clary knew that but looked at him worriedly all the same. He was closing and unclosing his hands, and murmuring under his breath. Finally he stopped. "Clary," he said. "You can make a Portal to the Seelie Court, right?"

"Yes," she said. "That I could do—I've been there; I remember it. But would we be safe? We haven't been invited, and the Fair Folk don't like incursions into their territory—"

"There's no 'we,'" Jace said. "None of you are coming. I'm going to do this alone."

Alec sprang to his feet. "I knew it, I bloody knew it, and absolutely not. Not a chance."

Jace cocked an eyebrow at him; he was outwardly calm, but Clary could see his tension in the set of his shoulders and the way he rocked forward slightly on the balls of his feet. "Since when do you say 'bloody'?"

"Since the situation *bloody* warrants it." Alec crossed his arms over his chest. "And I thought we were going to discuss telling the Clave?"

"We can't do that," Jace said. "Not if we're going to get to the demon realms through the Seelie Court. It's not like half the Clave can just pour into the Court; that would seem like an act of war against the Fair Folk."

"Whereas if it's just five of us we can sweet-talk them into letting us through?" Isabelle raised an eyebrow.

"We've parleyed with the Queen before," Jace said. "You went to the Queen when I—when Sebastian had me."

"And she tricked us into taking walkie-talkie rings she could listen in on," Simon said. "I wouldn't trust her further than I could throw a medium-sized elephant."

"I didn't say anything about trusting her. She'll do whatever's in her interest at the moment. We just have to make it her interest to let us have access to the road to Edom."

"We're still Shadowhunters," said Alec, "still representatives of the Clave. Whatever we do in Faerie, they'll answer for it."

"So we'll use tact and cleverness," said Jace. "Look, I'd love to make the Clave deal with the Queen and her court for us. But we don't have the time. They—Luke and Jocelyn and Magnus and Raphael—don't have the time. Sebastian's gearing up; he's speeding up his plans, his bloodlust. You don't know what he's like when he gets like this, but I do. *I do.*" He caught his breath; there was a thin sheen of sweat across his cheekbones. "Which is why I want to do this alone. Brother Zachariah said it to me: I *am* the heavenly fire. It's not like we can get another Glorious. We can't exactly summon another angel; we played that card."

"Fine," Clary said, "but even if you're the only source of heavenly fire, that doesn't mean you need to do this alone."

"She's right," Alec said. "We know that heavenly fire can hurt Sebastian. But we don't know it's the only thing that can hurt him."

"And it definitely doesn't mean you're the only one who can kill however many Endarkened Sebastian has standing around him," Clary pointed out. "Or that you can get yourself through the Seelie Court safely on your own or, after that, through some forsaken demon realm where you have to *find* Sebastian—"

"We can't track him because we're not in the same dimension," Jace said. He held up his wrist where Sebastian's silver bracelet glittered. "Once I'm in his world, I can track him. I've done it before—"

"*We* can track him," Clary said. "Jace, there's more to this than just finding him; this is huge, bigger than anything we've done. This isn't just about killing Sebastian; this is about the prisoners. It's a rescue mission. It's their lives on the line as well as ours." Her voice cracked.

Jace had paused his prowling; he looked from one of his friends to the other, almost pleading. "I just don't want anything to happen to you."

"Yeah, well, none of us want anything to happen to us either," said Simon. "But think ahead; what happens if you go and we stay? Sebastian wants Clary, wants her more than he wants you, and he can find her here in Alicante. Nothing's stopping him from coming again except a promise that he'll wait two days, and what are his promises worth? He could come for any of us at any time; he proved that with the Downworld representatives. We're sitting ducks here.

Better to go where he isn't expecting or looking for us."

"I will not hang back here in Alicante while Magnus is in danger," said Alec, in a surprisingly cold, adult voice. "Go without me, and you disrespect our *parabatai* oaths, you disrespect me as a Shadowhunter, and you disrespect the fact that this is my battle too."

Jace looked shocked. "Alec, I would never disrespect our oaths. You're one of the best Shadowhunters I know—"

"Which is why we come with you," said Isabelle. "You *need* us. You need Alec and me to back you up the way we always have. You need Clary's rune powers and Simon's vampire strength. This isn't just your fight. If you respect us as Shadowhunters and as your friends—all of us—then we go with you. It's that simple."

"I know," Jace said, softly. "I know I need you." He looked over at Clary, and she heard Isabelle's voice saying *you need Clary's rune powers* and remembered the first time she had ever seen him, Alec and Isabelle on either side of him, and how she had thought he looked dangerous.

It had never occurred to her that she was like him—that she was dangerous too.

"Thank you," he said, and cleared his throat. "Okay. Everyone get into gear, and pack bags. Pack for overland travel: water, what food you can grab, extra steles, blankets. And you," he added to Simon, "you might not need food, but if you have bottled blood, bring it. There might not be anything you can ... eat where we're going."

"There's always the four of you," Simon said, but he smiled a little, and Clary knew it was because Jace had included him among their number without a moment's hesitation. Finally Jace had accepted that where they went, Simon went too, whether he was a Shadowhunter or not.

"All right," Alec said. "Everyone meet back here in ten minutes.

Clary, get ready to create a Portal. And Jace?"

"Yes?"

"You'd better have a strategy for what we're going to do when we get to the Faerie Court. Because we're going to need it."

The maelstrom inside the Portal was almost a relief. Clary went last through the shining doorway, after the other four had stepped through, and she let the cold darkness take her like water pulling her down and under, stealing the breath from her lungs, making her forget everything but the clamor and the falling.

It was over too fast, the grip of the Portal releasing her to fall awkwardly, her backpack twisted underneath her, on the packed dirt floor of a tunnel. She caught her breath and rolled over, using a long, dangling root to pull herself upright. Alec, Isabelle, Jace, and Simon were picking themselves up around her, brushing off their clothes. It wasn't dirt they had fallen on, she realized, but a carpet of moss. More moss spread along the smooth brown tunnel walls, but it glowed with phosphorescent light. Small glowing flowers, like electric daisies, grew in among the moss, starring the green with white. Snaky roots dangled down from the roof of the tunnel, making Clary wonder what exactly was growing above ground. Various smaller tunnels branched off the main one, some of them too small to admit a human form.

Isabelle picked a piece of moss out of her hair and frowned. "Where are we exactly?"

"I aimed for just outside the throne room," Clary said. "We've been here. It just always looks different."

Jace had already moved down the main corridor. Even without the Soundless rune, he was as quiet as a cat on the soft moss. The others followed, Clary with her hand on the hilt of her sword. She was a little surprised at how short a time it had taken to become used to a weapon hovering at her side; if she reached for Heosphoros and found it not there, she thought, she would panic.

"Here," Jace said softly, motioning the rest of them to be quiet. They were in an archway, a curtain separating them from a larger room beyond. The last time Clary had been here, the curtain had been made out of living butterflies, and their struggles had made it rustle.

Today it was thorns, like the thorns that surrounded Sleeping Beauty's castle, thorns woven into one another so that they formed a dangling sheet. Clary could catch only glimpses of the room beyond—a glimmer of white and silver—but they could all hear the sound of laughing voices coming from the corridors around them.

Glamour runes didn't work on the Fair Folk; there was no way to hide from view. Jace was alert, his whole body tight. He carefully raised a dagger and parted the sheet of thorns as silently as he could. They all leaned in, staring.

The room beyond was a winter fairyland, the kind Clary had rarely seen, except in visits to Luke's farmhouse. The walls were sheets of white crystal, and the Queen reclined upon her divan, which was white crystal to match, shot through with veins of silver in the rock. The floor was covered in snow, and long icicles hung from the ceiling, each one bound around with ropes of gold-and-silver thorns. Bunches of white roses were piled around the room, scattered at the foot of the Queen's divan, wound through her red hair like a crown. Her dress was white and silver too, as diaphanous as a sheet of ice; one could glimpse her body through it, though not clearly. Ice and roses and the Queen. The effect was blinding. She was leaning back on her couch, her head tipped up, speaking to a heavily armored faerie knight. His armor was dark brown, the color of the trunk of a tree; one of his eyes was black, the other pale blue, almost white. For a moment Clary thought he had the head of a deer tucked under his big arm, but as she looked closer, she realized that it was a helmet, decorated with antlers.

"And how goes it with the Wild Hunt, Gwyn?" the Queen was asking. "The Gatherers of the Dead? I assume there were rich pickings for you at the Adamant Citadel the other night. I hear that the howls of the Nephilim tore the sky as they died."

Clary felt the Shadowhunters around her tense. She remembered lying beside Jace in a boat in Venice and watching the Wild Hunt go by overhead; a maelstrom of shouts and battle cries, horses whose hooves gleamed scarlet, hammering across the sky.

"So I have heard, my lady," Gwyn said in a voice so hoarse, it was barely understandable. It sounded like the scrape of a blade against rough bark. "The Wild Hunt comes when the ravens of the battlefield scream for blood: We gather our riders from among the dying. But we were not at the Adamant Citadel. The war games of Nephilim and Dark Ones are too rich for our blood. The Fair Folk mix poorly with demons and angels."

"You disappoint me, Gwyn," said the Queen, pouting. "This is a time of power for the Fair Folk; we gain, we rise, we achieve the world. We belong on the chessboards of power, as much as Nephilim do. I had hoped for your advice."

"Forgive me, lady," said Gwyn. "Chess is too delicate a game for us. I cannot advise you."

"But I gave you such a gift." The Queen sulked. "The Blackthorn boy. Shadowhunter and faerie blood together; it is rare. He will ride at your back, and demons will fear you. A gift from myself, and from Sebastian."

Sebastian. She said it comfortably, familiarly. There was fondness in her voice, if the Queen of Faeries could be said to be fond. Clary could hear Jace's breathing beside her: sharp and quick; the others were tense as well, panic chasing realization across their faces as the Queen's words sank in.

Clary felt Heosphoros grow cold in the grip of her hand. *A path to the demon realms that leads through faerie lands. The earth cracking open under Sebastian's feet. Sebastian bragging that he had allies.*

The Queen and Sebastian, giving the gift of a captured Nephilim child. Together.

"Demons already fear me, beautiful one," said Gwyn, and he smiled.

My beautiful one. The blood in Clary's veins was an icy river, singing down into her heart. Glancing down, she saw Simon move to cover Isabelle's hand with his, a quick reassuring gesture; Isabelle had gone white, and looked sick, as did Alec and Jace. Simon swallowed; the gold ring on his finger glittered, and she heard Sebastian's voice in her head:

Do you really think she'd let you get your hands on something that would let you communicate with your little friends without her being able to listen in? Since I took it from you, I've spoken to her, she's spoken to me—you were a fool to trust her, little sister. She likes to be on the winning side of things, the Seelie Queen. And that side will be ours, Clary. Ours.

"You owe me one favor, then, Gwyn, in exchange for the boy," said the Queen. "I know that the Wild Hunt serves its own laws, but I would request your presence at the next battle."

Gwyn frowned. "I am not sure one boy is worth such a weighty promise. As I have said, the Hunt has small desire to involve itself in the business of Nephilim."

"You need not fight," said the Queen, in a voice like silk. "I would ask only your assistance with the bodies afterward. And there will be bodies. The Nephilim will pay for their crimes, Gwyn. Everyone must pay."

Before Gwyn could reply, another figure strode into the room from the dark tunnel that curved away behind the Queen's throne. It was Meliorn, in his white armor, his black hair in a braid down his back. His boots were encrusted with what looked like blackish tar. He frowned when he saw Gwyn. "A Hunter never brings good tidings," he said.

"Subside, Meliorn," said the Queen. "Gwyn and I were only discussing an exchange of favors."

Meliorn inclined his head. "I bear news, my lady, but I would have counsel with you in private."

She turned to Gwyn. "Are we agreed?"

Gwyn hesitated, then nodded, curtly, and with a glance of dislike in Meliorn's direction, disappeared down the dark tunnel from which the faerie knight had come.

The Queen slid down in her divan, her pale fingers like marble against her gown. "Very well, Meliorn. What did you wish to speak of? Is it news of the Downworld prisoners?"

The Downworld prisoners. Clary heard Alec's sharp intake of breath behind her, and Meliorn's head whipped to the side. She saw his eyes narrow. "If I do not mistake myself," he said, reaching for the blade at his side, "my lady, we have visitors—"

Jace was already sliding his hand down his side, whispering, "*Gabriel.*" The seraph blade blazed up, and Isabelle leaped to her feet, sweeping her whip forward, slicing through the curtain of thorns, which collapsed, rattling, to the ground.

Jace darted past the thorns and advanced into the throne room, Gabriel blazing in his hand. Clary whipped her sword free.

They poured out into the room, arranging themselves in an arc behind Jace: Alec with his bow already strung, Isabelle with her whip out and glittering, Clary with her sword, and Simon—Simon had no better weapon than his own self, but he stood and smiled at Meliorn, and his teeth glittered.

The Queen drew herself upright with a hiss, quickly covered; it was the only time Clary had seen her flustered.

"How dare you enter the Court unbidden?" she demanded. "This is the highest of crimes, a breaking of Covenant Law—"

"How dare you speak of breaking Covenant Law!" Jace shouted, and the seraph blade burned in his hand. Clary thought Jonathan

Shadowhunter must have looked like that, so many centuries ago, when he drove the demons back and saved an unknowing world from destruction. "You, who have murdered, and lied, and taken Downworlders of the Council prisoner. You have allied yourself with evil forces, and you will pay for it."

"The Queen of the Seelie Court does not pay," said the Queen.

"Everyone pays," Jace said, and suddenly he was standing on the divan, over the Queen, and the tip of his blade was against her throat. She flinched back, but she was pinned in place, Jace standing over her, his feet braced on the couch. "How did you do it?" he demanded. "Meliorn swore that you were on the side of the Nephilim. Faeries can't lie. That's why the Council *trusted* you—"

"Meliorn is half-faerie. He can lie," said the Queen, shooting an amused glance at Isabelle, who looked shocked. Only the Queen could look amused with a blade to her throat, Clary thought. "Sometimes the simplest answer is the correct one, Shadowhunter."

"*That's* why you wanted him on the Council," said Clary, remembering the favor the Queen had asked of her what seemed so long ago now. "Because he can lie."

"A betrayal long-planned." Jace was breathing hard. "I should cut your throat right now."

"You would not dare," said the Queen, unmoving; the point of the sword against her throat. "If you touch the Queen of the Seelie Court, the Fair Folk will be ranged against you for all time."

Jace was breathing hard as he spoke, and his face was full of burning light. "Then what are you now?" he demanded. "We heard you. You spoke of Sebastian as an ally. The Adamant Citadel lies on ley lines. Ley lines are the province of the fey. *You* led him there, you opened the way, you let him ambush us. How are you not *already* ranged against us?"

An ugly look crossed Meliorn's face. "You may have heard us speaking, little Nephilim," he said. "But if we kill you before you return to the Clave to tell your tales, none others need ever know—"

The knight started forward. Alec let an arrow fly, and it plunged into Meliorn's leg. The knight toppled backward with a cry.

Alec strode forward, already notching another arrow to his bow. Meliorn was on the ground, moaning, the snow around him turning red. Alec stood over him, bow at the ready. "Tell us how to get Magnus—how to get the prisoners back," he said. "Do it, or I'll turn you into a pincushion."

Meliorn spat. His white armor seemed to blend into the snow around him. "I will tell you nothing," he said. "Torture me, kill me, I shall not betray my Queen."

"It doesn't matter what he says, anyway," said Isabelle. "He can lie, remember?"

Alec's face shut. "True," he said. "Die, then, liar." And he let the next arrow go.

It sank into Meliorn's chest, and the faerie knight fell back, the force of the arrow sending his body skidding back across the snow. His head hit the cave wall with a wet smack.

The Queen cried out. The sound pierced Clary's ears, snapping her out of her shock. She could hear the sound of faeries shouting, running feet in the corridors outside. "Simon!" she yelled, and he whirled around. "Come here!"

She jammed Heosphoros back into her belt, seized her stele, and darted toward the main door, now denuded of its ragged curtain of thorns. Simon was at her heels. "Lift me," she panted, and without asking, he put his hands around her waist and thrust her upward, his vampire strength nearly sending her hurtling to the roof.

She grabbed on tight to the top of the archway with her free hand, and looked down. Simon was staring up at her, obviously puzzled, but his grip on her was steady.

"Hold on," she said, and began to draw. It was the opposite of the rune she'd drawn on Valentine's boat: This was a rune for shutting and locking, for closing away all things, for hiding and safety.

Black lines spread from the tip of her stele as she drew, and she heard Simon say, "Hurry up. They're coming," just as she finished, and drew the stele back.

The ground underneath them jerked. They fell together, Clary landing on Simon—not the most comfortable landing, he was all knees and elbows—and rolling to the side as a wall of earth began to slide across the open archway, like a theater curtain being drawn. There were shadows rushing toward the door, shadows that began to take the shape of running faerie folk, and Simon jerked Clary upright just as the doorway that opened onto the corridor disappeared with a final rumble, shutting away the faeries on the other side.

"By the Angel," Isabelle said in an awed voice.

Clary turned around, stele in hand. Jace was on his feet, the Seelie Queen in front of him, his sword pointed at her heart. Alec stood over Meliorn's corpse; he was expressionless as he looked at Clary, and then at his *parabatai*. Behind him opened the passageway through which Meliorn had come and Gwyn had gone.

"Are you going to close the back tunnel?" Simon asked Clary.

She shook her head. "Meliorn had pitch on his shoes," she said. "'*And the streams of Edom shall be turned into pitch*,' remember? I think he came from the demon realms. I think they're that way."

"Jace," Alec said. "Tell the Queen what we want, and that if she does it, we will let her live."

The Queen laughed, a shrill sound. "Little archer boy," she said. "I underestimated you. Sharp are the arrows of a broken heart."

Alec's face tightened. "You underestimated all of us; you always have. You and your arrogance. The Fair Folk are an old people, a good people. You aren't fit to lead them. Under your rule they will all wind up like this," he said, jerking his chin toward Meliorn's corpse.

"You are the one who killed him," said the Queen, "not I."

"Everyone pays," Alec said, and his eyes on her were steady and blue and hard.

"We desire the safe return of the hostages Sebastian Morgenstern has taken," said Jace.

The Queen spread her hands. "They are not in this world, nor here in Faerie, nor in any land over which I have jurisdiction. There is nothing I can do to help you rescue them, nothing at all."

"Very well," said Jace, and Clary had the feeling he had expected that response. "There is one other thing you can do, one thing you can show us, that will make me spare you."

The Queen went still. "What is that, Shadowhunter?"

"The road to the demon realm of Edom," said Jace. "We want safe passage to it. We will walk it, and walk our way out of your kingdom."

To Clary's surprise the Queen seemed to relax. The tension bled from her posture, and a small smile tugged at the corner of her mouth—a smile that Clary did not like. "Very well. I will lead you to the road to the demon realm." The Queen lifted her diaphanous dress in her hands so that she could make her way down the steps that surrounded her divan. Her feet were bare, and as white as the snow. She began to make her way across the room to the dark passage that stretched away behind her throne.

Alec fell into step behind Jace, and Isabelle behind him; Clary and Simon made up the rear, a strange procession.

"I really, really hate to say this," Simon said in a low voice as they went out from the throne room and into the shadowed darkness of the underground passage, "but that kind of seemed too easy."

"That wasn't easy," Clary whispered back.

"I know, but the Queen—she's clever. She could have found a way out of doing this if she'd wanted to. She doesn't have to let us go to the demon realms."

"But she does want to," Clary said. "She thinks we'll die there."

Simon shot her a sideways look. "Will we?"

"I don't know," Clary said, and sped up her pace to catch up with the others.

The corridor wasn't as long as Clary had thought. Its darkness had made the distance seem impossible, but they had only been walking for a half hour or so when they broke out from the shadows and into a larger, lighted space.

They had been walking in silence and darkness, Clary lost in her thoughts—memories of the house she and Sebastian and Jace had shared, of the sound of the Wild Hunt roaring across the sky, of that piece of paper with the words "my beautiful one" on it. That hadn't been romance; that had been respect. The Seelie Queen, the beautiful one. *The Queen likes to be on the winning side of things, Clary, and that side will be ours,* Sebastian had said to her once; even when she had reported that to the Clave, she had taken it as part of his bluster. She had believed along with the Council that the Fair Folk's word that they were loyal was enough, that the Queen would at least wait to see which way the wind blew before she broke any alliances. She thought of the catch in Jace's breath when he'd said *a betrayal long-planned.* Maybe none of them had considered it because they hadn't been able to bear considering it: that the Queen would be so sure of Sebastian's eventual victory that she would hide him in Faerie, where he could not be tracked. That she would help him in battle. Clary thought of the earth opening at the Adamant Citadel and taking Sebastian and the Endarkened down into it; that had been faerie magic: The Courts lay underground, after all. Why else had the Dark Shadowhunters who had attacked the Los Angeles Institute taken Mark Blackthorn? Everyone had assumed Sebastian was afraid of the vengeance of the Fair Folk, but he wasn't. He was in league with them. He had taken Mark because he had faerie blood, and because of that blood, they thought Mark belonged to them.

In all her life she had never thought so much as she had in the past six months about blood and what it meant. Nephilim blood bred true; she was a Shadowhunter. Angel blood: It made her what she was, gifted her with the power of runes. It made Jace what he was, made him strong and fast and brilliant. Morgenstern blood: She had it, and so did Sebastian, and that was why he cared about her at all. It gave her a dark heart too, or did it? Was it Sebastian's blood—Morgenstern and demon, mixed—that made him a monster, or could he have been changed, fixed, made better, taught otherwise, as the Lightwoods had taught Jace?

"Here we are," said the Seelie Queen, and her voice was amused. "Can you guess the right road?"

They stood in a massive cave, the roof lost in shadow. The walls glowed with a phosphorescent shine, and four roads branched off from where they stood: the one behind them, and three others. One was clear and broad and smooth, leading directly ahead of them. The one on the left shone with green leaves and bright flowers, and Clary thought she saw the glimmer of blue sky in the distance. Her heart longed to go that way. And the last way, the darkest, was a narrow tunnel, the entrance wound about with spiked metal, and thornbushes lining the sides. Clary thought she could see darkness and stars at the end.

Alec laughed shortly. "We're Shadowhunters," he said. "We know the old tales. This is the Three Roads." At Clary's puzzled look he said, "Faeries don't like their secrets to get out, but sometimes human musicians have been able to encode faerie secrets into ancient ballads. There's one called 'Thomas the Rhymer,' about a man who was kidnapped by the Queen of Faerie—"

"Hardly kidnapped," objected the Queen. "He came quite willingly."

"And she took him to a place where three roads lay, and told him that one went to Heaven, and one went to Faerieland, and one went to Hell. '*And see ye not that narrow road, so thick beset with thorns and briars? That is the path of righteousness, though after it but few inquires.*'" Alec pointed toward the narrow tunnel.

"It goes to the mundane world," said the Queen sweetly. "Your folk find it heavenly enough there."

"That's how Sebastian got to the Adamant Citadel, and had warriors backing him up that the Clave couldn't see," said Jace in disgust. "He used this tunnel. He had warriors hanging back here in Faerie, where they couldn't be tracked. They came through when he needed them." He gave the Queen a dark look. "Many Nephilim are dead because of you."

"Mortals," said the Queen. "They die."

Alec ignored her. "There," he said, pointing to the leafy tunnel. "That goes farther into Faerie. And that"—he pointed ahead—"is the road to Hell. That's where we're going."

"I always heard it was paved with good intentions," said Simon.

"Place your feet upon the way and find out, Daylighter," said the Queen.

Jace twisted the tip of the blade in her back. "What will stop you from telling Sebastian we've come after him the moment we leave you?"

The Queen made no noise of pain; only her lips thinned. She looked old in that moment, despite the youth and beauty of her face. "You ask a fine question. And even if you kill me, there are those in my Court who will speak to him of you, and he will guess your intentions, for he is clever. You cannot evade his knowing, save you kill all the Fair Folk in my Court."

Jace paused. He held the seraph blade in his hand, the tip pressed up against the Seelie Queen's back. Its light flared up onto his face, carving out its beauty in peaks and valleys, the sharpness of cheekbones and the angle of jaw. It caught the tips of his hair and licked them with fire, as if he were wearing a crown of burning thorns.

Clary watched him, and the others did as well, silently, giving him their trust. Whatever decision he made, they would stand behind it.

"Come, now," said the Queen. "You do not have the stomach for so much killing. You were always Valentine's gentlest child." Her eyes lingered a moment on Clary, gleeful. *You have a dark heart in you, Valentine's daughter.*

"Swear," said Jace. "I know what promises mean to your people. I know you cannot lie. Swear you will say nothing of us to Sebastian, nor will you allow anyone in your court to do the same."

"I swear," said the Queen. "I swear that no one in my court by word or deed will tell him that you came here."

Jace stepped away from the Queen, lowering his blade to his side. "I know you think you are sending us to our deaths," he said. "But we will not die so easily. We will not lose this war. And when we are victorious, we shall make you and your people *bleed* for what you have done."

The Queen's smile left her face. They turned away from her and started down the path to Edom, silently; Clary looked over her shoulder once as they went, and saw only the outline of the Queen, motionless, watching them go, her eyes burning.

The corridor curved far away into the distance, seeming as if it had been hollowed out of the rock around it by fire. As the five of them went forward, moving in total silence, the pale stone walls around them darkened, stained here and there by streaks of charcoaled blackness, as if the rock itself had burned. The smooth floor began to give way to a rockier one, grit crunching under their boot heels. The phosphorescence in the walls started to dim, and Alec drew his witchlight from his pocket and raised it overhead.

As the light rayed out from between his fingers, Clary felt Simon, beside her, stiffen.

"What is it?" she whispered.

"Something moving." He jabbed a finger in the direction of the shadows ahead. "Up there."

Clary squinted but saw nothing; Simon's vampire eyesight was better even than a Shadowhunter's. As quietly as she could she drew Heosphoros from her belt and paced a few steps ahead, keeping to the shadows at the sides of the tunnel. Jace and Alec were deep in conversation. Clary tapped Izzy on the shoulder and whispered to her, "There's someone here. Or some*thing*."

Isabelle didn't reply, only turned to her brother and made a gesture at him—a complicated movement of fingers. Alec's eyes showed his comprehension, and he turned immediately to Jace. Clary remembered the first time she'd seen the three of them, in Pandemonium, years of practice melding them into a unit that thought together, moved together, breathed together, fought together. She couldn't help but wonder if, no matter what happened, no matter how dedicated a Shadowhunter she became, she would always be on the fringes—

Alec swung his hand down suddenly, dousing the light. A flash and a spark, and Isabelle was gone from Clary's side. Clary spun around, holding Heosphoros, and heard the sounds of a scuffle: a thump, and then a very human yelp of pain.

"Stop!" Simon called, and light exploded all around them. It was as if a camera flash had gone off. It took a moment for her eyes to adjust to the new brightness. The scene filled in slowly: Jace holding his witchlight, the glow radiating around him like the light of a small sun. Alec, his bow raised and notched. Isabelle, the handle of her whip tight in one hand, the whip itself curled around the ankles of a slight figure hunched against the cave wall—a boy, with pale-blond hair that curled over his slightly pointed ears—

"Oh, my God," Clary whispered, shoving her weapon back into her belt and pressing forward. "Isabelle—stop. It's all right," she said, moving toward the boy. His clothes were torn and dirty, his feet bare and black with filth. His arms were bare, too, and on them were the marks of runes. Shadowhunter runes.

"By the Angel." Izzy's whip slithered back into her grasp. Alec's bow fell to his side. The boy lifted his head and scowled.

"You're a Shadowhunter?" Jace said in an incredulous tone.

The boy scowled again, more ferociously. There was anger in his look, but more than that, there was grief and fear. There was no doubting who he was. He had the same fine features as his sister, the same angled chin and hair like bleached wheat, curling at the tips. He was about sixteen, Clary remembered. He looked younger.

"It's Mark Blackthorn," Clary said. "Helen's brother. Look at his face. Look at his *hand*."

For a moment, Mark looked confused. Clary touched her own ring finger, and his eyes lit with comprehension. He held out his thin right hand. On the fourth finger the family ring of the Blackthorns, with its design of intertwined thorns, glittered.

"How did you get here?" Jace said. "How did you know how to find us?"

"I was with the Hunters underground," Mark said in a low voice. "I heard Gwyn talking to some of the others about how you'd shown up in the Queen's chamber. I sneaked away from the Hunters; they weren't paying attention to me. I was looking for you and I ended up—here." He gestured to the tunnel around them. "I had to talk to you. I had to know about my family." His face was in shadow, but Clary saw his features tighten. "The faeries told me they were all dead. Is it true?"

There was a shocked silence, and Clary read the panic in Mark's expression as his eyes darted from Isabelle's downcast eyes, to Jace's blank expression, to Alec's tight posture.

"It's true," Mark said then, "isn't it? My family—"

"Your father was Turned. But your brothers and sisters are alive," Clary said. "They're in Idris. They escaped. They're fine."

If she had expected Mark to look relieved, she was disappointed. He went white. "What?"

"Julian, Helen, the others—they're all alive." Clary put her hand on his shoulder; he flinched away. "They're alive, and they're worried about you."

"Clary," Jace said, a warning in his voice.

Clary shot a look at him over her shoulder; surely telling Mark his siblings were alive was the most important thing?

"Have you eaten anything, drunk anything since the Fair Folk took you?" Jace asked, moving to peer into Mark's face. Mark jerked away, but not before Clary heard Jace's sharp intake of breath.

"What is it?" Isabelle demanded.

"His eyes," Jace said, raising his witchlight and shining it into Mark's face. Mark scowled again but allowed Jace to examine him.

His eyes were large, long-lashed, like Helen's; unlike hers, his were mismatched. One was Blackthorn blue, the color of water. The other was gold, hazed through with shadows, a darker version of Jace's own.

Jace swallowed visibly. "The Wild Hunt," he said. "You're one of them now."

Jace was scanning the boy with his eyes, as if Mark were a book he could read. "Put your hands out," Jace said finally, and Mark did so. Jace caught them and turned them over, baring the other boy's wrists. Clary felt her throat tighten. Mark was wearing only a T-shirt, and his bare forearms were striped with bloody whip marks. Clary thought of the way she had touched Mark's shoulder and he'd flinched away. God knew what his other injuries were, under his clothes. "When did this happen?"

Mark pulled his hands away. They were shaking. "Meliorn did

it," he said. "When he first took me. He said he'd stop if I ate and drank their food, so I did. I didn't think it mattered, if my family was dead. And I thought faeries couldn't lie."

"Meliorn can," said Alec grimly. "Or at least, he *could*."

"When did this all happen?" Isabelle demanded. "The faeries only took you less than a week ago —"

Mark shook his head. "I've been with the Folk for a long time," he said. "I couldn't say how long."

"Time runs differently in Faerie," Alec said. "Sometimes faster, sometimes slower."

Mark said, "Gwyn told me I belonged to the Hunt and I couldn't leave them unless they allowed me to go. Is that true?"

"It's true," Jace said.

Mark slumped against the cave wall. He turned his head toward Clary. "You saw them. You saw my brothers and sisters. And Emma?"

"They're all right, all of them, Emma, too," Clary said. She wondered if it helped. He had sworn to stay in Faerie because he thought his family was dead, and the promise held, though it was based on a lie. Was it better to think you had lost everything, and to start over? Or easier to know that the people you loved were alive, even if you could never see them again?

She thought of her own mother, somewhere in the world beyond the end of the tunnel. Better to know they were alive, she thought. Better for her mother and Luke to be alive and all right, and for her never to see them again, than for them to be dead.

"Helen can't take care of them. Not alone," Mark said a little desperately. "And Jules, he's too young. He can't take care of Ty; he doesn't know the things he needs. He doesn't know how to talk to him—" He took a shuddering breath. "You should let me come with you."

"You know you can't," said Jace, though he couldn't look Mark in the face; he was staring at the ground. "If you've sworn fealty to the Wild Hunt, you're one of them."

"Take me with you," Mark repeated. He had the stunned, bewildered look of someone who had been mortally injured but didn't yet realize the extent of the injury. "I don't want to be one of them. I want to be with my family—"

"We're going to Hell," Clary said. "We couldn't bring you with us, even if you could leave Faerie safely—"

"And you can't," Alec said. "If you try to leave, you'll die."

"I'd rather die," Mark said, and Jace's head whipped up. His eyes were bright gold, almost too bright, as if the fire inside him were spilling out through them.

"They took you because you have faerie blood, but also because you have Shadowhunter blood. They want to punish the Nephilim," Jace said, his gaze intent. "Show them what a Shadowhunter is made of; show them you aren't afraid. You can live through this."

In the wavering illumination of the witchlight, Mark looked at Jace. Tears had made their tracks through the dirt on his face, but his eyes were dry. "I don't know what to do," he said. "What do I do?"

"Find a way to warn the Nephilim," Jace said. "We're going into Hell, like Clary said. We might never come back. Someone has to tell the Shadowhunters the Fair Folk are not their allies."

"The Hunters will catch me if I try to send a message." The boy's eyes flashed. "They'll kill me."

"Not if you're fast and smart," said Jace. "You can do it. I know you can."

"Jace," Alec said, his bow at his side. "Jace, we need to let him go before the Hunt notice he's missing."

"Right," Jace said, and hesitated. Clary saw him take Mark's hand; he pressed his witchlight into the boy's palm, where it flickered, and then resumed its steady glow. "Take this with you," said

Jace, "for it can be dark in the land under the hill, and the years very long."

Mark stood for a moment, the rune-stone in his hand. He looked so slight in the wavering light that Clary's heart hammered a tattoo of disbelief—surely they could help him, they were Nephilim, they didn't leave their own behind—and then he turned and ran, away from them, on soundless bare feet.

"Mark—" Clary whispered, and cut herself off; he was gone. The shadows swallowed him up, only the darting will-o'-the-wisp light of the rune-stone visible, until it too blended with the darkness. She looked up at Jace. "What did you mean, 'the land under the hill'?" she asked. "Why did you say that?"

Jace didn't answer her; he looked stunned. She wondered if Mark, brittle and orphaned and alone, reminded him somehow of himself.

"The land under the hill is Faerie," said Alec. "An old, old name for it. He'll be all right," he said to Jace. "He will."

"You gave him your witchlight," Isabelle said. "You've always had that witchlight—"

"Screw the witchlight," Jace said violently, and slammed his hand against the wall of the cave; there was a brief flare of light, and he drew his arm back. The mark of his hand was burned black into the stone of the tunnel, and his palm still glowed, as if the blood in his fingers were phosphorus. He gave an odd, choked laugh. "I don't exactly need it, anyway."

"Jace," Clary said, and put her hand on his arm. He didn't move away from her, but he didn't react, either. She dropped her voice. "You can't save everyone," she said.

"Maybe not," he said as the light in his hand dimmed. "But it would be nice to save someone for a change."

"Guys," Simon said. He'd been oddly quiet throughout the encounter with Mark, and Clary was startled to hear him speak now.

"I don't know if you can see it, but there's something—something at the end of the tunnel."

"A light?" Jace said, his voice edged with sarcasm. His eyes glittered.

"The opposite." Simon moved forward, and after a hesitant moment Clary took her hand from Jace's arm, and followed him. The tunnel went straight on ahead and then jogged slightly; at the curve she saw what Simon must have seen, and stopped dead.

Darkness. The tunnel ended in a whirling vortex of darkness. Something moved in it, shaping the dark like the wind shaping clouds. She could hear it too, the purr and rumble of the dark, like the sound of jet engines.

The others joined her. Together they stood in a line, watching the dark. Watching it move. A curtain of shadow, and beyond it the utter unknown.

It was Alec who spoke, staring, awed, at the moving shadows. The air that blew down the corridor was stinging hot, like pepper thrown into the heart of a fire. "This," he said, "is the craziest thing we've ever done."

"What if we can't ever come back?" Isabelle said. The ruby around her neck was pulsing, glowing like a stoplight, illuminating her face.

"Then at least we'll be together," Clary said, and looked around at her companions. She reached out and took Jace's hand, and Simon's hand on the other side of her, and held them tight. "We go through together, and on the other side we *stay* together," she said. "All right?"

None of them answered, but Isabelle took Simon's other hand, and Alec took Jace's. They all stood for a moment, staring. Clary felt Jace's hand tighten on hers, a nearly imperceptible pressure.

They stepped forward, and the shadows swallowed them up.

* * *

"*Mirror, my mirror*," said the Queen, placing her hand upon the mirror. "Show me my Morning Star."

The mirror hung on the wall of the Queen's bedroom. It was surrounded by wreaths of flowers: roses from which no one had cut away the thorns.

The mist inside the mirror coalesced, and Sebastian's angular face looked out. "My beautiful one," he said. His voice was calm and composed, though there was blood on his face and clothes. He was holding his sword, and the stars along the blade were dimmed with scarlet. "I am ... somewhat occupied at the moment."

"I thought you might wish to know that your sister and adoptive brother have just left this place," said the Queen. "They found the road to Edom. They are coming to you."

His face transformed with a wolfish grin. "And they didn't make you promise not to tell me that they came to your court?"

"They did," said the Queen. "They said nothing about telling you of leaving."

Sebastian laughed.

"They killed one of my knights," said the Queen. "Spilled blood before my throne. They are beyond my reach now. You know my people cannot survive in the poison lands. You will have to take my revenge for me."

The light in his eyes changed. The Queen had always found what Sebastian felt for his sister, and Jace as well, to be something of a mystery, but then Sebastian himself was by far the greater mystery. Before he had come to make her his offer, she would never have considered a true alliance with Shadowhunters. Their peculiar sense of honor made them untrustworthy. It was Sebastian's very lack of honor that made her trust him. The fine craft of betrayal was second nature to Fair Folk, and Sebastian was an artist of lies.

"I will serve your interests in all ways, my Queen," he said. "In a short enough while your people and mine shall hold the reins of the world, and when we do, you may have revenge on any who have ever offended you."

She smiled at him. Blood still stained the snow in her throne room, and she still felt the jab of Jace Lightwood's blade against her throat. It was not a real smile, but she knew enough to let her beauty do her work for her, sometimes. "I do adore you," she said.

"Yes," said Sebastian, and his eyes flickered, their color like dark clouds. The Queen wondered idly if he thought of the two of them the way she did: lovers who, even while embracing, each held a knife to the other's back, ready to stab and to betray. "And I do like to be adored." He grinned. "I am glad they are coming. Let them come."

Part Two

That World Inverted

———◆———

And that the whole land thereof is brimstone, and salt,
and burning, that it is not sown, nor beareth,
nor any grass groweth therein.
—Deuteronomy 29:23

14

THE SLEEP OF REASON

Clary stood on a shady lawn that rolled away down a sloping hill. The sky overhead was perfectly blue, dotted here and there with white clouds. At her feet a stone walkway stretched to the front door of a large manor house, built of mellow golden stone.

She craned her head back, looking up. The house was lovely: The stones were the color of butter in the spring sunshine, covered in trellises of climbing roses in red and gold and orange. Wrought iron balconies curved out from the facade, and there were two large arched doors of bronze-colored wood, their surfaces wrought with delicate designs of wings. *Wings for the Fairchilds,* said a soft voice, reassuring, in the back of her mind. *This is Fairchild manor. It has stood for four hundred years and will stand four hundred more.*

"Clary!" Her mother appeared at one of the balconies, wearing an elegant champagne-colored dress; her red hair was down, and she looked young and beautiful. Her arms were bare, circled with black runes. "What do you think? Doesn't it look gorgeous?"

Clary followed her mother's gaze toward where the lawn flattened out. There was an archway of roses set up at the end of an aisle, on either side of which were rows of wooden benches. White flowers were scattered along the aisle: the white flowers that grew only in Idris. The air was rich with their honey scent.

She looked back up at her mother, who was no longer alone on the balcony. Luke was standing behind her, an arm around her waist. He was in rolled-up shirtsleeves and formal trousers, as if halfway dressed for a party. His arms too were twined with runes: runes for good luck, for insight, for strength, for love. "Are you ready?" he called down to Clary.

"Ready for what?" she said, but they didn't seem to hear her. Smiling, they disappeared back into the house. Clary took a few steps along the path.

"Clary!"

She whirled. He was coming toward her across the grass—slender, with white-pale hair that shone in the sunlight, dressed in formal black with gold runes at his collar and cuffs. He was grinning, a smudge of dirt on his cheek, and holding up a hand to block the brightness of the sun.

Sebastian.

He was entirely the same and yet entirely different: He was clearly himself, and yet the whole shape and set of his features seemed to have changed, his bones less sharp, his skin sun-darkened rather than pale, and his eyes—

His eyes shone, as green as spring grass.

He has always had green eyes, said the voice in her head. *People often marvel at how much alike you are, he and your mother and yourself. His name is Jonathan and he is your brother; he has always protected you.*

"Clary," he said again, "you're not going to believe—"

"Jonathan!" a small voice trilled, and Clary turned her wondering eyes to see a little girl dashing across the grass. She had red hair, the same shade as Clary's, and it flew out behind her like a banner. She was barefoot, wearing a green lace dress that had been so thoroughly torn to ribbons at the cuffs and hem that it resembled shredded lettuce. She might have been four or five years old, dirty-faced and adorable, and as she reached Jonathan, she held up her arms, and he bent down to swing her up into the air.

She shrieked in delight as he held her over his head. "Ouch, ouch—quit that, you demon child," he said as she pulled at his hair. "Val, I said stop it, or I'll hold you upside down. I mean it."

"Val?" Clary echoed. *But of course, her name is Valentina,* said the whispering voice in the back of her head. *Valentine Morgenstern was a great hero of the war; he died in battle against Hodge Starkweather, but not before he had saved the Mortal Cup, and the Clave along with it. When Luke married your mother, they honored his memory in the name of their daughter.*

"Clary, make him let me go, make him—owwww!" shrieked Val as Jonathan turned her upside down and swung her through the air. Val dissolved into giggles as he set her down on the grass, and she turned a pair of eyes the exact blue of Luke's up at Clary. "Your dress is pretty," she said matter-of-factly.

"Thank you," Clary said, still half in a daze, and looked at Jonathan, who was grinning down at his small sister. "Is that dirt on your face?"

Jonathan reached up and touched his cheek. "Chocolate," he said. "You'll never guess what I found Val doing. She had both fists in the wedding cake. I'm going to have to patch it up." He squinted at Clary. "Okay, maybe I shouldn't have mentioned that. You look like you're going to pass out."

"I'm fine," Clary said, tugging nervously at a lock of her hair.

Jonathan put his hands up as if to ward her off. "Look, I'll per-form surgery on it. No one will ever be able to tell that someone ate half the roses off." He looked thoughtful. "I could eat the other half of the roses, just so it's even."

"Yeah!" said Val from her place on the grass at his feet. She was busy yanking up dandelions, their white pods blowing on the wind.

"Also," Jonathan added, "I hate to bring this up, but you might want to put some shoes on before the wedding."

Clary looked down at herself. He was right, she was barefoot. Barefoot, and wearing a pale gold dress. The hem drifted around her ankles like a sunset-colored cloud. "I—What wedding?"

Her brother's green eyes widened. "*Your* wedding? You know, to Jace Herondale? About yea high, blond, all the girls looove him—" He broke off. "Are you having cold feet? Is that what this is?" He leaned in conspiratorially. "Because if it is, I'll totally smuggle you over the border into France. And I won't tell anyone where you went. Even if they stick bamboo shoots under my fingernails."

"I don't—" Clary stared at him. "Bamboo shoots?"

He shrugged eloquently. "For my only sister, not counting the creature currently sitting on my foot"—Val yelped—"I would do it. Even if it means not getting to see Isabelle Lightwood in a strapless dress."

"Isabelle? You like Isabelle?" Clary felt as if she were running a marathon and couldn't quite catch her breath.

He squinted at her. "Is that a problem? Is she a wanted criminal or something?" He looked thoughtful. "That would be kind of hot, actually."

"Okay, I don't need to know what you think is hot," Clary said automatically. "Bleh."

Jonathan grinned. It was an unconcerned, happy grin; the grin of someone who'd never really had much to worry about beyond pretty girls and whether one of his little sisters had eaten the other sister's wedding cake. Somewhere in the back of Clary's mind she saw black eyes and whip marks, but she didn't know why. *He's your brother. He's your brother, and he's always taken care of you.* "Right," he said. "Like I didn't have to suffer through years of 'Oooh, Jace is so cute. Do you think he liiikes me?'"

"I—" Clary said, and broke off, feeling a little dizzy. "I just don't remember him proposing."

Jonathan knelt down and tugged on Val's hair. She was humming to herself, bundling daisies together in a pile. Clary blinked—she'd been so sure they were dandelions. "Oh, I don't know if he ever did," he said casually. "We all just knew you'd end up together. It was inevitable."

"But I should have gotten to choose," she said, in a near whisper. "I should have gotten to say yes."

"Well, you would have, wouldn't you?" he said, watching the daisies blow across the grass. "Speaking of, do you think Isabelle would go out with me if I asked her?"

Clary's breath caught. "But what about Simon?"

He looked up at her, the sun bright in his eyes. "Who's Simon?"

Clary felt the ground give way under her. She reached out, as if to catch at her brother, but her hand went through him. He was as insubstantial as air. The green lawn and the golden mansion and the boy and the girl on the grass flew away from her, and she stumbled, hitting the ground hard, jarring her elbows with a pain she felt flare up her arms.

She rolled to her side, choking. She was lying on a patch of bleak ground. Broken cobblestones jutted up through the earth, and the burned-out shells of stone houses loomed over her. The sky was white-gray steel, shot through with black clouds like vampire veins. It was a dead world, a world with all the color leached out of it, and all the life. Clary curled up on the ground, seeing in front of her not the shell of a destroyed town but the eyes of the brother and the sister that she would never have.

Simon stood at the window, taking in the view of the city of Manhattan.

It was an impressive sight. From the penthouse floor of the

Carolina, you could see across Central Park, to the Met museum, to the high-rises of downtown. Night was falling, and the city lights were beginning to shine out one by one, a bed of electric flowers.

Electric flowers. He looked around, frowning thoughtfully. It was a nice turn of phrase; perhaps he should write it down. He never seemed to have time these days to really work on lyrics; time was swallowed up by other things: promotion, touring, signings, appearances. It was hard to remember sometimes that his main job was making music.

Still. A good problem to have. The darkening sky turned the window to a mirror. Simon smiled at his reflection in the glass. Tousled hair, jeans, vintage T-shirt; he could see the room behind him, vast acres of hardwood floor, gleaming steel, and leather furniture, a single elegant gold-framed painting on the wall. A Chagall— Clary's favorite, all soft roses and blues and greens, incongruous against the apartment's modernity.

There was a vase of hydrangeas on the kitchen island, a gift from his mother, congratulating him on playing a gig with Stepping Razor the week before. *I love you,* said the note attached. *I'm proud of you.*

He blinked at it. Hydrangeas; that was odd. If he had a favorite flower, it was roses, and his mother knew that. He turned away from the window and looked more closely at the vase. They *were* roses. He shook his head to clear it. White roses. They always had been. Right.

He heard the rattle of keys, and the door swung open, admitting a petite girl with long red hair and a brilliant smile. "Oh, my God," said Clary, half-laughing, half out of breath. She pushed the door shut behind her and leaned against it. "The lobby is a zoo. Press, photographers; it's going to be crazy going out tonight."

She came across the room, dropping her keys on the table. She was wearing a long dress, yellow silk printed with colorful butterflies, and a butterfly clip in her long red hair. She looked warm and open and loving, and as she neared him, she put her arms up, and he went to kiss her.

Just like he did every day when she came home.

She smelled like Clary, perfume and chalk, and her fingers were smudged with color. She wound her fingers in his hair as they kissed, tugging him down, laughing against his mouth as he nearly overbalanced.

"You're going to have to start wearing heels, Fray," he said, lips against her cheek.

"I hate heels. You'll either have to deal or buy me a portable ladder," she said, letting him go. "Unless you want to leave me for a really tall groupie."

"Never," he said, tucking a lock of her hair behind her ear. "Would a really tall groupie know all my favorite foods? Remember when I had a bed shaped like a race car? Know how to beat me mercilessly at Scrabble? Be willing to put up with Matt and Kirk and Eric?"

"A groupie would more than put up with Matt and Kirk and Eric."

"Be nice," he said, and grinned down at her. "You're stuck with me."

"I'll survive," she said, plucking his glasses off and setting them on the table. The eyes she turned up to him were dark and wide. This time the kiss was more heated. He wound his arms around her, pulling her against him as she whispered, "I love you; I've always loved you."

"I love you too," he said. "God, I love you, Isabelle."

He felt her stiffen in his arms, and then the world around him seemed to sprout black lines like shattered glass. He heard a high-pitched whine in his ears and staggered back, tripping, falling, not hitting the ground but spinning forever through the dark.

* * *

"Don't look, *don't* look..."

Isabelle laughed. "I'm *not* looking."

There were hands over her eyes: Simon's hands, slim and flexible. His arms were around her, and they were shuffling forward together, laughing. He'd grabbed her the moment she'd walked in the front door, wrapping his arms around her as her shopping bags dropped from her hands.

"I have a surprise for you," he'd said, grinning. "Close your eyes. No looking. No, really. I'm not kidding."

"I hate surprises," Isabelle protested now. "You know that." She could just see the edge of the rug under Simon's hands. She'd picked it out herself, and it was thick, bright pink, and fuzzy. Their apartment was small and cozy, a hodgepodge of Isabelle and Simon: guitars and katanas, vintage posters and hot-pink bedspreads. Simon had brought his cat, Yossarian, when they'd moved in together, which Isabelle had protested about but secretly liked: She'd missed Church after she'd left the Institute.

The pink rug vanished, and now Isabelle's heels clicked onto the tile floor of the kitchen. "Okay," Simon said, and withdrew his hands. "Surprise!"

"Surprise!" The kitchen was full of people: her mother and father, Jace and Alec and Max, Clary and Jordan and Maia, Kirk and Matt and Eric. Magnus was holding a silver sparkler and winking, waving it back and forth as the sparkles flew everywhere, landing on the stone counters and Jace's T-shirt, making him yelp. Clary was holding a clumsily lettered sign: HAPPY BIRTHDAY, ISABELLE. She held it up and waved.

Isabelle whirled on Simon accusingly. "You *planned* this!"

"Of course I did," he said, pulling her toward him. "Shadowhunters might not care about birthdays, but I do." He kissed her ear, murmuring, "You should have everything, Izzy," before he let her go, and her family descended.

There was a whirl of hugs, of presents and cake—baked by Eric, who actually had something of a flair for pastry creation, and decorated by Magnus with luminous frosting that tasted better than it looked. Robert had his arms around Maryse, who was leaning back against him, looking on proudly and contentedly as Magnus, one hand ruffling Alec's hair, tried to convince Max to put on a party hat. Max, with all the self-possession of a nine-year-old, was having none of it. He waved away Magnus's hand impatiently and said, "Izzy, I made the sign. Did you see the sign?"

Izzy glanced over at the hand-lettered sign, now liberally smeared with frosting, on the table. Clary winked at her. "It's awesome, Max; thank you."

"I was going to put what birthday it was on the sign," he said, "but Jace said that after twenty, you're just old, so it doesn't matter anyway."

Jace stopped with his fork halfway to his mouth. "I said that?"

"Way to make us all feel ancient," said Simon, pushing his hair back to smile at Isabelle. She felt a little twist of pain inside her chest—she loved him that much, for doing this for her, for always thinking of her. She couldn't remember a time when she hadn't loved him or trusted him, and he'd never given her a reason not to do either.

Isabelle slid off the stool she'd been sitting on, and knelt down in front of her little brother. She could see their reflection in the steel of the refrigerator: her own dark hair, cut to her shoulders now—she remembered vaguely years ago, when her hair had reached her waist—and Max's brown curls and glasses. "Do you know how old I am?" she said.

"Twenty-two," Max said, in the tone of voice that indicated he wasn't sure why she was asking him such a stupid question.

Twenty-two, she thought. She'd always been seven years older than Max, Max the surprise, Max the little brother she hadn't expected.

Max, who should be fifteen now.

She swallowed, suddenly cold all over. Everyone was still talking and laughing all around her, but the laughing sounded distant and echoing, as if it came from very far away. She could see Simon, leaning against the counter, his arms folded over his chest, his dark eyes unreadable as he watched her.

"And how old are you?" Isabelle said.

"Nine," said Max. "I've always been nine."

Isabelle stared. The kitchen around her was wavering. She could see through it, as if she were staring through printed fabric: everything going transparent, as mutable as water.

"Baby," she whispered. "My Max, my baby brother, please, please stay."

"I'll always be nine," he said, and touched her face. His fingers passed through her, as if he were passing his hand through smoke. "Isabelle?" he said in a fading voice, and disappeared.

Isabelle felt her knees give. She sank to the ground. There was no laughter around her, no pretty tiled kitchen, only gray, powdery ash and blackened rock. She put up her hands to stop her tears.

The Hall of Accords was hung with blue banners, each gilded with the flame blazon of the Lightwood family. Four long tables had been arranged facing one another. In the center was a raised speaker's lectern, decked with swords and flowers.

Alec sat at the longest table, in the highest of the chairs. On his left was Magnus, and on his right his family stretched out beside him: Isabelle and Max; Robert and Maryse; Jace; and beside Jace, Clary. There were Lightwood cousins there too, some of whom he hadn't seen since he'd been a child; all of them were beaming with pride, but no face glowed as brightly as his father's.

"My son," he kept saying, to anyone who would listen—he had buttonholed the Consul now, who'd been passing by their table with a glass of wine in hand. "My son won the battle; that's my son up there. Lightwood blood will tell; our family have always been fighters."

The Consul laughed. "Save it for the speech, Robert," she said, winking at Alec over the rim of her glass.

"Oh, God, the speech," Alec said, in horror, hiding his face in his hands.

Magnus rubbed his knuckles gently across Alec's spine, as if he were petting a cat. Jace looked over at them, and raised his eyebrows.

"As if we all haven't been in a room full of people telling us how amazing we are before," he said, and when Alec glared at him sideways, he grinned. "Ah, just me, then."

"Leave my boyfriend alone," Magnus said. "I know spells that could turn your ears inside out."

Jace touched his ears worriedly as Robert rose to his feet, his chair scraping backward, and tapped the side of his fork against his glass. The sound rang out in the room, and the Shadowhunters fell silent, looking up toward the Lightwood table expectantly.

"We gather here today," said Robert, reaching out his arms expansively, "to honor my son, Alexander Gideon Lightwood, who has single-handedly destroyed the forces of the Endarkened and who defeated in battle the son of Valentine Morgenstern. Alec saved the life of our third son, Max. Along with his *parabatai*, Jace Herondale, I am proud to say that my son is one of the greatest warriors I have ever known." He turned and smiled at Alec and Magnus. "It takes more than a strong arm to make a great warrior," he went on. "It takes a great mind and a great heart. My son has both. He is strong in courage, and strong in love. Which is why I also wanted to share our other good news with you. As of yesterday, my son became engaged to be married to his partner, Magnus Bane—"

A chorus of cheers broke out. Magnus accepted them with a modest wave of his fork. Alec slid down in his chair, his cheeks burning. Jace looked at him meditatively.

"Congratulations," he said. "I kind of feel like I missed an opportunity."

"W-what?" Alec stammered.

Jace shrugged. "I always knew you had a crush on me, and I kind of had a crush on you, too. I thought you should know."

"What?" Alec said again.

Clary sat up straight. "You know," she said, "do you think there's any chance that you two could..." She gestured between Jace and Alec. "It would be kind of hot."

"No," Magnus said. "I am a very jealous warlock."

"We're *parabatai*," Alec said, regaining his voice. "The Clave would—I mean—it's *illegal*."

"Oh, come on," said Jace. "The Clave would let you do anything you wanted. Look, everyone loves you." He gestured out at the room full of Shadowhunters. They were all cheering as Robert spoke, some of them wiping away tears. A girl at one of the smaller tables held up a sign that said, ALEC LIGHTWOOD, WE LOVE YOU.

"I think you should have a winter wedding," said Isabelle, looking longingly at the white floral centerpiece. "Nothing too big. Five or six hundred people."

"Isabelle," Alec croaked.

She shrugged. "You have a lot of fans."

"Oh, for God's sake," Magnus said, and snapped his fingers in front of Alec's face. His black hair stood up in spikes, and his gold-green eyes were brilliant with annoyance. "THIS IS NOT HAPPENING."

"What?" Alec stared.

"It's a hallucination," Magnus said, "brought on by your entry into the demon realms. Probably a demon that lurks near the entrance to the world and feeds on the dreams of travelers. Wishes have a lot of power," he added, examining his reflection in his spoon. "Especially the deepest wishes of our hearts."

Alec looked around the room. "This is the deepest wish of my heart?"

"Sure," Magnus said. "Your father, proud of you. You, the hero of the hour. Me, loving you. *Everyone* approving of you."

Alec looked over at Jace. "Okay, what about the Jace thing?"

Magnus shrugged. "I don't know. That part's just weird."

"So I have to wake up." Alec put his hands on the table, flat; the Lightwood ring shone on his finger. It all seemed real, felt real—but he couldn't remember what his father was talking about. Couldn't remember defeating Sebastian, or winning a war. Couldn't remember saving Max.

"Max," he whispered.

Magnus's eyes darkened. "I'm sorry," he said. "The wishes of our hearts are weapons that can be used against us. Fight, Alec." He touched Alec's face. "This isn't what you want, this dream. Demons don't understand human hearts, not well. They see as through a distorted glass and show you what you desire, but warped and wrong. Use that wrongness to push yourself out of the dream. Life is loss, Alexander, but it's better than this."

"God," Alec said, and closed his eyes. He felt the world around him crack, as if he were tapping his way out of a shell. The voices around him vanished, along with the feel of the chair underneath him, the smell of food, the clamor of applause, and lastly, the touch of Magnus's hand on his face.

His knees hit the ground. He gasped and his eyes snapped open. All around him was a gray landscape. The stink of garbage hit his nostrils, and he jerked back instinctively as something reared over him—a surging mass of inchoate smoke, a cluster of glittering yellow eyes hanging in the darkness. They glared out at him as he fumbled for his bow and drew it back.

The thing roared, and rushed forward, surging toward him like a wave breaking. Alec let the runed arrow fly—it flicked through the air and sank itself deep into the smoke demon. A shrilling scream cracked the air, the demon pulsing around the arrow buried deep inside it, tendrils of smoke flailing outward, clawing at the sky—

And the demon vanished. Alec scrambled to his feet, fumbling another arrow into position, and swung around, scanning the landscape. It looked like pictures he'd seen of the surface of the moon, pitted and ashy, and above was a scorched sky, gray and yellow, cloudless. The sun hung orange and low, a dead cinder. There was no sign of the others.

Fighting down panic, he jogged up the rise of the nearest hill, and down the other side. Relief hit him in a wave. There was a depression between two rises of ash and rock, and crouched in it was Isabelle, struggling to her feet. Alec scrambled down the steep side of the hill and caught her in a one-armed hug. "Iz," he said.

She made a sound suspiciously like a sniffle and pulled away from him. "I'm all right," she said. There were tear tracks on her face; he wondered what she had seen. *The wishes of our hearts are weapons that can be used against us.*

"Max?" he asked.

She nodded, her eyes bright with unshed tears and anger. Of course Isabelle would be angry. She hated to cry.

"Me too," he said, and then whirled at the sound of a footstep, half-pushing Isabelle behind him.

It was Clary, and beside her, Simon. They both looked shell-shocked. Isabelle moved out from behind Alec. "You two…?"

"Fine," Simon said. "We … saw things. Weird things." He wouldn't meet Isabelle's gaze, and Alec wondered what he'd imagined. What were Simon's dreams and desires? Alec had never given it much thought.

"It was a demon," Alec said. "The kind that feeds on dreams and wishes. I killed it." He glanced from them to Isabelle. "Where's Jace?"

Clary paled under the dirt on her face. "We thought he'd be with you."

Alec shook his head. "He's all right," he said. "I'd know if he weren't—"

But Clary had already spun back around and was half-running back the way she'd come; after a moment Alec followed her, and so did the others. She scrambled up the rise, and then up another rise. Alec realized she was heading for higher ground, where the view would be better. He could hear her coughing; his own lungs felt coated with ash.

Dead, he thought. *Everything in this world is dead and burned to dust. What* happened *here?*

At the top of the hill was a cairn of stones—a circle of smooth rocks, like a dried-out well. Seated on the edge of the cairn was Jace, staring at the ground.

"Jace!" Clary skidded to a halt in front of him, dropped to her knees, and caught at his shoulders. He looked at her blankly. "Jace," she said again, urgently. "Jace, snap out of it. It's not real. It's a demon, making us see the things we want. Alec killed it. Okay? It's not real."

"I know." He looked up, and Alec felt the look like a blow. Jace looked as if he'd been bleeding out, though he was obviously uninjured.

"What did you see?" Alec said. "Max?"

Jace shook his head. "I didn't see anything."

"It's all right, whatever you saw. It's all right," Clary said. She leaned in, touched Jace's face; Alec was reminded acutely of Magnus's fingers on his cheek in the dream. Magnus saying he loved him. Magnus, who might not even still be alive. "I saw Sebastian," she said. "I was in Idris. The Fairchild house was still standing. My mom was with Luke. I—there was going to be a wedding." She swallowed. "I had a little sister, too. She was named after Valentine. He was a hero. Sebastian was there but he was fine, he was normal. He loved me. Like a real brother."

"That's messed up," Simon said. He moved closer to Isabelle, and they stood shoulder to shoulder. Jace reached out and ran a careful finger down one of Clary's curls, letting it wind around his hand. Alec remembered the first time he'd realized Jace was in love with her: He'd been watching his *parabatai* across a room, watching Jace's eyes track her movements. He remembered thinking: *She's all he sees.*

"We all have dreams," Clary said. "It doesn't mean anything. Remember what I said before? We stay together."

Jace kissed her forehead and stood up, holding out a hand; after a moment Clary took it, and rose to her feet beside him. "I didn't see anything," he said gently. "All right?"

She hesitated, clearly not believing him; just as clearly, she didn't want to press the point. "All right."

"I hate to bring this up," Isabelle said, "but did anyone see a way *back*?"

Alec thought of his headlong rush over the desert hills, searching for the others, eyes raking the horizon. He saw his companions pale as they glanced around. "I think," he said, "that there is no way back. Not from here, not down the tunnel. I think it closed up after us."

"So this was a one-way trip," said Clary, with only a slight tremble to her voice.

"Not necessarily," said Simon. "We have to get to Sebastian— we always knew that. And once we get there, Jace can try to do his thing with the heavenly fire, whatever that is—no offense—"

"None taken," said Jace, casting his eyes up to the sky.

"And once we rescue the prisoners," said Alec, "Magnus can help us get back. Or we can figure out how Sebastian gets back and forth; this can't be the only way."

"That's optimistic," said Isabelle. "What if we can't rescue the prisoners, or we can't kill Sebastian?"

"Then he'll kill us," said Jace. "And it won't matter that we don't know how to get back."

Clary squared her small shoulders. "Then we'd better get to finding him, hadn't we?"

Jace tugged his stele free of his pocket, and took Sebastian's bracelet off his wrist. He closed his fingers around it, using the stele to draw a tracking rune on the back of his hand. A moment passed, and then another; a look of intense concentration passed over Jace's face, like a cloud. He lifted his head.

"He's not that far," he said. "A day, maybe two days of walking away." He slid the bracelet back onto his wrist. Alec looked at it pointedly, and then at Jace. *If I cannot reach Heaven, I will raise Hell.*

"Wearing it will keep me from losing it," Jace said, and when Alec said nothing, Jace shrugged and started off down the hill. "We should get moving," he called back over his shoulder. "We've got a long way to go."

15

BRIMSTONE AND SALT

"Please don't rip my hand off," Magnus said. "I like that hand. I *need* that hand."

"Hmph," said Raphael, who was kneeling beside him, his hands on the chain that ran between the manacle on Magnus's right hand and the *adamas* loop sunk deep into the floor. "I am only trying to help." He jerked, hard, on the chain, and Magnus yelped in pain and glared. Raphael had thin, boyish hands, but that was deceptive: He had a vampire's strength, and he was currently bending its power to the purpose of yanking Magnus's chains out by the roots.

The cell they were in was circular. The floor was made of granite flagstones, overlapping. Stone benches ran around the inside of the walls. There was no discernible door, though there were narrow windows—as narrow as arrow slits. There was no glass in them, and it was possible to see from their depth that the walls were at least a foot thick.

Magnus had woken up in this room, a circle of red-geared Dark Shadowhunters standing around him, affixing his chains to the floor. Before the door had clanged shut behind them, he'd seen Sebastian standing in the corridor outside, grinning in at him like a death's-head.

Now Luke stood at one of the windows, staring out. None of them had been given a change of clothes, and he still wore the suit trousers and shirt he'd worn to dinner in Alicante. The front of his shirt was splashed with rusty stains. Magnus had to keep reminding himself it was wine. Luke looked haggard, his hair rumpled, one of the lenses of his glasses cracked.

"Do you see anything?" Magnus asked now, as Raphael moved to his other side to see if the left-hand chain would be any easier to remove. Magnus was the only one chained. By the time he'd woken up, Luke and Raphael had already been awake, Raphael lounging against one of the benches while Luke called out for Jocelyn until he was hoarse.

"No," Luke said shortly. Raphael raised an eyebrow at Magnus. He looked tousled and young, teeth digging into his lower lip as his knuckles whitened around the chain links. They were long enough to allow Magnus to sit up, but not to stand. "Just fog. Gray-yellow fog. Maybe mountains in the distance. It's hard to tell."

"Do you think we're still in Idris?" Raphael asked.

"No," Magnus said shortly. "We're not in Idris. I can feel it in my blood."

Luke looked at him. "Where are we?"

Magnus could feel the burn in his blood, the beginning of fever. It prickled along his nerves, drying his mouth, making his throat ache. "We're in Edom," he said. "A demon dimension."

Raphael dropped the chain and swore in Spanish. "I cannot free you," he said, clearly frustrated. "Why have Sebastian's servants chained only you and not either of us?"

"Because Magnus needs his hands to do magic," said Luke.

Raphael looked at Magnus, surprised. Magnus wiggled his eyebrows. "Didn't know that, vampire?" he said. "I would have thought you would have figured it out by now; you've been alive long enough."

"Perhaps." Raphael sat back on his heels. "But I have never had much business with warlocks."

Magnus gave him a look, a look that said: *We both know that isn't true.* Raphael looked away.

"Too bad," Magnus said. "If Sebastian had done his research, he would have known I can't do magic in this realm. There's no need for this." He rattled his chains like Marley's ghost.

"So this is where Sebastian's been hiding all this time," Luke said. "This is why we couldn't track him. This is his base of operations."

"Or," said Raphael, "this is just some place he has abandoned us to die and rot."

"He wouldn't bother," Luke said. "If he wanted us dead, we'd be dead, the three of us. He's got some larger plan. He always does. I just don't know why—" He broke off, looking down at his hands, and Magnus remembered him suddenly much younger, flyaway hair and worried looks and his heart on his sleeve.

"He won't hurt her," Magnus said. "Jocelyn, I mean."

"He might," Raphael said. "He is very crazy."

"Why wouldn't he hurt her?" Luke sounded as if he were holding in a fear that threatened to explode. "Because she's his mother? It doesn't work that way. *Sebastian* doesn't work that way."

"Not because she's his mother," Magnus said. "Because she's Clary's mother. She's leverage. And he won't give that up easily."

They had been walking for what seemed like hours now, and Clary was exhausted.

The uneven ground made the walking harder. None of the hills were very high, but they were pathless, and covered in shale and jagged rock. Sometimes there were plains of sticky, tarry pitch to cross, and their feet sank in almost to the ankles, dragging down their steps.

They paused to put on runes for sure-footedness and strength, and to drink water. It was a dry place, all smoke and ashes, with the occasional bright river of molten rock sludging through the burned land. Their faces were already smeared with dirt and ash, their gear powdered with it.

"Ration the water," Alec warned, capping his plastic bottle. They had paused in the shadow of a small mountain. Its jagged top snarled up into peaks and crenellations that made it resemble a crown. "We don't know how long we'll be traveling."

Jace touched the bracelet on his wrist, and then his tracking rune. He frowned at the traced pattern on the back of his hand. "The runes we just put on," he said. "Someone show me one."

Isabelle made an impatient noise, then thrust out her wrist, where Alec had inked a speed rune earlier. She blinked down at it. "It's fading," she said, a sudden uncertainty in her voice.

"My tracking rune as well, and the others," said Jace, glancing over his skin. "I think runes fade more quickly here. We're going to have to be careful about using them. Check to make sure when they need to be applied again."

"Our Speed runes are fading," Isabelle said, sounding frustrated. "That could be the difference between two days of walking and three. Sebastian could be doing *anything* to the prisoners."

Alec winced.

"He won't," Jace said. "They're his insurance that the Clave will turn us over to him. He won't do anything to them unless he's sure that won't happen."

"We could walk all night," Isabelle said. "We could use Wakefulness runes. Keep applying them."

Jace glanced around. Dirt was smudged under his eyes, and across his cheeks and forehead where he'd rubbed the palm of his hand. The sky had deepened from yellow to dark orange, smeared with roiling black clouds. Clary guessed that meant that nightfall was near. She wondered if days and nights were the same in this place, or if the hours were different, the rotations of this planet subtly misaligned.

"When Wakefulness runes fade, you crash," Jace said. "Then we'll be facing Sebastian basically hungover—not a good idea."

Alec followed Jace's gaze around the deadly landscape. "Then we're going to have to find a place to rest. Sleep. Aren't we?"

Clary didn't hear whatever Jace said next. She'd already moved away from the conversation, clambering up the steep side of a ridge of rock. The effort made her cough; the air was foul, thick with smoke and ash, but she didn't feel like staying for an argument. She was exhausted, her head was pounding, and she kept seeing her mother, over and over, in her head. Her mother and Luke, standing on a balcony together, hand in hand, looking down at her fondly.

She dragged herself up to the top of the rise and paused there. It sloped down steeply on the other side, ending in a plateau of gray rock that stretched to the horizon, piled here and there with heaps of slag and shale. The sun had lowered in the sky, though it was still the same burned orange color.

"What are you looking at?" said a voice at her elbow; she started, and turned to find Simon there. He wasn't quite as grimy as the rest of them—dirt never seemed to stick to vampires—but his hair was full of dust.

She pointed to dark holes where they pocked the side of the nearby hill like gunshot wounds. "Those are cave entrances, I think," she said.

"Kind of looks like something out of World of Warcraft, doesn't it?" he said, gesturing around them at the blasted landscape, the ash-torn sky. "Only, you can't just turn it off to get away."

"I haven't been able to turn it off for a long time." Clary could see Jace and the other Lightwoods a distance away, still arguing.

"Are you all right?" Simon asked. "I haven't had a chance to talk to you since everything happened with your mother, and Luke—"

"No," Clary said. "I'm not all right. But I have to keep going. If I keep going, I can not think about it."

"I'm sorry." Simon put his hands into his pockets, his head down. His brown hair blew across his forehead, across the place where the Mark of Cain had been.

"Are you kidding? I'm the one who's sorry. For everything. The fact that you got turned into a vampire, the Mark of Cain—"

"That *protected* me," Simon protested. "That was a miracle. It was something only you could do."

"That's what I'm afraid of," Clary whispered.

"What?"

"That I don't have any more miracles in me," she said, and pressed her lips together as the others joined them, Jace looking curiously from Simon to Clary as if wondering what they had been talking about.

Isabelle gazed out over the plain, at the acres of bleakness ahead, the view choked with dust. "Did you see something?"

"What about those caves?" Simon asked, gesturing toward the dark entrances tunneling into the mountainside. "They're shelter—"

"Good idea," Jace said. "We're in a demon dimension, God knows what lives here, and you want to crawl into a narrow dark hole and—"

"All right," Simon interrupted. "It was just a suggestion. You don't need to get pissed off—"

Jace, who was clearly in a mood, gave him a cold look. "That wasn't me pissed off, vampire—"

A dark piece of cloud detached itself from the sky and darted suddenly downward, faster than any of them could follow. Clary caught a single horrible glimpse of wings and teeth and dozens of red eyes, and then Jace was rising up into the air, caught in the clawed grip of an airborne demon.

Isabelle screamed. Clary's hand went to her belt, but the demon had already shot back up into the sky, a whirl of leathery wings, emitting a high-pitched squeal of victory. Jace made no noise at all; Clary could see his boots dangling, motionless. Was he *dead*?

Her vision went white. Clary whirled on Alec, who already had his bow out, an arrow notched and ready.

"Shoot it!" she screamed.

He spun like a dancer, scanning the sky. "I can't get a clear shot; it's too dark—I could hit Jace—"

Isabelle's whip uncoiled from her hand, a glimmering wire, reaching up, up, impossibly up. Its shimmering light illuminated the clouded sky, and Clary heard the demon scream again, this time a shrill cry of pain. The creature was spinning through the air, tumbling over and over, Jace caught in its grip. Its claws were sunk deep into his back—or was he clinging to *it*? Clary thought she saw the gleam of a seraph blade, or it might only have been the shimmer of Izzy's whip as it reached up, and then fell back to earth in a brightening coil.

Alec swore, and let an arrow fly. It shot upward, piercing the darkness; a second later a heaving dark mass plummeted to earth and hit the ground with a *whump* that sent up a cloud of powdery ash.

They all stared. Splayed, the demon was large, almost the size of a horse, with a dark green, turtle-like body; limp, leathery wings; six centipede-like clawed appendages; and a long stem of a neck that ended in a circle of eyes and jagged, uneven teeth. The shaft of Alec's arrow protruded from its side.

Jace was kneeling on its back, a seraph blade in his hand. He plunged it down into the back of the creature's neck viciously, over and over, sending up small geysers of black ichor that sprayed his clothes and face. The demon gave a squealing gurgle and slumped, its multiple red eyes going blank and lightless.

Jace slid from its back, breathing hard. The seraph blade had already begun to warp and twist with ichor; he tossed it to the side and looked levelly at the small group of his friends, all staring at him with expressions of astonishment.

"*That*," he said, "was me pissed off."

Alec made a sound halfway between a groan and an expletive, and lowered his bow. His black hair was stuck to his forehead with sweat.

"You don't all have to look so worried," Jace said. "I was doing fine."

Clary, light-headed with relief, gasped. "*Fine?* If your definition of 'fine' suddenly includes becoming a snack for a flying death turtle, then we are going to have to have *words*, Jace Lightwood—"

"It didn't vanish," Simon interrupted, looking as stunned as the rest of them. "The demon. It didn't vanish when you killed it."

"No, it didn't," Isabelle said. "Which means its home dimension is here." Her head was craned back, and she was studying the sky. Clary could see the gleam of a newly applied Farsighted rune on her neck. "And apparently these demons can go out in the daylight. Probably because the sun here is almost burnt out. We need to get out of this area."

Simon coughed loudly. "What were you all saying about taking shelter in the caves being a bad idea?"

"Actually, that was just Jace," said Alec. "Seems like a fine idea to me."

Jace glared at them both, and scrubbed a hand across his face, succeeding in smearing the black ichor across his cheek. "Let's check the caves out. We'll find a small one, scout it thoroughly before we rest. I'll take first watch."

Alec nodded and started to move toward the nearest cave entrance. The rest of them followed; Clary fell into step beside Jace. He was silent, lost in thought; under the heavy cloud cover, his hair glinted a dull gold, and she could see the massive rips in the back of his gear jacket where the demon's claws had taken hold. The corner of his mouth quirked up suddenly.

"What?" Clary demanded. "Is something funny?"

"'Flying death turtle'?" he said. "Only you."

"'Only me'? Is that good or bad?" she asked as they reached the cave entrance, looming up before them like an open, dark mouth.

Even in the shadows his smile was quicksilver. "It's perfect."

They made it only a few feet into the tunnel before they found the way blocked with a metal gate. Alec cursed, looking back over his shoulder. The cave entrance was just behind them, and through it Clary could see orange sky and dark, circling shapes.

"No—this is good," Jace said, stepping closer to the gate. "Look. Runes."

Runes were indeed worked into the curves of the metal: some familiar, some Clary didn't know. Still, they spoke to her of protection, of the fending off of demonic forces, a whisper in the back of her head. "They're protection runes," she said. "Protection against demons."

"Good," said Simon, casting another anxious glance back over his shoulder. "Because the demons are coming—fast."

Jace shot a glance behind them, then seized the gate and yanked at it. The lock burst, shedding flakes of rust. He pulled again, harder, and the gate swung open; Jace's hands were shimmering with suppressed light, and the metal where he had touched it looked blackened.

He ducked into the darkness beyond, and the others followed, Isabelle reaching for her witchlight. Simon came after, then Alec last, reaching out to slam the gate shut behind them. Clary took a moment to add a locking rune, just to be sure.

Izzy's witchlight flared up, illuminating the fact that they were standing in a tunnel that snaked forward into darkness. The walls were smooth, marbled gneiss, carved over and over again with runes of protection, holiness, and defense. The floor was sanded stone, easy to walk on. The air grew clearer as they made their way deeper into the mountain, the taint of fog and demons slowly receding until Clary was breathing more easily than she had since they had come to this realm.

They emerged at last into a large circular space, clearly crafted by human hands. It looked like the inside of a cathedral dome: round, with a massive ceiling arching overhead. There was a fire pit in the center of the room, long gone cold. White stone gems had been set into the ceiling. They glowed softly, filling the room with dim illumination. Isabelle lowered her witchlight, letting it blink off in her hand.

"I think this was a place to hide," Alec said in a hushed voice. "Some sort of last barricade where whoever lived here once would be safe from the demons."

"Whoever lived here once knew rune magic," Clary said. "I don't recognize them all, but I can feel what they mean. They're holy runes, like Raziel's."

Jace slung his pack off his shoulders and let it slide to the ground. "We're sleeping here tonight."

Alec looked dubious. "Are you sure that's safe?"

"We'll scout the tunnels," Jace said. "Clary, come with me. Isabelle, Simon, take the east corridor." He frowned. "Well, we're going to call it the east corridor. Here's hoping this is still accurate in the demon realms." He tapped the compass rune on his forearm, which was one of the first Marks most Shadowhunters received.

Isabelle dropped her pack, took out two seraph blades, and slid them into holsters on her back. "Fine."

"I'll go with you," Alec said, looking at Isabelle and Simon with suspicious eyes.

"If you must," said Isabelle with exaggerated indifference. "I should warn you we'll be making out in the dark. Big, sloppy make-outage."

Simon looked startled. "We are—" he began, but Isabelle stomped on his toe, and he quieted.

"'Make-outage'?" said Clary. "Is that a word?"

Alec looked ill. "I suppose I could stay here."

Jace grinned and tossed him a stele. "Make a fire," he said. "Cook us a pie or something. This demon-hunting is hungry work."

Alec drove the stele into the sand of the pit and began drawing the rune for fire. He appeared to be muttering something about how Jace wouldn't like it if he woke up in the morning with all of his hair shaved off.

Jace grinned at Clary. Under the ichor and blood, it was a ghost of his old, impish grin, but good enough. She took out Heosphoros. Simon and Isabelle had already disappeared down the east-facing tunnel; she and Jace turned the other way, which sloped slightly downward. As they fell into step, Clary heard Alec yell from behind them, "And your eyebrows, too!"

Dryly, Jace chuckled.

Maia wasn't sure what she'd thought being pack leader would be like, but it hadn't been this.

She was sitting on the big desk in the lobby of the Second Precinct building, Bat in the swivel chair behind her, patiently explaining various aspects of wolf pack administration: how they communicated with the remaining members of the Praetor Lupus in England, how messages were sent back and forth from Idris, even how they managed orders placed at the Jade Wolf restaurant. They both looked up when the doors burst open and a blue-skinned warlock woman in nurse's scrubs stalked into the room, followed by a tall man in a sweeping black coat.

"Catarina Loss," Bat said, by way of introduction. "Our new pack leader, Maia Roberts—"

Catarina waved him away. She was *very* blue, almost a sapphire color, and had glossy white hair piled into a bun. Her scrubs had trucks on them. "This is Malcolm Fade," she said, gesturing to the tall man beside her. "High Warlock of Los Angeles."

Malcolm Fade inclined his head. He had angular features, hair the color of paper, and his eyes were purple. *Really* purple, a color no human eyes ever were. He was attractive, Maia thought, if you liked that sort of thing. "Magnus Bane is missing!" he announced, as if it were the title of a picture book.

"And so is Luke," said Catarina grimly.

"Missing?" Maia echoed. "What do you mean, missing?"

"Well, not missing exactly. Kidnapped," said Malcolm, and Maia dropped the pen she was holding. "Who knows where they could be?" He sounded as if the whole thing was rather exciting and he was sad not to be a greater part of it.

"Is Sebastian Morgenstern responsible?" Maia asked Caterina.

"Sebastian captured all the Downworld representatives. Meliorn, Magnus, Raphael, and Luke. And Jocelyn, too. He's holding them, he says, unless the Clave agrees to give him Clary and Jace."

"And if they don't?" asked Leila. Catarina's dramatic entrance had brought the pack out, and they were filing into the room, draping themselves over the stairwell, and huddling up to the desk in the curious manner of lycanthropes.

"Then he'll kill the representatives," said Maia. "Right?"

"The Clave must know that if they let him do that, then Downworlders will rebel," Bat said. "It would be tantamount to declaring that the lives of four Downworlders are worth less than the safety of two Shadowhunters."

Not just two Shadowhunters, Maia thought. Jace was difficult and prickly, and Clary had been reserved at first, but they had fought for her and with her; they had saved her life and she had saved theirs. "Handing Jace and Clary over would be murdering them," Maia said. "And with no real guarantee that we'd get Luke back. Sebastian lies."

Catarina's eyes flashed. "If the Clave doesn't at least make a gesture toward getting Magnus and the others back, they won't just lose the Downworlders on their Council. They'll lose the Accords."

Maia was quiet for a moment; she was conscious of all the eyes on her. The other wolves watching for her reaction. For their leader's reaction.

She straightened. "What is the word from the warlocks? What are they doing? What about the Fair Folk and the Night's Children?"

"Most of the Downworlders don't know," said Malcolm. "I happen to have an informant. I shared the news with Catarina because of Magnus. I thought she ought to know. I mean, this sort of thing doesn't happen every day. Kidnapping! Ransoms! Love, sundered by tragedy!"

"Shut up, Malcolm," said Catarina. "This is why no one ever takes you seriously." She turned to Maia. "Look. Most of Downworld knows that the Shadowhunters packed up and went to Idris, of course; they don't know *why*, though. They're waiting for news from their representatives, which of course hasn't come."

"But that situation can't hold," said Maia. "Downworld will find out."

"Oh, they'll find out," said Malcolm, looking as if he were trying hard to be serious. "But you know Shadowhunters; they keep themselves to themselves. Everyone knows about Sebastian Morgenstern, of course, and the Dark Nephilim, but the attacks on the Institutes have been kept fairly quiet."

"They have the warlocks of the Spiral Labyrinth working on a cure for the effects of the Infernal Cup, but even they don't know how urgent the situation is, or what's been happening in Idris,"

Catarina said. "I fear the Shadowhunters will wipe themselves out with their own secrecy." She looked even bluer than before; her color seemed to change with her mood.

"So why come here to us, to me?" Maia asked.

"Because Sebastian already brought his message to you through his attack on the Praetor," Catarina replied. "And we know you're close with the Shadowhunters—the Inquisitor's children and Sebastian's own sister, for instance. You know as much as we do, maybe more, about what's going on."

"I don't know that much," Maia admitted. "The wards around Idris have been making it hard for messages to get through."

"We can help with that," said Catarina. "Can't we, Malcolm?"

"Hmm?" Malcolm was idly wandering around the station, stopping to stare at things Maia thought of as everyday—a banister railing, a cracked tile in the wall, a pane of window glass—as if they were revelatory. The pack watched him in puzzlement.

Catarina sighed. "Don't mind him," she said to Maia in an undertone. "He's quite powerful, but something happened to him at the beginning of last century, and he's never been quite right since. He's pretty harmless."

"Help? Of course we can help," Malcolm said, turning around to face them. "You need to get a message through? There's always carrier kittens."

"You mean pigeons," said Bat. "Carrier pigeons."

Malcolm shook his head. "Carrier kittens. They're so cute, no one can deny them. Fix your mouse problem, too."

"We don't have a mouse problem," said Maia. "We have a megalomaniac problem." She looked at Catarina. "Sebastian's determined to drive wedges between Downworlders and Shadowhunters. Kidnapping the representatives, attacking the Praetor, he won't stop there. All of Downworld will know soon enough what's going on. The question is, where will they stand?"

"We will stand bravely with you!" Malcolm announced. Catarina looked darkly at him, and he quailed. "Well, we will stand bravely near you. Or at least within earshot."

Maia gave him a hard look. "So no guarantees, basically?"

Malcolm shrugged. "Warlocks are independent. And hard to get hold of. Like cats, but with fewer tails. Well, there are *some* tails. I don't have one myself—"

"*Malcolm*," said Catarina.

"The thing is," Maia said, "either the Shadowhunters win or Sebastian does, and if he does, he'll come for us, for all Downworlders. All he wants is to turn this world into a wasteland of ashes and bone. None of us will survive."

Malcolm looked faintly alarmed, though not anywhere near as alarmed, Maia thought, as he ought to. His overwhelming aspect was one of innocent, childlike glee; he had none of Magnus's wise mischief. She wondered how old he was.

"I don't think we can get into Idris to fight beside them, like we did before," Maia went on. "But we can try to get the word out. Reach other Downworlders before Sebastian does. He'll try to recruit them; we have to make them understand what joining up with him will mean."

"The destruction of this world," said Bat.

"There are High Warlocks in various cities; they'll probably consider the issue. But we're loners, like Malcolm said," replied Catarina. "The Fair Folk are unlikely to talk to any of us; they never do—"

"And who cares what the vampires do?" snapped Leila. "They turn on their own, anyway."

"No," said Maia after a moment. "No, they can be loyal. We need to meet with them. It's high time the leaders of the New York pack and vampire clan formed an alliance."

A shocked murmur ran around the room. Werewolves and

vampires didn't parley unless brought together by a larger outside force, like the Clave.

She reached her hand out to Bat. "Pen and paper," she said, and he gave it to her. She scrawled a quick note, tore off a sheet of paper, and handed it to one of the younger wolf pups. "Take this to Lily at the Dumort," she said. "Tell her I want to meet with Maureen Brown. She can pick a neutral location; we'll approve it before the meeting. Tell them it should be as soon as possible. The lives of both our representative and theirs might depend on it."

"I want to be mad at you," Clary said. They were making their way down the snaking tunnel; Jace was holding her witchlight, its illumination guiding them. She was reminded of the first time he had pressed one of the smooth carved stones into her hand. *Every Shadowhunter should have their own witchlight rune-stone.*

"Oh?" Jace said, casting a wary glance at her. The ground under their feet was polished smooth, and the walls of the corridor curved inward gracefully. Every few feet a new rune was carved into the stone. "What for?"

"Risking your life," she said. "Except you didn't, really. You were just standing there and the demon grabbed you. Admittedly, you were being obnoxious to Simon."

"If a demon grabbed me every time I was obnoxious to Simon, I'd have died the day you met me."

"I just..." She shook her head. Her vision was blurring with exhaustion, and her chest ached with longing for her mother, for Luke. For home. "I don't know how I got here."

"I could probably retrace our steps," Jace said. "Straight through the faerie corridor, left at the decimated village, right at the blasted plain of the damned, sharp U-turn at the heap of dead demon—"

"You know what I mean. I don't know how I got *here*. My life was ordinary. I was ordinary—"

"You've never been ordinary," Jace said, his voice very quiet. Clary wondered if she'd ever stop being dizzied by his sudden transformations from humor to seriousness and back again.

"I wanted to be. I wanted to have a normal life." She glanced down at herself, dusty boots and stained gear, her weapons glittering at her belt. "Go to art school."

"Marry Simon? Have six kids?" There was a slight edge to Jace's voice now. The corridor made a sharp right turn, and he disappeared around it. Clary quickened her step to catch up with him—

And gasped. They had come out of the tunnel into an enormous cavern, half-filled with an underground lake. The cavern stretched out into the shadows. It was beautiful, the first beautiful thing Clary had seen since they'd entered the demon realm. The roof of the cave was folded stone, formed by years of trickling water, and it glowed with the intense blue shimmer of bioluminescent moss. The water below was just as blue, a deep glowing twilight, with pillars of quartz jutting up here and there like rods of crystal.

The path opened out into a shallow beach of fine, very powdery sand, nearly as soft as ash, that led down to the water. Jace moved down the beach and crouched by the water, thrusting his hands into it. Clary came up behind him, her boots sending up puffs of sand, and knelt down as he splashed water over his face and neck, scrubbing at the stains of black ichor.

"Be careful—" She caught at his arm. "The water could be poisonous."

He shook his head. "It's not. Look under the surface."

The lake was clear, glassine. The bottom was smooth stone, carved all over with runes that emitted a faint glow. They were runes that spoke of purity, healing, and protection.

"I'm sorry," Jace said, snapping her out of her reverie. His hair was wet, plastered to the sharp curves of his cheekbones and temples. "I shouldn't have said that about Simon."

Clary put her hands into the water. Small ripples spread from the movement of her fingers. "You have to know I wouldn't wish for a different life," she said. "This life brought me you." She cupped her hands, bringing the water to her mouth. It was cold and sweet, reviving her flagging energy.

He gave her one of his real smiles, not just a quirk of the mouth. "Hopefully not just me."

Clary searched for words. "This life is real," she said. "The other life was a lie. A dream. It's just that..."

"You haven't really been drawing," he said. "Not since you started training. Not seriously."

"No," she said quietly, because it was true.

"I wonder sometimes," he said. "My father—Valentine, I mean—loved music. He taught me to play. Bach, Chopin, Ravel. And I remember once asking why the composers were all mundanes. There were no Shadowhunters who had written music. And he said that in their souls, mundanes have a creative spark, but our souls hold a warrior spark, and both sparks can't exist in the same place, any more than a flame can divide itself."

"So you think the Shadowhunter in me ... is driving out the artist in me?" Clary said. "But my mother painted—I mean, paints." She bit back the pain of having thought of Jocelyn in the past tense, even briefly.

"Valentine said that was what Heaven had given to mundanes, artistry and the gift of creation," said Jace. "That was what made them worth protecting. I don't know if there was any truth to any of that," he added. "But if people have a spark in them, then yours burns the brightest I know. You can fight *and* draw. And you will."

Impulsively Clary leaned in to kiss him. His lips were cool. He tasted like sweet water and like Jace, and she would have leaned farther into the kiss, but a sharp zap, like static electricity, passed between them; she sat back, her lips stinging.

"Ouch," she said ruefully. Jace looked wretched. She reached out to touch his damp hair. "Earlier, with the gate. I saw your hands spark. The heavenly fire—"

"I don't have it under control here, not like I did at home," Jace said. "There's something about this world. It feels like it's pushing the fire closer to the surface." He looked down at his hands, from which the glow was fading. "I think we both need to be careful. This place is going to affect us more than it does the others. Higher concentration of angel blood."

"So we'll be careful. You can control it. Remember the exercises Jordan did with you—"

"Jordan's dead." His voice was tight as he stood up, brushing sand from his clothes. He held out a hand to help her up from the ground. "Come on," he said. "Let's get back to Alec before he decides Isabelle and Simon are having sex off in the caves and starts freaking out."

"You know everyone thinks we're off having sex," said Simon. "They're probably freaking out."

"Hmph," Isabelle said. The glow of her witchlight bounced off the runed walls of the cave. "As if we'd have sex in a cave surrounded by hordes of demons. This is reality, Simon, not your fevered imagination."

"There was a time in my life when the idea that I might have sex one day seemed *more* likely than being surrounded by hordes of demons, I'll have you know," he said, maneuvering around a pile of tumbled rocks. The whole place reminded him of a trip to the Luray Caverns in Virginia that he'd taken with his mother and Rebecca in middle school. He could see the glitter of mica in the rocks with his vampire sight; he didn't need Isabelle's witchlight to guide him, but he imagined she did, so said nothing about it.

Isabelle muttered something; he wasn't sure what, but he had a feeling it wasn't complimentary.

"Izzy," he said. "Is there a reason you're so angry with me?"

Her next words came out on a sighing rush that sounded like "youerensupposedbhere." Even with his amplified hearing, he could make no sense of it. "What?"

She swung around on him. "You weren't supposed to be here!" she said, her voice bouncing off the tunnel walls. "When we left you in New York, it was so you would be *safe*—"

"I don't want to be safe," he said. "I want to be with you."

"You want to be with Clary."

Simon paused. They were facing each other across the tunnel, both of them still now, Isabelle's hands in fists. "Is that what this is about? Clary?"

She was silent.

"I don't love Clary that way," he said. "She was my first love, my first crush. But what I feel about you is totally different—" He held up a hand as she started to shake her head. "Hear me out, Isabelle," he said. "If you're asking me to choose between you and my best friend, then yes, I won't choose. Because no one who loved me would force to me make such a pointless choice; it would be like I asked you to choose between me and Alec. Does it bother me see-ing Jace and Clary together? No, not at all. In their own incredibly weird way they're great for each other. They belong together. I don't belong with Clary, not like that. I belong with you."

"Do you mean that?" She was flushed, color high up in her cheeks.

He nodded.

"Come here," she said, and he let her pull him toward her, until he was flush up against her, the rigidity of the cave wall behind them forcing her to curve her body against his. He felt her hand slide up under the back of his T-shirt, her warm fingers bumping gently over the knobs of his spine. Her breath stirred his hair, and his body stirred too, just from being this close to her.

"Isabelle, I love—"

She slapped his arm, but it wasn't an angry slap. "Not *now*."

He nuzzled down into her neck, into the sweet smell of her skin and blood. "Then when?"

She suddenly jerked back, leaving him feeling the unpleasant sensation of having had a bandage ripped away with no ceremony. "Did you hear that?"

He was about to shake his head, when he *did* hear it—what sounded like a rustle and a cry, coming from the part of the tunnel they hadn't explored yet. Isabelle took off at a run, her witchlight bouncing wildly off the walls, and Simon, cursing the fact that Shadowhunters were Shadowhunters above all else, followed her.

The tunnel had only one more curve before it ended in the remains of a shattered metal gate. Beyond what was left of the gate, a plateau of stone that sloped down to a blasted landscape. The plateau was rough, shingled with rock and heaps of weathered stone. Where it met the sand below, the desert started up again, dotted here and there with black, twisted trees. Some of the clouds had cleared, and Isabelle, looking up, made a little gasping noise. "Look at the moon," she said.

Simon looked—and started. It wasn't so much a moon as moons, as if the moon itself had been cracked apart into three pieces. They floated, jagged-edged, like shark's teeth scattered in the sky. Each gave off a dull glow, and in the broken moonlight Simon's vampire vision picked out the circling movements of *creatures*. Some seemed like the flying thing that had seized Jace earlier; others had a distinctly more insectile look. All were hideous. He swallowed.

"What can you see?" Isabelle asked, knowing that even a Farsighted rune wouldn't give her better vision than Simon's, especially here, where runes faded so quickly.

"There are demons out there. A lot. Mostly airborne."

Isabelle's tone was grim. "So they can come out during the day, but they're more active at night."

"Yeah." Simon strained his eyes. "There's more. There's a stone plateau that goes for a distance, and then it drops off and there's something behind it, something shimmering."

"A lake, maybe?"

"Maybe," Simon said. "It almost looks like—"

"Like what?"

"Like a city," he said reluctantly. "Like a demon city."

"Oh." He saw the implications hit Isabelle, and for a moment she paled; then, being Izzy, she straightened up and nodded, turning away, away from the wrecked and shattered ruins of a world. "We'd better get back and tell the others."

Stars carved out of granite hung from the ceiling on silver chains. Jocelyn lay on the stone pallet that served as a bed and stared up at them.

She'd already shouted herself hoarse, clawed at the door—thick, made out of oak with steel hinges and bolts—until her hands were bloody, searched her things for a stele, and slammed her fist against the wall so hard she had bruises down her forearm.

Nothing had happened. She'd hardly expected it. If Sebastian was anything like his father—and Jocelyn expected that he was a great deal like his father—then he was nothing if not thorough.

Thorough, and creative. She'd found the pieces of her stele in a heap in one of the corners, shattered and unusable. She still wore the same clothes she'd been wearing at Meliorn's parody of a dinner party, but her shoes had been taken. Her hair had been shorn to just below her shoulders, the ends ragged, as if it had been cut with a blunt razor.

Small, colorful cruelties that spoke of an awful, patient nature.

Like Valentine, Sebastian could wait to get what he wanted, but he would make the waiting hurt.

The door rattled and opened. Jocelyn leaped to her feet, but Sebastian was already in the room, the door shut securely behind him with the snick of a lock. He grinned at her. "Finally awake, Mother?"

"I've been awake," she said. She placed one foot carefully behind the other, giving herself balance and leverage.

He snorted. "Don't bother," he said. "I've no intention of attacking you."

She said nothing, just watched him as he paced closer. The light that flooded through the narrow windows was bright enough to reflect off his pale white hair, to illuminate the planes of his face. She could see little of herself there. He was all Valentine. Valentine's face, his black eyes, the gestures of a dancer or an assassin. Only his frame, tall and slender, was hers.

"Your werewolf is safe," he said. "For now."

Jocelyn resolutely ignored the quick skip of her heart. *Show nothing on your face.* Emotion was weakness—that had been Valentine's lesson.

"And Clary," he said. "Clary is also safe. If you care, of course." He paced around her, a slow, considering circle. "I never could be quite sure. After all, a mother heartless enough to abandon one of her children—"

"You weren't my child," she blurted, and then closed her mouth sharply. *Don't give in to him*, she thought. *Don't show weakness. Don't give him what he wants.*

"And yet you kept the box," he said. "You know what box I mean. I left it in the kitchen at Amatis's for you; a little gift, something to remind you of me. How did you feel when you found it?" He smiled, and there was nothing in his smile of Valentine, either. Valentine had been human; he had been a human monster. Sebastian was something else again. "I know you took it out every year and wept over it," he said. "Why did you do that?"

She said nothing, and he reached over his shoulder to tap the hilt of the Morgenstern blade, strapped to his back. "I suggest you answer me," he said. "I would have no compunction about cutting off your fingers, one by one, and using them to fringe a very small rug."

She swallowed. "I cried over the box because my child was stolen from me."

"A child you never cared about."

"That isn't true," she said. "Before you were born, I loved you, the idea of you. I loved you when I felt your heartbeat inside me. Then you were born and you were—"

"A monster?"

"Your soul was dead," she said. "I could see it in your eyes when I looked at you." She crossed her arms over her chest, repressing the impulse to shiver. "Why am I here?"

His eyes glittered. "You tell me, since you know me so well, Mother."

"Meliorn drugged us," she said. "I would guess from his actions that the Fair Folk are your allies. That they have been for some time. That they believe you will win the Shadowhunter war, and they wish to be on the winning side; besides, they have resented Nephilim for longer and more strongly than any other Downworlders. They have helped you attack the Institutes; they have swelled your ranks while you have recruited new Shadowhunters with the Infernal Cup. In the end, when you have grown powerful enough, you will betray and destroy them, for you despise them at heart." There was a long pause, while she looked at him levelly. "Am I right?"

She saw the pulse jump in his throat as he exhaled, and knew she had been. "When did you guess all that?" he said through his teeth.

"I didn't guess. I know you. I knew your father, and you are like him, in your nurture if not your nature."

He was still staring at her, his eyes fathomless and black. "If you hadn't thought I was dead," he said, "if you'd known I lived, would you have looked for me? Would you have kept me?"

"I would have," she said. "I would have tried to raise you, to teach you the right things, to change you. I do blame myself for what you are. I always have."

"You would have raised me?" He blinked, almost sleepily. "You would have raised me, hating me as you did?"

She nodded.

"Do you think I would have been different, then? More like her?"

It took her a moment before she realized. "Clary," she said. "You mean Clary." The name of her daughter hurt to say; she missed Clary fiercely, and at the same time was terrified for her. Sebastian loved her, she thought; if he loved anyone, he loved his sister, and if there was anyone who knew how deadly it was to be loved by someone like Sebastian, it was Jocelyn. "We'll never know," she said finally. "Valentine took that away from us."

"You should have loved me," he said, and now he sounded petulant. "I'm your son. You should love me now, no matter what I'm like, whether I'm like her or not—"

"Really?" Jocelyn cut him off midbreath. "Do *you* love *me*? Just because I'm your mother?"

"You're not my mother," he said, with a curl of his lip. "Come. Watch this. Let me show you what my *real* mother has given me the power to do."

He took a stele from his belt. It sent a jolt through Jocelyn— she forgot, sometimes, that he was a Shadowhunter and could use the tools of a Shadowhunter. With the stele he drew on the stone wall of the room. Runes, a design she recognized. Something all Shadowhunters knew how to do. The stone began to turn transparent, and Jocelyn braced herself to see what was beyond the walls.

Instead she saw the Consul's room at the Gard in Alicante. Jia sat behind her enormous desk covered in stacks of files. She looked exhausted, her black hair liberally sprinkled with strands of white. She had a file open on the desk before her. Jocelyn could see grainy photographs of a beach: sand, blue-gray sky.

"Jia Penhallow," Sebastian said.

Jia's head jerked up. She rose to her feet, the file sliding to the floor in a mess of paper. "Who is it? Who's there?"

"You don't recognize me?" Sebastian said, a smirk in his voice.

Jia stared desperately ahead of her. It was obvious that whatever she was looking at, the image wasn't clear. "Sebastian," she breathed. "But it hasn't been two days yet."

Jocelyn pushed past him. "Jia," she said. "Jia, don't listen to anything he says. He's a liar—"

"It's too soon," Jia said, as if Jocelyn hadn't spoken, and Jocelyn realized, to her horror, that Jia couldn't see or hear her. It was as if she weren't there. "I may not have an answer for you, Sebastian."

"Oh, I think you do," Sebastian said. "Don't you?"

Jia straightened her shoulders. "If you insist," she said icily. "The Clave has discussed your request. We will not deliver to you either Jace Lightwood or Clarissa Fairchild—"

"Clarissa *Morgenstern*," Sebastian said, a muscle in his cheek twitching. "She is my sister."

"I call her by the name she prefers, as I call you," said Jia. "We will not make a bargain in our blood with you. Not because we think it is more valuable than Downworlder blood. Not because we do not want our prisoners back. But because we cannot condone your tactics of fear."

"As if I sought your approval," Sebastian sneered. "You do understand what this means? I could send you Luke Garroway's head on a stick."

Jocelyn felt as if someone had punched her in the stomach.

"You could," Jia said. "But if you harm any of the prisoners, it will be war to the death. And we believe you have as much to fear from a war with us as we do from a war with you."

"You believe incorrectly," Sebastian said. "And I think, if you look, you will discover that it hardly matters that you've decided not to deliver Jace and Clary to me, all neatly wrapped up like an early Christmas present."

"What do you mean?" Jia's voice sharpened.

"Oh, it would have been *convenient* if you had decided to deliver them," said Sebastian. "Less trouble for me. Less trouble for all of us. But it's too late now, you see—they're already gone."

He twirled his stele, and the window he had opened to the world of Alicante closed on Jia's astonished face. The wall was a smooth blank canvas of stone once again.

"Well," he said, slipping the stele into his weapons belt. "That *was* amusing, don't you think?"

Jocelyn swallowed against a dry throat. "If Jace and Clary aren't in Alicante, where are they? Where are they, Sebastian?"

He stared at her for a moment, and then laughed: a laugh as pure and cold as ice water. He was still laughing when he went to the door and walked out of it, letting it lock shut behind him.

16

THE TERRORS
OF THE EARTH

Night had fallen over Alicante, and the stars shone down like bright sentinels, making the demon towers, and the water in the canals—half ice now—shimmer. Emma sat on the windowsill of the twins' bedroom and looked out over the city.

Emma had always thought she would come to Alicante for the first time with her parents, that her mother would show her the places she had known growing up, the now-closed Academy where her mother had gone to school, her grandparents' house. That her father would show her the monument to the Carstairs family he always spoke of proudly. She'd never imagined she would first look on the demon towers of Alicante with her heart so swelled up with grief that sometimes it felt like it was choking her.

Moonlight spilled in through the attic windows, illuminating the twins. Tiberius had spent the day in a vicious tantrum, kicking the bars of the baby's crib when he was told he couldn't leave the house, shrieking for Mark when Julian tried to calm him down, and finally smashing his fist through a glass jewelry box. He was too young for healing runes, so Livvy had wrapped her arms around him to keep him still while Julian picked the glass out of his younger brother's bloody hand with tweezers, and then carefully bandaged it.

Ty had collapsed into bed finally, though he hadn't slept until Livvy, as calm as always, had lain down beside him and put her hand over his bandaged one. He was asleep now, head on the pillow, turned toward his sister. It was only when Ty was sleeping that you could see how uncommonly beautiful a child he was, with his head of dark Botticelli curls and delicate features, anger and despair smoothed away by exhaustion.

Despair, Emma thought. It was the right word, for the loneliness in Tavvy's screaming, for the emptiness at the heart of Ty's anger and Livvy's eerie calm. No one who was ten should feel despair, but she supposed there was no other way to describe the words that pulsed through her blood when she thought of her parents, every heartbeat a mournful litany: Gone, gone, gone.

"Hey." Emma looked up at the sound of a quiet voice from the doorway, and saw Julian standing at the entrance to the room. His own dark curls, shades lighter than Ty's black, were tousled, and his face was pale and tired in the moonlight. He looked skinny, thin wrists protruding from the cuffs of his sweater. He was holding something furry in his hand. "Are they..."

Emma nodded. "Asleep. Yeah."

Julian stared at the twins' bed. Up close Emma could see Ty's bloody handprints on Jules's shirt; he hadn't had time to change his clothes. He was clutching a large stuffed bee that Helen had retrieved from the Institute when the Clave had gone back to search the place. It had been Tiberius's for as long as Emma could remember. Ty had been screaming for it before he'd fallen asleep. Julian crossed the room and bent down to tuck it against his little brother's chest, then paused to gently untangle one of Ty's curls before he drew back.

Emma took his hand as he moved it, and he let her. His skin was cold, as if he'd been leaning out the window into the night air. She turned his hand and drew with her finger on the skin of his forearm. It was something they'd done since they were small children and didn't want to get caught talking during lessons. Over the years they'd gotten so good at it that they could map out detailed messages on each other's hands, arms, even their shoulders through their T-shirts.

D-I-D Y-O-U E-A-T? she spelled out.

Julian shook his head, still staring at Livvy and Ty. His curls were sticking up in tufts as if he'd been raking his hands through his hair. She felt his fingers, light on her upper arm. *N-O-T H-U-N-G-R-Y.*

"Too bad." Emma slid off the windowsill. "Come on."

She shooed him out of the room, onto the hallway landing. It was a small space, with a steep set of stairs descending into the main house. The Penhallows had made it clear the children were welcome to food whenever they wanted it, but there were no set mealtimes, and certainly no family meals. Everything was eaten hastily at tables in the attic, with Tavvy and even Dru covering themselves in food, and only Jules responsible for cleaning them up afterward, for washing their clothes, and even for making sure they ate at all.

The moment the door closed behind them, Julian slumped against the wall, tipping his head back, his eyes closed. His thin chest rose and fell quickly under his T-shirt. Emma hung back, unsure what to do.

"Jules?" she said.

He looked toward her. His eyes were dark in the low light, fringed by thick lashes. She could tell that he was fighting not to cry.

Julian was part of Emma's earliest memories. They had been put in cribs together as babies by their parents; apparently she had crawled out, and bitten through her lip when she'd hit the ground.

She hadn't cried, but Julian had screamed at the sight of her bleeding, until their parents had come running. They had taken their first steps together: Emma first as always, Julian afterward, hanging determinedly on to her hand. They had started training at the same time, had gotten their first runes together: Voyance on his right hand and on her left. Julian never wanted to lie, but if Emma was in trouble, Julian lied for her.

Now they had lost their parents together. Julian's mother had died two years before, and watching the Blackthorns go through that loss had been terrible, but this was a different experience altogether. It was shattering, and Emma could feel the breakage, could feel them coming apart and being glued back together in a new and different way. They were becoming something else, she and Julian, something that was more than best friends but not family, either.

"Jules," she said again, and took his hand. For a moment it lay, still and cold, in hers; then he seized her wrist and gripped it tightly.

"I don't know what to do," he said. "I can't take care of them. Tavvy's just a baby, Ty hates me—"

"He's your brother. And he's only ten. He doesn't hate you."

Julian took a shuddering breath. "Maybe."

"They'll figure something out," Emma said. "Your uncle lived through the London attack. So when this is all over, you'll move in with him, and he'll look after you and the others. It won't be your responsibility."

Julian shrugged. "I barely remember Uncle Arthur. He sends us books in Latin; sometimes he comes from London for Christmas. The only one of us who can read Latin is Ty, and he just learned it to annoy everyone."

"So he gives bad gifts. He remembered you at Christmas. He cares enough to take care of you. They won't have to just send you to a random Institute or to Idris—"

Julian swung around to face her. "That's not what you think

is going to happen to you, is it?" he demanded. "Because it won't. You'll stay with us."

"Not necessarily," Emma said. She felt as if her heart were being squeezed. The thought of leaving Jules, Livvy, Dru, Tavvy—even Ty—made her feel sick and lost, like she was being swept out into the ocean, alone. "It depends on your uncle, doesn't it? Whether he wants me in the Institute. Whether he's willing to take me in."

Julian's voice was fierce. Julian was rarely fierce, but when he was, his eyes went nearly black and he shook all over, as if he were freezing. "It's not up to him. You're going to stay with us."

"Jules—" Emma began, and froze as voices drifted up from downstairs. Jia and Patrick Penhallow were passing through the corridor below. She wasn't sure why she was nervous; it wasn't as if they weren't allowed full run of the house, but the idea of being caught wandering around this late at night by the Consul made her feel awkward.

"... smirking little bastard was right, of course," Jia was saying. She sounded frayed. "Not only are Jace and Clary gone, but Isabelle and Alec along with them. The Lightwoods are absolutely frantic."

Patrick's deep voice rumbled an answer. "Well, Alec is an adult, technically. Hopefully he's looking after the rest of them."

Jia made a muffled, impatient noise in response. Emma leaned forward, trying to hear her. "... could have left a note at least," she was saying. "They were clearly furious when they fled."

"They probably thought we were going to deliver them to Sebastian."

Jia sighed. "Ironic, considering how hard we fought against that. We assume Clary made a Portal to get them out of here, but as to how they've blocked us from tracking them, we don't know. They're nowhere on the map. It's like they disappeared off the face of the earth."

"Just like Sebastian has," said Patrick. "Doesn't it make sense to assume they're wherever he is? That the place itself is shielding them, not runes or some other kind of magic?"

Emma leaned farther forward, but the rest of their words faded with distance. She thought she heard a mention of the Spiral Labyrinth, but she wasn't positive. When she straightened up again, she saw Julian looking at her.

"You know where they are," he said, "don't you?"

Emma put her finger to her lips and shook her head. *Don't ask.*

Julian huffed out a laugh. "Only you. How did you—No, don't tell me, I don't even want to know." He looked at her searchingly, the way he did sometimes when he was trying to tell if she was lying or not. "You know," he said, "there's a way they couldn't send you away from our Institute. They'd have to let you stay."

Emma raised an eyebrow. "Let's hear it, genius."

"We could—" he started, then stopped, swallowed, and started again. "We could become *parabatai*."

He said it shyly, half-turning his face away from her, so that the shadows partially hid his expression.

"Then they couldn't separate us," he added. "Not ever."

Emma felt her heart turn over. "Jules, being *parabatai* is a big deal," she said. "It's—it's forever."

He looked at her, his face open and guileless. There was no trickery in Jules, no darkness. "Aren't we forever?" he asked.

Emma thought. She couldn't imagine her life without Julian. It was just a sort of black hole of terrible loneliness: nobody ever understanding her the way he did, getting her jokes the way he did, protecting her the way he did—not protecting her physically but protecting her feelings, her heart. No one to be happy with or angry with or bounce ridiculous ideas off. No one to complete her sentences, or pick all the cucumbers out of her salad because she hated them, or eat the crusts off her toast, or find her keys when she lost them.

"I—" she began, and there was a sudden crash from the

bedroom. She exchanged panicked looks with Julian before they burst back into Ty and Livvy's room, to find Livia sitting up on the bed, looking sleepy and puzzled. Ty was at the window, a poker in his hand. The window had a hole punched through the middle of it, and the window glass was glittering across the floor.

"Ty!" Julian said, clearly terrified by the shards piled around his little brother's bare feet. "Don't move. I'll get a broom for the glass—"

Ty glared out at both of them from beneath his wild dark hair. He held up something in his right hand. Emma squinted in the moonlight—was it an acorn?

"It's a message," Ty said, letting the poker drop from his hand. "Faeries often choose objects from the natural world to send their messages in—acorns, leaves, flowers."

"You're saying that's a message from faeries?" Julian said dubiously.

"Don't be stupid," said Tiberius. "Of course it's not a message from faeries. It's a message from Mark. And it's addressed to the Consul."

It must be daytime here, Luke thought, for Raphael was curled in one corner of the stone room, his body tense even in sleep, his dusky curls pillowed on his arm. It was hard to tell, given that there was little to see beyond the window but thick mist.

"He needs to feed," Magnus said, looking at Raphael with a tense gentleness that surprised Luke. He hadn't thought there was much love lost between the warlock and the vampire. They had circled each other as long as he had known them, polite, occupying their different spheres of power within the Downworld of New York City.

"You know each other," Luke said, realizing. He was still leaning against the wall by the narrow stone window, as if the view outside—clouds and yellowish poison—could tell him anything.

Magnus raised an eyebrow, the way he did when someone asked an obviously stupid question.

"I mean," Luke clarified, "you knew each other. Before."

"Before what? Before you were born? Let me make something clear to you, werewolf; almost everything in my life happened before you were born." Magnus's eyes lingered on the sleeping Raphael; despite the sharpness in his tone, his expression was almost gentle. "Fifty years ago," he said, "in New York, a woman came to me and asked me to save her son from a vampire."

"And the vampire was Raphael?"

"No," said Magnus. "Her son was Raphael. I couldn't save him. It was too late. He was already Turned." He sighed, and in his eyes suddenly Luke saw his great, great age, the wisdom and sorrow of centuries. "The vampire had killed all his friends. I don't know why he Turned Raphael instead. He saw something in him. Will, strength, beauty. I don't know. He was a child when I found him, a Caravaggio angel painted in blood."

"He still looks like a child," said Luke. Raphael had always reminded him of a choirboy gone bad, with his sweet young face and his black eyes older than the moon.

"Not to me," said Magnus. He sighed. "I hope he survives this," he said. "The New York vampires need someone with sense to run their clan, and Maureen's hardly that."

"You hope Raphael survives this?" Luke said. "Come on—how many people has he killed?"

Magnus turned cold eyes on him. "Who among us has bloodless hands? What did you do, Lucian Graymark, to gain yourself a pack—two packs—of werewolves?"

"That was different. That was necessary."

"What did you do when you were in the Circle?" Magnus demanded.

At that, Luke was silent. Those were days he hated to think about. Days of blood and silver. Days of Valentine by his side, telling him everything was all right, silencing his conscience. "I'm worried about my family now," he said. "I'm worried about Clary and Jocelyn and Amatis. I can't worry about Raphael, too. And you—I thought you'd be worried about Alec."

Magnus breathed out through gritted teeth. "I don't want to talk about Alec."

"All right." Luke said nothing else, just rested against the cold stone wall and watched Magnus fiddle with his chains. A moment later Magnus spoke again.

"Shadowhunters," he said. "They get in your blood, under your skin. I've been with vampires, werewolves, faeries, warlocks like me—and humans, so many fragile humans. But I always told myself I wouldn't give my heart to a Shadowhunter. I've so nearly loved them, been charmed by them—generations of them, sometimes: Edmund and Will and James and Lucie ... the ones I saved and the ones I couldn't." His voice choked off for a second, and Luke, staring in amazement, realized that this was the most of Magnus Bane's real, true emotions that he had ever seen. "And Clary, too, I loved, for I watched her grow up. But I've never been in love with a Shadowhunter, not until Alec. For they have the blood of angels in them, and the love of angels is a high and holy thing."

"Is that so bad?" Luke asked.

Magnus shrugged. "Sometimes it comes down to a choice," he said. "Between saving one person and saving the whole world. I've seen it happen, and I'm selfish enough to want the person who loves me to choose me. But Nephilim will always choose the world. I look at Alec and I feel like Lucifer in *Paradise Lost*. '*Abashed the Devil stood, And felt how awful goodness is.*' He meant it in the classic sense. 'Awful' as in inspiring awe. And awe is well and good, but it's poison to love. Love has to be between equals."

"He's just a boy," said Luke. "Alec—he's not perfect. And you're not fallen."

"We're all fallen," said Magnus, and he wrapped himself up in his chains and was silent.

"You have got to be kidding me," Maia said. "Here? Seriously?"

Bat rubbed his fingers over the back of his neck, ruffling up his short hair. "Is that a Ferris wheel?"

Maia turned around in a slow circle. They were standing inside the darkened massive Toys"R"Us on Forty-Second Street. Outside the windows the neon glow of Times Square lit the night with blue, red, and green. The store stretched upward, level on level of toys: bright plastic superheroes, plush stuffed bears, pink and glittery Barbies. The Ferris wheel rose above them, each metal strut carrying a dangling plastic carriage decorated with decals. Maia had a dim memory of her mother taking her and her brother to ride on the wheel when they were ten years old. Daniel had tried to push Maia over the edge and had made her cry. "This is ... crazy," she whispered.

"Maia." It was one of the younger wolves, skinny and nervous, with dreadlocks. Maia had worked to cure them all of the habit of calling her "lady" or "madam" or anything else but Maia, even if she was temporary pack leader. "We've swept the place. If there were security guards, someone's taken them out already."

"Great. Thanks." Maia looked at Bat, who shrugged. There were about fifteen other pack wolves with them, looking incongruous among the Disney princess dolls and stuffed reindeer. "Could you—"

The Ferris wheel started up suddenly with a screech and a groan. Maia jumped back, almost knocking into Bat, who took her by the shoulders. They both stared as the wheel started to turn and music began to play—"It's a Small World," Maia was pretty sure, though there were no words, just tinny instrumentals.

"Wolves! Oooh! Wooolves!" sang out a voice, and Maureen, looking like a Disney princess in a pink gown and a rainbow tiara, tripped barefoot out from a stacked display of candy canes. She was followed by about twenty vamps, as pale-faced as dolls or mannequins in the sickly light. Lily strode just behind her, her black hair pinned back perfectly, her heels clicking on the floor. She looked Maia up and down as if she'd never seen her before. "Hello, hello!" Maureen burbled. "I'm so glad to meet you."

"Glad to meet you as well," Maia said stiffly. She put a hand out for Maureen to shake, but Maureen just giggled and seized up a sparkly wand from a nearby carton. She waved it in the air.

"So sorry to hear about Sebastian killing all your wolfie friends," Maureen said. "He's a nasty boy."

Maia flinched at a vision of Jordan's face, the memory of the heavy, helpless weight of him in her arms.

She steeled herself. "That's what I wanted to talk to you about," she said. "Sebastian. He's trying to threaten Downworlders..." She paused as Maureen, humming, began to climb to the top of a stack of boxes of Christmas Barbies, each one dressed in a red-and-white Santa miniskirt. "Trying to get us to turn against the Shadowhunters," Maia went on, slightly flummoxed. Was Maureen even paying attention? "If we unite..."

"Oh, yes," Maureen said, perching atop the highest box. "We should unite against Shadowhunters. Definitely."

"No, I said—"

"I heard what you said." Maureen's eyes flashed. "It was silly. You werewolves are always full of silly ideas. Sebastian isn't very nice, but the Shadowhunters are worse. They make up stupid rules and they make us follow them. They steal from us."

"Steal?" Maia craned her head back to see Maureen.

"They stole Simon from me. I had him, and now he's gone. I know who took him. Shadowhunters."

Maia met Bat's eyes. He was staring. She realized she'd forgotten to tell him about Maureen's crush on Simon. She'd have to catch him up later—if there was a later. The vampires behind Maureen were looking more than a little hungry.

"I asked you to come meet me so that we could form an alliance," Maia said, as gently as if she were trying not to spook an animal.

"I love alliances," said Maureen, and she hopped down from the top of the boxes. Somewhere she'd gotten hold of an enormous lollipop, the kind with multicolored swirls. She began to peel off the wrapping. "If we form an alliance, we can be part of the invasion."

"The invasion?" Maia raised her eyebrows.

"Sebastian's going to invade Idris," Maureen said, dropping the plastic wrap. "He'll fight them and he'll win, and then we'll divide up the world, all of us, and he'll give us all the people we want to eat..." She bit down on the lollipop, and made a face. "Ugh. Nasty." She spit out the candy, but it had already painted her lips red and blue.

"I see," Maia said. "In that case—absolutely, let us ally against the Shadowhunters."

She felt Bat tense at her side. "Maia—"

Maia ignored him, stepping forward. She offered her wrist. "Blood binds an alliance," she said. "So say the old laws. Drink my blood to seal our compact."

"Maia, no," Bat said; she shot him a quelling look.

"This is how it has to be done," Maia said.

Maureen was grinning. She tossed aside the candy; it shattered on the floor. "Oh, fun," she said. "Like blood sisters."

"Just like that," said Maia, bracing herself as the younger girl took hold of her arm. Maureen's small fingers interlaced with hers. They were cold and sticky with sugar. There was a click as Maureen's fang teeth snapped out. "Just like—"

Maureen's teeth sank into Maia's wrist. She was making no effort to be gentle: pain lanced up Maia's arm, and she gasped. The wolves behind her stirred uneasily. She could hear Bat, breathing hard with the effort not to lunge at Maureen and tear her away.

Maureen swallowed, smiling, her teeth still firmly seated in Maia's arm. The blood vessels in Maia's arm throbbed with pain; she met Lily's eyes over Maureen's head. Lily smiled coldly.

Maureen gagged suddenly and pulled away. She put a hand to her mouth; her lips were swelling, like someone who'd had an allergic reaction to bee stings. "Hurts," she said, and then fissuring cracks spread out from her mouth, across her face. Her body spasmed. "Mama," she whispered in a small voice, and she began to crumble: Her hair drifted to ashes, and then her skin, peeling away to show the bones underneath. Maia stepped back, her wrist throbbing, as Maureen's dress folded away to the ground, pink and sparkling and ... empty.

"Holy—What happened?" Bat demanded, and caught Maia as she stumbled. Her torn wrist was already beginning to heal, but she felt a little dizzy. The wolf pack was murmuring around her. More disturbing, the vampires had come together, whispering, their pale faces venomous, full of hate.

"What did you do?" demanded one of them, a blond boy, in a shrill voice. "What did you do to our leader?"

Maia stared at Lily. The other girl's expression was cool and blank. For the first time Maia felt a thread of panic unfurl beneath her rib cage. Lily...

"Holy water," said Lily. "In her veins. She put it there with a syringe, earlier, so Maureen would be poisoned with it."

The blond vampire bared his teeth, his fangs snapping into place. "Betrayal has consequences," he said. "Werewolves—"

"Stop," Lily said. "She did it because I asked her to."

Maia exhaled, almost surprised by the relief that hit her. Lily was looking around at the other vampires, who were staring at her in confusion.

"Sebastian Morgenstern is our enemy, as he is the enemy of all Downworlders," Lily said. "If he destroys the Shadowhunters, the next thing he will do is turn his attention on us. His army of Endarkened warriors would murder Raphael and then lay waste to all the Night's Children. Maureen would never have seen that. She would have driven us all to our destruction."

Maia shook out her wrist, and turned to the pack. "Lily and I agreed," she said. "This was the only way. The alliance between us, that was sincere. Now is our chance, when Sebastian's armies are at their smallest and the Shadowhunters are still powerful; now is the time we can make a difference. Now is the time we can revenge those who died at the Praetor."

"Who's going to lead us?" whined the blond vampire. "The one who kills the previous leader takes up the mantle of leadership, but we can't be led by a werewolf." He glanced at Maia. "No offense."

"None taken," she muttered.

"I am the one who killed Maureen," said Lily. "Maia was the weapon I wielded, but it was my plan, my hand behind it. I will lead. Unless anyone objects."

The vampires glanced around at one another in confusion. Bat, to Maia's surprise and amusement, cracked his knuckles loudly in the silence.

Lily's red lips curved. "I didn't think so." She took a step toward Maia, daintily avoiding the tulle dress and pile of ashes that were all that was left of Maureen. "Now," she said. "Why don't we discuss this alliance?"

"I did not make a pie," Alec announced when Jace and Clary returned to the large central chamber of the cave. He was lying on his back, on an unrolled blanket, with his head pillowed on a wadded-up jacket. There was a fire smoking in the pit, the flames casting elongated shadows against the walls.

He had spread out provisions: bread and chocolate, nuts and granola bars, water and bruised apples. Clary felt her stomach tighten, realizing only then how hungry she was. There were three plastic bottles next to the food: two of water, and a darker one of wine.

"I did not make a pie," Alec repeated, gesturing expressively with one hand, "for three reasons. One, because I do not have any pie ingredients. Two, because I don't actually know how to make a pie."

He paused, clearly waiting.

Removing his sword and leaning it against the cave wall, Jace said warily, "And three?"

"Because I am not your bitch," Alec said, clearly pleased with himself.

Clary couldn't help but smile. She undid her weapons belt and laid it down carefully by the wall; Jace, unbuckling his own, rolled his eyes.

"You know that wine is supposed to be for antiseptic purposes," Jace said, sprawling elegantly on the ground next to Alec. Clary sat beside him. Every muscle in her body protested—even months of training hadn't prepared her for the day's draining trek across the burning sand.

"There's not enough alcohol in wine to be able to use it for antiseptic purposes," said Alec. "Besides, I'm not drunk. I'm contemplative."

"Right." Jace swiped an apple, sliced it expertly in two, and offered half to Clary. She took a bite of the fruit, remembering. Their first kiss had tasted of apples.

"So," she said. "What are you contemplating?"

"What's going on at home," Alec said. "Now that they've

probably noticed we're gone and all that. I feel bad about Aline and Helen. I would have liked to warn them."

"You don't feel bad about your parents?" Clary said.

"No," Alec said after a long pause. "They had their chance to do the right thing." He rolled onto his side and looked at them. His eyes were very blue in the firelight. "I always thought being a Shadowhunter meant that I had to approve of what the Clave did," he said. "I thought otherwise I wasn't loyal. I made excuses for them. I always have. But I feel like whenever we have to fight, we're fighting a war on two fronts. We fight the enemy and we fight the Clave, too. I don't—I just don't know how I feel anymore."

Jace smiled at him fondly across the fire. "Rebel," he said.

Alec made a face and levered himself up onto his elbows. "Don't make fun of me," he snapped, with enough force that Jace looked surprised. Jace's expressions were unreadable to most people, but Clary knew him well enough to recognize the quick flash of hurt across his face, and the anxiety as he leaned forward to reply to Alec—just as Isabelle and Simon burst into the room. Isabelle looked flushed, but in the manner of someone who had been running rather than someone who had been giving in to passion. Poor Simon, Clary thought with amusement—amusement that vanished almost instantly when she saw the looks on their faces.

"The east corridor ends in a door," Isabelle said without preamble. "A gate, like the one we came in through, but it's broken. And there are demons, the flying kind. They're not coming near here, but you can see them. Someone should probably keep watch, just to be safe."

"I'll do it," Alec said, standing up. "I'm not going to sleep anyway."

"Me neither." Jace scrambled to his feet. "Besides, someone should keep you company." He looked at Clary, who offered an encouraging smile. She knew Jace hated it when Alec was angry at him. She wasn't sure if he could feel the discord through the *parabatai* bond or if it was just ordinary empathy, or a little of both.

"There are three moons," Isabelle said and sat down by the food, reaching for a granola bar. "And Simon thought he saw a city. A demon city."

"I wasn't sure," Simon added quickly.

"In the books Edom has a capital, called Idumea," said Alec. "There could be something. We'll keep an eye out." He bent to retrieve his bow and started off down the east corridor. Jace retrieved a seraph blade, kissed Clary quickly, and headed after him; Clary settled down on her side, staring into the fire, letting the soft murmur of Isabelle and Simon's conversation lull her to sleep.

Jace felt the sinews in his back and neck crack with exhaustion as he lowered himself down among the rocks, sliding back until he was sitting with his back to one of the larger ones, trying not to breathe too deeply in the bitter air. He heard Alec settle beside him, the rough material of his gear scratching against the ground. Moonlight sparked off his bow as he laid it across his lap and looked out over the landscape.

The three moons hung low in the sky; each fragment looked bloated and enormous, the color of wine, and they tinged the landscape with their bloody glow.

"Are you going to talk?" Jace asked. "Or is this one of those times where you're mad at me so you don't say anything?"

"I'm not mad at you," Alec said. He ran a leather-gauntleted hand over his bow, idly tapping his fingers against the wood.

"I thought you might be," Jace said. "If I'd agreed to look for shelter, I wouldn't have been attacked. I put us all in danger—"

Alec took a deep breath and let it out slowly. The moons had inched slightly higher in the sky, and they cast their dark glow across his face. He looked young, with his hair dirty and tangled, his shirt torn. "We knew the risks we were taking coming here with you. We signed up to die. I mean, obviously I'd rather survive. But we all chose."

"The first time you saw me," Jace said, looking down at his hands, looped around his knees, "I bet you didn't think, *He's going to get me killed.*"

"The first time I saw you, I wished you'd go back to Idris." Jace looked over at Alec incredulously; Alec shrugged. "You know I don't like change."

"I grew on you, though," Jace stated confidently.

"Eventually," Alec agreed. "Like moss, or a skin disease."

"You love me." Jace leaned his head back against the rock, looking out across the dead landscape through tired eyes. "You think we should have left a note for Maryse and Robert?"

Alec laughed dryly. "I think they'll figure out where we went. Eventually. Maybe I don't care if Dad ever figures it out." Alec threw his head back and sighed. "Oh, God, I'm a cliché," he said in despair. "Why do I care? If Dad decides he hates me because I'm not straight, he's not worth the pain, right?"

"Don't look at me," said Jace. "My adoptive father was a mass murderer. And I still worried about what he thought. It's what we're programmed to do. Your dad always seemed pretty great by comparison."

"Sure, he likes you," said Alec. "You're heterosexual and have low expectations of father figures."

"I think they'll probably put that on my gravestone. 'He Was Heterosexual and Had Low Expectations.'"

Alec smiled—a brief, forced flash of a smile. Jace looked at him narrowly. "Are you sure you're not mad? You seem kind of mad."

Alec looked up at the sky overhead. There were no stars visible through the cloud cover, only a smear of yellowish black. "Not everything is about you."

"If you're not doing okay, you should tell me," Jace said. "We're all under stress, but we have to keep it together as much as we—"

Alec whirled on him. There was disbelief in his eyes. "Doing okay? How would you be doing?" he demanded. "How would you be doing if it were Clary that Sebastian had taken? If it were her we were going to rescue, not knowing if she was dead or alive? How would you be doing?"

Jace felt as if Alec had slapped him. He also felt as though he deserved it. It took him several tries before he could get out the next words: "I—I would be in pieces."

Alec got to his feet. He was outlined against the bruise-colored sky, the glow of the broken moons reflecting off the ground; Jace could see every facet of his expression, everything he had been keeping pent up. He thought of the way Alec had killed the faerie knight in the Court; cold and quick and merciless. None of that was like Alec. And yet Jace had not paused to think about it, to think what drove that coldness: the hurt, the anger, the fear. "This," Alec said, gesturing toward himself. "This is me in pieces."

"Alec—"

"I'm not like you," Alec said. "I—I am not able to create the perfect facade at all times. I can tell jokes, I can try, but there are limits. I can't—"

Jace staggered to his feet. "But you don't have to create a facade," he said, bewildered. "You don't have to pretend. You can—"

"I can break down? We both know that's not true. We need to hold it together, and all those years I watched you, I watched you hold it together, I watched you after you thought your father died, I watched you when you thought Clary was your sister, I watched you, and this is how you survived, so if I have to survive, then I'm going to do the same thing."

"But you're not like me," Jace said. He felt as if the steady ground below him were cracking in half. When he was ten years old, he had built his life on the bedrock of the Lightwoods, Alec most of all. He had always thought that as *parabatai* they'd been there for each other, that he'd been there for Alec's broken heart as much as Alec had been there for his, but he realized now, and horribly, that he had given little thought to Alec since the prisoners had been taken, had not thought how each hour, each minute, must be for him, not knowing if Magnus was alive or dead. "You're better."

Alec stared at him, his chest rising and falling quickly. "What did you imagine?" he asked abruptly. "When we came through into this world? I saw your expression when we found you. You didn't envision 'nothing.' 'Nothing' wouldn't have made you look like that."

Jace shook his head. "What did *you* see?"

"I saw the Hall of Accords. There was a huge victory banquet, and everyone was there. Max—was there. And you, and Magnus, and everyone, and Dad was giving a speech about how I was the best warrior he'd ever known..." His voice trailed off. "I never thought I wanted to be the best warrior," he said. "I always thought I was happy being the dark star to your supernova. I mean, you have the angel's gift. I could train and train ... I'd never be you."

"You'd never want to," Jace said. "That's not you."

Alec's breathing had slowed. "I know," he said. "I'm not jealous. I always knew, from the first, that everyone thought you were better than me. My dad thought it. The Clave thought it. Izzy and Max looked up to you as the great warrior they wanted to be like. But the day you asked me to be your *parabatai*, I knew you meant that you trusted me enough to ask me to help you. You were telling me that you weren't the lone and self-sufficient warrior able to do everything alone. You needed me. So I realized that there was one person who didn't assume you were better than me. You."

"There all sorts of ways of being better," Jace said. "I knew that even then. I might be physically stronger, but you have the truest heart of anyone I've ever known, and the strongest faith in other people, and in that way you are better than I could ever hope to be."

Alec looked at him with surprised eyes.

"The best thing Valentine ever did for me was send me to you," Jace added. "Your parents, sure, but mainly you. You and Izzy and Max. If it hadn't been for you, I would have been—like Sebastian. Wanting this." He gestured at the wasteland in front of them. "Wanting to be king of a wasteland of skulls and corpses." Jace broke off, squinting into the distance. "Did you see that?"

Alec shook his head. "I don't see anything."

"Light, sparking off something." Jace searched among the shadows of the desert. He drew a seraph blade from his belt. Under the moonlight, even not yet activated, the clear *adamas* glowed with a ruby shine. "Wait here," he said. "Guard the entrance. I'm going to look."

"Jace—" Alec started, but Jace was already darting down the slope, springing from rock to rock. As he neared the foot of the rise, the rocks became paler in color, and began to crumble away under his feet as he landed on them. Eventually they gave way to powdery sand, dotted with massive arched boulders. There were a few growing things dotting the landscape: trees that looked as if they'd been fossilized in place by a sudden blast, a solar flare.

Behind him was Alec and the entrance to the tunnels. Ahead was desolation. Jace began to pick his way carefully among the broken rocks and dead trees. As he moved, he saw it again, a darting spark, something alive among the deadness. He turned toward it, placing each foot carefully, directly, in front of the other.

"Who's there?" he called, then frowned. "Of course," he added, addressing the darkness all around, "even I, as a Shadowhunter, have seen enough movies to know that anyone who yells 'Who's there?' is going to be instantly killed."

A noise echoed through the air—a gasp, a swallow of broken

breath. Jace tensed and moved forward swiftly. There it was: a shadow, evolving out of the dark into a human shape. A woman, crouched and kneeling, wearing a pale robe stained with dirt and blood. She seemed to be weeping.

Jace tightened his grip on the hilt of his blade. He had approached enough demons in his life who were pretending helplessness or who had otherwise disguised their true nature that he felt less sympathy than suspicion. *"Dumah,"* he whispered, and the blade flared up into light. He could see the woman more clearly now. She had long hair that fell to the ground and mixed with the scorched earth, and a circle of iron around her brow. Her hair was reddish in the shadows, the color of old blood, and for a moment, before she rose and turned to him, he thought of the Seelie Queen—

But it was not her. This woman was a Shadowhunter. She was more than that. She wore the white robes of an Iron Sister, bound under her breasts, and her eyes were the flat orange of flames. Dark runes disfigured her cheeks and brow. Her hands were clasped over her chest. She released them now, and let them fall to her sides, and Jace felt the air in his lungs turn cold as he saw the massive wound in her chest, the blood spreading across the white fabric of her dress.

"You know me, don't you, Shadowhunter?" she said. "I am Sister Magdalena of the Iron Sisters, whom you murdered."

Jace swallowed against his dry throat. "It's not her. You're a demon."

She shook her head. "I was cursed, for my betrayal of the Clave. When you killed me, I came here. This is my Hell, and I wander it. Never healing, always bleeding." She pointed backward, and he saw the footsteps behind her that led to this place, the marks of bare feet outlined in blood. "This is what you did to me."

"It wasn't me," he said hoarsely.

She cocked her head to the side. "Wasn't it?" she said. "Do you not remember?"

And he did remember, the small artist's studio in Paris, the Cup of *adamas*, Magdalena not expecting the attack as he drew his blade and stabbed her; the look on her face as she fell against the worktable, dying—

Blood on his blade, on his hands, on his clothes. Not demon's blood or ichor. Not the blood of an enemy. The blood of a Shadowhunter.

"You remember," said Magdalena, cocking her head to the side with a small smile. "How would a demon know the things I know, Jace Herondale?"

"Not—my name," Jace whispered. His blood felt hot in his veins, tightening his throat, choking off his words. He thought of the silver box with the birds on it, herons graceful in the air, the history of one of the great Shadowhunter families laid out in books and letters and heirlooms, and how he had felt as if he didn't deserve to touch the contents.

Her expression twitched, as if she didn't quite understand what he had said, but she went on smoothly, stepping toward him across the broken ground. "Then what are you? You have no real claim on the name of Lightwood. Are you a Morgenstern? Like Jonathan?"

Jace took a breath that scorched his throat like fire. His body was slick with sweat, his hands shaking. Everything in him screamed that he should lunge forward, should pierce the Magdalena creature with his seraph blade, but he kept seeing her falling, dying, in Paris, and himself standing over her, realizing what he had done, that he was a murderer, and how could you murder the same person twice—

"You liked it, didn't you?" she whispered. "Being bound to Jonathan, being one with him? It freed you. You can tell yourself now that everything you did was forced on you, that you weren't the one acting, that you didn't drive that blade into me, but we two know the truth. Lilith's bond was only an excuse for you to do the things you desired to do anyway."

Clary, he thought, achingly. If she were here, he would have her inexplicable conviction to cling to, her belief that he was intrinsically good, a belief that served as a fortress through which no doubt could travel. But she was not here and he was alone in a burned, dead land, the same dead land—

"You saw it, didn't you?" Magdalena hissed, and she was almost on him now, her eyes leaping and flaring orange and red. "This burned land, all destruction, and you ruling over it? That was your vision? The wish of your heart?" She caught at his wrist, and her voice rose, exultant, no longer quite human. "You think your dark secret is that you want to be like Jonathan, but I will tell you the true secret, the darkest secret. You already are."

"No!" Jace cried, and brought up his blade, an arc of fire across the sky. She jerked back, and for a moment Jace thought that the fire from the blade had caught the tip of her robe alight, for flame exploded across his vision. He felt the burn and twist of veins and muscles in his arms, heard Magdalena's scream turn guttural and inhuman. He staggered back—

And realized the fire was pouring from him, that it had burst from his hands and fingertips in waves that coursed across the desert, blasting everything in front of him. He saw Magdalena twist and writhe, becoming something hideous, tentacled and repulsive, before shivering away to ashes with a scream. He saw the ground blacken and shimmer as he fell to his knees, his seraph blade melting into the flames that rose to circle him. He thought, *I will burn to death here*, as the fire roared across the plain, blotting out the sky.

He was not afraid.

17

BURNT OFFERINGS

Clary dreamed of fire, a pillar of fire sweeping through a desert landscape, scorching everything in front of it: trees, brush, shrieking people. Their bodies turned black as they crumbled away before the force of the flames, and over them all hung a rune, hovering like an angel, a shape like two wings joined by a single bar—

A scream cut through the smoke and shadow, snapping Clary out of her nightmares. Her eyes flew open and she saw fire in front of her, bright and hot, and scrambled up, reaching for Heosphoros.

With the blade in her hand, her heartbeat ebbed slowly. This fire wasn't raging or out of control. It was contained, the smoke floating up toward the enormous roof of the cave. It illuminated the space around it. She could see Simon and Isabelle in the glow, Izzy lifting herself out of Simon's lap and blinking around, confused. "What—"

Clary was already on her feet. "Someone screamed," she said. "You two stay here—I'll go see what happened."

"No—no." Isabelle scrambled to her feet just as Alec burst into the chamber, panting hard.

"Jace," he said. "Something's happened—Clary, get your stele and come on." He turned around and darted back into the tunnel. Clary jammed Heosophoros through her belt and raced after him. She rocketed through the corridor, boots skimming over the uneven rocks, and exploded out into the night, her stele now in her hand.

The night was burning. The gray plateau of rocks tilted down toward the desert, and where the rocks met the sand there was fire—fire blasting up into the air, turning the sky gold, scorching the ground. She stared at Alec.

"Where's Jace?" she shouted over the crackle of the flames.

He looked away from her, at the heart of the fire. "There," he said. "Inside it. I saw it pour out of him and swallow him up."

Clary felt her heart seize up; she staggered back, away from Alec as if he'd hit her, and then he was reaching for her, saying, "Clary. He's not dead. If he were, I'd know it. I'd know—"

Isabelle and Simon burst out from the cave entrance behind them; Clary saw them both react to the heavenly fire, Isabelle with widened eyes, and Simon with a recoil of horror—fire and vampires didn't mix, even if he was a Daylighter. Isabelle caught at his arm as if to protect him; Clary could hear her shouting, her words lost against the roar of flames. Clary's arm burned and stung. She looked down to realize that she had begun drawing on her skin, the reflex taking over from her conscious mind. She watched as a *pyr* rune, for fireproofing, appeared on her wrist, bold and black against her skin. It was a strong rune: She could feel the force of it, radiating outward.

She started down the slope, turning when she sensed Alec behind her. "Stay back," she shouted at him, and held up her wrist, showing him the rune. "I don't know if it will work," she called. "Stay here; protect Simon and Izzy—the heavenly fire should keep the demons back, but just in case." And then she turned away, darting lightly among the rocks, closing the distance between herself and the blaze, as Alec stood on the path behind her, hands fisted at his sides.

Up close the fire was a wall of gold, moving and shifting, colors flickering in its heart: burning red, tongues of orange and green. Clary could see nothing *but* flames; the heat that poured off the blaze made her skin prickle and her eyes water. She took a breath that scorched her throat, and stepped into the fire.

It wrapped her like an embrace. The world turned red, gold, orange, and swam before her eyes. Her hair lifted and blew in the hot wind, and she couldn't tell what was its fiery strands and what was fire itself. She stepped forward carefully, staggering as if she were walking against a massive headwind—she could feel the Fireproof rune throbbing on her arm with each step—as the flames swirled up, around, and over her.

She took another scorching breath and pushed forward, her shoulders bent as if she were lifting a heavy weight. There was nothing around her but fire. She would die in the fire, she thought, burning up like a feather, not even a footprint left on the dirt of this alien world to mark that she had ever been there.

Jace, she thought, and took a final step. The flames parted around her like a curtain drawing back, and she gasped, falling forward, her knees hitting the earth hard. The Fireproof rune on her arm was fading, turning white, draining her energy along with its power. She lifted her head and stared.

The fire rose all around her in a circle, flames reaching for the scorched demon sky. In the center of the circle of flame knelt Jace; he was untouched by fire himself, on his knees, his golden head back, his eyes half-closed. His hands were flat on the ground, and from his palms poured a river of what looked like molten gold. It had threaded through the earth like tiny streams of lava, illuminating the ground. No, she thought, it was doing more than illuminating it. It was *crystallizing* the earth, turning it to a hard, golden material that shone like—

Like *adamas*. She crawled forward toward Jace, the ground under her turning from bumpy earth to a slippery glassine substance, like *adamas*, but the color of gold instead of white. Jace didn't move: Like the Angel Raziel rising from Lake Lyn streaming water, he remained still as fire poured from him, and all around the ground hardened and turned to gold.

Adamas. The power of it shuddered up and through Clary, making her bones shiver. Images bloomed in her mind: runes, looming up and then vanishing like fireworks, and she mourned their loss, so many runes she would never know the meaning of, the use of, but then she was inches from Jace, and the first rune she had ever imagined, the rune she had spent the last days dreaming of, rose up in her mind. *Wings, connected by a single bar—no, not wings—the hilt of a sword—it had always been the hilt of a sword—*

"Jace!" she cried, and his eyes flew open. They were more golden than even the fire. He looked at her in utter disbelief, and she realized immediately what he had thought he was doing—kneeling and waiting to die, waiting to be consumed by the fire like a medieval saint.

She wanted to slap him.

"Clary, *how*—"

She reached to catch at his wrist, but he was faster than she was, and dodged her grip. "No! Don't touch me. It isn't safe—"

"Jace, stop." She held up her arm, with the *pyr* rune on it, shimmering silver in the unearthly glow. "I walked through the fire to get to you," she said over the cry of the flames. "We're here. We're both here now, understand?"

His eyes were manic, desperate. "Clary, *get out*—"

"No!" She clutched at his shoulders, and this time he didn't move back. She fisted her hands in his gear. "*I know how to fix this!*"

she cried, and leaned forward to press her lips to his.

His mouth was hot and dry, his skin burning as she ran her hands up his neck to cup the sides of his face. She tasted fire and char and blood on his mouth and wondered if he tasted the same thing on her. "Trust me," she whispered against his lips, and though the words were swallowed up by the chaos around them, she felt him relax minutely and nod, leaning into her, letting the fire pass between them as they breathed each other's breath, tasting the sparks on each other's lips.

"Trust me," she whispered again, and reached for her blade.

Isabelle had her arms around Simon, holding him back. She knew that if she let him go, he would tear down the slope to the fire, where Clary had disappeared, and throw himself into it.

And he would go up like tinder, like gasoline-soaked tinder. He was a vampire. Isabelle held him, her hands clasped over his chest, and felt as if she could sense the hollowness under his ribs, the place where his heart *didn't* beat. Her own was racing. Her hair lifted and blew back in the hot wind from the immense fire burning at the foot of the plateau. Alec was halfway down the path, hovering; he was a black silhouette against the flames.

And the flames—they leaped toward the sky, blotting out the broken moon. Shifting and changing, a deadly beautiful wall of gold. As the flames trembled, Isabelle could make out shadows moving inside them—the shadow of someone kneeling, and then another, smaller shadow, bending and crawling. *Clary*, she thought, crawling toward Jace through the heart of the conflagration. She knew Clary had put a *pyr* rune on her arm, but Isabelle had never heard of a Fireproof rune that could withstand this kind of blaze.

"Iz," Simon whispered. "I don't—"

"Shh." She held him tighter, held him as if holding him would keep her from shattering apart herself. Jace was in there, in the heart of the fire, and she couldn't lose another brother, she couldn't—

"They're all right," she said. "If Jace were hurt, Alec would know. And if he's all right, then Clary's all right."

"They'll burn to death," Simon said, sounding lost.

Isabelle cried out as the flames leaped suddenly higher. Alec took a halting step forward and then fell to his knees, put his hands in the dirt. The curve of his back was a bow of pain. The sky was whorls of fire, spinning and dizzying.

Isabelle released Simon and bolted down the path to her brother. She bent over him, knotting her hands into the back of his jacket, hauling him upright. "Alec, *Alec*—"

Alec staggered to his feet, his face dead white except where it was smeared black with soot. He spun, turning his back to Isabelle, shrugging down his gear jacket. "My *parabatai* rune—can you see it?"

Isabelle felt her stomach drop; she thought for a moment she might faint. She grabbed at Alec's collar, pulled it down, and exhaled a hard breath of relief. "It's still there."

Alec shrugged his jacket back on. "I felt something change; it was like something in me *twisted*—" His voice rose. "I'm going down there."

"No!" Isabelle caught at his arm, and then Simon said sharply, from beside her:

"*Look.*"

He was pointing toward the fire. Isabelle gazed at it uncomprehendingly for a moment before realizing what he was indicating. The flames had begun to die down. She shook her head as if to clear it, her hand still on Alec's arm, but it wasn't an illusion. The fire was fading. The flames shrank down from towering orange pillars, fading to yellow, curling inward like fingers. She let go of Alec, and the three of them stood in a line, shoulder to shoulder, as the fire dwindled, revealing a circle of slightly darkened earth where the flames had burned, and inside it, two figures. Clary and Jace.

Both were hard to see through the smoke and the red glow of the still-burning embers, but it was clear they were alive and unharmed. Clary was standing, Jace kneeling in front of her, his hands in hers, almost as if he were being knighted. There was something ritualistic about the position, something that spoke of a strange, old magic. As the smoke cleared, Isabelle could see the bright glint of Jace's hair as he rose to his feet. They both began walking up the path.

Isabelle, Simon, and Alec broke formation and hurtled down toward them. Isabelle threw herself at Jace, who caught her and hugged her, reaching past her to clasp Alec's hand even as he held Isabelle tightly. His skin was cool against hers, almost cold. His gear was without a single scorch or burn mark, just as the desert earth behind them showed no trace that moments ago, a massive conflagration had burned there.

Isabelle turned her head against Jace's chest and saw Simon hugging Clary. He was holding her tightly, shaking his head, and as Clary turned a radiant smile up to him, Isabelle realized she didn't feel a single spark of jealousy. There was nothing different about the way Simon was hugging Clary from the way she was hugging Jace. There was love there, plain and clear, but it was a sisterly love.

She broke apart from Jace and flashed a smile at Clary, who smiled shyly back. Alec moved to hug Clary, and Simon and Jace eyed each other warily. Suddenly Simon grinned—that sudden, unexpected grin that flashed out even in the worst of circumstances, and which Isabelle loved—and held his arms out toward Jace.

Jace shook his head. "I don't care if I did just set myself on fire," he said. "I'm not hugging you."

Simon sighed and dropped his arms. "Your loss," he said. "If you'd gone in, I would've let you, but honestly it would've been a pity hug."

Jace turned to Clary, who was no longer embracing Alec but standing looking amused, with her hand on the hilt of Heosphoros. It seemed to shimmer, as if it had caught some of the light of the fire. "Did you hear that?" Jace demanded. "A *pity* hug?"

Alec held a hand up. Rather surprisingly, Jace fell silent.

"I recognize that we're all filled with the giddy joy of survival, thus explaining your current stupid behavior," Alec said. "But first"—he raised a finger—"I think the three of us are entitled to an explanation. What happened? How did you lose control of the fire? Were you attacked?"

"It was a demon," Jace said after a pause. "It took the form of a woman I—of someone I hurt, when Sebastian possessed me. It goaded me until I lost command over the heavenly fire. Clary helped me get it back under control."

"And that's it? You're both okay?" Isabelle said, half-disbelieving. "I thought—when I saw what was going on—I thought it was Sebastian. That he'd come for us somehow. That you'd tried to burn him and that you'd burned yourself up..."

"That won't happen." Jace touched Izzy's face gently. "I have the fire under control now. I know how to use it, and how not to use it. How to direct it."

"How?" Alec said, amazed.

Jace hesitated. His eyes flicked toward Clary, and seemed to grow darker, as if a shutter had come down over them. "You're just going to have to trust me."

"That's it?" Simon said in disbelief. "Just trust you?"

"Don't you?" Jace asked.

"I..." Simon looked at Isabelle, who glanced at her brother.

After a moment Alec nodded. "We trusted you enough to come here," he said. "We'll trust you to the end."

"Although it would be really awesome if you told us the plan, you know, a little before it," said Isabelle. "Before the end, I mean."

Alec raised an eyebrow at her. She shrugged innocently.

"Just a little before," she said. "I like to have some preparation."

Her brother's eyes met hers and then, a little hoarsely—as if he'd almost forgotten how to do it—he started to laugh.

***

To the Consul:
The Fair Folk are not your allies. They are your enemies. They hate the Nephilim and plan to betray them and bring them down. They have cooperated with Sebastian Morgenstern in attacking and destroying Institutes. Do not trust Meliorn or any other advisers from any Court. The Seelie Queen is your enemy. Do not try to respond to this message. I ride with the Wild Hunt now, and they will kill me if they think I have told you anything.

Mark Blackthorn

Jia Penhallow looked over her reading glasses at Emma and Julian, who stood nervously in front of the desk in the library of her house. A large picture window opened behind the Consul, and Emma could see the view of Alicante spread out: houses spilling down the hills, canals running toward the Accords Hall, Gard Hill rising against the sky.

Jia glanced down again at the paper they had brought her. It had been folded up with almost diabolical cleverness inside the acorn, and it had taken ages, and Ty's skilled fingers, to get it extricated. "Did your brother write anything else besides this? A private message to you?"

"No," Julian said, and there must have been something in the wounded tightness of his voice that made Jia believe him, because she didn't pursue it.

"You realize what this means," she said. "The Council will not want to believe it. They will say it's a trick."

"It's Mark's handwriting," said Julian. "And the way he signed it—" He pointed to the mark at the bottom of the page: a clear print of thorns, made in what looked like red-brown ink. "He rolled his family ring in blood and used it to make that," Julian said, his face flushed. "He showed me how to do it once. No one else would have the Blackthorn family ring, or know to do that with it."

Jia looked from Julian's clenched fists to Emma's set face, and nodded. "Are you all right?" she said more gently. "Do you know what the Wild Hunt is?"

Ty had lectured them rather extensively on it, but Emma found that now, with the Consul's compassionate dark gaze on her, she couldn't find words. It was Julian who spoke. "Faeries that are huntsmen," he said. "They ride across the sky. People think that if you follow them, they can lead you to the land of the dead, or to Faerie."

"Gwyn ap Nudd leads them," said Jia. "He has no allegiance; he is part of a wilder magic. He is called the Gatherer of the Dead. Though he is a faerie, he and his huntsmen are not involved with the Accords. They have no agreement with Shadowhunters and do not recognize our jurisdiction, and they will not abide by laws, any laws. Do you understand?"

They looked at her blankly. She sighed. "If Gwyn has taken your brother to be one of his Hunters, it might be impossible—"

"You're saying you won't be able to get him back," Emma said, and saw something in Julian's eyes shatter. The sight made her want to leap over the desk and clobber the Consul with her stack of neatly labeled files, each with a different name on it.

One leaped out at Emma like a sign lit up in neon. CARSTAIRS: DECEASED. She tried not to let the recognition of her family name show on her face.

"I'm saying I don't know." The Consul spread her hands flat over the surface of the desk. "There's so much we don't know right now," she said, and her voice sounded quiet and nearly broken. "To lose the Fair Folk as allies is a severe blow. Of all Downworlders, they are the subtlest enemies, and the most dangerous." She rose to her feet. "Wait here for a moment."

She left the room through a door in the paneling, and after a few moments of silence, Emma heard the sound of feet and the murmur of Patrick's voice. She caught individual words—"trial" and "mortal" and "betrayal."

She could sense Julian beside her, wound as tightly as a spring-loaded crossbow. She reached out to touch her hand lightly to his back, and drew between his shoulder blades with her finger: *A-R-E Y-O-U A-L-L R-I-G-H-T?*

He shook his head, without looking at her. Emma glanced toward the stack of files on the desk, then toward the door, then at Julian, silent and expressionless, and decided. She launched herself at the desk, plunging her hand into the stack of files, and pulled out the one labeled CARSTAIRS.

It was a bound file, not heavy, and Emma reached out to yank up Julian's shirt. She muffled his cry of surprise with a hand over his mouth, and used the other hand to stuff the file into the back of his jeans. She pulled his shirt down over it just as the door opened and Jia walked back in.

"Would you two be willing to testify before the Council one last time?" she asked, gazing from Emma, who guessed she was probably flushed, to Julian, who looked as if he had been electrified. His gaze hardened, and Emma marveled. Julian was so gentle, she sometimes forgot that those sea-colored eyes could turn as cold as the waves off the coast in winter. "No Mortal Sword," the Consul said. "I just want you to tell them what you know."

"If you promise you'll try to get Mark back," said Julian. "And you won't just say it, you'll actually do it."

Jia looked at him solemnly. "I promise that the Nephilim will not abandon Mark Blackthorn, not as long as he lives."

Julian's shoulders relaxed just a fraction. "Okay, then."

It bloomed like a flower against the clouded black sky: a sudden, silent explosion of flame. Luke, standing by the window, flinched back in surprise before pressing himself against the narrow opening, trying to identify the source of the radiance.

"What is it?" Raphael looked up from where he was kneeling by Magnus. Magnus appeared to be asleep, his eyes shadowed dark crescents against his skin. He had curled himself uncomfortably around the chains that held him, and looked ill, or at least exhausted.

"I'm not sure," Luke said, and held himself still as the vampire boy came to join him at the window. He had never felt entirely comfortable around Raphael. Raphael seemed to him like Loki or some other trickster god, sometimes working for good and sometimes for evil, but always in his own interests.

Raphael muttered something in Spanish and pushed past Luke. The flames reflected in the pupils of his dark eyes, red-gold.

"Sebastian's work, do you think?" Luke asked.

"No." Raphael's gaze was distant, and Luke was reminded that the boy in front of him, though he looked an ageless, angelic fourteen, was in fact older than he was, older than Luke's parents would have been, if they had lived—or in his mother's case, if she had remained mortal. "There is something holy about this fire. Sebastian's work is demon's work. This is like the way God appeared to the wanderers in the desert. 'By day the Lord went ahead of them in a pillar of cloud to guide them on their way and by night in a pillar of fire to give them light, so that they could travel by day or night.'"

Luke raised an eyebrow at him.

Raphael shrugged. "I was brought up a good Catholic boy." He cocked his head to the side. "I think our friend Sebastian will not like this very much, whatever it is."

"Can you see anything else?" Luke demanded; vampire vision was more powerful even than a werewolf's enhanced sight.

"Something—ruins, perhaps, like a dead city—" Raphael shook his head in frustration. "Look where the fire fades. It is dying away."

There was a soft murmur from the floor, and Luke glanced down. Magnus had rolled onto his back. His chains were long, giving him at least enough freedom of movement to curl his hands over his stomach, as if in pain. His eyes were open. "Speaking of fading..."

Raphael returned to his place by Magnus's side. "You must tell us, warlock," he said, "if there is something that we can do for you. I have not seen you so sick."

"Raphael..." Magnus pushed a hand through his sweaty black hair. His chain rattled. "It's my father," he said abruptly. "This is his realm. Well, one of them."

"Your father?"

"He's a demon," Magnus said shortly. "Which shouldn't be a huge surprise. Don't expect any more information than that."

"Fine, but why would being in your father's realm make you sick?"

"He's trying to get me to call on him," said Magnus, propping himself on his elbows. "He can reach me here easily. I can't do magic in this realm, so I can't protect myself. He can make me sick or make me well. He's making me sick because he thinks if I get desperate enough, I'll call on him for help."

"Will you?" asked Luke.

Magnus shook his head, and winced. "No. It wouldn't be worth the price. There's *always* a price, with my father."

Luke felt himself tense. He and Magnus weren't close, but he had always liked the warlock, respected him. Respected Magnus and warlocks such as Catarina Loss and Ragnor Fell and the others, those who had worked with Shadowhunters for generations. He didn't like the sound of despair in Magnus's voice now, or the echoing look in his eyes. "Wouldn't you pay it? If the choice were your life?"

Magnus looked at Luke wearily, and flopped back against the stone floor. "I might not be the one who pays it," he said, and shut his eyes.

"I—" Luke began, but Raphael shook his head at him, a scolding gesture. He had hunched up by Magnus's shoulder, his hands looped around his knees. Dark veins were visible at his temples and throat, signs that it had been too long since he had fed. Luke could only imagine the odd picture they made: the starving vampire, the dying warlock, and the werewolf keeping watch at the window.

"You know nothing of his father," said Raphael in a low voice. Magnus was still, clearly asleep again, his breathing labored.

"And I suppose you know who Magnus's father is?" Luke said.

"I paid a lot of money once to find it out."

"Why? What good would the knowledge do you?"

"I like to know things," Raphael said. "It can be useful. He knew my mother; it only seemed fair I know his father. Magnus saved my life once," added Raphael in an emotionless voice. "When I first became a vampire, I wanted to die. I thought I was a damned thing. He stopped me from throwing myself into the sunlight—Magnus showed me how to walk on holy ground, how to say the name of God, how to wear a cross. It wasn't magic he gave me, just patience, but it saved my life all the same."

"So you owe him," said Luke.

Raphael shrugged off his jacket and, in a single swift move, pushed it beneath Magnus's head. Magnus stirred but didn't wake. "You think about it however you would like to," he said. "I will not give up his secrets."

"Answer me one thing," Luke said, the stone wall cold against his back. "Is Magnus's father someone who could help us?"

Raphael laughed: a short, sharp bark without any real amusement in it. "You are very funny, werewolf," he said. "Go back to your watching at the window, and if you are the sort who prays, then perhaps you should pray that Magnus's father does not decide he wants to help us. If you trust me as regards nothing else, trust me about that, at least."

"Did you just eat *three* pizzas?" Lily was staring at Bat with a mixture of distaste and amazement.

"Four," said Bat, placing a now empty Joe's Pizza box on top of a stack of other boxes, and smiling serenely. Maia felt a rush of affection for him. She hadn't let him in on her plan for the meeting with Maureen, and he hadn't complained once, just complimented her on her poker face. He'd agreed to sit down with her and Lily to discuss the alliance, even though she knew he didn't much like vampires.

And he'd saved for her the pizza that had only cheese on it, since he knew she didn't like toppings. She was on her fourth slice. Lily, perched daintily on the edge of the desk in the police station lobby, was smoking a long cigarette (Maia guessed lung cancer wasn't that big a worry when you were dead already) and eyeing the pizza suspiciously. Maia didn't care how much Bat ate—something had to fuel all those muscles—as long as he seemed happy to keep her company during the meeting. Lily had stuck to their agreement about Maureen, but she still gave Maia the shivers.

"You know," Lily said, swinging her booted feet, "I must say I was expecting something a bit more—exciting. Less of a phone bank." She wrinkled her nose.

Maia sighed and looked around. The lobby of the police station was full of werewolves and vampires, probably for the first time since it had been built. There were stacks of papers listing what contact information for important Downworlders they'd managed to beg, borrow, steal, and dig up—it had turned out the vampires had pretty impressive records of who was in charge where—and everyone was on cell phones or computers, calling and texting and emailing the heads of clans and packs and every warlock they could track down.

"Thank goodness the faeries are centralized," said Bat. "One Seelie Court, one Unseelie Court."

Lily smirked. "The land under the hill stretches far and wide," she said. "The Courts are all we can reach in this world, that's all."

"Well, this world is what we're concerned with at the moment," said Maia, stretching and rubbing the back of her neck. She'd been calling and emailing and writing messages all day herself, and she was exhausted. The vampires had joined them only at nightfall, and were expected to work through till morning while the werewolves slept.

"You realize what Sebastian Morgenstern will do to us if his side wins," said Lily, looking thoughtfully around the crowded room. "I doubt he has much forgiveness for anyone who works against him."

"Maybe he'll kill us first," said Maia. "But he would kill us anyway. I know you vampires love the idea of reason and logic and clever, careful alliances, but that's not how he works. He wants to burn the world down. That's all he wants."

Lily exhaled smoke. "Well," she said. "That would be inconvenient, considering how we feel about fire."

"You're not having second thoughts, are you?" Maia said, trying hard to keep the worry from her voice. "You seemed very sure we should stand against Sebastian when we talked before."

"We walk a very dangerous line, that is all," said Lily. "Have you ever heard the expression 'When the cat is away, the mice will play'?"

"Of course," said Maia, glancing over at Bat, who muttered

something darkly in Spanish.

"For hundreds of years the Nephilim have kept their rules, and made sure that we kept to them as well," Lily said. "For that, they are much resented. Now they have gone to hide themselves away in Idris, and we cannot pretend that Downworlders will not enjoy certain ... advantages while they are gone."

"Being able to eat people?" Bat inquired, folding a piece of pizza in half.

"It is not just vampires," Lily said coldly. "The faeries love to tease and torment humans; only Shadowhunters prevent them. They will begin taking human babies again. The warlocks will sell their magic to the highest bidder, like—"

"Magical prostitutes?" They all looked up in surprise; Malcolm Fade had appeared in the doorway, brushing white flakes of snow from his already white hair. "It's what you were going to say, wasn't it?"

"I wasn't," said Lily, clearly caught off guard.

"Oh, say what you like. I don't mind," Malcolm said brightly. "Nothing against prostitution. It keeps civilization running." He shook snow off his coat. He was wearing a plain black suit and worn trench coat; there was nothing of Magnus's glittering eclecticism about him. "How do you people stand snow?" he demanded.

"'You people'?" Bat bristled. "Do you mean werewolves?"

"I mean East Coasters," said Malcolm. "Who would have weather if they could avoid it? Snow, hail, rain. I'd move to Los Angeles in a jiffy. Did you know that a jiffy is an actual measurement of time? It's a sixtieth of a second. You can't do anything in a jiffy, not really."

"You know," Maia said, "Catarina said you were pretty harmless—"

Malcolm looked pleased. "Catarina said I was pretty?"

"Can we stick to the point?" Maia demanded. "Lily, if what

you're worried about is that the Shadowhunters will take it out on all Downworlders if some of us go rogue while they're in Idris, well, that's why we're doing what we're doing. Assuring Downworlders that the Accords hold, that the Shadowhunters are trying to get our representatives back, that Sebastian is the real enemy here, will minimize the chances of chaos outside Idris affecting what happens in the case of a battle, or when all this is over—"

"Catarina!" Malcolm announced suddenly, as if remembering something pleasant. "I nearly forgot why I stopped by here in the first place. Catarina asked me to contact you. She's in the morgue at Beth Israel hospital, and she wants you to come as quickly as you can. Oh, and she said to bring a cage."

One of the bricks in the wall by the window was loose. Jocelyn had been passing the time by using the metal clip of her barrette to try to pry it free. She wasn't foolish enough to think that she could create a gap she could escape through, but she was hopeful that freeing a brick would give her a weapon. Something she could slam into Sebastian's head.

If she could make herself do it. If she wouldn't hesitate.

She had hesitated when he was a baby. She had held him in her arms and known there was something wrong with him, something irreparably damaged, but hadn't been able to act on her knowledge. She had believed in some small corner of her heart that he could still be saved.

The door rattled, and she around about, sliding the barrette back into her hair. It was Clary's barrette, something she had picked off her daughter's desk when she'd needed to keep her hair out of the paint. She hadn't returned it because it reminded her of her daughter, but it seemed wrong to even think of Clary here, in front of her other child, though she missed her, missed her so much that it hurt.

The door opened and Sebastian stepped through.

He wore a white knit shirt, and she was reminded again of his father. Valentine had liked to wear white. It had made him appear paler, his hair whiter, just that little bit more inhuman, and it did the same for Sebastian. His eyes looked like black paint dripped onto a white canvas. He smiled at her.

"Mother," he said.

She crossed her arms over her chest. "What are you doing here, Jonathan?"

He shook his head, still with the same smile on his face, and drew a dagger from his belt. It was narrow, with a thin blade like an awl. "If you call me that again," he said, "I will put your eyes out with this."

She swallowed. *Oh, my baby.* She remembered holding him, cold and still in her arms, not like a normal child at all. He hadn't cried. Not once. "Is that what you came to tell me?"

He shrugged. "I came to ask you a question." He glanced around the room, his expression bored. "And to show you something. Come. Walk with me."

She joined him as he left the room, with a mixture of reluctance and relief. She hated her cell, and surely it would be better to see more of the place where she was being kept? The size of it, the exits?

The corridor outside the room was stone, big blocks of limestone slotted together with concrete. The floor was smooth, worn down by footsteps. Yet there was a dusty feel to the place, as if no one had been in it for decades, even centuries.

There were doors set into the walls at random intervals. Jocelyn felt her heart begin to pound. Luke could be behind any of those doors. She wanted to dash at them, jerk them open, but the dagger was still in Sebastian's hand, and she didn't doubt for a moment that he knew that better than she did.

The corridor began to curve around, and Sebastian spoke.

"What," he said, "if I did tell you I loved you?"

Jocelyn clasped her hands loosely in front of her. "I suppose," she said carefully, "that I would say that you could no more love me than I could love you."

They had reached a set of double doors. They paused in front of them. "Aren't you supposed to pretend, at least?"

Jocelyn said, "Could you? Part of you is me, you know. The demon's blood changed you, but did you really think that everything in you otherwise comes from Valentine?"

Without answering, Sebastian shouldered the doors open and stepped inside. After a moment Jocelyn followed—and stopped in her tracks.

The room was huge and semicircular. A marble floor stretched out to a platform built of stone and wood rising against the western wall. In the center of the platform sat two thrones. There was no other word for them—massive ivory chairs overlaid with gold; each had a rounded back and six steps leading down from it. An enormous window, glass reflecting nothing but blackness, hung behind each throne. Something about the room was oddly familiar, but Jocelyn couldn't have said exactly what.

Sebastian bounded up onto the platform and beckoned her to follow him. Jocelyn moved slowly up the few steps to join her son, who stood in front of the two thrones with a look of gloating triumph on his face. She had seen the same look on his father's face, when he'd gazed down at the Mortal Cup. "'*He will be great,*'" Sebastian intoned, "'*and he will be called the Son of the Highest, and the Devil will give him the throne of his father. And he will reign over Hell forever, and of his kingdom there will be no end.*'"

"I don't understand," Jocelyn said, and her voice came out bleak and dead even to her own ears. "You want to rule this world? Some dead world of demons and destruction? You want to give orders to corpses?"

Sebastian laughed. He had Valentine's laugh: harsh and musical. "Oh, no," he said. "You misunderstand me entirely." He made a quick gesture with his fingers, something she had seen Valentine do when he had taught himself magic, and suddenly the two great windows behind the thrones were no longer blank.

One showed a blasted landscape: withered trees and scorched earth, vile winged creatures circling in front of a broken moon. A barren plateau of rocks spread out before the windows. It was populated by dark figures, each standing a little distance from the next, and Jocelyn realized that they were the Endarkened, keeping watch.

The other window showed Alicante, sleeping peacefully in the moonlight. A curve of moon, a sky full of stars, the shimmer of water in the canals. The view was one Jocelyn had seen before, and she realized with a jolt why the room she was in had seemed familiar.

It was the Council room in the Gard—transformed from an amphitheater to a throne room, but still the same arched roof, the same size, the same view of the City of Glass from what had been two great windows. Only, now one window looked out onto the world she knew, the Idris she had come from. And the other looked out onto the world she was in.

"This fortress of mine has doorways to both worlds," said Sebastian, his tone smug. "This world is drained dry, yes. A bloodless corpse of a place. Oh, but *your* world is ripe for ruling. I dream about it during the days as well as the nights. Do I burn the world slowly, with plague and famine, or should the slaughter be quick and painless—all that life, extinguished so quickly, imagine how it would *burn!*" His eyes were feverish. "Imagine the heights I could rise to, borne aloft on the screams of billions of people, raised up by the smoke of millions of burning hearts!" He turned to her. "Now," he said. "Tell me I got that from you. Tell me any of that is from you."

Jocelyn's head was ringing. "There are two thrones," she said.

A small crease appeared between his brows. "What?"

"*Two* thrones," she said. "And I'm not a fool; I know who you intend to have sit beside you. You need her there; you want her there. Your triumph means nothing if she isn't there to watch it. And that—that need for someone to love you—that *does* come from me."

He stared at her. He was biting his lip so hard, she was sure he would draw blood. "Weakness," he said, half to himself. "It's a weakness."

"It's human," she said. "But do you really think Clary could sit next to you here and be happy or willing?"

For a moment she thought she saw something spark in his eyes, but a moment later they were black ice again. "I'd rather have her happy and willing and here, but I'll take simply here," he said. "I don't care that much about willing."

Something seemed to explode inside Jocelyn's brain. She lunged forward, reaching for the dagger in his hand; he stepped back, evading her, and spun with a quick, graceful movement, knocking her legs out from under her. She hit the ground, rolled, and crouched. Before she could rise, she found a hand knotted in her jacket, yanking her to her feet.

"Stupid bitch," Sebastian snarled, inches from her face, the fingers of his left hand digging into the skin below her clavicle. "You think you could hurt me? My true mother's spell protects me."

Jocelyn jerked back. "Let me *go*!"

The leftmost window exploded with light. Sebastian reeled back, surprise blooming across his face as he stared. The blasted landscape of the dead world had suddenly lit up with fire, blazing golden fire, rising in a pillar toward the broken sky. The Dark Shadowhunters were running to and fro over the ground like ants. The stars were coruscating, reflecting the fire back, red and gold and blue and orange. It was as beautiful and terrible as an angel.

Jocelyn felt the hint of a smile touch the corners of her mouth. Her heart was lifting with the first hope she had felt since she had woken up in this world.

"Heavenly fire," she whispered.

"Indeed." A smile played around Sebastian's mouth. Jocelyn looked at him in dismay. She had expected him to be horrified, but instead he looked exalted. "As the Good Book says: *'This is the law of the burnt offering: It is the burnt offering, because of the burning upon the altar all night unto the morning, and the fire of the altar shall be burning in it,'*" he cried, and raised both arms, as if he meant to embrace the fire that burned so high and so bright beyond the window. "Waste your fire on the desert air, my brother!" he cried. "Let it pour into the sands like blood or water, and may you never stop coming—never stop coming until we are face-to-face."

18

BY THE WATERS
OF BABYLON

Energy runes were all well and good, Clary thought exhaustedly as she reached the top of yet another rise of sand, but they didn't begin to compete with a cup of coffee. She was pretty sure she could face another day of trudging, her feet sometimes slipping ankle-deep into heaps of ash, if she just had sweet caffeine pumping through her veins...

"Are you thinking what I'm thinking?" Simon said, coming up beside her. He looked drawn and tired, his thumbs hooked through the straps of his backpack. They all looked pretty drawn. Alec and Isabelle had taken watch after the incident with the heavenly fire, and had reported no demons or Dark Shadowhunters in the vicinity of their hideaway. Still, they were all jittery, and none of them had had more than a few hours of sleep. Jace seemed to be running on nerves and adrenaline, following the thread of the tracking spell on the bracelet around his wrist, sometimes forgetting to pause and wait for the others in his mad dash toward Sebastian, until they shouted or ran to catch up with him.

"That a massive latte from the Mud Truck would make

everything brighter just about now?"

"There's a vamp place not far from Union Square where they mix just the right amount of blood into the coffee," Simon said. "Not too sweet, not too salty."

Clary stopped; a dead branch, curling from the earth, had tangled itself in her bootlaces. "Remember when we talked about *not sharing?*"

"Isabelle listens to me talk about vampire things."

Clary drew out Heosphoros. The sword, with the new rune carved black into the blade, seemed to shimmer in her hand. She used the tip of it to pry the tough, thorny branch free. "Isabelle is your girlfriend," she said. "She *has* to listen to you."

"Is she?" Simon looked startled.

Clary threw her hands up and started down the hill. The ground slanted down, pocked here and there with cracked pits, everything covered over with the endless dull sheen of dust. The air was still bitter, the sky a sallow green. She could see Alec and Isabelle standing near Jace at the foot of the hill; he was touching the bracelet on his wrist and frowning into the distance.

Something glimmered at the corner of Clary's vision, and she stopped suddenly. She squinted, trying to see what it was. The shine of something silvery in the distance, past the stone and rubble heaps of the desert. She took out her stele and drew a quick Farsighted rune onto her arm, the burn and sting of the stele's dull tip cutting through the fog of exhaustion in her mind, sharpening her vision.

"Simon!" she said as he caught up with her. "Do you see that?"

He followed her gaze. "I caught a glimpse of it last night. Remember when Isabelle said I thought I'd seen a city?"

"Clary!" It was Jace, looking up at them, his face a pale hollow in the ashy air. She made a beckoning gesture. "What's going on?"

She pointed again, toward what she could now see as a definite shimmer, a cluster of shapes, in the distance. "There's something there," she called down. "Simon thinks it's a city—"

She broke off, because Jace had already started running in the direction she'd pointed. Isabelle and Alec looked startled before bolting after him; Clary exhaled an exasperated breath and, with Simon at her side, followed.

They started down the slope, which was covered in loose scree, half-running and half-sliding, letting the unmoored pebbles carry them. Not for the first time, Clary truly appreciated her gear: She could only imagine how the flying bits of gravel would have torn normal shoes and pants to shreds.

She hit the bottom of the slope at a run. Jace was some distance ahead, with Alec and Isabelle just behind him, moving fast, clambering over rock cairns, hopping small rivulets of molten slag. As Clary closed in on the three of them, she saw that they were heading toward a place where the desert seemed to drop away—the edge of a plateau? A cliff?

Clary sped up, scrambling over the last of the rock heaps and nearly rolling down the final one. She landed on her feet—Simon, far more graceful, just ahead of her—and saw that Jace was standing at the edge of a massive cliff that fell away before him like the edge of the Grand Canyon. Alec and Isabelle had moved to either side of him. All three were eerily silent, staring ahead in the dim bruised light.

Something in Jace's posture, the way he stood, told Clary even as she reached his side that there was something not right. Then she caught sight of his expression and mentally amended "not right" to "very wrong indeed."

He was staring down into the valley below as if he were staring into the grave of someone he had loved. In the valley were the ruins of a city. An old, old city that had once been built around a hillside. The top of the hillside was surrounded by gray clouds and fog. Heaps of rock were all that was left of the houses, and ash had settled over the streets and the jagged ruins of buildings. Tumbled among the ruins, like discarded matchsticks, were broken pillars made of shining pale stone, incongruously beautiful in this ruined land.

"Demon towers," she whispered.

Jace nodded grimly. "I don't know how," he said, "but somehow—this is Alicante."

"It is a dreadful burden, to have such responsibility visited upon those so young," said Zachariah as the door of the Council Hall closed behind Emma Carstairs and Julian Blackthorn. Aline and Helen had gone with them, to escort them back to the house where they were staying. Both children had been nearly swaying on their feet with exhaustion by the end of their interrogation by the Council, heavy dark shadows under their eyes.

There were only a few of the Council members still left in the room: Jia and Patrick, Maryse and Robert Lightwood, Kadir Safar, Diana Wrayburn, Tomas Rosales, and a scattering of Silent Brothers and heads of Institutes. Most were chattering among themselves, but Zachariah stood by Jia's lectern, looking at her with a deep sorrow in his eyes.

"They have endured much loss," said Jia. "But we are Shadowhunters; many of us endure great loss at a young age."

"They have Helen, and their uncle," said Patrick, standing not far away with Robert and Maryse, both of whom looked tense and drawn. "They will be well taken care of, and Emma Carstairs, as well, clearly considers the Blackthorns as family."

"Often those who raise us, who are our guardians, are not our blood," said Zachariah. Jia thought she had seen a special softness in his eyes when they rested on Emma, almost a regret. But perhaps she had imagined it. "Those who love us and who we love. So it was with me. As long as she is not parted from the Blackthorns, or the boy—Julian—that is the most important thing."

Jia distantly heard her husband reassuring the former Silent Brother, but her mind was on Helen. Down in the depths of her heart, Jia worried sometimes for her daughter, who had given her heart so completely to a girl who was part-faerie, a race known for their untrustworthiness. She knew that Patrick was not happy that Aline had chosen a girl at all rather than a boy, that he mourned—selfishly, she thought—for what he saw as the end of his branch of the Penhallows. She herself worried more that Helen Blackthorn would break her daughter's heart.

"How much credence do you give the claim of faerie betrayal?" asked Kadir.

"Entire credence," said Jia. "It explains a great deal. How the faeries were able to enter Alicante and abscond with the prisoners from the house given to the representative of the Fair Folk; how Sebastian was able to conceal troops from us at the Citadel; why he spared Mark Blackthorn—not out of fear of angering the faeries but out of respect for their alliance. Tomorrow I will confront the Faerie Queen and—"

"With all due respect," said Zachariah in his soft voice. "I don't think you should do that."

"Why not?" Patrick demanded.

Because you have information now that the Faerie Queen does not know you have, said Brother Enoch. *It is rare that that happens. In war there are advantages of power, but also advantages of knowledge. Do not squander this one.*

Jia hesitated. "Things may be worse than you know," she said, and drew something from the pocket of her coat. It was a fire-message, addressed to her from the Spiral Labyrinth. She handed it to Zachariah.

He seemed to freeze in place. For a moment he simply looked at it; then he brushed a finger over the paper, and she realized he was not reading it but rather tracing the signature of the writer of the letter, a signature that had clearly struck him like an arrow to the heart.

Theresa Gray.

"Tessa says," he said finally, and then cleared his throat, for his voice had emerged ragged and uneven. "She says that the warlocks of the Spiral Labyrinth have examined the body of Amalric Kriegsmesser. That his heart was shriveled, his organs desiccated. She says they are sorry, but there is absolutely nothing that can be done to cure the Endarkened. Necromancy might make their bodies move again, but their souls are gone forever."

"Only the power of the Infernal Cup keeps them alive," said Jia, her voice throbbing with sorrow. "They are dead inside."

"If the Infernal Cup itself could be destroyed…" Diana mused.

"Then it might kill them all, yes," said Jia. "But we do not have the Infernal Cup. Sebastian does."

"To kill them all in one sweep, it seems wrong," said Tomas, looking horrified. "They are Shadowhunters."

"They are not," said Zachariah, in a voice much less gentle than Jia had come to associate with him. She looked at him in surprise. "Sebastian counts on us thinking of them as Shadowhunters. He counts upon our hesitation, our inability to kill monsters that wear human faces."

"On our mercy," said Kadir.

"If I were Turned, I would want to be put out of my misery," said Zachariah. "*That* is mercy. That is what Edward Longford gave his *parabatai*, before he turned his sword on himself. That is why I paid my respects to him." He touched the faded rune at his throat.

"Then do we ask the Spiral Labyrinth to give up?" asked Diana. "To cease searching for a cure?"

"They have already given up. Did you not listen to what Tessa wrote?" said Zachariah. "A cure cannot always be found. At least, not in time. I know—that is, I have learned—that one cannot rely upon it. It cannot be our only hope. We must mourn the Endarkened as dead, and trust in what we are: Shadowhunters, warriors. We must do what we were made to do. Fight."

"But how do we defend ourselves against Sebastian? It was bad enough when it was just the Endarkened; now we must fight the Fair Folk as well!" Tomas snapped. "And you're just a boy—"

"I am a hundred and forty-six years old," said Zachariah. "And this is not my first unwinnable war. I believe we can turn the betrayal of the faeries into an advantage. We will require the help of the Spiral Labyrinth to do it, but if you will listen to me, I will tell you how."

Clary, Simon, Jace, Alec, and Isabelle picked their way in silence through the eerie ruins of Alicante. For Jace had been right: It *was* Alicante, unmistakably so. They had passed too much that was familiar for it to be anything else. The walls around the city, now crumbled; the gates, corroded with the scars of acid rain. Cistern Square. The empty canals, filled with spongy black moss.

The hill was blasted, a bare heap of rock. The marks where there had once been pathways were clearly visible like scars along the side. Clary knew that the Gard should be at the top of it, but if it still stood, it was invisible, hidden in gray fog.

At last they clambered over a high mound of rubble and found themselves in Angel Square. Clary took a breath of surprise— though most of the buildings that had ringed it had fallen, the square was surprisingly unharmed, cobblestones stretching away in the yellowish light. The Hall of Accords was still standing.

It wasn't white stone, though. In the human dimension, it looked like a Greek temple, but in this world it was lacquered metal. A tall square building, if something that looked like molten gold that had been poured out of the sky could be described as a building. Massive engravings ran around the structure, like ribbon wrapping a box; the whole thing glowed dully in the orange light.

"The Accords Hall." Isabelle stood with her whip coiled around her wrist, looking up at it. "Unbelievable."

They started up the steps, which were gold streaked with the black of ash and corrosion. At the top of the stairs, they paused to stare at the huge double doors. They were covered with squares of hammered metal. Each one was an engraved panel showing an image. "It's a story," Jace said, stepping closer and touching the engravings with a black-gloved finger. Writing in an unfamiliar language scrolled along the bottom of each illustration. He glanced over at Alec. "Can you read it?"

"Am I the *only* person who paid attention in language lessons?" Alec demanded wearily, but he stepped up to look more closely at the scrawl. "Well, first, the panels," he said. "They're a history." He pointed at the first one, which showed a group of people, barefoot and in robes, cowering as the clouds above them opened up and a clawed hand reached down toward them. "Humans lived here, or something like humans," Alec said, pointing at the figures. "They lived in peace, and then demons came. And then—" He broke off, his hand on a panel whose image was as familiar to Clary as the back of her own hand. The Angel Raziel, rising out of Lake Lyn, the Mortal Instruments in hand. "By the Angel."

"Literally," said Isabelle. "How—Is that *our* Angel? Our lake?"

"I don't know. This says the demons came, and the Shadowhunters were created to battle them," Alec went on, moving along the wall as the panels progressed. He jabbed his finger at the scrawl. "This word, here, it means 'Nephilim.' But the Shadowhunters rejected the help of Downworlders. The warlocks and the Fair Folk joined with their infernal parents. They sided with the demons. The Nephilim were defeated, and slaughtered. In their last days they created a weapon that was meant to hold the demons off." He indicated a panel showing a woman holding up a sort of iron rod with a burning stone set into the end of it. "They didn't have seraph blades; they hadn't developed them. It doesn't look like they had Iron Sisters or Silent Brothers, either. They had blacksmiths, and they developed some sort of weapon, something they thought might help them. The word here is '*skeptron*,' but it doesn't mean anything to me. Anyway, the *skeptron* wasn't enough." He moved to the next panel, which showed destruction: the Nephilim lying dead, the woman with the iron rod crumpled on the ground, the rod itself cast aside. "The demons—they're called *asmodei* here—burned away the sun and filled the sky with ash and clouds. They ripped fire from the earth and razed the cities to the ground. They killed everything that moved and breathed air. They drained the seas until everything in the water was dead too."

"*Asmodei*," echoed Clary. "I've heard that before. It was something Lilith said, about Sebastian. Before he was born. '*The child born with this blood in him will exceed in power the Greater Demons of the abysses between the worlds. He will be more mighty than the asmodei.*'"

"Asmodeus is one of the Greater Demons of the abysses between worlds," said Jace, meeting Clary's gaze. She knew he remembered Lilith's speech as well as she did. He had shared the same vision, shown to them by the angel Ithuriel.

"Like Abbadon?" Simon inquired. "He was a Greater Demon."

"Far more powerful than that. Asmodeus is a Prince of Hell— there are nine of them. The *Fati*. Shadowhunters cannot hope to defeat them. They can destroy angels in combat. They can remake worlds," said Jace.

"The *asmodei* are Asmodeus's children. Powerful demons. They drained this world dry and then left it for other, weaker demons to scavenge." Alec sounded sick. "This isn't the Accords Hall anymore. It's a tomb. A tomb for the life of this world."

"But is this *our* world?" Isabelle's voice rose. "Did we go forward in time? If the Queen tricked us—"

"She didn't. At least, not about where we are," said Jace. "We didn't go forward in time; we went sideways. This is a mirror dimension of our world. A place where history went slightly differently." He hooked his thumbs into his belt and glanced around. "A world with no Shadowhunters."

"It's like *Planet of the Apes*," said Simon. "Except that was the future."

"Yeah, well, this could be our future, if Sebastian gets what he wants," Jace said. He tapped the panel of the woman holding up the burning *skeptron*, and frowned, then pushed hard on the door.

It swung open with a shriek of hinges that cut the air like a knife. Clary winced. Jace drew his sword and peered cautiously through the gap in the door. There was a room beyond, filled with a grayish light. He shouldered the door open farther and slipped through the gap, gesturing for the others to wait.

Isabelle, Alec, Clary, and Simon exchanged glances, and without a word spoken, went after him immediately. Alec went first, bow drawn; then Isabelle with her whip, Clary with her sword, and Simon, eyes gleaming like a cat's in the dimness.

The inside of the Accords Hall was both familiar and unfamiliar. The floor was marble, cracked and broken. In many places great black blots spread across the stone, the remnants of ancient bloodstains. The roof above, which in their Alicante was glass, was long gone, only shards remaining, like clear knives against the sky.

The room itself was empty, save for a statue in the center. The place was filled with sickly yellow-gray light. Jace, standing facing the statue, whirled as they approached.

"I told you to wait," he snapped at Alec. "Don't you *ever* do anything I tell you to?"

"Technically you didn't actually say anything," Clary said. "You just gestured."

"Gesturing counts," Jace said. "I gesture very expressively."

"You're not in charge," Alec said, lowering his bow. Some of the tension had gone out of his posture. There were clearly no demons hiding in the shadows: Nothing blocked their view of the corroded walls, and nothing but the statue remained standing in the room. "You don't need to protect us."

Isabelle rolled her eyes at both of them and stepped closer to the statue, craning her head back. It was the statue of a man in armor; his feet, in mail boots, rested on a golden plinth. He wore an intricate hauberk of linked stone circlets, decorated with a motif of angel wings across the chest. In his hand he carried an iron replica of a *skeptron*, tipped by a circular metal ornament, into which a red jewel had been set.

Whoever had carved the statue had been skilled. The face was handsome, square-jawed, with a distant, clear gaze. But they had captured more than good looks: There was a certain harshness to the set of his eyes and jaw, a twist to his mouth that spoke of selfishness and cruelty.

There were words written on the plinth, and though they were not in English, Clary could read them.

JONATHAN SHADOWHUNTER. FIRST AND LAST OF THE NEPHILIM.

"First and last," Isabelle whispered. "This place *is* a tomb."

Alec crouched down. There were more words on the plinth, under Jonathan Shadowhunter's name. He read them out:

"*And he who overcomes, and he who keeps my deeds until the end, to him I will give authority over the nations; and he shall rule them with a rod of iron, and I will give him the Morning Star.*"

"What's that supposed to mean?" Simon asked.

"I think Jonathan Shadowhunter got cocky," said Alec. "I think he thought this *skeptron* thing would not just save them, but it would let him rule over the world."

"*And I will give him the Morning Star,*" said Clary. "That's from the Bible. Our Bible. And 'Morgenstern' means 'morning star.'"

"'The morning star' means a lot of things," said Alec. "It can mean 'the brightest star in the sky,' or it can mean 'heavenly fire,' or it can mean 'the fire that falls with angels when they're cast down out of Heaven.' It's also the name of Lucifer, the light-bringer, the demon of pride." He straightened up.

"Either way, it means that thing the statue is holding is a real weapon," said Jace. "Like in the door engravings. You said the *skeptron* is what they developed here, instead of seraph blades, to hold off the demons. Look at the marks on the handle. It's been in battle."

Isabelle tapped the pendant around her throat. "And the red stone. It looks like it's made from the same stuff as my necklace."

Jace nodded. "I think it is the same stone." Clary knew what he was going to say next before he said it. "That weapon. I want it."

"Well, you can't have it," Alec said. "It's attached to the statue."

"It's not." Jace pointed. "Look, the statue's gripping it, but they're actually two totally separate pieces. They carved the statue and then they put the scepter into its hands. It's *supposed* to be removable."

"I'm not sure that's exactly true—" Clary began, but Jace was already putting a foot up onto the plinth, preparing to climb. He had the glint in his eye she both loved and dreaded, the one that said, *I do what I want, and damn the consequences.*

"Wait!" Simon darted to block Jace from climbing farther. "I'm sorry, but does anyone else see what's going on here?"

"Nooo," Jace drawled. "Why don't you tell us all about it? I mean, we've got nothing but time."

Simon crossed his arms over his chest. "I've been in a lot of campaigns—"

"Campaigns?" Isabelle echoed, bewildered.

"He means Dungeons and Dragons games," Clary explained.

"*Games?*" Alec echoed in disbelief. "In case you haven't noticed, this is no game."

"That's not the point," Simon said. "The point is that when you're playing D&D and your group comes across a heap of treasure, or a big sparkly gem, or a magical golden skull, you should *never take it.* It's always a trap." He uncrossed his arms and waved them wildly. "*This* is a trap."

Jace was silent. He was looking at Simon thoughtfully, as if he'd never seen him before, or at least never considered him so closely. "Come here," he said.

Simon moved toward him, his eyebrows raised. "What—oof!"

Jace had dropped his sword into Simon's hands. "Hold this for me while I climb," Jace said, and leaped up onto the plinth. Simon's protests were drowned out by the sound of Jace's boots knocking against the stone as he scrambled up the statue, pulling himself up hand over hand. He reached the middle of the statue, where the carved hauberk offered footholds, and braced himself, reaching across the stone to close his hand around the handle of the *skeptron.*

It might have been an illusion, but Clary thought she saw the statue's smiling mouth twist into an even crueler grimace. The red stone flared up suddenly; Jace jerked back, but the room was already full of an earsplitting noise, the terrible combination of a fire alarm and a human scream, going on and on and on.

"Jace!" Clary raced to the statue; he had already dropped from it to the ground, wincing at the awful noise. The light of the red stone was increasing, filling the room with a bloody illumination.

"Goddamn it," Jace shouted over the noise. "I *hate* it when Simon is right."

With a glare Simon shoved Jace's sword back at him; Jace took it, his gaze darting around warily. Alec had raised his bow again; Isabelle stood ready with her whip. Clary drew a dagger from her belt.

"We'd better get out of here," Alec called. "It could be nothing, but—"

Isabelle cried out, and clapped her hand to her chest. Her pendant had begun to flash, slow steady bright pulses like a heartbeat.

"Demons!" she cried, just as the sky filled with flying things. And they were *things*—they had heavy round bodies, like huge pale grubs, pocked with rows of suckers. They had no faces: Both ends of them terminated in massive pink circular mouths rimmed with sharks' teeth. Rows of stubby wings lined their bodies, each wing tipped with a dagger-sharp talon. And there were a lot of them.

Even Jace paled. "By the Angel—*run!*"

They ran, but the creatures, despite their girth, were faster: They were landing all around them, with ugly wet sounds. Clary thought wildly that they sounded like giant spitballs falling from the sky. The light pouring from the *skeptron* had vanished the moment they'd appeared, and the room was now bathed in the ugly yellowish glow of the sky.

"Clary!" Jace shouted as one of the creatures heaved itself toward her, its circular mouth open. Ropes of yellow drool hung from it.

Thump. An arrow embedded itself in the roof of the demon's mouth. The creature reared back, spitting black blood. Clary saw Alec seize another arrow, fit it, let it fly. Another demon reeled back, and then Isabelle was on it, her whip slashing back and forth, slicing it to ribbons. Simon had seized another demon and was holding it, his hands sinking into its fleshy gray body, and Jace plunged his sword into it. The demon collapsed, knocking Simon back to the floor: he landed on his backpack. Clary thought she heard a sound like breaking glass, but a moment later Simon was back up on his feet, Jace steadying him with a hand to the shoulder before they both turned back to the fight.

Ice had descended over Clary: the silent coldness of battle. The demon Alec had shot was writhing, trying to spit out the arrow lodged in its mouth; she stepped over to it and plunged her dagger into its body, black blood spraying up from the wounds, soaking her gear. The room was full of the rotten-garbage stench of demons, laced through with the acid of ichor; she gagged as the demon gave a last spasm and collapsed.

Alec was backing up, steadily letting arrow after arrow fly, sending the demons reeling back, wounded. As they struggled, Jace and Isabelle fell on them, slashing them to pieces with sword and whip. Clary followed their lead, leaping on another wounded demon, sawing away at the soft band of flesh under its mouth, her hand, coated in oily demon blood, slipping on the hilt of her dagger. The demon collapsed in on itself with a hiss, sending her crashing to the ground. The blade skittered out of her hand, and she threw herself after it, seized it up, and rolled to the side just as another demon lunged with an uncoiling of its powerful body.

It hit the space where she'd just been lying, and curled itself around, hissing, so that Clary found herself facing two open, gaping mouths. She readied her blade to let it fly, when there was a flash of silver-gold and Isabelle's whip came down, slicing the thing in half.

It fell apart in two pieces, a jumbled mess of steaming internal organs pouring out. Even through the ice of battle, Clary was nearly sick. Demons usually died and vanished before you saw much of their insides. This one was still writhing, even in two pieces, twitching forward and back. Isabelle grimaced and raised her whip again—and the twitch turned into a sudden, violent jerk as half the monster twisted backward and sank its teeth into Isabelle's leg.

Izzy screamed, slashing down with the whip, and it released her; she fell back, her leg going out from under her. Clary leaped forward, stabbing at the other half of the demon, plunging her dagger into the creature's back until it crumbled apart under her and she found herself kneeling in a welter of demon blood, drenched blade in her hand, gasping.

There was silence. The ringing alarm had stopped, and the demons were gone. They had all been slaughtered, but there was no joy of victory. Isabelle was on the ground, her whip curled around her wrist, blood pouring from a crescent-shaped slash in her left leg. She was gasping, her eyelids fluttering.

"Izzy!" Alec dropped his bow and launched himself across the bloody floor at his sister. He fell to his knees, hauling her up into his lap. He yanked the stele from her belt. "Iz, Izzy, hold on—"

Jace, who had gathered up Alec's fallen bow, looked like he was going to throw up or fall; Clary saw with dull surprise that Simon had his hand on Jace's arm, his fingers digging in, as if he were holding Jace up.

Alec tore at the slashed fabric of Isabelle's gear, ripping her trouser leg open to the knee. Clary stifled a cry. Isabelle's leg was ribboned: it looked like pictures of shark bites Clary had seen, blood and pulped tissue surrounding deep indents.

Alec put his stele to the skin of her knee and drew an *iratze*, and then another an inch farther down. His shoulders were shaking, but his hand was steady. Clary wrapped her hand around Jace's and squeezed. His was ice-cold.

"Izzy," Alec whispered as the *iratzes* faded and sank into her skin, leaving white remnants behind. Clary remembered Hodge, how they had drawn healing rune after healing rune on him, but his wounds had been too great: the runes had faded, and he had bled out and died despite the runes' power.

Alec looked up. The shape of his face was awkward, twisted; there was blood on his cheek: Isabelle's, Clary thought. "Clary," he said. "Maybe if you try—"

Simon suddenly stiffened. "We need to get out of here," he said. "I can hear wings. There's going to be more of them."

Isabelle was no longer gasping. The bleeding from the slash in her leg had slowed, but Clary could see, with a sinking heart, that the wounds were still there, a puffed and angry red.

Alec rose, cradling his sister's limp body in his arms, her black hair hanging down like a flag. "Go *where*?" he said harshly. "If we run, they'll be on us—"

Jace whirled around. "Clary—"

His eyes were full of pleading. Clary's heart broke for him. Jace, who hardly ever pleaded for anything. For Isabelle, the bravest of them all.

Alec looked from the statue to Jace, to the pale face of his unconscious sister. "*Someone*," he said, his voice cracking, "do something—"

Clary spun on her heel and ran for the wall. She half-flung herself against it, yanking her stele free from her boot, and went for the stone. The contact of the instrument's tip with the marble sent a shock wave up her arm, but she pressed on, her fingers vibrating as she drew. Black lines fissured out across the stone, cracking into the shape of a door; the edges of the lines began to shimmer. Behind her Clary could hear the demons: the bellow of their voices, the flap of taloned wings, their hissing calls rising to shrieks as the door blazed up with light.

It was a silvery rectangle, as depthless as water but not water, framed with fiery runes. A Portal. Clary reached out with one hand, touched the surface. Every part of her mind concentrated on visualizing a single place. "Come *on*!" she screamed, her eyes fixed on it, not moving as Alec, carrying his sister, darted past her and disappeared into it, vanishing utterly. Simon followed him, and then Jace, catching at her free hand as he went. Clary only had a moment to turn and look behind her—a great black wing swept across her vision, a terrifying glimpse of teeth dripping poison—before the storm of the Portal took her and whirled her away into chaos.

Clary slammed into the ground hard, bruising her knees. The Portal had torn her away from Jace; she rolled to her feet quickly and looked around, breathing hard—what if the Portal hadn't worked? What if it had taken them to the wrong place?

But the cave roof rose above, familiar and towering, marked with runes. There was the fire pit, the scuff marks on the floor where they had all slept the night before. Jace, rising to his feet, Alec's bow falling from his hand, Simon—

And Alec, on his knees beside Isabelle. Any satisfaction Clary felt at her success with the Portal popped like a balloon. Isabelle lay still and drained-looking, gasping shallow breaths. Jace dropped down beside Alec and touched Isabelle's hair gently.

Clary felt Simon clasp her wrist. His voice was ragged. "If you can do anything—"

She moved forward as if in a dream, and knelt down on the other side of Isabelle, opposite Jace, stele slipping in her bloody fingers. She put the tip to Izzy's wrist, remembering what she had done outside the Adamant Citadel, how she had poured herself into healing Jace. *Heal, heal, heal,* she prayed, and finally the stele jerked to life and the black lines began to spiral sluggishly across Izzy's forearm. Izzy moaned and jerked in Alec's arms. He had his head down, his face buried against his sister's hair. "Izzy, please," he whispered. "Not after Max. Izzy, please, stay with me."

Isabelle gasped, her eyelids fluttering. She arched up—and then sank back as the *iratze* vanished from her skin. A dull pulse of blood oozed sluggishly from the wound in her leg: the blood looked tinted black. Clary's hand tightened so hard on her stele, she felt it bend in her hand. "I can't do it," she whispered. "I can't make one strong enough."

"It's not you; it's the poison," Jace said. "Demon poison. In her blood. Sometimes runes can't help."

"Try again," Alec said to Clary; his eyes were dry, but with a terrible brightness. "With the *iratze*. Or with a new rune; you could create a rune—"

Clary's mouth was dry. Never had she wanted to create a rune more, but the stele no longer felt like an extension of her arm; it felt like a dead thing in her hand. She had never felt more helpless.

Isabelle was taking rasping breaths. "Something has to help!" Simon shouted suddenly, his voice echoing off the walls. "You're Shadowhunters; you fight demons all the time. You have to be able to do something—"

"And we die all the time!" Jace shouted back at him, and then suddenly crumpled over Isabelle's body, doubling up as if he'd been punched in the stomach. "Isabelle, God, I'm sorry, I'm so sorry—"

"Move," Simon said, and suddenly he was on his knees next to Isabelle, all of them grouped around her, and Clary was reminded of the horrible tableau in the Accords Hall when the Lightwoods had gathered around Max's dead body, and it couldn't be happening again, it couldn't—

"Leave her alone," Alec snarled. "You're not her family, vampire—"

"No," Simon said, "I'm not." And his fangs snapped out, sharp and white. Clary sucked in her breath as Simon raised his own wrist to his mouth and tore at it, slicing open the veins, and blood ran in rivulets down his arm.

Jace's eyes widened. He stood up and backed away; his hands were in fists, but he didn't move to stop Simon, who held his wrist over the gash in Isabelle's leg and let his blood run down his fingers, spattering onto her, covering her wound.

"What ... are ... you ... doing?" Alec ground out between his teeth, but Jace flung up a hand, his eyes on Simon.

"Let him," Jace said, almost in a whisper. "It can work, I've heard of it working..."

Isabelle, still unconscious, arched back into her brother's arms.

Her leg was twitching. The heel of her boot dug into the ground as her ribboned skin began to knit itself back together. Simon's blood poured in a steady stream, covering the injury, but even beneath the blood Clary could see that new, pink skin was covering the torn mess of flesh.

Isabelle's eyes opened. They were wide and dark. Her lips had been almost white, but color was starting to come back into them. She stared at Simon uncomprehendingly, and then down at her leg.

The skin that had been torn and shredded looked clean and pale, only a faint half-moon of neatly spaced white scars left to show where the demon's teeth had gone in. Simon's blood was still dripping slowly from his fingers, though the wound in his wrist had mostly healed. He looked pale, Clary realized anxiously, much paler than usual, and his veins were standing out blackly against his skin. He lifted his wrist to his mouth, his teeth bared—

"Simon, no!" Isabelle said, struggling to sit up against Alec, who was staring down at her with shocked blue eyes.

Clary caught Simon's wrist. "It's all right," she said. Blood stained his sleeve, his shirt, the corners of his mouth. His skin was cold under her touch, his wrist pulseless. "It's okay—Isabelle's okay," she said, and drew Simon to his feet. "Let's give them a second," she said softly, and led him away to where he could lean against her by the wall. Jace and Alec were bending over Isabelle, their voices low and murmuring. Clary held Simon by the wrist as he slumped back against the stone, his eyes fluttering shut in exhaustion.

19

INTO THE SILENT LAND

The Endarkened woman had pale skin and long coppery hair. It might have been pretty once but was now tangled with dirt and twigs. She didn't appear to care, just placed the plates of food—gruel, soupy and gray-looking, for Magnus and Luke, and a bottle of blood for Raphael—on the floor and turned away from the prisoners.

Neither Luke nor Magnus moved toward their food. Magnus felt too sick to have much of an appetite. Besides, he was vaguely suspicious that Sebastian had poisoned the gruel, or drugged it, or both. Raphael, though, seized up the bottle and drank from it hungrily, swallowing until blood ran out of the corners of his mouth.

"Now, now, Raphael," said a voice from the shadows, and Sebastian Morgenstern appeared in the open doorway. The Endarkened woman bowed her head and hurried out past him, shutting the door behind her.

He really looked astonishingly like his father had at his age, Magnus thought. Those odd black eyes, entirely black without a hint of brown or hazel, the sort of feature that was beautiful because it was unusual. The same fanatic twitch to his smile. Jace had never had that—he had recklessness, and the anarchic joy of imagined self-annihilation, but he was not a zealot. Which, Magnus thought, was precisely why Valentine had sent him away. To crush your opposition, you needed a hammer, and Jace was a much more delicate weapon than that.

"Where's Jocelyn?" It was Luke, of course, his voice a low growl, his hands in fists at his sides. Magnus wondered what it was like for Luke to look at Sebastian, whether the resemblance to Valentine, who had once been his *parabatai*, was painful, or whether that loss had faded long ago. *"Where is she?"*

Sebastian laughed, and that was something that was different about him; Valentine had never been a man who laughed easily. Jace's sarcastic humor seemed to have been born into his blood, a distinctly Herondale trait. "She's fine," he said, "just fine, by which I mean she's still alive. Which is the best you can hope for, really."

"I want to see her," Luke said.

"Hmm," Sebastian said, as if considering it. "No. I don't see the advantage in it to me."

"She's your mother," said Luke. "You could be kind to her."

"It's none of your business, dog." For the first time there was a shadow of youth in Sebastian's voice, an edge of petulance. "You, with your hands all over my mother, making Clary believe you're her family—"

"I'm more her family than you are," said Luke, and Magnus shot him a warning look as Sebastian whitened, his fingers twitching toward his belt, where the hilt of the Morgenstern sword was visible.

"Don't," Magnus said in a low voice, and then, louder, "You know if you touch Luke, Clary will hate you. Jocelyn, too."

Sebastian drew his hand away from his sword with a visible effort. "I said I never intended to harm her."

"No, just hold her hostage," Magnus said. "You want some-thing—something from the Clave, or something from Clary and Jace. I'd guess the latter; the Clave has never interested you much, but you do care what your sister thinks. She and I are very close, by the way," he added.

"You're not that close." Sebastian's tone was withering. "I'm hardly going to spare the life of everyone she's ever met. I'm not that crazy."

"You seem very crazy," said Raphael, who had been silent up until that point.

"Raphael," Magnus said in a warning tone, but Sebastian didn't seem angry. He was regarding Raphael with a considering look.

"Raphael Santiago," he said. "Leader of the New York clan—or aren't you? No, it was Camille who held that position, and now the little mad girl. That must be quite frustrating for you. It really seems to me that the Shadowhunters of Manhattan ought to have stepped in before now. Neither Camille nor poor Maureen Brown were fit to be leaders. They broke the Accords—they cared nothing for the Law. But you do. It seems to me that of all the Downworld races, the vampires have been most ill treated by Shadowhunters. One only needs to look at your situation."

"*Raphael*," Magnus said again, and tried to lean forward, to catch the vampire's eye, but Magnus's chains pulled tight, rattling. He winced at the pain in his wrists.

Raphael was sitting back on his heels, his cheeks flushed from his recent feeding. His hair was tousled; he looked as young as he had when Magnus had first met him. "I do not see why you are tell-ing me this," he said.

"You can't say I've mistreated you more than your vampire leaders," said Sebastian. "I've fed you. I haven't put you in a cage. You know I'll win; you all know it. And on that day I'll be happy to make sure you, Raphael, rule all the vampires in New York—in fact, all the vampires in North America. You're welcome to them. All I need is for you to bring the other Night's Children to my side. The Fair Folk have already joined with me. The Court always picks the winning side. Shouldn't you?"

Raphael rose to his feet. There was blood on his hands; he frowned down at them. Raphael was nothing if not fastidious. "That seems reasonable," he said. "I shall join you."

Luke dropped his face into his hands. Through his teeth Magnus said, "Raphael, you have truly lived down to my lowest expectations of you."

"Magnus, it doesn't matter," said Luke; he was being protective, Magnus knew. Raphael had already gone to stand by Sebastian's side. "Let him go. He's no loss."

Raphael snorted. "No loss, you say," he said. "I am well quit of you idiots, flopping about this cell, whining about your friends and lovers. You are weak and have always been weak—"

"I should have let you walk into the daylight," Magnus said, and his voice was ice.

Raphael flinched—it was barely a movement, but Magnus saw it. Not that it brought him much satisfaction.

Sebastian saw the flinch, though, and the look in his dark eyes intensified. From his belt he produced a knife—thin, with a narrow blade. A misericord, a "mercy-killer," the kind of blade that was meant to pierce through the gaps in armor and deliver a killing stroke.

Raphael, seeing the flash of metal, stepped back quickly, but Sebastian only smiled and flipped the blade in his hand. He offered it to Raphael, hilt-first. "Take it," he said.

Raphael reached out a hand, his eyes suspicious. He took the knife and held it, dangling loosely—vampires had little use for weapons. They were their own weapons.

"Very good," said Sebastian. "Now let us seal our agreement in blood. Kill the warlock."

The blade dropped from Raphael's hand and clattered to the ground. With a look of irritation Sebastian bent and snatched it up, putting it back into the vampire's hand.

"We do not kill with knives," Raphael said, staring from the blade to Sebastian's cold expression.

"You do now," said Sebastian. "I won't have you tearing out his throat; too messy, too easy to get it wrong. Do as I tell you. Go to the warlock and stab him to death. Cut his throat, pierce his heart—however you like."

Raphael turned toward Magnus. Luke started forward; Magnus held up a warning hand. "Luke," he said. "Don't."

"Raphael, if you do this, there will be no peace between the pack and the Night's Children, not now or ever again," Luke said, his eyes gleaming with a green shine.

Sebastian laughed. "You can't imagine you'll ever hold sway over a pack again, can you, Lucian Graymark? When I win this war, and I will, I will rule with my sister beside me, and keep you in a cage for her to throw bones to when it amuses her."

Raphael took another step toward Magnus. His eyes were enormous. His throat had been kissed so many times by the crucifix he wore that the scar never left. The blade gleamed in his hand.

"If you think Clary would tolerate—" Luke began, and then turned away. He moved toward Raphael, but Sebastian was already in front of him, blocking his way with the Morgenstern blade.

With a strange detachment Magnus watched Raphael approach him. Magnus's heart was thudding in his chest, he was aware of that much, but he did not feel afraid. He had been close to death many times; so many that the idea no longer frightened him. Sometimes he thought some part of him longed for it, for that unknown country, the one place he had never been, that one experience as yet unlived.

The tip of the knife touched his neck. Raphael's hand was

shaking; Magnus felt the sting as the blade nicked the hollow of his throat.

"That's right," said Sebastian with a feral grin. "Cut his throat. Let the blood run out over the floor. He has lived too many years."

Magnus thought of Alec then, of his blue eyes and steady smile. He thought of walking away from Alec in the tunnels under New York. He thought of why he'd done it. Yes, Alec's willingness to see Camille had angered him, but it was more than that.

He remembered Tessa weeping in his arms in Paris, and thinking that he had never known the loss she felt, because he had never loved like she had, and that he was afraid that someday he would, and like Tessa he would lose his mortal love. And that it was better to be the one who died than the one who lived on.

He had dismissed that, later, as a morbid fantasy, and had not remembered it again until Alec. It had torn at him to walk away from Alec. But for an immortal to love a mortal, that had been the destruction of gods, and if gods had been destroyed by it, Magnus could hardly hope for better. He looked up at Raphael through his eyelashes. "You remember," he said in a low voice, so low he doubted Sebastian could hear him. "You know what you owe me."

"You saved my life," Raphael said, but his voice was numb. "A life I never wanted."

"Show me you're serious, Santiago," said Sebastian. "Kill the warlock."

Raphael's hand tightened on the hilt of the knife. His knuckles were white. He spoke to Magnus. "I have no soul," he said. "But I made you a promise on my mother's doorstep, and she was sacred to me."

"Santiago—" Sebastian began.

"I was a child then. I am not now." The knife fell to the floor. Raphael turned and looked at Sebastian, his wide dark eyes very clear. "I cannot," he said. "I will not. I owe him a debt from many years ago."

Sebastian was very still. "You disappoint me, Raphael," he said, and sheathed the Morgenstern sword. He stepped forward and picked up the knife at Raphael's feet, turning it over in his hand. A bit of light sparked along the blade, a singing teardrop of fire. "You disappoint me very much," he said, and then, too swiftly for the eye to follow, he drove the blade into Raphael's heart.

It was freezing inside the hospital morgue. Maia wasn't shivering, but she could feel it, like the points of needles against her skin.

Catarina was standing against the bank of steel compartments that held corpses, which ran along one wall. The yellowish fluorescent lights made her look washed-out, a pale blue blur in green scrubs. She was muttering under her breath in a strange language that made chills run up Maia's spine.

"Where is it?" Bat asked. He was holding a wicked-looking hunting knife in one hand and a large kennel-size cage in the other. He dropped the cage with a clang, his gaze sweeping the room.

Two bare steel tables stood in the center of the morgue. As Maia stared, one of them began inching forward. Its wheels dragged along the tiled floor.

Catarina pointed. "There," she said. Her gaze was on the cage; she made a gesture with her fingers and the cage seemed to vibrate and spark. "Under the table."

"You don't say," Lily drawled, clicking forward in her heels. She bent down to peer under the table, then leaped back with a shriek. She sailed through the air and landed on one of the countertops, where she perched like a bat, her black hair tumbling down out of its ponytail. "It's *hideous*," she said.

"It's a demon," said Catarina. The table had stopped moving. "Probably a Dantalion or some other ghoul type. They feed on the dead."

"Oh, for goodness' sake," said Maia, taking a step forward;

before she reached the table, Bat kicked it with a booted foot. It went over with a clang, revealing the creature underneath.

Lily had been right: it *was* hideous. It was about the size of a large dog, but it resembled a ball of grayish, pulsing intestines, studded with malformed kidneys and nodes of pus and blood. A single yellow, weeping eye glared out from among the jumble of organs.

"Ew," said Bat.

"I told you," said Lily, just as a long rope of intestine shot out from the demon and wrapped around Bat's ankle, jerking hard. He fell to the floor with a wince-inducing crash.

"Bat!" Maia cried, but before she needed to move, he whipped around and slashed with his knife through the pulsing matter that held him. He scrambled back as demon ichor sprayed across the floor.

"So *gross*," Lily said. She was seated on the counter now, holding up an oblong metal object—her phone—as if it would ward the demon off.

Bat scrambled to his feet as the demon skittered toward Maia. She kicked out at it, and it rolled back with an angry squishing noise. Bat looked down at his knife. The metal was melting, dissolved by the ichor. He dropped it with a noise of disgust.

"Weapons," he said, casting around. "I need a weapon—"

Maia seized a scalpel off a nearby table and flung it. It stuck into the creature with a slimy noise. The demon squealed. A moment later the scalpel shot back out of it as if it had been ejected from a particularly powerful toaster. It skidded along the floor, melting and sizzling.

"Ordinary weapons don't work on them!" Catarina stepped forward, raising her right hand. It was surrounded by blue flame. "Only runed blades—"

"Then let's get some of those!" Bat gasped, backing away as the pulsing creature scooted toward him.

"Only Shadowhunters can use them!" Catarina cried, and a bolt of blue fire shot from her hand. It struck the creature squarely, sending it rolling over and over. Bat seized hold of the cage and banged it down in front of the demon, yanking up the hatch just as the demon rolled inside.

Maia slammed the hatch down and threw the bolt, locking the demon inside. They all backed away, staring in horror as it hissed and threw itself around the confines of its warlock-strengthened prison. All except Lily, who was still pointing her phone at it.

"Are you *filming* this?" Maia demanded.

"Maybe," Lily said.

Catarina drew her sleeve across her brow. "Thanks for the help," she said. "Even warlock magic can't kill Dantalions; they're tough."

"*Why* are you filming this?" Maia said to Lily.

The vampire girl shrugged. "When the cat is away, the mice will play... Always good to remind the mice that in this case, when the cat is away, the mice will all be eaten by demons. I'm going to send this video file to every one of our Downworld contacts around the world. Just a reminder that there are demons we need Shadowhunters to destroy. That's why they exist."

"They won't exist for long," hissed the Dantalion demon. Bat yelled and jumped back another foot. Maia didn't blame him. The thing's mouth had opened. It looked like a slick black tunnel lined with teeth. "Tomorrow night is the attack. Tomorrow night is the war."

"What war?" Catarina demanded. "Tell us, creature, or when I get you home, I will set to torturing you in every way I can devise..."

"Sebastian Morgenstern," said the demon. "Tomorrow night he attacks Alicante. Tomorrow night the Shadowhunters cease to be."

A fire burned in the middle of the cave, the smoke furling up toward the high domed ceiling, lost in shadow. Simon could feel the heat from the fire, a tense crackling against his skin more than the real sensation of warmth. He guessed it was cold in the cave, from the fact that Alec had bundled himself up in a bulky sweater and carefully wrapped a blanket around Isabelle, who was sleeping stretched out across the floor, her head on her brother's lap. But Simon couldn't feel it, not really.

Clary and Jace had gone to check the tunnels and make sure they were still free of demons and other possible stray nasties. Alec hadn't wanted to leave Isabelle, and Simon had been too weak and dizzy to contemplate moving much. Not that he had let that fact be known. Technically he was on watch, listening for anything that might come at them from the shadows.

Alec was staring into the flames. The yellow light made him look tired, older. "Thanks," he said, suddenly.

Simon almost jumped. Alec hadn't said a word to him since *What are you doing?* "For what?"

"Saving my sister," said Alec. He brushed a hand through Isabelle's dark hair. "I know," he said, a little haltingly. "I mean, I knew, when we came here, that this could be a suicide mission. I know it's dangerous. I know I can't really expect us all to survive. But I thought it would be me, not Izzy…"

"Why?" Simon said. His head was pounding, his mouth dry.

"Because I'd rather it was me," Alec said. "She's—Isabelle. She's smart and tough and a good fighter. Better than me. She deserves to be all right, to be happy." He looked at Simon through the fire. "You have a sister, don't you?"

Simon was jolted by the question—New York seemed a world, a lifetime away. "Rebecca," he said. "That's her name."

"And what would you do to someone who made her unhappy?"

Simon eyed Alec warily. "I would reason with them," he said. "Talk it out. Maybe an understanding hug."

Alec snorted and seemed about to reply; then his head snapped around, as if he'd heard something. Simon raised an eyebrow. It wasn't often a human heard something before a vampire did. A moment later he recognized the sound himself, and understood: It was Jace's voice. Illumination danced at the end of the far tunnel, and Clary and Jace appeared, Clary holding a witchlight in her hand.

Even in her boots Clary barely came to Jace's shoulder. They weren't touching, but they moved together toward the fire. Simon thought that while they had seemed like a couple ever since the first time they'd come back from Idris, they seemed like something more now. They seemed like a team.

"Anything interesting?" Alec asked as Jace came to sit beside the fire.

"Clary put glamour runes on the cave entrances. No one should be able to see that there's any way in here."

"How long will they last?"

"Overnight, probably into tomorrow," said Clary, glancing at Izzy. "What with the runes wearing off quicker here, I'll have to check them later."

"And I've got a better idea of where we're positioned in terms of Alicante. I'm pretty sure that the rock wasteland where we were last night"—Jace pointed at the rightmost tunnel—"looks out over what I think used to be Brocelind Forest."

Alec half-closed his eyes. "That's depressing. The forest was—beautiful."

"Not anymore." Jace shook his head. "Just wasteland, as far as you can see." He bent and touched Isabelle's hair, and Simon felt a small pointless flare of jealousy—that he could touch her so carelessly, show his affection without thinking. "How is she?"

"Good. Sleeping."

"Think she'll be well enough to move by tomorrow?" Jace's voice was anxious. "We can't stay here. We've sent up enough warnings that we're present. If we don't get to Sebastian, he'll find us first. And we're running out of food."

Simon lost Alec's murmured response; a sudden stabbing pain shot through him, and he doubled up. He felt robbed of his breath, except he *didn't* breathe. Nevertheless his chest hurt, as if something had been ripped out of it.

"Simon. Simon!" Clary said sharply, her hand on his shoulder, and he looked up at her, his eyes streaming tears tinged with blood. "God, Simon, what's wrong?" she asked, frantic.

He sat up slowly. The pain was already starting to ebb. "I don't know. It was like someone stuck a knife into my chest."

Jace was swiftly on his knees in front of him, his fingers under Simon's chin. His pale gold gaze searched Simon's face. "Raphael," Jace said finally, in a flat voice. "He's your sire, the one whose blood made you a vampire."

Simon nodded. "So?"

Jace shook his head. "Nothing," he muttered. "When did you last feed?"

"I'm fine," Simon said, but Clary had already caught at his right hand and lifted it; the gold faerie ring shone on his finger. The hand itself was dead white, the veins under the skin showing black, like a network of cracks in marble. "You're not fine—haven't you fed? You lost all that blood!"

"Clary—"

"Where are the bottles you brought?" She cast around, looking for his bag, and found it shoved against the wall. She yanked it toward her. "Simon, if you don't start taking better care of yourself—"

"Don't." He grabbed the strap of the bag away from her; she glared at him. "They broke," he said. "The bottles broke, when we were fighting the demons in the Accords Hall. The blood's gone."

Clary stood up. "Simon Lewis," she said furiously. "Why didn't you *say something*?"

"Say something about what?" Jace moved away from Simon.

"Simon's starving," Clary explained. "He lost blood healing Izzy, and his supply was wrecked in the Hall—"

"Why *didn't* you say something?" Jace asked, rising and pushing back a lock of blond hair.

"Because," Simon said. "It's not like there's animals I can feed on here."

"There's us," Jace said.

"I don't want to feed on my friends' blood."

"Why not?" Jace stepped past the fire and looked down at Simon; his expression was open and curious. "We've been here before, haven't we? Last time you were starving, I gave you my blood. It was a little homoerotic, maybe, but I'm secure in my sexuality."

Simon sighed internally; he could tell that under the flippancy, Jace was completely serious in his offer. Probably less because it was sexy than because Jace had a death wish the size of Brooklyn.

"I'm not biting someone whose veins are full of heavenly fire," Simon said. "I have no desire to be toasted from the inside out."

Clary swept her hair back, baring her throat. "Look, drink my blood. I always said you were welcome to it—"

"No," Jace said immediately, and Simon saw him remembering the hold in Valentine's ship, the way Simon had said *I would have killed you*, and Jace had replied, wonderingly, *I would have let you*.

"Oh, for God's sake. I'll do it." Alec stood up, carefully repositioning Izzy on the blanket. He tucked the edge around her and straightened.

Simon let his head fall back against the wall of the cave. "You don't even like me. Now you're offering me your blood?"

"You saved my sister. I owe you." Alec shrugged, his shadow long and dark in the light of the flames.

"Right." Simon swallowed awkwardly. "Okay."

Clary reached her hand down. After a moment Simon took it

and let her haul him to his feet. He couldn't help staring across the room at Isabelle, asleep, half-wrapped in Alec's blue blanket. She was breathing, slow and steady. Izzy, still breathing, because of him.

Simon took a step toward Alec, and stumbled. Alec caught him and steadied him. His grip on Simon's shoulder was hard. Simon could feel Alec's tension in it, and he suddenly realized how bizarre the situation was: Jace and Clary gawking openly at them, Alec looking as if he were bracing himself to have a bucket of ice water dumped over his head.

Alec turned his head a little to the left, baring his throat. He was staring off fixedly at the opposite wall. Simon decided he looked less like someone who was about to have ice water dumped on their head and more like someone about to endure an embarrassing exam at the doctor's office.

"I am not doing this in front of everyone," Simon announced.

"It's not spin the bottle, Simon," said Clary. "It's just food. Not that you're food, Alec," she added when he glared. She held her hands up. "Never mind."

"Oh, for the Angel's—" Alec began, and closed his hand around Simon's upper arm. "Come on," he said, and dragged Simon partway down the tunnel that led back toward the gate, just far enough so that the others faded out of view, disappearing behind a jut of rock.

Though Simon did hear the last thing Jace said, just before they faded out of earshot. "What? They need privacy. It's an intimate moment."

"I think you should just let me die," Simon said.

"Shut up," Alec said, and pushed him up against the cave wall. He eyed Simon thoughtfully. "Does it have to be my neck?"

"No," Simon said, feeling as if he had wandered into a bizarre dream. "Wrists are okay too."

Alec began to push up the sleeve of his sweater. His arm was bare and pale except where the Marks were, and Simon could see his veins under his skin. Despite himself, he felt the sting of hunger, rousing him from exhaustion: He could smell blood, soft and salty, rich with the tang of daylight. Shadowhunter blood, like Izzy's. He ran his tongue along his upper teeth and was only a little surprised to feel his canines hardening and sharpening into fangs.

"I just want you to know," Alec said as he held his wrist out, "that I realize that to you vampires this feeding business sometimes equals sexy times."

Simon's eyes widened.

"My sister may have told me more than I wanted to know," Alec admitted. "Anyway, my point is that I am not attracted to you in the slightest."

"Right," Simon said, and took Alec's hand. He tried for a brotherly sort of grasp, but it didn't quite work, considering that he had to bend Alec's hand back to bare the vulnerable part of his wrist. "Well, you don't ring my bells either, so I guess we're even. Although, you could have faked it for five—"

"No, I couldn't," Alec said. "I hate it when straight guys think all gay guys are attracted to them. I'm not attracted to every guy any more than you're attracted to every girl."

Simon took a deep, purposeful breath. It was always a strange feeling, breathing when he didn't need to, but it was calming. "Alec," he said. "Chill. I don't think you're in love with me. In fact, most of the time I think you hate me."

Alec paused. "I don't hate you. Why would I hate you?"

"Because I'm a Downworlder? Because I'm a vampire who's in love with your sister and you think she's too good for me?"

"Don't *you*?" Alec said, but it was without rancor; after a moment he smiled a little, that Lightwood smile that lit up his face and made Simon think of Izzy. "She's my little sister. I think she's too good for everyone. But you—you're a good *person*, Simon. Regardless of whether you're a vampire, too. You're loyal and you're smart and you—you make Isabelle happy. I don't know why, but you do. I know I didn't like you when I met you. But that changed. And I'd hardly judge my sister for dating a Downworlder."

Simon stood very still. Alec was all right with warlocks, he thought. That much was obvious enough. But warlocks were born what they were. Alec was the most conservative of the Lightwood children—he wasn't chaos-loving or risk-taking like Jace and Isabelle—and Simon had always felt it in him, that sense that a vampire was a human transformed into something *wrong*.

"You wouldn't agree to being a vampire," Simon said. "Not even to be with Magnus forever. Right? You didn't want to live forever; you wanted to take his immortality away. That's why he broke up with you."

Alec flinched. "No," he said. "No, I wouldn't want to be a vampire."

"So you do think I'm less than you," Simon said.

Alec's voice cracked. "I'm *trying*," he said, and Simon felt it, felt how much Alec wanted to mean it, maybe even did mean it a little bit. And after all, if Simon hadn't been a vampire, he would still have been a mundane, still lesser. He felt Alec's pulse surge in the wrist he was holding. "Go ahead," Alec said, exhaling his words, clearly in an agony of waiting. "Just—do it."

"Brace yourself," Simon said, and lifted Alec's wrist to his mouth. Despite the tension between them, his body, hungry and deprived, responded. His muscles tightened and his fang teeth snapped out of their own accord. He saw Alec's eyes darken with surprise and fear. Hunger spread like a fire through Simon's body, and he spoke out of the drowning depths of it, struggling to try to say something human to Alec. He hoped he was audible enough to be understood around his fangs. "I'm sorry about Magnus."

"Me too. Now bite," Alec said, and Simon did, his fangs piercing fast and clean through the skin, the blood exploding into his mouth. He heard Alec gasp, and Simon gripped involuntarily tighter, as if to prevent Alec from trying to pull away. But Alec didn't try. His wild heartbeat was audible to Simon, pounding down through his veins like the tolling of a bell. Along with Alec's blood, Simon could taste the metal of fear, the spark of pain, and the eager flame of something else, something he had tasted the first time he had drunk Jace's blood on the filthy metal floor of Valentine's ship. Maybe all Shadowhunters did have a death wish, after all.

20

THE SERPENTS
OF THE DUST

When Alec and Simon returned to the central cave, they found
Isabelle still curled asleep among a pile of blankets. Jace was sitting
by the fire, leaning back on his hands, the play of light and shadow
dancing across his face. Clary lay with her head on his lap, though
Simon could see by the shimmer of her eyes as she watched them
approach that she wasn't asleep.

Jace raised his eyebrows. "Walk of shame, boys?"

Alec glowered. He stood with his left wrist turned in, hiding
the puncture marks, though they were mostly faded thanks to the
iratze he'd put on his wrist. He hadn't pushed Simon away, had let
him drink until Simon had stopped himself, and as a result he was
a little pale. "It wasn't sexy," he said.

"It was a little sexy," Simon said. He felt much better, having
fed, and couldn't help but poke at Alec a bit.

"It wasn't," said Alec.

"I had some feelings," said Simon.

"Do feel free to agonize about it on your own time," said Alec, and
bent down to grab the strap of his backpack. "I'm going to take watch."

Clary sat up with a yawn. "Are you sure? Do you need a blood replacement rune?"

"I already put on two," Alec said. "I'll be fine." He straightened up and glanced at his sleeping sister. "Just look after Isabelle, okay?" His gaze went to Simon. "Especially you, vampire."

Alec headed off down the corridor, his witchlight casting his shadow, long and spidery, against the cave wall. Jace and Clary exchanged a quick look before Jace scrambled to his feet and followed Alec into the tunnel. Simon could hear their voices—soft murmurs through the rock, though he couldn't make out any of the words.

Alec's words echoed in his head. *Look after Isabelle.* He thought of Alec in the tunnel. *You're loyal and you're smart and you—you make Isabelle happy. I don't know why, but you do.*

The idea of making Isabelle happy filled him with a sense of warmth. Simon sat down quietly beside her—she was like a cat, curled up in a ball of blankets, her head pillowed on her arm. He eased himself gently down to lie next to her. She was alive because of him, and her brother had done the closest thing he would probably ever do to giving them his blessing.

He heard Clary, over on the other side of the fire, laugh softly. "Good night, Simon," she said.

Simon could feel Isabelle's hair, as soft as spun silk, under his cheek. "Good night," he said, and closed his eyes, his veins full of Lightwood blood.

Jace caught up easily with Alec, who had paused where the cave corridor curved away toward the gate. The walls of the corridor were smooth as if worn away by years of water or wind, not chisels, though Jace had no doubt the passages were man-made.

Alec, leaning against the cave wall, clearly waiting for Jace, raised his witchlight. "Is something wrong?"

Jace slowed his pace as he neared his *parabatai*. "I just wanted to make sure you were all right."

Alec shrugged with one shoulder. "As much as I can be, I guess."

"I'm sorry," Jace said. "Again. I take stupid risks. I can't help it."

"We let you," said Alec. "Sometimes your risks pay off. We let you because we have to let you. Because if we didn't let you, nothing would ever get done." He rubbed at his face with his torn sleeve. "Isabelle would say the same thing."

"We never got to finish our conversation, before," Jace said. "I just wanted to say that you don't always have to be all right. I asked you to be my *parabatai* because I needed you, but you're allowed to need me, too. This"—he indicated his own *parabatai* rune—"means you are the better, other half of me, and I care about you more than I care about myself. Remember that. I'm sorry I didn't realize how much you were hurting. I didn't see it then, but I see it now."

Alec was very still for a moment, barely breathing. Then, to Jace's surprise, he reached out and ruffled Jace's hair, the way an older brother might ruffle his younger sibling's hair. His smile was cautious, but it was full of real affection. "Thanks for seeing me," he said, and walked off down the tunnel.

"*Clary.*"

She woke up slowly, out of mellow dreams of warmth and fire, the smell of hay and apples. In the dream she'd been on Luke's farm, hanging upside-down from a tree branch, laughing as Simon waved from below. Slowly she became aware of the hard stone under her hips and back, her head pillowed on Jace's legs.

"*Clary,*" he said again, still whispering. Simon and Isabelle were sprawled together some distance away, a dark heap in the shadows. Jace's eyes glimmered down at her, pale gold and dancing with reflected firelight. "I want a bath."

"Yeah, well, I want a million dollars," she said, rubbing at her eyes. "We all want something."

He cocked an eyebrow. "Come on, think about it," he said. "That cavern? The one with the lake? We could."

Clary thought of the cavern, the lovely blue water, as deep as twilight, and felt suddenly as if she were encrusted with a layer of grime—dirt and blood and ichor and sweat, her hair knotted back into a greasy tangle.

Jace's eyes danced, and Clary felt that familiar surge inside her chest, that pull she had felt since the first time she'd ever seen him. She couldn't pinpoint the exact moment she'd fallen in love with Jace, but there had always been something about him that reminded her of a lion, a wild animal unfettered by rules, the promise of a life of freedom. Never "I can't," but always "I can." Always the risk and the surety, never the fear or the question.

She scrambled to her feet as quietly as she could. "All right."

He was up instantly, taking her hand and tugging her down the west corridor that led away from the central cave. They went in silence, her witchlight lighting the way, a silence Clary felt almost afraid to break, as if she would be shattering the illusory calm of a dream or a spell.

The massive cavern opened in front of them suddenly, and she put her rune-stone away, dousing its light. The bioluminescence of the cave was enough: light shimmering out from the walls, from the glimmering stalactites that hung from the roof like electrified icicles. Knives of light pierced the shadows. Jace let go of her hand and walked the last steps of the path down to the edge of the water, where the small beach was powdery and fine, glittering with mica. He paused a few feet from the water and said, "Thank you."

She looked over at him in surprise. "For what?"

"Last night," he said. "You saved me. The heavenly fire would have killed me, I think. What you did—"

"We still can't tell the others," she said.

"I didn't last night, did I?" he asked. It was true. Jace and Clary had maintained the fiction that Clary had simply helped Jace control and dissipate the fire, and that nothing else had changed.

"We can't risk them giving it away, even by the wrong kind of glance or expression," she said. "You and I, we've had some practice hiding things from Sebastian, but they haven't. It wouldn't be fair to them. I almost wish *we* didn't know..."

She trailed off, unnerved by his lack of response. Jace was looking at the water, blue and depthless, his back to her. She took a step forward and tapped him lightly on the shoulder. "Jace," she said. "If you want to do something different, if you think we should make another plan—"

He turned, and suddenly she was in the circle of his arms. It sent a shock through her whole body. His hands cupped her shoulder blades, his fingers stroking lightly along the material of her shirt. She shivered, thoughts flying out of her head like feathers scattered on the wind.

"When," he said, "did you get so careful?"

"I'm not careful," she said as he touched his lips to her temple. His warm breath stirred the curls by her ear. "I'm just not you."

She felt him laugh. His hands slid down her sides, gripped her waist. "That, you are definitely not. *Much* prettier."

"You must love me," she said, breath hitching as his lips traveled excruciatingly slowly along her jaw. "I never thought you'd admit anyone was prettier than you." She started as his mouth found her own, his lips parting to taste hers, and she leaned up and into the kiss, determined to take back some control. She wound her arms around his neck, opening her mouth to him, and nipped gently at his bottom lip.

It had more of an effect than she'd bargained for; his hands tightened on her waist and he groaned low into her mouth. A moment later he'd broken away, flushed, his eyes glittering. "You're all right?" he said. "You want this?"

She nodded, swallowing. Her whole body felt as if it were vibrating like a plucked string. "Yes, I do. I—"

"It's just, for so long I haven't really been able to touch you, and now I can," he said. "But maybe this isn't the place—"

"Well, we are filthy," she admitted.

"'Filthy' seems a bit judgmental."

Clary raised her hands, palms-up. There was dirt embedded in her skin and under her nails. She grinned at him. "I mean *literally*," she said, and indicated the water nearby with a jerk of her chin. "Weren't we going to wash off? In the water?"

The sparkle in his eyes darkened them to amber. "Right," he said, and reached up to unzip his jacket.

Clary almost squeaked, *What are you doing?* but it was perfectly obvious what he was doing. She'd said "in the water," and it wasn't like they could wade in with their gear on. She just hadn't quite thought this far ahead.

He dropped the jacket and pulled his T-shirt off over his head; the collar caught for a moment, and Clary just stared, suddenly hyperaware of the fact that they were alone, and of his body: honey-colored skin mapped with old and new Marks, a fading scar just under the curve of his left pectoral muscle. Flat, ridged stomach tapering to narrow hips; he'd lost weight, and his weapons belt hung loose. Legs, arms, graceful like a dancer's; he pulled free of the shirt and shook out his bright hair, and she thought with a sudden sinking in her stomach that it just wasn't possible that he was hers, he wasn't the sort of person ordinary people got to be near, much less touch, and then he looked up at her, hands on his belt, and smiled his familiar crooked smile.

"Keeping your clothes on?" he said. "I could promise not to look, but I'd be lying."

Clary unzipped her gear jacket and threw it at him. He caught it and dropped it onto the pile of his clothes, grinning. He unlooped his belt, dropped it as well. "Pervert," she said. "Though you get points for being honest about it."

"I'm seventeen; we're all perverts," he said, kicking his shoes off and stepping out of his pants. He was wearing black boxer shorts, and to Clary's mixed relief and slight regret, he kept them on as he stepped into the water, wading in knee-deep. "Or, at least, I'll be seventeen in a few weeks," he called back over his shoulder. "I did the math, with my father's letters and the time of the Uprising. I was born in January."

Something about the complete normalcy of his tone set Clary at ease. She toed off her boots, pulled her T-shirt off and then her pants, and went to the edge of the water. It was cool but not cold, lapping up to her ankles.

Jace looked up at her and smiled. Then his eyes traveled down from her face to her body, her plain cotton panties and bra. She wished she'd worn something prettier, but it wasn't like "fancy lingerie" had been on her packing list for the demon realms. Her bra was pale blue cotton, the totally boring kind you could buy at the supermarket, though Jace was looking at it like it was something exotic and amazing.

He flushed suddenly, and averted his eyes, backing away so that the water rose to cover him, up to his shoulders. He ducked under and resurfaced again, looking less flustered but a lot wetter, his hair dark gold and streaming rivulets. "It's easier if you get in fast," he said.

Clary took a breath and dived forward, the water closing over her head. And it was gorgeous—dark blue, shot with threads of silver from the light above. The powdery stone had mixed with the water, giving it a heavy, soft texture. It was easy to float; the moment she let herself, she bobbed to the surface, shaking water from her hair.

She sighed in relief. There was no soap, but she rubbed her hands together, watching the flakes of dirt and blood melt away into the water. Her hair floated on the surface, red mixing with blue.

A spray of water droplets made her look up. Jace was a few feet away, shaking out his hair. "I guess that makes me a year older than you," he said. "I'm cradle-robbing."

"Six months," Clary corrected. "And you're a Capricorn, huh? Stubborn, reckless, bends the rules—sounds about right."

He caught hold of her hips and pulled her toward him through the water. It was just deep enough that his feet touched the ground, but hers didn't quite; she clenched her hands on his shoulders to keep herself upright as he drew her legs around his waist. She stared down at him, heat coiling in her stomach, at the sleek wet lines of his neck and shoulders and chest, the water droplets caught in his eyelashes like stars.

He rose up to kiss her just as she leaned in; their lips crashed together with a force that sent a shock of pleasure-pain through her. His hands slid up her skin; she cupped the back of his head, fingers tangling in wet curls. He parted her lips, stroked inside with his tongue. They were both shuddering and she was gasping, her breath mingling with his.

He reached behind himself with one hand to steady them on the wall of the cave, but it was slick with water and he half-slipped; Clary broke away from kissing him as he found his footing, his left arm still wrapped tightly against her, pressing her body to his. His pupils were blown wide, his heart hammering against her.

"That was," he gasped, and pressed his face to the juncture of her neck and shoulder and breathed as if he were breathing her in; he was shaking a little, although his grip on her was steady and firm. "That was—intense."

"It's been a while," she murmured, touching his hair gently, "since we could, you know—let go. At all."

"I can't believe it," he said, "I still can't, that I can kiss you now, touch you, actually touch you, without being afraid—" He pressed a kiss to her throat, and she jumped; he tipped his head back to look up at her. Water trickled down his face like tears, outlining the sharp edges of cheekbones, the curve of his jaw.

"Reckless," he said. "You know, when I first showed up at the Institute, Alec called me reckless so many times that I went and looked it up in the dictionary. Not that I didn't already know what it meant, but—I always kind of thought it meant brave. It actually meant 'someone who doesn't care about the consequences of their actions.'"

Clary felt stung on behalf of small Jace. "But you do care."

"Not enough, maybe. Not all the time." His voice shook. "Like the way I love you. I loved you recklessly from the moment I knew you. I never cared about the consequences. I told myself I did, I told myself you wanted me to, and so I tried, but I never did. I wanted you more than I wanted to be good. I wanted you more than I wanted anything, ever." His muscles were rigid under her grip, his body thrumming with tension. She leaned in to brush her lips across his, to kiss the tension away, but he pulled back, biting against his lower lip hard enough to whiten the skin.

"Clary," he said, roughly. "Wait, just—wait."

Clary felt momentarily dazed. Jace loved kissing; he could kiss for hours, and he was *good* at it. And he wasn't uninterested. He was *very* interested. She braced her knees on either side of his hips and said, uncertainly, "Is everything all right?"

"I have to tell you something."

"Oh, no." She dropped her head onto his shoulder. "Okay. What is it?"

"Remember when we came through into the demon realm, and everyone saw something?" he asked. "And I said I didn't."

"You don't have to tell me what you saw," Clary said gently. "It's your business."

"I do," he said. "You should know. I saw a room with two thrones in it—gold and ivory thrones—and through the window I could see the world, and it was ashes. Like this world, but the destruction was newer. The fires were still burning, and the sky was full of horrible flying things. Sebastian was sitting on one of the thrones and I was sitting on the other. You were there, and Alec and Izzy, and Max—" He swallowed. "But you were all in a cage. A big cage with a massive lock on the door. And I knew I had put you in it, and turned the key. But I didn't feel regret. I felt—triumph." He exhaled, hard. "You can shove me away in disgust now. It's fine."

But of course it wasn't fine; nothing about his tone—flat and dead, and devoid of hope—was fine. Clary shivered in his arms; not from horror but from pity, and from the tension of knowing how delicate Jace's faith in himself was, and how careful her answer had to be.

"The demon showed us what it thought we wanted," she said finally. "Not what we actually want. It got things wrong; that's how we all managed to break free. By the time we found you, you'd already broken free on your own. So what it showed you, that wasn't what you want. When Valentine raised you, he controlled everything—nothing was ever safe, and nothing you loved was safe. So the demon looked inside you and saw that, that child's fantasy of completely controlling the world so nothing bad can happen to the people he loves, and it tried to give you that, but it wasn't what you want, not really. So you woke up." She touched his cheek. "Some part of you is still that little boy who thinks to love is to destroy, but you're learning. You're learning every day."

For a moment he just looked at her in astonishment, his lips parted slightly; Clary felt her cheeks flush. He was looking at her like she was the first star that had ever come out in the sky, a miracle painted across the face of the world that he could barely believe in. "Let me—" he said, and broke off. "Can I kiss you?"

Instead of nodding, she leaned down to press her lips to his. If their first kiss in the water had been a sort of explosion, this was like a sun going supernova. It was a hard, hot, driving kiss, a nip at her lower lip and the clash of tongues and teeth, both of them pressing as hard as they could to get close, closer. They were glued together, skin and fabric, a heady mix of the chill of the water, the heat of their bodies, and the frictionless slide of damp skin.

His arms wrapped her completely, and suddenly he was lifting her as he walked them both out of the lake, water pouring off them in streams. He went down on his knees on the powdery sand beach, laying her as gently as he could on top of the pile of their heaped clothes. She scrabbled for purchase for a moment and then gave up, lying back and pulling him down on top of her, kissing him fiercely until he groaned and whispered, "Clary, I can't—you have to tell me—I can't *think*—"

She wound her hands into his hair, drawing back just enough to see his face. He was flushed, his eyes black with desire, his hair, beginning to curl as it dried, hanging into his eyes. She tugged lightly at the strands wound between her fingers. "It's okay," she whispered back. "It's okay, we don't have to stop. I want to." She kissed him, slow and hard. "I want to, if you do."

"If I want to?" There was a wild edge to his soft laugh. "Can't you tell?" And then he was kissing her again, sucking her lower lip into his mouth, kissing her throat and mouthing her collarbone as she ran her hands all over him, free in the knowledge that she could touch him, as much as she liked, however she liked. She felt as if she were drawing him, her hands mapping his body, the slope of his back, flat stomach, the indentations above his hips, the muscles in his arms. As if, like a painting, he were coming to life under her hands.

When his hands slid underneath her bra, she gasped at the sensation, then nodded at him when he froze, his eyes questioning. *Go on.* He stopped at each moment, stopped before removing each piece of clothing from either of them, asking her with eyes and words if he should keep going, and each time she nodded and said, *Yes, go on, yes.* And when finally there was nothing between them but skin, she stilled her hands, thinking that there was no way to ever be closer to another person than this, that to take another step would be like cracking open her chest and exposing her heart.

She felt Jace's muscles flex as he reached past her for something, and heard the crackle of foil. Suddenly everything seemed very real; she felt a sudden flash of nerves: This was really happening.

He stilled. His free hand was cradling her head, his elbows dug deep into the sand on either side of her, keeping his weight off her body. All of him was tense and shaking, and the pupils of his eyes were wide, the irises just rims of gold. "Is something wrong?"

Hearing Jace sound uncertain—she thought maybe her heart *was* cracking, shattering into pieces. "No," she whispered, and pulled him down again. They both tasted salt. "Kiss me," she pleaded, and he did, hot languorous slow kisses that sped up as his heartbeat did, as the movement of their bodies quickened against each other. Each kiss was different, each rising higher and higher like a spark as a fire grew: quick soft kisses that told her he loved her, long slow worshipful kisses that said that he trusted her, playful light kisses that said that he still had hope, adoring kisses that said he had faith in her as he did in no one else. Clary abandoned herself to the kisses, the language of them, the wordless speech that passed between the two of them. His hands were shaking, but they were quick and skilled on her body, light touches maddening her until she pushed and pulled at him, urging him on with the mute appeal of fingers and lips and hands.

And even at the final moment, when she did flinch, she pressed him to go on, wrapping herself around him, not letting him go. She kept her eyes wide open as he shuddered apart, his face against her neck, saying her name over and over, and when finally she closed her eyes, she thought she saw the cavern blaze up in gold and white, wrapping them both in heavenly fire, the most beautiful thing she had ever seen.

Simon was vaguely aware of Clary and Jace standing up and leaving the cavern, whispering to each other as they went. *Not as subtle as you think you are,* he thought at them, half-amused, but he hardly grudged them the time together, considering what they were all going to face the next day.

"Simon." It was barely a whisper, but Simon propped himself up on his elbow and looked down at Isabelle. She turned onto her back and gazed up at him. Her eyes were very huge and dark, her cheeks flushed—his chest tightened with anxiety.

"Are you all right?" he said. "Are you feverish?"

She shook her head and wiggled partway out of her cocoon of blankets. "Just warm. Who wrapped me up like a mummy?"

"Alec," Simon said. "I mean, maybe—you should stay in them."

"I'd rather not," Isabelle said, wrapping her arms around his shoulders and pulling him close to her.

"I can't warm you up. No body heat." His voice sounded a little tinny.

She nuzzled her way into the juncture of his collarbone and shoulder. "I think we have established in so many ways that I am hot enough for the both of us."

Unable to help it, Simon reached out to run his hands up her back. She had shed her gear and wore only a black thermal top, the material thick and soft under his fingers. She felt substantial and real, human and breathing, and he silently thanked the God whose name he could now say that she was all right.

"Is there anyone else here?"

"Jace and Clary snuck off, and Alec took first watch," Simon said. "We're alone. I mean, not *alone* alone, like I wouldn't—" He gasped as she rolled over so that she was on top of him, pinning him to the ground. She laid an arm delicately across his chest. "I wouldn't maybe do *that*," he said. "Not that you should stop."

"You saved my life," she said.

"I didn't—" He broke off as she narrowed her eyes. "I am a brave heroic rescuer?" he tried.

"Mmm-hmm." She nudged his chin with hers.

"No Lord Montgomery stuff," he warned. "Anyone could walk in."

"What about regular kissing?"

"Seems all right," he said, and immediately Isabelle was kissing him, her lips almost unbearably soft. His hands found their way up under her shirt and smoothed up her spine, tracing the line of her shoulder blades. When she broke away, her lips were reddened, and he could see the blood pounding in her throat—Isabelle's blood, salty-sweet, and even though he wasn't hungry, he *wanted*—

"You can bite me," she whispered.

"No." Simon wriggled back slightly. "No—you've lost too much blood. I can't." He could feel his chest heaving with unnecessary breath. "You were asleep when we were talking about it, but we can't stay here. Clary put glamour runes on the entrances, but they won't hold that long, and we're running out of food. The atmosphere's making everyone sicker and weaker. And Sebastian will find us. We have to go to him—tomorrow—at the Gard." He raked curled fingers through her soft hair. "And that means you need all your strength."

She pressed her lips together, her eyes darting over him. "When we came through from the Faerie Court, into this world, what did you see?"

He touched her face lightly, not wanting to lie, but the

truth—the truth was hard and awkward. "Iz, we don't have to—"

"I saw Max," she said. "But I saw you, too. You were my boyfriend. We lived together and my whole family accepted you. I can tell myself I don't want you to be part of my life, but my heart knows differently," she said. "You weaseled your way into my life, Simon Lewis, and I don't know how or why or even when but it happened, and I kind of hate it but I can't change it, and here it is."

He made a small choking sound. "Isabelle—"

"Now tell me what you saw," she said, and her eyes glittered like mica.

Simon braced his hands against the stone floor of the cave. "I saw me being famous, a rock star," he said slowly. "I was rich, my family was together, and I was with Clary. She was my girlfriend." He felt Isabelle tense on top of him, felt her start to roll away, and he caught at her arms. "Isabelle, listen. *Listen.* She was my girlfriend, and then when she came to tell me she loved me, I said, 'I love you, too—Isabelle.'"

She stared at him.

"Isabelle," he said. "It snapped me out of the vision, when I said your name. Because I knew the vision was wrong. It wasn't what I really wanted."

"Why do you tell me you love me only when you're drunk or dreaming?" she asked.

"I have awful timing," said Simon. "But it doesn't mean I don't mean it. There are things we want, down under what we know, under even what we feel. There are things our souls want, and mine wants you."

He felt her exhale. "Say it," she said. "Say it sober."

"I love you," he said. "I don't want you to say it back unless you mean it, but I love you."

She leaned back over him, and pressed the pads of her fingertips against his. "I mean it."

He raised himself up on his elbows just as she leaned down, and their lips met. They kissed, long and soft and sweet and gentle, and then Isabelle pulled back slightly, her breathing ragged, and Simon said, "So have we DTRed now?"

Isabelle shrugged. "I have no idea what that means."

Simon hid the fact that he was inordinately pleased by this. "Are we officially boyfriend and girlfriend? Is there a Shadowhunter ritual? Should I change my Facebook status from 'it's complicated' to 'in a relationship'?"

Isabelle screwed up her nose adorably. "You have a book that's also a face?"

Simon laughed, and Isabelle bent down and kissed him again. This time he reached up to draw her down, and they wrapped themselves around each other, tangled in blankets, kissing and whispering. He lost himself in the pleasure of the taste of her mouth, the curve of her hip under his hand, the warm skin of her back. He forgot that they were in a demon realm, that they were going into battle the next day, that they might never see home again: Everything faded away and was Isabelle.

"WHY DOES THIS KEEP HAPPENING?" There was a sound of shattering glass, and they both sat up to see Alec glaring at them. He had dropped the empty bottle of wine he had been carrying, and there were bits of sparkly glass all over the cave floor. "WHY CAN'T YOU GO SOMEWHERE ELSE TO DO THESE HORRIBLE THINGS? MY EYES."

"It's a demon realm, Alec," Isabelle said. "There's nowhere for us to go."

"And you said I should look after her—" Simon began, then realized that would not be a productive line of conversation, and shut up.

Alec flopped down on the opposite side of the fire and glared at them both. "And where have Jace and Clary gone?"

"Ah," said Simon delicately. "Who can say..."

"Straight people," Alec declared. "Why can't they control themselves?"

"It's a mystery," Simon agreed, and lay back down to sleep.

Jia Penhallow sat on the desk in her office. It felt so casual, she couldn't help but wonder if it would be frowned on, the Consul sitting irreverently on the ancient desk of power—but she was alone in the room, and tired beyond all measures of tired.

In her hand she gripped a note that had come from New York: a warlock's fire-message, powerful enough to bypass the wards around the city. She recognized the handwriting as Catarina Loss's, but the words were not Catarina's.

> Consul Penhallow,
> This is Maia Roberts, temporary leader of the New York pack.
> We understand you are doing what you can to bring our Luke
> and the other prisoners back. We appreciate that. As a sign of
> our good faith, I wish to pass on a message to you. Sebastian
> and his forces will attack Alicante tomorrow night. Please do
> what you can to be ready. I wish we could be there, fighting by
> your side, but I know that isn't possible. Sometimes it is only
> possible to warn, and wait, and hope.
> Remember that the Clave and the Council—Shadowhunters
> and Downworlders together—are the light of the world.
>   With hope,
>   Maia Roberts

With hope. Jia folded the letter again and slipped it into her pocket. She thought of the city out there, under the night sky, the pale silver of the demon towers soon to turn to the red of war. She thought of her husband and her daughter. She thought of the boxes and boxes that had arrived from Theresa Gray only a short while ago, rising up through the earth in Angel Square, each box stamped with the spiral symbol of the Labyrinth. She felt a stirring in her heart—some fear, but also some relief, that finally the time was coming, finally the waiting would be over, finally they would have their chance. She knew that the Shadowhunters of Alicante would fight to the last: with determination, with bravery, with stubbornness, with vengeance, with glory.

With hope.

21

THE KEYS OF DEATH
AND HELL

"God, my head," Alec said as he and Jace knelt beside a ridge of
rock that crowned the top of a gray, scree-covered hill. The rock
gave them cover, and past it, using Farsighted runes, they could
see the half-ruined fortress, and all around it, Dark Shadowhunters
clustered like ants.

It was like a warped mirror of Alicante's Gard Hill. The structure atop it resembled the Gard they knew, but with a massive
wall around it, the fortress enclosed within like a garden in a
cloister.

"Maybe you shouldn't have drunk so much last night," Jace
said, leaning forward and narrowing his eyes. All around the wall
the Endarkened stood in concentric rings, a tight group in front of
the gates that led inside. There were smaller groups of them at stra-
tegic points up and down the hill. Alec could see Jace computing
the numbers of the enemy, considering and discarding strategies
in his head.

"Maybe you should try looking a little less smug about what
you did last night," said Alec.

Jace nearly fell off the ridge. "I do not look smug. Well," he amended, "no more than usual."

"Please," Alec said, pulling out his stele. "I can read your face like a very open, very pornographic book. I wish I couldn't."

"Is this your way of telling me to shut my face?" Jace inquired.

"Remember when you mocked me for sneaking around with Magnus and asked me if I'd fallen on my neck?" Alec asked, placing the tip of the stele against his forearm and starting to draw an *iratze*. "This is payback."

Jace snorted and grabbed the stele from Alec. "Give me that," he said, and finished off the *iratze* for him, with his usual messy flourish. Alec felt the numbing kick as his headache started to recede. Jace turned his attention back to the hill.

"You know what's interesting?" he said. "I've seen a few flying demons, but they're staying well away from the Dark Gard—"

Alec raised an eyebrow. "Dark Gard?"

"Got a better name?" Jace shrugged. "Anyway, they're staying away from the Dark Gard and the hill. They serve Sebastian, but they seem to be respecting his space."

"Well, they can't be too far away," said Alec. "They got to the Accords Hall pretty fast when you triggered that alarm."

"They could be *inside* the fortress," said Jace, voicing what they were both thinking.

"I wish you'd managed to get the *skeptron*," Alec said, in a subdued voice. "I got the feeling it could take out a lot of demons. If it still worked, after all these years." Jace had an odd expression on his face. Alec hastened to add, "Not that anyone could have gotten it. You tried—"

"I'm not so sure," Jace said, his expression both calculating and faraway. "Come on. Let's get back to the others."

There was no time to reply; Jace was already retreating. Alec followed him, crawling backward, out of range of sight of the Dark

Gard. Once they had gone enough of a distance, they straightened up and half-slid down the scree slope to where the others were waiting. Simon was standing by Izzy, and Clary had her sketchpad and a pen out and was drawing runes. From the way she was shaking her head, tearing out the pages and crumpling them up in her hand, it wasn't going as well as she might have liked.

"Are you littering?" Jace demanded as he and Alec jogged to a stop beside the other three.

Clary gave him what was probably meant to be a withering look, but which came out fairly soppy. Jace returned it just as soppily. Alec wondered what would happen if he made a sacrifice to the dark demon gods of this world in exchange for not being constantly reminded that he was single. And not just single. He didn't only *miss* Magnus; he was terrified for him, with a deep constant aching terror that never went away completely.

"Jace, this world has been burned to a cinder, and every living creature is dead," Clary said. "I'm fairly sure there's no one left to recycle."

"So what did you see?" Isabelle demanded. She hadn't been at all pleased to be left behind while Alec and Jace did recon, but Alec had insisted that she save her strength. She was listening to him more these days, Alec thought, in that way that Izzy only listened to people whose opinions she respected. It was nice.

"Here." Jace pulled his stele from his pocket and knelt down, shrugging off his gear jacket. The muscles of his back moved under his shirt as he used the pointed tip of the stele to draw in the yellowish dirt. "Here's the Dark Gard. There's one way in, and that's through the gate in the outer wall. It's closed, but an Open rune should take care of that. The question is how to get to the gate. The most defensible positions are here, here, and here"—his stele made quick swipes in the dirt—"so we go around and up the back. If the geography here is like it is in our Alicante, and it looks like it is, there's a natural pathway up the back of the hill. Once we get closer, we split here and here"—the stele made swirls and patterns as he drew, and a patch of sweat darkened between his shoulder blades—"and we try to herd any demons or Endarkened toward the center." He sat back, worrying at his lip. "I can take out a lot of them, but I'll need you to keep them contained while I do it. Do you understand the plan?"

They all stared for a few silent moments. Then Simon pointed. "What's that wobbly thing?" he said. "Is it a tree?"

"Those are the *gates*," Jace said.

"Ohh," said Isabelle, pleased. "So what are the swirly bits? Is there a moat?"

"Those are trajectory lines—Honestly, am I the only person who's ever seen a strategy map?" Jace demanded, throwing his stele down and raking his hand through his blond hair. "Do you understand *anything* I just said?"

"No," Clary said. "Your strategy is probably awesome, but your drawing skills are terrible; all the Endarkened look like trees, and the fortress looks like a frog. There has to be a better way to explain."

Jace sank back on his heels and crossed his arms. "Well, I'd love to hear it."

"I have an idea," Simon said. "Remember how before, I was talking about Dungeons and Dragons?"

"Vividly," Jace said. "It was a dark time."

Simon ignored him. "All the Dark Shadowhunters dress in red gear," he said. "And they're not enormously bright or self-driven. Their wills seem to be subsumed, at least in part, by Sebastian's. Right?"

"Right," Isabelle said, and gave Jace a quelling look.

"In D&D, my first move, when you're dealing with an opposing army like that, would be to lure away a group of them—say five— and take their clothes."

"Is this so they have to go back to the fortress naked and their embarrassment will negatively affect morale?" said Jace. "Because that seems complicated."

"I'm pretty sure he means take their clothes and wear them as disguises," Clary said. "So that we can sneak up to the gates unobserved. If the other Endarkened aren't very perceptive, they might not notice." Jace looked at her in surprise. She shrugged. "It's in every movie, like, ever."

"We don't watch movies," said Alec.

"I think the question is whether *Sebastian* watches movies," said Isabelle. "Is our strategy when we actually see him still 'trust me,' by the way?"

"It's still 'trust me,'" Jace said.

"Oh, good," Isabelle said. "For a second there I was worried there was going to be an actual plan with, like, steps we could follow. You know, something reassuring."

"There is a plan." Jace slid his stele into his belt and rose fluidly to his feet. "Simon's idea for how we get into Sebastian's fortress. We're going to do it."

Simon stared at him. "Seriously?"

Jace retrieved his jacket. "It's a good idea."

"But it's *my* idea," Simon said.

"And it was good, so we're doing it. Congratulations. We're going up the hill the way I outlined, and then we're going to enact your plan when we get toward the top. And when we get there..." He turned to Clary. "That thing you did in the Seelie Court. The way you jumped up and drew the rune on the wall; could you do it again?"

"I don't see why not," Clary said. "Why?"

Jace began to smile.

Emma sat on the bed in her small attic room, surrounded by papers. She had finally liberated them from the folder she had taken from the Consul's office. They were spread out on her blanket, illuminated by the light of the sun coming through the small window, though she could hardly bring herself to touch them.

There were grainy photographs, taken under a bright Los Angeles sky, of the bodies of her parents. She could see now why they hadn't been able to bring the bodies to Idris. They had been stripped, their skin gray like ash except where it was marked all over with ugly black scrawls, not like Marks at all but hideous. The sand around them was wet, as if it had rained; they were far back from the tide line. Emma fought back the urge to throw up as she tried to force herself to absorb the information: when the bodies had been found, when they had been identified, and how they had crumbled away in clumps when the Shadowhunters had tried to lift them—

"Emma." It was Helen, standing in the doorway. The light that spilled in through the window turned the edges of her hair to the color of silver, the way it had always done to Mark's. She looked more like Mark than ever; in fact, stress had made her thinner and revealed more clearly the delicate arches of her cheekbones, the points at the tops of her ears. "Where did you get those?"

Emma raised her chin defiantly. "I took them from the Consul's office."

Helen sat down on the edge of the bed. "Emma, you have to put them back."

Emma jabbed a finger at the papers. "They're not going to look to find out what happened to my parents," she said. "They're saying it's just a random attack by the Endarkened, but it wasn't. I know it wasn't."

"Emma, the Endarkened and their allies didn't just kill the Shadowhunters of the Institute. They wiped out the Los Angeles Conclave. It makes sense they'd go after your parents, too."

"Why wouldn't they Turn them?" Emma demanded. "They needed every warrior they could get. When you say they wiped out the Conclave, they didn't leave *bodies*. They Turned them all."

"Except the young and the very old."

"Well, my parents were neither of those things."

"Would you rather they'd been Turned?" Helen said quietly, and Emma knew she was thinking of her own father.

"No," Emma said. "But are you really saying that it doesn't matter who killed them? That I shouldn't even want to know *why*?"

"Why what?" Tiberius was standing in the door, his mop of unruly black curls tumbling into his eyes. He looked younger than his ten years, an impression helped by the fact that his stuffed bee was dangling from one hand. His delicate face was smudged with tiredness. "Where's Julian?"

"He's down in the kitchen getting food," Helen said. "Are you hungry?"

"Is he angry with me?" Ty asked, looking at Emma.

"No, but you know he gets upset when you yell at him, or hurt yourself," Emma said carefully. It was hard to know what might frighten Ty or send him into a tantrum. In her experience it was better to always tell him the unvarnished truth. The sort of lies people routinely told children, of the "This injection won't hurt a bit" variety, were disastrous when told to Ty.

Yesterday, Julian had spent quite a bit of time picking broken glass out of his brother's bloody feet and had explained to him rather sternly that if he ever walked on broken glass again, Julian would tell on him to the adults and he'd have to take whatever punishment he got. Ty had kicked him in response, leaving a bloody footprint on Jules's shirt.

"Jules wants you to be okay," Emma said now. "That's all he wants."

Helen reached out her arms for Ty—Emma didn't blame her. Ty looked small and huddled, and the way he was clutching his bee made her worried for him. She would have wanted to hug him too. But he didn't like to be touched, not by anyone but Livvy. He flinched away from his half sister and moved over to the window. After a moment Emma joined him there, being careful to give him his space.

"Sebastian can get in and out of the city," said Ty.

"Yes, but he's only one person, and he's not that interested in us. Besides, I believe the Clave has a plan to keep us safe."

"I believe the same thing," Ty muttered, looking down and out the window. He pointed. "I just don't know if it'll work."

It took Emma a moment to realize what he was indicating. The streets were crowded, and not with pedestrians. Nephilim in the uniforms of the Gard, and some in gear, were moving back and forth in the streets, carrying hammers and nails and boxes of objects that made Emma stare—scissors and horseshoes, knives and daggers and assorted weapons, even boxes of what looked like earth. One man carried several burlap sacks marked SALT.

Each box and bag had a symbol stamped on it: a spiral. Emma had seen it before in her *Codex*: the sigil of the Spiral Labyrinth of the warlocks.

"Cold iron," said Ty thoughtfully. "Wrought, not heated and shaped. Salt, and grave dirt."

There was a look on Helen's face, that look adults got when they knew something but didn't want to tell you what it was. Emma looked over at Ty, quiet and composed, his serious gray eyes tracking up and down the streets outside. Beside him stood Helen, who had risen up off the bed, her expression anxious.

"They sent for magical ammunition," said Ty. "From the Spiral Labyrinth. Or maybe it was the warlocks' idea. It's hard to know."

Emma stared through the glass and then back at Ty, who looked up at her through his long lashes. "What does it mean?" she asked.

Ty smiled his rare, unpracticed smile. "It means what Mark said in his note was true," he said.

* * *

Clary didn't think she'd ever been so heavily runed, or had ever seen the Lightwoods covered in as many of the magical sigils as they were now. She had done them all herself, putting everything she had into them—all of her desire for them all to be safe, all her yearning to find her mother and Luke.

Jace's arms looked like a map: runes spread down onto his collarbones and chest, the backs of his hands. Clary's own skin looked foreign to her when she caught sight of it. She remembered once having seen a boy who had the elaborate musculature of the human body tattooed onto his skin, and thinking it was as if he had been turned to glass. It was a bit like that now, she thought, looking around at her companions as they toiled up the hill toward the Dark Gard: the road map of their bravery and hopes, their dreams and desires, marked clearly on their bodies. Shadowhunters weren't always the most forthcoming of people, but their skins were honest.

Clary had covered herself with healing runes, but they weren't enough to keep her lungs from aching from the constant dust. She remembered what Jace had said about the two of them suffering more than the others because of their higher concentration of angel blood. She stopped to cough now and turned away, spitting up black. She wiped her hand across her mouth quickly, before Jace could turn and see.

Jace's drawing skills might have been poor, but his strategy was faultless. They were making their way upward in a sort of zigzag formation, darting from one heap of blackened stone to another. With the foliage all gone, the stone was the only cover the hill provided. The hill was mostly stripped of trees, only a few dead stumps here and there. They had met only a single Endarkened, quickly dispatched, blood soaking into the ashy earth. Clary remembered the path up to the Gard in Alicante, green and lovely, and looked with hatred at the wasteland around her.

The air was heavy and hot, as if the burned-orange sun were pressing down on them. Clary joined the others behind a high cairn. They had refilled their bottles that morning from the lake in the cave, and Alec was sharing around some water, his grim face streaked with black dust. "This is the last of it," he said, and handed it to Isabelle. She took a tiny sip and passed it to Simon, who shook his head—he didn't need water—and passed it on to Clary.

Jace looked at Clary. She could see herself reflected in his eyes, looking small and pale and dirty. She wondered if she looked different to him after last night. She had almost expected him to look different to her, when she woke up in the morning by the cold remains of the fire, with his hand in hers. But he was the same Jace, the Jace she had always loved. And he looked at her as he always had, as if she were a small miracle, the kind you kept close to your heart.

Clary took a mouthful of water and passed the thermos to Jace, who tipped his head back and swallowed. She watched the muscles move in his throat with a brief fascination and then looked away before she could blush—okay, maybe some things *had* changed, but this really wasn't the time to be thinking about it.

"That's it," Jace said, and dropped the now empty thermos. They all watched it roll among the rocks. *No more water.* "One less thing to carry," he added, trying to sound light, but his voice came out sounding as dry as the dust around them.

His lips were cracked and bleeding slightly despite his *iratze*s. Alec had shadows under his eyes, and a nervous twitch in his left hand. Isabelle's eyes were red with dust, and she blinked and rubbed at them when she thought no one was watching. They all looked pretty terrible, Clary thought, with the possible exception of Simon, who mostly looked the same. He was standing close to the cairn, his fingers resting lightly on a ledge of stone. "These are graves," he said suddenly.

Jace looked up. "What?"

"These rock piles. They're graves. Old ones. People fell in battle and they buried them by covering their bodies with stones."

"Shadowhunters," Alec said. "Who else would die defending Gard Hill?"

Jace touched the stones with a leather-gloved hand, and frowned. "We burn our dead."

"Maybe not in this world," Isabelle said. "Things are different. Maybe they didn't have time. Maybe it was their last stand—"

"Stop," Simon said. He had frozen, a look of intense concentration on his face. "Someone's coming. Someone human."

"How do you know they're human?" Clary dropped her voice.

"Blood," he said succinctly. "Demon blood smells different. These are people—Nephilim, but not."

Jace made a quick, quieting gesture with his hand, and they all fell silent. He pressed his back to the cairn and peered around the side. Clary saw his jaw tighten. "Endarkened," he said in a low voice. "Five of them."

"Perfect number," said Alec with a surprisingly wolfish grin. His bow was in his hands almost before Clary could see the movement, and he stepped sideways, out of the shelter of the rocks, and let his arrow fly.

She saw Jace's surprised expression—he hadn't been expecting Alec to move first—and then he caught hold of one of the rocks of the cairn and flung himself up and over. Isabelle sprang after him like a cat, and Simon followed, fast and unerring, his hands bare. It was as if this world had been made for those who were already dead, Clary thought, and then she heard a long gurgling cry, cut abruptly short.

She reached for Heosphoros, thought better of it, and seized a dagger from her weapons belt before hurling herself around the side of the cairn. There was an incline behind it, the Dark Gard looming black and ruined above them. Four Shadowhunters dressed in red were looking around in shock and surprise. One of their company, a blond woman, was sprawled on the ground, her body pointing uphill, an arrow protruding from her throat.

That explains the gurgling noise, Clary thought a little dizzily as Alec notched his bow again and sent another arrow flying. A second man, dark-haired and paunchy, staggered back with a yell, the arrow in his leg; Isabelle was on him in an instant, her whip slicing across his throat. As the man went down, Jace leaped and rode his body to the ground, using the force of the fall to hurl his own body forward. His blades flashed with a scissoring motion, slicing the head off a bald man whose red gear was splotched with patches of dried blood. More blood fountained, drenching the scarlet gear with another layer of red as the headless corpse slid to the ground. There was a shriek, and the woman who had been standing behind him lifted a curved blade to slice at Jace; Clary whipped her dagger forward and let it fly. It buried itself in the woman's forehead and she folded silently to the ground without another cry.

The last of the Endarkened began to run, stumbling uphill. Simon flashed past Clary, a movement too swift to see, and sprang like a cat. The Endarkened man went down with a gasp of terror, and Clary saw Simon rear up over him and strike like a snake. There was a sound like tearing paper.

They all looked away. After a few long moments Simon rose from the still body and came down the hill toward them. There was blood on his shirt, and blood on his hands and face. He turned his face to the side, coughed, and spat, looking sick.

"Bitter," he said. "The blood. It tastes like Sebastian's."

Isabelle looked ill, in a way she hadn't when she'd been cutting the Dark Shadowhunter's throat. "I hate him," she said suddenly. "Sebastian. What he's done to them, it's worse than murder. They're not even people anymore. When they die, they can't be buried in the Silent City. And no one will mourn for them. They've already been mourned for. If I loved someone and they were Turned like this—I'd be happy if they were dead."

She was breathing hard; no one said anything. Finally Jace looked up at the sky, gold eyes gleaming in his dirt-smudged face. "We'd better get moving—the sun's going down, and besides, someone might have heard us." They stripped the gear from the bodies, silently and quickly. There was something sickening about the work, something that hadn't seemed quite so horrible when Simon had described the strategy but that now seemed very horrible. Clary had killed—demons and Forsaken; she would have killed Sebastian, if she had been able to do it without harming Jace. But there was something grim and butcher-like about stripping the clothes from the dead bodies of Shadowhunters, even those Marked with the runes of death and Hell. She couldn't stop herself from looking at the face of one of the dead Shadowhunters, a man with brown hair, and wondering if he could be Julian's father.

She put on the gear jacket and trousers of the smaller of the women, but they were still too big. Some quick work with her knife shortened the sleeves and hems, and her weapons belt held the pants up. There wasn't much Alec could do: He'd wound up with the largest of the Shadowhunters' jackets, and it bulked on him. Simon's sleeves were too short and tight; he cut the seams at the shoulders to allow himself more movement. Jace and Isabelle both managed to wind up with clothes that fit them, though Isabelle's were spotted with drying blood. Jace managed to look handsome in the dark red, which was nothing short of annoying.

They hid the bodies behind the rock cairn and started their way back up the hill. Jace had been right, the sun *was* going down, bathing the realm in the colors of fire and blood. They fell into step with one another as they drew closer and closer to the great silhouette of the Dark Gard.

The upward slope suddenly leveled out, and they were there,

on a plateau in front of the fortress. It was like looking at one photo negative overlapping another. Clary could see in her mind's eye the Gard as it was in her world, the hill covered in trees and greenery, the gardens surrounding the keep, the glow of witchlight illuminating the whole place. The sun shining down on it during the day, and the stars at night.

Here the top of the hill was barren and swept with wind cold enough to cut through the material of Clary's stolen jacket. The horizon was a red line like a slit throat. Everything was bathed in that bloody light, from the crowd of Endarkened who milled around the plateau, to the Dark Gard itself. Now that they were close, they could see the wall that surrounded it, and the sturdy gates.

"You'd better pull your hood up," Jace said from behind her, taking hold of the item in question and drawing it up and over her head. "Your hair's recognizable."

"To the Endarkened?" said Simon, who looked incredibly strange to Clary in his red gear. She had *never* imagined Simon in gear.

"To Sebastian," said Jace shortly, and drew his own hood up. They had taken their weapons out: Isabelle's whip gleamed in the red light, and Alec's bow was in his hands. Jace was looking toward the Dark Gard. Clary almost expected him to say something, to make a speech, to mark the occasion. He didn't. She could see the sharp angle of his cheekbones under the hood of the gear, the tight set of his jaw. He was ready. They all were.

"We go to the gates," he said, and moved forward.

Clary felt cold all over—battle-coldness, keeping her spine straight, her breath even. The dirt here was different, she noticed almost distantly. Unlike the rest of the sand of the desert world, it had been churned by the passage of feet. A red-clad warrior passed her then, a brown-skinned man, tall and muscular. He paid no attention to them. He appeared to be walking a beat, as were several of the rest of the Endarkened, a sort of assigned path back and forth. A white woman with graying hair was a few feet behind him. Clary felt her muscles tighten—*Amatis?*—but as she passed closer, it was clear that her face was not familiar. Clary thought she felt the woman's eyes on them, just the same, and was relieved when they passed out of her sight.

The Gard was looming up in front of them now, the gates massive and made of iron. They were carved with a pattern of a hand holding a weapon—an orb-tipped *skeptron*. It was clear the gates had been subjected to years of desecration. Their surfaces were chipped and scarred, splashed here and there with ichor and what looked disturbingly like dried human blood.

Clary stepped up to place her stele against the gates, ready with an Open rune already in her head—but the gates swung wide at her touch. She cast a surprised look back at the others. Jace was chewing his lip; she raised a questioning eyebrow at him, but he only shrugged, as if to say: *We go forward. What else can we do?*

They went. Past the gates was a bridge over a narrow ravine. Darkness roiled at the bottom of the chasm, thicker than fog or smoke. Isabelle crossed first, with her whip, and Alec took up the rear, facing behind them with his bow and arrow. As they went over the bridge in single file, Clary chanced a glance downward into the crevasse, and nearly flinched back—the darkness had limbs, long and hooked like spider's legs, and what looked like gleaming yellow eyes.

"*Don't* look," Jace said in a low voice, and Clary snapped her eyes back to Isabelle's whip, gold and gleaming ahead of them. It lit the darkness so that when they arrived at the front doors of the keep, Jace was able to find the latch easily, and to swing the door open.

It opened on darkness. They all looked at one another, a brief paralysis none of them could break. Clary found she was staring at the others, trying to memorize them; Simon's brown eyes, the curve of Jace's collarbone under the red jacket, the arch of Alec's eyebrow, Isabelle's worried frown.

Stop, she told herself. *This isn't the end. You'll see them again.*

She glanced behind her. Past the bridge were the gates, wide open, and past that were the Endarkened, standing motionless. Clary had the sense they were watching too, everything caught in stillness in this one breathless moment before the fall.

Now. She stepped forward, into the darkness; she heard Jace say her name, very low, almost a whisper, and then she was over the threshold, and light was all around her, blinding in its suddenness. She heard the murmur of the others as they took their places at her side, and then the cold rush of air as the door slammed shut behind them.

She raised her eyes. They were standing in an enormous entry-way, the size of the inside of the Accords Hall. A massive double spiral stone staircase led upward, twisting and winding, two sets of stairs that interwove with each other but never met. Each was lined on either side by a stone balustrade, and Sebastian was leaning against one of the near balustrades, smiling down at them.

It was a positively feral smile: delighted and anticipatory. He wore spotless scarlet gear, and his hair shone like iron. He shook his head. "Clary, Clary," he said. "I really thought you were much smarter than this."

Clary cleared her throat. It felt clotted from dust, and from fear. Her skin was buzzing as if she'd swallowed adrenaline. "Smarter than what?" she said, and nearly winced at the echo of her own voice, bouncing off the bare stone walls. There were no tapestries, no paintings, nothing to soften the harshness.

Though she didn't know what else she would have expected from a demon world. Of course there was no art.

"We are here," she said. "Inside your fortress. There are five of us, and one of you."

"Oh, right," he said. "Am I supposed to look surprised?" He twisted his face up into a mocking grimace of false astonishment that made Clary's gut twist. "Who could *believe* it?" he said mockingly. "I mean, never mind that obviously I found out from the Queen that you'd come here, but since you've arrived, you've set an enormous fire, tried to steal a demon-protected artifact—I mean you've done everything other than put up an enormous flashing arrow pointing directly to your location." He sighed. "I've always known most of you were terribly stupid. Even Jace, well, you're pretty but not too bright, are you? Maybe if Valentine had had a few more years with you—but no, probably not even then. The Herondales have always been a family more prized for their jawlines than their intelligence. As for the Lightwoods, the less said the better. Generations of idiots. But Clary—"

"You forgot me," Simon said.

Sebastian dragged his gaze over to Simon, as if he were distasteful. "You do keep turning up like a bad penny," he said. "Tedious little vampire. I killed the one who made you, did you know that? I thought vampires were supposed to feel that sort of thing, but you seem indifferent. Terribly callous."

Clary felt Simon stiffen minutely beside her, remembered him in the cave, doubling over as if he were in pain. Saying he felt as if someone had stuck a knife in his chest.

"Raphael," Simon whispered; beside him Alec had paled markedly.

"What about the others?" he demanded in a rough voice. "Magnus—Luke—"

"Our mother," Clary said. "Surely even you wouldn't hurt her."

Sebastian's smirk turned brittle. "She's not *my* mother," he said, and then shrugged with a sort of exaggerated exasperation. "She's alive," he said. "As for the warlock and the werewolf, I couldn't say. I haven't checked on them in a while. The warlock wasn't looking so well the last time I saw him," he added. "I don't think this dimension's been good for him. He might be dead by now. But you really can't expect me to have foreseen *that*."

Alec lifted his bow in a single swift motion. "Foresee this," he said, and let an arrow fly.

It shot straight toward Sebastian—who moved like lightning, plucking the arrow out of the air, fingers closing around it as it vibrated in his grasp. Clary heard Isabelle's sudden intake of breath, felt the rush of blood and dread in her own veins.

Sebastian pointed the sharp end of the arrow toward Alec as if he were a teacher wielding a ruler, and made a clucking noise of disapproval. "Naughty," he said. "Try to harm me here in my own stronghold, will you, at the heart of my power? As I said, you're a fool. You all are fools." He made a sudden gesture, a twist of the wrist, and the arrow snapped, the sound like a gunshot.

The double doors at both ends of the entryway flew open, and demons poured in.

Clary had expected it, had braced herself, but there was no real bracing oneself for something like this. She had seen demons, quantities of them, and yet as the flood poured in from both sides—spider-creatures with fat, poisonous bodies; skinless humanoid monsters dripping blood; things with talons and teeth and claws, massive praying mantises with jaws that dropped open as if unhinged—her skin felt as if it wanted to crawl away from her body. She forced herself still, her hand on Heosphoros, and looked up at her brother.

He met her gaze with his own dark one, and she remembered the boy in her vision, the one with green eyes like hers. She saw a furrow appear between his eyes.

He raised his hand; snapped his fingers. "Stop," he said.

The demons froze, midmotion, on either side of Clary and the others. She could hear Jace's harsh breathing, felt him press his fingers against the hand she was holding behind her back. A silent signal. The others were rigid, surrounding her.

"My sister," Sebastian said. "Don't hurt her. Bring her to me here. Kill the others." He narrowed his eyes at Jace. "If you can."

The demons surged forward. Isabelle's necklace pulsed like a strobe light, sending out blazing tongues of red and gold, and in the fiery light Clary saw the others turn to hold the demons off.

It was her chance. She spun and darted toward the wall, feeling the Agility rune on her arm burn as she launched herself up, caught at the rough stone with her left hand, and swung forward, slamming the tip of her stele into the granite as if it were an axe going into tree bark. She felt the stone shudder: small fissures appeared, but she clung on grimly, dragging her stele across the wall's surface, swift and slashing. She felt the grind and drag of it distantly. Everything seemed to have receded, even the screech and crash of fighting behind her, the stink and howl of demons. She could only feel the power of the familiar runes echoing through her as she drew, and drew, and drew—

Something seized her ankle and yanked. A bolt of pain shot up her leg; she glanced down and saw a ropy tentacle wrapped around her boot, dragging her down. It was attached to a demon that looked like a massive molting parrot with tentacles exploding out from where its wings should have been. She clung on harder to the wall, whipping her stele back and forth, the rock shivering as the black lines ate into the stone.

The pressure on her ankle increased. With a cry Clary let go, her stele falling as she tumbled, hitting the ground hard. She gasped and rolled to the side just as an arrow flew past her head and sank deep into the grasping demon's flesh. She whipped her head up and saw Alec, reaching back for another arrow, just as the runes on the wall behind her blazed up like a map of heavenly fire. Jace was beside Alec, his sword in his hand, his eyes fixed on Clary.

She nodded, minutely. *Do it.*

The demon that had been holding her roared; the tentacle loosed its grasp, and Clary staggered up and to her feet. She hadn't been able to draw a rectangular doorway, so the entrance scrawled on the wall was blazing in a ragged circle, like the opening to a tunnel. Within the blaze she could see the shimmer of the Portal—it rippled like silver water.

Jace hurtled by her and threw himself into it. She caught a brief glimpse of what was beyond—the blasted Accords Hall, the statue of Jonathan Shadowhunter—before she flung herself forward, pressing her hand to the Portal, keeping it open so that Sebastian couldn't close it. Jace needed only a few seconds—

She could hear Sebastian behind her, screaming in a language she didn't know. The stench of demons was all around; she heard a hiss and a rattle and turned to see a Ravener scuttling toward her, its scorpion tail raised. She flinched back, just as it fell apart into two pieces, Isabelle's metal whip scissoring down to slice it in half. Stinking ichor flooded across the floor; Simon grabbed Clary and dragged her back, just as the Portal swelled with a sudden, incredible light and Jace came through it.

Clary sucked in a breath. Never had Jace looked so much like an avenging angel, hurtling through cloud and fire. His bright hair seemed to burn as he landed lightly and raised the weapon he was holding in his hand. It was Jonathan Shadowhunter's *skeptron*. The orb at the center was shining. Through the Portal behind Jace, just before it closed, Clary saw the dark shapes of flying demons, heard their shrieks of disappointment and rage as they arrived to find the weapon gone and the thief nowhere to be seen.

As Jace raised the *skeptron*, the demons around them began to scuttle backward. Sebastian was leaning over the balustrade, his hands clenched on it, dead white. He was staring at Jace. "Jonathan," he said, and his voice rose and carried. "Jonathan, I *forbid*—"

Jace thrust the *skeptron* skyward, and the orb burst into flame. It was a brilliant, contained, icy flame, more light than heat, but a piercing light that shot through the whole room, limning everything in brilliance. Clary saw the demons turned to flaming silhouettes before they shuddered and exploded into ash. The ones closest to Jace crumbled first, but the light ran through all of them like a fissure opening in the earth, and one by one they shrieked and dissolved, leaving a thick layer of gray-black ash on the floor.

The light intensified, burning brighter until Clary closed her eyes, still seeing the burst of last brilliance through the eyelids. When she opened them again, the entryway was almost empty. Only she and her companions remained. The demons were gone—and Sebastian was there, still, standing pale and shocked on the stairway.

"*No,*" he ground out through clenched teeth.

Jace was still standing with the *skeptron* in his hand; the orb had turned black and dead, like a lightbulb that had burned out. He looked up at Sebastian, his chest rising and falling fast. "You thought we didn't know you were expecting us," he said. "But we were *counting* on it." He took a step forward. "*I know you,*" he said, still breathlessly, his hair wild and his golden eyes blazing. "You took me over, took control of me, forced me to do whatever you wanted, *but I learned from you.* You were in my head, and I remember. I remember how you think, how you plan. I remember all of it. I knew you'd underestimate us, think we didn't guess it was a trap, think we wouldn't have planned for that. You forget I know you; down to the last corner of your arrogant little mind I know you—"

"Shut *up,*" Sebastian hissed. He pointed at them with a shaking hand. "You will pay in blood for this," he said, and then he turned and ran up the steps, vanishing so quickly that even Alec's arrow, winging after him, couldn't catch him up. It hit the curve of the staircase instead and snapped on impact with the stone, then fell to the ground in two neat pieces.

"Jace," Clary said. She touched his arm. He seemed frozen in place. "Jace, when he says we'll pay in blood, he doesn't mean our blood. He means theirs. Luke and Magnus and Mom. We *have* to go find them."

"I agree." Alec had lowered his bow; his red gear jacket had been torn from him in the fight, and the bracer on his arm was stained with blood. "Each staircase leads to a different level. We're going to have to split up. Jace, Clary, you take the east staircase; the rest of us will take the other."

No one protested. Clary knew Jace would never have agreed to split off from her, and neither would Alec have left his sister, or Isabelle and Simon have left each other. If they had to separate, this was the only way to do it.

"*Jace,*" Alec said, again, and this time the word seemed to snap Jace out of his fugue state. He tossed the dead *skeptron* aside, let it clatter to the ground, and looked up with a nod.

"Right," he said, and the door behind them burst open. Dark Shadowhunters in red gear began to pour into the room. Jace seized Clary's wrist and they ran, Alec and the others pounding along beside them until they reached the stairway and broke apart. Clary thought she heard Simon say her name as she and Jace lunged for the east staircase. She turned around to look for him, but he was gone. The room was full of the Endarkened, several of them raising weapons—crossbows, even slingshots—to take aim. She ducked her head and continued to run.

Jia Penhallow stood on the balcony of the Gard and looked down over the city of Alicante.

The balcony was rarely used. There had been a time when the Consul had often spoken to the populace from this spot high above them, but the habit had fallen out of favor in the nineteenth century when Consul Fairchild had decided that the action smacked too much of the behavior of a pope or a king.

Twilight had come, and the lights of Alicante had begun to burn: witchlight in the windows of every house and storefront, witchlight illuminating the statue in Angel Square, witchlight pouring from the Basilias. Jia took a deep breath, holding the note from Maia Roberts that spoke of hope in her left hand as she readied herself.

The demon towers flared up blue, and Jia began to speak. Her voice echoed from tower to tower, dispersing itself through the city. She could see people stopped in the street, their heads craned back to look at the demon towers, people arrested on the doorsteps of their houses, listening as her words rolled over them like a tide.

"Nephilim," she said. "Children of the Angel, warriors, tonight we ready ourselves, for tonight Sebastian Morgenstern will bring his forces against us." The wind coming across the hills that surrounded Alicante was icy; Jia shivered. "Sebastian Morgenstern is trying to destroy what we are," she said. "He will bring against us warriors who wear our own faces but are not Nephilim. We cannot hesitate. When we face them, when we look at an Endarkened, we cannot see brother or mother or sister or wife, but a creature in torment. A human from whom all humanity has been stripped. We are what we are because our will is free: We are free to choose. We choose to stand and fight. We choose to defeat Sebastian's forces. They have the darkness; we have the strength of the Angel. Fire tests gold. In this fire we will be tested, and we will shine out. You know the protocol; you know what to do. Go forth, children of the Angel.

"Go forth and light the lights of war."

22

THE ASHES OF OUR FATHERS

The sound of a sudden, wailing siren split the air, and Emma started up in bed, scattering the papers to the floor. Her heart was pounding.

Through the open window of her bedroom, she could see the demon towers, flashing gold and red. The colors of war.

She staggered to her feet, reaching for her gear, which was on a peg by the bed. She had just slid into it and was bending down to tie up her boots when the door to her room burst open. It was Julian. He skidded halfway inside before catching himself. He stared at the papers on the floor, and then at her. "Emma—didn't you hear the announcement?"

"I was napping." She clipped out the words as she attached the harness that held Cortana to her back, then slipped the blade into the scabbard.

"The city's under attack," he said. "We have to get to the Accords Hall. They're going to lock us inside—all the kids—it's the safest place in the city."

"I won't go," Emma said.

Julian stared at her. He was wearing jeans and a gear jacket and sneakers; there was a shortsword stuck through his belt. His soft brown curls were wild and unbrushed. "What do you mean?"

"I don't want to hide in the Accords Hall. I want to fight."

Jules pushed his hands through his tangled hair. "If you fight, I fight," he said. "And that means nobody carries Tavvy to the Accords Hall, and nobody protects Livvy or Ty or Dru."

"What about Helen and Aline?" Emma demanded. "The Penhallows—"

"Helen's waiting for us. All the Penhallows are up at the Gard, Aline included. There's no one home but Helen and us," said Julian, holding out a hand for Emma. "Helen can't protect us all on her own and carry the baby, too; she's only one person." He looked at her, and she could see the fear in his eyes, the fear he was usually so careful to shield from the younger children.

"Emma," he said. "You're the best, the best fighter of all of us. You're not just my friend, and I'm not just their older brother. I'm their *father*, or the closest thing to it, and they need me, and I need you." The hand he was holding out was shaking. His sea-colored eyes were huge in his pale face: He didn't look like anyone's father. "Please, Emma."

Slowly Emma reached out and took his hand, wrapping her fingers around his. She saw him let out a minute breath of relief, and felt her chest tighten. Behind him, through the open door, she could glimpse them: Tavvy and Dru, Livia and Tiberius. Her responsibility. "Let's go," she said.

At the top of the stairs Jace released Clary's hand. She clutched at the balustrade, trying not to cough, though her lungs felt like they wanted to tear their way out of her chest. He looked at her—*What's wrong?*—but then he stiffened. Audible behind them was the sound of racing feet. The Endarkened were on their heels.

"Come on," Jace said, and started to run again.

Clary forced herself after him. Jace seemed to know where he was going, unerringly; she supposed he was using the map of the Gard in Alicante that he had in his head, burrowing in toward the center of the keep.

They turned into a long corridor; halfway down it Jace stopped in front of a set of metal doors. They were slashed with unfamiliar runes. Clary would have expected death runes, something that spoke of Hell and darkness, but these were runes of grieving and sorrow for a world destroyed. Who had etched them here, she wondered, and in what excess of mourning? She had seen runes of grief before. Shadowhunters wore them like badges when someone they loved had died, though they did nothing to ease suffering. But there was a difference between grief for a person and grief for a world.

Jace ducked his head, kissed her hard and fast on the mouth. "Are you ready?"

She nodded, and he swung the door open and stepped inside. She followed.

The room beyond was as large as the Council room in Alicante's Gard, if not larger. The ceiling rose high above them, though instead of rows of seats a wide bare marble floor stretched toward a dais at the end of the room. Behind the dais were two massive, separate windows. Sunset light poured through each of them, though one sunset was the color of gold, and the other was the color of blood.

In the bloody golden light Sebastian knelt in the center of the room. He was etching runes into the floor, a circle of dark connected sigils. Realizing what he was doing, Clary started toward him—and then lurched back with a scream as a massive gray shape loomed up in front of her.

It looked like an enormous maggot, the only gap in its slick gray body its mouth full of jagged teeth. Clary recognized it. She'd seen one before in Alicante, rolling its slippery body over a pile of blood and glass and icing sugar. A Behemoth demon.

She reached for her dagger, but Jace was already leaping, sword in hand. He flew through the air and landed on the back of the demon, stabbing down through its eyeless head. Clary backed away as the Behemoth demon thrashed, spraying stinging ichor, a loud, ululating wail coming from its open throat. Jace clung to its back, ichor spraying up over him as he brought the sword down, and down, and down again until the demon, with a gurgling scream, collapsed to the ground with a thud. Jace rode it down, knees clamped to its sides, until the last moment. He rolled off and hit the ground standing.

For a moment there was silence. Jace looked around the room as if he expected another demon to lunge out at them from the shadows, but there was nothing, only Sebastian, who had risen to his feet in the center of his now completed circle of runes.

He began to clap slowly. "Lovely work," he said. "Really excellent demon-dispatching. I bet Dad would have given you a gold star. Now. Shall we dispense with the pleasantries? You recognize where we are, don't you?"

Jace's eyes moved around the room, and Clary followed his gaze. The light outside the windows had dimmed slightly, and she could see the dais more clearly. On it sat two immense—well, the only word for them was "thrones." They were ivory and gold, with gold steps leading up to them. Each had a curved back embossed with a single key.

"*I am he that liveth, and was dead,*" said Sebastian, "*and behold, I am alive for evermore, and have the keys of hell and of death.*" He made a sweeping gesture toward the two chairs, and Clary realized with a sudden jolt that there was someone kneeling beside the left-most chair—a Dark Shadowhunter in red gear. A woman on her knees, her hands clasped in front of her. "These are the keys, made over in the shapes of thrones and given to me by the demons who rule this world, Lilith and Asmodeus."

His dark eyes moved to Clary, and she felt his gaze like cold fingers walking up her spine. "I don't know why you're showing me this," she said. "What do you expect? Admiration? You won't get it. You can threaten me if you want; you know I don't care. You can't threaten Jace—he has the fire of Heaven in his veins; you can't hurt him."

"Can't I?" he said. "Who knows how much of Heaven's fire he has still in his veins, after that fireworks display he put on the other night? That demon got to you, didn't she, brother? I knew you could never quite bear the knowledge of it, that you had killed your own kind."

"You forced me to murder," Jace said. "It wasn't my hand holding the knife that killed Sister Magdalena; it was yours."

"If you like." Sebastian's smile turned cold. "Regardless, there are others I can threaten. Amatis, rise, and bring Jocelyn here."

Clary felt tiny daggers of ice shoot through her veins; she tried to keep her face from showing any expression as the woman kneeling by the throne rose. It was indeed Amatis, with her disconcerting Luke-blue eyes. She smiled. "With pleasure," she said, and stalked out of the room, the hem of her long red coat sweeping behind her.

Jace stepped forward with an inarticulate growl—and stopped in his tracks, several feet from Sebastian. He put his hands out, but they seemed to collide with something translucent, an invisible wall.

Sebastian snorted. "As if I'd let you get near me—you, with that fire burning in you. Once was enough, thank you."

"So you know I can kill you," Jace said, facing him, and Clary couldn't help but think how alike they were and how different—like ice and fire, Sebastian all white and black, and Jace burning up with red and gold. "You can't hide in there forever. You'll starve."

Sebastian made a quick gesture with his fingers, the way Clary had seen Magnus gesture when casting a spell—and Jace flew up and back, and slammed into the wall behind them. Her breath caught in a gasp as she spun to see him crumple to the ground, a bloody gash across the side of his head.

Sebastian hummed in delight and lowered his hand. "Don't worry," he said conversationally, and turned his gaze back to Clary. "He'll be fine. Eventually. If I don't change my mind about what to do with him. I'm sure you understand, now that you've seen what I can do."

Clary held herself still. She knew how important it was to keep her face blank, not to look at Jace in panic, not to show Sebastian her anger or her fear. Deep down in her heart she knew what he wanted, better than anyone else; she knew what he was *like*, and that was the best weapon she had.

Well, maybe the second-best.

"I've always known you had power," she said, deliberately not looking toward Jace, deliberately not analyzing his motionlessness, the thick trickle of blood that was making its way down the side of his face. This was always going to happen; it was always going to be her facing Sebastian with no one else, not even Jace, by her side.

"*Power*," he echoed, as if it were an insult. "Is that what you call it? Here I have more than power, Clary. Here in this keep I can shape what is real." He had begun to pace inside the circle he had drawn, his hands looped casually behind his back, like a professor delivering a lecture. "This world is connected only by the thinnest threads to the one where we were born. The road through Faerie is one such thread. These windows are another. Step through that one"—he pointed to the window on the right, through which Clary could see dark blue twilight sky, and stars—"and you will return to Idris. But it's not that simple." He regarded the stars through the window. "I came to this world because it was a place to hide. And then I began to realize. I am sure our father quoted these words to you many times"—he spoke to Jace, as if Jace could hear him—"but it is better to rule in Hell than serve in Heaven. And here I rule. I have my Dark

Ones and my demons. I have my keep and citadel. And when the borders of this world are sealed, everything here will be my weapon. Rocks, dead trees, the ground itself will come to my hand and wield its power for me. And the Great Ones, the old demons, will look down on my work, and they will reward me. They will raise me up in glory, and I will rule the abysses between worlds and the spaces between all the stars."

"'*And he shall rule them with a rod of iron,*'" said Clary, remembering Alec's words in the Accords Hall, "'*and I will give him the Morning Star.*'"

Sebastian whirled on her, his eyes bright. "Yes!" he said. "Yes, very good, you're understanding now. I thought I wanted our world, to bring it down in blood, but I want more than that. I want the legacy of the Morgenstern name."

"You want to be the devil?" Clary said, half-baffled and half-terrified. "You want to rule Hell?" She spread her hands out. "Go ahead, then," she said. "None of us will stop you. Let us go home, promise you'll leave our world alone, and you can *have* Hell."

"Alas," said Sebastian. "For I have discovered one other thing that perhaps sets me apart from Lucifer. I do not want to rule alone." He extended his arm, an elegant gesture, and indicated the two great thrones on the dais. "One of those is for me. And the other—the other is for you."

The streets of Alicante turned and twisted back in on themselves like the currents of a sea; if Emma hadn't been following Helen, who was carrying a witchlight in one hand and her crossbow in the other, she would have been hopelessly lost.

The last of the sun was vanishing from the sky, and the streets were dark. Julian was carrying Tavvy, the baby's arms locked around his neck; Emma held Dru by the hand, and the twins clung together in silence.

Dru wasn't fast, and kept stumbling; she fell several times, and Emma had to drag her to her feet. Jules called out to Emma to be careful, and she *was* trying to be careful. She couldn't imagine how Julian did it, holding Tavvy so carefully, murmuring so reassuringly that the little boy didn't even cry. Dru was sobbing silently; Emma brushed the tears off the younger girl's cheeks as she helped her up for the fourth time, murmuring nonsense comforting words the way her mother once had to her when she'd been a child and had fallen.

She had never missed her parents more agonizingly than she did now; it felt like a knife under her ribs.

"Dru," she began, and then the sky lit up red. The demon towers had flamed to the color of pure scarlet, all the gold of warning gone.

"The city walls are broken," Helen said, staring up at the Gard. Emma knew she was thinking about Aline. The red glow of the towers turned her pale hair the color of blood. "Come on—quickly."

Emma wasn't sure they *could* go any more quickly; she got a tighter hold of Drusilla's wrist and yanked the little girl nearly off her feet, muttering apologies as she went. The twins, hand in hand, were faster, even as they raced up a jagged set of stairs toward Angel Square, led by Helen.

They were almost at the top step when Julian gasped out, "Helen, behind us!" and Emma spun around to see a faerie knight in white armor approaching the foot of the stairs. He carried a bow made from a curved branch, and his hair was long and bark-colored.

For a moment his eyes met Helen's. The expression on his face changed, and Emma couldn't help wondering if he recognized the Fair Folk in her blood—and then Helen raised her right arm and shot her crossbow directly at him.

He whirled away. The bolt hit the wall behind him. The faerie smirked, and leaped up the first step, then the second—and screamed. Emma watched in shock as his legs buckled under him; he fell and howled as his skin came into contact with the edge of the step. For the first time Emma noticed that corkscrews, nails, and other hunks of cold-forged iron had been hammered into the step edges. The faerie warrior reeled back, and Helen shot again. The bolt went through his armor and into his chest. He crumpled.

"They've *faerie-proofed*," Emma said, remembering looking out the window at the Penhallows' with Ty and Helen. "All the metal, the iron." She pointed at a nearby building, where a long row of scissors hung from cords connected to the edge of the roof. "That's what the guards were doing—"

Suddenly Dru shrieked. Another figure raced up the street. A second faerie knight, this one a woman with armor of pale green, carrying a shield of overlapping carved leaves.

Emma whipped a knife from her belt and threw it. Instinctively the faerie raised her shield to block the knife—which sailed past her head, and severed the cord holding a pair of scissors to the roof above. The scissors fell, blade-first, and plunged between the faerie woman's shoulders. She fell to the ground with a shriek, her body spasming.

"Good job, Emma," said Helen in a hard voice. "Come on, all of you—"

She broke off with a cry as three Endarkened surged from a side street. They wore the red gear that had appeared so often in Emma's nightmares, dyed even redder by the light from the demon towers.

The children were as silent as ghosts. Helen raised her crossbow and shot a bolt. It struck one of the Endarkened in the shoulder, and he spun away, staggering but not falling. She fumbled to reload the bow; Julian struggled to hold Tavvy while reaching for the blade at his side. Emma put her hand on Cortana—

A spinning circle of light hurtled through the air and buried itself in the throat of the first Endarkened, blood spattering the wall behind him. He clawed at his throat, once, and fell. Two more circles flew, one after the other, and sliced into the chests of the other Dark Nephilim. They crumpled silently, more blood spreading in a pool along the cobblestones.

Emma whirled and looked up. Someone stood at the top of the stairs: a young Shadowhunter with dark hair, a gleaming *chakhram* still in his right hand. Several others were hooked to his weapons belt. In the red light of the demon towers he seemed to glow—a tall, thin figure in dark gear against the darker black of night, the Accords Hall rising like a pale moon behind him.

"*Brother Zachariah?*" said Helen in amazement.

"What's going on?" Magnus asked hoarsely. He was no longer able to sit up, and was lying, half-propped on his elbows, on the floor of the cell. Luke was standing with his face pressed to the arrow-slit window. His shoulders were tense, and he'd barely moved since the first screams and shouting had begun.

"Light," Luke said, finally. "There's some kind of light pouring out of the keep—it's burning the mist away. I can see the plateau down below, and some of the Endarkened running around. I just don't know what's caused it."

Magnus laughed under his breath, and tasted metal in his mouth. "Come on," he said. "Who do you think?"

Luke looked at him. "The Clave?"

"The *Clave?*" Magnus said. "I hate to break it to you, but they don't care enough about us to come here." He tipped his head back. He felt worse than he could remember ever feeling—well, maybe not ever. There had been that incident with the rats and the quicksand around the turn of the century. "Your daughter, though," he said. "She does."

Luke looked horrified. "Clary. No. She shouldn't be here."

"Isn't she always where she isn't supposed to be?" Magnus said in a reasonable voice. At least, he thought he sounded reasonable. It was hard to tell when he felt so dizzy. "And the rest of them. Her constant companions. My..."

The door burst open. Magnus tried to sit up, couldn't, and fell back onto his elbows. He felt a dull sense of annoyance. If Sebastian had come to kill them, he'd rather die on his feet than his elbows. He heard voices: Luke, exclaiming, and then others, and then a face swam into view, hovering over his, eyes like stars in a pale sky.

Magnus exhaled—for a moment he no longer felt ill, or afraid of dying, or even angry or bitter. Relief washed over him, as profound as sorrow, and he reached up to brush the cheek of the boy leaning over him with the back of his bruised knuckles. Alec's eyes were huge and blue and full of anguish.

"Oh, my Alec," he said. "You've been so sad. I didn't know."

As they forged their way farther into the center of the city, the crowd thickened: more Nephilim, more Endarkened, more faerie warriors—though the faeries moved sluggishly, painfully, many of them weakened by contact with the iron, steel, rowan wood, and salt that had been liberally deployed around the city as protection against them. The might of faerie soldiers was legendary, but Emma saw many of them—who might otherwise have been victorious—fall beneath the flashing swords of the Nephilim, their blood running across the white flagstones of Angel Square.

The Endarkened, however, were not weakened. They seemed unconcerned with the troubles of their faerie companions, hacking and slashing their way through the Nephilim jamming Angel Square. Julian had Tavvy zipped into his jacket; the little boy was screaming now, his cries lost among the shrieks of battle. *"We have to stop!"* Julian shouted. *"We're going to be separated! Helen!"*

Helen was pale and ill-looking. The closer they got to the Hall of Accords, now looming above them, the thicker the clusters of faerie protection spells were; even Helen, with her partial heritage, was beginning to feel it. It was Brother Zachariah—just Zachariah now, Emma reminded herself, just a Shadowhunter like they were—in the end who moved to fashion them all into a line, Blackthorns and Carstairs, everyone hand in hand. Emma hung on to Julian's belt since his other hand was supporting Tavvy. Even Ty was forced to hold hands with Drusilla, though he scowled at her when he did it, bringing fresh tears to her eyes.

They made their way toward the Hall, clinging together, Zachariah in front of them; he was out of throwing blades and had taken out a long-bladed spear. He swept the crowd with it as they went, efficiently and icily hacking a pathway through the Endarkened.

Emma burned to seize Cortana out of its scabbard, to run forward and stab and slash at the enemies who had murdered her parents, who had tortured and Turned Julian's father, who had taken Mark away from them. But that would have meant letting go of Julian and Livvy, and that she would not do. She owed the Blackthorns too much, Jules especially, Jules who had kept her alive, who had brought her Cortana when she had thought she would die of grief.

Finally they stumbled up the front steps of the Hall behind Helen and Zachariah, and reached the massive double doors of the entryway. There was a guard on either side, one holding an enormous wooden bar. Emma recognized one of them as the woman with the koi tattoo who sometimes spoke out in meetings: Diana Wrayburn. "We're about to shut the doors," said the one holding the bar. "You two, you're going to have to leave them here; only children are allowed inside—"

"Helen," said Dru in a trembling little voice. The line broke into pieces then, with the Blackthorn children swarming Helen; Julian standing a little aside, his face blank and ashen, his free hand stroking Tavvy's curls.

"It's all right," Helen was saying in a choked voice. "This is the safest place in Alicante. Look, there's salt and grave dirt all up and down the steps to keep the faeries out."

"And cold iron under the flagstones," said Diana. "The instructions of the Spiral Labyrinth were followed to the letter."

At the mention of the Spiral Labyrinth, Zachariah took in a sharp breath and knelt down, bringing his eyes on a level with Emma's. "Emma Cordelia Carstairs," he said. He looked both very young and very old at the same time. There was blood at his throat where his faded rune stood out, but it wasn't his. He seemed to be searching her face, though for what, she couldn't tell. "Stay with your *parabatai*," he said finally, so quietly that no one else could hear them. "Sometimes it's braver not to fight. Protect them, and save your vengeance for another day."

Emma felt her eyes widen. "But I don't have a *parabatai*—and how did you—"

One of the guards cried out and fell, a red-fletched arrow in his chest. "Get *inside!*" shouted Diana, seizing hold of the children and half-throwing them into the Hall. Emma felt herself caught and tossed inside; she spun to get one last look at Zachariah and Helen, but it was too late. The double doors had slammed shut after her, the massive wooden latch falling into place with a sound of echoing finality.

"No," Clary said, looking from the terrifying throne to Sebastian and back again. *Blank your mind*, she told herself. *Focus on Sebastian, on what's happening here, on what you can do to stop him. Don't think about Jace.* "You must know I won't stay here. Maybe you'd rather rule Hell than serve in Heaven, but I don't want either—I just want to go home and live my life."

"That isn't possible. I've already sealed the pathway that brought you here. No one can return through it. All that's left is this, here"—he gestured at the window—"and in a short time that will be sealed too. There will be no returning home, not for you. You belong here, with me."

"Why?" she whispered. "Why me?"

"Because I love you," Sebastian said. He looked—uncomfortable. Tense and strained, as if he were reaching for something he couldn't quite touch. "I don't want you hurt."

"You don't—You *have* hurt me. You tried to—"

"It doesn't matter if *I* hurt you," he said. "Because you belong to me. I can do what I want with you. But I don't want other people touching you or owning you or hurting you. I want you to be around, to admire me and to see what I've done, what I've accomplished. That's love, isn't it?"

"No," Clary said, in a soft sad voice. "No, it isn't." She took a step toward him, and her boot knocked against the invisible force field of his circle of runes. She could go no farther. "If you love someone, then you want them to love you back."

Sebastian's eyes narrowed. "Don't patronize me. I know what you think love is, Clarissa; I happen to think you're wrong. You will ascend the throne, and you will reign beside me. You have a dark heart in you, and it is a darkness we share. When I am all there is in your world, when I am all that is left, you *will* love me back."

"I don't understand—"

"I can't imagine you would," Sebastian smirked. "You aren't exactly in possession of all the information. Let me guess, you know nothing of what's happened in Alicante since you departed?"

A cold feeling began to spread in Clary's stomach. "We're in another dimension," she said. "There's no way *to* know."

"Not exactly," said Sebastian, and his voice was rich with delight, as if she had fallen into precisely the trap he had wanted. "Look into the window above the eastern throne. Look, and see Alicante now."

Clary looked. When she had come into the room, she had seen only what seemed like the starred night sky through the eastern window, but now, as she concentrated, the surface of the glass shimmered and rippled. She thought of the story of Snow White suddenly, the magic mirror, its surface shimmering and changing to reveal the outside world...

She was looking at the inside of the Accords Hall. It was full of children. Shadowhunter children sat and stood and clung together. There were the Blackthorns, the children huddled tightly in a group, Julian sitting with the baby on his lap, his free arm stretched out as if he could encompass the rest of his siblings, could pull them all in and protect them. Emma sat close by him, her expression stony, her golden sword gleaming behind her shoulder—

The scene resolved into Angel Square. All around the Hall of Accords was a boiling mass of Nephilim, and ranged against them were the Endarkened in their scarlet gear, bristling with weapons— and not just the Endarkened but figures that Clary recognized with a sinking heart as faerie warriors. A tall faerie with hair of mixed blue and green strands was battling Aline Penhallow, who stood in front of her mother, her sword drawn as if ready to fight to the death. Across the square Helen was trying to push her way through the crowd toward Aline, but the crush was too great. The fighting penned her back, but so did the bodies—bodies of Nephilim warriors, fallen and dying, so many more in black gear than red. They were losing the battle, losing it—

Clary whirled on Sebastian as the scene began to fade. *"What's happening?"*

"It's over," he said. "I requested that the Clave turn you over to me; they didn't. Admittedly because you'd run off, but nevertheless, they were no further use to me. My forces have invaded the city. The Nephilim children are hiding in the Accords Hall, but when all the others are dead, the Hall will be taken. Alicante will be mine. All of Idris will be mine. The Shadowhunters have lost the war—not that there was much of one. I really thought they'd put up more of a fight."

"That's hardly all the Shadowhunters that exist," Clary said. "That was just who was in Alicante. There are still Nephilim scattered all over the world—"

"All the Shadowhunters you see there will drink from the Infernal Cup soon enough. Then they will be my servants, and I will send them out to find their brethren in the world, and those who remain will be Turned or killed. I will slay the Iron Sisters and the Silent Brothers in their citadels of stone and silence. Inside of a month the race of Jonathan Shadowhunter will be wiped from the world. And then..." He smiled a terrible smile, and gestured toward the western window, which looked out on the dead and blasted world of Edom. "You've seen what happens to a world without protectors," he gloated. "Your world will die. Death on death, and blood in the streets."

Clary thought of Magnus. *I saw a city all of blood, with towers made of bone, and blood ran in the streets like water.*

"You can't imagine," she said in a dead voice, "that if you do this, if what you're telling me is going to happen does actually happen, that there is *any* chance I would sit on a throne beside you. I'd rather be tortured to death."

"Oh, I don't think it," he said breezily. "That's why I've waited, you see. To give you a choice. All those Fair Folk who are my allies, all the Endarkened you see there, they wait on my orders. If I give the signal, they will stand down. Your world will be safe. You'll never be able to return there, of course—I'll seal the borders between this world and that, and never again will anyone, demon or human, travel between them. But it will be safe."

"A choice," Clary said. "You said you were giving me a choice?"

"Of course," he said. "Rule beside me, and I will spare your world. Refuse, and I will give the order to annihilate it. Choose me, and you can save millions, billions of lives, my sister. You could save a whole world by damning a single soul. Your own. So tell me, what is your decision?"

"Magnus," Alec said desperately, reaching to feel the *adamas* chains, sunk deep into the floor, that connected to the manacles on the warlock's wrists. "Are you all right? Are you hurt?"

Isabelle and Simon were checking Luke for injuries. Isabelle kept glancing back at Alec, her face anxious; Alec deliberately didn't meet her gaze, not wanting her to see the fear in his eyes. He touched the back of his hand to Magnus's face.

Magnus looked sunken and sallow, his lips dry, ashy shadows beneath his eyes.

My Alec, Magnus had said, *you've been so sad. I didn't know.* And then he had sunk back against the floor, as if the effort of speaking exhausted him.

"Hold still," Alec said now, and drew a seraph blade from his belt. He opened his mouth to name it, and felt a sudden touch at his wrist. Magnus had wrapped his slender fingers around Alec's wrist.

"Call it Raphael," Magnus said, and when Alec looked at him in puzzlement, Magnus glanced toward the blade in Alec's hand. His eyes were half-closed, and Alec remembered what Sebastian had said in the entryway, to Simon: *I killed the one who made you.* Magnus's mouth quirked at the corner. "It *is* an angel's name," he said.

Alec nodded. *"Raphael,"* he said softly, and when the blade blazed up, he brought it down hard on the *adamas* chain, which splintered under the touch of the knife. The chains fell away, and Alec, dropping the blade to the floor, reached forward to take Magnus by the shoulders and help him up.

Magnus reached for Alec, but instead of rising to his feet,

he pulled Alec against him, his hand sliding up Alec's back to knot in his hair. Magnus pulled Alec down and against him, and kissed him, hard and awkward and determined, and Alec froze for a moment and then abandoned himself to it, to kissing Magnus, something he'd thought he'd never get to do again. Alec ran his hands up Magnus's shoulders to the sides of his neck and cupped his hands there, holding Magnus in place while he kissed him thoroughly breathless.

Finally Magnus drew back; his eyes were shining. He let his head fall onto Alec's shoulder, arms encircling him, keeping them tightly together. "Alec..." he began softly.

"Yes?" Alec said, desperate to know what Magnus wanted to ask him.

"Are you being chased?"

"I—ah—some of the Endarkened are looking for us," Alec said carefully.

"Pity," Magnus said, closing his eyes again. "It would be nice if you could just lie down with me here. Just ... for a little while."

"Well, you can't," said Isabelle, not unkindly. "We have to get out of here. The Endarkened will be here any second, and we've got what we came for—"

"Jocelyn." Luke drew away from the wall, straightening up. "You're forgetting Jocelyn."

Isabelle opened her mouth, then closed it again. "You're right," she said. Her hand went to her weapons belt, and she unfastened a sword; taking a step across the room, she handed it to Luke, then bent down to pick up Alec's still-burning seraph blade.

Luke took the sword and held it with the careless competence of someone who had handled blades all their life; sometimes it was hard for Alec to remember that Luke had been a Shadowhunter once, but he remembered now.

"Can you stand?" Alec said to Magnus gently, and Magnus

nodded, and let Alec lift him to his feet.

He lasted almost ten seconds before his knees buckled and he collapsed forward, coughing. "Magnus!" Alec exclaimed, and threw himself down by the warlock's side, but Magnus waved him away and struggled up to his knees.

"You should go without me," he said, in a voice made gravelly by hoarseness. "I'll slow you down."

"I don't understand." Alec felt as if a vise were compressing his heart. "What happened? What did he do to you?"

Magnus shook his head; it was Luke who answered. "This dimension is killing Magnus," he said, voice flat. "There's something about it—about his father—that's destroying him."

Alec glanced at Magnus, but Magnus only shook his head again. Alec fought down an irrational burst of anger—*still withholding things, even now*—and took a deep breath. "The rest of you go find Jocelyn," he said. "I'll stay with Magnus. We'll head toward the center of the keep. When you find her, come looking for us there."

Isabelle looked wretched. "Alec—"

"Please, Izzy," said Alec, and he saw Simon put his hand on Isabelle's back, and whisper something into her ear. She nodded, finally, and turned toward the door; Luke and Simon followed her, both pausing to look back at Alec before they went, but it was the image of Izzy that stuck in his mind, carrying her blazing seraph blade in front of her like a star.

"Here," he said to Magnus as gently as he could, and reached down to lift him up. Magnus stumbled to his feet, and Alec managed to get one of the warlock's long arms slung over his shoulder. Magnus was thinner than he had ever been; his shirt clung to his ribs, and the spaces under his cheekbones looked sunken, but there was still a lot of warlock to contend with: a lot of skinny arms and legs and long, bony spine.

"Hold on to me," Alec said, and Magnus gave him the sort of

smile that made Alec feel like someone had taken an apple corer to his heart and tried to dig out the center.

"I always do, Alexander," he said. "I always do."

The baby had fallen asleep in Julian's lap. He was holding Tavvy tightly, carefully, great dark hollows under his eyes. Livvy and Ty were huddled together on one side of him, Dru curled against him on the other.

Emma sat behind him, her back against his, giving him something to lean on to balance the weight of the baby. There were no free pillars to sit against, no bare space of wall; dozens, hundreds of children were prisoned in the Hall.

Emma leaned her head back against Jules's. He smelled the way he always did: soap, sweat, and the tang of ocean, as if he carried it in his veins. It was comforting and not comforting in its familiarity. "I hear something," she whispered. "Do you?"

Julian's eyes flicked immediately to his brothers and sisters. Livvy was half-asleep, her chin propped on her hand. Dru was looking all around the room, her big blue-green eyes taking everything in. Ty was tapping his finger against the marble floor, obsessively counting from one to a hundred and backward again. He had kicked and screamed when Julian had tried to look at a welt on his arm where he had fallen. Jules had let it go, and allowed Ty to go back to his counting and rocking. It soothed him to quietness, which was what mattered.

"What do you hear?" Jules asked, and Emma's head fell back then as the sound rose, a sound like a great wind or the crackle of a massive bonfire. People started to move and cry out, looking up at the glass ceiling of the Hall.

Through it clouds were visible, moving across the face of the moon—and then from the clouds burst a wild assortment of riders: riders of black horses, whose hooves were flame, riders of massive black dogs with orange-burning eyes. More modern forms of transport were mixed in as well—black carriages drawn by skeletal steeds, and motorcycles gleaming with chrome and bone and onyx.

"The Wild Hunt," Jules whispered.

The wind was a living thing, whipping the clouds into peaks and valleys that the horsemen hurtled up and down, their cries audible even over the gale, their hands bristling with weapons: swords and maces and spears and crossbows. The front doors of the Hall began to shake and tremble; the wooden bar that had been placed across them exploded into splinters. The Nephilim stared toward the doors with terrified eyes. Emma heard the voice of one of the guards among the crowd, speaking in a harsh whisper:

"The Wild Hunt are chasing away our warriors outside the Hall," she said. "The Endarkened are clearing away the iron and the grave dirt. They'll break down the doors if the guards don't get rid of them!"

"The Raging Host has come," said Ty, breaking off his counting briefly. "The Gatherers of the Dead."

"But the Council protected the city against faeries," Emma protested. "Why..."

"They're not ordinary faeries," said Ty. "The salt, the grave dirt, the cold iron; it won't work on the Wild Hunt."

Dru whipped round and looked up. "The Wild Hunt?" she said. "Does that mean Mark's here? Has he come to save us?"

"Don't be a fool," Ty said witheringly. "Mark is with the Huntsmen now, and the Wild Hunt *want* there to be battles. They come to gather the dead when it's all over, and the dead serve them."

Dru screwed up her face in confusion. The doors of the Hall were shuddering violently now, the hinges threatening to tear free of the walls. "But if Mark isn't coming to save us, then who will?"

"No one," said Ty, and only the nervous tapping of his fingers on marble showed that the idea bothered him at all. "No one is coming to save us. We're going to die."

* * *

Jocelyn flung herself once more against the door. Her shoulder was already bruised and bloody, her nails torn where she'd gouged at the lock. She had been hearing the sounds of fighting for a quarter of an hour now, the unmistakable sounds of running feet, of demons screaming...

The knob of the door began to turn. She scrambled back, and seized up the brick she'd managed to loosen from the wall. She couldn't kill Sebastian; she knew that much, but if she could hurt him, slow him—

The door swung open, and the brick flew from her hand. The figure in the doorway ducked; the brick hit the wall, and Luke straightened up and looked at her curiously. "I hope when we're married, that's not the way you greet me every day when I come home," he said.

Jocelyn hurled herself at him. He was filthy and bloody and dusty, his shirt torn, a sword in his right hand, but his left arm came around her and held her close. "Luke," she said into his neck, and for a moment she thought she might shake apart from relief and happiness and delirium and fear, the way she'd shaken apart in his arms when she'd found out he'd been bitten. If only she'd known then, had realized then, that the way she loved him was the way you loved someone you wanted to spend your life with, everything would have been different.

But then there would never have been Clary. She pulled back, looking up into his face, his blue eyes steady on hers. "Our daughter?" she asked.

"She's here," he said, and stepped back so that she could see past him to where Isabelle and Simon waited in the corridor. Both looked very uncomfortable, as if seeing two adults embrace was about the worst thing you could glimpse, even in the demon realms. "Come with us—we're going to find her."

***

"It's not certain," Clary said desperately. "The Shadowhunters might not lose. They could rally."

Sebastian smiled. "That's a chance you could take," he said. "But listen. They have come to Alicante now, those who ride the winds between the worlds. They are drawn to places of slaughter. Can you see?"

He gestured toward the window that opened out onto Alicante. Through it Clary could see the Hall of Accords under the moonlight, clouds moving restlessly to and fro in the background—and then the clouds resolved themselves, and became something else. Something she had seen once before, with Jace, lying in the bottom of a boat in Venice. The Wild Hunt, racing across the sky: dark-clothed and ragged warriors, bristling with weapons, howling as their ghostly steeds pounded across the sky.

"The Wild Hunt," she said, numb, and remembered Mark Blackthorn suddenly, the whip marks on his body, his broken eyes.

"The Gatherers of the Dead," said Sebastian. "The carrion crows of magic, they go where great slaughter is. A slaughter only you can prevent."

Clary closed her eyes. She felt as if she were adrift, floating on dark water, seeing the lights of the shore recede and recede in the distance. Soon she would be alone on the ocean, the icy sky above her and eight miles of empty darkness below.

"Go and take the throne," he said. "If you do it, you can save them all."

She looked at him. "How do I know you'll keep your word?"

He shrugged. "I'd be a fool not to. You'd know immediately that I'd lied to you, and then you'd fight me, which I don't want. Besides. To fully come into my power here, I must seal the borders between our world and this one. Once the borders are closed, the Endarkened in your world will be weakened, cut off from me, their source. The Nephilim will be able to defeat them." He smiled, ice-white and blinding. "It will be a miracle. A miracle performed for them by us—by me. Ironic, don't you think? That I should be their saving angel?"

"What about everyone who's here? Jace? My mom? My friends?"

"They can all live. It makes no difference to me," Sebastian said. "They cannot harm me, not now, and doubly not when the borders are sealed."

"And all I have to do is ascend that throne," Clary said.

"And promise to stay beside me for as long as I live. Which, admittedly, will be a long time. When this world is sealed, I will not just be invulnerable; I will live forever. '*And behold, I am alive for evermore, and have the keys of hell and of death.*'"

"You're willing to do this? Give up the whole world of Earth, your Dark Shadowhunters, your revenge?"

"It was beginning to bore me," said Sebastian. "This is more interesting. To be honest, you're beginning to bore me a bit too. Do decide whether you're going to get up on the throne or not, will you? Or do you need persuasion?"

Clary knew Sebastian's methods of persuasion. Knives under the fingernails, a hand to the throat. Part of her wished he would kill her, take this decision away from her. No one could help her. In this she was utterly alone.

"I will not be the only one who lives forever," Sebastian said, and to her surprise his voice was almost gentle. "Ever since you discovered the Shadow World, haven't you secretly wanted to be a hero? To be the most special of a special people? In our own way we each wish to be the hero of our kind."

"Heroes save worlds," Clary said. "They don't *destroy* them."

"And I am offering you that chance," said Sebastian. "When you ascend that throne, you save the world. You save your friends. You have power unlimited. I am giving you a great gift, because I love you. You can embrace your own darkness and yet always tell yourself that you did the right thing. How is that for getting everything you want?"

Clary closed her eyes for one heartbeat, and then another. Only enough time to see faces flash behind her eyelids: Jace, her mother, Luke, Simon, Isabelle, Alec. And so many more: Maia and Raphael and the Blackthorns, little Emma Carstairs, the faeries of the Seelie Court, the faces of the Clave, even the ghostly memory of her father.

She opened her eyes, and walked toward the throne. She heard Sebastian, behind her, draw a sharp breath. So, for all the surety in his voice, he had doubted, hadn't he? He had not been sure of her. Behind the thrones the two windows flickered like video screens: one showing desolation, the other Alicante under attack. She caught glimpses of the inside of the Accords Hall as she reached the steps and walked up them. She moved steadily. She had made her decision; there was no faltering now. The throne was huge; it was like climbing up onto a platform. The gold of it was icy cold to her touch. She reached the last step, turned, and took her seat.

She seemed to be looking down for miles from the top of a mountain peak. She saw the Council Hall spread out before her; Jace, lying motionless by the wall. Sebastian, looking up at her with a smile spreading over his face.

"Well done," he said. "My sister, my queen."

23

JUDAS KISS

The doors of the Hall exploded inward with a blast of splinters; shards of marble and wood flew like shattered bone.

Emma stared numbly as red-clad warriors began to spill into the Hall, followed by faeries in green and white and silver. And after them came the Nephilim: Shadowhunters in black gear, desperate to protect their children.

A wave of guards raced to meet the Endarkened at the door, and were cut down. Emma watched them fall in what felt like slow motion. She knew she had risen to her feet, and so had Julian, thrusting Tavvy into Livia's arms; they both moved to block the younger Blackthorns, as hopeless as Emma knew the gesture was.

This is how it ends, she thought. They had run from Sebastian's warriors in Los Angeles, had fled to the Penhallows', and from the Penhallows to the Hall, and now they were trapped like rats and they would die here and they might as well never have run at all.

She reached for Cortana, thinking of her father, of what he would have said if she gave up. Carstairs didn't give up. They suffered and survived, or they died on their feet. At least if she died, she thought, she'd see her parents again. At least she'd have that.

The Endarkened surged into the room, parting the desperately fighting Shadowhunters like blades parting a field of wheat, driving toward the center of the Hall. They seemed a murderous blur, but Emma's vision sharpened suddenly as one of them moved out of the crowd, directly toward the Blackthorns.

It was Julian's father.

His time as a servant of Sebastian's had not been good to him. His skin looked dull and gray, his face welted with bloody cuts, but he was striding forward purposefully, his eyes on his children.

Emma froze. Julian, beside her, had caught sight of his father; he seemed mesmerized, as if by a snake. He had seen his father forced to drink from the Infernal Cup, Emma realized, but he hadn't seen him after, hadn't seen him raise a blade to his own son, or laugh about the idea of his son's death, or force Katerina to her knees to be tortured and Turned...

"Jules," she said. "Jules, that *isn't your father*—"

His eyes widened. "Emma, look out—"

She whirled, and screamed. A faerie warrior was looming above her, decked in silver armor; his hair was not hair at all, but a ropy tangle of thorned branches. Half his face was burned and bubbling where he must have been sprayed with iron powder or rock salt. One of his eyes was rolling, white and blinded, but the other fixed on Emma with murderous intent. Emma saw Diana Wrayburn, her dark hair whirling as she spun toward them, her mouth open to cry a warning. Diana moved toward Emma and the faerie, but there was no way she was going to make it in time. The faerie raised his bronze sword with a savage snarl—

Emma lunged forward, sinking Cortana into his chest.

His blood was like green water. It sprayed out over her hand as she let go of her sword in shock; he fell like a tree, striking the marble floor of the Hall with a heavy clang. She sprang forward, reaching for the hilt of Cortana, and heard Julian cry out:

"*Ty!*"

She whipped around. Amid the chaos of the Hall, she could see the small space in which the Blackthorns stood. Andrew Blackthorn stopped in front of his children, an odd little smile on his face, and reached out a hand.

And Ty—Ty, of all of them, the least trusting, the least sentimental—was moving forward, his eyes fixed on his father, his own hand outstretched. "Dad?" he said.

"Ty?" Livia reached for her twin, but her hand closed on air. "Ty, don't—"

"Don't listen to her," said Andrew Blackthorn, and if there had been any doubt that he was no longer the man who had been Julian's father, it was gone when Emma heard his voice. There was no kindness in it, only ice, and the savage edge of a cruel glee. "Come here, my boy, my Tiberius..."

Ty took another step forward, and Julian pulled the shortsword from his belt and threw it. It sang through the air, straight and true, and Emma remembered, with a bizarre clarity, that last day in the Institute, and Katerina showing them how to throw a blade as direct and graceful as a line of poetry. How to throw a blade so that it never missed its mark.

The blade whipped past Tiberius and sank into Andrew Blackthorn's chest. The man's eyes flew open in shock, his gray hand fumbling for the hilt protruding from his rib cage—and then he fell, crumpling to the ground. His blood smeared across the marble floor as Tiberius gave a cry, whirling to lash out at his brother, pounding his fists against Julian's chest.

"No," Ty panted. "Why did you do that, Jules? I hate you, I *hate* you—"

Julian hardly seemed to feel it. He was staring at the place where his father had fallen; the other Endarkened were already moving forward, trampling the body of their fallen comrade. Diana Wrayburn stood a distance away: She had begun to move toward the children and then stopped, her eyes full of sorrow.

Hands came up and caught at the back of Tiberius's shirt, pulling him away from Julian. It was Livvy, her face set. "Ty." Her arms went around her twin, pinning his fists to his sides. "Tiberius, stop it right now." Ty stopped, and sagged against his sister; slight as she was, she supported his weight. "Ty," she said again, softly. "He had to. Don't you understand? He had to."

Julian stepped back, his face as white as paper, stepped back and back until he hit one of the stone pillars and slid down it, crumpling, his shoulders shaking with silent gasps.

My sister. My queen.

Clary sat rigid on the ivory and gold throne. She felt like a child in an adult's chair: the thing had been built for someone massive, and her feet dangled above the top step. Her hands gripped the arms of the throne, but her fingers didn't come close to reaching the carved handrests—though, since each was shaped like a skull, she had no desire to touch them anyway.

Sebastian was pacing inside his protective circle of runes; every once in a while he would pause to look up at her and smile the sort of uninhibited, gleeful smile she associated with the Sebastian from her vision, the boy with guiltless green eyes. He drew a long, sharp dagger from his belt as she watched, and ran the blade along the inside of his palm. His head fell back, his eyes half-closing as he stretched his hand out; blood ran down his fingers and splattered onto the runes.

Each began to glow with a dawning spark as the blood struck it. Clary pressed herself against the solid back of the throne. The runes were not Gray Book runes; they were alien and strange.

The door to the room opened, and Amatis strode in, followed by two moving lines of Endarkened warriors. Their faces were blank as they silently ranged themselves along the walls of the room, but Amatis looked worried. Her gaze skipped past Jace, motionless on the floor beside the body of the dead demon, to focus on her master. "Lord Sebastian," she said. "Your mother is not in her cell."

Sebastian frowned and tightened his bleeding hand into a fist. All around him the runes were burning fiercely now, with a cold ice-blue flame. "Vexing," he said. "The others must have let her out."

Clary felt a surge of hope mixed with terror; she forced herself to remain silent, but saw Amatis's eyes flick toward her. She didn't seem surprised to see Clary on the throne: on the contrary, her lips curved into a smirk. "Would you like me to set the rest of the army to searching for them?" she said to Sebastian.

"There's no need." He glanced up toward Clary and smiled; there was a sudden explosive shattering sound, and the window behind her, the one that had looked out on Alicante, splintered into a spider-web of mazed lines. "The borders are closing," Sebastian said. "I will bring them to me."

"The walls are closing in," Magnus said.

Alec tried to pull Magnus farther upright; the warlock slumped heavily against him, his head almost on Alec's shoulder. Alec had absolutely no idea where they were going—he had lost track of the twisting corridors what felt like ages ago, but he had no desire to communicate that to Magnus. Magnus seemed to be doing badly enough as it was—his breathing ragged and shallow, his heartbeat rapid. And now this.

"Everything's fine," Alec soothed, his arm sliding around Magnus's waist. "We just have to make it to—"

"Alec," Magnus said again, his voice surprisingly firm. "I am *not hallucinating*. The walls are moving."

Alec stared—and felt a flutter of panic. The corridor was heavy with dusty air; the walls seemed to shimmer and tremble. The floor warped as the walls began to slide toward each other, the corridor narrowing from one end like a trash compactor slamming closed. Magnus slipped and hit one of the buckling walls with a hiss of pain. Panicked, Alec seized his arm and pulled Magnus toward him.

"Sebastian," Magnus gasped as Alec began to drag him down the hall, away from the collapsing stone. "He's doing this."

Alec managed an incredulous look. "How would that even be possible? He doesn't control everything!"

"He could—if he sealed the borders between the dimensions." Magnus took a rattling breath as he pushed himself into a run. "He could control this whole world."

Isabelle shrieked as the ground opened up behind her; she threw herself forward just in time to avoid toppling into the chasm that was splitting the corridor apart. "Isabelle!" Simon shouted, and reached to catch her by the shoulders.

He forgot, sometimes, the strength that his vampire blood flooded through his body. He wrenched Isabelle up with such force that they both toppled backward and Izzy landed on top of him. Under other circumstances, he might have enjoyed it, but not with the stone keep shuddering itself apart around them.

Isabelle sprang to her feet, pulling him up after. They had lost Luke and Jocelyn back in one of the other corridors as a wall had split apart, shedding mortarless rocks like scales. Everything since then had been a mad dash, dodging splintering wood and falling stones, and now chasms opening up in the ground. Simon was fighting despair—he couldn't help but feel that this was the end; the fortress would fall apart around them, and they would die and be buried here.

"Don't," Isabelle said, breathless. Her dark hair was full of dust, her face bloody where flying rock had cut her skin.

"Don't what?" The ground heaved, and Simon half-ducked,

half-fell forward into another corridor. He couldn't rid himself of the thought that somehow the fortress was *herding* them. There seemed a purpose to its dissolution, as if it were directing them somehow...

"Don't give *up*," she gasped, flinging herself against a set of doors as the corridor behind them began to crumble; the doors swung open, and she and Simon tumbled into the next room.

Isabelle sucked in a gasp, quickly cut off as the doors slammed behind them, shutting away the explosive noise of the keep. For a moment Simon simply thanked God that the ground under his feet was steady and the walls weren't moving.

Then he registered where he was, and his relief vanished. They were in an enormous room, semicircular in shape, with a raised platform at the curved end half cast in shadow. The walls were lined with Endarkened warriors in red gear, like a row of scarlet teeth.

The room stank like pitch and fire, sulfur and the unmistakable taint of demon blood. The body of a bloated demon lay sprawled against one wall, and near it was another body. Simon felt his mouth go dry. Jace.

Within a circle of glowing runes etched on the floor stood Sebastian. He grinned as Isabelle gave a cry, ran to Jace, and dropped down by his side. She put her fingers to his throat; Simon saw her shoulders relax.

"He's alive," Sebastian said, sounding bored. "Queen's orders."

Isabelle looked up. Some of the strands of her dark hair were stuck to her face with blood. She looked fierce, and beautiful. "The Seelie Queen? When has she ever cared about Jace?"

Sebastian laughed. He seemed to be in an enormously good mood. "Not the Seelie Queen," he said. "The queen of this realm. You may know her."

With a flourish he gestured toward the platform at the far end of the room, and Simon felt his unbeating heart contract. He had barely glanced at the dais when he had come into the room. He saw now that on it were two thrones, of ivory bone and melted gold, and on the right-hand throne sat Clary.

Her red hair was incredibly vivid against the white and gold, like a banner of fire. Her face was pale and still, expressionless.

Simon took an involuntary step forward—and was immediately blocked by a dozen Endarkened warriors, Amatis at their center. She carried a massive spear and wore an expression of frightening venom. "Stop where you are, vampire," she said. "You will not approach the lady of this realm."

Simon staggered back; he could see Isabelle staring incredulously from Clary, to Sebastian, to him. "Clary!" he called; she didn't flinch or move, but Sebastian's face darkened like a thunderstorm.

"You will not say my sister's *name*," he hissed. "You thought she belonged to you; she belongs to me now, and I will not *share*."

"You're insane," Simon said.

"And you're dead," Sebastian said. "Does any of it matter now?" His eyes raked up and down Simon. "Dear sister," he said, pitching his voice loudly enough for the whole room to hear it. "Are you absolutely sure you want to keep this one intact?"

Before she could answer, the entryway to the room burst open and Magnus and Alec spilled in, followed by Luke and Jocelyn. The doors slammed behind them, and Sebastian clapped his hands together. One hand was bloody, and a drop of blood fell at his feet, and sizzled where it hit the glowing runes, like water sizzling on a hot skillet.

"Now everyone's here," he declared, his voice delighted. "It's a party!"

In Clary's life she had seen many things that were wonderful and beautiful, and many things that were terrible. But none were as terrible as the look on her mother's face as Jocelyn stared at her daughter, seated on the throne beside Sebastian's.

"Mom," Clary breathed, so softly that no one could hear her. They were all staring at her—Magnus and Alec, Luke and her mother, Simon and Isabelle, who had moved to hold Jace in her lap, her dark hair falling down over him like the fringe of a shawl. It was every bit as bad as Clary had imagined it would be. Worse. She had expected shock and horror; she hadn't thought of hurt and betrayal. Her mother staggered back; Luke's arms went around her, to hold her up, but his gaze was on Clary, and he looked as if he were staring at a stranger.

"Welcome, citizens of Edom," said Sebastian, his lips curling up like a bow being drawn. "Welcome to your new world."

And he stepped free of the burning circle that held him. Luke's hand went to his belt; Isabelle began to rise, but it was Alec who moved fastest: one hand to his bow and the other to the quiver at his back, the arrow nocked and flying before Clary could shape the cry for him to stop.

The arrow flew straight toward Sebastian and buried itself in his chest. He staggered back from the force of it, and Clary heard a gasp ripple down the line of Dark Shadowhunters. A moment later Sebastian regained his balance and, with a look of annoyance, pulled the arrow from his chest. It was stained with blood.

"Fool," he said. "You can't hurt me; nothing under Heaven can." He flung the arrow at Alec's feet. "Did you think you were an exception?"

Alec's eyes flicked toward Jace; it was minute, but Sebastian caught the glance, and grinned.

"Ah, yes," he said. "Your hero with the heavenly fire. But it's gone, isn't it? Spent on rage in the desert at a demon of my sending." He snapped his fingers, and a spark of ice blue shot from them, rising like a mist. For a moment Clary's view of Jace and Isabelle was obscured; a moment later she heard a cough and gasp, and Isabelle's arms were sliding away from Jace as he sat up, then rose to his feet. Behind Clary the window was still splintering, slowly; she could hear the grind of the glass. Through the now-crazed glass spilled a lacelike quilting of light and shadow.

"Welcome back, brother," said Sebastian equably, as Jace stared around him with a face that was rapidly draining of color as he took in the room full of warriors, his friends standing horrified around him, and lastly: Clary, on her throne. "*Would* you like to try to kill me? You have plenty of weapons there. If you feel like you'd like to try slaying me with the heavenly fire, now is your chance." He opened his arms wide. "I won't fight back."

Jace stood facing Sebastian. They were the same height, almost the same build, though Sebastian was thinner, more wiry. Jace was filthy and bloodstained, his gear torn, his hair tangled. Sebastian was elegant in red; even his bloody hand seemed intentional. Sebastian's wrists were bare; around Jace's left wrist, a silver circlet gleamed.

"You're wearing my bracelet," Sebastian observed. "'*If I cannot reach Heaven, I will raise Hell.*' Apt, don't you think?"

"Jace," Isabelle hissed. "Jace, do it. Stab him. Go on—"

But Jace was shaking his head. His hand had been at his weapons belt; slowly he lowered it to his side. Isabelle gave a cry of despair; the look on Alec's face was just as bleak, though he stayed silent.

Sebastian lowered his arms to his sides and held out his hand. "I believe that it's time you returned my bracelet, brother. Time you rendered unto Caesar what is Caesar's. Give me back my possessions, including my sister. Do you renounce her to my keeping?"

"No!" It wasn't Jace; it was Jocelyn. She pulled away from Luke and launched herself forward, hands reaching out for Sebastian. "You hate me—so kill me. Torture me. Do what you want to me, but leave Clary alone!"

Sebastian rolled his eyes. "I *am* torturing you."

"She's just a girl," Jocelyn panted. "My child, my daughter—"

Sebastian's hand shot out and gripped Jocelyn's jaw, half-lifting her off the floor. "*I* was your child," he said. "Lilith gave me a realm; you gave me your curse. You are no kind of mother, and you will stay away from my sister. You are alive on her sufferance. You all are. Do you understand?" He let go of Jocelyn; she staggered back, the bloody print of his hand marked on her face. Luke caught her. "You all are alive because Clarissa wants you alive. There is no other reason."

"You told her you wouldn't kill us if she ascended that throne," Jace said, unclasping the silver bracelet from around his wrist. His voice was without inflection. He hadn't met Clary's eyes. "Didn't you?"

"Not exactly," said Sebastian. "I offered her something much more ... substantial than that."

"The world," Magnus said. He appeared to be upright through sheer force of will. His voice sounded like gravel tearing his throat. "You're sealing the borders between our world and this one, aren't you? That's what this rune circle is for, not just protection. So you could work your spell. That's what you've been doing. If you close the gateway, you are no longer splitting your powers between two worlds. All your force will be concentrated here. With all your power concentrated in this dimension, you will be well-nigh invincible here."

"If he seals the borders, how will he get back to our world?" Isabelle demanded. She had risen to her feet; her whip gleamed on her wrist, but she made no move to use it.

"He won't," said Magnus. "None of us will. The gates between the worlds will close forever, and we will be trapped here."

"Trapped," Sebastian mused. "Such an ugly word. You'll be ... guests." He grinned. "Trapped guests."

"That's what you offered her," Magnus said, raising his eyes to Clary. "You told her if she would agree to rule beside you here, you would close the borders and leave our world in peace. Rule in Edom, save the world. Right?"

"You're very perceptive," Sebastian said after a brief pause. "It's annoying."

"Clary, *no!*" Jocelyn cried; Luke tugged her back, but she was paying attention to nothing but her daughter. "Don't do this—"

"I have to," Clary said, speaking for the first time. Her voice caught and carried, incredibly loud in the stone room. Suddenly everyone was looking at her. Everyone but Jace. He was staring down at the bracelet held between his fingers.

She straightened. "I have to. Don't you understand? If I don't, he'll kill everyone in our world. Destroy everything. Millions, billions of people. He'll turn our world to *this.*" She gestured toward the window that looked out onto the burned plains of Edom. "It's worth it. It has to be. I'll learn to love him. He won't hurt me. I believe it."

"You think you can change him, temper him, make him better, because you're the only thing he cares about," Jocelyn said. "I *know* Morgenstern men. It doesn't work. You'll regret—"

"You never held the life of a whole world in your hand, Mom," said Clary, with infinite tenderness and infinite sorrow. "There's only so much advice you can give me." She looked at Sebastian. "I choose what he chooses. The gift he gave me. I accept it."

She saw Jace swallow. He dropped the bracelet into Sebastian's open palm. "Clary is yours," he said, and stepped back.

Sebastian snapped his fingers. "You heard her," he said. "All of you. Kneel to your queen."

No! Clary thought, but she forced herself into stillness, silence. She watched as the Endarkened began to kneel, one by one, their heads bowed; the last to kneel was Amatis, and she did not bow her head. Luke was staring at his sister, his face flayed open. It was the first time he had seen her like this, Clary realized, though he had been told of it.

Amatis turned and looked over her shoulder at the

Shadowhunters. Her gaze caught on her brother's for just a moment; her lip curled. It was a vicious look. "Do it," she said. "Kneel, or I will kill you."

Magnus knelt first. Clary would never have guessed that. Magnus was so proud, but then it was a pride that transcended the emptiness of gestures. She doubted it would shame him to kneel when it meant nothing to him. He went down on his knees, gracefully, and Alec followed him down; then Isabelle, then Simon, then Luke, drawing Clary's mother down beside him. And lastly Jace, his blond head bowed, went to his knees, and Clary heard the window behind her shatter into pieces. It sounded like her breaking heart.

Glass rained down; behind it was bare stone. There was no longer any window that led to Alicante.

"It is done. The paths between the worlds are closed." Sebastian wasn't smiling, but he looked—incandescent. As if he were blazing. The circle of runes on the floor was shimmering with blue fire. He ran toward the platform, took the steps two at a time, and reached up to catch Clary's hands; she let him draw her down from the throne, until she stood in front of him. He was still holding her. His hands felt like bracelets of fire around her wrists. "You accept it," he said. "You accept your choice?"

"I accept it," she said, forcing herself to look at him with absolute directness. "I do."

"Then kiss me," he said. "Kiss me like you love me."

Her stomach tightened. She had been expecting this, but it was like expecting a blow to the face: Nothing could prepare you. Her face searched his; in some other world, some other time, some other brother was smiling across the grass at her, eyes as green as springtime. She tried to smile. "In front of everyone? I don't think—"

"We have to show them," he said, and his face was as immovable as an angel pronouncing a sentencing. "That we are unified. Prove yourself, Clarissa."

She leaned toward him; he shivered. "Please," she said. "Put your arms around me."

She caught a flash of something in his eyes—vulnerability, surprise at being asked—before his arms came up around her. He drew her close; she laid one hand on his shoulder. Her other hand slid to her waist, where Heosphoros rested with its scabbard tucked into the belt of her gear. Her fingers curled around the back of his neck. His eyes were wide; she could see his heartbeat, pulsing in his throat.

"Now, Clary," he said, and she leaned up, touching her lips to his face. She felt him shudder against her as she whispered, her lips moving against his cheek.

"Hail, master," she said, and saw his eyes widen, just as she pulled Heosphoros free and brought it up in a bright arc, the blade slamming through his rib cage, the tip positioned to pierce his heart.

Sebastian gasped, and spasmed in her arms; he staggered back, the hilt of the blade protruding from his chest. His eyes were wide, and for a moment she saw the shock of betrayal in them, shock and *pain*, and it actually hurt; it hurt somewhere down deep in a place she thought she had buried long ago, a place that mourned the brother he might have been.

"Clary," he gasped, starting to straighten, and now the look of betrayal in his eyes was fading, and she saw the beginning spark of rage. It hadn't worked, she thought in terror; it hadn't worked, and even if the borders between the worlds were sealed now, he would take it out on her, on her friends, her family, on Jace. "You *know better*," he said, reaching down to grasp the hilt of the sword in his hand. "I can't be hurt, not by any weapon under Heaven—"

He gasped, and broke off. His hands had closed around the hilt, just above the wound in his chest. There was no blood, but there was a flash of red, a spark—fire. The wound was beginning to burn.

"What—is—this?" he demanded through clenched teeth.

"*And I will give him the Morning Star,*" Clary said. "It's not a weapon that was made under Heaven. It *is* Heaven's fire."

With a scream he pulled the sword free. He gave the hilt, with its hammered pattern of stars, one incredulous look before he blazed up like a seraph blade. Clary staggered back, tripped over the edge of the steps to the throne, and threw one arm partly over her face. He was burning, burning like the pillar of fire that went before the Israelites. She could still see Sebastian within the flames, but they were around him, consuming him in their white light, turning him to an outline of dark char within a flame so bright, it seared her eyes.

Clary looked away, burying her face in her arm. Her mind raced back through that night when she had come to Jace through the flames, and kissed him and told him to trust her. And he had, even when she had knelt down in front of him and driven the point of Heosphoros into the ground. All around it she had drawn the same rune over and over with her stele—the rune she had once seen, it felt like so long ago now, on a rooftop in Manhattan: the winged hilt of an angel's sword.

A gift from Ithuriel, she guessed, who had given her so many gifts. The image had rested in her mind until she'd needed it. The rune for shaping Heaven's fire. That night on the demon plain, the blaze all around them had evaporated, drawn into the blade of Heosphoros, until the metal had burned and glowed and sung when she'd touched it, the sound of angelic choruses. The fire had left behind only a wide circle of sand fused into glass, a substance that had glowed like the surface of the lake she had so often dreamed about, the frozen lake where Jace and Sebastian had battled to the death in her nightmares.

This weapon could kill Sebastian, she had said. Jace had been more dubious, careful. He had tried to take it from her, but the light had died in it when he'd touched it. It reacted only to her, the one who had created it. She had agreed that they had to be cautious, in case it didn't work. It seemed the height of hubris to imagine she had trapped holy fire in a weapon, the way that fire had been trapped in the blade of Glorious...

But the Angel gave you this gift to create, Jace had said. *And do we not have his blood in our veins?*

Whatever the blade had sung with, it was gone now, gone into her brother. Clary could hear Sebastian screaming, and over that, the cries of the Endarkened. A burning wind blew past her, carrying with it the tang of ancient deserts, of a place where miracles were common and the divine was manifest in fire.

The noise stopped as suddenly as it had started. The dais shook under Clary as a weight collapsed onto it. She looked up and saw that the fire was gone, though the ground was scarred and both thrones looked blackened, the gold on them no longer bright but charred and burned and melted.

Sebastian lay a few feet away from her, on his back. There was a great blackened hole across the front of his chest. He turned his head toward her, his face taut and white with pain, and her heart contracted.

His eyes were green.

The strength in her legs gave out. She collapsed to the dais on her knees. "You," he whispered, and she stared at him in horrified fascination, unable to look away from what she had wrought. His face was utterly without color, like paper stretched over bone. She didn't dare to look down at his chest, where his jacket had fallen away; she could see the stain of blackness across his shirt, like a spill of acid. "You put ... the heavenly fire ... into the blade of the sword," he said. "It was ... cleverly done."

"It was a rune, that's all," she said, kneeling over him, her eyes searching his. He looked different, not just his eyes but the whole shape of his face, his jawline softer, his mouth without its cruel twist. "Sebastian..."

"No. I'm not him. I'm—Jonathan," he whispered. "I'm Jonathan."

"Go to Sebastian!" It was Amatis, rising, with all the Endarkened behind her. There was grief on her face, and rage. "Kill the girl!"

Jonathan struggled to sit upright. "No!" he shouted hoarsely. "Get back!"

The Dark Shadowhunters, who had begun to surge forward, froze in confusion. Then, pushing between them, came Jocelyn; she shoved by Amatis without a look and dashed up the steps to the dais. She moved toward Sebastian—Jonathan—and then froze, standing over him, staring down with a look of amazement, mixed with a terrible horror.

"Mother?" Jonathan said. He was staring, almost as if he couldn't quite focus his eyes on her. He began to cough. Blood ran from his mouth. His breath rattled in his lungs.

I dream sometimes, of a boy with green eyes, a boy who was never poisoned with demon blood, a boy who could laugh and love and be human, and that is the boy I wept over, but that boy never existed.

Jocelyn's face hardened, as if she were steeling herself to do something. She knelt down by Jonathan's head and drew him up into her lap. Clary stared; she didn't think she could have done it. Could have brought herself to touch him like that. But then her mother had always blamed herself for Jonathan's existence. There was something in her determined expression that said that she had seen him into the world, and she would see him out.

The moment he was propped up, Jonathan's breathing eased. There was bloody foam on his lips. "I am sorry," he said with a gasp. "I am so..." His eyes tracked to Clary. "I know there is nothing I could do or say now that would allow me to die with even a shred of grace," he said. "And I would hardly blame you if you cut my throat. But I am ... I regret. I'm ... sorry."

Clary was speechless. What could she say? *It's all right?* But it wasn't all right. Nothing he had done was all right, not in the world, not to her. There were things you could not forgive.

And yet he had not done them, not exactly. This person, the boy her mother was holding as if he were her penance, was not Sebastian, who had tormented and murdered and wrought destruction. She remembered what Luke had said to her, what felt like years ago: *The Amatis that is serving Sebastian is no more my sister than the Jace who served Sebastian was the boy you loved. No more my sister than Sebastian is the son your mother ought to have had.*

"Don't," he said, and half-closed his eyes. "I see you trying to puzzle it out, my sister. Whether I ought to be forgiven the way Luke would forgive his sister if the Infernal Cup released her now. But you see, she *was* his sister once. She was human once. I—" And he coughed, more blood appearing on his lips. "I never existed at all. Heavenly fire burns away that which is evil. Jace survived Glorious because he is good. There was enough of him left to live. But I was born to be all corruption. There is not enough left of me to survive. You see the ghost of someone who could have been, that is all."

Jocelyn was crying, tears falling silently down her face as she sat very still. Her back was straight.

"I must tell you," he whispered. "When I die—the Endarkened will rush at you. I won't be able to hold them back." His gaze flicked to Clary. "Where's Jace?"

"I'm here," Jace said. And he was, already up on the dais, his expression hard and puzzled and sad. Clary met his eyes. She knew how hard it must have been for him to play along with her, to let Sebastian think he had her, to let Clary risk herself at the last. And she knew how this must be for him, Jace who had wanted revenge so badly, to look at Jonathan and realize that the part of Sebastian that could have been—should have been—punished was gone. Here was another person, someone else entirely, someone who had never been given a chance to live, and now never would.

"Take my sword," said Jonathan, his breath coming in gasps, indicating Phaesphoros, which had fallen some feet away. "Cut—cut it open."

"Cut what open?" Jocelyn said in puzzlement, but Jace was already moving, bending to seize Phaesphoros, flipping himself down from the dais. He strode across the room, past the huddled Dark Shadowhunters, past the ring of runes, to where the Behemoth demon lay dead in its ichor.

"What is he doing?" Clary asked, though as Jace raised the sword and sliced cleanly down into the demon's body, it seemed obvious. "How did he know..."

"He—knows me," Jonathan breathed.

A tide of stinking demon guts poured across the floor; Jace's expression twisted with disgust—and then surprise, and then realization. He bent down and, with his bare hand, picked up something lumpy, glistening with ichor—he held it up, and Clary recognized the Infernal Cup.

She looked over at Jonathan. His eyes were rolling back, shudders racking his body. "T-tell him," he stuttered. "Tell him to throw it into the ring of runes."

Clary lifted her head. "Throw it into the circle!" she cried to Jace, and Amatis whipped around.

"No!" she cried. "If the Cup is ruined, so shall we all be!" She spun toward the dais. "Lord Sebastian! Do not let your army be destroyed! We are loyal!"

Jace looked at Luke. Luke was gazing at his sister with an expression of ultimate sadness, a sadness as profound as death. Luke had lost his sister forever, and Clary had only just gotten back her brother, the brother who had gone from her all her life, and still it was death on both sides.

Jonathan, half-supported against Jocelyn's shoulder, looked

at Amatis; his green eyes were like lights. "I'm sorry," he said. "I should never have made you."

And he turned his face away.

Luke nodded, once, at Jace, and Jace flung the Cup as hard as he could into the circle of runes. It struck the ground and shattered into pieces.

Amatis gasped, and put her hand to her chest. For a moment— just a moment—she stared at Luke with a look of recognition in her eyes: a look of recognition, even love.

"Amatis," he whispered.

Her body slumped to the ground. The other Endarkened followed, one by one, collapsing where they stood, until the room was full of corpses.

Luke turned away, too much pain in his eyes for Clary to be able to bear to look at him. She heard a cry—distant and harsh—and wondered for a moment if it was Luke, or even one of the others, horrified to see so many Nephilim fall, but the cry rose and rose and became a great shrieking howl that rattled the glass and swirled the dust outside the window that looked out on Edom. The sky turned a red the color of blood, and the cry went on, fading now, a gasping exhalation of sorrow as if the universe were weeping.

"Lilith," Jonathan whispered. "She weeps for her dead children, the children of her blood. She weeps for them and for me."

Emma pulled Cortana free of the body of the dead faerie warrior, heedless of the blood that slicked her hands. Her only thought was to get to Julian—she had seen the terrible look on his face as he'd slid to the ground, and if Julian was broken, then the whole world was broken and nothing would be right again.

The crowd was spinning around her; she barely saw them as she pushed through the melee toward the Blackthorns. Dru was huddled against the pillar beside Jules, her body curled protectively around Tavvy; Livia was still holding Ty by the wrist, but now she was staring past him, her mouth open. And Jules—Jules was still slumped against the pillar, but he had begun to raise his head, and as Emma realized that he was staring, she turned to see what he was looking at.

All around the room the Endarkened had begun to crumple. They fell like toppling chess pieces, silent and without crying out. They fell locked in battle with Nephilim, and their faerie brethren turned to stare as one by one the Endarkened warriors' bodies dropped to the floor.

A harsh shout of victory rose from a few Shadowhunter throats, but Emma barely heard it. She stumbled toward Julian and went down on her knees beside him; he looked at her, his blue-green eyes wretched. "Em," he said hoarsely. "I thought that faerie was going to kill you. I thought—"

"I'm fine," she whispered. "Are you?"

He shook his head. "I killed him," he said. "I killed my father."

"That wasn't your father." Her throat was too dry to speak anymore; instead she reached out and drew on the back of his hand. Not a word, but a sigil: the rune for bravery, and after it, a lopsided heart.

He shook his head as if to say, *No, no, I don't deserve that*, but she drew it again, and then leaned into him, even covered in blood as she was, and put her head on his shoulder.

The faeries were fleeing the Hall, abandoning their weapons as they went. More and more Nephilim were flooding into the Hall from the square outside. Emma saw Helen heading toward them, Aline beside her, and for the first time since they had left the Penhallows', Emma let herself believe that they might survive.

"They're dead," Clary said, looking around the room in wonder at the remains of Sebastian's army. "They're all dead."

Jonathan gave a half-choking laugh. "*Some good I mean to do, despite of my own nature,*" he murmured, and Clary recognized the quote from English class. *King Lear.* The most tragic of all the tragedies. "That was something. The Dark Ones are gone."

Clary leaned over him, urgency in her voice. "Jonathan," she said. "Please. Tell us how to open the border. How to go home. There must be some way."

"There's—there's no way," Jonathan whispered. "I shattered the gateway. The path to the Seelie Court is closed; all paths are. It's—it's impossible." His chest heaved. "I'm sorry."

Clary said nothing. She could taste only bitterness in her mouth. She had risked herself, had saved the world, but everyone she loved would die. For a moment her heart swelled with hatred.

"Good," Jonathan said, his eyes on her face. "Hate me. Rejoice when I die. The last thing I would want now would be to bring you more grief."

Clary looked at her mother; Jocelyn was still and upright, her tears falling silently. Clary took a deep breath. She remembered a square in Paris, facing Sebastian across a small table, him saying: *Do you think you can forgive me? I mean, do you think forgiveness is possible for someone like me? What would have happened if Valentine had brought you up along with me? Would you have loved me?*

"I don't hate you," she said finally. "I hate Sebastian. I don't know you."

Jonathan's eyes fluttered closed. "I dreamed of a green place once," he whispered. "A manor house and a little girl with red hair, and preparations for a wedding. If there are other worlds, then maybe there is one where I was a good brother and a good son."

Maybe, Clary thought, and ached for that world for a moment, for her mother, and for herself. She was aware of Luke standing by the dais, watching them; aware that there were tears on Luke's face. Jace, the Lightwoods, and Magnus were standing well back, and

Alec had his hand in Isabelle's. All around them lay the dead bodies of Endarkened warriors.

"I didn't think you could dream," said Clary, and she took a deep breath. "Valentine filled your veins with poison, and then he raised you to hate; you never had a choice. But the sword burned away all that. Maybe this is who you really are."

He took a ragged, impossible breath. "That would be a beautiful lie to believe," he said, and, incredibly, the ghost of a smile, bitter and sweet, passed over his face. "The fire of Glorious burned away the demon's blood. All my life it has scorched my veins and cut at my heart like blades, and weighed me down like lead—all my life, and I never knew it. I never knew the difference. I've never felt so ... light," he said softly, and then he smiled, and closed his eyes, and died.

Clary rose slowly to her feet. She looked down. Her mother was kneeling, holding Jonathan's body sprawled across her lap.

"Mom," Clary whispered, but Jocelyn didn't look up. A moment later someone brushed by Clary: It was Luke. He gave her hand a squeeze, and then knelt down by Jocelyn, his hand gentle on her shoulder.

Clary turned away; she couldn't bear it anymore. The sadness felt like a crushing weight. She heard Jonathan's voice in her head as she descended the stairs: *I've never felt so light.*

She moved forward through the corpses and ichor on the floor, numb and heavy with the knowledge of her failure. After everything she had done, there was still no way to save them. They were waiting for her: Jace and Simon and Isabelle, and Alec and Magnus. Magnus looked ill and pale and very, very tired.

"Sebastian's dead," she said, and they all looked at her, with their tired, dirty faces, as if they were too exhausted and drained to feel anything at the news, even relief. Jace stepped forward and took her hands, lifted them and kissed them quickly; she closed her eyes, feeling as if just a fraction of warmth and light had been returned to her.

"Warrior hands," he said quietly, and let her go. She stared down at her fingers, trying to see what he saw. Her hands were just her hands, small and callused, stained with dirt and blood.

"Jace was telling us," said Simon. "What you did, with the Morgenstern sword. That you were faking Sebastian out the whole time."

"Not there at the end," she said. "Not when he turned back into Jonathan."

"I wish you'd told us," Isabelle said. "About your plan."

"I'm sorry," Clary whispered. "I was afraid it wouldn't work. That you'd just be disappointed. I thought it was better—not to hope too much."

"Hope is all that keeps us going sometimes, biscuit," said Magnus, though he didn't sound resentful.

"I needed him to believe it," Clary said. "So I needed you to believe it too. He had to see your reactions and think he'd won."

"Jace knew," Alec said, looking up at her; he didn't sound angry either, just dazed.

"And I never looked at her from the time she got up onto the throne to the time she stabbed that bastard in the heart," Jace said. "I couldn't. Handing over that bracelet to him, I—" He broke off. "I'm sorry. I shouldn't have called him a bastard. Sebastian was, but Jonathan isn't, *wasn't*, the same person—and your mother—"

"It is like she lost a child twice," said Magnus. "I can think of few worse things."

"How about being trapped in a demon realm with no way to get out?" Isabelle said. "Clary, we need to get back to Idris. I hate to ask, but did Seb—did Jonathan say anything about how to unseal the borders?"

Clary swallowed. "He said it wasn't possible. That they're closed forever."

"So we're trapped here," Isabelle said, her dark eyes shocked. "Forever? That can't be. There must be a spell—Magnus—"

"He wasn't lying," Magnus said. "There's no way for us to reopen the paths from here to Idris."

There was an awful silence. Then Alec, whose gaze had been resting on Magnus, said, "No way for *us*?"

"That's what I said," Magnus replied. "There's no way to open the borders."

"No," said Alec, and there was a dangerous note in his voice. "You said there was no way for *us* to do it, meaning there might be someone who could."

Magnus drew away from Alec and looked around at them all. His expression was unguarded, stripped of its usual distance, and he looked both very young and very, very old. His face was a young man's face, but his eyes had seen centuries pass, and never had Clary been more aware of it. "There are worse things than death," Magnus said.

"Maybe you should let us be the judge of that," said Alec, and Magnus scrubbed a despairing hand across his face and said, "Dear God. Alexander, I have gone my whole life without ever taking recourse to this path, save once, when I learned my lesson. It is not a lesson I want the rest of you to learn."

"But you're alive," said Clary. "You lived through the lesson."

Magnus smiled an awful smile. "It wouldn't be much of a lesson if I hadn't," he said. "But I was duly warned. Playing dice with my own life is one thing; playing with all of yours—"

"We'll die here anyway," said Jace. "It's a rigged game. Let us take our chances."

"I agree," Isabelle said, and the others chimed in their agreement as well. Magnus looked toward the dais, where Luke and Jocelyn still knelt, and sighed.

"Majority vote," he said. "Did you know there's an old Downworlder saying about mad dogs and Nephilim never heeding a warning?"

"Magnus—" Alec began, but Magnus only shook his head and drew himself weakly to his feet. He still wore the rags of the clothes he must have put on for that long-ago dinner at the Fair Folk's refuge in Idris: the incongruous shreds of a suit jacket and tie. Rings sparkled on his fingers as he brought his hands together, as if in prayer, and closed his eyes.

"My father," he said, and Clary heard Alec suck in his breath with a gasp. "My father, who art in Hell, unhallowed be thy name. Thy kingdom come, thy will be done, in Edom as it is in Hell. Forgive not my sins, for in that fire of fires there shall be neither loving kindness, nor compassion, nor redemption. My father, who makes war in high places and low, come to me now; I call you as your son, and incur upon myself the responsibility of your summoning."

Magnus opened his eyes. He was expressionless. Five shocked faces looked back at him.

"By the Angel—" Alec started.

"No," said a voice just beyond their huddled group. "*Definitely* not by your Angel."

Clary stared. At first she saw nothing, just a shifting patch of shadow, and then a figure evolved out of the darkness. A tall man, as pale as bone, in a pure white suit; silver cuff links gleamed at his wrists, carved in the shape of flies. His face was a human face, pale skin pulled tight over bone, cheekbones sharp as blades. He didn't have hair so much as a sparkling coronet of barbed wires.

His eyes were gold-green, and slit-pupilled like a cat's.

"Father," said Magnus, and the word was an exhalation of sorrow. "You came."

The man smiled. His front teeth were sharp, pointed like feline teeth. "My son," he said. "It has been a long time since you called on me. I was beginning to despair that you ever would again."

"I hadn't planned to," Magnus said dryly. "I called on you once, to determine that you were my father. That once was enough."

"You wound me," said the man, and he turned his pointed-tooth smile on the others. "I am Asmodeus," he said. "One of the Nine Princes of Hell. You may know my name."

Alec made a short sound, quickly muffled.

"I was a seraphim once, one of the angels indeed," continued Asmodeus, looking pleased with himself. "Part of an innumerable company. Then came the war, and we fell like stars from Heaven. I followed the Light-Bringer down, the Morning Star, for I was one of his chief advisers, and when he fell, I fell with him. He raised me up in Hell and made me one of the nine rulers. In case you were wondering, it *is* preferable to rule in Hell than serve in Heaven—I've done both."

"You're—Magnus's father?" said Alec in a strangled voice. He turned to Magnus. "When you held the witchlight in the subway tunnel, it flared up in colors—is that because of *him*?" He pointed at Asmodeus.

"Yes," Magnus said. He looked very tired. "I warned you, Alexander, that this was something you would not like."

"I don't see what the fuss is about. I have been the father of many warlocks," said Asmodeus. "Magnus has made me the most proud."

"Who are the others?" Isabelle asked, her dark eyes suspicious.

"What he's not saying is that they're mostly dead," Magnus said. He met his father's eyes briefly and then looked away, as if he couldn't stand prolonged eye contact. His thin, sensitive mouth was set in a hard line. "He's also not telling you that all princes of Hell have a realm they rule; this is his."

"Since this place—Edom—is *your* realm," Jace said, "then you're responsible for—for what happened here?"

"It is my realm, though I am rarely here," said Asmodeus with a martyred sigh. "Used to be an exciting place. The Nephilim of this realm put up quite the fight. When they invented the *skeptron*, I rather thought they might win out at the last moment, but the Jonathan Shadowhunter of this world was a divider, not a uniter, and in the end they destroyed themselves. Everyone does, you know. We demons get the blame, but we only open the door. It is humanity who steps through it."

"Don't excuse yourself," Magnus snapped. "You as much as murdered my mother—"

"She was a willing little piece, I assure you," said Asmodeus, and Magnus flushed red across his cheekbones. Clary felt a dull pang of shock that it was actually possible to *do* that to Magnus, to hurt him with barbs about his family. It had been so long, and he was so collected.

But then, perhaps your parents could always hurt you, no matter how old you were.

"Let's cut to the business part of this," said Magnus. "You can open a door, correct? Send us through to Idris, back to our world?"

"Would you like a demonstration?" Asmodeus asked, flicking his fingers toward the dais, where Luke was on his feet, looking toward them. Jocelyn seemed about to rise, too. Clary could see the expression of concern on both their faces—just before they winked out of existence. There was a shimmer of air and they both vanished, taking Jonathan's body with them. Just as they vanished, for a moment, Clary glimpsed the inside of the Accords Hall, the mermaid fountain and the marble floor, and then it was gone, like a tear in the universe sewing itself back up again.

A cry broke from Clary's throat. *"Mom!"*

"I sent them back to your world," said Asmodeus. "Now you know." He examined his nails.

Clary was panting, half with panic, half with rage. "How dare you—"

"Well, it's what you wanted, isn't it?" said Asmodeus. "There, you got the first two for free. The rest, well, it'll cost you." He sighed at the looks on the faces around him. "I'm a *demon*," he said pointedly. "Really, what do they teach Nephilim these days?"

"I know what you want," Magnus said in a strained voice. "And you can have it. But you must swear on the Morning Star to send all my friends back to Idris, *all* of them, and never to bother them again. They will owe you *nothing*."

Alec stepped forward. "Stop," he said. "No—Magnus, what do you mean, what he wants? Why are you talking like you're not coming back to Idris with us?"

"There is a time," said Asmodeus, "when we must all return to live in the houses of our fathers. Now is Magnus's time."

"'*In my father's house are many mansions*,'" Jace whispered; he looked very pale, and as if he might throw up. "Magnus. He can't mean—he doesn't want to take you back with him? Back to—"

"To Hell? Not precisely," Asmodeus said. "As Magnus said, Edom is my realm. I shared it with Lilith. Then her brat took it over and laid waste to the grounds, destroyed my keep—it's in slivers out there. And *you* murdered half the populace with the *skeptron*." The last was addressed to Jace, rather petulantly. "It takes great energy to fuel a realm. We draw from the power of what we have left behind, the great city of Pandemonium, the fire we fell into, but there is a time when life must fuel us. And immortal life is the best of all."

The numb heaviness weighing Clary's limbs vanished as she snapped to attention, moving in front of Magnus. She nearly collided with the others. They had all moved just as she had, to block the warlock from his demon father, even Simon. "You want to take his *life*?" Clary asked. "That's just cruel and stupid, even if you're a demon. How could you want to kill your own *child*—"

Asmodeus laughed. "Delightful," he said. "Look at them,

Magnus, these children who love you and want to protect you! Who would ever have thought it! When you are buried, I will make sure they inscribe it on your tomb: *Magnus Bane, beloved of Nephilim.*"

"You won't touch him," Alec said, his voice like iron. "Maybe you've forgotten what it is we do, us Nephilim, but we kill *demons.* Even princes of Hell."

"Oh, I know well what you do; my kinsman Abbadon you slew, and our princess Lilith you scattered to the winds of the void, though she will return. She always has a place in Edom. That is why I allowed her son to set himself up here, though I admit I did not realize what a mess he'd make." Asmodeus rolled his eyes; Clary suppressed a shudder. Around the gold-green pupils the sclerae of his eyes were as black as oil. "I do not plan to kill Magnus. That would be messy and silly, and besides I could have had his death arranged at any time. It is his life freely given I want, for the life of an immortal has power, great power, and it will help me fuel my kingdom."

"But he's your son," Isabelle protested.

"And he will remain with me," said Asmodeus with a grin. "In spirit, you might say."

Alec whirled on Magnus, who stood with his hands in his pockets, scowling. "He wants to take your immortality?"

"Exactly," Magnus said.

"But—you'd survive? Just not be immortal anymore?" Alec looked wretched, and Clary couldn't help feeling awful for him. After the reason Alec and Magnus had broken up, Alec certainly didn't want or need to be reminded that he had once wanted Magnus's immortality taken away.

"My immortality would be gone," Magnus said. "All the years of my life would come on me at once. I would be unlikely to survive it. Almost four hundred years is quite a lot to take, even if you moisturize regularly."

"You can't," Alec said, and there was a plea in his voice. "He said 'a life given willingly.' Say no."

Magnus raised his head and looked up and over at Alec; it was a look that made Clary flush and glance away. There was so much love in it, mixed with exasperation and pride and despair. It was an unguarded look, and it felt wrong to see it. "I can't say no, Alexander," he said. "If I do, we all remain here; we'll die anyway. We'll starve, our ashes turned to dust to plague the demons of the realm."

"Fine," Alec said. "There isn't any one of us who would give up your life to save ours."

Magnus glanced around at the faces of his companions, dirty and exhausted and brutalized and despairing, and Clary saw the look on Magnus's face change as he realized that Alec was right. None of them would give up his life to save theirs, even all of theirs.

"I've lived a *long* time," Magnus said. "So many years, and no, it doesn't feel like enough. I won't lie and say it does. I want to live on—partly because of you, Alec. I have never wanted to live so much as I have these past few months, with you."

Alec looked stricken. "We'll die together," he said. "Let me stay at least, with you."

"You have to go back. You have to go back to the world."

"I don't want the world. I want you," Alec said, and Magnus closed his eyes, as if the words almost hurt. Asmodeus watched as they spoke, avidly, almost hungrily, and Clary remembered that demons fed on human emotions—fear and joy and love and pain. Most of all, pain.

"You can't stay with me," Magnus said after a pause. "There will be no me; the demon will take my life force, and my body will crumble away. Four hundred years, remember."

"'The demon,'" Asmodeus said, and sniffed. "You could say my name, at least, while you're boring me."

Clary resolved then and there that she might hate Asmodeus more than any other demon she had ever met.

"Get on with it, my boy," Asmodeus added. "I haven't got all eternity to wait—and neither have you, anymore."

"I have to save you, Alec," Magnus said. "You and everyone you love; it's a small price to pay, isn't it, in the end, for all of that?"

"Not *everyone* I love," Alec whispered, and Clary felt tears pressing behind her eyes. She had tried, tried so hard, to be the one who paid the price. It was not fair that Magnus should pay it; Magnus, who had the least part in the story of Nephilim and angels and demons and vengeance, compared to any of the rest of them; Magnus, who was only a part of it all because he loved Alec. "No," Alec said. Through her tears Clary could see them clinging to each other; there was tenderness even in the curve of Magnus's fingers around Alec's shoulder as he bent to kiss him. It was a kiss of desperation and clutching more than passion; Magnus held on tightly enough for his fingers to bite into Alec's arms, but in the end he stepped away, and turned toward his father.

"All right," Magnus said, and Clary could tell he was bracing himself, nerving himself up as if he were about to throw his body onto a pyre. "All right, take me. I give you my life. I am—"

Simon—Simon, who had been silent till that moment; Simon, who Clary had almost forgotten was there—stepped forward. "I am willing."

Asmodeus's eyebrows shot up. "What was that?"

Isabelle seemed to catch on before anyone else. She paled and said, "No, Simon, no!" but Simon went on, his back straight, his chin lifted.

"I also have an immortal life," he said. "Magnus isn't the only one. Take mine; take my immortality."

"Ahhhh," breathed Asmodeus, his eyes suddenly shining. "Azazel told me of you. A vampire is not interesting, but a *Daylighter*!

You carry the power of the world's sun in your veins. Sunlight and eternal life, that is a power indeed."

"Yes," Simon said. "If you'll take my immortality instead of Magnus's, then I give it to you. I am—"

"*Simon!*" Clary said, but it was already too late.

"I am willing," he finished, and with a glance around at the rest of the group, he set his jaw, with a look that said, *I've said it. It's done.*

"God, Simon, no," said Magnus, in a voice of terrible sadness, and he closed his eyes.

"I'm only seventeen," Simon said. "If he takes my immortality, I'll live out my life—I won't die here. I never wanted immortality, I never wanted to be a vampire, I never wanted any of it."

"You won't live out your life!" There were tears in Isabelle's eyes. "If Asmodeus takes your immortality, then you'll be a corpse, Simon. You're undead."

Asmodeus made a rude noise. "You're a very stupid girl," he said. "I am a Prince of Hell. I can break down the walls between worlds. I can build worlds and destroy them. You think I can't reverse the transformation that Turns a human to a vampire? You think I can't make his heart beat again? Child's play."

"But why would you do that?" Clary said, bewildered. "Why would you make it so that he lived? You're a demon. You don't care—"

"I don't care. But I want," said Asmodeus. "There is one more thing I want from you. One more item to sweeten the deal." He grinned, and his teeth glimmered like sharp crystals.

"What?" Magnus's voice shook. "What is it you want?"

"His memories," said Asmodeus.

"Azazel took a memory from each of us, as payment for a favor," Alec said. "What is it with you demons and memories?"

"Human memories, freely given, are like food to us," said Asmodeus. "Demons live on the cries and agony of the damned in torment. Imagine then, how nice a change of pace a feast of happy memories is. Mixed together, they are delicious, the sour and the sweet." He looked around, his cat's eyes glittering. "And I can already tell there will be many happy memories to take, little vampire, for you are much loved, are you not?"

Simon looked strained. He said, "But if you take my memories, who will I be? I don't—"

"Well," said Asmodeus. "I could take every memory you have and leave you a drooling idiot, I suppose, but really, who wants the memories of a baby? Dull, dull. The question is, what would be the *most* fun? Memories are delicious, but so is pain. What would cause the most pain to your friends, here? What would remind them to fear the power and the wit of demons?" He clasped his hands behind his back. Each of the buttons of his white suit was carved in the shape of a fly.

"I promised my immortality," Simon said. "Not my memories. You said 'freely given'—"

"God in Hell, the banality," said Asmodeus, and he moved, as swift as a lick of flame, to seize Simon by the forearm. Isabelle darted forward, as if to catch hold of Simon, and then flinched back with a gasp. A red welt had appeared across her cheek. She put her hand to it, looking shocked.

"Leave her alone," Simon snapped, and wrenched his arm out of the demon's grip.

"Downworlder," the demon breathed, and touched his long, spidery fingers to Simon's cheek. "You must have had a heart that beat so strong in you, when it still beat."

"Let him go," Jace said, drawing his sword. "He is ours, not yours; the Nephilim protect what belongs to us—"

"No!" Simon said. He was shivering all over, but his back was straight. "Jace, don't. This is the only way."

"Indeed it is," said Asmodeus. "For none of you can fight a

Prince of Hell in his place of power; not even you, Jace Herondale, child of angels, or you, Clarissa Fairchild, with your tricks and runes." He moved his fingers, slightly; Jace's sword clattered to the ground, and Jace jerked his hand back, grimacing in pain as if he'd been burned. Asmodeus spared him only a glance before raising his hand again.

"There is the gateway. Look." He gestured toward the wall, which shimmered and came clear. Through it Clary could see the hazy outlines of the Hall of Accords. There were the bodies of the Endarkened, lying on the ground in heaps of scarlet, and there were the Shadowhunters, running, stumbling, hugging, embracing one another—victory after the battle.

And there were her mother and Luke, looking around in bewilderment. They were still in the same position they had been in on the dais: Luke standing, Jocelyn kneeling with her son's body in her arms. Other Shadowhunters were only just beginning to glance toward them, surprised, as if they had appeared out of nowhere—which they had.

"There is everything you want," said Asmodeus, as the gateway flickered and went dark. "And in return I shall take the Daylighter's immortality, and along with it, his memories of the Shadow World—all his memories of all of you, of all he has learned, of all he has been. That is my desire."

Simon's eyes widened; Clary felt her heart give a terrible lurch. Magnus looked as if someone had stabbed him. "There it is," he whispered. "The trick at the heart of the game. There always is one, with demons."

Isabelle looked incredulous. "Are you saying you want him to *forget* us?"

"Everything about you, and that he ever knew you," said Asmodeus. "I offer you this in exchange. He will live. He will have the life of an ordinary mundane. He will have his family back; his mother, his sister. Friends, school, all the trappings of a *normal* human life."

Clary looked at Simon desperately. He was shaking, clenching and unclenching his hands. He said nothing.

"Absolutely not," said Jace.

"Fine. Then you'll all die here. You really don't have much leverage, little Shadowhunter. What are memories when weighed against such a great cost of life?"

"You're talking about who Simon *is*," said Clary. "You're talking about taking him away from us forever."

"Yes. Isn't it delightful?" Asmodeus smiled.

"This is ridiculous," said Isabelle. "Say you do take his memories. What's to stop us from tracking him down and telling him about the Shadow World? Introducing him to magic? We did it before, we can do it again."

"Before, he knew you, knew and trusted Clary," said Asmodeus. "Now he will know none of you. You will all be strangers to him, and why should he listen to mad strangers? Besides, you know Covenant Law as well as I do. You will be breaking it, telling him about the Shadow World for no reason at all, endangering his life. There were special circumstances before. Now there will not be. The Clave will strip all your runes if you try it."

"Speaking of the Clave," said Jace. "They're not going to be too pleased if you toss a mundane back out into a life where everyone he knows thinks he's a *vampire*. All Simon's friends know! His family knows! His sister, his mother. *They'll* tell him, even if we don't."

"I see." Asmodeus looked displeased. "That does complicate things. Perhaps I should take Magnus's immortality after all—"

"*No*," Simon said. He looked shocked, sick on his feet, but his voice was determined. Asmodeus looked at him with covetous eyes.

"Simon, shut up," Magnus said desperately. "Take me instead, Father—"

"I want the Daylighter," said Asmodeus. "Magnus, Magnus. You've never quite understood what it is to be a demon, have you? To feed on pain? But what is pain? Physical torment, that's so dull; any garden-variety demon can do that. To be an *artist* of pain, to create agony, to blacken the soul, to turn pure motives to filth, and love to lust and then to hate, to turn a source of joy to a source of torture, *that* is what we exist for!" His voice rang out. "I shall go forth into the mundane world. I will strip the memories of those close to the Daylighter. They will remember him only as mortal. They will not remember Clary at all."

"No!" Clary shouted, and Asmodeus threw his head back and laughed, a dazzling laugh that made her remember that once he had been an angel.

"You can't take our memories," said Isabelle furiously. "We're Nephilim. It would be tantamount to an attack. The Clave—"

"Your memories you may keep," said Asmodeus. "Nothing about your remembering Simon will get me in trouble with the Clave, and besides, it will torment you, which only doubles my pleasure." He grinned. "I shall rip a hole through the heart of your world, and when you feel it, you will think on me and remember me. Remember!" Asmodeus pulled Simon close, his hand sliding up to press against Simon's chest, as if he could reach through his rib cage into his heart. "We begin here. Are you ready, Daylighter?"

"Stop!" Isabelle stepped forward, her whip in hand, her eyes burning. "We know your name, demon. Do you think I am afraid to slay even a Prince of Hell? I would hang your head on my wall like a trophy, and if you dare touch Simon, I will hunt you down. I will spend my *life* hunting you—"

Alec wrapped his arms around his sister, and held her tightly. "Isabelle," he said quietly. "No."

"What do you mean, no?" Clary demanded. "We can't let this happen—Jace—"

"This is Simon's choice." Jace stood stock-still; he was ashy pale but unmoving. His eyes were locked on Simon's. "We have to honor it."

Simon looked back at Jace, and inclined his head. His gaze was moving slowly over all of them, flicking from Magnus to Alec, to Jace, to Isabelle, where it stopped and rested, and was so full of broken possibilities that Clary felt her own heart break.

And then his gaze moved to Clary, and she felt the rest of her shatter. There was so much in his expression, so many years of so much love, so many whispered secrets and promises and shared dreams. She saw him reach down, and then something bright arced through the air toward her. She reached up and caught it, reflexively. It was the golden ring Clary had given him. Her hand tightened around it, feeling the bite of metal against her palm, welcoming the pain.

"Enough," said Asmodeus. "I hate good-byes." And he tightened his grip on Simon. Simon gasped, his eyes flying wide open; his hand went to his chest.

"My heart—" he gasped, and Clary knew, knew from the look on his face, that it had started beating again. She blinked against her tears as a white mist exploded up around them. She heard Simon cry out in pain; her own feet moved without volition and she ran forward, only to be hurled back as if she had struck an invisible wall. Someone caught her—Jace, she thought. There were arms around her, even as the mist circled Simon and the demon like a small tornado, half-blocking them from view.

Shapes began to appear in the mist as it thickened. Clary saw herself and Simon as children, holding hands, crossing a street in Brooklyn; she had barrettes in her hair and Simon was adorably rumpled, his glasses sliding off his nose. There they were again, throwing snowballs in Prospect Park; and at Luke's farmhouse, tanned from summer, hanging upside down from tree branches.

She saw them in Java Jones, listening to Eric's terrible poetry, and on the back of a flying motorcycle as it crashed into a parking lot, with Jace there, looking at them, his eyes squinted against the sun. And there was Simon with Isabelle, his hands curved around her face, kissing her, and she could see Isabelle as Simon saw her: fragile and strong, and so, so beautiful. And there was Valentine's ship, Simon kneeling on Jace, blood on his mouth and shirt, and blood at Jace's throat, and there was the cell in Idris, and Hodge's weathered face, and Simon and Clary again, Clary etching the Mark of Cain onto his forehead. Maureen, and her blood on the floor, and her little pink hat, and the rooftop in Manhattan where Lilith had raised Sebastian, and Clary was passing him a gold ring across a table, and an Angel was rising out of a lake before him, and he was kissing Isabelle ...

All Simon's memories, his memories of magic, his memories of all of them, being drawn out and spun into a skein. It shimmered, as white-gold as daylight. There was a sound all around them, like a gathering storm, but Clary barely heard it. She reached her hands out, beseeching, though she didn't know who she was begging. *"Please—"*

She felt Jace's arms tighten around her, and then the edge of the storm caught her. She was lifted up, whirled away. She saw the stone room recede into the distance at a terrible speed, and the storm took her cries for Simon and turned them into a sound like the ragged tearing of wind. Jace's hands were torn from her shoulders. She was alone in the chaos, and for a moment she thought Asmodeus had lied to them after all, that there was no gateway, and that they would float in this nothingness forever until they died.

And then the ground came up, fast. She saw the floor of the Accords Hall, hard marble veined with gold, before she hit it. The collision was hard, rattling her teeth; she rolled automatically, as she'd been taught, and came to a stop at the side of the mermaid fountain in the center of the room.

She sat up and looked around. The room was full of utterly silent, staring faces, but they didn't matter. She wasn't looking for strangers. She saw Jace first; he had landed in a crouch, poised to fight. She saw his shoulders relax as he looked around, realizing where they were, that they were in Idris, and the war was over. And there was Alec; he had his hand still in Magnus's. Magnus looked sick and exhausted, but he was alive.

And there was Isabelle. She had come through the closest to Clary, only a foot or so away. She was already on her feet, her gaze scanning the room, once, twice, a desperate third time. They were all there, all of them, all except one.

She looked down at Clary; her eyes were shining with tears. "Simon's not here," she said. "He's really gone."

The silence that had held the assembly of Shadowhunters in its grip seemed to break like a wave: Suddenly there were Nephilim running toward them. Clary saw her mother and Luke, Robert and Maryse, Aline and Helen, even Emma Carstairs, moving to surround them, to embrace them and heal them and help them. Clary knew they meant well, that they were running to the rescue, but she felt no relief. Her hand tightening on the gold ring in her palm, she curled up against the floor and finally allowed herself to cry.

24

CALL IT PEACE

"Who stands, then, to represent the Faerie Courts?" said Jia Penhallow.

The Hall of Accords was draped with the blue banners of victory. They looked like pieces cut out of the sky. Each was stamped with a golden rune of triumph. It was a clear winter day outside, and the light that poured through the windows shimmered across the long lines of chairs that had been set up facing the raised dais at the center of the room, where the Consul and the Inquisitor sat at a long table. The table itself was decorated with more gold and blue: massive golden candlesticks that nearly obscured Emma's view of the Downworlders who also shared the table: Luke, representing the werewolves; a young woman named Lily, representing the vampires; and the very famous Magnus Bane, the representative for the warlocks.

No seat had been placed at the table for a representative of Faerie. Slowly, from among the seated crowd, a young woman rose to her feet. Her eyes were entirely blue with no white, her ears pointed like Helen's. "I am Kaelie Whitewillow," she said. "I will stand for the Seelie Court."

"But not for the Unseelie?" said Jia, her pen hovering above a scroll of paper.

Kaelie shook her head, her lips pressed together. A murmur ran through the room. For all the brightness of the banners, the mood in the room was tense, not joyful. In the row of seats in front of the Blackthorns sat the Lightwoods: Maryse with her back ramrod-straight, and beside her, Isabelle and Alec, their dark heads bent together as they whispered.

Jocelyn Fairchild sat beside Maryse, but there was no sign anywhere of Clary Fray or Jace Lightwood.

"The Unseelie Court declines a representative," said Jia, noting it down with her pen. She looked at Kaelie over the rims of her glasses. "What word do you bring us from the Seelie Court? Do they agree to our terms?"

Emma heard Helen, at the end of her row of seats, take a deep breath. Dru and Tavvy and the twins had been considered too young to come to the meeting; technically no one under eighteen was allowed, but special considerations had been made for those, like her and Julian, who had been directly affected by what was coming to be called the Dark War.

Kaelie moved to the aisle between the rows of seats and began to walk toward the dais; Robert Lightwood rose to his feet. "You must ask permission to approach the Consul," he said in his gravelly voice.

"Permission is not given," said Jia tightly. "Stay where you are, Kaelie Whitewillow. I can hear you perfectly well."

Emma felt a sudden brief burst of pity for the faerie girl—everyone was staring at her with eyes like knives. Everyone except Aline and Helen, who sat pressed close together; they were holding each other's hands, and their knuckles were white.

"The Faerie Court asks for your mercy," Kaelie said, clasping her slim hands in front of her. "The terms you have set down are too harsh. The faeries have always had their own sovereignty, our own kings and queens. We have always had warriors. We are an ancient people. What you ask for will crush us completely."

A low murmur ran around the room. It was not a friendly noise. Jia picked up the paper lying on the table in front of her. "Shall we review?" she said. "We ask that the Faerie Courts accept all responsibility for the loss of life and damage sustained by Shadowhunters and Downworlders in the Dark War. The Fair Folk shall be responsible for the costs of rebuilding broken wards, for the reestablishment of the Praetor Lupus on Long Island, and the rebuilding of what in Alicante has been destroyed. You will spend your own riches upon it. As for the Shadowhunters taken from us—"

"If you mean Mark Blackthorn, he was taken by the Wild Hunt," Kaelie said. "We have no jurisdiction over them. You will have to negotiate with them yourselves, though we will not prevent it."

"He was not all that was taken from us," said Jia. "There is that for which there can be no reparation—the loss of life sustained by Shadowhunters and lycanthropes in battle, those who were torn from us by the Infernal Cup—"

"That was Sebastian Morgenstern, not the Courts," Kaelie protested. "He was a *Shadowhunter*."

"And that's why we are not punishing you with a war that you would inevitably lose," said Jia coldly. "Instead we insist merely that you disband your armies, that there be no more Fair Folk warriors. You may no longer bear arms. Any faerie found carrying a weapon without a dispensation from the Clave will be killed on sight."

"The terms are too severe," Kaelie protested. "The Fair Folk cannot abide under them! If we are weaponless, we cannot defend ourselves!"

"We will put it to a vote, then," said Jia, setting her paper down. "Any not in favor of the terms set down for the Fair Folk, please speak now."

There was a long silence. Emma could see Helen's eyes roving the room, her mouth pinched at the sides; Aline was holding her wrist tightly. Finally there was the sound of a chair scraping back, echoing in the silence, and one lone figure rose to his feet.

Magnus Bane. He was still pale from his ordeal in Edom, but his gold-green eyes burned with an intensity that Emma could see from across the room. "I know that mundane history is not of enormous interest to most Shadowhunters," he said. "But there was a time before the Nephilim. A time when Rome battled the city of Carthage, and over the course of many wars was victorious. After one of the wars, Rome demanded that Carthage pay them tribute, that Carthage abandon their army, and that the land of Carthage be sowed with salt. The historian Tacitus said of the Romans that 'they make a desert and call it peace.'" He turned to Jia. "The Carthaginians never forgot. Their hatred of Rome sparked another war in the end, and that war ended in death and slavery. That was not peace. *This* is not peace."

At that, there were catcalls from the assembly.

"Perhaps we don't want peace, warlock!" someone shouted.

"What's your solution, then?" shouted someone else.

"Leniency," said Magnus. "The Fair Folk have long hated the Nephilim for their harshness. Show them something other than harshness, and you will receive something other than hate in return!"

Noise burst out again, louder than ever this time; Jia raised a hand, and the crowd quieted. "Does anyone else speak for the Fair Folk?" she asked.

Magnus, taking his seat again, glanced sideways at his fellow Downworlders, but Lily was smirking and Luke was staring down at the table with a fixed look on his face. It was common knowledge that his sister had been the first taken and Endarkened by Sebastian Morgenstern, that many of the wolves in the Praetor had been his friends, including Jordan Kyle—and yet there was doubt on his face—

"Luke," Magnus said in a soft voice that somehow managed to echo through the room. "Please."

The doubt vanished. Luke shook his head grimly. "Don't ask for what I can't give," he said. "The whole Praetor was slaughtered, Magnus. As the representative of the werewolves, I cannot speak against what they all want. If I did, they would turn against the Clave, and nothing would be accomplished by that."

"There it is, then," Jia said. "Speak, Kaelie Whitewillow. Will you agree to the terms, or will there be war between us?"

The faerie girl bowed her head. "We agree to the terms."

The assembly burst into applause. Only a few did not clap: Magnus, the row of Blackthorns, the Lightwoods, and Emma herself. She was too busy watching Kaelie as the faerie sat down. Her head might have been bowed submissively, but her face was full of a white-hot rage.

"So it is done," said Jia, clearly pleased. "Now we move to the subject of—"

"Wait." A thin Shadowhunter with dark hair had risen to his feet. Emma didn't recognize him. He could have been anyone. A Cartwright? A Pontmercy? "There remains the question of Mark and Helen Blackthorn."

Helen's eyes closed. She looked like someone who had been half-expecting a guilty sentence in a trial and half-hoping for a reprieve, and this was the moment after the guilty sentence had fallen.

Jia paused, her pen in her hand. "What do you mean, Balogh?"

Balogh drew himself up. "There's already been discussion of the fact that Morgenstern's forces penetrated the Los Angeles Institute so easily. Both Mark and Helen Blackthorn have the blood of faeries in them. We know the boy's already joined up with the Wild Hunt, so he's beyond us, but the girl shouldn't be among Shadowhunters. It isn't decent."

Aline shot to her feet. "That's ridiculous!" she spat. "Helen's a Shadowhunter; she's always been one! She's got the blood of the Angel in her—you can't turn your back on that!"

"And the blood of faeries," said Balogh. "She can lie. We've already been tricked by one of her sort, to our sorrow. I say we strip her Marks—"

Luke brought his hand down on the table with a loud slam; Magnus was hunched forward, his long-fingered hands covering his face, his shoulders slumped. "The girl's done nothing," Luke said. "You can't punish her for an accident of birth."

"Accidents of birth make us all what we are," said Balogh stubbornly. "You can't deny the faerie blood in her. You can't deny she can lie. If it comes down to a war again, where will her loyalties stand?"

Helen got to her feet. "Where they stood this time," she said. "I fought at the Burren, and at the Citadel, and in Alicante, to protect my family and protect Nephilim. I've never given anyone reason to question my loyalty."

"This is what happens," Magnus said, raising his face. "Can't you see, this is how it begins *again*?"

"Helen is right," said Jia. "She's done nothing wrong."

Another Shadowhunter rose to her feet, a woman with dark hair piled on her head. "Begging your pardon, Consul, but you are not objective," she said. "We all know of your daughter's relationship with the faerie girl. You should recuse yourself from this discussion."

"Helen Blackthorn is needed, Mrs. Sedgewick," said Diana Wrayburn, standing. She looked outraged; Emma remembered her in the Accords Hall, the way she had tried to get to Emma, to help her. "Her parents have been murdered; she has five younger brothers and sisters to care for—"

"She is not needed," snapped Sedgewick. "We are reopening the Academy—the children can go there, or they can be split up among various Institutes—"

"No," Julian whispered. His hands were in fists on his knees.

"Absolutely not," Helen shouted. "Jia, you must—"

Jia met her eyes and nodded, a slow, reluctant nod. "Arthur Blackthorn," she said. "Please rise."

Emma felt Julian, beside her, freeze in shock as a man on the other side of the room, hidden among the crowd, rose to his feet. He was slight, a paler, smaller version of Julian's father, with thinning brown hair and the Blackthorn eyes, half-hidden behind spectacles. He leaned heavily on a wooden cane, with a discomfort that made her think the injury that required the cane was recent.

"I wished to wait until after this meeting, that the children might meet their uncle properly," Jia said. "I summoned him immediately on news of the attack on the Los Angeles Institute, of course, but he had been injured in London. He arrived in Idris only this morning." She sighed. "Mr. Blackthorn, you may introduce yourself."

The man had a round, pleasant face, and looked extremely uncomfortable being stared at by so many people. "I am Arthur Blackthorn, Andrew Blackthorn's brother," he said. His accent was British; Emma always forgot that Julian's father had originally come from London. He had lost his accent years before. "I will be moving into the Los Angeles Institute as soon as possible and bringing my nieces and nephews with me. The children will be under my protection."

"Is that really your uncle?" Emma whispered, staring.

"Yes, that's him," Julian whispered back, clearly agitated. "It's just—I was hoping—I mean, I was really starting to think he wouldn't come. I'd—I'd rather have Helen look after us."

"While I'm sure we're all immeasurably relieved that you'll be looking after the Blackthorn children," said Luke, "Helen is one of them. Are you saying, by claiming responsibility for the younger siblings, that you agree that her Marks should be stripped?"

Arthur Blackthorn looked horrified. "Not at all," he said. "My brother may not have been wise in his ... dalliances ... but all records show that the children of Shadowhunters are Shadowhunters. As they say, *ut incepit fidelis sic permanet*."

Julian slid down in his seat. "More Latin," he muttered. "Just like Dad."

"What does it mean?" Emma asked.

"'She begins loyal and ends loyal'—something like that." Julian's eyes flicked around the room; everyone was muttering and glaring. Jia was in muted conference with Robert and the Downworld representatives. Helen was still standing, but it looked as if Aline was all that was holding her up.

The group at the dais broke apart, and Robert Lightwood stepped forward. His face was thunderous. "So that there is no discussion that Jia's personal friendship with Helen Blackthorn will have influenced her decision, she has recused herself," he said. "The rest of us have decided that, as Helen is eighteen, at the age where many young Shadowhunters are posted to other Institutes to learn their ways, she will be posted to Wrangel Island to study the wards."

"For how long?" said Balogh immediately.

"Indefinitely," said Robert, and Helen sank down into her chair, Aline at her side, her face a mask of grief and shock. Wrangel Island might have been the seat of all the wards that protected the world, a prestigious posting in many ways, but it was also a tiny island in the frozen Arctic sea north of Russia, thousands of miles from Los Angeles.

"Is that good enough for you?" Jia said in a cold voice. "Mr. Balogh? Mrs. Sedgewick? Shall we vote on it? All in favor of assigning Helen Blackthorn to a posting on Wrangel Island until her loyalty is determined, say 'aye.'"

A chorus of "aye," and a quieter chorus of "nay," ran around the room. Emma said nothing, and neither did Jules; both of them were too young to vote. Emma reached her hand over and took Julian's, squeezed it tightly; his fingers were like ice. He had the look of someone who had been hit so many times that they no longer even wanted to get up. Helen was sobbing softly in Aline's arms.

"There remains the question of Mark Blackthorn," said Balogh.

"*What* question?" demanded Robert Lightwood, sounding exasperated. "The boy has been taken by the Wild Hunt! In the unlikely event that we are able to negotiate his release, shouldn't this be a problem to worry about then?"

"That's just it," said Balogh. "As long as we don't negotiate his release, the problem takes care of itself. The boy is likely better off with his own kind anyway."

Arthur Blackthorn's round face paled. "No," he said. "My brother wouldn't have wanted that. He'd have wanted the boy at home with his family." He gestured toward where Emma and Julian and the rest were sitting. "They've had so much taken away from them. How can we take more?"

"We're protecting them," snapped Sedgewick. "From a brother and sister who will only betray them as time passes and they realize their true loyalty to the Courts. All in favor of permanently abandoning the search for Mark Blackthorn, say 'aye.'"

Emma reached to hold Julian as he hunched forward in his chair. She clung awkwardly to his side. All his muscles were rigid, as hard as iron, as if he were readying himself for a fall or a blow. Helen leaned toward him, whispering and murmuring, her own face streaked with tears. As Aline reached past Helen to stroke Jules's hair, Emma caught sight of the Blackthorn ring sparkling on Aline's finger. As the chorus of "aye" went around the room in a terrible symphony, the gleam made Emma think of the shine of a distress signal far out at sea, where no one could see it, where there was no one to care.

If this was peace and victory, Emma thought, maybe war and fighting were better after all.

Jace slid from the back of the horse and reached up a hand to help Clary down after him. "Here we are," he said, turning to face the lake.

They stood on a shallow beach of rocks facing the western edge of Lake Lyn. It was not the same beach where Valentine had stood when he had summoned the Angel Raziel, not the same beach where Jace had bled his life out and then regained it, but Clary had not been back to the lake since that time, and the sight of it still sent a shiver through her bones.

It was a lovely place, there was no doubt about that. The lake stretched into the distance, tinted with the color of the winter sky, limned in silver, the surface brushed and rippled so that it resembled a piece of metallic paper folding and unfolding under the wind's touch. The clouds were white and high, and the hills around them were bare.

Clary moved forward, down to the edge of the water. She had thought her mother might come with her, but at the last moment Jocelyn had refused, saying that she had bidden good-bye to her son a long time ago and that this was Clary's time. The Clave had burned his body—at Clary's request. The burning of a body was an honor, and those who died in disgrace were buried at crossroads whole and unburned, as Jace's mother had been. The burning had been more than a favor, Clary thought; it had been a sure way for the Clave to be absolutely certain that he was dead. But still Jonathan's ashes were never to be taken to the abode of the Silent Brothers. They would never form a part of the City of Bones; he would never be a soul among other Nephilim souls.

He would not be buried among those he had caused to be murdered, and that, Clary thought, was only fair and just. The Endarkened had been burned, and their ashes buried at the cross-roads near Brocelind. There would be a monument there, a necropolis to recall those who had once been Shadowhunters, but there would be no monument to recall Jonathan Morgenstern, whom no one wanted to remember. Even Clary wished she could forget, but nothing was that easy.

The water of the lake was clear, with a slight rainbow sheen to it, like a slick of oil. It lapped against the edges of Clary's boots as she opened the silver box she was holding. Inside it were ashes, powdery and gray, flecked with bits of charred bone. Among the ashes lay the Morgenstern ring, glimmering and silver. It had been on a chain around Jonathan's throat when he had been burned, and it remained, untouched and unharmed by the fire.

"I never had a brother," she said. "Not really."

She felt Jace place his hand on her back, between her shoulder blades. "You did," he said. "You had Simon. He was your brother in all the ways that matter. He watched you grow up, defended you, fought with and for you, cared about you all your life. He was the brother you chose. Even if he's ... gone now, no one and nothing can take that away from you."

Clary took a deep breath and flung the box as far as she could. It flew far, over the rainbow water, black ashes arcing out behind it like the plume of a jet plane, and the ring fell along with it, turning over and over, sending out silver sparks as it fell and fell and disappeared beneath the water.

"*Ave atque vale*," she said, speaking the full lines of the ancient poem. "*Ave atque vale in perpetuum, frater*. Hail and farewell forever, my brother."

The wind off the lake was cold; she felt it against her face, icy on her cheeks, and only then did she realize that she had been crying, and that her face was cold because it was wet with tears. She had wondered since she had found out that Jonathan was alive why her mother had cried on the day of his birth every year. Why cry, if she had hated him? But Clary understood now. Her mother had been crying for the child she would never have, for all the dreams that had been wrapped up in her imagination of having a son, her imagination of what that boy would be like. And she'd been crying for the bitter chance that had destroyed that child before he had ever been born. And so, as Jocelyn had for so many years, Clary stood at the side of the Mortal Mirror and wept for the brother she would never have, for the boy who had never been given the chance to live. And she wept as well for the others lost in the Dark War, and she wept for her mother and the loss she had endured, and she wept for Emma and the Blackthorns, remembering how they had fought back tears when she had told them that she had seen Mark in the tunnels of Faerie, and how he belonged to the Hunt now, and she wept for Simon and the hole in her heart where he had been, and the way she would miss him every day until she died, and she wept for herself and the changes that had been wrought in her, because sometimes even change for the better felt like a little death.

Jace stood by her side as she cried, and held her hand silently, until Jonathan's ashes had sunk under the water's surface without a trace.

"Don't eavesdrop," said Julian.

Emma glared at him. All right, so she could hear the raised voices through the thick wood of the Consul's office door, now shut but for a crack. And maybe she *had* been leaning toward the door, tantalized by the fact that she could hear the voices, could nearly make them out, but not quite. So? Wasn't it better to know things than to not know them?

She mouthed "So what?" at Julian, who raised his eyebrows

at her. Julian didn't exactly *like* rules, but he obeyed them. Emma thought rules were for breaking, or bending at the very least.

Plus, she was bored. They had been led to the door and left there by one of the Council members, at the end of the long corridor that stretched nearly the length of the Gard. Tapestries hung all around the office entrance, threadbare from the passing of years. Most of them showed passages from Shadowhunter history: the Angel rising from the lake with the Mortal Instruments, the Angel passing the Gray Book to Jonathan Shadowhunter, the First Accords, the Battle of Shanghai, the Council of Buenos Aires. There was another tapestry as well, this one looking newer and freshly hung, which showed the Angel rising out of the lake, this time without the Mortal Instruments. A blond man stood at the edge of the lake, and near him, almost invisible, was the figure of a slight girl with red hair, holding a stele...

"There'll be a tapestry about you someday," said Jules.

Emma flicked her eyes over to him. "You have to do something really big to get a tapestry about you. Like win a war."

"You could win a war," he said confidently. Emma felt a little tightening around her heart. When Julian looked at her like that, like she was brilliant and amazing, it made the missing-her-parents ache in her heart a little less. There was something about having someone care about you like that that made you feel like you could never be totally alone.

Unless they decided to take her away from Jules, of course. Move her to Idris, or to one of the Institutes where she had distant relatives—in England, or China or Iran. Suddenly panicked, she took out her stele and carved an audio rune into her arm before pressing her ear to the wood of the door, ignoring Julian's glare.

The voices immediately came clear. She recognized Jia's first, and then the second after a beat: The Consul was talking to Luke Garroway.

"... Zachariah? He is no longer an active Shadowhunter," Jia was saying. "He left today before the meeting, saying he had some loose ends to tie up, and then an urgent appointment in London in early January, something he couldn't miss."

Luke murmured an answer Emma didn't hear; she hadn't known Zachariah was leaving, and wished she could have thanked him for the help he'd given them the night of the battle. And asked him how he'd known her middle name was Cordelia.

She leaned in more closely to the door, and heard Luke, halfway through a sentence. "... should tell you first," he was saying. "I'm planning to step down as representative. Maia Roberts will take my place."

Jia made a surprised noise. "Isn't she a little young?"

"She's very capable," said Luke. "She hardly needs my endorsement—"

"No," Jia agreed. "Without her warning before Sebastian's attack, we would have lost many more Shadowhunters than we did."

"And as she'll be leading the New York pack from now on, it makes more sense for her to be your representative than for me." He sighed. "Besides, Jia. I've lost my sister. Jocelyn lost her son—again. And Clary's still devastated over what happened with Simon. I'd like to be there for my daughter."

Jia made an unhappy noise. "Maybe I shouldn't have let her try to call him."

"She had to know," said Luke. "It's a loss. She has to come to terms with it. She has to grieve. I'd like to be there to help her through it. I'd like to get married. I'd like to be there for my family. I need to step away."

"Well, you have my blessing, of course," she said. "Though I could have used your help in reopening the Academy. We have lost so many. It has been a long time since death undid so many Nephilim. We must reach out into the mundane world, find those who might

Ascend, teach and train them. There will be a great deal to do."

"And many to help you do it." Luke's tone was inflexible.

Jia sighed. "I'll welcome Maia, no fear. Poor Magnus, surrounded by women."

"I doubt he'll mind or notice," said Luke. "Though, I should say that you know he was right, Jia. Abandoning the search for Mark Blackthorn, sending Helen Blackthorn to Wrangel Island—that was unconscionable cruelty."

There was a pause, and then, "I know," said Jia in a low voice. "You think I don't know what I did to my own daughter? But letting Helen stay—I saw the hate in the eyes of my own Shadowhunters, and I was afraid for Helen. Afraid for Mark, should we be able to find him."

"Well, I saw the devastation in the eyes of the Blackthorn children," said Luke.

"Children are resilient."

"They've lost their brother and their father, and now you're leaving them to be raised by an uncle they've seen only a few times—"

"They will come to know him; he is a good man. Diana Wrayburn has requested the position of their tutor as well, and I am inclined to give it to her. She was impressed by their bravery—"

"But she isn't their mother. My mother left when I was a child," Luke said. "She became an Iron Sister. Cleophas. I never saw her again. Amatis raised me. I don't know what I would have done without her. She was—all I had."

Emma glanced quickly over at Julian to see if he'd heard. She didn't think he had; he wasn't looking at her but was staring off into nothing, blue-green eyes as distant as the ocean they resembled. She wondered if he was remembering the past or fearing for the future; she wished she could rewind the clock, get her parents back, give Jules back his father and Helen and Mark, unbreak what was broken.

"I'm sorry about Amatis," said Jia. "And I am worried about the Blackthorn children, believe me. But we have always had orphans; we're Nephilim. You know that as well as I do. As for the Carstairs girl, she will be brought to Idris; I'm worried she might be a little headstrong—"

Emma shoved the door of the office open; it gave much more easily than she had anticipated, and she half-fell inside. She heard Jules give a startled yelp and then follow her, grabbing at the back of the belt on her jeans to pull her upright. "No!" she said.

Both Jia and Luke looked at her in surprise: Jia's mouth partly open, Luke beginning to crack a smile. "A little?" he said.

"Emma Carstairs," Jia began, rising to her feet, "how dare you—"

"How dare *you*." And Emma was utterly surprised that it was Julian who had spoken, his verdigris eyes blazing. In five seconds he had turned from worried boy to furious young man, his brown hair standing out wildly as if it were angry too. "How dare you shout at Emma when you're the one who promised. You promised the Clave would never abandon Mark while he was living—*you promised!*"

Jia had the grace to look ashamed. "He is one of the Wild Hunt now," she said. "They are neither the dead nor the living."

"So you knew," said Julian. "You knew when you promised that it didn't mean anything."

"It meant saving Idris," said Jia. "I am sorry. We needed the two of you, and I..." She sounded as if she were choking out the words. "I would have fulfilled the promise if I could. If there were any way—if it could be done—I would see it done."

"Then you owe us," Emma said, planting her feet firmly in front of the Consul's desk. "You owe us a broken promise. So you have to do *this* now."

"Do what?" Jia looked bewildered.

"I won't be moved to Idris. I won't. I belong in Los Angeles."

Emma felt Jules freeze up behind her. "Of course they're not moving you to Idris," he said. "What are you talking about?"

Emma pointed an accusing finger at Jia. "She said it."

"Absolutely not," Julian said. "Emma lives in L.A.; it's her *home*. She can stay at the Institute. That's what Shadowhunters *do*. The Institute is supposed to be a refuge."

"Your uncle will be running the Institute," said Jia. "It's up to him."

"What did he say?" Julian demanded, and behind those four words were a wealth of feeling. When Julian loved people, he loved them forever; when he hated them, he hated them forever. Emma had the feeling the question of whether he was going to hate his uncle forever hung in the balance at exactly this moment.

"He said he would take her in," Jia said. "But really, I think there's a place for Emma at the Shadowhunter Academy here in Idris. She's exceptionally talented, she'd be surrounded by the best instructors, there are many other students there who've suffered losses and could help her with her grief—"

Her grief. Emma's mind suddenly swam through images: the photos of her parents' bodies on the beach, covered in markings. The Clave's clear lack of interest in what had happened to them. Her father bending to kiss her before he walked off to the car where her mother waited. Their laughter on the wind.

"*I've* suffered losses," Julian said through clenched teeth. "I can help her."

"You're twelve," said Jia, as if that answered everything.

"I won't be always!" Julian shouted. "Emma and I, we've known each other all our lives. She's like—she's like—"

"We're going to be *parabatai*," said Emma suddenly, before Julian could say that she was like his sister. For some reason she didn't want to hear that.

Everyone's eyes snapped wide open, including Julian's.

"Julian asked me, and I said yes," she said. "We're twelve; we're old enough to make the decision."

Luke's eyes sparked as he looked at her. "You can't split up *parabatai*," he said. "It's against the Clave's Law."

"We need to be able to train together," Emma said. "To take the examinations together, to do the ritual together—"

"Yes, yes, I understand," said Jia. "Very well. Your uncle doesn't mind, Julian, if Emma lives in the Institute, and the institution of *parabatai* trumps all other considerations." She looked from Emma to Julian, whose eyes were shining. He looked happy, actually happy, for the first time in so long that Emma nearly couldn't remember the last time she'd seen him smile like that. "You're sure?" the Consul added. "Becoming *parabatai* is serious business, nothing to be undertaken lightly. It's a commitment. You'll have to look out for each other, protect each other, care for the other one more than you care for yourself."

"We already do," said Julian confidently. It took Emma a moment more to speak. She was still seeing her parents in her head. Los Angeles held the answers to what had happened to them. Answers she needed. If no one ever avenged their deaths, it would be as if they had never lived at all.

And it wasn't as if she didn't want to be Jules's *parabatai*. The thought of a whole life spent without ever being separated from him, a promise that she would never be alone, trumped the voice in the back of her head that whispered: *Wait...*

She nodded firmly. "Absolutely," she said. "We're absolutely sure."

Idris had been green and gold and russet in the autumn, when Clary had first been there. It had a stark grandeur in the late winter, so close to Christmas: The mountains rose in the distance, capped white with snow, and the trees along the side of the road that led back to Alicante from the lake were stripped bare, their leafless branches making lacelike patterns against the bright sky.

They rode without haste, Wayfarer treading lightly along the path, Clary behind Jace, her arms clasped around his torso. Sometimes he would slow the horse to point out the manor houses of the richer Shadowhunter families, hidden from the road when the trees were full but revealed now. She felt his shoulders tense as they passed one whose ivy-covered stones nearly melded with the forest around it. It had clearly been burned to the ground and rebuilt. "Blackthorn manor," he said. "Which means that around this bend in the road is..." He paused as Wayfarer summited a small hill, and then Jace reined him in so they could look down to where the road split in two. One direction led back toward Alicante—Clary could see the demon towers in the distance—while the other curled down toward a large building of mellow golden stone, surrounded by a low wall. "Herondale manor," Jace finished.

The wind picked up; icy, it ruffled Jace's hair. Clary had her hood up, but he was bareheaded and bare-handed, having said he hated wearing gloves when horseback riding. He liked to feel the reins in his hands. "Did you want to go and look at it?" she asked.

His breath came out in a white cloud. "I'm not sure."

She pressed closer to him, shivering. "Are you worried about missing the Council meeting?" She had been, though they were returning to New York tomorrow and there had been no other time she could think of to secretly lay her brother's ashes to rest; it was Jace who had suggested taking the horse from the stables and riding to Lake Lyn when nearly everyone else in Alicante was sure to be in the Accords Hall. Jace understood what it meant to her to bury the idea of her brother, though it would have been hard to explain to almost anyone else.

He shook his head. "We're too young to vote. Besides, I think they can manage without us." He frowned. "We'd have to break in," he said. "The Consul told me that as long as I want to call myself Jace Lightwood, I've got no legal right to the Herondale properties. I don't even have a Herondale ring. One doesn't exist. The Iron Sisters would have to craft a new one. In fact, when I turn eighteen, I'll lose the right to the name entirely."

Clary sat still, holding on to his waist lightly. There were times when he wanted to be prompted and asked questions, and times when he didn't; this was one of the latter. He would get there on his own. She held him and breathed quietly until he suddenly tensed under her hold and dug his heels into Wayfarer's sides.

The horse headed down the path toward the manor house at a trot. The low gates—decorated with an iron motif of flying birds—were open, and the path opened out into a circular gravel drive, in the center of which was a stone fountain, now dry. Jace drew up in front of the wide steps that led up to the front door, and stared up at the blank windows.

"This is where I was born," he said. "This is where my mother died, and Valentine cut me out of her body. And Hodge took me and hid me, so no one would know. It was winter then, too."

"Jace..." She splayed her hands over his chest, feeling his heart beat under her fingers.

"I think I want to be a Herondale," he said abruptly.

"So be a Herondale."

"I don't want to betray the Lightwoods," he said. "They're my family. But I realized that if I don't take the Herondale name, it'll end with me."

"It's not your responsibility—"

"I know," he said. "In the box, the one Amatis gave me, there was a letter from my father to me. He wrote it before I was born. I read it a few times. The first times I read it, I just hated him, even though he said he loved me. But there were a few sentences I couldn't get rid of in my head. He said, *'I want you to be a better man than I was. Let no one else tell you who you are or should be.'"* He tipped his head back, as if he could read his future in the curl of the manor's eaves. "Changing your name, it doesn't change your nature. Look at Sebastian—Jonathan. Calling himself Sebastian didn't make any difference in the end. I wanted to spurn the Herondale name because I thought I hated my father, but I don't hate him. He might have been weak and have made the wrong decisions, but he knew it. There's no reason for me to hate him. And there have been generations of Herondales before him—it's a family that's done a lot of good—and to let their whole house fall just to get back at my father would be a waste."

"That's the first time I've heard you call him your father and sound like that," Clary said. "Usually you only say it about Valentine."

She felt him sigh, and then his hand covered hers where it lay on his chest. His fingers were cool, long and slender, so familiar, she would have known them in the dark. "We might live here someday," he said. "Together."

She smiled, knowing he couldn't see her, but unable to help it. "Think you can win me over with a fancy house?" she said. "Don't get ahead of yourself, Jace. Jace *Herondale*," she added, and wrapped her arms around him in the cold.

Alec sat at the edge of the roof, dangling his feet over the side. He supposed that if either of his parents came back to the house and looked up, they'd see him and he'd get shouted at, but he doubted Maryse or Robert would return soon. They'd been called to the Consul's office after the meeting and were probably still there. The new treaty with the Fair Folk would be hammered out over the next week, during which they'd stay in Idris, while the rest of the Lightwoods went back to New York and celebrated the New Year without them. Alec would, technically, be running the Institute for that week. He was surprised to find that he was actually looking forward to it.

Responsibility was a good way to take your mind off other things. Things like the way Jocelyn had looked when her son had died, or the way Clary had stifled her silent sobs against the floor when she'd realized that they'd come back from Edom, but without Simon. The way Magnus's face had looked, bleak with despair, as he'd said his father's name.

Loss was part of being a Shadowhunter, you expected it, but that didn't help the way Alec had felt when he'd seen Helen's expression in the Council Hall as she'd been exiled to Wrangel Island.

"You couldn't have done anything. Don't punish yourself." The voice behind him was familiar; Alec squeezed his eyes shut, trying to steady his breathing before he replied.

"How'd you get up here?" he asked. There was a rustle of fabric as Magnus settled himself down next to Alec at the edge of the roof. Alec chanced a sideways glance at him. He'd seen Magnus only twice, briefly, since they'd returned from Edom—once when the Silent Brothers had released them from quarantine, and once again today in the Council Hall. Neither time had they been able to talk. Alec looked him over with a yearning he suspected was poorly disguised. Magnus was back to his normal healthy color after the drained look he had had in Edom; his bruises were largely healed, and his eyes were bright again, glinting under the dimming sky.

Alec remembered throwing his arms around Magnus in the demon realm, when he'd found him chained up, and wondered why things like that were always so much easier to do when you thought you were about to die.

"I should have said something," Alec said. "I voted against sending her away."

"I know," said Magnus. "You and about ten other people. It was overwhelmingly in favor." He shook his head. "People get scared, and they take it out on anyone they think is different. It's the same cycle I've seen a thousand times."

"It makes me feel so useless."

"You're anything but useless." Magnus tipped his head back, his eyes searching the sky as the stars began to make their appearances, one by one. "You saved my life."

"In Edom?" Alec said. "I helped, but really—you saved your own life."

"Not just in Edom," Magnus said. "I was—I'm almost four hundred years old, Alexander. Warlocks, as they get older, they start to calcify. They stop being able to *feel* things. To care, to be excited or surprised. I always told myself that would never happen to me. That I'd try to be like Peter Pan, never grow up, always retain a sense of wonder. Always fall in love, be surprised, be open to being hurt as much as I was open to being happy. But over the last twenty years or so I've felt it creeping up on me anyway. There was nobody before you for a long time. Nobody I loved. No one who surprised me or took my breath away. Until you walked into that party, I was starting to think I'd never feel anything that strongly again."

Alec caught his breath and looked down at his hands. "What are you saying?" His voice was uneven. "That you want to get back together?"

"If you want to," Magnus said, and he actually sounded uncertain, enough that Alec looked at him in surprise. Magnus looked very young, his eyes wide and gold-green, his hair brushing his temples in wisps of black. "If you..."

Alec sat, frozen. For weeks he'd sat and daydreamed about Magnus saying these exact words, but now that Magnus was, it didn't feel the way he'd thought it would. There were no fireworks in his chest; he felt empty and cold. "I don't know," he said.

The light died out of Magnus's eyes. He said, "Well, I can understand that you—I wasn't very kind to you."

"No," Alec said bluntly. "You weren't, but I guess it's hard to break up with someone kindly. The thing is, I *am* sorry about what I did. I was wrong. Incredibly wrong. But the reason I did it, that isn't going to change. I can't go through my life feeling like I don't know you at all. You keep saying the past is the past, but the past made you who you are. I want to know about your life. And if you're not willing to tell me about it, then I shouldn't be with you. Because I know me, and I won't ever be okay with it. So I shouldn't put us both through that again."

Magnus pulled his knees up to his chest. In the darkening twilight he looked gangly against the shadows, all long legs and arms and thin fingers sparkling with rings. "I love you," he said quietly.

"Don't—" Alec said. "Don't. It's not fair. Besides—" He glanced away. "I doubt I'm the first one who ever broke your heart."

"My heart's been broken more times than the Clave's Law about Shadowhunters not engaging in romances with Downworlders," Magnus said, but his voice sounded brittle. "Alec … you're right."

Alec cut his eyes sideways. He didn't think he'd ever seen the warlock look so vulnerable.

"It's not fair to you," Magnus said. "I've always told myself I was going to be open to new experiences, and so when I started to—to harden—I was shocked. I thought I'd done everything right, not closed my heart off. And then I thought about what you said, and I realized why I was starting to die inside. If you never tell anyone the truth about yourself, eventually you start to forget. The love, the heartbreak, the joy, the despair, the things I did that were good, the things I did that were shameful—if I kept them all inside, my memories of them would start to disappear. And then I would disappear."

"I…" Alec wasn't sure what to say.

"I had a lot of time to think, after we broke up," Magnus said. "And I wrote this." He pulled a notebook out of the inside pocket of his jacket: just a very ordinary spiral-bound notebook of lined paper, but when the wind flapped it open, Alec could see that the pages were covered with thin, looping handwriting. Magnus's handwriting. "I wrote down my life."

Alec's eyes widened. "Your whole life?"

"Not all of it," Magnus said carefully. "But some of the incidents that have shaped me. How I first met Raphael, when he was very young," Magnus said, and sounded sad. "How I fell in love with Camille. The story of the Hotel Dumort, though Catarina had to help me with that. Some of my early loves, and some of my later ones. Names you might know—Herondale—"

"Will Herondale," said Alec. "Camille mentioned him." He took the notebook; the thin pages felt bumpy, as if Magnus had pressed the pen very hard into the paper while writing. "Were you ... *with* him?"

Magnus laughed and shook his head. "No—though, there are a lot of Herondales in the pages. Will's son, James Herondale, was remarkable, and so was James's sister, Lucie, but I have to say Stephen Herondale rather put me off the family until Jace came along. That guy was a pill." He noticed Alec staring at him, and added quickly, "No Herondales. No Shadowhunters at all, in fact."

"No Shadowhunters?"

"None in my heart like you are," Magnus said. He tapped the notebook lightly. "Consider this a first installment of everything I want to tell you. I wasn't sure, but I hoped—if you wanted to be with me, as I want to be with you, you might take this as evidence. Evidence that I am willing to give you something I have never given anyone: my past, the truth of myself. I want to share my life with you, and that means today, and the future, and all of my past, if you want it. If you want me."

Alec lowered the notebook. There was writing on the first page, a scrawled inscription: *Dear Alec...*

He could see the path in front of him very clearly: He could hand back the book, walk away from Magnus, find someone else, some Shadowhunter to love, be with him, share the kinship of predictable days and nights, the daily poetry of an ordinary life.

Or he could take the step out into nothingness and choose Magnus, the far stranger poetry of him, his brilliance and anger, his sulks and joys, the extraordinary abilities of his magic and the no less breathtaking magic of the extraordinary way he loved.

It was hardly a choice at all. Alec took a deep breath, and jumped.

"All right," he said.

Magnus whipped toward him in the dark, all coiled energy now, all cheekbones and shimmering eyes. "Really?"

"Really," Alec said. He reached out a hand, and interlinked his fingers with Magnus's. There was a glow being woken in Alec's chest, where all had been dark. Magnus cupped his long fingers under Alec's jawline and kissed him, his touch light against Alec's skin: a slow and gentle kiss, a kiss that promised more later, when they were no longer on a roof and could be seen by anyone walking by.

"So I'm your first ever Shadowhunter, huh?" Alec said when they separated at last.

"You're my first so many things, Alec Lightwood," Magnus said.

The sun was setting when Jace dropped Clary off at Amatis's house, kissed her, and headed back down the canal toward the Inquisitor's. Clary watched him walk away before turning back to the house with a sigh; she was glad they were leaving the next day.

There were things she loved about Idris. Alicante was still the loveliest city she had seen: Over the houses, now, she could see the sunset striking sparks off the clear tops of the demon towers. The rows of houses along the canal were softened by shadow, like velvet silhouettes. But it was heart-achingly sad being inside Amatis's house, knowing now, with certainty, that she would never come back to it.

Inside, the house was warm and dimly lit. Luke was sitting on the sofa, reading a book. Jocelyn was asleep beside him, curled up with a throw rug over her. Luke smiled at Clary as she came in, and he pointed toward the kitchen, making a bizarre gesture that Clary translated as an indication that there was food in there if she wanted it.

She nodded and tiptoed up the stairs, careful not to wake her mother. She went into her room, already pulling off her coat; it took her a moment to realize that there was someone else there.

The room was chilly, the cold air pouring in through the half-open window. On the windowsill sat Isabelle. She wore high boots zipped over jeans; her hair was loose, blowing slightly in the breeze. She looked over at Clary as she came into the room, and smiled tightly.

Clary went over to the window and pulled herself up beside Izzy. There was enough room for both of them, but barely; the toes of her shoes nudged up against Izzy's leg. She folded her hands over her knees and waited.

"Sorry," Isabelle said, finally. "I probably should have come in through the front door, but I didn't want to deal with your parents."

"Was everything okay at the Council meeting?" Clary asked. "Did something happen—"

Isabelle laughed shortly. "The faeries agreed to the Clave's terms."

"Well, that's good, right?"

"Maybe. Magnus didn't seem to think so." Isabelle exhaled. "It just—There were nasty pointy angry bits sticking out everywhere. It didn't seem like a victory. And they're sending Helen Blackthorn to Wrangel Island to 'study the wards.' Get that. They want to get her away because she's got faerie blood."

"That's horrible! What about Aline?"

"Aline's going with her. She told Alec," Isabelle said. "There's some uncle that's coming to take care of the Blackthorn kids and the girl—the one who likes you and Jace."

"Her name's Emma," Clary said, poking Isabelle's leg with her toe. "You could *try* to remember it. She did help us out."

"Yeah, it's a little hard for me to be grateful right now." Isabelle ran her hands down her denim-clad legs and took a deep breath. "I know there was no other way it could have played out. I keep trying to imagine one, but I can't think of anything. We had to go after Sebastian, and we had to get out of Edom or we all would have died anyway, but I just *miss* Simon. I miss him all the time, and I came here because you're the only one who misses him as much as I do."

Clary stilled. Isabelle was playing with the red stone at her throat, staring out the window with the sort of fixed stare Clary was familiar with. It was the kind of stare that said, *I'm trying not to cry*.

"I know," Clary said. "I miss him all the time too, just in a different way. It feels like waking up missing an arm or a leg, like there's something that's always been there that I relied on, and now it's gone."

Isabelle was still staring out the window. "Tell me about the phone call," she said.

"I don't know." Clary hesitated. "It was bad, Iz. I don't think you really want to—"

"*Tell me*," Isabelle said through her teeth, and Clary sighed and nodded.

It wasn't as if she didn't remember; every second of what had happened was burned into her brain.

It had been three days after they had come back, three days during which all of them had been quarantined. No Shadowhunter had survived a trip to a demon dimension before, and the Silent Brothers had wanted to be absolutely sure that they were carrying no dark magic with them. It had been three days of Clary screaming at the Silent Brothers that she wanted her stele, she wanted a Portal, she wanted to see Simon, she wanted someone to just *check* on him and make sure he was all right. She hadn't seen Isabelle or any of the others during those days, not even her mother or Luke, but they must have done their own fair share of screaming, because the moment they had all been cleared by the Brothers, a guard had appeared and guided Clary to the Consul's office.

Inside the office of the Consul, in the Gard on top of Gard Hill, was the only working telephone in Alicante.

It had been enchanted to work sometime around the turn of the century by the warlock Ragnor Fell, a little before the development of fire-messages. It had survived various attempts to remove it on the theory that it might disrupt the wards, as it had shown no sign of ever doing so.

The only other person in the room was Jia Penhallow, and she gestured for Clary to sit. "Magnus Bane has informed me about what happened with your friend Simon Lewis in the demon realms," she said. "I wished to say that I am so sorry for your loss."

"He isn't *dead*," Clary ground out through her teeth. "At least he isn't supposed to be. Has anyone bothered to check? Has anyone looked to see if he's all right?"

"Yes," Jia said, rather unexpectedly. "He is fine, living at his home with his mother and sister. He seems entirely well: no longer a vampire, of course, but simply a mundane leading a very ordinary life. He appears from observation to have no recollection of the Shadow World."

Clary flinched, then straightened up. "I want to talk to him."

Jia thinned her lips. "You know the Law. You cannot tell a mundane about the Shadow World unless he is in danger. You cannot reveal the truth, Clary. Magnus said the demon who freed you told you as much."

The demon who freed you. So Magnus hadn't mentioned it was his father—not that Clary blamed him. She wouldn't reveal his secret either. "I won't tell Simon anything, all right? I just want to hear his voice. I need to know he's okay."

Jia sighed and pushed the phone toward her. Clary grabbed it, wondering how you dialed out of Idris—how did they pay their phone bills?—then decided screw it, she was just going to dial as if she were in Brooklyn already. If that didn't work, she could ask for guidance.

To her surprise the phone rang, and was picked up almost immediately, the familiar voice of Simon's mother echoing down the line. "Hello?"

"Hello." The receiver almost slipped in Clary's hand; her palm was damp with sweat. "Is Simon there?"

"What? Oh, yes, he's in his room," said Elaine. "Can I tell him who's calling?"

Clary closed her eyes. "It's Clary."

There was a short silence, and then Elaine said, "I'm sorry, who?"

"Clary Fray." She tasted bitter metal in the back of her throat. "I—I go to Saint Xavier's. It's about our English homework."

"Oh! Well, all right, then," said Elaine. "I'll go get him." She put the phone down, and Clary waited, waited for the woman who had thrown Simon out of her house and called him a monster, had left him to throw up blood on his knees in the gutter, to go and see if he would pick up a phone call like a normal teenager.

It wasn't her fault. It was the Mark of Cain, acting on her without her knowledge, turning Simon into a Wanderer, cutting him away from his family, Clary told herself, but it didn't stop the burn of anger and anxiety flooding her veins. She heard Elaine's footsteps going away, the murmur of voices, more footsteps—

"Hello?" Simon's voice, and Clary almost dropped the phone. Her heart was pounding itself into pieces. She could picture him so clearly, skinny and brown-haired, propping himself against the table in the narrow hallway just past the Lewises' front door.

"Simon," she said. "Simon, it's me. It's Clary."

There was a pause. When he spoke again, he sounded bewildered. "I—Do we know each other?"

Each word felt like a nail being pounded into her skin. "We have English class together," she said, which was true enough in a way—they had had most of their classes together when Clary had still gone to mundane high school. "Mr. Price."

"Oh, right." He sounded not unfriendly; cheerful enough, but baffled. "I'm really sorry. I have a total mental block for faces and names. What's up? Mom said it was something about homework, but I don't think we have any homework tonight."

"Can I ask you something?" Clary said.

"About *A Tale of Two Cities*?" He sounded amused. "Look, I haven't read it yet. I like the more modern stuff. *Catch-22*, *The Catcher in the Rye*—anything with 'catch' in the title, I guess." He was flirting a little, Clary thought. He must have thought she'd called him up out of the blue because she thought he was cute. Some random girl at school whose name he didn't even know.

"Who's your best friend?" she asked. "Your best friend in the whole world?"

He was silent for a moment, then laughed. "I should have guessed this was about Eric," he said. "You know, if you wanted his phone number, you could have just asked him—"

Clary hung the phone up and sat staring at it as if it were a poisonous snake. She was aware of Jia's voice, asking her if she was all right, asking what had happened, but she didn't answer, just set her jaw, absolutely determined not to cry in front of the Consul.

"You don't think maybe he was just faking it?" Isabelle said now. "Pretending he didn't know who you were, you know, because it would be dangerous?"

Clary hesitated. Simon's voice had been so blithe, so banal, so *completely ordinary*. Nobody could fake that. "I'm totally sure," she said. "He doesn't remember us. He can't."

Izzy looked away from the window, and Clary could clearly see the tears standing in her eyes. "I want to tell you something," Isabelle said. "And I don't want you to hate me."

"I couldn't hate you," Clary said. "Not possible."

"It's almost worse," Isabelle said. "Than if he were dead. If he were dead, I could grieve, but I don't know what to think—he's safe, he's alive, I should be grateful. He isn't a vampire anymore, and he *hated* being a vampire. I should be happy. But I'm not happy. He told me he loved me. He told me he loved me, Clary, and now he doesn't even know who I am. If I were standing in front of him, he wouldn't recognize my face. It feels like I never mattered. None of it ever mattered or ever happened. He never loved me at all." She swiped angrily at her face. "I *hate* it!" she broke out suddenly. "I hate this feeling, like there's something sitting on my chest."

"Missing someone?"

"Yes," Isabelle said. "I never thought I'd feel it about some *boy*."

"Not some boy," Clary said. "Simon. And he did love you. And it did matter. Maybe he doesn't remember, but you do. I do. The Simon who's living in Brooklyn now, that's Simon the way he used to be six months ago. And that's not a terrible thing. He was wonderful. But he changed when you knew him: He got stronger, and he got hurt, and he was different. And *that* Simon was the one you fell in love with and who fell in love with you, so you are grieving, because he's gone. But you can keep him alive a little by remembering him. We both can."

Isabelle made a choking sound. "I *hate* losing people," she said, and there was a savage edge to her voice: the desperation of someone who had lost too much, too young. "I hate it."

Clary put her hand out and took Izzy's—her thin right hand, the one with the Voyance rune stretched across her knuckles. "I know," Clary said. "But remember the people you've gained, too. I've gained you. I'm grateful for that." She pressed Izzy's hand, hard, and for a moment there was no response. Then Isabelle's fingers tightened on hers. They sat in silence on the windowsill, their hands locked across the distance between them.

Maia sat on the couch in the apartment—her apartment now. Being pack leader paid a small salary, and she had decided to use it for rent, to keep what once had been Jordan and Simon's place, keep their things from being thrown into the street by an angry, evicting landlord. Eventually she would go through their belongings, pack up what she could, sort through the memories. Exorcise the ghosts.

For today, though, she was content to sit and look at what had arrived for her from Idris in a small package from Jia Penhallow. The Consul hadn't thanked her for the warning she'd been given, though she had welcomed her as the new and permanent leader of the New York pack. Her tone had been cool and distant. But wrapped in the letter was a bronze seal, the seal of the head of the Praetor Lupus, the seal with which the Scott family had always signed their letters. It had been retrieved from the ruins on Long Island. There was a small note attached, with two words written on it in Jia's careful hand.

Begin again.

"You're going to be all right. I promise."

It was probably the six hundredth time Helen had said the same thing, Emma thought. It would probably have helped more if she didn't sound like she was trying to convince herself.

Helen was nearly finished packing the belongings that she had brought with her to Idris. Uncle Arthur (he had told Emma to call him that too) had promised to send on the rest. He was waiting downstairs with Aline to escort Helen to the Gard, where she would take the Portal to Wrangel Island; Aline would follow her the next week, after the last of the treaties and votes in Alicante.

It all sounded boring and complicated and horrible to Emma. All she knew was that she was sorry for ever having thought that Helen and Aline were soppy. Helen didn't seem soppy to her at all now, just sad, her eyes red-rimmed and her hands shaking as she zipped up her bag and turned to the bed.

It was an enormous bed, big enough for six people. Julian was sitting up against the headboard on one side, and Emma was on the other. You could have fit the rest of the family between them, Emma thought, but Dru, the twins, and Tavvy were asleep in their rooms. Dru and Livvy were cried out; Tiberius had accepted the news of Helen's departure with wide-eyed confusion, as if he didn't know what was happening or how he was expected to respond. At the last he'd shaken her hand and solemnly wished her good luck, as if she were a colleague leaving on a business trip. She'd burst into tears. "Oh, Ty," she'd said, and he'd slunk away, looking horrified.

Helen knelt down now, bringing herself almost eye level with Jules where he sat on the bed. "Remember what I said, okay?"

"We're going to be all right," Julian parroted.

Helen squeezed his hand. "I hate leaving you," she said. "I'd take care of you if I could. You know that, right? I'd take over the Institute. I love you all so much."

Julian squirmed in the manner that only a twelve-year-old boy could squirm upon hearing the word "love."

"I know," he managed.

"The only reason I can leave is that I'm sure I'm leaving you all in good hands," she said, her eyes boring into his.

"Uncle Arthur, you mean?"

"I mean you," she said, and Jules's eyes widened. "I know it's a lot to ask," she added. "But I also know I can depend on you. I know you can help Dru with her nightmares, and take care of Livia and Tavvy, and maybe even Uncle Arthur could do that too. He's a nice enough man. Absentminded, but he seems to want to try..." Her voice trailed off. "But Ty is—" She sighed. "Ty is special. He ... translates the world differently from how the rest of us do. Not everyone can speak his language, but you can. Take care of him for me, all right? He's going to be something amazing. We just have to keep the Clave from understanding how special he is. They don't like people who are different," she finished, and there was bitterness in her tone.

Julian was sitting up straight now, looking worried. "Ty hates me," he said. "He fights me all the time."

"Ty *loves* you," said Helen. "He sleeps with that bee you gave him. He watches you all the time. He wants to be like you. He's just—it's hard," she finished, not sure how to say what she wanted to: that Ty was jealous of the way Julian so easily navigated the world, so easily made people love him, that what Julian did every day without thinking seemed to Ty like a magic trick. "Sometimes it's hard when you want to be like someone but you don't know how."

A sharp furrow of confusion appeared between Julian's brows, but he looked up at Helen and nodded. "I'll take care of Ty," he said. "I promise."

"Good." Helen stood up and kissed Julian quickly on the top of his head. "Because he's amazing and special. You all are." She smiled over his head at Emma. "You, too, Emma," she said, and her voice tightened on Emma's name, as if she were going to cry. She closed her eyes, hugged Julian one more time, and fled out of the room, grabbing her suitcase and coat as she went. Emma could hear her running downstairs, and then the front door closing amid a murmur of voices.

Emma looked over at Julian. He was sitting rigidly upright, his chest rising and falling as if he'd been running. She reached over quickly and took his hand, traced onto the inside of his palm: W-H-A-T-S W-R-O-N-G?

"You heard Helen," he said in a low voice. "She trusts me to take care of them. Dru, Tavvy, Livvy, Ty. My whole family, basically. I'm going to be—I'm twelve, Emma, and I'm going to have four kids!"

Anxiously she started to write: N-O Y-O-U W-O-N-T—

"You don't have to do that," he interrupted. "It's not like there are any parents to overhear us." It was an unusually bitter thing for Jules to say, and Emma swallowed hard.

"I know," she said finally. "But I like having a secret language with you. I mean, who else can we talk about this stuff with, if we don't talk to each other?"

He slumped down against the headboard, turning to face her. "The truth is, I don't know Uncle Arthur at all. I've only seen him at holidays. I know Helen says she does and he's great and fine and everything, but they're *my* brothers and sisters. I know them. He doesn't." He curled his hands into fists. "I'll take care of them. I'll make sure they have everything they want and nothing ever gets taken away from them again."

Emma reached for his arm, and this time he gave it to her, letting his eyes fall half-closed as she wrote on the inside of his wrist with her index finger.

I-L-L H-E-L-P Y-O-U.

He smiled at her, but she could see the tension behind his eyes. "I know you will," he said. He reached his hand out and clasped it around hers. "You know the last thing Mark said to me before he was taken?" he asked, leaning against the headboard. He looked absolutely exhausted. "He said, 'Stay with Emma.' So we'll stay with each other. Because that's what *parabatai* do."

Emma felt as if the breath had been pulled out of her lungs. *Parabatai*. It was a big word—for Shadowhunters, one of the biggest, encompassing one of the most intense emotions you could ever have, the most significant commitment you could ever make to another person that wasn't about romantic love or marriage.

She had wanted to tell Jules when they got back to the house, had wanted to tell him somehow that when she had burst out with the words in the Consul's office that they were going to be *parabatai* bonded, it had been about more than wanting to be his *parabatai*. *Tell him*, said a little voice in her head. *Tell him you did it because you needed to stay in Los Angeles; tell him you did it because you need to be there to find out what happened to your parents. To get revenge.*

"Julian," she said softly, but he didn't move. His eyes were closed, his dark lashes feathering against his cheeks. The moonlight coming in through the window outlined him in white and silver. The bones of his face were already beginning to sharpen, to lose the softness of childhood. She could suddenly imagine how he was going to look when he was older, broader and rangier, a grown-up Julian. He was going to be so handsome, she thought; girls would be all over him, and one of them would take him away from her forever, because Emma was his *parabatai*, and that meant she could never be one of those girls now. She could never love him like that.

Jules murmured and shifted in his fitful sleep. His arm was stretched out toward her, his fingers not quite touching her shoulder. His sleeve was rucked up to his elbow. She reached out her hand and carefully scrawled on the bare skin of his forearm, where the skin was pale and tender, unmarked yet by any scars.

I-M S-O S-O-R-R-Y J-U-L-E-S, she wrote, and then sat back, holding her breath, but he didn't feel it, and he didn't wake up.

EPILOGUE:
THE BEAUTY
OF A THOUSAND STARS

May 2008

The air was beginning to show the first warm promise of sum-
mer: The sun shone, hot and bright, down on the corner of Carroll
Street and Sixth Avenue, and the trees that lined the brownstoned
block were thick with green leaves.

Clary had stripped off her light jacket on the way out of the subway, and stood in her jeans and tank top across from the entrance
to St. Xavier's, watching as the doors opened and the students
streamed out onto the pavement.

Isabelle and Magnus lounged against the tree opposite her,
Magnus in a velvet jacket and jeans and Isabelle in a short silver
party dress that showed her Marks. Clary supposed her own Marks
were pretty visible too: all up and down her arms, at her belly where
the tank top rode up, on the back of her neck. Some permanent,
some temporary. All of them marking her out as different—not just
different from the students milling around the school's entrance,
exchanging their good-byes for the day, making plans to walk to the

park or to meet up later at Java Jones, but different from the self she had once been. The self who had been one of them.

An older woman with a poodle and a pillbox hat was whistling her way down the street in the sunshine. The poodle waddled over to the tree where Isabelle and Magnus were leaning; the old woman paused, whistling. Isabelle, Clary, and Magnus were completely invisible to her.

Magnus gave the poodle a ferocious glare, and it backed off with a whimper, half-dragging its owner down the street. Magnus looked after them. "Invisibility glamours do have their drawbacks," he remarked.

Isabelle quirked a smile, which disappeared almost immediately. Her voice when she spoke was tight with repressed feeling. "There he is."

Clary's head snapped up. The school doors had opened again, and three boys had stepped out onto the front stairs. She recognized them even from across the street. Kirk, Eric, and Simon. Nothing had changed about Eric or Kirk; she felt the Farsighted rune on her arm spark as her eyes skipped over them. She stared at Simon, drinking in every detail.

It had been December when she'd seen him last, pale and dirty and bloody in the demon realm. Now he was aging, getting older, no longer frozen in time. His hair had gotten longer. It fell over his forehead, down the back of his neck. He had color in his cheeks. He stood with one foot up on the bottom step of the stairs, his body thin and angular as always, maybe a little more filled out than she had remembered him. He wore a faded blue shirt he'd had for years. He pushed up the frames of his square-rimmed glasses as he gestured animatedly with his other hand, in which he held a wad of rolled-up papers.

Without taking her eyes off him, Clary fumbled her stele out of her pocket and drew on her arm, canceling out her glamour runes.

She heard Magnus mutter something about being more careful. If anyone had been looking, they would have seen her suddenly pop into existence in between the trees. Nobody seemed to be, though, and Clary stuffed the stele back into her pocket. Her hand was shaking.

"Good luck," Isabelle said without asking her what she was doing. Clary supposed it was obvious. Isabelle was still leaning back against the tree; she looked drawn and tense, her back very straight. Magnus was busy twirling a blue topaz ring on his left hand; he just winked at Clary as she stepped off the curb.

Isabelle would never go talk to Simon, Clary thought, starting across the street. She would never risk the blank look, the lack of recognition. She would never endure the evidence that she had been forgotten. Clary wondered if she wasn't some kind of masochist, to throw herself into the path of it herself.

Kirk had wandered off, but Eric saw her before Simon did; she tensed for a moment, but it was clear his memory of her had been wiped away too. He gave her a confused, appreciative look, clearly wondering if she was heading toward him. She shook her head and pointed her chin at Simon; Eric raised an eyebrow and gave Simon a *Later, man* clap on the shoulder before making himself scarce.

Simon turned to look at Clary, and she felt it like a punch to the stomach. He was smiling, brown hair blowing across his face. He used his free hand to push it back.

"Hi," she said, coming to a stop in front of him. "Simon."

Dark brown eyes shadowed by confusion, he stared at her. "Do I—Do we know each other?"

She swallowed back the sudden bitter tang in her mouth. "We used to be friends," she said, and then clarified: "It was a long time ago. Kindergarten."

Simon raised a doubtful eyebrow. "I must have been a really charming six-year-old, if you still remember me."

"I do remember you," she said. "I remember your mom, Elaine, and your sister, Rebecca, too. Rebecca used to let us play with her Hungry Hungry Hippos game, but you ate all the marbles."

Simon had gone a little pale under his slight tan. "How do you—that did happen, but I was alone," he said, his voice shading past bewilderment into something else.

"No, you weren't." She searched his eyes, willing him to remember, remember *something*. "I'm telling you, we were friends."

"I'm just ... I guess I don't ... remember," he said slowly, though there were shadows, a darkness in his already dark eyes, that made her wonder.

"My mom's getting married," she said. "Tonight. I'm on my way there, actually."

He rubbed at his temple with his free hand. "And you need a date to the wedding?"

"No. I have one." She couldn't tell if he looked disappointed or just more confused, as if the only logical reason he could imagine for her to be talking to him had disappeared. She could feel her cheeks burning. Somehow embarrassing herself like this was harder than facing down a gaggle of Husa demons in Glick Park. (She ought to know; she'd done it the night before.) "I just—you and my mom used to be close. I thought you should know. It's an important day, and if things were right, then you would have been there."

"I..." Simon swallowed. "I'm sorry?"

"It's not your fault," she said. "It never was your fault. Not any of it." She leaned up on her tiptoes, the back of her eyelids burning, and kissed him quickly on the cheek. "Be happy," she said, and turned away. She could see the blurred figures of Isabelle and Magnus, waiting for her across the street.

"Wait!"

She turned. Simon had hurried after her. He was holding

something out. A flyer he'd pulled from the rolled stack he was carrying. "My band…" he said, half-apologetically. "You should come to a show, maybe. Sometime."

She took the flyer with a silent nod, and dashed back across the street. She could feel him staring after her, but she couldn't bear to turn around and see the look on his face: half confusion and half pity.

Isabelle detached herself from the tree as Clary hurtled toward them. Clary slowed down just enough to retrieve her stele and slash the glamour rune back onto her arm; it hurt, but she welcomed the sting. "You were right," she said to Magnus. "That was pointless."

"I didn't say it was pointless." He spread his hands wide. "I said he wouldn't remember you. I said you should do it only if you were okay with that."

"I'll *never* be okay with it," Clary snapped, and then took a deep, hard breath. "I'm sorry," she said. "I'm sorry. It's not your fault, Magnus. And, Izzy—that can't have been fun for you, either. Thank you for coming with me."

Magnus shrugged. "No need to apologize, biscuit."

Isabelle's dark eyes scanned Clary quickly; she reached out a hand. "What's that?"

"Band flyer," Clary said, and shoved it toward Isabelle. Izzy took it with an arched eyebrow. "I can't look at it. I used to help him Xerox those and pass them out—" She winced. "Never mind. Maybe I'll be glad we came, later." She gave a wobbly smile, shrugging her jacket back on. "I'm heading out. I'll see you guys at the farmhouse."

Isabelle watched Clary go, a small figure making its way up the street, unnoticed by other pedestrians. Then she glanced down at the flyer in her hand.

SIMON LEWIS,
ERIC HILLCHURCH, KIRK DUPLESSE,
AND MATT CHARLTON

"THE MORTAL INSTRUMENTS"

MAY 19, PROSPECT PARK
BAND SHELL

BRING THIS FLYER,
GET $5 OFF YOUR ENTRANCE FEE!

Isabelle's breath hitched in her throat. "*Magnus.*"

He had been watching Clary too; he glanced over now, and his glance fell on the flyer. They both stared at it.

Magnus whistled between his teeth. "The Mortal Instruments?"

"His band name." The paper shook in Isabelle's hand. "Okay, Magnus, we *have* to—you said if he remembered *anything*—"

Magnus glanced after Clary, but she was long gone. "All right," he said. "But if it doesn't work, if he doesn't want it, we can never tell her."

Isabelle was crumpling the paper in her fist, already reaching for her stele with her other hand. "Whatever you say. But we have to at least try."

Magnus nodded, shadows chasing shadows in his gold-green eyes. Isabelle could tell he was worried about her, afraid that she'd be hurt, disappointed, and she wanted to be angry at him and grateful to him all at once. "We will."

It had been another weird day, Simon thought. First the lady behind the counter in Java Jones who'd asked him where his friend was, the pretty girl who always came in with him and always ordered her coffee black. Simon had stared—he didn't really have any close girl friends, certainly no one whose coffee preferences he might be expected to know. When he'd told the barista she must have been thinking of someone else, she'd looked at him like he was crazy.

And then the redheaded girl who'd come up to him on the steps of St. Xavier's.

The front of the school was deserted now. Eric had been supposed to give Simon a ride home, but he'd disappeared when the girl had come up to Simon, and he hadn't reappeared. It was nice that Eric thought he could pick up ladies with such blithe ease, Simon thought, but annoying when it meant he was going to have to take the subway home.

Simon hadn't even thought about trying to hit on her, not really. She'd seemed so fragile, despite the fairly badass tattoos that decorated her arms and collarbone. Maybe she *was* crazy—the evidence pointed that way—but her green eyes had been huge and sad when she'd looked at him; he'd been reminded of the way he'd looked himself, the day of his father's funeral. Like something had punched a hole right through his rib cage and squeezed his heart. Loss like that—no, she hadn't been hitting on him. She'd really believed they'd meant something important to each other, once.

Maybe he *had* known that girl, he thought. Maybe it was something he'd forgotten—who remembered the friends you had in kindergarten? And yet he couldn't shake an image of her, not looking sad but smiling over her shoulder at him, something in her hand— a drawing? He shook his head in frustration. The image was gone like a silver-quick fish slipping off a line.

He cast his mind back, desperately trying to remember. He found himself doing that a lot lately. Bits of memories would come to him, fragments of poetry he didn't know how he'd learned, glancing recollections of voices, dreams he'd wake up from shaking and sweating and unable to recall what had happened in them. Dreams of desert landscapes, of echoes, the taste of blood, a bow and arrow in his hands. (He'd learned archery in summer camp, but he'd never cared *that* much about it, so why was he dreaming about it now?) Not being able to get back to sleep, the aching sense that there was something missing, he didn't know what but *something*, like a weight in the middle of his chest. He'd put it down to too many late-night D&D campaigns, junior year stress, and worrying about colleges. As his mother said, once you started worrying about the future, you started obsessing about the past.

"Anyone sitting here?" said a voice. Simon looked up and saw a tall man with spiky black hair standing over him. He wore a velvet prep school blazer with a crest emblazoned on it in glittering thread, and at least a dozen rings. There was something odd about his features…

"What? I, uh. No," Simon said, wondering how many strangers were going to accost him today. "You can sit, if you want."

The man glanced down and made a face. "I see that many pigeons have pooped upon these stairs," he remarked. "I shall remain standing, if that's not too rude."

Simon shook his head mutely.

"I'm Magnus." He smiled, showing blinding white teeth. "Magnus Bane."

"Are we long-lost friends, by any chance?" Simon said. "Just wondering."

"No, we never got along all that well," said Magnus. "Long-lost acquaintances? Compadres? My cat liked you."

Simon scrubbed his hands over his face. "I think I'm going crazy," he remarked, to no one in particular.

"Well, then, you should be all right with what I'm about to tell you." Magnus turned his head slightly to the side. "Isabelle?"

Out of nowhere, a girl appeared. Maybe the most beautiful girl Simon had ever seen. She had long black hair that spilled over a silver dress and made him want to write bad songs about starry nights. She also had tattoos: the same ones the other girl had sported, black and swirling, covering her arms and bare legs.

"Hello, Simon," she said.

Simon just stared. It was entirely out of the realm of anything he had ever imagined that a girl who looked like *this* would ever say his name like *that*. Like it was the only name that mattered. His brain sputtered to a stop like an old car. "Mgh?" he said.

Magnus held out a long-fingered hand, and the girl placed something into it. A book, bound in white leather with the title stamped on it in gold. Simon couldn't quite see the words, but they were etched in an elegant calligraphic hand. "This," Magnus said, "is a book of spells."

There didn't seem to be a response for that, so Simon didn't try for one.

"The world is full of magic," said Magnus, and his eyes were sparkling. "Demons and angels, werewolves and faeries and vampires. You knew all this, once. You had magic, but it was taken from you. The idea was that you would live out the rest of your life without it, without remembering it. That you would forget the people you loved, if they knew about magic. That you would spend the rest of your life ordinary." He turned the book over in his slim fingers, and Simon caught sight of a title in Latin. Something about the sight sent a zing of energy through his body. "And there's something to be said for that, for being relieved of the burden of greatness. Because you were great, Simon. You were a Daylighter, a warrior. You saved lives and slew demons, and the blood of angels rocketed through your veins like sunlight." Magnus was grinning now, a little manically. "And I don't know, it just strikes me as a little fascist to take all that away."

Isabelle tossed her dark hair back. Something glittered at the hollow of her throat. A red ruby. Simon felt the same zing of energy, stronger this time, as if his body were yearning toward something his mind couldn't recall. "Fascist?" she echoed.

"Yes," Magnus said. "Clary was born special. Simon here had specialness thrust upon him. He adapted. Because the world isn't divided into the special and the ordinary. Everyone has the potential to be extraordinary. As long as you have a soul and free will, you can be anything, do anything, choose anything. Simon should get to choose."

Simon swallowed against his dry throat. "I'm sorry," he said. "But what are you talking about?"

Magnus tapped the book in his hand. "I've been searching for a way out of this spell, this curse on you," he said, and Simon almost protested that he wasn't cursed, but subsided. "This thing that made you forget. Then I figured it out. I ought to have figured it out a lot sooner, but they've always been so strict about Ascensions. So particular. But then Alec mentioned to me: They're *desperate* for new Shadowhunters now. They lost so many in the Dark War, it would be easy. You've got so many people to vouch for you. You could be a Shadowhunter, Simon. Like Isabelle. I can do a little with this book; I can't fix it completely, and I can't make you what you were before, but I can prepare you to be able to Ascend, and once you do, once you're a Shadowhunter, *he* can't touch you. You'll have the Clave's protection, and the rules about not telling you about the Shadow World, those will be gone."

Simon looked at Isabelle. It was a little like looking at the sun, but the way she was looking back at him made it easier. She was looking at him as if she had missed him, though he knew that wasn't possible. "There's really magic?" he asked. "Vampires and werewolves and wizards—"

"Warlocks," Magnus corrected.

"And all of that? It exists?"

"It exists," Isabelle said. Her voice was sweet, a little husky and—familiar. He remembered the smell of sunlight and flowers suddenly, a taste like copper in his mouth. He saw desert landscapes stretching out under a demon sun, and a city with towers that shimmered as if they were made of ice and glass. "It's not a fairy tale, Simon. Being a Shadowhunter means being a warrior. It's dangerous, but if it's right for you, it's amazing. I wouldn't ever want to be anything else."

"It's your decision, Simon Lewis," said Magnus. "Remain in the existence you have, go to college, study music, get married. Live your life. Or—you can have an uncertain life of shadows and dangers. You can have the joy of reading the stories of incredible happenings, or you can be part of the story." He leaned closer, and Simon saw the light spark off his eyes, and realized why he'd thought they were odd. They were gold-green and slit-pupilled like a cat's. Not human eyes at all. "The choice is up to you."

It was always a surprise that werewolves turned out to have such a deft touch with floral arrangements, Clary thought. Luke's old pack—Maia's now—had pitched in to decorate the grounds around the farmhouse, where the reception was being held, and the old barn where the ceremony had taken place. The pack had overhauled the entire structure. Clary remembered playing with Simon in the old hayloft that creaked, the cracked and peeling paint, the uneven floorboards. Now everything had been sanded down and refinished, and the post-and-beam room glowed with the soft glow of old wood. Someone had a sense of humor, too: The beams had been wrapped with chains of wild lupine.

Big wooden vases held arrays of cattails and goldenrod and lilies. Clary's own bouquet was wildflowers, though it had gone a bit limp from being clutched in her hand for so many hours. The whole ceremony had gone by in something of a blur: vows, flowers, candlelight, her mother's happy face, the glow in Luke's eyes. In the end Jocelyn had eschewed a fancy dress and gone with a plain white sundress and her hair up in a messy bun with, yes, a colored pencil stuck through it. Luke, handsome in dove gray, didn't seem to mind at all.

The guests were all milling about now. Several werewolves were efficiently clearing away the rows of chairs and stacking the presents on a long table. Clary's own gift, a portrait she had painted of her mother and Luke, hung on one wall. She had loved drawing it; had loved having the brush and paints in her hands again—drawing not to make runes, but only to make something lovely that someone might someday enjoy.

Jocelyn was busy hugging Maia, who looked amused at Jocelyn's enthusiasm. Bat was chatting with Luke, who seemed dazed, but in a good way. Clary smiled in their direction and slipped out of the barn, onto the path outside.

The moon was high, shining down on the lake at the foot of the property, making the rest of the farm glow. Lanterns had been hung in all the trees, and they swung in the faint wind. The paths were lined with tiny glowing crystals—one of Magnus's contributions, though where *was* Magnus? Clary hadn't seen him in the crowd at the ceremony, though she'd seen nearly everyone else: Maia and Bat, Isabelle in silver, Alec very serious in a dark suit, and Jace having defiantly discarded his tie somewhere, probably in some nearby foliage. Even Robert and Maryse were there, suitably gracious; Clary had no idea what was going on with their relationship, and didn't want to ask anyone.

Clary headed down toward the largest of the white tents; the DJ station was set up for Bat, and some of the pack and other guests were busy clearing a space for dancing. The tables were draped with long white cloths and set with old china from the farmhouse, sourced from Luke's years of scouring flea markets in the small towns around the farm. None of it matched, and the glasses were old jam jars, and the centerpieces were hand-picked blue asters and clover floating in mismatched pottery bowls, and Clary thought it was the prettiest wedding she'd ever seen.

A long table was set up with champagne glasses; Jace was standing near it, and as he saw her, he raised a glass of champagne and winked. He had gone the disheveled route: rumpled blazer and tousled hair and now no tie, and his skin was all gold from the beginning of summer, and he was so beautiful that it made her heart hurt.

He was standing with Isabelle and Alec; Isabelle looked stunning with her hair swept up in a loose knot. Clary knew she'd never be able to pull off that sort of elegance in a million years, and she didn't care. Isabelle was Isabelle, and Clary was grateful she existed, making the world a little fiercer with every one of her smiles. Isabelle whistled now, shooting a look across the tent. "Look at that."

Clary looked—and looked again. She saw a girl who seemed about nineteen years old; she had loose brown hair and a sweet face. She wore a green dress, a little old-fashioned in its style, and a jade necklace around her throat. Clary had seen her before, in Alicante, talking to Magnus at the Clave's party in Angel Square.

She was holding the hand of a very familiar, very handsome boy with mussed dark hair; he looked tall and rangy in an elegant black suit and white shirt that set off his high-cheekboned face. As Clary watched, he leaned over to whisper something into her ear, and she smiled, her face lighting up.

"Brother Zachariah," Isabelle said. "Months January through December of the Hot Silent Brothers Calendar. What's he doing here?"

"There's a Hot Silent Brothers Calendar?" said Alec. "Do they sell it?"

"Quit that." Isabelle elbowed him. "Magnus will be here any minute."

"Where *is* Magnus?" Clary asked.

Isabelle smiled into her champagne. "He had an errand."

Clary looked back over toward Zachariah and the girl, but they had melted back into the crowd. She wished they hadn't—there was something about the girl that fascinated her—but a moment later Jace's hand was around her wrist, and he was setting down his glass. "Come dance with me," he said.

Clary looked over at the stage. Bat had taken his place at the DJ booth, but there was no music yet. Someone had placed an upright piano in the corner, and Catarina Loss, her skin glowing blue, was tinkling at the keys.

"There's no music," she said.

Jace smiled at her. "We don't need it."

"Aaaand that's our cue to leave," Isabelle said, seizing Alec by the elbow and hauling him off into the crowd. Jace grinned after her.

"Sentimentality gives Isabelle hives," said Clary. "But, seriously, we can't dance with no music. Everyone will stare at us—"

"Then let's go where they can't see us," Jace said, and drew her away from the tent. It was what Jocelyn called "the blue hour" now, everything drenched in twilight, the white tent like a star and the grass soft, each blade shimmering like silver.

Jace drew her back against him, fitting her body to his, wrapping his arms around her waist, his lips touching the back of her neck. "We could go in the farmhouse," he said. "There are bedrooms."

She turned around in his arms and poked him in the chest, firmly. "This is my mother's wedding," she said. "We're not going to have sex. At all."

"But 'at all' is my favorite way to *have* sex."

"The house is full of vampires," she told him cheerfully. "They were invited, and they came last night. They've been waiting in there for the sun to go down."

"Luke invited *vampires*?"

"Maia did. Peace gesture. They're trying to all get along."

"Surely the vampires would respect our privacy."

"Surely not," said Clary, and she drew him firmly away from the path to the farmhouse, into a copse of trees. It was shaded in here, and hidden, the ground all packed earth and roots, mountain mint with its starry white flowers growing around the trunks of the trees in clusters.

She backed up against a tree trunk, pulling Jace with her, so that he leaned against her, his hands on either side of her shoulders, and she rested in the cage of his arms. She smoothed her hands down over the soft fabric of his jacket. "I love you," she said.

He looked down at her. "I think I know what Madame Dorothea meant," he said. "When she said I'd fall in love with the wrong person."

Clary's eyes widened. She wondered if she was about to be broken up with. If so, she would have a thing or two to say to Jace about his timing, after she drowned him in the lake.

He took a deep breath. "You make me question myself," he said. "All the time, every day. I was brought up to believe I had to be perfect. A perfect warrior, a perfect son. Even when I came to live with the Lightwoods, I thought I had to be perfect, because otherwise they would send me away. I didn't think love came with forgiveness. And then you came along, and you broke everything I believed into pieces, and I started to see everything differently. You had—so much love, and so much forgiveness, and so much faith. So I started to think that maybe I was worth that faith. That I didn't have to be perfect; I had to try, and that was good enough." He lowered his eyelids; she could see the faint pulse at his temple, feel the tension in him. "So I think you were the wrong person for the Jace that I was, but not the Jace that I am now, the Jace you helped make me. Who is, incidentally, a Jace I like much better than the old one. You've changed me for the better, and even if you left me, I would still have that." He paused. "Not that you should leave me," he added hastily, and leaned his head against hers, so their foreheads touched. "Say something, Clary."

His hands were on her shoulders, warm against her cool skin; she could feel them trembling. His eyes were gold even in the blue light of twilight. She remembered when she had found them hard and distant, even frightening, before she had grown to realize that what she was looking at was the expert shielding of seventeen years of self-protection. Seventeen years of protecting his heart. "You're shaking," she said, with some wonder.

"You make me," he said, his breath against her cheek, and he slid his hands down her bare arms, "every time—every time."

"Can I tell you a boring science fact?" she whispered. "I bet you didn't learn it in Shadowhunter history class."

"If you're trying to distract me from talking about my feelings, you're not being very subtle about it." He touched her face. "You know I make speeches. It's okay. You don't have to make them back. Just tell me you love me."

"I'm not trying to distract you." She held up her hand and wiggled the fingers. "There are a hundred trillion cells in the human body," she said. "And every single one of the cells of my body loves you. We shed cells, and grow new ones, and my new cells love you more than the old ones, which is why I love you more every day than I did the day before. It's science. And when I die and they burn my body and I become ashes that mix with the air, and part of the ground and the trees and the stars, everyone who breathes that air or sees the flowers that grow out of the ground or looks up at the stars will remember you and love you, because I love you *that much*." She smiled. "How was that for a speech?"

He stared at her, rendered wordless for one of the first times in his life. Before he could answer, she stretched up to kiss him—a chaste press of lips to lips at first, but it deepened quickly, and soon he was parting her lips with his, tongue stroking into her mouth, and she could taste him: the sweetness of Jace spiked with the bite of champagne. His hands were feverishly running up and down her back, over the bumps of her spine, the silk straps of her dress, the bare wings of her shoulder blades, pressing her into him. She slid her hands under his jacket, wondering if maybe they should have gone to the farmhouse after all, even if it *was* full of vampires—

"Interesting," said an amused voice, and Clary pulled back from Jace quickly to see Magnus, standing in a gap between two trees. His tall figure was limned in moonlight; he had eschewed anything particularly outrageous and was dressed in a perfectly cut black suit that looked like a spill of ink against the darkening sky.

"*Interesting?*" Jace echoed. "Magnus, what are you doing here?"

"Came to get you," Magnus said. "There's something I think you should see."

Jace closed his eyes as if praying for patience. "WE ARE BUSY."

"Clearly," said Magnus. "You know, they say life is short, but it isn't all that short. It can be quite long, and you have all your lives to spend together, so I *really* suggest you come with me, because you're going to be sorry if you don't."

Clary broke away from the tree, her hand still in Jace's. "Okay," she said.

"Okay?" said Jace, following her. "Seriously?"

"I trust Magnus," Clary said. "If it's important, it's important."

"And if it's not, I'm going to drown him in the lake," Jace said, echoing Clary's earlier, unspoken thought. She hid her grin in the dark.

Alec stood at the edge of the tent, watching the dancing. The sun was down enough now to simply be a red stripe painted across the distant sky, and the vampires had come out from the farmhouse and joined the party. Some discreet accommodation had been made for their tastes, and they mingled among the others holding sleek metal flutes, plucked from the champagne table, whose opacity hid the liquid inside.

Lily, the head of the vampire clan of New York, was at the ivory keys of the piano, filling the room with the sounds of jazz. Over the music a voice said in Alec's ear, "It was a lovely ceremony, I thought."

Alec turned and saw his father, his big hand clasped around a fragile champagne flute, staring out at the guests. Robert was a large man, broad-shouldered, never at his best in a suit: He looked like an overgrown schoolboy who'd been forced into it by an annoyed parent.

"Hi," Alec said. He could see his mother, across the room, talking to Jocelyn. Maryse had more streaks of gray in her dark hair than he remembered; she looked elegant, as she always did. "It was nice of you to come," he added grudgingly. Both his parents had been almost painfully grateful that he and Isabelle had returned to them after the Dark War—too grateful to be angry or scolding. Too grateful for Alec to say much of anything to either of them about Magnus; when his mother had returned to New York, he'd gathered the rest of his possessions from the Institute and moved into the loft in Brooklyn. He was still in the Institute nearly every day, still saw his mother often, but Robert had remained in Alicante, and Alec hadn't tried to contact him. "Pretend to be civil with Mom, all of that—really nice."

Alec saw his father flinch. He'd meant to be gracious, but he'd never done gracious well. It always seemed like lying. "We're not pretending to be civil," said Robert. "I still love your mother; we care about each other. We just—can't be married. We should have ended it earlier. We thought we were doing the right thing. Our intentions were good."

"Road to Hell," said Alec succinctly, and looked down at his glass.

"Sometimes," Robert said, "you choose whom you want to be with when you're too young, and you change, and they don't change with you."

Alec took in a slow breath; his veins were suddenly sizzling with anger. "If that's meant to be a dig at me and Magnus, you can shove it," he said. "You gave up your right to have any jurisdiction over me and my relationships when you made it clear that as far as you were concerned, a gay Shadowhunter wasn't really a Shadowhunter." He set his glass down on a nearby speaker. "I'm not interested—"

"Alec." Something about Robert's voice made Alec turn; he didn't sound angry, just ... broken. "I did, I said—unforgivable things. I know that," he said. "But I have always been proud of you, and I am no less proud now."

"I don't believe you."

"When I was your age, younger, I had a *parabatai*," said Robert.

"Yes, Michael Wayland," said Alec, not caring that he sounded bitter, not caring about the look on his father's face. "I know. It's why you took Jace in. I always thought you two must not have been particularly close. You didn't seem to miss him much, or mind that he was dead."

"I didn't believe he was dead," said Robert. "I know that must seem hard to imagine; our bond had been severed by the sentence of exile passed down by the Clave, but even before that, we had grown apart. There was a time, though, when we were close, the best of friends; there was a time when he told me that he loved me."

Something about the weight his father put on the words brought Alec up short. "Michael Wayland was *in love* with you?"

"I was—not kind to him about it," said Robert. "I told him never to say those words to me again. I was afraid, and I left him alone with his thoughts and feelings and fears, and we were never close again as we had been. I took Jace in to make up, in some small measure, for what I had done, but I know there is no making up for it." He looked at Alec, and his dark blue eyes were steady. "You think that I am ashamed of you, but I am ashamed of myself. I look at you, and I see the mirror of my own unkindness to someone who never deserved it. We find in our children our own selves again, who might be made better than we are. Alec, you are so much a better man than I ever was, or will be."

Alec stood frozen. He remembered his dream in the demon lands, his father telling everyone how brave he was, what a good Shadowhunter and warrior, but he had never imagined his father telling him that he was a good *man*.

It was a much better thing, somehow.

Robert was looking at him with the lines of strain plain around his eyes and mouth. Alec couldn't help but wonder if he'd ever told anyone else about Michael, and what it had cost him to say it just now.

He touched his father's arm lightly, the first time he had willingly touched him in months, and then dropped his hand.

"Thank you," he said. "For telling me the truth."

It wasn't forgiveness, not exactly, but it was a start.

The grass was damp from the chill of the oncoming night; Clary could feel the cold soaking through her sandals as she made her way back toward the tent with Jace and Magnus. Clary could see the rows of tables being set up, china and silverware flashing. Everyone had pitched in to help out, even the people she usually thought of as almost unassailable in their reserve: Kadir, Jia, Maryse.

Music was coming from the tent. Bat was lounging up at the DJ station, but someone was playing jazz piano. She could see Alec standing with his father, talking intently, and then the crowd parted and she saw a blur of other familiar faces: Maia and Aline chatting, and Isabelle standing near Simon, looking awkward—

Simon.

Clary came up short. Her heart skipped a beat, and then another; she felt hot and cold all over, as if she were about to faint. It couldn't be Simon; it had to be someone else. Some other skinny boy with messy brown hair and glasses, but he was wearing the same faded shirt she'd seen him in that morning, and his hair was still too long and in his face, and he was smiling at her a little uncertainly across the crowd and it was Simon and it was Simon and it was *Simon.*

She didn't even remember starting to run, but suddenly Magnus's hand was on her shoulder, a grip like iron holding her back. "Be *careful*," he said. "He doesn't remember everything. I could give him a few memories, not much. The rest will have to wait, but, Clary—remember that he *doesn't* remember. Don't expect everything."

She must have nodded, because he let her go, and then she was tearing across the lawn and into the tent, hurling herself at Simon so hard that he staggered back, almost falling over. *He doesn't have vampire strength anymore; go easy, go easy,* her mind said, but the rest of her didn't want to listen. She had her arms around him, and she was half-hugging him and half-sobbing into the front of his coat.

She was aware of Isabelle and Jace and Maia standing near them, and Jocelyn, too, hurrying over. Clary pulled back from Simon just enough to look up into his face. And it was definitely Simon. This close up she could see the freckles on his left cheekbone, the tiny scar on his lip from a soccer accident in eighth grade. "Simon," she whispered, and then, "Do—you know me? Do you know who I am?"

He pushed his glasses up the bridge of his nose. His hand was shaking slightly. "I..." He looked around. "It's like a family reunion where I barely know anyone but everyone knows me," he said. "It's..."

"Overwhelming?" Clary asked. She tried to hide the chime of disappointment, deep down in her chest, that he didn't recognize her. "It's all right if you don't know me. There's time."

He looked down at her. There was uncertainty and hope in his expression, and a slightly dazed look, as if he'd just woken up from a dream and wasn't entirely sure where he was. Then he smiled. "I don't remember everything," he said. "Not yet. But I remember you." He brought her hand up, touched the gold ring on her right index finger, the Fair Folk metal warm to the touch. "Clary," he said. "You're Clary. You're my best friend."

Alec made his way up the hill to where Magnus stood on the pathway overlooking the tent. He was leaning against a tree, hands in his pockets, and Alec joined him to watch as Simon, looking as bewildered as a newborn duckling, was swarmed by friends: Jace and Maia and Luke, and even Jocelyn, crying with happiness as she hugged him, smearing her makeup. Only Isabelle stood apart from the group, her hands clasped in front of her, her face almost expressionless.

"You'd almost think she didn't care," said Alec as Magnus reached out to straighten his tie. Magnus had helped him pick out the suit he was wearing, and was very proud of the fact that it had a slender stripe of blue that brought out Alec's eyes. "But I'm pretty sure she does."

"You're correct," Magnus said. "She cares too much; that's why she's standing apart."

"I would ask you what you did, but I'm not sure I want to know," Alec said, leaning his back against Magnus, taking comfort in the solid warmth of the body behind him. Magnus put his chin down on Alec's shoulder, and for a moment they stood motionless together, looking down at the tent and the scene of happy chaos below. "It was good of you."

"You make the choice you have to make at the time," Magnus said in his ear. "You hope for no consequences, or no serious ones."

"You don't think your father will be angry, do you?" Alec said, and Magnus laughed dryly.

"He has a great deal more to pay attention to than me," Magnus said. "What about you? I saw you talking to Robert."

Alec felt Magnus's posture tense as he repeated what his father had told him. "You know, I would *not* have guessed that," Magnus said when Alec was done. "And I've met Michael Wayland." Alec felt him shrug. "Goes to show. 'The heart is forever inexperienced' and all that."

"What do you think? Should I forgive him?"

"I think what he told you was an explanation, but it wasn't an excuse for how he behaved. If you forgive him, do it for yourself, not for him. It's a waste of your time to be angry," Magnus said, "when you're one of the most loving people I've known."

"Is that why you forgave me? For me, or you?" Alec said, not angry, just curious.

"I forgave you because I love you and I hate being without you. I hate it, my cat hates it. And because Catarina convinced me I was being stupid."

"Mmm. I like her."

Magnus's hands reached around Alec and flattened against his chest, as if he were feeling for his heartbeat. "And you forgive me," he said. "For not being able to make you immortal, or end my own immortality."

"There's nothing to forgive," Alec said. "I don't want to live forever." He laid one of his hands over Magnus's, twining their fingers together. "We might not have that much time," said Alec. "I'll get old and I'll die. But I promise I won't leave you until then. It's the only promise I *can* make."

"A lot of Shadowhunters don't get old," Magnus said. Alec

could feel the thrum of his pulse. It was strange, Magnus like this, without the words that usually came to him so easily.

Alec turned around in Magnus's embrace so that they faced each other, taking in all the details that he never got tired of: the sharp bones of Magnus's face, the gold-green of his eyes, the mouth that always seemed about to smile, though he looked worried now. "Even if it were just days, I would want to spend them all with you. Does that mean anything?"

"Yes," Magnus said. "It means that from now on we make every day matter."

They were dancing.

Lily was playing something slow and soft on the piano, and Clary drifted among the other wedding guests, Jace's arms around her. It was exactly the kind of dancing she liked: not too complicated, mostly a matter of holding on to your partner and not doing anything to trip them up.

She had her cheek against Jace's shirtfront, the fabric rumpled and soft under her skin. His hand played idly with the curls that had fallen from her chignon, fingers tracing the back of her neck. She couldn't help but remember a dream she'd had a long time ago, in which she had been dancing with Jace in the Hall of Accords. He had been so removed back then, so often cold; it amazed her sometimes now when she looked at him, that this was the same Jace. *The Jace you helped make me*, he had said. *A Jace I like much better.*

But he was not the only one who had changed; she had changed too. She opened her mouth to tell him so, when there was a tap on her shoulder. She turned to see her mother, smiling at them both.

"Jace," Jocelyn said. "If I could ask you a favor?"

Jace and Clary had both stopped dancing; neither said anything. Jocelyn had come to like Jace much better in the past six months than she had liked him before; she was even, Clary would venture to say, fond of him, but she still wasn't always thrilled about Clary's Shadowhunter boyfriend.

"Lily's tired of playing, but everyone's enjoying the piano so much—and you play, don't you? Clary told me how talented you are. Would you play for us?"

Jace swept a glance toward Clary, so quick that she saw it only because she knew him well enough to look. He had manners, though, exquisite ones, when he chose to use them. He smiled at Jocelyn like an angel, and then went over to the piano. A moment later the strains of classical music filled the tent.

Tessa Gray and the boy who had been Brother Zachariah sat at the farthest table in the corner and watched as Jace Herondale's light fingers danced over the keys of the piano. Jace wore no tie and his shirt was partly unbuttoned, his face a study in concentration as he abandoned himself to the music with a passion.

"Chopin." Tessa identified the music with a soft smile. "I wonder—I wonder if little Emma Carstairs will play the violin someday."

"Careful," her companion said with a laugh in his voice. "You can't force these things."

"It's hard," she said, turning to look at him earnestly. "I wish you could tell her more of the connection between the two of you, that she might not feel so alone."

Sorrow turned down the corners of his sensitive mouth. "You know I cannot. Not yet. I hinted at it to her. That was all I could do."

"We will keep an eye on her," said Tessa. "We will always keep an eye on her." She touched the marks on his cheeks, remnants of his time as a Silent Brother, almost reverently. "I remember you said this war was a story of Lightwoods and Herondales and Fairchilds, and it is, and Blackthorns and Carstairs as well, and it's amazing to see them. But when I do, it's as if I see the past that stretches out behind them. I watch Jace Herondale play, and I see the ghosts that rise up in the music. Don't you?"

"Ghosts are memories, and we carry them because those we love do not leave the world."

"Yes," she said. "I just wish *he* were here to see this with us, just here with us one more time."

She felt the rough silk of his black hair as he bent to kiss her fingers lightly—a courtly gesture from a bygone age. "He is with us, Tessa. He can see us. I believe it. I *feel* it, the way I used to know sometimes if he was sad or angry or lonely or happy."

She touched the pearl bracelet at her wrist, and then his face, with light, adoring fingers. "And what is he now?" she whispered. "Happy or wistful or sad or lonely? Do not tell me he is lonely. For you must know. You always knew."

"He is happy, Tessa. It gives him joy to see us together, as it always gave me joy to see the two of you." He smiled, that smile that had all the truth of the world in it, and slid his fingers from hers as he sat back. Two figures were approaching their table: a tall, redheaded woman, and a girl with the same red hair and green eyes. "And speaking of the past," he said, "I think there's someone here who wants to talk to you."

Clary was watching Church with amusement when her mother sidled up to her. The cat had been festooned with dozens of tiny silver wedding bells and, in a vengeful rage, was gnawing a hole in one of the piano legs.

"Mom," Clary said suspiciously. "What are you up to?"

Her mother stroked her hair, looking fond. "There's someone I want you to meet," she said, taking Clary's hand. "It's time."

"Time? Time for what?" Clary let herself be pulled along, only half-protesting, to a white-draped table in the corner of the tent. At it sat the brown-haired girl she had seen earlier. The girl looked up as Clary approached. Brother Zachariah was rising from her side; he gave Clary a soft smile and moved across the room to talk to Magnus, who had come down from the hill holding hands with Alec.

"Clary," Jocelyn said. "I want you to meet Tessa."

"Isabelle."

She looked up; she had been leaning against the side of the piano, letting Jace's playing (and the faint sound of Church gnawing wood) lull her. It was music that reminded her of her childhood, of Jace spending hours in the music room, filling the halls of the Institute with a cascade of notes.

It was Simon. He had unbuttoned his denim jacket in the warmth of the tent, and she could see the flush of heat and awkwardness across his cheekbones. There was something alien about it, a Simon who blushed and was cold and hot and grew up and grew away—from her.

His dark eyes were curious as they rested on her; she saw some recognition in them, but it wasn't total. It wasn't the way Simon had looked at her before, longing and that sweet ache and sense that here was someone who *saw* her, saw Isabelle, the Isabelle she presented to the world and the Isabelle she hid away, tucked into the shadows where only a very few could see her.

Simon had been one of those few. Now he was—something else.

"Isabelle," he said again, and she sensed Jace looking over at her, his eyes curious as his hands darted over the piano keys. "Would you dance with me?"

She sighed and nodded. "All right," she said, and let him draw her onto the dance floor. In her heels she was as tall as he was; their eyes were on a level. Behind the glasses his were the same dark coffee brown.

"I've been told," he said, and cleared his throat, "or at least, I get the sense, that you and I—"

"Don't," she said. "Don't talk about it. If you don't remember, then I don't want to hear it."

One of his hands was on her shoulder, the other on her waist. His skin was warm against hers, not cool as she remembered it. He seemed incredibly human, and fragile.

"But I want to remember it," he said, and she remembered how argumentative he'd always been; that, at least, hadn't changed. "I remember some of it—it's not like I don't know who you are, Isabelle."

"You would call me Izzy," she said, suddenly feeling very tired. "Izzy, not Isabelle."

He leaned in, and she felt his breath against her hair. "Izzy," he said. "I remember kissing you."

She shivered. "No, you don't."

"Yes, I do," he said. His hands slid to her back, fingers brushing the space just below her shoulder blade that always made her squirm. "It's been months now," he said, in a low voice. "And nothing's felt quite right. I've always felt like something was missing. And now I know it was this, all of this, but it was also *you*. I didn't remember during the day. But I dreamed at night about you, Isabelle."

"You dreamed about us?"

"Just you. The girl with the dark, dark eyes." He touched the edge of her hair with light fingers. "Magnus tells me I was a hero," he said. "And I see on your face when you're looking at me that you're searching for that guy. The guy you knew who was a hero, who did great things. I don't remember doing those things. I don't know if that makes me not a hero anymore. But I'd like to try to be that guy again. That guy who gets to kiss you because he earned it. If you'll be patient enough to let me try."

It was such a *Simon* thing to say. She looked up at him, and for the first time felt a swell of hope in her chest and didn't immediately move to crush it down. "I might let you," she said. "Try, that is. I can't promise anything."

"I wouldn't expect you to." His face lit up, and she saw the shadow of a memory move behind his eyes. "You're a heartbreaker, Isabelle Lightwood," he said. "I remember that much, at least."

"Tessa is a warlock," said Jocelyn, "although a very unusual kind of warlock. Remember what I told you, that I was panicked about how to put the spell on you that all Shadowhunters receive when they're born? The protection spell? And that Brother Zachariah and a female warlock stood in and helped with the ceremony? This is the warlock I was talking about. Tessa Gray."

"You told me that was where you got the idea for the name Fray." Clary sank down in the seat opposite Tessa at the round table. "F for Fairchild," she said, realizing aloud. "And the rest for Gray."

Tessa smiled, and her face lit up. "It was an honor."

"You were a baby; you wouldn't recall it," said Jocelyn, but Clary thought of the way Tessa had looked familiar to her the first time she had seen her, and wondered.

"Why are you just telling me now?" Clary demanded, looking up at her mother, who was standing by her chair, twisting her new wedding ring around her finger anxiously. "Why not before?"

"I had asked to be there when she told you, if she chose to," said Tessa; her voice was musical, soft and sweet, with the trace of an English accent. "And I fear I have long separated myself from the Shadowhunter world. My memories of it are sweet and bitter, sometimes more bitter than sweet."

Jocelyn dropped a kiss onto Clary's head. "Why don't you two talk?" she said, and walked away, toward Luke, who was chatting with Kadir.

Clary looked at Tessa's smile, and said, "You're a warlock, but you're friends with a Silent Brother. More than friends—that's a little odd, isn't it?"

Tessa leaned her elbows onto the table. A pearl bracelet gleamed around her left wrist; she touched it idly, as if through force of habit. "Everything about my life is quite out of the ordinary, but then, the same could be said for you, couldn't it?" Her eyes sparkled. "Jace Herondale plays the piano very well."

"And he knows it."

"That sounds like a Herondale." Tessa laughed. "I must tell you, Clary, that I learned only recently that Jace had decided that he wished to be a Herondale and not a Lightwood. Both are honorable families, and both I have known, but my fate has always been most entwined with that of the Herondales." She looked over at Jace, and there was a sort of wistfulness in her expression. "There are families—the Blackthorns, the Herondales, the Carstairs—for whom I have always felt a special affinity: I have watched over them from a distance, though I have learned not to interfere. That is in part why I retreated to the Spiral Labyrinth after the Uprising. It is a place so far from the world, so hidden, I thought I could find peace there from my knowledge of what had happened to the Herondales. And then after the Mortal War I asked Magnus if I should approach Jace, speak to him of the past of the Herondales, but he said to give him time. That to bear the burden of the knowledge of the past was a heavy one. So I returned to the Labyrinth." She swallowed. "This was a dark year, such a dark year for Shadowhunters, for Downworlders, for all of us. So much loss and grief. In the Spiral Labyrinth we heard rumors, and then there were the Endarkened, and I thought the best thing I could do to help was to find a cure, but there was none. I wish we could have found one. Sometimes there is not always a cure." She looked toward Zachariah with a light in her eyes. "But then, sometimes there are miracles. Zachariah told me of the way in which he became mortal again. He said it was 'A story of

Lightwoods and Herondales and Fairchilds.'" She glanced over at Zachariah, who was busy patting Church. The cat had climbed up onto the champagne table and was gleefully knocking over glasses. Her look was one of exasperation and fondness mixed together. "You don't know what it means to me, how grateful I am for what you did for my—for Zachariah, what you all of you did for him."

"It was Jace, more than anyone else. It was— Did Zachariah just pick up Church?" Clary stared in astonishment. Zachariah was holding the cat, who had gone boneless, his tail curled around the former Silent Brother's arm. "That cat hates everybody!"

Tessa gave a small smile. "I wouldn't say everybody."

"So he is—Zachariah is mortal now?" Clary asked. "Just—an ordinary Shadowhunter?"

"Yes," Tessa said. "He and I have known each other a long time. We had a standing meeting every year in early January. This year, when he arrived for it, to my shock, he was mortal."

"And you didn't know before he just showed up? I would have killed him."

Tessa grinned. "Well, that would have somewhat defeated the point. And I think he wasn't sure how I would receive him, mortal as he is, when I am not mortal." Her expression reminded Clary of Magnus, that look of old, old eyes in a young face, reminded her of a sorrow that was too still and too deep for those with short human lives to understand. "He will age and die, and I will remain as I am. But he has had a long life, longer than most, and understands me. Neither he nor I are the age we seem. And we love each other. That is the important thing."

Tessa closed her eyes, and for a moment seemed to let the notes of the piano music wash over her.

"I have something for you," she said, opening her eyes—they were gray, the color of rainwater. "For both of you—for you, and for Jace as well." She slid something out of her pocket and held it out to Clary. It was a dull silver circlet, a family ring, glimmering with the pattern of engraved birds in flight. "This ring belonged to James Herondale," she said. "It is a true Herondale ring, many years old. If Jace has decided that he wishes to be a Herondale, he should have it to wear."

Clary took the ring; it just fit onto her thumb. "Thank you," she said, "though you could give it to him yourself. Maybe now is the time to talk to him."

Tessa shook her head. "Look how happy he is," she said. "He is deciding who he is and who he wants to be, and finding joy in it. He should have a bit more time, to be happy like that, before he picks up any burdens again." She took up something that had been lying on the chair beside her, and held it out to Clary. It was a copy of *The Shadowhunter's Codex*, bound in blue velvet. "This is for you," she said. "I am sure you have your own, but this was dear to me. There is an inscription on the back—see?" And she turned the book over, so that Clary could see where words had been stamped in gold against the velvet.

"*Freely we serve, because we freely love,*'" Clary read out, and looked up at Tessa. "Thank you; this is a lovely thing. Are you sure you want to give it away?"

Tessa smiled. "The Fairchilds, too, have been dear to me in my life," she said, "and your red hair and your stubbornness recall to me people I once loved. Clary," she said, and leaned forward across the table so that her jade pendant swung free, "I feel a kinship with you, too, you who have lost both brother and father. I know you have been judged and spoken of as the daughter of Valentine Morgenstern, and now the sister of Jonathan. There will always be those who want to tell you who you are based on your name or the blood in your veins. Do not let other people decide who you are. Decide for yourself." She looked over at Jace, whose hands were dancing over the piano keys. Light from the tapers caught like stars in his hair and made his skin shine. "That freedom is not a gift; it is a birthright. I hope that you and Jace will use it."

"You sound so grave, Tessa. Don't frighten her." It was Zachariah, coming to stand behind Tessa's chair.

"I'm not!" Tessa said with a laugh; she had her head tipped back, and Clary wondered if that was how she herself looked, looking up at Jace. She hoped so. It was a safe and happy look, the look of someone who was confident in the love they gave and received. "I was just giving her advice."

"Sounds terrifying." It was odd how Zachariah's speaking voice sounded both like and unlike his voice in Clary's mind—in life his English accent was stronger than Tessa's. He also had laughter in his voice as he reached down and helped Tessa up out of her chair. "I'm afraid we must go; we have a long journey ahead of us."

"Where are you going?" Clary asked, holding the *Codex* carefully on her lap.

"Los Angeles," Tessa said, and Clary recalled her saying that the Blackthorns were a family in which she had a particular interest. Clary was glad to hear it. She knew that Emma and the others were living in the Institute with Julian's uncle, but the idea that they might have someone special to watch over them, a guardian angel of sorts, was reassuring.

"It was good to meet you," Clary said. "Thank you. For everything."

Tessa smiled radiantly and disappeared into the crowd, saying she was going to bid Jocelyn good-bye; Zachariah gathered up his coat and her wrap, Clary watching him curiously. "I remember once you told me," she said, "that you had loved two people more than anything else in the world. Was Tessa one of them?"

"She *is* one of them," he said agreeably, shrugging himself into his coat. "I have not stopped loving her, nor my *parabatai*; love does not stop when someone dies."

"Your *parabatai*? You lost your *parabatai*?" Clary said, feeling a sense of shocked hurt for him; she knew what that meant to Nephilim.

"Not from my heart, for I have not forgotten," he said, and she heard a whisper of the sadness of ages in his voice, and remembered him in the Silent City, a wraith of parchment smoke. "We are all the pieces of what we remember. We hold in ourselves the hopes and fears of those who love us. As long as there is love and memory, there is no true loss."

Clary thought of Max, of Amatis, of Raphael and Jordan and even of Jonathan, and felt the prickle of tears in her throat.

Zachariah slung Tessa's scarf around his shoulders. "Tell Jace Herondale that he plays Chopin's Concerto no. 2 very well," he said, and vanished after Tessa, into the crowd. She stared after him, clutching the ring and the *Codex*.

"Has anyone seen Church?" said a voice in her ear. It was Isabelle, her fingers tucked around Simon's arm. Maia stood beside them, fiddling with a gold clasp in her curly hair. "I think Zachariah just stole our cat. I swear I saw him putting Church into the backseat of a car."

"There's no way," said Jace, appearing beside Clary; he had his sleeves rolled up to the elbows and was flushed from the effort of playing. "Church hates everyone."

"Not everyone," Clary murmured with a smile.

Simon was looking at Jace as if he were both fascinating and also a little alarming. "Did I—did we ever—did I *bite* you?"

Jace touched the scar on his throat. "I can't believe you remember *that*."

"Did we ... roll around on the bottom of a boat?"

"Yes, you bit me, yes, I kind of liked it, yes, let's not talk about it again," said Jace. "You're not a vampire anymore. Focus."

"To be fair, you bit Alec, too," said Isabelle.

"When did *that* happen?" Maia asked, her face lighting with amusement as Bat came up behind her; without a word he took the clip out of her hand and slid it back into her hair. He snapped the clasp efficiently. His hands lingered a moment, gentle against her hair.

"What happens in the demon realms stays in the demon realms," said Jace. He glanced over at Clary. "Do you want to go for a walk?"

"A walk or a *walk*?" Isabelle inquired. "Like, are you going to—"

"I think we should all go down to the lake," Clary said, standing up, the *Codex* in one hand and the ring in the other. "It's beautiful down there. Especially at night. I'd like my friends to see it."

"I remember it," Simon said, and gave her a smile that made her heart feel like it was expanding in her chest. The farmhouse was where they had gone every summer; it would always be tied to Simon in her mind. That he remembered it made her happier than she could have imagined being that morning.

She slid her hand into Jace's as they all headed away from the tent, Isabelle darting off to tell her brother to go fetch Magnus along as well. Clary had wanted to be alone with Jace earlier; now she wanted to be with everyone.

She had loved Jace for what felt like a long time now, loved him so much that sometimes she felt like she might die from it, because it was something she needed and couldn't have. But that was gone now: desperation replaced by peace and a quiet happiness. Now that she no longer felt that every moment with him was snatched from the possibility of disaster, now that she could imagine a whole lifetime of times with him that were peaceful or funny or casual or relaxed or kind, she wanted nothing more than to walk down to the farmhouse lake with all of her friends and celebrate the day.

As they passed down over the ridge onto the path to the lake, she glanced behind her. She saw Jocelyn and Luke standing by the tent, watching after them. She saw Luke smile at her and her mother raise her hand in a wave before lowering it to clasp her new husband's. It had been the same for them, she thought, years of separation and sadness, and now they had a lifetime. *A lifetime of times.* She raised her hand in an answering wave, and then hurried to catch up with her friends.

Magnus was leaning against the outside of the barn, watching Clary and Tessa deep in conversation, when Catarina came up to him. She had blue flowers in her hair that set off her sapphire-blue skin. He glanced out across the orchard, down toward where the lake shimmered like water held in the cup of a hand.

"You look worried," said Catarina, placing her hand on his shoulder companionably. "What is it? I saw you kissing that Shadowhunter boy of yours earlier, so it can't be that."

Magnus shook his head. "No. Everything with Alec is fine."

"I saw you speaking to Tessa, too," Catarina said, craning her neck to look. "Strange to have her here. Is that what's bothering you? Past and future colliding; it must feel a bit strange."

"Maybe," Magnus said, though he didn't think it was that. "Old ghosts, the shadows of might-have-beens. Though I always liked Tessa and her boys."

"Her son was a piece of work," said Catarina.

"As was her daughter." Magnus laughed, though it was as brittle as twigs in winter. "I feel the past weighing on me heavily these days, Catarina. The repetition of old mistakes. I hear things, rumblings in Downworld, the rumor of coming strife. The Fair Folk are a proud people, the proudest; they will not take the shaming from the Clave without retaliation."

"They are proud but patient," said Catarina. "They may wait a long time, generations, for vengeance. You cannot fear it coming now, when the shadow may not descend for years yet."

Magnus didn't look at her; he was looking down at the tent, where Clary sat talking with Tessa, where Alec stood side by side with Maia and Bat, laughing, where Isabelle and Simon were dancing to the music Jace was playing on the piano, the haunting sweet notes of Chopin reminding him of another time, and the sound of a violin at Christmas.

"Ah," said Catarina. "You worry about them; you worry about the shadow descending upon those you love."

"Them, or their children." Alec had broken away from the others and was heading up the hill toward the barn. Magnus watched him come, a dark shadow against the darker sky.

"Better to love and fear than feel nothing. That is how we petrify," said Catarina, and she touched his arm. "I am sorry about Raphael, by the way. I never got a chance to say it. I know you saved his life once."

"And then he saved mine," Magnus said, and looked up as Alec reached them. Alec gave Catarina a courteous nod.

"Magnus, we're going down to the lake," he said. "Do you want to come?"

"Why?" Magnus inquired.

Alec shrugged. "Clary says it's pretty," he said. "I mean, I've seen it before, but there was a huge angel rising out of it, and that was distracting." He held his hand out. "Come on. Everyone's going."

Catarina smiled. "Carpe diem," she said to Magnus. "Don't waste your time fretting." She picked up her skirts and wandered off toward the trees, her feet like blue flowers in the grass.

Magnus took Alec's hand.

There were fireflies down by the lake. They illuminated the night with their winking flashes as the group spread out jackets and blankets, which Magnus produced from what he claimed was thin air, though Clary suspected that they had been illegally summoned from Bed Bath & Beyond.

The lake was a silver dime, reflecting back the sky and all its thousands of stars. Clary could hear Alec naming off the constellations to Magnus: the Lion, the Bow, the Winged Horse. Maia had kicked off her shoes and was walking barefoot along the lakeshore. Bat had followed her, and as Clary watched, he took her hand hesitantly.

She let him.

Simon and Isabelle were leaning together, whispering. Every once in a while Isabelle would laugh. Her face was brighter than it had been in months.

Jace sat down on one of the blankets and drew Clary with him, his legs on either side of her. She leaned her back against him, feeling the comforting beat of his heart against her spine. His arms reached around her, and his fingers touched the *Codex* in her lap. "What's this?"

"A gift, for me. And there's one for you, too," she said, and took his hand, unfolding his fingers one by one until his hand was open. She placed the slightly battered silver ring onto it.

"A Herondale ring?" He sounded bewildered. "Where did you..."

"It used to belong to James Herondale," she said. "I don't have a family tree around, so I don't know what that means exactly, but he was clearly one of your ancestors. I remember you saying the Iron Sisters would have to make you a new ring because Stephen hadn't left you one—but now you have one."

He slid it onto the ring finger of his right hand.

"Every time," he said quietly. "Every time I think I'm missing a piece of me, you give it back."

There were no words, so she didn't say any; just turned around in his arms and kissed him on the cheek. He was beautiful under the night sky, the stars shedding their light down over him, gleaming against his hair and eyes and the Herondale ring shining on his finger, a reminder of everything that had been, and everything that would be.

We are all the pieces of what we remember. We hold in ourselves the hopes and fears of those who love us. As long as there is love and memory, there is no true loss.

"Do you *like* the name Herondale?" he asked.

"It's your name, so I love it," she said.

"There are some pretty bad Shadowhunter names I could have ended up with," he said. "Bloodstick. Ravenhaven."

"Bloodstick can't possibly be a name."

"It may have fallen out of favor," he acknowledged. "Herondale, on the other hand, is melodic. Dulcet, one might say. Think of the sound of 'Clary Herondale.'"

"Oh, my God, that sounds *horrible*."

"We all must sacrifice for love." He grinned, and reached around her to pick up the *Codex*. "This is old. An old edition," he said, turning it over. "The inscription on the back is Milton."

"Of course you know that," she said fondly, and leaned against him as he turned the book over in his hands. Magnus had started a fire, and it was burning merrily at the lakeside, sending up sparks into the sky. The reflection of the burning raced along the scarlet of Isabelle's necklace as she turned to say something to Simon, and it shone in the sharp gleam of Magnus's eyes and along the water of the lake, turning the ripples to lines of gold. It picked out the inscription written on the back of the *Codex*, as Jace read the words aloud to Clary, his voice as soft as music in the glittering dark.

"Freely we serve
Because we freely love, as in our will
To love or not; in this we stand or fall."